DAVID FALKAYN: STAR TRADER

THE TECHNIC CIVILIZATION SAGA

POUL ANDERSON

BAEN

DAVID FALKAYN: STAR TRADER

A Baen Book

Baen Publishing Enterprises
P.O. Box 1403
Riverdale, NY 10471
www.baen.com

ISBN 10: 1-4391-3294-1
ISBN 13: 978-1-4391-3294-4

Cover art by David Seeley

First Baen printing, January 2009

Distributed by Simon & Schuster
1230 Avenue of the Americas
New York, NY 10020

Library of Congress Cataloging-in-Publication Data

Anderson, Poul, 1926-2001.
David Falkayn : star trader / by Poul Anderson.
p. cm. -- (Technic civilization saga ;v bk. 2)
Sequel to: The Van Rijn method, 2008.
ISBN 978-1-4165-5520-9 (hc) -- ISBN 978-1-4391-3294-4 (trade pb)
1. Life on other planets--Fiction. 2. Human-alien encounters--Fiction. 3. Interplanetary voyages--Fiction. I. Davis, Hank. II. Miesel, Sandra, 1941- III. Title.

PS3551.N378D38 2009
813'.54--dc22

2008044410

Printed in the United States of America

10 9 8 7 6 5 4 3 2 1

CONTENTS

Acknowledgements

"A Historical Reflection" (excerpt from "Margin of Profit") first appeared in this form in *Trader to the Stars*, Doubleday, 1966. Copyright 1956 by Street & Smith Publications, Inc.

"Territory," first published in *Analog*, June 1963, copyright 1963 by Condé Nast Publications Incorporated.

"Plus Ça Change, Plus C'est la Même Chose," first published in *The Trouble Twisters*, Doubleday, 1966. Copyright 1966 by Poul Anderson.

"The Trouble Twisters," first published in Analog, July and August 1965, copyright 1965 by Condé Nast Publications Incorporated.

Introduction to "Day of Burning," first published in *The Earth Book of Stormgate*, Berkley Putnam, 1978. Copyright 1978 by Poul Anderson.

"Day of Burning," first published as "Supernova" in *Analog*, January 1967, copyright 1967 by Condé Nast Publications Incorporated.

"The Master Key," first published in *Analog*, July, 1964, copyright 1964 by Condé Nast Publications Incorporated.

Satan's World, first published in Analog, May, June, July and August 1968, copyright 1968 by Condé Nast Publications Incorporated.

Introduction to "A Little Knowledge," first published in *The Earth Book of Stormgate*, Berkley Putnam, 1978. Copyright 1978 by Poul Anderson.

"A Little Knowledge," first published in *Analog*, August 1971, copyright 1971 by Condé Nast Publications Incorporated.

Introduction to "Lodestar," first published in *The Earth Book of Stormgate*, Berkley Putnam, 1978. Copyright 1978 by Poul Anderson.

"Lodestar," first published in *Astounding: John W. Campbell Memorial Anthology*, ed. Harry Harrison, Random House, 1973. Copyright 1973 by Random House, Inc.

"Afterword," first published in *Astounding: John W. Campbell Memorial Anthology*, ed. Harry Harrison, Random House, 1973. Copyright 1973 by Random House, Inc.

"Chronology of Technic Civilization" by Sandra Miesel, copyright 2008 by Sandra Miesel.

HIGH PROFITS AND HIGH ADVENTURE

And now the second volume in the Technic Civilization saga, with young David Falkayn taking center stage. Not that Nicholas van Rijn is through having a few more adventures of his own (including—literally—one armchair adventure), adventures which he would just as soon have delegated to someone else, such as in the first story in this book, but Falkayn is now not the only one front and center, but his trader team is ready for action.

Team leader is David Falkayn, a member of the aristocracy on the planet Hermes, where he had the misfortune (or, perhaps, not misfortune at all) of being the younger son of a baronial house, a spare part in case something happens to the older son who's the rightful heir, and consequently obliged to strike out on a career of his own. The reader will have met him in the first volume, *The van Rijn Method* (and if the reader hasn't read that book, the reader should hasten to the local bricks-and-mortar bookstore, or else get online and acquire it; it won't be on sale forever, even if it certainly should be). As detailed therein, he had a trial-by-fire (not to mention trial-by-alien-arrows), acquitted himself well, and was given assignments of increasing importance and authority. And now he has his own ship, and a most unusual crew.

Besides Falkayn, there's Chee Lan, a tempestuous felinesque being, considerably smaller than a human but with enough attitude for a whole battalion of monkey-boys (or girls), covered with silky-white fur, and a crack shot with a blaster. Better not beat her at poker—or do anything else to get her mad. But she keeps a cool head in a crisis: "glacially self-possessed," as Poul Anderson puts it.

Then there's Adzel, as imperturbable as Chee Lan is high-strung, and I suspect that his imperturbability has less to do with his being a Buddhist than with his reptilian species' having evolved on a planet where they're the biggest life form—not quite elephant sized. They are dragonlike, but also centaurlike, with four legs and an additional two arms. He abhors violence, but has no problem with self-defense—or defense of his comrades.

Muddlehead completes the team. Their ship, *Muddlin' Through*, has an intelligent computer that tends to show initiative at the most unexpected times, sometimes exasperatingly so, but at other times with highly welcome ingenuity, outsmarting the bad guys. Now if only it didn't sound so smug, particularly when it wins at poker. . . .

Their first adventure, between these covers as "The Trouble Twisters," finds Poul Anderson having some more fun with space opera stereotypes, much as he did with *The Man Who Counts* (included in *The van Rijn Method*). This time, it's the intrepid space-farer who has to rescue a woman (human, that is) from pursuing alien bad guys. The whole thing is straight out of the stories that writers for *Planet Stories* (and Anderson was a frequent contributor to that marvelous pulp magazine) wrote with a straight face. This time the author has his tongue at least in the vicinity of his cheek, and even Falkayn comments, "No. . . . Such things don't happen." The author gives a solid reason for finding a human damsel in distress on an alien planet, and there's just as much adventure as *Planet* could have boasted, plus a bit of humor. But that's enough from me—go read the story.

In fact, I should shut up now and say, "Go read the book." But I'll make a few more comments, beginning with "Day of Burning," which is a pivotal moment in the Technic Civilization universe. A planet is menaced by a nearby supernova, and the Polesotechnic League, with Falkayn's trader team first on the scene, is going to help the planet's race as much as possible to survive. But no good deed goes unpunished, and not only do things get dangerously complicated for a member of the team, but the planet happens to be Merseia. And centuries later, Dominic Flandry and the Terran Empire would have ample reason to regret that good deed.

Then, there's "The Master Key," which has van Rijn back on Earth, in the lap of comfort, while he listens to his agents describe *their* adventures on a troublesome planet. He listens to their story, takes in all the facts, then solves a mystery without getting out of his chair, making me wonder if perhaps centuries ago he might have had a similarly rotund ancestor whose name was Wolfe.

But, though he'd rather stay back on Earth while paying others to face danger and have adventures, it's not that kind of universe, and in the novel *Satan's World*, van Rijn and the trader team are together again for the first time, facing a menace not just to van Rijn's beloved profits, but to Earth itself.

And while they're both in action in the concluding novella in this volume, they're not really together. Dark times are coming, though the real darkness hasn't fallen yet (but it will in the third volume, *Rise of the Terran Empire*), and it's not always easy to stuff a genie back into the bottle. Poul Anderson's universes, that of the Polesotechnic League and Technic Civilization included, are places with love, joy and heroisms—but they are never cozy. The center may hold for a time, but never holds forever. The darkness is always lurking out there, waiting to descend. James Blish once noted Anderson's strong sense of tragedy: ". . . as a physicist, he knows that the entropy gradient goes inexorably in only one direction, and he wastes no time sniveling about it."

Neither do Anderson's heroes snivel. It's not a friendly universe, but those heroes and heroines do what they must, bringing forth light for a time and driving back the darkness in their corner of an uncaring cosmos. Even if they finally are defeated, they still fought the good fight. While Poul Anderson claimed no loftier status than a craftsman whose object was to entertain the audience—a role he fulfilled admirably—his SF often had a larger dimension; a dimension which is very much on display in the Technic Civilization saga.

The van Rijn Method made use of the introductory material that Poul Anderson had written for the stories appearing in the earlier collections *Trader to the Stars*, *The Trouble Twisters*, and *The Earth*

Book of Stormgate. This time, the novel had no introduction in any edition that I'm aware of, "The Master Key" was preceded by a quote from Shelley's poem "Hellas," and "Territory" was prefaced by an excerpt from the first van Rijn story, "Margin of Profit." Since "Margin of Profit" (the revised version) was included in *The van Rijn Method* (and the original, unrevised version was added as an appendix to the online version of the book), I was at first uncertain about including the excerpt, but finally decided that: (1) Poul Anderson had decided to include it back in 1964 and, being much more intelligent than I (and most other people), he must have had a good reason, (2) You don't *have* to read it, if you've read either or both of the full-length versions, (3) Even so, it won't *hurt* you to read it again, and (4) It doesn't add anything to the *cost* of the book. (When all other arguments fail, hit 'em in the wallet.)

As for three of the introductions, I'll reiterate (for the reader who hasn't read *The van Rijn Method*) that *The Earth Book of Stormgate* had introductions to its stories (and one novel) which were written as if by Hloch, a member of the winged race called Ythrians. And I'll add that, while the Ythrians are not represented as fully in this second volume as they were in the first, they will occupy a whole novel in the third. Stay tuned.

Finally, the story "Lodestar" has an introduction (by Hloch) and also an afterword by the author, which was originally a foreword when it first appeared in an anthology of all-original stories. The anthology was called *Astounding*, edited by Harry Harrison, and subtitled *John W. Campbell Memorial Anthology.* Unfortunately, almost four decades after John W. Campbell's death, it's possible that some readers may not know who he was. This is not the place for a complete treatment of the man who was *the* pivotal figure in SF in the 1940s, editing *Astounding Science Fiction* (later and presently, *Analog*), the leading magazine in the field, raising the standards for sf almost overnight and discovering writers who would become titans of the field, such as Heinlein, Sturgeon, Asimov—and, a few years later, Anderson. While the afterword doesn't add much to our understanding of the Technic Civilization series, it does have a touching anecdote, it indicates that Poul Anderson was considering writing no more Polesotechnic League stories after "Lodestar" (but apparently changed his mind, fortunately), and it emphasizes that the series might have been *much* shorter, except for Campbell's liking for the Polesotechnic League stories. Thank you, Mr. Campbell.

And thank *you*, Mr. Anderson.

—Hank Davis, 2008

A HISTORICAL REFLECTION

It is a truism that the structure of a society is basically determined by its technology. Not in an absolute sense—there may be totally different cultures using identical tools—but the tools settle the possibilities: you can't have interstellar trade without spaceships. A race limited to one planet, possessing a high knowledge of mechanics but with all its basic machines of commerce and war requiring a large capital investment, will inevitably tend toward collectivism under one name or another. Free enterprise needs elbow room.

Automation made manufacturing cheap, and the cost of energy nose-dived when the proton converter was invented. Gravity control and the hyperdrive opened a galaxy to exploitation. They also provided a safety valve: a citizen who found his government oppressive could usually emigrate elsewhere, which strengthened the libertarian planets; their influence in turn loosened the bonds of the older world.

Interstellar distances being what they are, and intelligent races all having their own ideas of culture, there was no universal union. Neither was there much war: too destructive, with small chance for either side to escape ruin, and too little to fight about. A race doesn't get to be intelligent without an undue share of built-in ruthlessness, so all was not sweetness and brotherhood—but the balance of power remained fairly stable. And there was a brisk demand for trade goods. Not only did colonies want the luxuries of home, and the home planets want colonial produce, but the old worlds themselves had much to swap.

Under such conditions, an exuberant capitalism was bound to strike root. It was also bound to find mutual interests, to form alliances, and settle spheres of influence. The powerful companies joined together to squeeze out competition, jack up prices, and generally make the best of a good thing. Governments were limited to a few planetary systems each, at most; they could do little to control their cosmopolitan merchants. One by one, through bribery, coercion, or sheer despair, they gave up the attempt.

Selfishness is a potent force. Governments, officially dedicated to altruism, remained divided; the Polesotechnic League became a super-government, sprawling from Canopus to Polaris, drawing its membership from a thousand species. It was a horizontal society, cutting across all political and cultural boundaries. It set its own policies, made its own treaties, established its own bases, fought its own minor wars—and, in the course of milking the Milky Way, did more to spread a truly universal civilization and enforce a lasting *Pax* than all the diplomats in the galaxy.

But it had its troubles.

—"Margin of Profit"

TERRITORY

Joyce Davisson awoke as if she had been stabbed.

The whistle came again, strong enough to penetrate mortar and metal and insulation, on into her eardrums. She sat up in the dark with a gasp of recognition. When last she heard that wildcat wail, it was in the Chabanda, and it meant that two bands were hunting each other. But then she had been safely aloft in a flitter, armed men on either side of her and a grave Ancient for guide. What she saw and heard came to her amplified by instruments that scanned the ice desert glittering beneath. Those tiger-striped warriors who slew and died were only figures in a screen. She had felt sorry for them, yet somehow they were not quite real: individuals only, whom she had never met, atoms that perished because their world was perishing. Her concern was with the whole.

Now the whistle was against her station.

It couldn't be!

An explosion went *crump.* She heard small things rattle on her desk top and felt her bed shaken. Suddenly the glissandos were louder in her head, and a snarl of drumtaps accompanied them, a banging on metal and a crashing as objects were knocked off shelves. The attackers must have blown down the door of the machine section and swarmed through. Only where could they have gotten the gunpowder?

Where but in Kusulongo the City?

That meant the Ancients had decided the humans were better killed. The fear of death went through Joyce in a wave. It passed on, leaving bewilderment and pain, as if she were a child struck for no reason. Why had they done this to her, who came for nothing but to help them?

Feet pounded in the hall just outside the Terrestrialized section of the dome. The mission's native staff had roused and were coming out of their quarters with weapons to hand. She heard savage yells. Then, farther off among the machines, combat broke loose. Swords clattered, tomahawks cracked on bone, the pistol she had given Uulobu spoke with an angry snap. But her gang couldn't hold out long. The attackers had to be Shanga, from the camp in the oasis just under Kusulongo the Mountain. No other clan was near, and the Ancients themselves never fought aggressively. But there were hundreds of male Shanga in the oasis, while the mission had scarcely two dozen trustworthy t'Kelans.

Heavily armored against exterior conditions, the human area would not be entered as easily as the outside door of the machine section had been destroyed. But once the walls were cracked—

Joyce bounded to her feet. One hand passed by the main switch plate on its way to her gear rack, and the lights came on. The narrow, cluttered room, study as well as sleeping place, looked somehow distorted in that white glow. Because I'm scared, she realized. I'm caught in a living nightmare. Nerve and muscle carried on without her mind. She leaped into the form-fitting Long John and the heavy fabricoid suit. Drawing the skin-thin gloves over her hands, she connected their wiring to the electric net woven into the main outfit. Now: kerofoam-soled boots; air renewal tank and powerpack on the back; pistol and bandolier; pouched belt of iron rations; minicom in breast pocket; vitryl helmet snugged down on the shoulders but face-plate left open for the time being.

Check all fasteners, air system, heat system, everything. The out-doors is lethal on t'Kela. The temperature, on this summer night in the middle latitudes, is about sixty degrees below zero Celsius. The partial pressure of nitrogen will induce narcosis, the ammonia will burn out your lungs. There is no water vapor that your senses can detect; the air will suck you dry. None of these factors differ enough from Earth to kill you instantly. No, aided by an oxygen content barely sufficient to maintain your life, you will savor the process for minutes before you even lose consciousness.

And the Shanga out there, now busily killing your native assistants, have gunpowder to break down these walls.

Joyce whirled about. The others! There was no intercom; two dozen people in one dome didn't need any. She snatched at the door of the room adjoining hers. Nothing happened. "Open up, you idiot!" she heard herself scream above the noise outside. "Come along! We've got to get away—"

A hoarse basso answered through the panels, "What you mean, open up? You locked yourself in, by damn!"

Of course, of course, Joyce's mind fumbled. Her pulse and the swelling racket of battle nearly drowned thought. She'd fastened this door on her own side. During her time with the mission itself, there had never been any reason to do so. But then Nicholas van Rijn landed, and got himself quartered next to her, and she had enough trouble by day fending off his ursine advances . . . She pushed the switch.

The merchant rolled through. Like most Esperancians, Joyce was tall, but she did not come up to his neck. His shoulders filled the doorway and his pot belly strained the fabricoid suit that had been issued him. Hung about with survival equipment, he looked still more monstrous than he had done when snorting his way around the dome in snuff-stained finery of lace and ruffles. The great hooked nose jutted from an open helmet, snuffing the air as if for a scent of blood.

"Hah!" he bawled. Greasy black hair, carefully ringleted to shoulder length, swirled as he looked from side to side; the waxed mustache and goatee threatened every corner like horns. "What in the name of ten times ten to the tenth damned souls on a logarithmic spiral to hell is going on here for fumblydiddles? I thought, me, you had any-hows the trust of those natives!"

"The others—" Joyce choked. "Come on, let's get together with them."

Van Rijn nodded curtly, so that his several chins quivered, and let her take the lead. Personal rooms in the human section faced the same corridor, each with a door opening onto that as well as onto its two neighbors. Joyce's room happened to be at the end of the row, with the machine storage section on its farther side. Unmarried and fond of privacy, she had chosen that arrangement when she first came here. The clubroom was at the hall's other terminus, around the curve of the dome. As she emerged from her quarters, Joyce saw door after door gaping open. The only ones still closed belonged to chambers which nobody occupied, extras built in the anticipation of outside visitors like van Rijn's party. So everyone else had already gotten into their suits and down to the clubroom, the fixed emergency rendezvous. She broke into a run. van Rijn's ponderous jog trot made a small earthquake behind her. Gravity on t'Kela was about the same as on Earth or Esperance.

The only thing that's the same, Joyce thought wildly. For an instant she was nearly blinded by the recollection of her home on the green planet of the star called Pax—a field billowing with grain, remote blue mountains, the flag of the sovereign world flying red and gold against a fleecy sky, and that brave dream which had built the Commonalty.

It roared at her back. The floor heaved underfoot. As she fell, the boom came again, and yet again. The third explosion pierced through. A hammerblow of concussion followed.

Striking the floor, she rolled over. Her head rattled from side to side of her helmet. The taste of blood mixed with smoke in her mouth. She looked back down the corridor through ragged darknesses that came and went before her eyes. The wall at the end, next to her own room, was split and broken. Wild shadowy figures moved in the gloom beyond the twisted structural members.

"They blew it open," she said stupidly.

"Close your helmet," van Rijn barked. He had already clashed his own faceplate to. The amplifier brought her his gravelly tones, but a dullness would not let them through to her brain.

"They blew it open," she repeated. The thing seemed too strange to be real.

A native leaped into the breach. He could stand Terrestrial air and temperature for a while if he held his breath. And t'Kelan atmosphere, driven by a higher pressure, was already streaming past him. The stocky, striped figure poised in a tension like that of the strung bow he aimed. Huge slit-pupiled eyes glared in the light from the fluoros.

An Esperancian technician came running around the bend of the corridor. "Joyce!" he cried. "Freeman van Rijn! Where—" The bow twanged. A barbed arrowhead ripped his suit. A moment afterward the air seemed full of arrows, darts, spears, hurled from the murk. Van Rijn threw himself across Joyce. The technician spun on his heel and fled.

Van Rijn's well-worn personal blaster jumped into his fist. He fired from his prone position. The furry shape in the breach tumbled backward. The shadows behind withdrew from sight. But the yell and clatter went on out there.

A first ammoniacal whiff stung Joyce's nostrils. "Pox and pestilence," van Rijn growled. "You like maybe to breathe that dragon belch?" He rose to his knees and closed her faceplate. His little black close-set eyes regarded her narrowly. "So, stunned, makes that the way of it? Well, hokay, you is a pretty girl with a nice figure and stuff even if you should not cut your hair so short. Waste not, want not. I rescue you, ha?"

He dragged her across one shoulder, got up, and backed wheezily along the hall, his blaster covering the direction of the hole. "Ugh, ugh," he muttered, "this is not a job for a poor old fat man who should be at home in his nice office on Earth with a cigar and maybe a wee glass Genever. The more so when those misbegotten snouthearts he must use for help will rob him blind. *Ja,* unscrew his eyeballs they will, so soon as he isn't looking. But all the factors at all the trading posts are such gruntbrains that poor Nicholas van Rijn must come out his own selfs, a hundred light-years in the direction of Orion's bellybutton he must come, and look for new trading possibilities. Else the wolves-with-rabies competition tears his Solar Spice & Liquors Company in shreds and leaves him prostitute in his old age . . . Ah, here we is. Downsy-daisy."

Joyce shook her head as he eased her to the floor. Full awareness had come back, and her knees didn't wobble much. The clubroom door was in front of her. She pushed the switch. The barrier didn't move. "Locked," she said.

Van Rijn pounded till it shivered. "Open up!" he bellowed. "Thunder and thighbones, what is this farce?"

A native raced around the curve of the hall. Van Rijn turned. Joyce shoved his blaster aside. "No, that's Uulobu." The t'Kelan must have exhausted his pistol and thrown it away, for a tomahawk now dripped in his hand. Three other autochthones bounded after him, swords and hatchets aloft. Their kilts were decorated with the circle-and-square insigne of the Shanga clan. "Get them!"

Van Rijn's blaster spat fire. One of the invaders flopped over. The others whirled to escape. Uulobu yowled and threw his tomahawk. The keen obsidian edge struck a Shanga and knocked him down, bleeding. Uulobu yanked the cord that ran between his weapon and wrist, retrieved the ax, and threw it again to finish the job.

Van Rijn returned to the door. "You termite-bitten cowards, let us in!" As his language got bluer, Joyce realized what must have happened. She pounded his back with her fists, much as he was pounding the door, until he stopped and looked around.

"They wouldn't abandon us," Joyce said. "But they must think we've been killed. When Carlos saw us, back there in the hall, we were both lying on the floor, and there were so many missiles . . . They aren't in the clubroom any longer. They locked the door to delay the enemy while they took a different way to the spaceships."

"Ah, *ja, ja,* must be. But what do we do now? Blast through the door to follow?"

Uulobu spoke in the guttural language of the Kusulongo region. "All of us are slain or fled, sky-female. No more battle. The noise you hear now is the Shanga plundering. If they find us, they will fill us with arrows. Two guns cannot stop that. But I think if we go back among the iron-that-moves, we can slip out that way and around the dome."

"What's he besputtering about?" van Rijn asked.

Joyce translated. "I think he's right," she added. "Our best chance is to leave through the machine section. It seems deserted for the time being. But we'd better hurry."

"So. Let this pussycat fellow go ahead, then. You stay by me and cover my back, *nie?*"

They trotted back the way they had come. Hoarfrost whitened the walls and made the floor slippery, as water vapor condensed in the t'Kelan cold. The breach into the unlighted machine section gaped like a black mouth. Remotely through walls, Joyce heard ripping, smashing, and exultant shouts. The work of years was going to pieces around her. *Why?* she asked in pain, and got no answer.

Uulobu's eyes, more adaptable to dark than any human's, probed among bulky shapes as they entered the storage area. Vehicles were parked here: four groundcars and as many flitters. In addition, this long chamber housed the specialized equipment of the studies the Esperancians had made, seeking a way to save the planet. Most lay in wreckage on the floor.

An oblong of dim light, up ahead, was the doorway to the outside. Joyce groped forward. Her boot struck something, a fallen instrument. It clanked against something else.

There came a yammer of challenge. The entrance filled with a dozen shapes. They whipped through and lost themselves among shadows and machines before van Rijn could fire. Uulobu hefted his tomahawk and drew his knife. "Now we must fight for our passage," he said unregretfully.

"Cha-a-a-arge!" van Rijn led the way at a run. Several t'Kelans closed in on him. Metal and polished stone whirled in the murk. The Earthman's blaster flared. A native screamed. Another native got hold of the gun arm and dragged it downward. Van Rijn tried to shake him loose. The being hung on, though the human clubbed him back and forth against his fellows.

Uulobu joined the ruckus, stabbing and hacking with carnivore glee. Joyce could not do less. She had her own pistol out, a slugthrower. Something bumped into the muzzle. Fangs and eyes gleamed at her in what light there was. A short spear poised, fully able to pierce her suit. Even so, she had never done anything harder than to pull the trigger. The crack of the gun resounded in her own skull.

Then for a while it was jostling, scrabbling, firing, falling, and wrestling lunacy. Now and again Joyce recognized Uulobu's screech, the battle cry of his Avongo clan. Van Rijn's voice sounded above the din like a trumpeted, "St. Dismas help us! Down with mangy dogs!" Suddenly it was over. The guns had been too much. She lay on the floor, struggling for breath, and heard the last few Shanga run out. Somewhere a wounded warrior groaned, until Uulobu cut his throat.

"Up with you," van Rijn ordered between puffs. "We got no time for making rings around the rosies."

Uulobu helped her rise. He was too short to lean on very well, but van Rijn offered her an arm. They staggered out of the door, into the night.

There was no compound here, only the dome and then t'Kela

itself. Overhead glittered unfamiliar constellations. The larger moon was aloft, nearly full, throwing dim coppery light on the ground. West and south stretched a rolling plain, thinly begrown with shrubs not unlike Terrestrial sagebrush in appearance: low, wiry, silvery-leaved. Due north rose the sheer black wall of Kusulongo the Mountain, jagged against the Milky Way. The city carved from its top could be seen only as a glimpse of towers like teeth. Some kilometers eastward, at its foot, ran the sacred Mangivolo River. Joyce could see a red flash of moonlight on liquid ammonia. The trees of that oasis where the Shanga were camped made a blot of shadow. The hills that marched northward from Kusulongo gleamed with ice, an unreal sheen.

"Hurry," van Rijn grated. "If the other peoples think we are dead, they will raise ship more fast than we can."

His party rounded the dome at the reeling pace of exhaustion. Two tapered cylinders shimmered under the moon, the mission's big cargo vessel and the luxury yacht which had brought van Rijn and his assistants from Earth. A couple of dead Shanga lay nearby. The night wind ruffled their fur. It had been a fight to reach safety here. Now the ramps were retracted and the air locks shut. As van Rijn neared, the whine of engines shivered forth.

"Hey!" he roared. "You clabberbrains, wait for me!"

The yacht took off first, hitting the sky like a thunderbolt. The backwash of air bowled van Rijn over. Then the Esperancian craft got under way The edge of her drive field caught van Rijn, picked him up, and threw him several meters. He landed with a crash and lay still.

Joyce hurried to him. "Are you all right?" she choked. He was a detestable old oaf, but the horror of being marooned altogether alone seized upon her.

"Oo-oo-oo," he groaned. "St. Dismas, I was going to put a new stained-glass window in your chapel at home. Now I think I will kick in the ones you have got."

Joyce glanced upward. The spaceships flashed like rising stars, and vanished. "They didn't see us," she said numbly.

"Tell me more," van Rijn snorted.

Uulobu joined them. "The Shanga will have heard," he said. "They will come out here to make sure, and find us. We must escape."

Van Rijn didn't need that translated. Shaking himself gingerly, as if afraid something would drop off, he crawled to his feet and lurched back toward the dome. "We get a flitter, *nie?*" he said.

"The groundcars are stocked for a much longer period," Joyce answered. "And we'll have to survive until someone comes back here."

"With the pest-riddled planeteezers chasing us all the while," van Rijn muttered. "Joy forever, unconfined!"

"We go west, we find my people," Uulobu said. "I do not know where the Avongo are, but other clans of the Rokulela Horde must surely be out between the Narrow Land and the Barrens."

They entered the machine section. Joyce stumbled on a body and shuddered. Had she killed that being herself?

The groundcars were long and square-built; the rear four of the eight wheels ran on treads. The accumulators were fully charged, energy reserve enough to drive several thousand rough kilometers and maintain Earth-type conditions inside for a year. There were air recyclers and sufficient food to keep two humans going at least four months. Six bunks, cooking and sanitary facilities, maps, navigation equipment, a radio transceiver, spare parts for survival gear—everything was there. It had to be, when you traveled on a planet like this.

Van Rijn heaved his bulk through the door, which was not locked, and settled himself in the driver's seat. Joyce collapsed beside him. Uulobu entered with uneasy eyes and quivering whiskers. Only the Ancients, among t'Kelans, liked riding inside a vehicle. That was no problem, though, Joyce recalled dully. On field trips, once you had established a terrestroid environment within, your guides and guards rode on top of the car, talking with you by intercom. Thus many kilometers had been covered, and much had been learned, and the plans had been drawn that would save a world . . . and now!

Van Rijn's ham hands moved deftly over the controls. "In my company we use Landmasters," he said. "I like not much these Globetrotters. But sometimes our boys have to—um—borrow one from the competition, so we know how to . . . Ah." The engine purred to life. He moved out through the door, riding the field drive at its one-meter ceiling instead of using the noisier wheels.

But he could have saved his trouble. Other doors in the dome were spewing forth Shanga. There must be a hundred of them, Joyce thought. Van Rijn's lips skinned back from his teeth. "You want to play happy fun games yet, ha?" He switched on the headlights.

A warrior was caught in the glare, dazzled by it so that he stood motionless, etched against blackness. Joyce's eyes went over him, back and forth, as if something visible could explain why he had turned on her. He was a typical t'Kelan of this locality; races varied elsewhere, as on most planets, but no more than among humans.

The stout form was about 150 centimeters tall, heavily steatopygous to store as much liquid as the drying land afforded. Hands and feet were nearly manlike, except for having thick blue nails and only four digits apiece. The fur that covered the whole body was a vivid orange, striped with black, a triangle of white on the chest. The head was round, with pointed ears and enormous yellow cat-eyes, two fleshy tendrils on the forehead, a single nostril crossing the broad nose, a lipless mouth full of sharp white teeth framed in restless cilia. This warrior carried a sword—the bladelike horn of a *gondyanga* plus a wooden handle—and a circular shield painted in the colors of the Yagola Horde to which the Shanga clan belonged.

"Beep, beep!" van Rijn said. He gunned the car forward.

The warrior sprang aside, barely in time. Others tried to attack. Joyce glimpsed one with a bone piston whistle in his mouth. The Yagola never used formal battle cries, but advanced to music. A couple of spears clattered against the car sides. Then van Rijn was through, bounding away at a hundred KPH with a comet's tail of dust behind.

"Where we go now?" he demanded. "To yonder town on the mountain? You said they was local big cheeses."

"The Ancients? No!" Joyce stiffened. "They must be the ones who caused this."

"Ha? Why so?"

"I don't know, I don't know. They were so helpful before . . . But it has to be them. They incited . . . No one else could have. W—we never made any enemies among the clans. As soon as we had their biochemistry figured out, we synthesized medicines and—and helped them—" Joyce found suddenly that she could cry. She leaned her helmet in her hands and let go all emotional holds.

"There, there, everything's hunky-dunky," van Rijn said. He patted her shoulder. "You been a brave girl, as well as pretty. Go on, now, relax, have fun."

✲ ✲ ✲

T'Kela rotated once in thirty hours and some minutes, with eight degrees of axial tilt. Considerable night remained when the car stopped, a hundred kilometers from Kusulongo, and the escapers made camp. Uulobu took a sleeping bag outside while the others Earth-conditioned the interior, shucked their suits, and crawled into bunks. Not even van Rijn's snores kept Joyce awake.

Dawn roused her. The red sun climbed from the east with a glow like dying coals. Though its apparent diameter was nearly half again that of Sol seen from Earth or Pax from Esperance, the light was dull to human eyes, shadows lay thick in every dip and gash, and the horizon was lost in darkness. The sky was deep purple, cloudless, but filled to the south with the yellow plumes of a dust storm. Closer by, the plain stretched bare, save for sparse gray vegetation, strewn boulders, a coldly shimmering ice field not far northward. One scavenger fowl wheeled overhead on leathery-feathered wings.

Joyce sat up. Her whole body ached. Remembering what had happened made such an emptiness within that she hardly noticed. She wanted to roll over in the blankets, bury her head, and sleep again. Sleep till rescue came, if it ever did.

She made herself rise, go into the bath cubicle, wash, and change into slacks and blouse. With refreshment came hunger. She returned to the main body of the car and began work at the cooker.

The smell of coffee wakened van Rijn. "Ahhh!" Whalelike in the long john he hadn't bothered to remove, he wallowed from his bunk and snatched at a cup. "Good girl." He sniffed suspiciously. "But no brandy in it? After our troubles, we need brandy."

"No liquor here," she snapped.

"*What?*" For a space the merchant could only goggle at her. His jowls turned puce. His mustaches quivered. "Nothings to drink?" he strangled. "Why—why—why, this is extrarageous. Who's responsible? By damn, I see to it he's blacklisted from here to Polaris!"

"We have coffee, tea, powdered milk and fruit juices," Joyce said. "We get water from the ice outside. The chemical unit removes ammonia and other impurities. One does not take up storage space out in the field with liquor, Freeman van Rijn."

"One does if one is civilized. Let me see your food stocks." He rummaged in the nearest locker. "Dried meat, dried vegetables, dried—Death and destruction!" he wailed. "Not so much as one jar caviar? You want me to crumble away?"

"You might give thanks you're alive."

"Not under this condition. . . . Well, I see somebody had one brain cell still functional and laid in some cigarettes." Van Rijn grabbed a handful and crumbled them into a briar pipe he had stuffed in his bosom. He lit it. Joyce caught a whiff, gagged, and returned to work at the cooker, banging the utensils about with more ferocity than was needful.

Seated at the folding table next to one of the broad windows, van Rijn crammed porridge down his gape and peered out at the dim landscape. "Whoof, what a place. Like hell with the furnaces on the fritz. How long you been here, anyways?"

"Myself, about a year, as a biotechnician." She decided it was best to humor him. "Of course, the Esperancian mission has been operating for several years."

"*Ja,* that I know. Though I am not sure just how. I was only here a couple of days, you remember, before the trouble started. And any planet is so big and complicated a thing, takes long to understand it even a little. Besides, I had some other work along I must finish before investigating the situation here."

"I admit being puzzled why you came. You deal in spices and things, don't you? But there's nothing here that a human would like. We could digest some of the proteins and other biological compounds—they aren't all poisonous to us—but they lack things we need, like certain amino acids, and they taste awful."

"My company trades with nonhumans too," van Rijn explained. "Not long ago, my research staff at home came upon the original scientific reports, from the expedition who found this planet fifteen years ago. This galaxy is so big no one can keep track of everything while it happens. Always we are behind. But anyhows, was mention of some wine that the natives grow."

"Yes, *kungu.* Most of the clans in this hemisphere make it. They raise the berries along with some other plants that provide fiber. Not that they're farmers. A carnivorous race, nomadic except for the Ancients. But they'll seed some ground and come back in time to harvest it."

"Indeed. Well, as you know, the first explorers here was from

Throra, which is a pretty similar planet to this only not so ugh. They thought the *kungu* was delicious. They even wanted to take seeds home, but found because of ecology and stuffs, the plant will only grow on this world. Ah-ha, thought Nicholas van Rijn, a chance maybe to build up a very nice little trade with Throra. So because of not having nobody worth trusting that was on Earth to be sent here, I came in my personals to see. Oh, how bitter to be so lonely!" Van Rijn's mouth drooped in an attempt at pathos. One hairy hand stole across the table and closed on Joyce's.

"Here comes Uulobu," she exclaimed, pulling free and jumping to her feet. In the very nick of time, bless both his hearts! she thought.

The t'Kelan loped swiftly across the plain. A small animal that he had killed was slung across his shoulders. He was clad differently from the Shanga: in the necklace of fossil shells and the loosely woven blue kilt of his own Avongo clan and Rokulela Horde. A leather pouch at his waist had been filled with liquid.

"I see he found an ammonia well," Joyce chattered, brightly and somewhat frantically, for van Rijn was edging around the table toward her. "That's what they have those tendrils for, did you know? Sensitive to any trace of ammonia vapor. This world is so dry. Lots of frozen water, of course. You find ice everywhere you go on the planet. Very often hundreds of square kilometers at a stretch. You see, the maximum temperature here is forty below zero Celsius. But ice doesn't do the indigenous life any good. In fact, it's one of the things that are killing this world."

Van Rijn grumped and moved to the window. Uulobu reached the car and said into the intercom, "Sky-female, I have found spoor of hunters passing by, headed west toward the Lubambaru. They can only be Rokulela. I think we can find them without great trouble. Also I have quenched my thirst and gotten meat for my hunger. Now I must offer the Real Ones a share."

"Yes, do so for all of us," Joyce answered.

Uulobu began gathering sticks for a fire. "What he say?" van Rijn asked. Joyce translated. "So. What use to us, making league with savages out here? We only need to wait for rescue."

"If it comes," Joyce said. She shivered. "When they hear about this at Esperance, they'll send an expedition to try and learn what went wrong. But not knowing we're alive, they may not hurry it enough."

"My people will," van Rijn assured her. "The Polesotechnic League looks after its own, by damn. So soon as word gets to Earth, a warship comes for full investigation. Inside a month."

"Oh, wonderful," Joyce breathed. She went limp and sat down again.

Van Rijn scowled. "Natural," he ruminated, "they cannot search a whole planet. They will know I was at that bestinkered Kusulongo place, and land there. I suppose those Oldsters or Seniles or whatever you call them is sophisticated enough by now in interstellar matters to fob the crew off with some story, if we are not nearby to make contact. So . . . we must remain in their area, in radio range. And radio range has to be pretty close on a red dwarf's planet, where ionosphere characteristicals are poor. But close to our enemies we cannot come so well, if they are whooping after us the whole time. They can dig traps or throw crude bombs or something . . . one way or other, they can kill us even in this car. Ergo, we must establish ourselves as too strong to attack, in the very neighborhood of Kusulongo. This means we need allies. So you have right, we must certain go along to your friend's peoples."

"But you can't make them fight their own race!" Joyce protested.

Van Rijn twirled his mustache. "Can't I just?" he grinned.

"I mean . . . I don't know how, in any practical sense . . . but even if you could, it would be wrong."

"Um-m-m." He regarded her for a while. "You Esperancers is idealists, I hear. Your ancestors settled your planet for a Utopian community, and you is still doing good for everybody even at this low date, *nie?* Your mission to help this planet here was for no profit, except it makes you feel good . . ."

"And as a matter of foreign policy," Joyce admitted, under the honesty fetish of her culture. "By assisting other races, we gain their goodwill and persuade them, a little, to look at things our way. If Esperance has enough such friends, we'll be strong and influential without having to maintain armed services."

"From what I see, I doubt very much you ever make nice little vestrymen out of these t'Kelans."

"Well . . . true . . . they *are* out-and-out carnivores. But then, man started as a carnivorous primate, didn't he? And the t'Kelans in this area did achieve an agricultural civilization once, thousands of years ago. That is, grain was raised to feed meat animals. Kusulongo the City is the last remnant. The ice age wiped it out otherwise, leaving savagery—barbarism at most. But given improved conditions, I'm sure the autochthones could recreate it. They'll never have unified nations or anything, as we understand such things. They aren't gregarious enough. But they could develop a world order and adopt machine technology."

"Except, from what you tell me, those snakes squatting on top of the mountain don't want that."

Joyce paused only briefly to wonder how a snake could squat, before she nodded. "I guess so. Though I can't understand why. The Ancients were so helpful at first."

"Means they need to have some sense beaten into their skull-bones. Hokay, so for the sake of t'Kela's long-range good, we arrange to do the beating, you and I."

"Well . . . maybe . . . but still . . ."

Van Rijn patted her head. "You just leave the philosophizings to me, little girl," he said smugly. "You only got to cook and look beautiful."

Uulobu had lit his fire and thrown the eyeballs of his kill onto it. His chant to his gods wailed eerily through the car wall. Van Rijn clicked his tongue. "Not so promising materials, that," he said. "You civilize them if you can. I am content to get home unpunctured by very sharp-looking spears, me." He rekindled his pipe and sat down beside her. "To do this, I must understand the situation. Suppose you explain. Some I have heard before, but no harm to repeat." He patted her knee. "I can always admire your lips and things while you talk."

Joyce got up for another cup of coffee and reseated herself at a greater distance. She forced an impersonal tone.

"Well, to begin with, this is a very unusual planet. Not physically. I mean, there's nothing strange about a type M dwarf star having a planet at a distance of half an A.U., with a mass about forty percent greater than Earth's."

"So much? Must be low density, then. Metal-poor."

"Yes. The sun is extremely old. Fewer heavy atoms were available at the time it formed with its planets. T'Kela's overall specific gravity is only four-point-four. It does have some iron and copper, of course . . . As I'm sure you know, life gets started slowly on such worlds. Their suns emit so little ultraviolet, even in flare periods, that the primordial organic materials aren't energized to interact very fast. Nevertheless, life does start eventually, in oceans of liquid ammonia."

"*Ja.* And usual goes on to develop photosynthesis using ammonia and carbon dioxide, to make carbohydrates and the nitrogen that the animals breathe." Van Rijn tapped his sloping forehead. "So much I have even in this dumb old bell. But why does evolution go different now and then, like on here and Throra?"

"Nobody knows for sure. Some catalytic agent, perhaps. In any event, even at low temperatures like these, all the water isn't solid. A certain amount is present in the oceans, as part of the ammonium hydroxide molecule. T'Kelan or Throran plant cells have an analogue of chlorophyll, which does the same job: using gaseous carbon dioxide and 'dissolved' water to get carbohydrates and free oxygen. The animals reverse the process, much as they do on Earth. But the water they release isn't exhaled. It remains in their tissues, loosely held by a specialized molecule. When an organism dies and decays, this water is taken up by plants again. In other words, H-two-O here acts very much like nitrogenous organic material on our kind of planets."

"But the oxygen the plants give off, it attacks ammonia."

"Yes. The process is slow, especially since solid ammonia is denser than the liquid phase. It sinks to the bottom of lakes and oceans, which protects it from the air. Nevertheless, there is a gradual conversion. Through a series of steps, ammonia and oxygen yield free nitrogen and water. The water freezes out. The seas shrink; the air becomes poorer in oxygen; the desert areas grow."

"This I know from Throra. But there a balance was struck. Nitrogen-fixing bacteria evolved and the drying-out was halted, a billion years ago. So they told me once."

"Throra was lucky. It's a somewhat bigger planet than t'Kela, isn't it? Denser atmosphere, therefore more heat conservation. The greenhouse effect on such worlds depends on carbon dioxide and ammonia vapor. Well, several thousand years ago, t'Kela passed a critical point. Just enough ammonia was lost to reduce the greenhouse effect sharply. As the temperature fell, more and more liquid ammonia turned solid and went to the bottom, where it's also quite well protected against melting. This made the climatic change catastrophically sudden. Temperatures dropped so low that now carbon dioxide also turns liquid, or even solid, through part of the year. There's still some vapor in the atmosphere, in equilibrium, but very little. The greenhouse effect *really* dropped off!

"Plant life was gravely affected, as you can imagine. It can't grow without carbon dioxide and ammonia to build its tissues. Animal life died out with it. Areas the size of a Terrestrial continent became utterly barren, almost overnight. I told you that the native agricultural civilization was wiped out. Worse, though, we've learned from geology that the nitrogen-fixing bacteria were destroyed. Completely. They couldn't survive the winter temperatures. So there's no longer any force to balance the oxidation of ammonia. The deserts encroach everywhere, year by year . . . and t'Kela's year is only six-tenths Standard. Evolution has worked hard, adapting life to the change, but the pace is now too rapid for it. We estimate that all higher animals, including the natives, will be extinct within another millennium. In ten thousand years there'll be nothing alive here."

Though she had lived with the realization for months, it still shook Joyce to talk about. She clamped fingers around her coffee cup till they hurt, stared out the window at drifting dust, and strove not to cry.

Van Rijn blew foul clouds of smoke a while in silence. Finally he rumbled almost gently, "But you have a cure program worked out, *ja?*"

"Oh . . . oh, yes. We do. The research is completed and we were about ready to summon engineers." She found comfort in proceeding.

"The ultimate solution, of course, is to reintroduce nitrogen-fixing bacteria. Our labs have designed an extremely productive strain. It will need a suitable ecology, though, to survive: which means a lot of work with soil chemistry, a microagricultural program. We can hasten everything—begin to show results in a decade—by less subtle methods. In fact, we'll have to do so, or the death process will outrun anything that bacteria can accomplish.

"What we'll do is melt and electrolyze water. The oxygen can be released directly into the air, refreshing it. But some will go to burn local hydrocarbons. T'Kela is rich in petroleum. This burning will generate carbon dioxide, thus strengthening the greenhouse effect. The chemical energy released can also supplement the nuclear power stations we'll install: to do the electrolysis and to energize the combination of hydrogen from water with nitrogen from the atmosphere, recreating ammonia."

"A big expensive job, that," van Rijn said.

"Enormous. The biggest thing Esperance has yet undertaken. But the plans and estimates have been drawn up. We know we can do it."

"If the natives don't go potshotting engineers for exercise after lunch."

"Yes." Joyce's blond head sank low. "That would make it impossible. We have to have the good will of all of them, everywhere. They'll have to cooperate, work with us and each other, in a planet-wide effort. And Kusulongo the City influences a quarter of the whole world! What have we done? I thought they were our friends . . ."

"Maybe we get some warriors and throw sharp things at them till they appreciate us," van Rijn suggested.

The car went swiftly, even over irregular ground. An hour or so after it had started again, Uulobu shouted from his seat on top. Through the overhead window the humans saw him lean across his windshield and point. Looking that way, they saw a dust cloud on the northwestern horizon, wider and lower than the one to the south. "Animals being herded," Uulobu said. "Steer thither, sky-folk."

Joyce translated and van Rijn put the control bar over. "I thought you said they was hunters only," he remarked. "Herds?"

"The Horde people maintain an economy somewhere between that of ancient Mongol cattlekeepers and Amerind bison-chasers," she explained. "They don't actually domesticate the *iziru* or the *bambalo.* They did once, before the glacial era, but now the land couldn't support such a concentration of grazers. The Hordes do still exercise some control over the migrations of the herds, though, cull them, and protect them from predators."

"Um-m-m. What are these Hordes, anyhows?"

"That's hard to describe. No human really understands it. Not that t'Kelan psychology is incomprehensible. But it is nonhuman, and our mission has been so busy gathering planetographical data that we never found time to do psychological studies in depth. Words like 'pride,' 'clan,' and 'Horde' are rough translations of native terms—not very accurate, I'm sure—just as t'Kela' is an arbitrary name of ours for the whole planet. It means 'this earth' in the Kusulongo language."

"Hokay, no need beating me over this poor old eggnoggin with the too-obvious. I get the idea. But look you, Freelady Davisson . . . I can call you Joyce?" van Rijn buttered his tones. "We is in the same boat, sink or swim together, except for having no water to do it in, so let us make friends, ha?" He leaned suggestively against her. "You call me Nicky."

She moved aside. "I cannot prevent your addressing me as you wish, Freeman van Rijn," she said in her frostiest voice.

"Heigh-ho, to be young and not so globulous again! But a lonely old man must swallow his sorrows." Van Rijn sighed like a self-pitying tornado. "Apropos swallowing, *why* is there not so much as one little case beer along? Just one case; one hour or maybe two of sips, to lay the sandstorms in this mummy gullet I got; is that so much to ask, I ask you?"

"Well, there isn't." She pinched her mouth together. They drove on in silence.

Presently they raised the herd: *iziru,* humpbacked and spike-tailed, the size of Terran cattle. Those numbered a few thousand, Joyce estimated from previous experience. With vegetation so sparse, they must needs spread across many kilometers.

A couple of natives had spied the car from a distance and came at a gallop. They rode *basai,* which looked not unlike large stocky antelope with tapir faces and a single long horn. The t'Kelans wore kilts similar to Uulobu's, but leather medallions instead of his shell necklace. Van Rijn stopped the car. The natives reined in. They kept weapons ready, a strung bow and a short throwing-spear.

Uulobu jumped off the top and approached them, hands out-spread. "Luck in the kill, strength, health, and offspring!" he wished them in the formal order of importance. "I am Tola's son Uulobu, Avongo, Rokulela, now a follower of the sky-folk."

"So I see," the older, grizzled warrior answered coldly. The young one grinned and put his bow away with an elaborate flourish.

Uulobu clapped hand to tomahawk. The older being made a somewhat conciliatory gesture and Uulobu relaxed a trifle.

Van Rijn had been watching intently. "Tell me what they say," he ordered. "Everything. Tell me what this means with their weapon foolishness."

"That was an insult the archer offered Uulobu," Joyce explained unhappily. "Disarming before the ceremonies of peace have been completed. It implies that Uulobu isn't formidable enough to be worth worrying about."

"Ah, so. These is rough peoples, them. Not even inside their own Hordes is peace taken for granted, ha? But why should they make nasty at Uulobu? Has he got no prestige from serving you?"

"I'm afraid not. I asked him about it once. He's the only t'Kelan I could ask about such things."

"*Ja?* How come that?"

"He's the closest to a native intimate that any of us in the mission have had. We saved him from a pretty horrible death, you see. We'd just worked out a cure for a local equivalent of tetanus when he caught the disease. So he feels gratitude toward us, as well as having an economic motive. All our regular assistants are—were impoverished, for one reason or another. A drought had killed off too much game in their territory, or they'd been dispossessed, or something like that." Joyce bit her lip. "They . . . they did swear us fealty . . . in the traditional manner . . . and you know how bravely they fought for us. But that was for the sake of their own honor. Uulobu is the only t'Kelan who's shown anything like real affection for humans."

"Odd, when you come here to help them. By damn, but you was a bunch of mackerel heads! You should have begun with depth psychology first of all. That fool planetography could wait . . . Rotten, stinking mackerel, glows blue in the dark . . ." Van Rijn's growl trailed into a mumble. He shook himself and demanded further translation.

"The old one is called Nyaronga, head of this pride," Joyce related. "The other is one of his sons, of course. They belong to the Gangu clan, in the same Horde as Uulobu's Avongo. The formalities have been concluded, and we're invited to share their camp. These people are hospitable enough, in their fashion . . . after bona fides has been established."

The riders dashed off. Uulobu returned. "They must hurry," he reported through the intercom. "The sun will brighten today, and cover is still a goodly ways off. Best we trail well behind so as not to stampede the animals, sky-female." He climbed lithely to the cartop. Joyce passed his words on as van Rijn got the vehicle started.

"One thing at a time, like the fellow said shaking hands with the octopus," the merchant decided. "You must tell me much, but we begin with going back to why the natives are not so polite to anybody who works for your mission."

"Well . . . as nearly as Uulobu could get it across to me, those who came to us were landless. That is, they'd stopped maintaining themselves in their ancestral hunting grounds. This means a tremendous loss of respectability. Then, too, he confessed—very bashfully—that our helpers' prestige suffered because we never involved them in any fights. The imputation grew up that they were cowards."

"A warlike culture, ha?"

"N-no. That's the paradox. They don't have wars, or even vendettas, in our sense. Fights are very small-scale affairs, though they happen constantly. I suppose that arises from the political organization. Or does it? We've noticed the same thing in remote parts of t'Kela, among altogether different societies from the Horde culture."

"Explain that, if you will be so kind as to make me a little four-decker sandwich while you talk."

Joyce bit back her annoyance and went to the cooker table. "As I said, we never did carry out intensive xenological research, even locally," she told him. "But we do know that the basic social unit is the same everywhere on this world, what we call the pride. It springs from the fact that the sex ratio is about three females to one male. Living together you have the oldest male, his wives, their offspring of subadult age. All males, and females unencumbered with infants, share in hunting, though only males fight other t'Kelans. The small—um—children help out in the work around camp. So do any widows of the leader's father that he's taken in. The size of such a pride ranges up to twenty or so. That's as many as can make a living in an area small enough to cover afoot, on this desert planet."

"I see. The t'Kelan pride answers to the human family. It is just as universal, too, right? I suppose larger units get organized in different ways, depending on the culture."

"Yes. The most backward savages have no organization larger than the pride. But the Kusulongo society, as we call it—the Horde people—the biggest and most advanced culture, spread over half the northern hemisphere—it has a more elaborate superstructure. Ten or twenty prides form what we call a clan, a cooperative group claiming descent from a common male ancestor, controlling a large territory through which they follow the wild herds. The clans in turn are loosely federated into Hordes, each of which holds an annual get-together in some traditional oasis. That's when they trade, socialize, arrange marriages—newly adult males get wives and start new prides—yes, and they adjudicate quarrels, by arbitration or combat, at such times. There's a lot of squabbling among clans, you see, over points of honor or practical matters like ammonia wells. One nearly always marries within one's own Horde; it has its own dress, customs, gods, and so forth."

"No wars between Hordes?" Van Rijn asked.

"No, unless you want to call the terrible things that happen during a *Völkerwanderung* a war. Normally, although individual units from different Hordes may clash, there isn't any organized campaigning. I suppose they simply haven't the economic surplus to maintain armies in the field."

"Um-m-m. I suspect, me, the reason goes deeper than that. When humans want to have wars, by damn, they don't let any little questions of if they can afford it stop them. I doubt t'Kelans would be any different. Um-m-m." Van Rijn's free hand tugged his goatee. "Maybe here is a key that goes tick-a-lock and solves our problem, if we know how to stick it in."

"Well," Joyce said, "the Ancients are also a war preventive. They settle most inter-Horde disputes, among other things."

"Ah, yes, those fellows on the mountain. Tell me about them."

Joyce finished making the sandwich and gave it to Van Rijn. He wolfed it noisily. She sat down and stared out at the scene: brush and boulders and swirling dust under the surly red light, the dark mass of the herd drifting along, a rider who galloped back to head off some stragglers. Far ahead now could be seen the Lubambaru, a range of ice, sharp peaks that shimmered against the crepuscular sky. Faintly to her, above the murmur of the engine, came yelps and the lowing of the animals. The car rocked and bumped; she felt the terrain in her bones.

"The Ancients are survivors of the lost civilization," she said. "They hung on in their city, and kept the arts that were otherwise forgotten. That kind of life doesn't come natural to most t'Kelans. I gather that in the course of thousands of years, those who didn't like it there wandered down to join the nomads, while occasional nomads who thought the city would be congenial went up and were adopted into the group. That would make for some genetic selection. The Ancients are a distinct psychological type. Much more reserved and . . . intellectual, I guess you'd call it . . . than anyone else."

"How they make their living?" Van Rijn asked around a mouthful.

"They provide services and goods for which they are paid in kind. They are scribes, who keep records; physicians; skilled metallurgists; weavers of fine textiles; makers of gunpowder, though they only sell fireworks and keep a few cannon for themselves. They're credited with magical powers, of course, especially because they can predict solar flares."

"And they was friendly until yesterday?"

"In their own aloof, secretive fashion. They must have been plotting the attack on us for some time, though, egging on the Shanga and furnishing the powder to blow open our dome. I still can't imagine why. I'm certain they believed us when we explained how we'd come to save their race from extinction."

"*Ja,* no doubt. Only maybe at first they did not see all the implications." Van Rijn finished eating, belched, picked his teeth with a fingernail, and relapsed into brooding silence. Joyce tried not to be too desperately homesick.

After a long time, van Rijn smote the control board so that it rang. "By damn!" he bellowed. "It fits together!"

"What?" Joyce sat straight.

"But I still can't see how to use it," he said.

"What do you mean?"

"Shut up, Freelady." He returned to his thoughts. The slow hours passed.

Late in the afternoon, a forest hove into sight. It covered the foothills of the Lubambaru, where an ammonia river coursed thinly and seepage moistened the soil a little. The trees were low and gnarled, with thorny blue trunks and a dense foliage of small greenish-gray leaves. Tall shrubs sprouted in thickets between them. The riders urged their *iziru* into the wood, posted a few pickets to keep watch, and started northward in a compact group, fifteen altogether, plus pack animals and a couple of fuzzy infants in arms. The females were stockier than the males and had snouted faces. Though hairy and homeothermic, the t'Kelans were not mammals; mothers regurgitated food for children who had not yet cut their fangs.

Old Nyaronga led the band, sword rattling at his side, spear in hand and shield on arm, great yellow eyes flickering about the landscape. His half-grown sons flanked the party, arrows nocked to bows. Van Rijn trundled the car in their wake. "They expect trouble?" he asked.

Joyce started from her glum thoughts. "They always expect trouble," she said. "I told you, didn't I, what a quarrelsome race this is—no wars, but so many bloody set-tos. However, their caution is just routine today. Obviously they're going to pitch camp with the other prides of their clan. A herd this size would require all the Gangu to control it."

"You said they was hunters, not herders."

"They are, most of the time. But you see, *iziru* and *bambalo* stampede when the sun flares, and many are so badly sunburned that they die. That must be because they haven't developed protection against ultraviolet since the atmosphere began to change. Big animals with long generations evolve more slowly than small ones, as a rule. The clans can't afford such losses. In a flare season like this, they keep close watch on the herds and force them into areas where there is some shade and where the undergrowth hinders panicky running."

Van Rijn's thumb jerked a scornful gesture at the lowering red disc. "You mean that ember ever puts out enough radiation to hurt a sick butterfly?"

"Not if the butterfly came from Earth. But you know what type M dwarfs are like. They flare, and when they do, it can increase their luminosity several hundred percent. These days on t'Kela, the oxygen content of the air has been lowered to a point where the ozone layer doesn't block out as much ultraviolet as it should. Then, too, a planet like this, with a metal-poor core, has a weak magnetic field. Some of the charged particles from the sun get through also—adding to an already high cosmic-ray background. It wouldn't bother you or me, but mankind evolved to withstand considerably more radiation than is the norm here."

"*Ja*, I see. Maybe also there not being much radioactive minerals locally has been a factor. On Throra, the flares don't bother them. They make festival then. But like you say, t'Kela is a harder luck world than Throra."

Joyce shivered. "This is a cruel cosmos. That's what we believe in on Esperance—fighting back against the universe, all beings together."

"Is a very nice philosophy, except that all beings is not built for it. You is a very sweet child, anyone ever tell you that?" Van Rijn laid an arm lightly across her shoulder. She found that she didn't mind greatly, with the gloom and the brewing star-storm outside.

In another hour they reached the camp site. Humpbacked leather tents had been erected around a flat field where there was an ammonia spring. Fires burned before the entrances, tended by the young. Females crouched over cooking pots, males swaggered about with hands on weapon hilts. The arrival of the car brought everyone to watch, not running, but strolling up with an elaborate pretense of indifference.

Or is it a pretense? Joyce wondered. She looked out at the crowd, a couple of hundred unhuman faces, eyes aglow, spearheads a-gleam, fur rumpled by the whimpering wind, but scarcely a sound from anyone. They've acted the same way, she thought, every clan and Horde, everywhere we encountered them: wild fascination at first, with our looks and our machines; then a lapse into this cool formal courtesy, as if we didn't make any real difference for good or ill. They've thanked us, not very warmly, for what favors we could do, and often insisted on making payment, but they've never invited us to their merrymakings or their rites, and sometimes the children throw rocks at us.

Nyaronga barked a command. His pride began pitching their own camp. Gradually the others drifted away.

Van Rijn glanced at the sun. "They sure it flares today?" he asked.

"Oh, yes. If the Ancients have said so, then it will," Joyce assured him. "It isn't hard to predict, if you have smoked glass and a primitive telescope to watch the star surface. The light is so dim that the spots and flare phenomena can easily be observed—unlike a type-G star—and the patterns are very characteristic. Any jackleg astronomer can predict a flare on an M class dwarf, days in advance. Heliograph signals carry the word from Kusulongo to the Hordes."

"I suppose the Old Fogies got inherited empirical knowledge from early times, like the Babylonians knew about planetary movements, *ja* . . . Whoops, speak of the devil, here we go!"

The sun was now not far above the western ridges, which stood black under its swollen disc. A thin curl of clearer red puffed slowly out of it on one side. The *basai* reared and screamed. A roar went through the clansfolk. Males grabbed the animals' bridles and dragged them to a standstill. Females snatched their pots and their young into the tents.

The flame expanded and brightened. Light crept along the shadowy hills and the plains beyond. The sky began to pale. The wind strengthened and threshed in the woods on the edge of camp.

The t'Kelans manhandled their terrified beasts into a long shelter of hides stretched over poles. One bolted. A warrior twirled his lariat, tossed, and brought the creature crashing to earth. Two others helped drag it under cover. Still the flame from the solar disc waxed and gathered luminosity, minute by minute. It was not yet too brilliant for human eyes to watch unprotected. Joyce saw how a spider web of forces formed and crawled there, drawn in fiery loops. A gout of radiance spurted, died, and was reborn. Though she had seen the spectacle before, she found herself clutching van Rijn's arm. The merchant stuffed his pipe and blew stolid fumes.

Uulobu got down off the car. Joyce heard him ask Nyaronga, "May I help you face the angry Real One?"

"No," said the patriarch. "Get in a tent with the females."

Uulobu's teeth gleamed. The fur rose along his back. He unhooked the tomahawk at his waist.

"Don't!" Joyce cried through the intercom. "We are guests!"

For an instant the two t'Kelans glared at each other. Nyaronga's spear was aimed at Uulobu's throat. Then the Avongo sagged a little. "We are guests," he said in a choked voice. "Another time, Nyaronga, I shall talk about this with you."

"You—landless?" The leader checked himself. "Well, peace has been said between us, and there is no time now to unsay it. But we Gangu will defend our own herds and pastures. No help is needed."

Stiff-legged, Uulobu went into the nearest tent. Presently the last *basai* were gotten inside the shelter. Its flap was laced shut, to leave them in soothing darkness.

The flare swelled. It became a ragged sheet of fire next the sun disc, almost as big, pouring out as much light, but of an orange hue. Still it continued to grow, to brighten and yellow. The wind increased.

The heads of prides walked slowly to the center of camp. They formed a ring; the unwed youths made a larger circle around them. Nyaronga himself took forth a brass horn and winded it. Spears were raised aloft, swords and tomahawks shaken. The t'Kelans began to dance, faster and faster as the radiance heightened. Suddenly Nyaronga blew his horn again. A cloud of arrows whistled toward the sun.

"What they doing?" van Rijn asked. "Exorcising the demon?"

"No," said Joyce. "They don't believe that's possible. They're defying him. They always challenge him to come down and fight. And he's not a devil, by the way, but a god."

Van Rijn nodded. "It fits the pattern," he said, half to himself. "When a god steps out of his rightful job, you don't try to bribe him back, you threaten him. *Ja,* it fits."

The males ended their dance and walked with haughty slowness to their tents. The doorflaps were drawn. The camp lay deserted under the sun.

"Ha!" Van Rijn surged to his feet. "My gear!"

"What?" Joyce stared at him. She had grown so used to wan red light on this day's travel that the hue now pouring in the windows seemed ghastly on his cheeks.

"I want to go outside," van Rijn told her. "Don't just stand there with tongue unreeled. Get me my suit!"

Joyce found herself obeying him. By the time his gross form was bedecked, the sun was atop the hills and had tripled its radiance. The flare was like a second star, not round but flame-shaped, and nearly white. Long shadows wavered across the world, which had taken on an unnatural brazen tinge. The wind blew dust and dead leaves over the ground, flattened the fires, and shivered the tents till they thundered.

"Now," van Rijn said, "when I wave, you fix your intercom to full power so they can hear you. Then tell those so-called males to peek out at me if they have the guts." He glared at her. "And be unpolite about it, you understand me?"

Before she could reply he was in the air lock. A minute afterward he had cycled through and was stumping over the field until he stood in the middle of the encampment. Curtly, he signaled.

Joyce wet her lips. What did that idiot think he was doing? He'd never heard of this planet a month ago. He hadn't been on it a week. Practically all his information about it he had from her, during the past ten or fifteen hours. And he thought he knew how to conduct himself? Why, if he didn't get his fat belly full of whetted iron, it would only be because there was no justice in the universe. Did he think she'd let herself be dragged down with him?

Etched huge and black against the burning sky, van Rijn jerked his arm again.

Joyce turned the intercom high and said in the vernacular, "Watch, all Gangu who are brave enough! Look upon the male from far places, who stands alone beneath the angered sun!"

Her tones boomed hollowly across the wind. Van Rijn might have nodded. She must squint now to see what he did. That was due to the contrast, not to the illumination per se. It was still only a few percent of what Earth gets. But the flare, with an effective temperature of a million degrees or better, was emitting in frequencies to which her eyes were sensitive. Ultraviolet also, she thought in a corner of her mind: too little to turn a human baby pink, but enough to bring pain or death to these poor dwellers in Hades.

Van Rijn drew his blaster. With great deliberation, he fired several bolts at the star. Their flash and noise seemed puny against the rage up there. Now what—?

"No!" Joyce screamed.

Van Rijn opened his faceplate. He made a show of it, sticking his countenance out of the helmet, into the full light. He danced grotesquely about and thumbed his craggy nose at heaven.

But . . .

The merchant finished with an unrepeatable gesture, closed his helmet again, fired off two more bolts, and stood with folded arms as the sun went under the horizon.

The flare lingered in view for a while, a sheet of ghostly radiance above the trees. Van Rijn walked back to the car through twilight. Joyce let him in. He opened his helmet, wheezing, weeping, and blaspheming in a dozen languages. Frost began to form on his suit.

"Hoo-ee!" he moaned. "And not even a little hundred cc. of whiskey to console my poor old mucky membranes!"

"You could have died," Joyce whispered.

"Oh, no. No. Not that way does Nicholas van Rijn die. At the age of a hundred and fifty, I plan to be shot by an outraged husband. The cold was not too bad, for the short few minutes I could hold my breath. But letting in that ammonia—Terror and taxes!" He waddled to the bath cubicle and splashed his face with loud snortings.

The last flare-light sank. The sky remained hazy with aurora, so that only the brightest stars showed. The most penetrating charged particles from the flare would not arrive for hours; it was safe outside. One by one, the t'Kelans emerged. Fires were poked up, sputtering and glaring in the dark.

Van Rijn came back. "Hokay, I'm set," he said. "Now put on your own suit and come out with me. We got to talk at them."

As she walked into the circle around which stood the swart outlines of the tents, Joyce pushed her way through females and young. Their ring closed behind her, and she saw fireglow reflected from their eyes and knew she was hemmed in. It was comforting to have van Rijn's bulk so near and Uulobu's *pad-pad* at her back.

Thin comfort, though, when she looked at the males who waited by the ammonia spring. They had gathered as soon as they saw the humans coming. To her vision they were one shadow, like the night behind them. The fires on either side, that made it almost like day for a t'Kelan, hardly lit the front rank for her. Now and then a flame jumped high in the wind, or sparks went showering, or the dull glow on the smoke was thrown toward the group. Then she saw a barbed obsidian spearhead, a horn sword, an ax or an iron dagger, drawn. The forest soughed beyond the camp and she heard the frightened bawling of *iziru* as they blundered around in the dark. Her mouth went dry.

The fathers of the prides stood in the forefront. Most were fairly young; old age was not common in the desert. Nyaronga seemed to have primacy on that account. He stood, spear in hand, fangs showing in the half-open jaws, tendrils astir. His kilt fluttered in the unrestful air.

Van Rijn came to a halt before him. Joyce made herself stand close and meet Nyaronga's gaze. Uulobu crouched at her feet. A murmur like the sigh before a storm went through the warriors.

But the Earthman waited imperturbable, until at last Nyaronga must break the silence. "Why did you challenge the sun? No sky-one has ever done so before."

Joyce translated, a hurried mumble. Van Rijn puffed himself up visibly, even in his suit. "Tell him," he said, "I came just a short time ago. Tell him the rest of you did not think it was worth your whiles to make defiance, but I did."

"What do you intend to do?" she begged. "A misstep could get us killed."

"True. But if we don't make any steps, we get killed for sure, or starve to death because we don't dare come in radio range of where the rescue ship will be. Not so?" He patted her hand. "Damn these gloves! This would be more fun without. But in all kinds of cases, you trust me, Joyce. Nicholas van Rijn has not got old and fat on a hundred rough planets, if he was not smart enough to outlive everybody else. Right? Exact. So tell whatever I say to them, and use a sharp tone. Not unforgivable insults, but be snotty, hokay?"

She gulped. "Yes. I don't know why, b-but I will let you take the lead. If—" She suppressed fear and turned to the waiting t'Kelans. "This sky-male with me is not one of my own party," she told them. "He is of my race, but from a more powerful people among them than my people. He wishes me to tell you that though we sky-folk have hitherto not deigned to challenge the sun, he has not thought it was beneath him to do so."

"You never deigned?" rapped someone. "What do you mean by that?"

Joyce improvised. "The brightening of the sun is no menace to our people. We have often said as much. Were none of you here ever among those who asked us?"

Stillness fell again for a moment, until a scarred one-eyed patriarch said grudgingly, "Thus I heard last year, when you—or one like you—were in my pride's country healing sick cubs."

"Well, now you have seen it is true," Joyce replied.

Van Rijn tugged her sleeve. "Hoy, what goes on? Let me talk or else our last chance gets stupided away."

She dared not let herself be angered, but recounted the exchange. He astonished her by answering, "I am sorry, little girl. You was doing just wonderful. Now, though, I have a speech to make. You translate as I finish every sentence, ha?"

He leaned forward and stabbed his index finger just beneath Nyaronga's nose, again and again, as he said harshly, "You ask why I went out under the brightening sun? It was to show you I am not afraid of the fire it makes. I spit on your sun and it sizzles. Maybe it goes out. My sun could eat yours for breakfast and want an encore, by damn! Your little clot hardly gives enough light to see by, not enough to make bogeyman for a baby in my people."

The t'Kelans snarled and edged closer, hefting their weapons. Nyaronga retorted indignantly, "Yes, we have often observed that you sky-folk are nearly blind."

"You ever stood in the light from our cars? You go blind then, *nie?* You could not stand Earth, you. Pop and sputter you'd go, up in a little greasy cloud of smoke."

They were taken aback at that. Nyaronga spat and said, "You must even bundle yourselves against the air."

"You saw me stick my head out in the open. You care to try a whiff of my air for a change? I dare you."

A rumble went through the warriors, half wrath and half unease. Van Rijn chopped contemptuously with one hand. "See? You is more weakling than us."

A big young chieftain stepped forward. His whiskers bristled. "I dare."

"Hokay, I give you a smell." Van Rijn turned to Joyce. "Help me with this bebloodied air unit. I don't want no more of that beetle venom they call air in my helmet."

"But—but—" Helplessly, she obeyed, unscrewing the flush valve on the recycler unit between his shoulders.

"Blow it in his face," van Rijn commanded.

The warrior stood bowstring taut. Joyce thought of the pain he must endure. She couldn't aim the hose at him. "Move!" van Rijn barked. She did. Terrestrial atmosphere gushed forth.

The warrior yowled and stumbled back. He rubbed his nose and streaming eyes. For a minute he wobbled around, before he collapsed into the arms of a follower. Joyce refitted the valve as Van Rijn chortled, "I knew it. Too hot, too much oxygen, and especial the water vapor. It makes Throrans sick, so I thought sure it would do the same for these chaps. Tell them he will get well in a little while."

Joyce gave the reassurance. Nyaronga shook himself and said, "I have heard tales about this. Why must you show that poor fool what was known, that you breathe poison?"

"To prove we is just as tough as you, only more so, in a different way," van Rijn answered through Joyce. "We can whip you to your kennels like small dogs if we choose."

That remark brought a yell. Sharpened stone flashed aloft. Nyaronga raised his arms for silence. It came, in a mutter and a grumble and a deep sigh out of the females watching from darkness. The old chief said with bleak pride, "We know you command weapons we do not. This means you have arts we lack, which has never been denied. It does not mean you are stronger. A t'Kelan is not stronger than a *bambalo* simply because he has a bow to kill it from afar. We are a hunter folk, and you are not, whatever your weapons."

"Tell him," van Rijn said, "that I will fight their most powerful man barehanded. Since I must wear this suit that protects from his bite, he can use armaments. They will go through fabricoid, so it is fair, *nie?*"

"He'll kill you," Joyce protested.

Van Rijn leered. "If so, I die for the most beautifullest lady on this planet." His voice dropped. "Maybe then you is sorry you was not more kind to a nice old man when you could be."

"I won't!"

"You will, by damn!" He seized her wrist so strongly that she winced. "I know what I am making, you got me?"

Numbly, she conveyed the challenge. Van Rijn drew his blaster and threw it at Nyaronga's feet. "If I lose, the winner can keep this," he said.

That fetched them. A dozen wild young males leaped forth, shouting, into the firelight. Nyaronga roared and cuffed them into order. He glared from one to another and jerked his spear at an individual. "This is my own son Kusalu. Let him defend the honor of pride and clan."

The t'Kelan was overtopped by van Rijn, but was almost as broad. Muscles moved snakishly under his fur. His fangs glistened as he slid forward, tomahawk in right hand, iron dagger in left. The other males fanned out, making a wide circle of eyes and poised weapons. Uulobu drew Joyce aside. His grasp trembled on her arm. "Could I but fight him myself," he whispered.

While Kusalu glided about van Rijn turned, ponderous as a planet. His arms hung apelike from hunched shoulders. The fires tinged his crude features where they jutted within the helmet. "Nya-a-ah," he said.

Kusalu cursed and threw the tomahawk with splintering force. Van Rijn's left hand moved at an impossible speed. He caught the weapon in mid air and threw himself backward. The thong tautened. Kusalu went forward on his face. Van Rijn plunged to the attack.

Kusalu rolled over and bounced to his feet in time. His blade flashed. Van Rijn blocked it with his right wrist. The Earthman's left hand took a hitch in the thong and yanked again. Kusalu went to one knee. Van Rijn twisted that arm around behind his back. Every t'Kelan screamed.

Kusalu slashed the thong across. Spitting, he leaped erect again and pounced. Van Rijn gave him an expert kick in the belly, withdrawing the foot before it could be seized. Kusalu lurched. Van Rijn closed in with a karate chop to the side of the neck.

Kusalu staggered but remained up. Van Rijn barely ducked the rip of the knife. He retreated. Kusalu stood a moment regaining his wind. Then he moved in one blur.

Things happened. Kusalu was grabbed as he charged and sent flailing over van Rijn's shoulder. He hit ground with a thump. Van Rijn waited. Kusalu still had the dagger. He rose and stalked near. Blood ran from his nostril.

"*Là ci darem la mano,*" sang Van Rijn. As Kusalu prepared to smite, the Earthman got a grip on his right arm, whirled him around, and pinned him.

Kusalu squalled. Van Rijn ground a knee in his back. "You say, 'Uncle?'" he panted.

"He'll die first," Joyce wailed.

"Hokay, we do it hard fashion." Van Rijn forced the knife loose and kicked it aside. He let Kusalu go. But the t'Kelan had scarcely raised himself when a gauntleted fist smashed into his stomach. He reeled. Van Rijn pushed in relentlessly, blow after blow, until the warrior sank.

The merchant stood aside. Joyce stared at him with horror. "Is all in order," he calmed her. "I did not damage him permanent."

Nyaronga helped his son climb back up. Two others led Kusalu away. A low keening went among the massed t'Kelans. It was like nothing Joyce had ever heard before.

Van Rijn and Nyaronga confronted each other. The native said very slowly, "You have proven yourself, sky-male. For a landless one, you fight well, and it was good of you not to slay him."

Joyce translated between sobs. Van Rijn answered, "Say I did not kill that young buck because there is no need. Then say I have plenty territory of my own." He pointed upward, where stars glistened in the windy, hazy sky. "Tell him there is my hunting grounds, by damn."

When he had digested this, Nyaronga asked almost plaintively, "But what does he wish in our land? What is his gain?"

"We came to help—" Joyce stopped herself and put the question to van Rijn.

"Ha!" the Earthman gloated. "Now we talk about turkeys." He squatted near a fire. The pride fathers joined him; their sons pressed close to listen. Uulobu breathed happily, "We are taken as friends."

"I do not come to rob your land or game," van Rijn said in an oleaginous tone. "No, only to make deals, with good profit on both sides. Surely these folks trade with each other. They could not have so much stuffs as they do otherwise."

"Oh, yes, of course." Joyce settled weakly beside him. "And their relationship to the city is essentially quid pro quo, as I told you before."

"Then they will understand bargains being struck. So tell them those Gaffers on the mountain has got jealous of us. Tell them they sicced the Shanga onto our camp. The whole truths, not varnished more than needful."

"What? But I thought—I mean, didn't you want to give them the impression that we're actually powerful? Should we admit we're refugees?"

"Well, say we has had to make a . . . what do the military communiqués say when you has got your pants beaten off? . . . an orderly rearward advance for strategic reasons, to previously prepared positions."

Joyce did. Tendrils rose on the native heads, pupils narrowed, and hands raised weapons anew. Nyaronga asked dubiously, "Do you wish shelter among us?"

"No," said van Rijn. "Tell him we is come to warn them, because if they get wiped out we can make no nice deals with profit. Tell them the Shanga now has your guns from the dome, and will move with their fellow clans into Rokulela territory."

Joyce wondered if she had heard aright. "But we don't . . . we didn't . . . we brought no weapons except a few personal sidearms. And everybody must have taken his own away with him in the retreat."

"Do they know that, these peoples?"

"Why . . . well . . . would they believe you?"

"My good pretty blonde with curves in all the right places, I give you Nicholas van Rijn's promise they would not believe anythings else."

Haltingly, she spoke the lie. The reaction was horrible. They boiled throughout the camp, leaped about, brandished their spears, and ululated like wolves. Nyaronga alone sat still, but his fur stood on end.

"Is this indeed so?" he demanded. It came as a whisper through the noise.

"Why else would the Shanga attack us, with help from the Ancients?" Van Rijn countered.

"You know very well why," Joyce said. "The Ancients bribed them, played on their superstitions, and probably offered them our metal to make knives from."

"*Ja,* no doubt, but you give this old devil here my rhetorical just the way I said it. Ask him does it not make sense, that the Shanga would act for the sake of blasters and slugthrowers, once the Geezers put them up to it and supplied gunpowder? Then tell him this means the Graybeards must be on the side of the Shanga's own Horde . . . what's they called, now?"

"The Yagola."

"So. Tell him that, things you overheard give you good reason to believe the Shanga clan will put themselves at the head of the Yagola to move west and push the Rokulela out of this fine country."

Nyaronga and the others, who fell into an ominous quiet as Joyce spoke, had no trouble grasping the concept. As she had told Van Rijn, war was not a t'Kelan institution. But she was not conveying the idea of a full-dress war—rather, a *Völkerwanderung* into new hunting grounds. And such things were frequent enough on this dying planet. When a region turned utterly barren, its inhabitants must displace someone else, or die in the attempt.

The difference now was that the Yagola were not starved out of their homes. They were alleged to be anticipating that eventuality, plotting to grab off more land with their stolen firearms to give them absolute superiority.

"I had not thought them such monsters," Nyaronga said.

"They aren't," Joyce protested in Anglic to van Rijn. "You're maligning them so horribly that—that—"

"Well, well, all's fair in love and propaganda," he said. "Propose to Nyaronga that we all return to Kusulongo, collecting reinforcements as we go, to see for ourselves if this business really is true and use numerical advantage while we have still got it."

"You *are* going to set them at each other's throats! I won't be party to any such thing. I'll die first."

"Look, sweet potato, nobody has got killed yet. Maybe nobody has to be. I can explain later. But for now, we have got to strike while the fat is in the fire. They is wonderful excited. Don't give them a chance to cool off till they has positive decided to march." The man laid a hand on his heart. "You think old, short of breath, comfort-loving, cowardly Nicholas van Rijn wants to fight a war? You think again. A formfitting chair, a tall cool drink, a Venusian cigar, *Eine Kleine Nachtmusik* on the taper, aboard his ketch while he sails with a bunch of dancing girls down Sunda Straits, that is only which he wants. Is that much to ask? Be like your own kind, gentle selfs and help me stir them up to fight."

Trapped in her own bewilderment, she followed his lead. That same night, riders went out bearing messages to such other Rokulela clans as were known to be within reach.

✲ ✲ ✲

The first progress eastward was in darkness, to avoid the still flaring sun. Almost every male, grown or half-grown, rode along, leaving females and young behind in camp. They wore flowing robes and burnooses, their *bāsai* were blanketed, against the fierce itch that attacked exposed t'Kelan skin during such periods. Most of the charged particles from the star struck the planet's day side, but there was enough magnetic field to bring some around to the opposite hemisphere. Even so, the party made surprisingly good speed. Peering from the car windows, Joyce glimpsed them under the two moons, shadowy shapeless forms that slipped over the harsh terrain, an occasional flash of spearheads. Through the engine's low voice she heard them calling to each other, and the deep earth-mutter of unshod hoofs.

"You see," van Rijn lectured, "I am not on this world long, but I been on a lot of others, and read reports about many more. In my line of business this is needful. They always make parallels. I got enough clues about these t'Kelans to guess the basic pattern of their minds, from analogizings. You Esperancers, on this other hand, has not had so much experience. Like most colonies, you is too isolated from the galactic mainstream to keep *au courant* with things, like for instance the modern explorer techniques. That was obvious from the fact you did not make depth psychology studies the very first thing, but instead took what you found at face valuation. Never do that, Joyce. Always bite the coin that feeds you, for this is a hard and wicked universe."

"You seem to know what you're about, Nick," she admitted. He beamed and raised her hand to his lips. She made some confused noise about heating coffee and retreated. She didn't want to hurt his feelings; he really was an old dear, under that crust of his.

When she came back to the front seat, placing herself out of his reach, she said, "Well, tell me, what pattern did you deduce? How do their minds work?"

"You assumed they was like warlike human primitives, in early days on Earth," he said. "On the topside, that worked hokay. They is intelligent, with language; they can reason and talk with you; this made them seem easy understood. What you forgot, I think, me, was conscious intelligence is only a small part of the whole selfness. All it does is help us get what we want. But the wanting itself—food, shelter, sex, everything—our motives—they come from deeper down. There is no logical reason even to stay alive. But instinct says to, so we want to. And instinct comes from very old evolution. We was animals long before we became thinkers and, uh—" van Rijn's beady eyes rolled piously ceilingward—"and was given souls. You got to think how a race evolved before you can take them . . . I mean understand them.

"Now humans, the experts tell me, got started way back when, as ground apes that turned carnivore when the forests shrank up in Africa for lots of megayears. This is when they started to walking erect the whole time, and grew hands fully developed to make weapons because they had not claws and teeth like lions. Hokay, so we is a mean lot, we Homo Sapienses, with killer instincts. But not exclusive. We is still omnivores who can even survive on Brussels sprouts if we got to. Pfui! But we can. Our ancestors been peaceful nut-pluckers and living off each other's fleas a long, longer time than they was hunters. It shows.

"The t'Kelans, on the other side, has been carnivores since they was still four-footers. Not very good carnivores. Unspecialized, with no claws and pretty weak biting apparatus even if it is stronger than humans'. That is why they also developed hands and made tools, which led to them getting big brains. Nevertheleast, they have no vegetarian whatsolutely in their ancestors, as we do. And they have much powerfuller killing instincts than us. And is not so gregarious. Carnivores can't be. You get a big concentration of hunters in one spot, and by damn, the game goes away. Is that coffee ready?"

"I think so." Joyce fetched it. Van Rijn slurped it down, disregarding a temperature that would have taken the skin off her palate, steering with one bare splay foot as he drank.

"I begin to see," she said with growing excitement. "That's why they never developed true nations or fought real wars. Big organizations are completely artificial things to them, commanding no loyalty. You don't fight or die for a Horde, any more than a human would fight for . . . for his bridge club."

"Um-m-m, I have known some mighty bloodshot looks across bridge tables. But *ja,* you get the idea. The pride is a natural thing here, like the human family. The clan, with blood ties, is only one step removed. It can excite t'Kelans as much, maybe, as his country can excite a man. But Hordes? *Nie.* An arrangement of convenience only.

"Not that pride and clan is loving-kindness and sugar candy. Humans make family squabbles and civil wars. T'Kelans have still stronger fighting instincts than us. Lots of arguments and bloodshed. But only on a small scale, and not taken too serious. You said to me, is no vendettas here. That means somebody killing somebody else is not thought to have done anything bad. In fact, whoever does not fight—male, anyhow—strikes them as unnatural, like less than normal."

"Is . . . that why they never warmed up to us? To the Esperancian mission, I mean?"

"Partly. Not that you was expected to fight at any specifical time. Nobody went out to pick a quarrel when you gave no offense and was even useful. But your behavior taken in one lump added up to a thing they couldn't understand. They figured there was something wrong with you, and felt a goodly natured contempt. I had to prove I was tough as they or tougher. That satisfied their instincts, which then went to sleep and let them listen to me with respects."

Van Rijn put down his empty cup and took out his pipe. "Another thing you lacked was territory," he said. "Animals on Earth, too, has an instinct to stake out and defend a piece of ground for themselves. Humans do. But for carnivores this instinct has got to be very, very, very powerful, because if they get driven away from where the game is, they can't survive on roots and berries. They die.

"You saw yourselfs how those natives what could not maintain a place in their ancestral hunting grounds but went to you instead was looked downwards on. You Esperancers only had a dome on some worthless nibble of land. Then you went around preaching how you had no designs on anybody's country. Ha! They had to believe you was either lying—maybe that is one reason the Shanga attacked you—or else was abnormal weaklings."

"But couldn't they understand?" Joyce asked. "Did they expect us, who didn't even look like them, to think the same way as they do?"

"Sophisticated, civilized t'Kelans could have caught the idea," van Rijn said. "However, you was dealing with naive barbarians."

"Except the Ancients. I'm sure they realize—"

"Maybe so. Quite possible. But you made a deadly threat to them. Could you not see? They has been the scribes, doctors, high-grade artisans, sun experts, for ages and ages. You come in and start doing the same as them, only much better. What you expect them to do? Kiss your foots? Kiss any part of your anatomy? Not them! They is carnivores, too. They fight back."

"But we never meant to displace them!"

"Remember," van Rijn said, wagging his pipe stem at her, "reason is just the lackey for instinct. The Gaffers is more subtle than anybody else's. They can sit still in one place, between walls. They do not hunt. They do not claim thousands of square kilometers for themselves. But does this mean they have no instinct of territoriality? Ha! Not bloody likely! They has only sublimed it. Their work, *that* is their territory—and you moved in on it!"

Joyce sat numbly, staring out into night. Time passed before she could protest. "But we explained to them—I'm sure they understood—we explained this planet will die without our help."

"*Ja, ja.* But a naturally born fighter has less fear of death than other kinds animals. Besides, the death was scheduled for a thousand years from now, did you not say? That is too long a time to feel with emotions. Your own threat to them was real, here and now."

Van Rijn lit his pipe. "Also," he continued around the mouthpiece, "your gabbing about planet-wide cooperation did not sit so well. I doubt they could really comprehend it. Carnivores don't make cooperations except on the most teensy scale. It isn't practical for them. They haven't got such instincts. The Hordes—which, remember, is not nations in any sense—they could never get what you was talking about, I bet. Altruism is outside their mental horizontals. It only made them suspicious of you. The Ancients maybe had some vague notion of your motives, but didn't share them in the littlest. You can't organize these peoples. Sooner will you build a carousel on Saturn's rings. It does not let itself be done."

"You've organized them to fight!" she exclaimed in her anguish.

"No. Only given them a common purpose for this time being. They believed what I said about weapons left in the dome. With minds like that, they find it much the easiest thing to believe. Of course you had an arsenal—everybody does. Of course you would have used it if you got the chance—anybody would. Ergo, you never got the chance; the Shanga captured it too fast. The rest of the story, the Yagola plot against the Rokulela, is at least logical enough to their minds that they had better investigate it good."

"But what are you going to make them do?" She couldn't hold back the tears any longer. "Storm the mountain? They can't get along without the Ancients."

"Sure, they can, if humans substitute."

"B-b-but—but—no, we can't, we mustn't—"

"Maybe we don't have to," van Rijn said. "I got to play by my ear of tinned cauliflower when we arrive. We will see." He laid his pipe aside. "There, there, now, don't be so sad. But go ahead and cry if you want. Papa Nicky will dry your eyes and blow your nose." He offered her the curve of his arm. She crept into it, buried her face against his side, and wept herself to sleep.

Kusulongo the Mountain rose monstrous from the plain, cliff upon gloomy cliff, with talus slopes and glaciers between, until the spires carved from its top stood ragged across the sun-disc. Joyce had seldom felt the cold and murk of this world as she did now, riding up the path to the city on a horned animal that must be blanketed against the human warmth of her suit. The wind went shrieking through the empty dark sky, around the crags, to buffet her like fists and snap the banner which Uulobu carried on a lance as he rode ahead. Glancing back, down a dizzying sweep of stone, she saw Nyaronga and the half-dozen other chiefs who had been allowed to come with the party. Their cloaks streamed about them; spears rose and fell with the gait of their mounts; the color of their fur was lost in this dreary light, but she thought she made out the grimness on their faces. Immensely far below, at the mountain's foot, lay their followers, five hundred armed and angry Rokulela. But they were hidden by dusk, and if she died on the heights they could give her no more than a vengeance she didn't want.

She shuddered and edged her *basai* close to the one which puffed and groaned beneath van Rijn's weight. Their knees touched. "At least we have some company," she said, knowing the remark was moronic but driven to say anything that might drown out the wind. "Thank God the flare died away so fast."

"*Ja,* we made good time," the merchant said. "Only three days from the Lubambaru to here, that's quicker than I fore-waited. And lots of allies picked up."

She harked back wistfully to the trek. Van Rijn had spent the time being amusing, and had succeeded better than she would have expected. But then they arrived, and the Shanga scrambled up the mountain one jump ahead of the Rokulela charge; the attackers withdrew, unwilling to face cannon if there was a chance of avoiding it; a parley was agreed on; and she couldn't imagine how it might end other than in blood. The Ancients might let her group go down again unhurt, as they'd promised—or might not—but, however that went, before sundown many warriors would lie broken for the carrion fowl. Oh, yes, she admitted to herself, I'm also afraid of what will happen to me, if I should get back alive to Esperance. Instigating combat! Ten years' corrective detention if I'm lucky . . . unless I run away with Nick and never see home again, never, never—But to make those glad young hunters die!

She jerked her reins, half minded to flee down the trail and into the desert. The beast skittered under her. Van Rijn caught her by the shoulder. "Calm, there, if you please," he growled. "We has got to outbluff them upstairs. They will be a Satan's lot harder to diddle than the barbarians was."

"Can we?" she pleaded. "They can defend every approach. They're stocked for a long siege, I'm certain, longer than . . . than we could maintain."

"If we bottle them for a month, is enough. For then comes the League ship."

"But they can send for help, too. Use the heliographs." She pointed to one of the skeletal towers above. Its mirror shimmered dully in the red luminance. Only a t'Kelan could see the others, spaced out in several directions across the plains and hills. "Or messengers can slip between our lines—we'd be spread so terribly thin—they could raise the whole Yagola Horde against us."

"Maybe so, maybe not. We see. Now peep down and let me think."

They jogged on in silence, except for the wind. After an hour they came to a wall built across the trail. Impassable slopes of detritus stretched on either side. The archway held two primitive cannon. Four members of the city garrison poised there, torches flickering near the fuses. Guards in leather helmets and corselets, armed with bows and pikes, stood atop the wall. The iron gleamed through the shadows.

Uulobu rode forth, cocky in the respect he had newly won from the clans. "Let pass the mighty sky-folk who have condescended to speak with your patriarchs," he demanded.

"Hmpf!" snorted the captain of the post. "When have the sky-folk ever had the spirit of a gutted *yangulu?*"

"They have always had the spirit of a *makovolo* in a rage," Uulobu said. He ran a thumb along the edge of his dagger. "If you wish proof, consider who dared cage the Ancients on their own mountain."

The warrior made a flustered noise, collected himself, and stated loudly, "You may pass, then, and be safe as long as the peace between us is not unsaid."

"No more fiddlydoodles there," van Rijn rapped. "We want by, or we take your popguns and stuff them in a place they do not usually go." Joyce forebore to interpret. Nick had so many good qualities; if only he could overcome that vulgarity! But he had had a hard life, poor thing. No one had ever really taken him in hand. . . . Van Rijn rode straight between the cannon and on up the path.

It debouched on a broad terrace before the city wall. Other guns frowned from the approaches. Two score warriors paced their rounds with more discipline than was known in the Hordes. Joyce's eyes went to the three shapes in the portal. They wore plain white robes, and fur was grizzled with age. But their gaze was arrogant on the newcomers.

She hesitated. "I . . . this is the chief scribe—" she began.

"No introduction to secretaries and office boys," van Rijn said. "We go straight to the boss."

Joyce moistened her lips and told them: "The head of the sky-folk demands immediate parley."

"So be it," said one Ancient without tone. "But you must leave your arms here."

Nyaronga bared his teeth. "There is no help for it," Joyce reminded him. "You know as well as I, by the law of the fathers, none but Ancients and warriors born in the city may go through this gate with weapons." Her own holster and van Rijn's were already empty.

She could almost see the heart sink in the Rokulela, and remembered what the Earthman had said about instinct. Disarming a t'Kelan was a symbolic emasculation. They put a bold face on it, clattering their implements down and dismounting to stride with stiff backs at van Rijn's heels. But she noticed how their eyes flickered about, like those of trapped animals, when they passed the gateway.

Kusulongo the City rose in square tiers, black and massive under the watchtowers. The streets were narrow guts twisting between, full of wind and the noise of hammering from the metalsmiths' quarters. Dwellers by birthright stood aside as the barbarians passed, drawing their robes about them as if to avoid contact. The three councillors said no word; stillness fell everywhere as they walked deeper into the citadel, until Joyce wanted to scream.

At the middle of the city stood a block full twenty meters high, windowless, only the door and the ventholes opening to air. Guards hoisted their swords and hissed in salute as the hierarchs went through the entrance. Joyce heard a small groan at her back. The Rokulela followed the humans inside, down a winding hall, but she didn't think they would be of much use. The torchlit cave at the end was cleverly designed to sap a hunter's nerve.

Six white-robed oldsters were seated on a semicircular dais. The wall behind them carried a mosaic, vivid even in this fluttering dimness, of the sun as it flared. Nyaronga's breath sucked between his teeth. He had just been reminded of the Ancients' power. True, Joyce told herself, he knew the humans could take over the same functions. But immemorial habit is not easily broken.

Their guides sat down too. The newcomers remained standing. Silence thickened. Joyce swallowed several times and said, "I speak for Nicholas van Rijn, patriarch of the sky-folk, who has leagued himself with the Rokulela clans. We come to demand justice."

"Here there is justice," the gaunt male at the center of the dais replied. "I, Oluba's son Akulo, Ancient-born, chief in council, speak for Kusulongo the City. Why have you borne a spear against us?"

"Ha!" snorted van Rijn when it had been conveyed to him. "Ask that old hippopotamus why he started these troubles in the first place."

"You mean hypocrite," Joyce said automatically.

"I mean what I mean. Come on, now. I know very well why he has, but let us hear what ways he covers up."

Joyce put the question. Akulo curled his tendrils, a gesture of skepticism, and murmured, "This is strange. Never have the Ancients taken part in quarrels below the mountains. When you attacked the Shanga, we gave them refuge, but such is old custom. We will gladly hear your dispute with them and arrange a fair settlement, but this is no fight of ours."

Joyce anticipated van Rijn by snapping in an upsurge of indignation. "They blew down our walls. Who could have supplied them the means but yourselves?"

"Ah, yes." Akulo stroked his whiskers. "I understand your thinking, sky-female. It is very natural. Well, as this council intended to explain should other carriers of your people arrive here and accuse us, we do sell fireworks for magic and celebration. The Shanga bought a large quantity from us. We did not ask why. No rule controls how much may be bought at a time. They must have emptied the powder out themselves, to use against you."

"What's he say?" van Rijn demanded.

Joyce explained. Nyaronga muttered—it took courage with the Ancients listening—"No doubt the Shanga pride-fathers will support that tale. An untruth is a low price for weapons like yours."

"What weapons speak you of?" a councillor interrupted.

"The arsenal the sky-folk had, which the Shanga captured for use against my own Horde," Nyaronga spat. His mouth curled upward. "So much for the disinterestedness of the Ancients."

"But—No!" Akulo leaned forward, his voice not quite as smooth as before. "It is true that Kusulongo the City did nothing to discourage an assault on the sky-ones' camp. They are weak and bloodless—legitimate prey. More, they were causing unrest among the clans, undermining the ways of the fathers—"

"Ways off which Kusulongo the City grew fat," Joyce put in.

Akulo scowled at her but continued addressing Nyaronga. "By their attack, the Shanga did win a rich plunder of metal. They will have many good knives. But that is not enough addition to their power that they could ever invade new lands when desperation does not lash them. We thought of that too, here on the mountain, and did not wish to see it happen. The concern of the Ancients was ever to preserve a fitting balance of things. If the sky-folk went away, that balance would actually be restored which they endangered. A little extra metal in Yagola hands would not upset it anew. The sky-folk were never seen to carry any but a few hand-weapons. Those they took with them when they fled. There never was an armory in the dome for the Shanga to seize. Your fear was for nothing, you Rokulela."

Joyce had been translating for van Rijn *sotto voce.* He nodded. "Hokay. Now tell them what I said you should."

I've gone too far to retreat, she realized desolately. "But we did have weapons in reserve!" she blurted. "Many of them, hundreds, whole boxes full, that we did not get a chance to use before the attack drove us outside."

Silence cracked down. The councillors stared at her in horror. Torch flames jumped and shadows chased each other across the walls. The Rokulela chiefs watched with a stern satisfaction that put some self-confidence back into them.

Finally Akulo stuttered, "B-b-but you said—I asked you once myself, and you denied having—having more than a few . . ."

"Naturally," Joyce said, "we kept our main strength in reserve, unrevealed."

"The Shanga reported nothing of this sort."

"Would you expect them to?" Joyce let that sink in before she went on. "Nor will you find the cache if you search the oasis. They did not resist our assault with fire, so the guns cannot have been in this neighborhood. Most likely someone took them away at once into the Yagola lands, to be distributed later."

"We shall see about this." Another Ancient clipped off the words. "Guard!" A sentry came in through the doorway to the entry tunnel. "Fetch the spokesman of our clan guests."

Joyce brought van Rijn up to date while they waited. "Goes well so far," the merchant said. "But next comes the ticklish part, not so much fun as tickling you."

"Really!" She drew herself up, hot in the face. "You're impossible."

"No, just improbable . . . Ah, here we go already."

A lean t'Kelan in Shanga garb trod into the room. He folded his arms and glowered at the Rokulela. "This is Batuzi's son Masotu," Akulo introduced. He leaned forward, tense as his colleagues. "The sky-folk have said you took many terrible weapons from their camp. Is that truth?"

Masotu started. "Certainly not! There was nothing but that one emptied handgun I showed you when you came down at dawn."

"So the Ancients were indeed in league with the Shanga," rasped a t'Kelan in van Rijn's party.

Briefly disconcerted, Akulo collected himself and said in a steel tone, "Very well. Why should we deny it, after all? Kusulongo the City seeks the good of the whole world, which is its own good; and these sly strangers were bringing new ways that rotted old usage. Were they not softening you for the invasion of their own people? What other reason had they to travel about in your lands? What other reason could they have? Yes, this council urged the Shanga to wipe them out as they deserve."

Though her heartbeat nearly drowned her words, Joyce managed to interpret for van Rijn. The merchant's lips thinned. "Now they confess it to our facing," he said. "Yet they have got to have some story ready to fob off Earthships and make humans never want to come here again. They do not intend to let us go down this hill alive, I see, and talk contradictions afterwards." But he gave her no word for the natives.

Akulo pointed at Masotu. "Do you tell us, then, that the sky-folk have lied and you found no arsenal?"

"Yes." The Shanga traded stares with Nyaronga. "Ah, your folk fretted lest we use that power to overrun your grasslands," he deduced shrewdly. "There was no need to fear. Go back in peace and let us finish dealing with the aliens."

"We never *feared*," Nyaronga corrected. Nonetheless his glance toward the humans was doubtful.

An Ancient stirred impatiently on the dais. "Enough of this," he said. "Now we have all seen still another case of the sky-folk brewing trouble. Call in the guards to slay them. Let peace be said between Shanga and all Rokulela. Send everyone home and have done."

Joyce finished her running translation as Akulo opened his mouth. "Botulism and bureaucrats!" van Rijn exploded. "Not this fast, little chum." He reached under the recycler tank on his back and pulled out his blaster. "Please to keep still."

No t'Kelan stirred, though a hiss went among them. Van Rijn

backed toward the wall so he could cover the doorway as well. "Now we talk more friendly," he smiled.

"The law has been broken," Akulo sputtered.

"Likewise the truce which you said between us," Joyce answered, though no culture on this planet regarded oath-breaking as anything but a peccadillo. She felt near fainting with relief. Not that the blaster solved many problems. It wouldn't get them out of a city aswarm with archers and spear-casters. But—

"Quiet!" boomed van Rijn. Echoes rang from wall to stony wall. A couple of sentries darted in. They pulled up short when they saw the gun.

"Come on, join the party," the Earthman invited. "Lots of room and energy charges for everybodies."

To Joyce he said, "Hokay, now is where we find out whether we have brains enough to get out of being heroes. Tell them that Nicholas van Rijn has a speech to make, then talk for me as I go along."

Weakly, she relayed the message. The least relaxation showed on the tigery bodies before her. Akulo, Nyaronga, and Masotu nodded together. "Let him be heard," the Ancient said. "There is always time to fight afterward."

"Good." Van Rijn's giant form took a step forward. He swept the blaster muzzle around in an oratorical gesture. "First, you should know I caused all this hullabaloo mainly so we could talk. If I come back here alone, you would have clobbered me with pointy little rocks, and that would not be so good for any of us. Ergo, I had to come in company. Let Nyaronga tell you I can fight like a hungry creditor if needful. But maybe there is no need this time, ha?"

Joyce passed on his words, sentence by sentence, and waited while the Gangu pride-father confirmed that humans were tough customers. Van Rijn took advantage of the general surprise to launch a quick verbal offensive.

"We have got this situation. Suppose the Shanga are lying and have really coppered a modern arsenal. Then they can gain such power that even this city becomes a client of theirs instead of being *primus inter pares* like before. *Nie?* To prevent this, a common cause is needful between Ancients, Rokulela, and us humans who can get bigger weapons to stop the Yagola when our rescue ship comes in."

"But we have no such booty," Masotu insisted.

"So you say," Joyce replied. She was beginning to get van Rijn's general idea. "Ancients and Rokulela, dare you take his word on so weighty a matter?"

As indecision waxed on the dais, van Rijn continued. "Now let us on the other hands suppose I am the liar and there never was any loose zappers in the dome. Then Shanga and Ancients must keep on working together. For my people's ship that will come from our own territory, which is the whole skyful of stars, they must be told some yarn about why their dome was destroyed. Everybody but me and this cute doll here got safe away, so it will be known the Shanga did the job. Our folks will be angry at losing such a good chance for profit they have been working on for a long time. They will blame the Ancients as using Shanga for pussyfoots, and maybe blow this whole mountain to smitherlets, unless a good story that Shanga corroborate in every way has been cooked beforehand to clear the Ancients. Right? *Ja*. Well, then, for years to come, the Shanga—through them, all Yagola—must be in close touch with Kusulongo town. And they will not take the blame for no payment at all, will they? So hokay, you Rokulela, how impartial you think the Ancients will be to you? How impartial can the Ancients be, when the Shanga can blackmail them? You need humans here to make a balance."

Uulobu clashed his teeth together and cried, "This is true!" But Joyce watched Nyaronga. The chief pondered a long while, trading looks with his colleagues, before he said, "Yes, this may well be. At least, one does not wish to risk being cheated, when disputes come here for judgment. Also, the bad years may come to Yagolaland next, when they must move elsewhere . . . and a single failure to predict a flare for us could weaken our whole country for invasion."

Stillness stretched. Joyce's phone pickup sent her only the sputter of torches and the boom of wind beyond the doorway. Akulo stared down van Rijn's gun muzzle, without a move. At last he said, "You sow discord with great skill, stranger. Do you think we can let so dangerous a one, or these pride-fathers whom you have now made into firm allies, leave here alive?"

"*Ja*," answered van Rijn complacently through Joyce. "Because I did not really stir up trouble, only prove to your own big benefits that you can't trust each other and need human peoples to keep order.

For see you, with humans and their weapons around, who have an interest in peace between clans and Hordes, some Yagola with a few guns can't accomplish anything. Or if they truly don't have guns, there is still no reason for the city to work foot in shoe with them if humans return peacefully and do not want revenge for their dome. So either way, the right balance is restored between herders and town. Q.E.D."

"But why should the sky-folk wish to establish themselves here?" Akulo argued. "Is your aim to take over the rightful functions of Kusulongo the City? No, first you must slay each one of us on the mountain!"

"Not needful," van Rijn said. "We make our profit other ways. I have asked out the lady here about the facts while we was en route, and she dovetails very pretty, let me tell you. Uh . . . Joyce . . . you take over now. I am not sure how to best get the notion across when they haven't much chemical theory."

Her mouth fell open. "Do you mean—Nick, do you have an answer?"

"*Ja, ja, ja.*" He rubbed his hands and beamed. "I worked that out fine. Like follows: My own company takes over operations on t'Kela. You Esperancers help us get started, natural, but after that you can go spend your money on some other planet gone to seed . . . while Nicholas van Rijn takes money out of this one."

"What, what are you thinking?"

"Look, I want *kungu* wine, and a fur trade on the side might also be nice to have. The clans everywhere will bring me this stuff. I sell them ammonia and nitrates from the nitrogen-fixing plants we build, in exchange. They will need this to enrich their soils—also they will need to cultivate nitrogen-fixing bacteria the way you show them—to increase crop yields so they can buy still more ammonia and nitrates. Of course, what they will really do this for is to get surplus credit for buying modern gadgets. Guns, especial. Nobody with hunter instincts can resist buying guns; he will even become a part-time farmer to do it. But also my factors will sell them tools and machines and stuff, what makes them slowly more civilized the way you want them to be. On all these deals, Solar Spice & Liquors turns a pretty good profit."

"But we didn't come to exploit them!"

Van Rijn chuckled. He reached up to twirl his mustache, clanked a hand against his helmet, made a face, and said, "Maybe you Esperancers didn't, but I sure did. And don't you see, this they can understand, the clans. Charity is outside their instincts, but profit is not, and they will feel good at how they swindle us on the price of wine. No more standoffishness and suspicion about humans—not when humans is plainly come here on a money hunt. You see?"

She nodded, half dazed. They weren't going to like this on Esperance; the Commonalty looked down from a lofty moral position on the Polesotechnic League; but they weren't fanatical about it, and if this was the only way the job could be done—Wait. "The Ancients," she objected. "How will you conciliate them? Introducing so many new elements is bound to destroy the basis of their whole economy."

"Oh, I already got that in mind. We will want plenty of native agents and clerks, smart fellows who keep records and expand our market territory and cetera. That takes care of many young Ancients . . . silly name. . . . As for the rest, though, maintaining the power and prestiges of the city as a unit, that we can also do. Remember, there are oil wells to develop and electrolysis plants to build. The electrolyzer plants will sell hydrogen to the ammonia plants, and the oil-burning operation can sell electricity. Hokay, so I build these oil and electrolyzer plants, turn them over to the Ancients to run, and let the Ancients buy them from me on a long-term mortgage. So profitable and key facilities should suit them very well, *nie?*" He stared thoughtfully into a dark corner. "Um-m-m . . . do you think I can get twenty percent interest, compounded annual, or must I have to settle for fifteen?"

Joyce gasped a while before she could start searching for Kusulongo phrases.

They went down the mountain toward sunset, with cheers at their back and campfires twinkling below to welcome them. Somehow the view seemed brighter to Joyce than ever ere now. And there was beauty in that illimitable westward plain, where a free folk wandered through their own lives. The next few weeks, waiting for the ship, won't be bad at all, she thought. In fact, they should be fun.

"Another advantage," van Rijn told her smugly, "is that making a commercial operation with profit for everybody out of this is a much better guarantee the job will be continued for long enough to save the planet. You thought your government could do it. Bah! Governments is dayflies. Any change of ideology, of mood, even, and poof goes your project. But private action, where everybody concerned is needful to everybody else's income, that's stable. Politics, they come and go, but greed goes on forever."

"Oh, no, that can't be," she denied.

"Well, we got time in the car to argue about it, and about much else," van Rijn said. "I think I can rig a little still to get the alcohol out of *kungu*. Then we put it in fruit juice and have a sort of wine with our meals like human beings, by damn!"

"I . . . I shouldn't, Nicky . . . that is, well, us two alone—"

"You is only young once. You mean a poor old man like me has got to show you how to be young?" Van Rijn barely suppressed a leer. "Hokay, fine by me."

Joyce looked away, flushing. She'd have to maintain a strict watch on him till the ship arrived, she thought. And on herself, for that matter.

Of course, if she did happen to relax just the littlest bit . . . after all, he really was a very interesting person . . .

PLUS ÇA CHANGE PLUS C'EST LA MÊME CHOSE

Did I ever meet Noah Arkwright? Did *I* ever meet *Noah Arkwright*? Just pull up a chair and tune up an ear. No, better not that chair. We keep it in case the Gratch should pay us a call. Glowberry wood, the tree concentrates uranium salts, so less'n you're wearing lead diapers . . .

Sure, we'd heard of that skyhoot Noah Arkwright wanted to do. Space pilots flit the jaw, even this far out the spokes. We wanted no more snatch at his notion than any other men whose brains weren't precessing. Figured the Yonder could wait another couple hundred years; got more terry incog already than we can eat, hey? But when he bunged down his canster here, he never jingled a word about it. He had a business proposition to make, he said, and would those of us who had a dinar or two to orbit be interested?

Sounded right sane, he did; though with that voice I compute he could've gotten jewelry prices for what he'd call dioxide of ekacarbon. See you, nigh any planet small enough for a man to dig on has got to have its Victory Heads—Golcondas, Mesabis, Rands, if you want to go back to Old Earth—anyhow, its really rich mineral deposits. The snub always was, a planet's one gorgo of a big place. Even with sonics and spectros, you'll sniff around a new one till entropy overhauls you before you have a white dwarf chance of making the real find. But he said he had a new hypewangle that'd spot from satellite altitude. He needed capital to proceed, and they were too stuffnoggin on Earth to close him a circuit, so why not us?

Oh, we didn't arc over. Not that we saw anything kinked in his not telling us how the dreelsprail worked; out here, secrets are property. But we made him demonstrate, over on Despair. Next planet spaceward, hardly visited at all before, being as useless a little glob as ever was spunged off God's thumbnail. Dis if his meters didn't swing a cory over what developed into the biggest rhenium strike since Ignatz.

Well, you know how it is with minerals. The rich deposits have an edge over extraction methods, like from sea water, but not so much of an edge that you can count your profits from one in exponentials. Still, if we had a way to find any number of 'em, quick and cheap, in nearby systems— We stood in line to capitalize his company. And me, I was so tough and smart I rammed my way to the head of the line!

I do think, though, his way of talking did it. He could pull Jupiter from Sol with, oh, just one of his rambles through xenology or analytics or Shakespeare or history or hypertheory or anything. Happen I've still got a tape, like I notice you making now. You cogno yours stays private, for your personal journal, right? I wouldn't admit the truth about this to another human. Not to anybeing, if I wasn't an angstrom drunk. But listen, here's Noah Arkwright.

"—isn't merely that society in the large goes through its repetitions. In fact, I rather doubt the cliché that we are living in some kind of neo-Elizabethan age. There are certain analogies, no more. Now a *life* has cycles. Within a given context, the kinds of event that can happen to you are of a finite number. The permutations change, the elements remain the same.

"Consider today's most romantic figure, the merchant adventurer. Everyone, especially himself, thinks he leads a gorgeously variegated existence. And yet, how different can one episode be from the next? He deals with a curious planetary environment, natives whose inwardness he must try to understand, crafty rivals, women tempting or belligerent, a few classes of dangers, the eternal problems of making his enterprise pay off—what more, ever? What I would like to do is less spectacular on the surface. But it would mean a breaking of the circle: an altogether new order of experience. Were you not so obsessed with your vision of yourself as a bold pioneer, you would see what I mean."

Yah. Now I do.

We didn't see we'd been blued till we put the articles of partnership through a semantic computer. He must have used symbolic logic to write them, under all the rainbow language. The one isolated fusing thing he was legally committed to do was conduct explorations on our behalf. He could go anywhere, do anything, for any reason he liked. So of course he used our money to outfit his damned expedition! He'd found that rhenium beforehand. He didn't want to wait five years for the returns to quantum in; might not've been enough anyway. So he dozzled up that potburning machine of his and— On Earth they call that swindle the Gypsy Blessing.

Oh, in time we got some sort of profit out of Despair, though not half what we should've dragged on so big an investment. And he tried to repay us in selfcharge if not in cash. But—the output of the whole works is—here I am, with a whole star cluster named after me, and there's not a fellow human being in the universe that I can tell why!

—Recorded in the diary of Urwain
the Wide-Faring

THE TROUBLE TWISTERS

✲I✲

Poker is not a very good three-handed game, so the crew of the trade pioneer ship *Muddlin' Through* had programmed her computer to play with them. It bought chips with IOUs. Being adjusted to an exactly average level of competence, it just about balanced winnings and losses in the course of a mission. This freed the crew to go after each other's blood.

"Two cards," said its mechanical voice. David Falkayn dealt them onto a scanner plate that he had rigged at one end of the saloon table. An arm projecting from a modified waldo box shoved the discards aside. Down in their armored tank, at the middle of the ship, think cells assessed the new odds.

"One," said Chee Lan.

"None for me, thank you," rumbled Adzel.

Falkayn gave himself three and picked up his hand. He'd improved: a pair of treys to match his kings. Adzel might well stand pat on nothing better, and Chee had probably tried to complete a flush; the first round of betting, opened by the machine, had been unenthusiastic. But Muddlehead itself, now—

The steel arm dropped a blue chip into the pot.

"*Damn!*" shrieked Chee. Her tail bottled out to twice its normal size, the silky-white fur stood erect over her whole small body, and she threw her cards down so hard that the tabletop ought to have rung. "Pestilence upon you! I hate your cryogenic guts!"

Imperturbably, Adzel doubled the bet. Falkayn sighed and folded.

Chee's fury ebbed as fast as it had come. She settled down on her elevated stool and began washing, cat-fashion. Falkayn reached for a cigarette.

Muddlehead raised back. Adzel's dragon countenance wasn't able to change expression, except for the rubbery lips, but his huge scaly form, sprawled across the cabin, grew tense. He studied his cards again.

A bell tone interrupted him. That part of the computer which was always on watch had observed something unusual.

"I'll go," Falkayn said. He rose and went quickly down the forward passageway: a tall and muscled young man, yellow-haired, blue-eyed, snub-nosed, and high of cheekbone. Even here, light-years from the nearest fellow human, he wore lounging pajamas that would not have been out of place in Tycho Lodge. He told himself that he was obliged to maintain standards—younger son of a baronial house on Hermes, currently a representative of the Polesotechnic League, and all that sort of thing—but the fact was that he had not quite outgrown a certain vanity.

At the midsection scanner turret, he punched controls. No oddities appeared in the screen. What the devil had the observer units noticed? So much computer capacity was engaged in the game that the ship herself couldn't tell him. Maybe he'd better— He shifted the cigarette in his mouth and increased the magnification.

Westward in a deep purplish sky, the sun stood at eternal late afternoon. It was a K_0 dwarf, barely one-tenth as luminous as man's home star, furnace red. But at a mere third of an astronomical unit from Ikrananka, it showed nearly three and a half times the angular diameter and gave about as much irradiation. Through the dull light and thin air, a few other stars were visible. Spica, little more than three parsecs away, shone like a white jewel. Otherwise the heavens held nothing but a flock of leathery-winged flying beasties and, above the northern heights, the yellow cloud of a dust storm.

Halfway up a hill, *Muddlin' Through* commanded a wide overlook of the Chakora. That former sea bottom stretched ruddy-green and indigo shadowed, densely planted with low succulent crops. Here and there on it Falkayn could see clusters of buildings, woven in patterns from gaily colored fibers, each surrounding a stone tower: the thorps and defensive keeps of agricultural families. Wherever a spring seeped forth, the vegetation became intensely verdant and gold. And there thickets of long stalks, like plumed bamboo, the closest this world had ever come to trees, swayed in the wind.

The hill itself was craggy, eroded, with little except scrub growing between the boulders. On its top loomed the ramparts of Haijakata. At the foot was a tower guarding the town's well, accessible from above through a tunnel. Nearby, a dirt road from the east twisted to enter the gates. Falkayn didn't see any natives abroad.

No, wait. Dust smoked on that highway, three or four kilometers off but rapidly nearing. Somebody was bound here in an awful hurry.

Falkayn adjusted the scanner. The scene leaped at him.

Half a dozen Ikranankans were urging their zandaras on. The big, brown-furred, thick-tailed bipeds rose in soaring arcs, touched earth, instantly gathered their leg muscles and sprang again. The riders shook lances and sabers aloft. Their open beaks showed that they screamed.

A breeze blew aside the dust and Falkayn saw what they were pursuing. He just avoided swallowing his cigarette.

"No," he heard himself feebly say. "Such things don't happen, I swear they don't."

His paralysis broke. He whirled and ran back aft. At a mere sixty-five percent of Terrestrial gravity, he moved like a scared comet. He burst into the saloon, skidded to a halt, and roared, "Emergency!"

Chee Lan hopped across the table and switched the computer back to normal function. Adzel thrust a final chip into the pot and turned over his cards. He had a straight. "What is the matter?" Chee asked, glacially self-possessed as always when trouble showed.

"A . . . a woman," Falkayn panted. "Being chased."

"By whom?"

"Not me, dammit. But listen, it's so! Bunch of native cavalry after a human female. Her zandara looks tired. They'll catch her before she gets here, and Lord knows what they'll do."

While Falkayn was blurting, Adzel looked at Muddlehead's hand. Full house. He sighed philosophically and shoved the pot over. Rising, he said, "Best we go remonstrate with them. Chee, stand by."

The Cynthian nodded and pattered off to the bridge. Adzel followed Falkayn to the lower exit. His cloven hooves clanged on the deck. At the locker, the man slipped on a gun belt and stuck a radio transceiver into a pocket of the coat he grabbed. They valved through.

To avoid delays when going out, they maintained interior air pressure at local norm, about three-fourths of Earth sea level. But they preferred more warmth and moisture. Swift, dry, and chill, the wind struck savagely at Falkayn's mucous membranes. His eyes needed a moment to adapt. Adzel picked him up in two great horny hands and set him on his own back, just behind the centauroid torso. The Wodenite had had one of the sharp plates which jutted from his head, along his spine to the end of his tail, removed for that purpose. He started downhill in a smooth gallop. His musky odor blew back around Falkayn.

"One supposes that another ship has come," he said, his basso as placid as if they were still dealing cards. "By accident?"

"Must be." Falkayn squinted ahead. "She's dressed funny, though. Could she have run afoul of barbarian raiders? We do keep getting hints of war in the Sundhadarta mountains."

He could barely make out the highest peaks of that range, glooming above the eastern horizon. On his left marched the tawny cliffs which had once been a continental shelf. To the right lay only the evergreen fields of the Chakora. Behind him reared Haijakata hill, and his ship like a shining spearhead. But the view here had grown deadly familiar. He wasn't sorry for a bit of action. No danger to speak of; that gang would probably head for home and mother the minute they saw Adzel.

Muscles rippled between his thighs. The cloven air shrilled and nipped his ears. Hoofbeats drummed. And now, ahead, he could clearly see the girl and her pursuers. Harsh nonhuman yelps reached him.

She waved and spurred her flagging zandara to a last rush. The Ikranankans shouted to each other. Falkayn caught a few words—why, they spoke the Katandaran language perfectly—

One of them halted his beast and unshipped a crossbow from his saddle. It was a slender weapon. His arms had merely half a man's strength to cock it. But the darts it threw were needle sharp and traveled far in this gravity. He fired. The missile zipped within centimeters of her loosened auburn braids. He cried an order while he fitted another dart. Two more riders unlimbered their own bows.

"Judas on Pluto!" Falkayn gasped. "They mean to kill her!"

Every sense he had surged to full alertness. He looked through red-tinged dust and ruby light as if he were face to face with the closest autochthon.

The being stood some one hundred fifty centimeters tall. In body he resembled a barrel-chested, wasp-waisted man with unduly long, thin limbs. Sleek brown fur covered him; he was warm-blooded and omnivorous, and his mate brought forth her young alive; but for all that, he was no mammal. Atop a slender neck, his bowling-ball head sported a black ruff, pale eyes, donkeylike ears, and a corvine beak that might have been molded in amber. His padded feet were bare so the three long toes on each could grip stirrups. Otherwise he wore tight cross-gartered pants, a leather cuirass with iron shoulder pieces and a zigzag insigne on the breast, and a wide belt from which there hung dagger and saber. Three sharp-nailed fingers and a thumb cranked the bow taut. His right hand lifted the stock.

Falkayn snatched forth his blaster and fired upward. It was a warning; also, the beam dazzled native eyes and spoiled their aim. The girl cheered.

The squad at her back scattered. They were all accoutered more or less alike. The kinship symbol they shared was not familiar to Falkayn. Their leader screeched a command. They rallied and charged on. A dart buzzed near the man. Another broke on Adzel's scales.

"Why—why—they have decided to kill us, too," the Wodenite stammered. "They must have been prepared for the sight of us."

"*Get going!*" Falkayn howled.

He was born and bred an aristocrat on a planet where they still needed soldiers. Boyhood training took over in him. Gone metal steady, he narrowed his fire beam for maximum range and dropped one zandara in its tracks.

Adzel opened up. His ton of mass accelerated to a sprint of one hundred fifty KPH. Wind whipped blindingly in Falkayn's eyes. But he wasn't needed any more. Adzel had gotten in among the Ikranankans. He simply bowled over the first animal and rider. Two others spun through the air in a bow wave. His tail struck to one side, and that flattened a fourth. The last two bolted off across the fields.

Adzel braked himself and trotted back. A couple of the opposition were hotfooting it elsewhere, the other casualties seemed barely able to move. "Oh, dear," he said. "I do hope we did not injure them seriously."

Falkayn shrugged. A race of giants could afford to be gentler than men. "Let's get back to the ship," he said.

The girl had stopped further down the road. As they neared her, his lips shaped a whistle.

Perhaps she was a little too muscular for his taste. But what a figure! Tall, full, long-legged and straight-backed . . . and her outfit showed delightfully much of it, what with half-length boots, fur kilt hiked up for riding, doublet appropriately curved over a sleeveless blouse, and a short blue cloak. She was armed with cutlery similar to the natives', had a painted shield hung by her saddle and a flat helmet over her rusty coils of hair. Her skin was very white. The features had an almost Hellenic clearness, with big gray eyes and wide mouth to soften them.

"What *ho!*" Falkayn murmured. "And where are you from, lass?"

She wiped sweat off her brow and breathed hard, which was pleasant to see. Adzel continued lumbering down the road. She clucked to her zandara. It walked alongside, too exhausted to be skittish of his enormousness.

"You . . . are . . . are in truth from Beyond-the-World?" she asked. Her husky Anglic held an accent he had never met before.

"Yes. I suppose so." Falkayn pointed to the ship.

She traced a sign. "*Algat* is good!" The word was local, meaning approximately "magic."

Recovering some composure, she peered after her enemies. They had restored order, but weren't giving chase. Even as she watched, one of them on an unharmed animal started off, hell for leather, toward the far side of the hill. The rest followed slowly.

She reached out to touch Falkayn's hand, as if to make sure he was real. "Only rumors drifted usward," she said low. "We heard a strange Ershokh had arrived in a flying chariot, and the Emperor forbade anyone to come near. But the story could've grown in telling. You are truly from Beyond-the-World? Even from Earth?"

"I said yes," he answered. "But what are you talking about? What do you mean, Ershokh?"

"Humans. Did you not know? They call us Ershoka in

Katandara." She considered him, and it was as if a mask slid over her. With a slowness and caution he did not understand, she ventured: "Ever since our ancestors came, over four hundred years ago."

"Four hundred?" Falkayn's jaw hit his Adam's apple. "But the hyperdrive wasn't invented then!"

"Obviously she means Ikranankan years," said Adzel, who was hard to surprise. "Let me see, with a revolution period of seventy-two standard days . . . yes, that makes about seventy-five Terrestrial years."

"But—I say, how the deuce—"

"They were bound elsewhere, to . . . what is the word? . . . to be colonists," the girl said. "Robbers captured them and left them here, the whole five hundred."

Falkayn tried to make his mind stop whirling. Vaguely he heard Adzel say, "Ah, yes, doubtless a squadron from the Pirate Suns, venturing so far from their bases in the hope of just such valuable booty as a large ship. They were not interested in ransom. But it was meritorious of them to find a habitable planet and maroon rather than kill their prisoners." He patted her shoulder. "Do not fret, small female. The Polesotechnic League has long since taught the Pirate Sun dwellers the error of their ways."

Falkayn decided that any comforting should be done by him. "Well!" he beamed. "What a sensation this will make! As soon as we tell Earth, they'll send transportation for you."

Still she watched him, strangely and disappointingly careful. A damsel lately in distress ought not to act that way. "You are an Ersho—I mean an Earthman?"

"Actually I'm a citizen of the Grand Duchy of Hermes, and my shipmates are from other planets. But we operate out of Earth. David Falkayn's my name."

"I am Stepha Carls, a lieutenant in the household troops of—" She broke off. "No matter now."

"Why were those klongs chasing you?"

She smiled a little. "One thing at a time, I beg. So much to tell each other, truth?" But then she did drop her reserve. Her eyes widened, her smile went up to about fifty megawatts, she clapped her hands and cried: "Oh, this is purest wonder! A man from Earth—my own rescuer!"

Well, now, Falkayn thought, a bit stunned, *that's more like it.* He dropped his questions and simply admired the scenery. After all, he'd been away from humankind for a good many weeks.

At the ship they tethered the zandara to a landing jack. Falkayn bowed Stepha up the ramp to the lock. Chee Lan came springing to meet them. "What a darling pet," the girl exclaimed.

Chee bristled. In some respects she was not unlike Master Beljagor. "You try to kitchy-koo me, young lady, and you'll be lucky to get your fingers back." She swung on her fellows. "What in the name of nine times nine to the ninety-ninth devils is going on?"

"Didn't you watch the fight?" Falkayn said. Under Stepha's eyes, he preened himself. "I thought we did a rather good job on those bandits."

"What bandits?" Chee snapped. "From here I could see them go right into town. If you ask me—if you have the wit to ask me, you pair of vacuum-headed louts—you've clobbered a squad of Imperial soldiers—the same Emperor's that we came here to deal with!"

II

They hied themselves to the saloon. Going into town might lead to being shot at. Let Gujgengi come and ask for an explanation. Besides, they had a lot of mutual explaining to get out of the way first.

Falkayn poured Scotch for himself and Stepha. Adzel took a four-liter bucket of coffee. His Buddhistic principles did not preclude drinking, but no ship on an extended mission could carry enough liquor to do him much good. Chee Lan, who was not affected by alcohol, kindled a mildly narcotic cigarette in an interminable ivory holder. They were all in bad need of soothing.

The girl squinted and scowled simultaneously at her glass—she wasn't used to Earth illumination—raised it to her lips, and tossed it off. "Whoo-oo-oo!" she spluttered. Falkayn pounded her back. Between coughs and wheezes, her oaths made him blush. "I thought you were being niggard," she said weakly.

"I suppose you would have lost most of your technology in three generations, at that," Adzel said. "Five hundred people, children included, have insufficient knowledge between them to maintain a modern civilization, and a colony ship would not have carried a full microlibrary."

Stepha wiped her eyes and looked at him. "I always thought Great Granther was an awful liar," she said. "But reckon he must really have seen some things as a youngling. Where are you from?"

He was certainly an impressive sight. Counting the tail, his quadrupedal body was a good four and a half meters long, and the torso had arms, chest, and shoulders to match. Blue-gray scales shimmered overall, save where scutes protected the belly and plates the back; those were umber. The crocodilian head sat on a meter of neck, with bony ears and shelves over the eyes. But those eyes were large, brown, and wistful, and the skull bulged backward to hold a considerable brain.

"Earth," he said. "That is, Zatlakh, which means 'earth' in my language. Humans dubbed it Woden. That was before they ran out of Terrestrial names for planets. Nowadays, for the most part, one uses whatever term is found in the language of what seems the most advanced local culture: as, for instance, 'Ikrananka' here."

"Wouldn't *you* be good in combat?" Stepha mused. One hand dropped to her dagger.

Adzel winced. "Please. We are most peaceful. We are only so large and armored because Woden breeds giant animals. The sun is type F5, you see, in the Regulus sector. It puts out so much energy that, in spite of a surface gravity equal to two and a half times Earth's, life can grow massive and—"

"Shut your gas jet, you blithering barbarian," Chee Lan cut in. "We've work on hand."

Adzel came near losing his temper. "My friend," he growled, "it is most discourteous to denigrate other cultures. Granted that my own people are simple hunters, nevertheless we would dare set our arts against anyone's. And when I got a scholarship to study planetology on Earth, I earned extra money by singing Fafnir in the San Francisco Opera."

"Also by parading at Chinese New Year's," said Chee poisonously.

Falkayn struck the table with his fist. "That'll do for both of you," he rapped.

"But where in truth is the, ah, lady from?" Stepha asked.

"The second planet of O_2 Eridani A," Falkayn said. "Cynthia, its human discoverers named it, after the captain's wife."

"I have heard that she was not exactly his wife," Chee murmured.

Falkayn blushed again and stole a glance at Stepha. But she didn't look embarrassed; and considering those cusswords she'd ripped out—"They'd reached about an Alexandrine level of technology on one continent, at the time," he said, "and had invented the scientific method. But they didn't have cities. A nation was equal to a trade route. So they've fitted very well into League activities." He realized that now he was blithering, and stopped short.

Chee tapped the ash from her cigarette with one delicate six-digited hand. She herself was a mere ninety centimeters tall when she stood fully erect. Mostly she crouched on muscular legs and equally long arms, her magnificent brush curled over the back. Her head was big in proportion, round, with a short black-nosed muzzle, neat little ears, and cat whiskers. Save for a dark mask around the huge luminous-golden eyes, she was entirely covered by white Angora fur. Her thin voice turned brisk: "Let us begin by reviewing your situation, Freelady Carls. No, pardon me, Lieutenant Carls, isn't it? I assume your ancestors were marooned in this general area."

"Yes," Stepha nodded. She picked her words with renewed care. "They soon made touch with the natives, sometimes violent, sometimes not. The violence taught them humans have more strength and endurance than Ikranankans. And here is always war. Better, easier, to be the best soldiers than sweat in fields and mines, not so? Ever since, every Ershokh has grown into the—body?—the corps. Those who can't fight are quartermasters and such." Falkayn observed a scar on her arm. *Poor kid,* he thought in pity. *This is all wrong. She should be dancing and flirting on Earth, with me, for instance. A girl is too sweet and gentle a creature in her heart to—*

Stepha's eyes glittered. "I heard old people tell of wars in Beyond-the-World," she said eagerly. "Could we hire out?"

"What? Well—er—"

"I'm good. You should have seen me at the Battle of the Yanjeh. Ha! They charged our line. One zandara spitted itself on my pike, ran right up." Stepha jumped to her feet, drew her saber and whizzed it through the air. "I took the rider's head off with one sweep. It bounced. I turned and split the fellow beside him from gullet to guts.

A dismounted trooper attacked on my left. I gave him my shield boss, crunch, right in the beak. Then—"

"Please!" roared Adzel, and covered his ears.

"We do have to find out the situation," Falkayn added hastily. "Are you or are you not an enemy of the Emperor in Katandara?"

Stepha checked her vehemence, sat down again, and held out her glass for a refill. Once more she was speaking with great caution. "The Ershoka hired out to the first Jadhadi, when the old Empire fell apart. They helped set him on the Beast in Katandara, and rebuild the Empire and expand it, and since then they've been the household troops of each Emperor and the core of his army. Of late, some of them were the capturers of Rangakora, in Sundhadarta to the east on the edge of the Twilight. And that's a most important place to hold. Not alone does it command the chief pass through the mountains, but the water thereabouts makes that country the richest in the Chakora."

"To chaos with your pus-bleeding geopolitics!" Chee interrupted. "Why were you being chased by Imperial soldiers?"

"Um-m-m . . . I am not sure." Stepha sipped for a moment's silence. "Best might be if you tell me of yourselves first. Then maybe between us we can find why the third Jadhadi has you off here instead of in Katandara. Or do you know?"

Adzel shook his ponderous head. "We do not," he answered. "Indeed, we were unaware of being quarantined. We did have intimations. It seemed curious that we have not yet been invited to the capital, and that so few came to visit us even among local dwellers. When we took the flitter out for a spin, we observed military encampments at some distance. Then Gujgengi requested that we refrain from flying. He said the unfamiliar sight produced too much consternation. I hesitate to accuse anyone of prevaricating, but the reason did seem rather tenuous."

"You are truth-told walled away, by Imperial order," Stepha said grimly. "Haijakata has been forbidden to any outsiders, and no one may leave these parts. It hurts trade, but—" Falkayn was about to ask why she had violated the ban, when she continued: "Tell me, though—how come you to be here, in this piddling little corner of nowhere? Why did you come to Ikrananka at all?"

"She's stalling," Chee hissed to Falkayn in League Latin.

"I know," he answered likewise. "But can you blame her? Here we are, total strangers, and the last contact her people had with galactic civilization was that piracy. We've got to be kind, show her we really mean well."

Chee threw up her hands. "Oh, cosmos!" she groaned. "You and your damned mating instinct!"

Falkayn turned his back on her. "Pardon us," he said in Anglic. "We, uh, had something personal to discuss."

Stepha smiled, patted his hand, and leaned quite close to breathe, "I do understand, David. . . . So pretty a name, David. And you from Beyond-the-World! I'm strangling to hear everything about you."

"Well, uh, that is," stuttered Falkayn, "we're trade pioneers. Something new." He hoped his grin was modest rather than silly. "I, er, helped work out the idea myself." With due regard for preserving the basic secret, he explained.

Nicholas van Rijn left his desk and waddled across to the transparency that made one entire wall of his office. From this height, he could overlook a sweep of slim city towers, green parkscape, Sunda Straits flashing under Earth's lordly sky. For a while he stood puffing his cigar, until, without turning around, he said:

"*Ja,* by damn, I think you has here the bacteria of a good project with much profit. And you is a right man to carry it away. I have watched you like a hog, ever since I hear what you did on Ivanhoe when you was a, you pardon the expression, teen-ager. Now you got your Master's certificate in the League, uh-huh, you can be good working for the Solar Spice & Liquors Company. And I need good men, poor old fat lonely me. You bring home the bacon and eggs scrambled with turmeric, I see you get rich."

"Yes, sir," Falkayn mumbled.

"You come speak of how you like to help open new places, for new stuffs to sell here and natives to buy from us what have not yet heard what the market prices are. Hokay. Only I think you got more possibilities, boy. I been thinking a lot, me, these long, long nights when I toss and turn, getting no sleep with my worries."

Falkayn refrained from telling van Rijn that everybody knew the cause of the merchant's current insomnia was blond and curvy. "What do you mean, sir?" he asked.

Van Rijn faced about, tugged his goatee, and studied him out of beady eyes set close to the great hook nose. "I tell you confidential," he said at length. "You not violate my confidence, ha? I got so few friends. You break my old gray heart and I personal wring your neck. Understand? Fine, fine. I like a boy what has got good understandings.

"My notion is, here the League finds new planets, and everybody jumps in with both feets and is one cutthroat scramble. You thought you might go in at this. But no, no, you is too fine, too sensitive. I can see that. Also, you is not yet one of the famous space captains, and nobody spies to see where you is bound next. So . . . for Solar Spice & Liquors, you go find us our private planets!" He advanced and dug a thumb into Falkayn's ribs. The younger man staggered. "How you like that, ha?"

"But—but—that is—"

Van Rijn tapped two liters of beer from his cooler, clinked glasses, and explained.

The galaxy, even this tiny fragment of one spiral arm which we have somewhat explored, is inconceivably huge. In the course of visiting and perhaps colonizing worlds of obvious interest to them, space travelers have leapfrogged past literally millions of others. Many are not even catalogued. Without a special effort, they are unlikely to become known for millennia. Yet from statistics we can predict that thousands of them are potentially valuable, as markets and sources of new exotic goods. Rather than continue to exploit the discovered planets, why not find new ones . . . and keep the fact quiet as long as possible?

A sector would be chosen, out where the traffic is still thin: Spica, for instance. A base would be established. Small, cheap automated craft would be dispatched by the hundreds. Whenever they found a world that, from their standardized observations of surface conditions, seemed promising, they would report back. The trade pioneer crew would go for a closer look. If they struck pay dirt, they would collect basic information, lay the groundwork for commercial agreements, and notify van Rijn.

"Three in a ship, I think, is enough," he said. "Better be enough, what wages and commissions your pest-be-damned Brotherhood charges! You, the Master merchant, trained in culture comparisons and swogglehorning. A planetologist and a xenobiologist. They should be nonhumans. Different talents, you see, also not so much nerve-scratching when cooped together. Nicer to have a lovingly girl along, I know, but when you get back again, ha, ha!—you make up good. Or even before. You got just invited to my next little orgy, boy, if you take the job."

"So you knew there was a civilization here with metal," Stepha nodded. "Of course your robots—jeroo, to think I never believed Great Granther when he talked about robots!—they didn't see us few Ershoka. But what did they tell you was worth coming here for?"

"An Earthlike planet is always worth investigating," Falkayn said.

"What? This is like Earth? Great Granther—"

"Any planet where men can live without special apparatus is Earthlike. They're not too common, you see. The physical conditions, the biochemistry, the ecology . . . never mind. Ikrananka has plenty of differences from Earth or Hermes, true."

(Mass, 0.394 Terrestrial, density 0.815, diameter 0.783. But though its sun is feeble, it orbits close. To be sure, then tidal action has forced one hemisphere constantly to face the primary. But this slow rotation in turn means a weak magnetic field, hence comparatively little interaction with stellar charged particles, which are not emitted very strongly from a red dwarf anyway. Thus it keeps a reasonable atmosphere. Granted, most of the water has been carried to the cold side and frozen, making the warm side largely desert. But this took time, during which life based on proteins in water solution could evolve and adapt. Indeed, the chemistry remains startlingly like home.)

"What is there to get here?"

"Lots. The robots brought back pictures and samples. At least two new intoxicants, several antibiotics, potential spices, some spectacular furs, and doubtless much else. Also a well-developed civilization to gather the stuff for us, in exchange for trade goods that they're far enough advanced to appreciate."

Chee smacked her lips. "The commissions to be gotten!"

Stepha sighed. "I wish you'd speak Anglic. But I'll take your word for true. Why did you land at Haijakata? You must have known Katandara is the biggest city."

"It's complicated enough being a visitor from space, without getting swarmed over from the start," Falkayn replied. "We've been learning the local language, customs, the whole setup, in this backwater. It goes pretty quick, with modern mnemonic techniques. And the Emperor sent Gujgengi as a special teacher, once he heard of us. We were going to the capital before now; but as soon as we announced that, the professor started finding excuses for delay. That was three or four weeks back."

"I wonder how much we really have learned," Chee muttered.

"What are weeks?" Stepha asked.

"Forget it," Chee said. "See here, female, you have involved us in trouble that may cost us our whole market."

"What a stupid!" the girl barked impatiently. "Conquer them."

"A highly immoral procedure," Adzel scolded. "Also it is against policy: as much, I confess, because of being economically unfeasible as for any other reason."

"Will you get to the point, you yattertongues?" Chee screamed. "Why were those soldiers after you?"

The alarm bell toned. The computer said, "A party is approaching from the town."

III

Falkayn decided he had better be courteous and meet the Imperial envoy-instructor at the air lock. He kept his blaster conspicuously on one hip.

Waiting, he could look up to the walls on the hillcrest. They were of dry-laid stone; water was too precious to use in mortar. Their battlements, and the gaunt towers at their corners, enclosed a few score woven houses. Haijakata was a mere trading center for the local farmers and for caravans passing through. A rather small garrison was maintained. The northern highlands had been cleared of those barbarian raiders who haunted most deserts, Gujgengi admitted, so Falkayn suspected the troops were quartered here mainly as a precaution against revolt. What little he had found out of Ikranankan history sounded turbulent.

Which is still another worry, he fretted. *Old Nick isn't going to invest in expensive facilities unless there's a reasonably stable social order to keep the trade routes open. And the Katandaran Empire looks like the only suitable area on the whole planet. No trading post on Ikrananka, no commissions for me. What a jolly, carefree, swashbuckling life we explorers lead!*

His gaze shifted to the oncoming party. There were a couple of dozen soldiers, in leather breastplates, armed to the teeth they didn't have with swords, knives, crossbows, and big ugly halberds. All wore the curlicue insigne of the Tirut phratry; everyone in the garrison did. At their head stalked Gujgengi. He was tall for an Ikranankan, skinny, his blue-black fur grizzled, a pair of gold-rimmed spectacles perched precariously on his beak. A scarlet robe swept to his feet, emblazoned with the crest of the Deodakh, the Imperial, phratry. At his tasseled belt hung a long snickersnee. Falkayn had not yet seen any native male without a weapon.

The human made the knee bend with arms crossed on breast that did duty here for a salaam. "To the most noble Gujgengi and his relatives, greeting," he intoned ritually. He'd never be able to pronounce this guttural language right. His speaking apparatus was not designed for it. And his grammar was still ramshackle. But by now he was reasonably fluent.

Gujgengi did not use the formula, "Peace between our kindred," but rather, "Let us talk," which implied there was a serious matter on hand that he *hoped* could be settled without bloodshed. And he made signs against evil, which he hadn't done of late.

"Honor my house," Falkayn invited, since the native tongue had no word for ship and "wagon" was ridiculous.

Gujgengi left his followers posted and stiffly climbed the ramp. "I do wish you would put in decent lighting," he complained. Since he saw no wavelength shorter than yellow, though his visual spectrum included the near infrared, the fluoros were dim to him; his horizontal-pupiled eyes had little dark adaptation, which was scarcely needed on the sunward hemisphere.

Falkayn guided him to the saloon. Gujgengi grumbled the whole way. This place was too hot, one might as well be in Subsolar country, and it stank and the air was wet and would Falkayn please quit breathing damp on him. Ikranankans didn't exhale water vapor. What their metabolism produced went straight into the bloodstream.

Stepha sat for a moment in a silence deepened by the rustle of air in ventilators, the impatient tap of Chee's cigarette holder on the table, and Gujgengi's asthmatic breathing. She scowled at the deck and tugged her chin. Abruptly she reached a decision, straightened, and said:

"Yes, truth, this has hurt the Ershoka in Katandara. They know they're under suspicion. Let the Emperor get too bloody suspicious, and he may even try to have 'em massacred. I don't think that'd be so wise of him—any bets who'd come out of the fracas alive?—but we don't want to rip the Empire apart. At the same time, we've got to look out for our own. So we heard rumors about these new-come strangers. Bound to happen, you know. Haijakatans would've carried the news around before the ban was laid on. Now and then, a planter may still sneak past the guard posts. We had to find out, in the Iron House, what these yarns meant. Else we'd be like blind men on a cliff trail. I reckoned to reach this place. My own idea, I true-speak you. None else knew. But a patrol eyeballed me."

Gujgengi did not seize on the obvious opportunity to bluster about loyalty and subordination. Or maybe there was no such chance. More and more during the weeks, Falkayn had gotten the impression that Ikranankans were loyal to their own blood kindred and anything else was a mere bond of convenience.

But wait!

Excited, he sprang up. Gujgengi reached for his sword, but the man only paced, back and forth, feet jarring on the deck, as he rattled out:

"Hey, this whole thing is a turn of magic for us." No word for good luck. "Your Emperor was wrong to suspect us. We're traders. Our interest lies in a secure realm that we can deal with. The weapons on this ship can blow down any wall ever built. We'll take Rangakora for him."

"No!" Stepha shouted. She boiled to her own feet, saber gleaming forth. "You filthy—"

Falkayn let her run down, in Adzel's grasp, before he asked, "Why, what's wrong? Aren't you on the Imperial side?"

"Before I let you kill a thousand Ershoka," she said between her teeth, "I'll—" and she was off again, in quite a long and anatomical catalogue of what she would do to David Falkayn.

"Oh, but honey chil'," he protested. "You don't understand. I'm not going to kill anybody. Just knock down a wall or two, and overawe the garrison."

"Then Jadhadi's soldiers will take care of them," she said bleakly.

"Uh-uh. We'll protect them. Make some arrangement."

"See here," Gujgengi objected, "the Emperor's prerogatives—"

Falkayn told him where the Emperor could store his prerogatives, but in Latin. In Katandaran he said, "An amnesty is our price for helping. With safeguards. I don't think it's too high. But that's for the Emperor to decide. We'll fly to him and discuss the matter."

"Now, wait!" Gujgengi cried. "You cannot—"

"Precisely how do you plan to stop us, sonny boy?" Chee leered.

Gujgengi fell back on argument. The Emperor would be displeased if his orders were flouted. There was no suitable place in Katandara for landing the ship. The populace was so uneasy that the sight could provoke a riot. Et cetera, et cetera.

"Best we compromise," Adzel whispered. "Arrogance breeds resistance."

After considerable haggling, Gujgengi agreed that, under the circumstances, the flitter might go. It was small, could dart in before many people saw it and sit unseen in the palace gardens. And indeed a message to Katandara by land would take an awkwardly long time.

"As well, at that, to keep the ship here," Chee remarked. "A reserve, in case you have trouble."

"In case *we* do?" Adzel pounced.

"You don't think I intend to go live in that dust pot of an atmosphere, do you? Not if I can help it. And I can play my tapes in peace while you and your cast-iron ear are gone."

"If you intend to play what, for lack of a suitably malodorous word, is called Cynthian music, then I will most certainly not be here."

"We'll take you home with us," Falkayn offered Stepha.

She had held oddly aloof, watching with the mask back in place. Now she hesitated. "You won't get into trouble, will you?" he asked.

"N-n-no," she said in Anglic, which Gujgengi didn't speak. "My barrack mates will have covered my disappearance, even if they didn't know the reason for it. Not hard to do, when these stupid Ikranankans think all Ershoka look alike. But we must be—I mean, we're confined to the city for the time being. I can't walk right in the gates, and if I arrived openly with you, I'd be watched." She pondered. "You land quick, right in front of the Iron House, and I can dash in. If they ask you why, afterward, tell them you mistook it for the palace."

"Why do you care if you're watched?"

"I don't like the idea." She grasped his hands and leaned close. "Please, David. You've been so good a friend till now."

"Well—"

She waggled her eyelashes. "I hope we can become still better friends."

"All right, dammit!"

Arrangements were quickly made. Falkayn changed into a warm tunic, trousers, and boots, with a white cloak and a bejeweled cap tilted rakishly across his brow to add class. Two guns snugged at his waist, blaster and stunner. Into a breast pocket he slipped a transceiver; the planet had sufficient ionosphere for radio to reach between here and Katandara. He stuffed a bag with extra gear and gifts for the Emperor. Adzel took no more than a communicator hung about his neck.

"We'll call in regularly, Chee," Falkayn said. "If you don't hear from either of us for eight hours straight, haul gravs and come a-running."

"I still don't know why you bother," the Cynthian grumbled. "That wretched female has already spoiled this whole mission."

"The secrecy angle? We may solve that somehow. At worst, even with competitors swarming in, Old Nick will get some good out of a stable Empire. And, uh, in any event we can't let bloodshed go on."

"Why not?" She gave up. "Very well, be off. I'll continue our sessions with Gujgengi. The more information we have, the better."

The Imperial agent had already gone back to town with his escort. But Haijakata's parapets were dark with natives clustered to see the takeoff.

"Oh-h-h!" Stepha gasped and clutched Falkayn's arm. He resisted the temptation to do some aerial acrobatics and lined off for Katandara, a little north of west. The preliminary survey had made excellent maps, and Gujgengi had identified points of interest on them.

Kilometer after kilometer, the Chakora fled beneath them. They rode in a humming bubble over endless red-green fields, tiny thorps, once a strung-out caravan of laden four-footed karikuts guarded by warriors on zandara-back. "Those must be Shekhej," Stepha remarked. "Their phratry does most of the hauling in these parts."

Adzel, squeezing the trio together by his bulk (not that Falkayn minded), asked, "Is every trade a family affair?"

"Why, yes," Stepha said. "You're born a Shekhej, you're a caravaneer. All Deodaka used to be hunters till they conquered Katandara; now they're officials. The Tiruts and others, like we Ershoka, are soldiers. The Rahinjis are scribes. And so it goes."

"But suppose one is born with the wrong sort of talent?"

"Oh, each phratry has lots of different things to do. The main job is the most honorable one. But somebody has to keep house, keep accounts, keep farms if the group owns any—everything. You'd not trust that to outsiders, would you?

"Also, a youth at the age when he's to begin learning the phratry secrets, he can be adopted into a different one if he wants and if it'll take him. That's one reason we Ershoka are so apart. We couldn't marry with any Ikranankans"—Stepha giggled and made a vulgar joke—"so we have to stay in the corps. On t'other hand, for that same reason, we know we can trust our young. They've no place else to go. So we initiate them early."

"I understand most phratries are very ancient."

"Yes. Kingdoms come and go, none last more'n a few generations, but a bloodline is forever."

Her words confirmed what Falkayn had already gathered. It bespoke an ingrained clannishness that worried him. If the attitude was instinctive, this was a poor world in which to set up operations. But if it could be altered—if the Ikranankans could be made to feel loyalty toward something larger than a cluster of families—

Katandara hove into view. The city lay no more than two hundred kilometers from Haijakata, which in turn was halfway to Rangakora. The Empire's great extent was west and south, through the fertile Chakora.

Winding from the northeast came the Yanjeh River, a silver gleam surrounded by a belt of vegetation that glowed against stark eastern hills and tawny western ranchlands. Where it ran down the former continental shelf and emptied into broad, muddy Lake Urshi, Katandara was built. That was an impressive city, which must house half a million. Whole civilizations had possessed it, one after the other, as Rome and Constantinople, Peking and Mexico City, had been possessed: each adding to walls and towers and buildings, until now the ramparts enclosed a sprawl built almost entirely in stone. Old were those stones, the hewn outlines crumbling, and old were the narrow streets that twisted between facades gray, square, and secretive. Only at the landward end, where the ground rose steeply, was there anything not scoured by millennia of desert sand—the works of the newest rulers, marble-veneered and dome-topped, roofed with copper and decorated with abstract mosaics. That section, like those of earlier overlords, had a wall of its own, to protect masters from people.

With a magnifying scanner, Stepha could point out details at such a distance that the flitter was yet unseen. Falkayn went into a dive. Air shrieked. The controls thrummed beneath his hands. At the last instant, he threw in reverse grav and came to a bone-jarring halt.

"Farewell, David . . . till we meet again." Stepha leaned over and brushed her lips across his. Blood beat high in her face. He caught the sweet wild odor of her hair. Then she was out the lock.

The Ershoka were barracked in a single great building near the palace. It fronted on a cobbled square, along with the homes of the wealthy. Like them, it was built around a courtyard and turned a blank entry to the world. But some memory of Earth lingered in peaked iron roof, gable ends carved into monster heads, even the iron doors. A few Ikranankans gaped stupefied at the flitter. So did the sentries at the barrack entrance, big bearded men in chain mail, helmets gilt and plumed, cloaks that the wind flung about in rainbow stripes. But at once their weapons snapped up and they shouted.

Stepha sped toward them. Falkayn took off. He had a last glimpse of her being hustled inside.

"Now ho for Ol' Massa's," he said. "Let's hope he asks questions first and shoots later."

IV

A gong rang outside the guest apartment. "Come in," said Falkayn. A servant in close-fitting livery parted the thick drapes which served for interior doors in this wood-poor country. He saluted and announced that the Emperor wished audience with the delegates of the 'Olesotechnic' gir. His manner was polite but unservile, and he used no special titles for the ruler, like His Majesty or His Potency or His Most Awe-Inspiring Refulgence. The system of hereditary jobs did not amount to a caste hierarchy; backed by his kin, a janitor was as proudly independent as a soldier or scribe.

"My associate has gone out," Falkayn said, "but I suppose I'll do."

Do what? he wondered to himself. *We've been cooling our motors for a week by my watch. Maybe one of those couriers that keep scurrying back and forth has put a firecracker in Jadhadi's pants, at last. Or maybe this time I can, when he isn't looking. Sure wish so. All right, I'll do, and I'll do, and I'll do.*

He went to get a suitably fancy tunic for the occasion. The rooms lent him were spacious, except for low ceilings, and luxurious in their fashion. Too bad the fashion wasn't his. He liked hangings of gorgeous orange fur, especially when he estimated what such pelts would fetch on Earth. But the murals were not only in an alien artistic idiom; half the colors registered on him as mere black. The bare floor was always cold. And he couldn't fit himself comfortably onto the gaunt settees or into a shut-bed designed for an Ikranankan.

The third-story balcony gave him a view of the palace gardens. They suggested an Old Japanese layout: rocks, low subtly hued plants, the extravagance of a fountain—which played inside a glass column, to control evaporation. Little but roofs were visible above the estate walls. To the west, the sun shone dull and angry crimson through a dust veil. Another storm, Falkayn thought; more trouble for the ranchers out yonder.

A week inside an imperial palace could have been interesting, if the Imperium had been human and reasonably decadent. Katandara was neither. In sheer despair, he had been improving his language by reading what was billed as the greatest epic in the world. It had more begats than the Bible. He made a face at the codex and thumbed his transceiver. "Hullo, Adzel," he said in Latin, "how're you doing?"

"We are about to enter what I assume is a tavern," the Wodenite's voice replied. "At least, the legend says this is The House of Exquisite Pleasures and Ferocious Booze."

"Oh, Lord, and I have to mind the store. Listen, the big red wheel has summoned me. Probably just for more quizzing and more postponement of any decision, but you never know. So maintain radio silence, huh?" As far as the galactics could tell, the Ikranankans were ignorant of this means of communication. It was as well to keep some aces in the hole.

Unless the Ershoka had told—No, that seemed unlikely. Set down with nothing more than clothes and a few hand tools, caught up almost at once in this tumultuous culture, their ancestors had rapidly forgotten the arts of home. Why build guns or anything else that would prove an equalizer, even if you found time and skill to do so, when you lived by being twice as tough as the locals? Except for a few gadgets useful in everyday life, the humans had introduced nothing, and their knowledge dwindled away into fable.

"Very well," Adzel said. "I will assure Captain Padrick it is harmless magic. I have to calm him anyway. Good luck."

Falkayn returned to the main room and followed the servant down long corridors and sweeping ramps. A hum of activity surrounded him, footfalls, voices, rustling robes and papers. Ikranankans passed: gowned officials, hooded merchants, uniformed flunkies, planters in kilts, ranchers in chaps and spurred boots, visitors from afar, even a trader from the warm lands of Subsolar, shivering in a hairy cloak—the ebb and flow of life through this crown on the queen city. Cooking odors reminded Falkayn he was hungry. He had to admit regional cuisine was excellent, auguring well for van Rijn. If.

At the entrance to the throne room, four Ershoka stood guard, as gaudily outfitted as the men before the Iron House. They weren't at attention. That hadn't been invented here, and the humans had been smart enough not to suggest the idea. But they and their gleaming halberds scarcely moved. Flanking them were a dozen Tirut archers. Falkayn felt pretty sure those had been added since the troubles began in Rangakora. You couldn't blame Jadhadi for a soured attitude, when he could no longer trust his own *Sicherheitsdienst.*

Still, there was something downright paranoid about his wariness. Instead of jumping at Falkayn's offer to recover the stolen town, he'd interrogated for a week. Since he had nothing to lose by accepting, or at least hadn't given any such reasons, it must be due to exaggerated xenophobia. But what caused that, and what could be done about it?

Falkayn's attendant switched the drapes aside, and he passed through.

Jadhadi III waited on the Beast, a chimera in gilt bronze whose saddle he bestrode. Falkayn stopped at the required distance of seven paces (which, he suspected, gave the Ershoka by the thone time to intervene if he should make an assassin's lunge) and saluted. "Where is your companion?" asked the Emperor sharply. He was middle-aged, his fur still sleekly red-black, his beginning paunch hidden under a scarlet robe. One hand clutched a jeweled scepter which was also a businesslike spear.

"An officer of the household troops invited us on a tour of your city, most noble," Falkayn explained. "Not wishing to be both absent—"

"What officer?" Jadhadi leaned forward. The nearest of his Ershoka, a woman who would have made a better Valkyrie were she not battle-scarred, gray-haired, and built like a brick washtub, dropped hand to sword. The others in attendance, scribes, advisers, magicians, younger sons learning the business of government, edged closer. Their eyes glowed in the murky light.

"Why . . . Hugh Padrick, his name was, most noble."

"Ak-krrr. Will they be back soon?"

"I don't know, most noble. Is there any haste?"

"No. Perhaps not. Yet I mislike it." Jadhadi turned to a native guards officer. "Have them found and returned." To a scribe: "Post a notice that all Ershoka are forbidden contact with the delegates of the 'Olesotechnic' gir."

"Most noble!" The one other human not on sentry-go in the room—its length, between the polished malachite columns, was filled with alternate Ershoka and Otnakaji—stepped out from the courtiers. He was an old man, with beard and shoulder-length hair nearly white, but erect in his tunic. Falkayn had met him at other audiences: Harry Smit, senior of the phratry and its spokesman before the Emperor. "I protest."

The chamber grew suddenly very still. Shadows wove beneath the silver chandeliers, whose luminance shimmered on marble and fur and rich dark fabrics. Bitter incense smoked snakishly from braziers. The harpists at the far end of the chamber stopped their plangent chords, the ornate clock behind them seemed to tick louder.

Jadhadi stiffened in his saddle. The diamond eyes of the Beast glittered as hard as his own. "What say you?" the Emperor rasped.

Smit stood soldierly in front of him and answered: "Most noble, we Ershoka of your household also rage at Bobert Thorn's insubordination. He is no longer one of us, nor will we receive his followers among us again." (The woman guard acquired a look at those words, even more harsh than the situation warranted.) "Only let us march to Rangakora, and we will show you that the house of Ershokh stands by the house of Deodakh no less now than in the years of the first Jadhadi. But you trust us not. You keep us idle, you spy on our every step, you assign other phratries to join us in the duties that were ours since this palace was raised. This we have borne in patience, knowing you cannot be sure how strong the call of blood may be. Nonetheless, we chafe. They grumble in the Iron House. Insult them so openly, and I may not be able to restrain them."

For a moment glances clashed. Then Jadhadi looked away, toward his chief magician. "What say you, Nagagir?" he asked sullenly.

That stooped Ikranankan in the habit emblemed with devices of power refrained from saying the obvious—that this room held fifty Ershoka who wouldn't stand for any rough treatment of their phratry chief. Instead, he croaked shrewdly, "The matter seems slight, most noble. Very few guards will find their way to your distinguished guests. If they feel so strongly about it, what difference?"

"I was speaking in your own best interests," Harry Smit added in a mild voice.

Falkayn thought he saw an opening. "If we don't linger here, most noble, the issue hardly arises, does it?" he said. "Take my offer, and we'll be off to Rangakora; refuse, and we'll go home. What about a decision?"

"Krrr-ek." The Emperor gave in. "Cancel those orders," he said. To Falkayn: "I cannot decide blindly. We know so little about you. Even with friendly intentions, you could somehow bring bad luck. That was what I summoned you for today. Explain your rites to Nagagir, that he can evaluate them."

Oh no! Falkayn groaned to himself.

However, he found the session interesting. He'd wondered before about what seemed a total absence of religion but hadn't gotten around to querying Gujgengi. While he couldn't ask Nagagir to explain things point by point—might be as dangerous to reveal ignorance as to keep it—he gathered a certain amount of information indirectly. By claiming, sometimes falsely, not to understand various questions, he drew the magician out on the key items.

Only a moron or a tourist would generalize about an entire planet from a single culture. But you could usually figure that the most advanced people on a world had at least one of the more sophisticated theologies. And Katandara's was astoundingly crude. Falkayn wasn't sure whether to call that mishmash a religion or not. There weren't any gods: merely a normal order of things, an expected course of events, which had maintained ever since primordial Fire and Ice happened to get together and condense into the universe. But there were vaguely personified demons, powers, call them what you will; and they were forever trying to restore chaos. Their modus operandi was to cause disasters. They could only be held at bay through magic, ranging from a hundred everyday observances and taboos to the elaborate arcana which Nagagir and his college practiced.

And magicians weren't uniformly good, either. You never knew if somebody hadn't been corrupted and was lending his abilities to the service of Destruction.

The mythology sounded as paranoid as the rest of Ikranankan thought. Falkayn began to despair of getting a trade treaty okayed.

"Yes, indeed," he fended, "we of the Polesotechnic League are mighty wizards. We have studied deeply those laws of chance that govern the world. I'll be glad to teach you a most educational rite we call poker. And for keeping off bad luck, why, we can sell you talismans at unbelievably low prices, such as those precious herbs named four-leaved clovers."

Nagagir, though, wanted details. Falkayn's magic could be less effective than the human believed; Destruction sometimes lured people thus to their doom. It could even be black magic; the most noble would understand that this possibility had to be checked.

Not being Martin Schuster, to upset a whole cult by introducing the Kabbalah, Falkayn must needs stall. "I'll prepare an outline, most noble, which we can study together." *Lord help me,* he said to himself. *Or, rather, Chee Lan help me. Not Adzel—a Buddhist convert isn't good for much in this connection except soothing noises—but I've seen Chee tell fortunes at parties. I'll call her and we'll work out something.* "If you would make a similar outline of your own system for me, that would be valuable."

Nagagir's beak dropped open. Jadhadi rose in his golden stirrups, poised his spear, and screeched, "You pry into our secrets?"

"No, no, no!" Falkayn spread his hands and sweated. "Not your classified information—I mean, not anything hidden from the uninitiated of the sorcerer phratries. Just the things that everybody knows, except a foreigner like me."

Nagagir cooled off. "That shall be done," he said, "albeit the writing will take time."

"How long?"

Nagagir shrugged. Nobody else was much more helpful. While mechanical clocks had been around for some centuries, and the Ershoka had made improvements, Katandara used these simply to equalize work periods. Born to a world without nights or seasons, the people remained vague about any interval shorter than one of their seventy-two-day years. Matters were worse in the boondocks where *Muddlin' Through* sat. There, the Ikranankans just worked at whatever needed doing till they felt ready to knock off. Doubtless their attitude made for a good digestion. But Falkayn's innards curdled.

"May I go, most noble?" he asked. Jadhadi said yes, and Falkayn left before he spat in most noble's eye.

"Have some dinner brought me," he instructed the servant who guided him back, "and writing materials, and a jug of booze. A large jug."

"What kind of booze?"

"Ferocious, of course. Scat!" Falkayn dropped the curtain across his door.

An arm closed around his throat. "Guk!" he said, and reached for his guns while he kicked back.

His heel struck a heavy calf-length boot. The mugger's free hand clamped on his right wrist. Falkayn was strong, but he couldn't unlimber a weapon with that drag on him, nor the one on his left hip when another brawny Ershokh clung to that arm. He struggled for air. A third human glided into view before him. He lashed out with a foot, hit a shield, and would have yelped in anguish had he been able. The shield pressed him back against the mugger. And behind it was the face of Stepha Carls. Her right hand pushed a soaked rag over his nostrils. The strangler eased off; reflex filled Falkayn's lungs; an acrid smell hit him like a blow and whirled him toward darkness.

V

Ordinarily, Hugh Padrick said, Old City wasn't the safest area in the world. Aside from being the home of phratries specializing in murder, theft, strong-arm robbery—plus less antisocial occupations like gambling and prostitution—it was a skulking place for the remnants of earlier cycles, who resented the Deodakh conquest. Ershoka went down there in groups. However, Adzel counted as a group by himself.

"But I don't want to provoke a conflict," the Wodenite said.

"Hardly reckon you will," Padrick grinned. In undress uniform, tunic, trousers, boots, cloak, sword and knife, he was a big young man. His curly brown hair framed rugged features, where a new-looking beard grew beneath a Roman nose. His conversation had been interesting on the several occasions when he dropped in at the apartment. And Adzel, whose bump of curiosity was in proportion to the rest of him, couldn't resist the guardsman's offer of a conducted tour.

They strolled out the palace gates and across New City. The Wodenite drew stares but caused no sensation. News had gotten around about the Emperor's guests. And the educated class had some knowledge of astronomy.

"Did you humans teach them that?" Adzel asked when Padrick remarked on it.

"A little, I reckon," the Ershokh replied. "Though I'm told they already knew about the planets going around the sun and being worlds, even had a notion the stars are other suns."

"How could they? In this perpetual daylight—"

"From the Rangakorans, I think. That's a city with more arts than most. And close enough to Twilight that their explorers could go clear into the Dark for charting stars."

Adzel nodded. Atmospheric circulation must keep the far side reasonably warm. Even the antipodes of Subsolar would hardly get below minus fifty degrees or so. For the same reason, as well as the planet being smaller and the sun having a larger angular diameter, there was less edge effect here than on Earth. Neither the poles nor the border of Twilight differed radically in climate from the temperate zones.

Natives who ventured into the frozen lands would be handicapped by poor night vision. But after establishing fuel depots, they'd have fire on hand. Probably the original motive for such a base had been mining. Scientific curiosity came later.

"In fact," Padrick murmured, "Rangakora's a lot better town than this. More comfortable and more, uh, civilized. Sometimes I wish our ancestors had met the Rangakorans before they joined with a slew of barbarians invading a busted empire." He clipped his mouth shut and glanced around to make sure he hadn't been overheard.

Beyond the inner wall, the ground fell abruptly. Buildings grew progressively older, weathered gray blocks crowding each other, shut doors marked with the symbols of long-dead civilizations. In market sections, females occupied booths, crying their husbands' wares, food, drink, cloth, pelts, handicrafts. In the workshops behind them, iron rang, potters' wheels whirred, pedal-driven looms whickered. But the shops themselves were locked away from public sight, lest a demon or a wicked magician find ways to cause an accident.

Traffic was brisk, raucous, aggressive in fighting its way through the narrow sand streets. Planters' carts, drawn by spans of karikuts, loaded with Chakoran produce, creaked past near-naked porters with burdens on their shaven heads, but yielded to swaggering Shekheji caravaneers. A flatbed wagon was guarded by none less than several Tiruts, for it carried stalks spliced and glued together to make timber, more costly than bronze. Awkward when they must walk rather than leap, a dozen zandaras bore Lachnakoni come to trade hides for city goods; the desert dwellers gripped their lances tight and peered warily from behind their veils. Noise surfed around, harsh Ikranankan babble, rumblings, groanings, footfalls, clangor, and dust and smoke swirled with a thousand sharp smells.

No one disputed Adzel's right of way. Indeed, quite a few tried to climb straight up the nearest wall. A hundred beaked faces goggled fearfully off the verge of every flat roof. Padrick carried high a staff with the Deodakh flag, and of course *some* word about the strangers had penetrated this far. But the ordinary Katandaran didn't seem very reassured.

"Why is that one in the brown robe making signs at us, from yonder alley?" Adzel asked.

"He's a wizard. Taking your curse off the neighborhood. Or so he hopes." Padrick was hard to hear above the voice-roar that was rising toward a collective shriek.

"But I wouldn't curse anybody!"

"He doesn't know that. Anyhow, they reckon anything new is likely black-magical."

An attitude which evidently prevailed in high society, too, Adzel reflected. That would help account for Jadhadi's reluctance to ally himself with the League envoys. *I must discuss this with David when I get back.*

Padrick spent some time showing points of interest: a statue five thousand Earth-years old, the palace of a former dynasty turned into a warehouse, a building whose doorway was an open beak . . . museum stuff. Adzel paid more attention to the imposing houses of several great phratries, where the seniors lived and member families held council. Though they took part in the present government, these blood groups had not changed their headquarters to New City. Why should they? Empires, languages, civilizations, the march and countermarch of history, all were ephemeral. Only the phratry endured.

"The House of the Stone Ax," Padrick pointed. "Belongs to the Dattagirs. Their senior still carries that ax. Flint head; nobody knows when it was made, except must've been before metalworking." He yawned. "You getting bored? Let's go where we can find some life. Old City."

"Won't they avoid me there, too?" Adzel asked. He hoped not. It pained him that mothers should snatch their cubs and run when he appeared—such cute, fuzzy little infants, he'd love to hold one for a while.

"Not so much," Padrick said. "Less scared of black magic, seeing as a lot of them are black magicians themselves."

Down they went, past a ruined wall and into the casbah. The houses they found were more tall and narrow than those of later eras, shoulder to shoulder with overhanging balconies so that a bare strip of plum-colored sky showed overhead and shadows were thick purple. Living in a more prosperous time, when the land was not quite as arid, the builders had cobbled their streets. Adzel's hooves rang loud on the stones, for this was a silent quarter, where cloaked dwellers passed on furtive errands and only the keening of a hidden harp resounded. Along the way, that toppled toward the sea bed, Adzel could look back to the red-tinged cliffs above the whole city; and down, to the remnants of wharves among the reeds where Lake Urshi glimmered. Padrick stopped. "What say you of a drink?"

"Well, I like your brew—" Adzel broke off. The transceiver at his neck had come alive with Falkayn's voice.

"What the demons!" Padrick sprang back. His sword hissed from the scabbard. A pair of Ikranankans, squatting before a doorway across the lane, gathered their ragged capes around them and vanished inside.

Adzel waved a soothing hand and finished his Latin conversation with Falkayn. "Don't be alarmed," he said. "A bit of our own magic, quite safe. A, ah, a spell against trouble, before entering a strange house."

"That could be useful, I grant." Padrick relaxed. "'Specially hereabouts."

"Why do you come if you find danger?"

"Booze, gambling, maybe a fight. Gets dull in barracks. C'mon."

"I, ah, believe I had better return to the palace."

"What? When the fun's only beginning?" Padrick tugged Adzel's arm, though he might as well have tried to haul a mountain.

"Another time, perhaps. The magic advised me—"

Padrick donned a hurt expression. "You're no friend of mine if you won't drink my liquor."

"Forgive me," Adzel capitulated. "After your great kindness, I would not be discourteous." And he was thirsty; and Falkayn hadn't intimated there was any hurry.

Padrick led the way through a half-rotted leather curtain. A wench sidled toward him with a croaked invitation, saw he was human, and withdrew. He chuckled. "The stews are no use to an Ershokh, worse luck," he remarked. "Oh, well, things are free and easy in the Iron House."

As the Wodenite entered, stillness fell on the crowded, smoky room. Knives slid forth at the wicker tables where the patrons sat. Torches guttering in sconces threw an uneasy light—dim and red to Adzel, bright to a native—on sleazy garments, avian faces, unwinking eyes. Padrick set down his flag and raised his hands. "Peace between our kindred," he called. "You know me, Hugh of the Household, I've stood many a round. This is the Emperor's guest. He's big but gentle, and no demon's trailing him. Any demon 'ud be scared to."

A drunk in a corner cackled laughter. That eased the atmosphere somewhat. The customers returned to their drinks, though they kept looking sideways and doubtless their mutterings were now chiefly about this dragonish alien. Padrick found a backless chair and Adzel coiled on the dirt floor across from him. The landlord gathered courage to ask what they wanted. When Padrick pointed to Adzel and said munificently, "Fill him up," the Ikranankan cocked his head, calculated probable capacity, and rubbed his hands.

The brandy, or gin or arrack or whatever you wanted to call a liquor distilled from extraterrestrial fruits, was no more potent than concentrated sulfuric acid. But it had a pleasant dry flavor. Adzel tossed off half a liter or so. "I must not be greedy," he said.

"Don't be shy. This is on me." Padrick slapped a fat purse. "We draw good pay, I must say that for him on the Beast."

"I have been wondering. Surely not all the Ershoka live in the Iron House."

"No, no. You serve there between getting your commission, if you do, and getting married. And it's phratry headquarters. But families take homes throughout New City, or they go to one of our ranches, or whatever they like. After marrying, women usually lay down their arms. Men go drill once a year and naturally join the colors in an important war."

"How then did Bobert Thorn's contingent dare revolt? Their families at home were hostage to the Emperor."

"Not so. If he touched a one of those left behind, we'd all rise, from Harry Smit on down to the youngest drummer boy, and set his head on a pike. But anyhow, a lot of the wives and kids went along. That's usual, if there's a siege or an extended campaign. Women make perfectly good camp guards, against these flimsy Ikranankans, and they're our quartermasters and—" Padrick finished listing their functions.

That wouldn't have been feasible, under such primitive conditions, if this were Earth. But few if any native germs affected humans. It made another reason why the Ershoka were prime soldiers. Before preventive medicine becomes known, disease thins armies more cruelly than battle.

"I sympathize with your plight," Adzel said. "It cannot be easy, when you are so close-knit, to be in conflict with your own relatives."

"Who said we were?" Padrick bridled. "That doddering Smit? The phratry bonds weren't so strong when he was growing up. He'd never get anyone my age to march against Thorn." He drained his beaker and signaled for more. "But seems the Iron House will obey its officers enough to stay neutral."

To change a difficult subject, Adzel asked if he had seen Stepha Carls since her return. "I sure to curses have!" Padrick said enthusiastically. "What a girl!"

"A pleasant, if impulsive personality," Adzel agreed.

"I wasn't talking about personality. Though truth, she's tough and smart as any man. Here's to Stepha!"

Beakers clunked together. Seeing the dragon so convivial, the house relaxed yet more. Presently an Ikranankan drinking buddy of Padrick's drifted over to his table and said hello. "Siddown!" the Ershokh bawled. "Have one on me."

"I really should return," Adzel said.

"Don't be stupid. And don't insult my good friend Rakshni. He'd like to make your 'quaintance."

Adzel shrugged and accepted more booze. Others came to join the party. They started yarning, then they started arguing about the Rangakora situation—not very heatedly, since nobody in Old City cared what happened to the parvenu Emperor—and then they had a short brawl between three or four cutthroats that broke the last ice, and then they began toasting. They toasted their phratries and they toasted the wenches cuddling in among them and they toasted the memory of good King Argash and they toasted the Yanjeh River that kept Katandara alive and they toasted Lake Urshi that took charge of so many inconvenient corpses and they toasted Hugh Padrick often because he was buying and about then they lost track and the tetrahedral dice commenced to rattle and all in all they had quite a time. Booze was cheap and Padrick's purse was full. The party ended at last more because the majority had passed out on the floor than because he went broke.

"I . . . mus' . . . really must . . . go back," said Adzel. His legs seemed more flexible than he preferred, and his tail had made up its own mind to wag. That demolished most of the furniture, but the landlord didn't object. He had passed out, too.

"Uh, yeh, yeh, reckon so." Padrick lurched erect. "Duty calls."

"In a shrill unpleasant voice," Adzel said. "My friend, you have uh—hic!—wrong concep'. If you were at one wi' the universe—now please don' fall inna common error iden'ifying Nirvana with annihilation, matterfack's t' be achieved in this life—" He was no zealot, but he felt this fine chap reeling beside him deserved at least to have an accurate understanding of Mahayana Buddhism. So he lectured the whole way back. Padrick sang songs. Natives scurried out of the way.

"—an' so," Adzel droned, "you see reincarnation not at all necesshry to the idea uh Karma—"

"Wait." Padrick halted. Adzel bent his neck down to regard him. They were near the gates of New City.

"Why, whuzzuh mazzuh?"

"Remembered an errand." The Ershokh was acting sober with unexpected swiftness. Had he really matched the others drink for drink? Adzel hadn't noticed. "You go on."

"But I uz jus' coming to the mos' in'eresting part."

"Later, later." Wind ran down the empty street, driving sand, and ruffled the bronze hair. No one else was in sight. Odd, thought Adzel hazily. The citizens had retreated from him before, but not to that extent. And there was no equivalent of night time; the same proportion were always awake.

"Well, thank you f'r a (whoops!) ver' inshuck—insturruck—insurrect—in-structive 'shperience." Adzel offered his hand. Padrick took it hurriedly, almost embarrassedly, and loped off. The sword jingled at his belt.

A strange place, this. Adzel's thoughts turned sentimentally back to Woden, the dear broad plains under the brilliant sun, where his hooves spurned kilometers . . . and after the chase, the fellowship of the campfire, friends, children, females. . . . But that was long behind him. His family having been close associates of the League factor, they had wanted him to get a modern education; and he'd gotten one, and now he was so changed that he would never feel at home among the hunters. The females he didn't miss, being sexually stimulated only by the odor of one in rutting season. But a certain sense of belonging, an innocence, was forever gone. He wiped his eyes and trotted on, weaving from side to side of the street.

"*There he comes!*"

Adzel jerked to a stop. The space before the New City wall was a broad plaza. It swarmed with soldiers. He had some trouble estimating how many, for they kept doubling when he looked at them, like amoebas; but a lot, and every one a native. The gates were shut, with a line of catapults in front.

A cavalry troop bounded forward. "Halt, you!" shouted the leader. His lance head flashed bloody in the red light.

"I awready halted," said Adzel reasonably.

Though uneasy, the Imperial zandaras were well disciplined. They moved to encircle him. "Most noble," called the troop leader, in a rather nervous tone, "let us talk. Trouble is afoot and the Emperor, ak-krrr, desires your presence."

Adzel clapped a hand to his stomach—the scutes rang—and bowed. His neck kept on going till his snout hit the ground. That annoyed him, but he hung on to urbanity. "Why, sure, any ol' thing t' oblizhe. Le's go."

"Uk-k-k, as a matter of form only, most noble, the Emperor wishes you to, krrr-ek, wear these badges of dignity." The officer waved forward a foot soldier, who obeyed without visible happiness. He carried a set of chains.

"What?" Adzel backed off. His mind wobbled.

"Hold, there!" the officer cried. "Hold or we shoot!" The catapult crews swiveled their weapons about. One of those engines could drive a steel-headed shaft through even a Wodenite.

"Bu-bu-buh wah's wrong?" Adzel wailed.

"Everything. The demons must have broken all barriers. Your associate has vanished, with a good score of Ershoka. When he learned this, the Emperor sensed treachery and had the Iron House surrounded. Those inside grew angry and would not surrender. They shot at our own people!" The officer ran clawlike fingers through his ruff. His cloak flapped in the wind, his zandara made a skittish leap.

Crossbows cocked where lances were not couched; his troopers held their ring about the Wodenite.

"What?" Confound that liquor! And no anti-intoxicants on hand. Adzel thumbed the switch of his transceiver. "David! Where are you? Whuh happen?"

Silence answered.

"David! 'Merzh'ncy! Help!"

"Now keep still," the officer chattered. "Hold out your wrists first. If you are blameless, you shall not be harmed."

Adzel switched to the ship's wavelength. "Chee! You there?"

"Of course I am there," said the waspish voice. "Where else would I be but where I am?"

Adzel recited a mantra or two under his breath. The beneficent influence cleared some of his private fog. He blurted out an explanation. "I'll go 'long wi'm," he said. "Peaceful. You come in uh ship. They'll got . . . they will have to lemme go then, an' we'll look f' David."

"At once," said Chee.

A squad of magicians made frantic passes. Adzel turned to the officer. "Yes, 'course I'll hic th' Emperor." From the radio came an indistinct mumble. Chee must be talking with someone else. He extended his arms and opened his mouth. It was meant for a smile, but it showed an alarming array of fangs.

The officer pricked the chain-bearing infantryman with his lance. "Go on," he said. "Do your duty."

"You do it," whimpered the other.

"What do I hear? Do you contradict an order?"

"Yes." The infantryman backed away. His mounted comrades opened a sympathetic way for him.

"Oh, come now," said Adzel. He wanted to see Jadhadi and get to the bottom of this as fast as possible. He sprang forward. The cavalry yelped and scuttled aside.

"But I on'y wanna help!" Adzel roared. He caught the soldier, removed the chains, and set him down again. The Ikranankan curled into a little ball.

Adzel hunkered on his tail and considered. The links had gotten fouled. "How yuh 'spec' me to fasten these?" he asked pettishly. The more he tried to unsnarl the mess, the worse it got. The Imperial army watched in fascination.

A shout broke from the transceiver. "Adzel! Get away! The unsanctified creature of unmentionable habits has caught me!"

There followed sounds of scuffling, a sharp blow, and nothing.

For a lunatic instant Adzel thought he was back on the ship playing Lord Love a Duck: seven card stud, low hole card wild. He had a trey in reserve, which with another trey on the board completed a royal flush, and he raised till his pay was hocked for the next six months, and then came the final draw and he got a deuce. The alcohol fumes blew out of him and he realized he wasn't actually in that situation. It merely felt that way.

The League trained its spacemen to react fast. He continued fumbling with the chains while his eyes flicked back and forth, assessing the terrain. Given a quick—yes, in yonder direction—and a certain amount of luck, he could make a break. But he mustn't hurt any of these poor misguided souls, if that could possibly be avoided.

He gathered his thews and leaped.

A cavalry trooper was in his way. He scooped the Ikranankan up, zandara and all, and threw him into the detachment of spearmen beyond. Their line of grounded pikes broke apart. He bounded through. Yells exploded around him, with a sleet of crossbow quarrels. A catapult shaft buzzed his ears. The mounted officer laid lance in rest and charged from the side. Adzel didn't see him in time. The steel point smote. It didn't go in but met the radio at the Wodenite's throat and smashed the case open. Adzel brushed past, still gathering speed. The zandara spun like a top, the rider went off in an arc.

A blank wall loomed ahead, four stories high. Adzel hit it at full velocity. Momentum carried him upward. He grabbed the verge and hauled himself over. The rough-surfaced stones gave sufficient grip. A catapult bolt struck by his flank, knocking out splinters of rock. Adzel crossed the roof, jumped to the next, dropped into an alley, and headed back toward Old City.

No help for him there, of course, except that he'd be hard to track through that maze. He'd get to Lake Urshi. They had nothing to chase a swimmer but clumsy rafts that he could easily outdistance. Once on the far shore, he'd strike across the Chakora. No word could reach Haijakata ahead of him—but damn the loss of his transceiver!

Well, Chee's would serve, after he'd bailed the little fluffbrain out of whatever trouble she'd gotten into. They'd raise ship, retrieve their flitter at the palace, and start looking for David. If David was alive. If they themselves stayed alive.

VI

Perhaps there was something to the Katandaran theory that supernatural beings were uniformly malevolent. If Chee Lan had been aboard the spacecraft when Adzel called—But she herself, an uncompromising rationalist, would have said her luck, though bad, involved no great improbability. She had been spending almost half her time with Gujgengi. Both were anxious to learn as much as possible about each other's civilizations.

One new idea she introduced, not entirely to his liking, was that of regular appointments. Haijakata's lone clock kept such slapdash time that she presented him with a watch. After that, drums rolled and flags got replaced to signal a change of guard with some predictability; and she knew when to go uphill for another session.

The computer, which she had set to remind her, did so. "You might be more respectful," she grumbled, laying down her book. She had pretty well convinced her shipmates that the Cynthian volumes she had along were philosophical works (in fact, they were slushy love novels) but still she enjoyed the chance to read without inane interruptions.

"You did not program me to be respectful," said the mechanical voice.

"Remind me to. No, cancel that. Who cares about a machine's opinions?"

"No one," said Muddlehead, which did not have rhetorical units.

Chee hopped off her bunk and made ready. Transceiver and taper in one hand, a ladylike needle gun at her waist, were all she needed. "Standby orders as usual," she said, and went out the lock.

Muddlehead hummed quietly to itself. Standby meant that, although the Katandaran language had been added to its memory bank, it would only obey commands—voice, radio, or code—from one of the crew. However, Chee had connected the external speaker, in case she ever wanted to ask from the outside what the sensors observed.

The entry valve locked behind her and she scampered down the ramp. One hatch remained open immediately above the landing jacks, for an extra bolt-hole. There was no danger of natives wandering in and causing damage. Apart from their awe of the ship, the hatch merely led to the empty No. 4 hold, which no Ikranankan could harm, and *Muddlin' Through* wouldn't operate the door from it to 'tween-decks for anyone but a crew member. Chee prided herself on thinking ahead.

The crimson sun was whiter and brighter to her eyes than to Falkayn's or Adzel's. Nonetheless she found the landscape shadowy, swore when an unseen twig snagged the fur she had spent an hour grooming, and was glad to reach the highway. And the air drank moisture from her nose like Falkayn drinking after a cruise when the Scotch gave out; and the wind was as cold as van Rijn's heart; and it carried from the Chakora scents of vegetation akin to creosote and Gorgonzola. Oh, to be back on Ta-chih-chien-pi, Lifehome-under-Sky, again in a treetop house among forest perfumes! Why had she ever left?

Money, of course. Which she was currently not making, at a furious rate. She bottled her tail and hissed.

The sentries at the gate touched sword to beak in salute as her small form passed. After she was safely beyond, they fingered charms and whispered incantations. True, the newcomers had not caused any trouble so far, and in fact promised great benefits. But demons are notorious liars.

Chee would not have been surprised, or even offended, had she seen. More and more she was discovering how immensely conservative these Ikranankans were, how suspicious of everything new. That accounted for their being still prescientific, in spite of a fantastically long recorded history. She hadn't yet developed any explanation for the attitude itself.

She sprang lithely among the plaid-woven huts. A female sat outside one, putting food in the mouth of an infant. To that extent, Ikranankans were like Cynthians. Neither had mammary glands, the young being born equipped to eat solid food. (Cynthians use their lips to suck, not suckle.) But there the resemblance ended. An Ikranankan's wife was little, ruffless, drab, and subservient. A female Cynthian, who must carry her cub through the trees—though not strictly arboreal, among endless forests the race has made the branches a second environment—is bigger than her mate, and every bit as tough a carnivore. Matrilineal descent is the norm, polyandry occurs in numerous cultures, and the past has known some outright matriarchies. Chee supposed that was why her planet was so progressive.

She popped in the door of the large cabin where Gujgengi had quartered himself. The envoy was seated at a table with his host, garrison commandant Lalnakh. They were playing some game that involved dropping colored sticks onto a board divided in squares.

Chee soared to the tabletop, nearly upsetting the frail wicker structure. "What's that?" she asked.

Lalnakh scowled. Gujgengi, more used to her unceremonious ways, said, "It is called *akritel*," and explained. The rules were rather complicated, but in essence the game amounted to betting on how the sticks would fall. "Quite popular," Gujgengi added.

"Do you want to make your play or do you not?" Lalnakh snapped.

"Indeed, indeed. Give me time." Gujgengi adjusted his spectacles and pondered the distribution of rods that had already been dropped. The less likely a configuration he made, the more he would win; but if he failed to get a score within the range he declared, he would lose correspondingly. "I do believe my luck is normal today," he said, nodding at the stack of coins already before him. A galactic would have spoken of a run of good luck. "I will try to—" He chose his sticks and made his declaration.

"You shouldn't guess," Chee said. "You should know."

Lalnakh glared. "What do you mean?"

"Not the actual outcome," Chee said. "But what the chances are. Whether the chance of winning is good enough to justify the bet you make."

"How in Destruction can that be calculated?" Gujgengi asked.

"Play, curse you!" Lalnakh said.

Gujgengi rattled his sheaf of sticks and let them drop. He made his point.

"Arrr-k!" Lalnakh growled. "That does for me." He shoved his last coins across the table.

Gujgengi counted. "You appear to owe more," he said.

Lalnakh made a vile remark and fished in the pouch below his doublet. He threw a dull-white disk into Gujgengi's stack. "Will you take that? Rangkoran work. I've carried it for a talisman. But the demons were too strong for it today."

Gujgengi wiped his glasses and squinted. Chee had a look herself. The medallion bore a pleasing design, a wreath on the obverse and a mountainscape on the reverse. But part of the silver had rubbed off. "Why, this is plated bronze," she said.

"An art they have there, among others," Gujgengi replied. "They put the metal in a bath and—I know not what. Strong magic. I was there once on an embassy, and they had me grip two copper threads coming out of a box, and something *bit* me. They laughed." He recollected his dignity. "But at any rate, being so magical, objects like this are prized. That makes yet another reason why the conquest of Rangakora is desirable."

"Which we could accomplish for you," Chee pointed out. "And, incidentally, we can sell you any amount of plated stuff ourselves."

"Ak-krrr. Understand, most noble, I have no authority to make so, uk-k-k, momentous?—yes, so momentous a decision. I am simply the Emperor's representative."

"You can make recommendations, can't you?" Chee pursued. "I know messengers go back and forth all the time."

"Uk-k-k, indeed. Shall we continue our previous discussions?"

"I'm going," Lalnakh said surlily.

That was when the transceiver spoke.

"Chee! You there?"

Adzel's voice, in badly slurred Anglic. Was the big slubber drunk? Chee hoped no Ershoka were present. Her skin prickled. "Of course—" she began, more tartly than she felt.

Lalnakh sprang aside, yanking out his dagger. Gujgengi rose and made industrious signs against evil. His glasses slipped off his beak to interrupt him.

"What the plague is this?" Lalnakh demanded.

"Where are my spectacles?" Gujgengi complained from the floor. "I cannot see my spectacles. Has a demon run away with them?"

"Protective magic," said Chee quickly in Katandaran, while the radio muttered with noise of a large crowd. "Nothing to fear."

"Help me find my spectacles," Gujgengi quacked. "I need my spectacles."

Lalnakh swore and retrieved them. Chee heard Adzel out. Her fur stood on end. But the self-possession of trouble came upon her, and her mind raced like a cryogenic calculator.

"At once," she said, and looked at the Ikranankans. They stared back, stiff and hostile.

"I must go," she said. "My magic has warned me of trouble."

"What kind of trouble?" Lalnakh rapped.

Gujgengi, more accustomed by now to outworld marvels, pointed a lean finger. "That was the monster's voice," he said. "But he is in the capital!"

"Well, yes," Chee said. Before she could improvise a story, Gujgengi went on:

"That must be a thing for speaking across distances. I had begun to suspect you possessed some such ability. Now, now, most noble, please do not insult me by denying the obvious. He has called you to his assistance, has he not?"

Chee could only nod. The Ikranankans trod closer, towering above her. She didn't want to be caught, later, in an outright lie; bad for future relations, which were ticklish enough already. "The Ershoka have rebelled," she said. "They are barricaded in the, what you call it, the Iron House. Adzel wants me to come and oversee them."

"No, you don't," Lalnakh told her; and Gujgengi: "I am distressed, most noble, but since your fellows arrived at the palace, I have been sent explicit orders that your conveyance is to remain in place."

"Sandstorms and pestilence!" Chee exclaimed. "Do you want a civil war? That's what you'll get, if the Ershoka aren't brought into line, and fast." The racket from the radio grew louder. "Use your judgment for a change. If we wanted Jadhadi's ruin, would I not sit here and let it happen?"

They paused. Lalnakh looked uncertain. Gujgengi scratched beneath his beak. "A point," he murmured. "Yes, a distinct point."

The set broke into a roar. Metal belled, voices howled, thuds and bumps shivered the speaker. A thin Ikranankan cry: "Help, the beast is killing me!"

Lalnakh started. Sunlight slanting into the gloomy room touched his knife with red. "Is that friendly?" the officer said, low in his throat.

Chee pulled her gun. "Some misunderstanding," she chattered. "I true-speak that we are your friends, and I'll shoot anyone who calls me a liar." Adzel's mild basso hiccuped forth, above an iron rattle. "Hear that? He isn't fighting, is he?"

"No," Lalnakh said. "Feeding."

Chee poised on the table. "I shall go," she started. "I suggest you do not try to stop me."

Gujgengi surprised her. She had taken him for a mere bumbling professor. He drew his sword and said quietly, "I am a Deodakh. Did I fail to try, they would read my ghost out of the phratry."

Chee hesitated. She didn't want to kill him. That would also louse up future negotiations. A disabling shot?

Her attention was distracted from Lalnakh. The officer's hand swept through an arc. His knife smashed into her weapon. The impact tore it from her hand. He threw himself over her. She had barely time to cry a warning, then she was on the floor, pinioned.

"Hak-k-k," Lalnakh grated. "Keep still, you!" He cuffed her so that her head rang, snatched off her transceiver and threw it aside.

"Now, now," Gujgengi chided. "No violence, most noble, no violence until we learn whether violence is necessary. This is all most unfortunate." He saluted Chee, where she lay in Lalnakh's grasp. Simultaneously, he crushed the radio under his foot. "I shall dispatch a messenger at once. Until word comes, you shall be treated as honorably as circumstances allow."

"Wait a bit!" Lalnakh said. "I am the garrison chief."

"But my dear friend, it may conceivably turn out that some accommodation can be reached."

"I doubt it. These creatures are demons, or demon-possessed. But jail her any way you like, as long as I can inspect your security arrangements. What I am going to do is post a guard on that flying house. With catapults, in case the giant arrives, and orders to kill if he does."

"Well," said Gujgengi, "that is not a bad idea."

VII

Falkayn didn't black out. Rather, consciousness fragmented, as if he were at a final stage of intoxication. His mind went off on a dozen different tracks, none involving willpower.

Sagging against the wall as the Ershoka released him, he was dizzily aware of its hardness at his back; of how the floor pressed with a planet's mass on his boot soles; of air chill and dry in his nostrils, soughing in his lungs, and the bitter drug odor; of his heart slamming; of red light a-sheen on the naked floor, and the dusky sky in a window across its expanse, which seemed to be tilting; of the big blond man who had mugged him, and the equally big redhead who supported him; of the redhead's nose, whose shape had some comic and probably sinister significance— He thought once that the Ikranankan stuff he'd breathed must have pharmaceutical possibilities; then he thought of his father's castle on Hermes and that he really must write home more often; but in half a second he was remembering a party at Ito Yamatsu's place in Tokyo Integrate; and this, by an obvious association, recalled several young women to him; which in turn led him to wonder—

"Give me a hand, Owen," Stepha Carls muttered. "His batman'll be back soon. Or anybody might chance by."

She began to strip off Falkayn's clothes. The process could have been embarrassing if he weren't too muzzy to care, or fun if she'd been less impersonal. And, of course, if the blond warrior hadn't assisted. Falkayn did try to observe various curves as she handled him, but his brain wouldn't stay focused.

"All right." Stepha jerked her thumb at a bundle on the floor. The yellow-haired man unrolled it, revealing Ershoka garb. The cloth was coarse, the pants reinforced with leather: a cavalry field outfit. She started to dress Falkayn. Her job wasn't easy, the way he lolled in the redhead's arms.

The stupor was leaving, though. Almost, he tried to shout. But drilled-in caution, rather than wit, stopped him. Not a chance, yet. However, strength flowed back, the room no longer whirled, and presently they'd buckle on his dagger belt. . . .

Stepha did so. He could have whipped out the knife and driven it into her back where she squatted before him. But that would be a dreadful waste. He lurched, sliding aside from the redhead. His hand brushed across the dagger haft, his fingers clamped, he drew and stabbed at the man's chest.

At! There was no blade, only a squared-off stub barely long enough to keep the thing in its sheath. The Ershokh took a bruise, no doubt; he recoiled with a whispered curse. Falkayn, still wobbly, staggered for the doorway. He opened his mouth to yell. The blond grabbed his arms and Stepha her wet rag. Tiger swift, she bounded forward and crammed it down his gape.

As he spun into pieces again, he saw her grin and heard her murmur genially, "Nice try. You're a man of parts in more ways than one. But we reckoned you might be."

She bent to take his guns. Light coursed along her braids. "Hoy!" said the blond. "Leave those."

"But they're his weapons," Stepha said. "I told you what they can do."

"We don't know what else they're good for, what black magic might be in 'em. Leave them be, I said."

The redhead, rubbing his sore ribs, agreed. Stepha looked mutinous. But there was scarcely time to argue. She sighed and rose. "Put the stuff in his cabinet, then, so they'll think he just stepped out, and let's go."

With a man on either side supporting him by his elbows, Falkayn lurched into the hall. He was too loaded to remember what the fuss was about and obeyed their urging mechanically. In this residential part of the palace, few were abroad. On the downramp they passed his servant, returning with a jug of ferocious booze. The Ikranankan didn't recognize him in his new clothes. Nor did anyone in the more crowded passages below. One official asked a question. "He got drunk and wandered off," Stepha said. "We're taking him to barracks."

"Disgraceful!" said the bureaucrat. Confronted by three armed and touchy Ershoka who were sober, he did not comment more.

After some time Falkayn was so far recovered that he knew they'd come to a sally port in the north wall. Cityward, the view was blocked by a row of houses. Some twenty Ershoka, most of them men, waited impatiently in battle dress. Four Tiruts, the sentries, lay bound, gagged, and indignant. The humans slipped out.

The canyon of the Yanjeh lay west of town, marked by leafy sides and the loud clear rush of water. There, too, the upland highway entered. Here was sheer desert, which rose sharply in crags, cliffs, and talus slopes, ruddy with iron oxide and sun, to the heights. In such a wilderness, the Ershoka vanished quickly.

"Move, you!" The blond jerked Falkayn's arm. "You're undoped by now."

"Uh-h-h, somewhat," he admitted. Normality progressed with every stone-rattling stride. Not that that did him much good, hemmed in by these thugs.

After a while they found a gulch. A good fifty zandaras milled about in the care of two Ikranankan riders. Several were pack animals, most were mounts and remounts. The band swung into their saddles. Falkayn got on more gingerly. The natives headed back toward town.

Stepha took the lead. They climbed until they were above the cliffs, on dunes where nothing lived but a few bushes. At their backs, and northward, Yanjeh Belt shone green. The city gloomed below them, and beyond, the Chakora reached flat and murky to the horizon. But they pointed themselves east and broke into full gallop.

No, hardly the word! Falkayn's zandara took off with an acceleration that nearly tore him from his seat. He knew a sick moment of free fall, then the saddle and his lower jaw rose and hit him. He flopped to the right. The man alongside managed to reach over and keep him from going off. By then the zandara was once more aloft. Falkayn bounced backward. He saved himself by grabbing the animal's neck. "Hoy, you want to strangle your beast?" someone yelled.

"As . . . a . . . matter . . . of . . . fact . . . yes," Falkayn gusted between bounces.

Around him gleamed helmets, byrnies, spearheads, gaudy shields, and flying cloaks. Metal clattered, leather creaked, footfalls drummed. Sweat and zandara musk filled the air. So did fine sand, whirled up in a cloud. Falkayn had a glimpse of Stepha, across the wild pack. The she-troll was laughing!

He gritted his teeth. (He had only meant to set them, but his mouth was full of sand.) If he was to survive this ride, he'd have to learn the technique.

Bit by bit, he puzzled it out. You rose slightly in the stirrups as the zandara came down, to take the shock with flexed knees. You swayed your body in rhythm with the pace. And, having thought yourself athletic, you discovered that this involved muscles you never knew you had, and that said muscles objected. His physical misery soon overwhelmed any speculation as to what this escapade meant.

A few times they stopped to rest and change steeds, and after some eternities to camp. That amounted to gulping down iron rations from the saddlebags, with a miserly drink of water from your canteens. Then you posted guards, got into your bedroll, and slept.

Falkayn didn't know how long he had been horizontal when Stepha roused him. "Go 'way," he mumbled, and burrowed back into the lovely dark. She grabbed a handful of hair and yanked. Eventually she dragged him to breakfast.

Their pace was easier now, though, and some of the aches worked themselves out of Falkayn. He began to notice things. The desert was getting hillier all the time, and a little more fertile, too. The sun behind him was lower, shadows stretched enormous in front, toward the Sundhadarta mountains, whose slate-blue bulk was slowly lifting over the world's edge. The Ershoka had relaxed, they joked and laughed and sang some rather bloodthirsty songs.

Near the end of the "day," a lone rider with a few spare animals overtook them. Falkayn started. Hugh Padrick, by Satan! The Ershokh waved affably at him and rode to the head of the parade to confer with Stepha.

Those two were still talking when the second camp was made, on a hilltop among scattered vividly yellow bushes. The Ershoka didn't go to sleep at once but built small fires and lounged about in companionable groups. Falkayn let another man unsaddle his zandaras, hobble them and turn them out to graze. Himself, he sat down with the intention of sulking but got up fast.

A shadow in the long light fell across him. Stepha stood there. He must admit she was a handsome sight, big, full-bodied, queenly featured. More used to the chill than he, she'd stripped to blouse and kilt, which further lightened his mood.

"Come join us," she invited.

"Do I have a choice?" he said hoarsely.

The gray eyes were grave on his. She touched his hand in an almost timid fashion. "I'm sorry, David. No way to treat you. Not only after what you did for me. No, you deserve better'n this in your own right. But won't you let me explain?"

He followed her less grudgingly than he made out, to a fire where

Padrick sat toasting some meat on a stick. "Hullo," the Ershokh said. A grin flashed white in his grimy beard. "Hope you liked the ride so far."

"What's become of Adzel?" Falkayn demanded.

"Dunno. Last I saw, he was headed for the palace, drunk's a brewmaster. Reckoned I'd better get out of town before the fun started, so I went back to Lake Urshi where I'd hid my animals and took off after you. Saw your dust a long ways off." Padrick lifted a leather bottle. "Took some booze."

"Do you suppose I'll drink with you, after—"

"David," Stepha pleaded. "Hear us out. I don't think your big friend can have gotten into deep trouble. They'd not dare hurt him when the little one still has your flyer. Or Jadhadi may decide right away you were snatched, 'stead of leaving of your will."

"I doubt that," Falkayn said. "A galactic might, but those Ikranankans see a conspiracy under every bed."

"We've made trouble for our own mates, too, in the Iron House," Stepha reminded him. "Could come to blows between them and the beak faces, what with nerves being strung so tight on both sides."

"That's a hell of a way to run a phratry," Falkayn said.

"No! We're working for their good. Only listen to us."

Stepha gestured at a saddle blanket spread over the ground. Falkayn yielded and lowered himself, reclining Roman fashion. The girl sat down beside him. Across the fire, Padrick chuckled tolerantly. "Dinner coming soon," he promised. "How about that drink?"

"Oh, the devil, all right!" Falkayn glugged. The thermonuclear liquid scorched some of the aches from him and blunted his worry about Adzel.

"You're Bobert Thorn's people, aren't you?" he asked.

"We are now," Stepha said. "Me alone, at first. You see, Thorn sends out spies, Ikranankans, that is. If they must be conquered, the Rangakorans would mostly rather have Ershoka than Deodaka; we seem to get along better. So some of their units are fighting on our side, and then there are the merchants and—Anyhow, it's not hard for one to sneak out and mingle with the besiegers, claiming to be a highland trader come to see if he can peddle anything. Or whatever."

Rotten security, Falkayn reflected. How come, in a race that suspected everyone not an in-law of being an outlaw? . . . Well, yes, such clannishness would make for poor liaison between different kin-regiments. Which invited, if not espionage, at least the gathering of intelligence.

"Jadhadi's people also got wind of you," Stepha said. "I reckon he alerted his top officers, and somebody blabbed." Falkayn could imagine the process: a Tirut or Yandaji ordered by a Deodakh to have secrets from his own relatives, getting mad and spilling the beans on principle. "Just dim, scary rumors seeped down to the ranks, you understand. But our spies heard them, too. We didn't know what they meant, and had to find out. Twilight was still over the area, so I got clear without being seen, rustled me a couple of zandaras, and headed off. A patrol near Haijakata did notice me, though. My spare mount took a quarrel. I bloody near did myself." She laughed and rumpled Falkayn's hair. "Thanks, David."

"And, of course, when you sounded us out and learned we were on Jadhadi's side, you pretended to be likewise," he nodded, mainly to rub his head against her palm. "But why'd you take the risk of coming back to Katandara with us?"

"Had to do something, didn't I? You meant to break us. I didn't know what I could swing, but I did know there must be a lot of people who wished they'd been sent to Rangakora, too. And I knew nobody in the Iron House would give me away to the Ikranankans." Stepha grinned mischievously. "Oh, but old Harry Smit was mad! He wanted to court-martial me on the spot. But too many others wouldn't have it. He settled for confining me to barracks while he tried to figure out some answer to the whole mess. That was a mistake. I could sit there and talk, whenever he wasn't around. I could guess who to talk most with, too—old friends and lovers that I knew well."

"Huh?" said Falkayn. Padrick looked smug.

"So we plotted," Stepha said. "We waited for a chance to act. Hugh hired a couple of his Old City buddies to buy animals and supplies and keep them stashed. We'd money enough between us, our gang. Then he went and got to know you. Plain, we'd never snatch you from Adzel. Would've been simpler if you'd gone out with Hugh. But when you let Adzel go first, we reckoned we'd better not lose more time. One by one, our people found excuses to stroll into town. Owen and Ross smuggled me out the back. We headed for your apartment. Nasty shock when you weren't there! But you must've gone to an Imperial audience, so we waited and hoped. Glad we did."

Falkayn took another comforting swig, rolled over on one elbow, and looked hard at the girl. "What's the point of this fantastic stunt?" he demanded.

"To stop you from helping Jadhadi," Padrick said. "Maybe even get you to help us. We're your fellow humans, after all."

"So are the Ershoka back in Katandara."

"But we're doing this for them also," Stepha insisted. "Why should our phratry be hirelings, and have to live under law and custom never meant for them, when they could be masters of their own country?"

"A better country than back yonder, anyhow," Padrick said.

"Bobert Thorn's thought," Stepha agreed. "He hoped the Ershoka would break from Jadhadi and come join him as soon as they learned what he'd done. Be tough, we know, cutting a way through the Imperial army. There'd be lives lost. But it could be done"—her voice rang forth—"and well worth the price!"

"You may have provoked matters so far by snatching me that the Ershoka won't have any choice," Falkayn admitted bitterly. "And for what? Didn't I tell you that you can all be returned to Earth?"

Stepha's eyes widened. Her hand went to her mouth. "Oh! I forgot!"

"Too late now," Padrick laughed. "Besides, take time to fetch your flyers, right, David? Meanwhile, what's to happen at Rangakora? And . . . I'm not sure I'd want to leave. Earth ways may be too different, worse than Katandara."

"Very well," Falkayn said. "You've succeeded this far. You've made trouble in the capital. You've prevented our ship taking action till my mates find what's become of me. You may have driven a wedge between us and Jadhadi. But don't think we'll do your dirty work for you."

"I wish you would, though," Stepha murmured, and stroked his cheek.

"Now cut that out, girl! I come to curry Caesarism, not to raze it."

"No matter," said Padrick. "Long's your, uh, ship keeps hands off"—Falkayn had a brief giddy vision of *Muddlin' Through* with hands—"we'll manage. And it'll sure do that while we've got you."

"Unless she rescues me, knocking down your damned walls in the process."

"They try," said Padrick, "and they'll find you in two pieces. We'll let 'em know that, if they do show up." He didn't even have the decency to sound grim.

"It'd be such a pity," Stepha cooed. "We've hardly begun our friendship, David."

"Meat's cooked," said Padrick.

Falkayn resigned himself. He didn't mean to stay passive longer than he must. However, food, drink, and a pretty woman constituted a situation which he could accept with an equanimity that would make Adzel proud of him. *(Adzel, you scaly old mutt, are you safe? Yes. You've got to be. All you need do is radio Chee for help.)* The conversation at dinner was amicable and animated. Padrick was a fine fellow after several drinks, and Stepha was a supernova. The only fault he could find, at length, was that they insisted on switching off the party to rest for the next stage. Dismal attitude.

His watch had been left behind with everything else, but as near as he could tell, the Ershoka had a well-developed time sense. The ancient cycles of Earth still governed them. An hour to get started, sixteen hours—with short breaks—to travel, an hour to make camp and relax, six hours' sleep, divided roughly between two changes of guard. Not that there was much to fear, in this wasteland.

But the country grew yet greener as the sun sank, until the Sundhadarta foothills were carpeted with mosslike growth, brooks rilled, and forests of plumed stalks swayed in the wind. Once clouds massed in the north, colored hot gold. The mountains rose sheer to east, aglow in the level red light. Falkayn saw snow peaks and glaciers. Above them the sky was a royal purple deepening toward black, where fifty stars and a planet glimmered. They were at the edge of the Twilight Zone.

Not only did the atmosphere diffuse enough light to make a belt of dusk; Ikrananka had a rather eccentric orbit, and so librated. The gloaming swept back and forth across these lands, once in each seventy-two-day year. At present it had withdrawn, and the sun stood a little above the western piedmont. The slopes reflected so much heat, and so much infrared got through at this altitude, that the region was actually warmer than Katandara. The precipitation of the cold season was melting, and rivers foamed down the cliffs. Falkayn understood now why Rangakora was coveted.

He estimated that the party had traveled about five Terrestrial days, covering some four hundred kilometers, when they turned south toward the eastern end of the Chakora. A shoulder thrust huge before them and they must climb, up toward the snow cone of Mount Gundra. Falkayn had gotten used to the saddle and let his zandara do the struggling while he admired the tremendous view and reminisced about his last session by the campfire. Padrick had gone off with some other girl, leaving him and Stepha alone. Well, not exactly alone; no privacy, with people scattered around; but still, he reflected, his captivity might turn out to have compensations. . . .

They rounded a precipice and Rangakora stood above them.

The city was built athwart a pass over the range, on a small plateau. A road of sorts wound heavenward from it, and on this side precipitously down toward the sea bottom. That glimmered misty, marshy, intensely green and gold. A river coursed near the wall. For the most part it was hidden by forest, but just above Rangakora it leaped over a sheer cliff and thundered in a waterfall crowned by rainbows. Falkayn caught his breath.

The Ershoka halted and drew together. Shields went onto arms, sabers into hands, crossbows were cocked and lances couched. Falkayn realized with a gulp that now was no time to contemplate scenery.

The plateau's verdure was scarred by feet. Campfires smoked around the city's rough walls, tents crowded and banners flew. Tiny at this remove, Jadhadi's people sat in clumps before the prize from which they had been expelled. "We'll make a rush," Padrick said. The wind and the cataract boomed around his words. "Thorn's folk'll see us and sally forth to fetch us in."

Stepha brought her animal next to Falkayn's. "I'd not want you to get ideas about bolting and surrendering to the others," she smiled sweetly.

"Oh, hell," said Falkayn, who already had them.

She looped a cord from her saddlebow to his zandara's bridle. Another girl tied his right ankle to the stirrup. He had often been told about the moral and psychological value of absolute commitment, but this seemed a bit extreme.

"Battle formation!" Padrick called. His sword flew clear. "Charge!"

The beasts bounded forward. Drums beat staccato alarms from the Imperial outposts. A cavalry squadron marshaled themselves and started full tilt to intercept. Their lances flashed intolerably bright.

VIII

Being as prone to disorderly conduct as most races, the Ikranankans needed jails. Haijakata's was a one-room cabin near the market square. An interior grid of stout stalks, closely lashed together, protected the woven outside walls against any tenants. If a prisoner wanted light, he could draw back the door curtain; but the wooden-barred gate beyond would remain locked. Furniture amounted to a straw tick and some clay utensils. Chee had broken one of these and tried to cut her way out with a shard. It crumbled, showing that while her captors might be crazy, they were not stupid.

A click and rattle snapped her out of a rather enjoyable reverie. The gate creaked open, the curtain was pulled aside, relieving the purplish dusk, and Gujgengi's spectacles glittered. "I was just thinking about you," Chee said.

"Indeed?" The mandarin sounded flattered. "May I ask what?"

"Oh, something humorous, but lingering, with either boiling oil or melted lead. What do you want?"

"I . . . uk-k-k . . . may I come in?" The curtain drew wider. Behind the gaunt, robed form, Chee saw a couple of armed and alert guards, and beyond them a few civilians haggling at the market booths. The quarantine had reduced trade to a minimum. "I wish to ascertain if you are satisfactorily provided for."

"Well, the roof keeps off the rain."

"But I have told you that rainfall is unknown west of Sundhadarta."

"Exactly." Chee's glance fell wistful on the saber at Gujgengi's side. Could she lure him in alone and snatch that—No, he need only fend off an attack and holler. "And why can't I have my cigarettes? That is, those fire-tubes you have seen me put in my mouth."

"They are inside your house, most noble, and while the house does not appear to resent being guarded, it refuses to open for us. I asked."

"Take me there, and I will give it orders."

Gujgengi shook his head. "No, I regret. That involves too many unknown powers you might unleash. When the present, ak-krrr, deplorable misunderstanding has been cleared up, yes, indeed, most noble. I have dispatched couriers posthaste to Kantandara, and we should receive word before long." Taking an invitation for granted, he stepped through. The soldiers closed the awkward padlock.

"Meanwhile poor Adzel arrives and gets himself killed by your hotheads," Chee said. "Pull that curtain, you dolt! I don't want those yokels gaping in at me."

Gujgengi obeyed. "Now I can scarcely see," he complained.

"Is that my fault? Sit down. Yes, there's the bedding. Do you want some booze? They gave me a crockful."

"Ek-k-k, well, I ought not."

"Come on," Chee urged. "As long as we drink together, we are at least not deadly enemies." She poured into a clay bowl.

Gujgengi tossed off the dose and accepted a refill. "I do not perceive you drinking," he said in a heavy-footed attempt at humor. "Do you plan to get me intoxicated, perhaps?"

Well, Chee thought with a sigh, *it was worth trying.*

Briefly, she grew rigid. The jolt passed, her mind hummed into overdrive, she relaxed her body and said, "There isn't much else to do, is there?" She took the vessel and drank. Gujgengi couldn't see what a face she made. Pah!

"You malign us, you know," she said. "We have none but the friendliest intentions. However, if my comrade is killed when he arrives, expect revenge."

"Krrr-ek, he will be only if he grows violent. Somewhat against Commandant Lalnakh's wish, I have posted criers who will shout warnings that he is to stay away. I trust he will be sensible."

"Then what do you plan to do about him? He has to eat." Gujgengi winced. "Here, have another drink," Chee said.

"We, ak-krrr, we can try for some accommodation. Everything depends on what message I get from the capital."

"But if Adzel has headed this way, he will be here well before that. Come on, drink and I'll recharge the bowl."

"No, no, really, this is quite enough for an oldster like me."

"I don't like to drink alone," Chee urged.

"You have not taken much," Gujgengi pointed out.

"I'm smaller than you." Chee drained the vessel herself and glugged out some more from the crock. "Though you would be astonished at my capacity," she added.

Gujgengi leaned forward. "Very well. As an earnest of my own wish for friendship, I will join you." Chee could practically read his thought: *Get her drunk and she may reveal something.* She encouraged him with a slight hiccup.

He kept his own intake low, while she poured the stuff down at an ever mounting rate. Nonetheless, in the course of the next hour or so, his speech grew a little slurred.

He remained lucid, however, in contrast to Chee. He was not unsubtle about trying to trap her into an admission that Falkayn must have engineered the trouble in Katandara. When her denials grew belligerent, he abandoned that line. "Let us discuss something else," he said. "Your capabilities, for example."

"I'm'sh capable'sh you," Chee said.

"Yes, yes, of course."

"More sho."

"Well, you have certainly revealed—"

"Prettier, too."

"Uk-k-k, tastes vary, you know, tastes vary. But I must concede you an intrinsic—"

"So I'm not beautiful, huh?" Chee's whiskers dithered.

"On the contrary, most noble. Please, I beg you—"

"Sing real good, too. Lisshen." Chee rose to her feet, bowl in hand, and staggered about waving her tail and caterwauling. Gujgengi folded his ears.

"*Ching, chang, guli, guli vassa,*
Ching, chang, guli, guli bum."

"Most melodious! Most melodious! I fear I must be on my way." Gujgengi stirred where he sat on the mattress.

"Don' go, ol' frien'," Chee pleaded. "Don' lea' me 'lone."

"I will be back. I—"

"Oops!" Chee reeled against him. The bowl swept across his glasses. They fell. Chee grabbed after them. She came down on top, with the bowl. There was a splintering.

"Help!" Gujgengi cried. "My spectacles!"

"Sho shorry, sho shorry." Chee fumbled around after the pieces.

The guards got in as fast as they could. Chee retreated. Gujgengi blinked in the sudden brightness. "What's wrong, most noble?" asked a soldier. His sword was out.

"Li'l accshiden'," Chee babbled. "Ver' shorry. I fix you up."

"Stand back!" The saber poked in her direction. The other guard stooped and collected the pieces.

"It was doubtless unintentional," Gujgengi said, making signs against demons. "I think you had best get some sleep now."

"Fix you up. Got doctors, we do, fix your eyes sho you never need glasshes." Chee was surprised at her own sincerity. The Imperial envoy wasn't such a bad sort, and doubtless he'd have a devil of a time getting replacements. Katandaran optometry must be a crude cut-and-try business.

"I have spares," Gujgengi said. "Conduct me to my residence." He saluted Chee and shuffled out. She rolled over on her tick and closed her eyes.

"Too mush light," she complained. "Draw 'at curtain."

They obeyed, before locking the gate again. She waited a few minutes until she rose, though, and continued to emit realistic snores.

The liquor made her stomach uneasy. But it hadn't affected her mind. Ethanol is a normal product of Cynthian metabolism. And . . . unseen in murk, by Gujgengi's weak eyes, she had palmed a couple of the largest fragments and slipped them under the mattress.

She ripped the ticking with her teeth, for rags to protect her hands, and got busy at the far end of the hut.

The glass wasn't very hard. As edges wore down, it sawed with ever less efficiency on the lashings of the framework. She could use pressure flaking to resharpen—a League academy gives a broad practical education—but only a few times before the chunks got too small to handle. "Hell and damnation!" she shouted when one of them broke completely.

"What's that?" called a voice from outside.

"Z-z-z-z," snored Chee.

A human would have sweated through that slow hour, but she was philosophical about the possibility of failing. Also, she needed less of an opening than a man would. Nonetheless, she barely finished before her tools wore to uselessness.

Now, arch your spine, pour through your arms and legs the strength they won leaping from branch to branch in the forests of home . . . ugh! . . . the canes bent aside, she squirmed through, they snapped back into position and she was caught against the outer wall. Its fabric was rough against her nose. Panting, shivering in the chill gloom, she attacked with teeth and nails. One by one, the fibers gave way.

Quick, though, before somebody noticed!

A rent appeared, ruddy sunlight and a windowless carpet wall across a deserted lane. Chee wriggled out and ran.

The city gates might or might not be watched too closely. But in either case, crossing that much distance, she'd draw half the town after her. Somebody could intercept her; or a crossbow could snap. She streaked around the jail and onto the plaza.

The natives screeched. A foodwife ducked behind her wares. A smith emerged from his shop, hammer in hand. Her guards took off after her. Ahead was a kiosk, at the center of the square. Chee sprang through its entrance.

Rough-hewn steps wound downward into the hill. A dank draft blew in her face. The entrance disappeared from sight and she was in a tunnel, dug from earth and stone, lit at rare intervals by shelved lamps. She stopped to pinch the wicks of the first two. Though she must then slow, groping until she reached the next illuminated spot, the Ikranankans were more delayed. Their cries drifted to her, harsh and distorted by echoes. Not daring to meet the unknown in the dark, they'd have to go back for torches.

By that time she was out at the bottom of the hill. A short stone passage led to a room with a well in the middle. A female let go the windlass handle and jumped onto the coping with a scream. Chee ignored her. The gate here was open and unguarded when the town faced no immediate threat. She'd seen that before, at the time Gujgengi gave her party the grand tour. She bounded from the tower, forth into brush and sand.

A glance behind showed turmoil at Haijakata's portals. She also glimpsed *Muddlin' Through,* nose thrusting bright into the sky. For a moment she debated whether to try regaining the ship. Once aboard, she'd be invincible. Or a shouted command for the vessel to lift and come get her would suffice.

No. Spears and shields ringed in the hull. Catapults crouched skeletal before them. She'd never get within "earshot" without being seen, nor finish a wigwag sentence before a quarrel pierced her. And Muddlehead hadn't been programmed to do anything without direct orders, no matter what the detectors observed.

Oh, well. Adzel could set that right. Chee started off. Before long she was loping parallel to the Haijakata road, hidden by the farm crops that lined it, all pursuit shaken.

The air was like mummy dust—thin mummy dust—and she grew thirstier by the minute. She managed to suppress most symptoms by concentrating on how best to refute a paper she'd seen in the *Journal of Xenobiology* before they left Earth. The author obviously had hash for brains and fried eggs for eyes.

Even so, eventually she had to get a drink and a rest. She slanted across the fields toward a canebrake that must mark a spring. There she glided cautiously, a shadow among shadows, until she peered out at the farmstead it enclosed.

Adzel was there. He stood with a pig-sized animal, from a pen of similar beasts, hooting in his arms, and said plaintively to the barred and shuttered central keep: "But my good fellow, you must give me your name."

"For you to work magic on?" said a hoarse male voice from within.

"No, I promise you. I only wish to give you a receipt. Or, at least, know whom to repay when I am able. I require food, but I do not intend to steal."

A dart whined from an arrow slot. He sighed. "Well, if you feel that way—"

Chee came forth. "Where's some water?" she husked.

Adzel started. "You! Dear friend, what in the universe has happened to you?"

"Don't 'dear friend' me, you klong. Can't you see I'm about to dry up and blow away?"

Adzel tried to bristle. Having no hair, he failed. "You might keep a civil tongue in your head. You would be astonished at how much less detested that can make you. Here I have been traveling day and night—"

"What, clear around the planet?" Chee gibed. Adzel surrendered and showed her the spring. The water was scant and muddy, but she drank with some understanding of what Falkayn meant by vintage champagne. Afterward she sat and groomed herself. "Let's catch up on our news," she proposed.

Adzel butchered the animal while she talked. He had no tools for the job, but didn't need them either. In the end, he looked forlorn and said: "Now what shall we do?"

"Call the ship, of course."

"How?"

Chee noticed for the first time that his transceiver was also broken. They stared at each other.

Gujgengi adjusted his spare glasses. They didn't fit as well as the old ones had. The view was fuzzy to his eyes. *This might be preferable, though,* he thought. *The thing is so* huge. *And so full of sorcery. Yes, I do believe that under present circumstances I am quite satisfied not to see it too clearly.*

He gulped, mustered his whole courage, and tottered a step closer. At his back, the soldiers watched him with frightened expressions. That nerved him a trifle. *Must show them we Deodaka are uniformly fearless and so forth.* Though he would never have come except for Lalnakh. Really, the Commandant had behaved like a desert savage. One knew the Tiruts weren't quite one's equals—who was?—but one had at least taken them for a civilized phratry. Yet Lalnakh had stormed and raved so about the prisoner escaping that . . . well, from a practical standpoint, too, it would not help Gujgengi's reputation. But chiefly for the honor of the bloodline, one must answer the Tirut's unbridled tirade with stiff dignity and an offer to go consult the flying house. Would the Commandant care to be along? No? Excellent. One did not say so immediately, for fear of provoking him into changing his mind, but when one returned, one might perhaps drop a hint or two that most noble Lalnakh had not *dared* come. Yes, one must maintain a proper moral superiority, even at the risk of one's life.

Gujgengi swallowed hard. "Most noble," he called. His voice sounded strange in his ears.

"Are you addressing me?" asked the flat tones from overhead.

"Ak-krrr, yes." Gujgengi had already had demonstrated to him, before the present wretched contretemps, that the flying house (no, the word was *shi'*, with some unpronounceable consonant at the end, was it not?) could speak and think. Unless, to be sure, the strangers had deceived him, and there was really just someone else inside. If so, however, the someone had a peculiar personality, with little or no will of its own.

"Well?" said Gujgengi when the silence had stretched too far.

"I wait for you to proceed," said the shi'.

"I wish, most noble, to ask your intentions."

"I have not yet been told what to intend."

"Until then you do nothing?"

"I store away whatever data I observe, in case these are required at a later time."

Gujgengi let out a hard-held breath. He'd hoped for something like this. Greatly daring, he asked: "Suppose you observed one of your crew in difficulties. What would you do?"

"What I was ordered to do, within the limits of capability."

"Nothing else? I mean, krrr-ek, would you take no action on your own initiative?"

"None, without verbal or code orders. Otherwise there are too many possibilities for error."

Still more relieved, Gujgengi felt a sudden eagerness to explore. One had one's intellectual curiosity. And, of course, whatever was learned might conceivably find practical application. If the newly come Ershokh and his two eldritch companions were killed, well, the shi' would still be here. Gujgengi turned to the nearest officer. "Withdraw all personnel a distance," he said. "I have secrets to discuss."

The Tirut gave him a suspicious glance but obeyed. Gujgengi turned back to the shi'. "You are not totally passive," he pointed out. "You answer me in some detail."

"I am so constructed. A faculty of logical judgment is needed."

"Ak-krrr, do you not get, shall we say, bored sitting here?"

"I am not constructed to feel tedium. The rational faculty of me remains automatically active, analyzing data. When no fresh data are on hand, I rehearse the logical implications of the rules of poker."

"What?"

"Poker is a game played aboard my hull."

"I see. Uk-k-k, your responsiveness to me is most pleasing."

"I have been instructed to be nonhostile to your people. 'Instructed' is the closest word I can find in my Katandaran vocabulary. I have not been instructed not to reply to questions and statements. The corollary is that I should reply."

Excitement coursed high in Gujgengi. "Do you mean—do I understand you rightly, most noble—you will answer any question I ask?"

"No. Since I am instructed to serve the interests of my crew, and since the armed force around me implies that this may have come into conflict with your interests, I will release no information which might enhance your strength."

The calmness was chilling. And Gujgengi felt disappointed that the shi' was not going to tell him how to make blasters. Still, a shrewd interrogator might learn something. "Would you advise me about harmless matters, then?"

The wind blew shrill, casting whirls of grit and tossing the bushes, while the hidden one considered. Finally: "This is a problem at the very limits of my faculty of judgment. I can see no reason not to do so. At the same time, this expedition is for the purpose of gaining wealth. The best conclusion I can draw is that I should charge you for advice."

"But, but how?"

"You may bring furs, drugs, and other valuables, and lay them in that open doorway you presumably see. What do you wish me to compute?"

Taken aback, Gujgengi stuttered. He had a potential fortune to make, he knew, if only he could think. . . . Wait. He remembered a remark Chee Lan had made in Lalnakh's house before her arrest. "We play a game called *akritel,*" he said slowly. "Can you tell me how to win at it?"

"Explain the rules."

Gujgengi did so. "Yes," the shi' said, "this is simple. There is no way to win every time without cheating. But by knowing the odds on various configurations that may be achieved, you can bet according to those odds and therefore be ahead in the long run, assuming your opponents do not. Evidently they do not, since you ask, and since Drunkard's Walk computations involve comparatively sophisticated mathematics. Bring writing materials and I will dictate a table of odds."

Gujgengi restrained himself from too much eagerness. "What do you want for this, most noble?"

"I cannot be entirely certain. Let me weigh what information I have, in order to estimate what the traffic will bear." The shi' pondered awhile, then named what it said was a fair amount of trade goods. Gujgengi screamed that this would impoverish him. The shi' pointed out that in that case he need not buy the information. It did not wish to haggle. Doubtless there were others who would not find the fee excessive.

Gujgengi yielded. He'd have to borrow a sum to pay for that much stuff; still, with the market depressed by the quarantine, the cost wouldn't be unmanageable. Once he left this miserable hamlet and returned to Katandara, where they gambled for real stakes—

"Did you learn anything, most noble?" asked the officer as Gujgengi started uphill again.

"Yes," he said. "Most potent information. I will have to pay a substantial bribe, but this I will do out of my own pocket, in the interests of the Emperor. Ak-krrr . . . see to it that no one else discourses with the shi'. The magic involved could so easily get out of hand."

"Indeed, most noble!" shuddered the officer.

IX

The heroes of adventure fiction can go through any harrowing experience and—without psychochemicals, usually without sleep, always without attending to bodily needs—are at once ready to be harrowed all over again. Real people are built otherwise. Even after a possible twelve hours in the sack, Falkayn felt tired and sore. He hadn't been hurt during that wild ride through the Katandaran lines, but bolts zipped nastily close, and Stepha sabered an enemy rider seconds before he reached the Hermetian. Then Bobert Thorn's people sallied, beat off the opposition, and brought the newcomers into Rangakora. Falkayn wasn't used to coming that near death. His nerves were still tied in knots.

It didn't help that Stepha was utterly cheerful as she showed him around the palace. But he must admit that the building fascinated him. Not only was it more light and airy than anything in Katandara, not only did it often startle him with beauty; it held the accumulated wealth of millennia less violent than farther west. There were even interior doors such as he knew at home, of bronze cast in bas-reliefs; reasonably clear glass windows; steam heating.

They left the electroplating shop, a royal monopoly operated in the palace, and strolled to a balcony. Falkayn was surprised at how far the grave philosophers had progressed: lead-acid batteries, copper wire, early experimentation with a sort of Leyden jar. He could understand why this was a more congenial society for humans than Katandara.

"Jeroo, there's Thorn himself, and the King," Stepha exclaimed. She led Falkayn to the rail where they stood. His two guards tramped behind. They were friendly young chaps, but they never left him and their weapons were loose in the scabbards.

Thorn put down the brass telescope through which he had been looking and nodded. "That camp gets sloppier every watch," he said. "They're demoralized, right enough."

Falkayn glanced the same way. The palace was a single unit, many-windowed, several stories high. He was near the top. No wall surrounded it, simply a garden, and beyond that the city. Like Katandara, Rangakora was so old as to be almost entirely stone-built. But the houses here were a symphony of soft whites, yellows, and reds. Facing outward rather than inward, with peaked tile roofs and graceful lines, they reminded him somewhat of First Renaissance architecture on Earth. Traffic moved on comparatively wide, paved avenues, distance-dwarfed figures, a faint rumble of wheels and clatter of feet. Smoke drifted into a Tyrian sky where a few clouds wandered. Behind, the heights soared gray-blue to Mount Gundra, whose snowcap glowed gold with perpetual sunset. The falls tumbled on his right, white and green and misted with rainbows, querning their way down to a Chakora which here was brilliant with fertility.

His gaze stopped short, at the besiegers. Beyond the city ramparts, their tents and campfires dotted the plateau, their animals grazed in herds and metal flashed where the soldiers squatted. Jadhadi must have sent powerful reinforcements when he learned of the rebellion. "I'd still not like to take them on, the way they outnumber your effectiveness," he said.

Bobert Thorn laughed. He was a stocky, grizzle-bearded man with fierce blue eyes. Old battle scars and well-worn saber stood out against his embroidered scarlet tunic and silky trousers. "No hurry," he said. "We've ample supplies, more than they're able to strip off the country. Let 'em sit for a while. Maybe the rest of the Ershoka will arrive. If not, come next twilight they'll be so hungry and diseased, and half blinded to boot, we can rout 'em. They know that themselves, too. They haven't much guts left." He turned to the slim red-pelted young Ikranankan in saffron robe and gilt chaplet. "King Ursala, this here's the man from Beyond-the-World I told you about."

The monarch inclined his avian head. "Greeting," he said, in a dialect not too thick to follow. "I have been most anxious to meet you. Would the circumstances had been friendlier."

"They might be yet," Falkayn hinted.

"Not so, if your comrades carry out their threat to bring us under Katandara," said Ursala. His mild tone softened the import.

Falkayn felt ashamed. "Well, uh, there we were, strangers with no real knowledge. And what's so bad about joining the Empire? Nobody there seemed to be ill treated."

Ursala tossed his ruff and answered haughtily: "Rangakora was ancient when Katandara was a village. The Deodaka were desert barbarians a few generations ago. Their ways are not ours. We do not set phratry against phratry, nor decree that a son is necessarily born into his father's profession."

"That so?" Falkayn was taken aback.

Stepha nodded. "Phratries here're just family associations," she said. "Guilds cut right across them."

"That's what I keep telling you, most noble," said Thorn self-righteously. "Once under the protection of the Ershoka—"

"Which we did not ask for," Ursala interrupted.

"No, but if I hadn't decided to take over, Jadhadi's viceroy would be here now."

"I suppose you are the best of a hard bargain," sighed the King. "The Irshari may have favored us too long; we seem to have lost skill in war. But let us be honest. You will exact a price for your protection, in land, treasure, and power."

"Of course," said Thorn.

To break an uncomfortable silence, Falkayn asked who or what the Irshari might be. "Why, the makers and rulers of the universe," said Ursala. "Are you as superstitious in Beyond-the-World as they are in the Westlands?"

"Huh?" Falkayn clenched his fists. A shiver ran through him. He burst into questions.

The responses upset every preconception. Rangakora had a perfectly standard polytheistic religion, with gods that wanted sacrifices and flattery but were essentially benevolent. The only major figure of evil was he who had slain Zuriat the Bright, and Zuriat was reborn annually while the other gods kept the bad one at bay.

But then the Ikranankans were not paranoid by instinct!

What, then, had made the western cultures think that the cosmos was hostile?

Falkayn's mind leaped: not at a conclusion, he felt sure, but at a solution that had been staring him in the face for weeks. Ikrananka's dayside *had no seasons.* There was no rhythm to life, only an endless struggle to survive in a slowly worsening environment. Any change in nature was a disaster, a sandstorm, a plague, a murrain, a drying well. No wonder the natives were suspicious of everything new, and so by extension of each other. No wonder that they only felt at ease with fully initiated members of their own phratries. No wonder that civilizations were unstable and the barbarians free to come in so often. Those poor devils!

Rangakora, on the edge of the Twilight Zone, knew rain and snow and quickening, in the alternation of day and dusk. It knew, not just a few isolated stars, but constellations; after its people had ventured into the night land, it knew them well. In short, Falkayn thought, while the local citizens might be S.O.B.s, they were Earth's kind of S.O.B.s.

But then—

No. Rangakora was small and isolated. It simply hadn't the capability of empire. And, with the factions and wild raiders on this planet, van Rijn would deal with nothing less than an empire. Turning coat and helping out this city might be a quixotic gesture, but the Polesotechnic League didn't go in for tilting at windmills. A liberated Rangakora would be gobbled up again as soon as the spaceship left; for there would be no further visits.

Yet its steadying influence could prove invaluable to outworld traders. Wasn't some compromise possible?

Falkayn glanced despairingly heavenward. When in hell was *Muddlin' Through* going to arrive? Surely Chee and Adzel would look first for him here. Unless something dreadful had happened to them.

He grew aware that Ursala had spoken to him and climbed out of his daze. "Beg pardon, most noble?"

"We use no honorifics," the King said. "Only an enemy needs to be placated. I asked you to tell me about your home. It must be a marvelous place, and the Irshari know I could use some distraction."

"Well—uh—"

"I'm interested, too," said Thorn. "After all, if we Ershoka are to leave Ikrananka, that throws everything off the wagon. We might as well pull out of Rangakora now." He didn't look too happy about it.

Falkayn gulped. When the humans were evacuated to Earth, he himself would be a public hero, but van Rijn would take him off trade pioneering. No doubt he'd still have a job: a nice, safe position as third officer on some milk run, with a master's berth when he was fifty and compulsory retirement on a measured pension ten years later.

"Uh, the sun is more bright," he said. "You saw how our quarters were lit, Stepha."

"Damn near blinded me," the girl grumbled.

"You'd get used to that. You'd have to be careful at first anyway, going outdoors. The sun could burn your skin."

"The plague you say!" exploded one of Falkayn's guards.

The Hermetian decided he was giving a poor impression. "Only for a while," he stumbled. "Then you're safe. Your skin turns tough and brown."

"What?" Stepha raised a hand to her own clear cheek. Her mouth fell open.

"It must be hot there," said Ursala shrewdly.

"Not so much," Falkayn said. "Warmer than here, of course, in most places."

"How can you stand it?" Thorn asked. "I'm sweating right now."

"Well, in really hot weather you can go indoors. We can make a building as warm or cool as we please."

"D'you mean to say I'd have to just *sit,* till the weather made up its own confounded mind to change?" Thorn barked.

"I remember," Stepha put in. "The air you had was muggier'n a marsh. Earth like that?"

"Depends on where you are," Falkayn said. "And actually, we control the weather cycle pretty well on Earth."

"Worse and worse," Thorn complained. "If I'm to sweat, I sure don't want to do it at somebody else's whim." He brightened. "Unless you can fight them when you don't like what they're up to?"

"Good Lord, no!" Falkayn said. "Fighting is forbidden on Earth."

Thorn slumped back against the rail and gaped at him. "But what am I going to do then?"

"Uh . . . well, you'll have to go to school for a number of years. That's Earth years, about five times as long as Ikranankan. You'll have to learn, oh, mathematics and natural philosophy and history and—now that I think about it, the total is staggering. Don't worry, though. They'll find you work, once you've finished your studies."

"What sort of work?"

"M-m-m, couldn't be too highly paid, I fear. Not even on a colony planet. The colonies aren't primitive, you realize, and you need a long education to handle the machines we use. I suppose you could become a—" Falkayn groped for native words—"a cook or a machine tender's helper or something."

"Me, who ruled a city?" Thorn shook his head and mumbled to himself.

"You must have some fighting to do," Stepha protested.

"Yes, unfortunately," Falkayn said.

"Why 'unfortunately'? You're a strange one." Stepha turned to Thorn. "Cheer up, Cap'n. We'll be soldiers. If Great Granther didn't lie, those places are stuffed with plunder."

"Soldiers aren't allowed to plunder," Falkayn said. They looked positively shocked. "And anyway, they also need more skill with machines than I think you can acquire at your present ages."

"Balls . . . of . . . fire," Thorn whispered.

"We've got to hold a phratry council about this," said a guard in an alarmed voice.

Thorn straightened and took command of himself again. "That wouldn't be easy right now," he pointed out. "We'll carry on as we were. When the siege is broken and we get back in touch with our people, we'll see what we want to do. Ursala, you and I were going to organize that liaison corps between our two forces."

"Yes, I suppose we must," said the King reluctantly. He dipped his head to Falkayn. "Farewell. I trust we can talk later at length." Thorn's good-by was absentminded; he was in a dark brown study. They wandered off.

Stepha leaned her elbows on the rail. She wore quite a brief tunic, and her hair was unbound. A breeze fluttered the bronze locks. Though her expression had gone bleak, Falkayn remembered certain remarks she had let drop earlier. His pulse accelerated. Might as well enjoy his imprisonment.

"I didn't mean to make Earth sound that bad," he said. "You'd like it. A girl so good-looking, with so exotic a background—you'd be a sensation."

She continued to stare at the watchtowers. The scorn in her voice dismayed him. "Sure, a novelty. For how long?"

"Well—my dear, to me you will always be a most delightful novelty."

She didn't respond. "What the deuce are you so gloomy about all of a sudden?" Falkayn asked.

Her lips compressed. "What you said. When you rescued me, I reckoned you for a big piece of man. Should've seen right off, nothing to that fracas, when you'd a monster to ride and a, a *machine* in your hand! And unfair, maybe, to call you a rotten zandaraman. You never were trained to ride. But truth, you are no good in the saddle. Are you good for anything, without a machine to help?"

"At least one thing," he tried to grin.

She shrugged. "I'm not mad, David. Only dis'pointed. My fault, truth, for not seeing before now 'twas just your being different made you look so fine."

My day, Falkayn groaned to himself.

"Reckon I'll go see if Hugh's off duty," Stepha said. "You can look 'round some more if you want."

Falkayn rubbed his chin as he stared after her. Beginning bristles scratched back. Naturally, this would be the time when his last dose of antibeard enzyme started to wear off. Outside the ship, there probably wasn't a razor on all Ikrananka. He was in for days of itchiness, until the damned face fungus had properly sprouted.

The girl had not spoken without justification, he thought bitterly. He had indeed been more sinned against than sinning, this whole trip. If Chee Lan and Adzel had come to grief, the guilt was his; he was the captain. In another four months, if they hadn't reported back, the travel plan they'd left at base would be unsealed and a rescue expedition dispatched. That might bail him out, assuming he was still alive. At the moment, he wasn't sure he wanted to be.

A shout spun him around. He stared over the rail and the city wall. Thunder seemed to crash through his head.

Adzel!

The Wodenite came around the bend of the lower road at full gallop. Scales gleamed along the rippling length of him; he roared louder than the waterfall. A shriek lifted from the enemy camp. Drums rolled from Rangakora's towers. Men and Ikranankans swarmed beweaponed to the parapets.

"Demons alive!" gasped at Falkayn's back. He glanced, and saw his two guards goggling ashen-faced at the apparition. It flashed through him: a chance to escape. He slipped toward the door.

Stepha returned. She seized his arm and threw her weight against him. "Look aware!" she yelled. The men broke from their paralysis, drew blade, and herded him back. He felt sick.

"What's going on?" he choked. "Where's the spaceship?"

Now he could only watch. A Katandaran cavalry troop rallied and charged. Adzel didn't stop. He plowed on through. Lances splintered against his armor, riders spilled and zandaras fled in panic. He might have been halted by catapult fire. But the field artillery had not been briefed on extraplanetary beings, nor on what to do when an actual, visible demon made straight for them. They abandoned their posts.

Terror spread like hydrogen. Within minutes, Jadhadi's army was a howling, struggling mob, headed downhill for home. Adzel chased them awhile, to make sure they kept going. When the last infantry soldier had scuttled from view, the Wodenite came back, across a chaos of dropped weapons, plunging zandaras and karikuts, idle wagons, empty tents, smoldering fires. His tail wagged gleefully.

Up to the gates he trotted. Falkayn couldn't hear what he bellowed but could well imagine. The human's knees felt liquid. He struggled for air. No time seemed to pass before a messenger hastened out to say he was summoned. But the walk through hollow streets—Rangakora's civilian population had gone indoors to wail at the gods—and onto the parapet, took forever.

The walk calmed him somewhat, though. When he stood with Thorn, Ursala, Stepha, and a line of soldiers, looking down on his friend, he could again think. This close, he saw Chee's furry form on the great shoulders. At least they were both alive. Tears stung his eyes.

"David!" bawled Adzel. "I hoped so much you'd be here. Why don't they let me in?"

"I'm a prisoner," Falkayn called back in Latin.

"No, you don't," said Thorn. "Talk Anglic or Katandaran, that I can understand, or keep mouth shut."

Because the spearheads bristling around looked so infernally sharp, Falkayn obeyed. It added to the general unpleasantness of life that everybody should learn how his ship was immobilized. And now he really was stuck here. His gullet lumped up.

Thorn said eagerly: "Hoy, look, we've got common cause. Let's march on Haijakata together, get that flying thing of yours away from them, and then on to Katandara."

Ursala's tone grew wintry. "In other words, my city is to be ruled from there in spite of everything."

"We've got to help our brethren," Thorn said.

"I intercepted a courier on my way here," Adzel told them. "I am afraid I lost merit by frightening him, but we read his dispatches. The Ershoka who were in town but not in the Iron House assembled and attacked from the rear. Thus combined, their forces crumpled the siege lines and fought their way out of the city. They took over—what was the name now? a Chakoran village—and sent for outlying families to come and be safer. Jadhadi does not dare attack them with his available troops. He is calling for reinforcements from the various Imperial garrisons."

Thorn tugged his beard. "If I know my people," he said, "they'll march out before that can happen. And where would they march but to us?" His countenance blazed. "By Destruction! We need but sit, and we'll get everything I wanted!"

"Besides," Stepha warned, "we couldn't trust Falkayn. Soon's he got back that flying machine of his, he could do what he felt like." She gave the Hermetian a hostile look. "Reckon you'd bite on us."

"The one solitary thing I wish for is to get away from this planet," he argued. "Very far away."

"But afterward? Your stinking merchant's interest does lie with Katandara. And could well be others like you, coming later on. No, best we keep you, my buck." She leaned over the battlements, cupped her hands, and shouted: "Go away, you, or we'll throw your friend's head at you!"

Chee stood up between the spinal plates. Her thin voice barely reached them through the cataract's boom: "If you do that, we'll pull your dungheap of a town down around your ears."

"Now, wait, wait," Ursala pleaded. "Let us be reasonable."

Thorn ran an eye along the faces crowding the wall. Sweat glistened and tongues moistened lips; beaks hung open and ruffs drooped. "We can't well sally against him," he said *sotto voce.* "Our people are too scared right now, and besides, most zandaras would bolt. But we can keep him at his distance. When the whole phratry arrives—yes, that'll be too many. We can wait."

"And keep me alive for a bargaining counter," said Falkayn quickly.

"Sure, sure," Stepha sneered.

Thorn issued an order. Engineers began to wind catapult skeins. Adzel heard the creaking and drew back out of range. "Have courage, David!" he called. "We shall not abandon you."

Which was well meant but not so useful, Falkayn reflected in a gray mood. Thorn not only desired to keep Rangakora, he had to, for the sake of his kinfolk. The Ershoka had been sufficiently infected by the chronic suspiciousness of Katandara that they'd never freely let Falkayn back on his ship. Rather, they'd make him a permanent hostage, against the arrival of other spacecraft. And once firmly established here, they'd doubtless try to overthrow the Deodakh hegemony. Might well succeed, too. The most Falkayn could hope for was that a rescue expedition could strike a bargain: in exchange for him, the League would stay off Ikrananka. The treaty would be observed, he knew; it didn't pay to trade with a hostile population. And when he learned this market must not merely be shared, but abandoned, van Rijn would bounce Falkayn clear to Luna.

What a fine bouillabaisse he'd gotten himself into!

His guards hustled him off toward the palace apartment which was his jail. Adzel collected what few draft animals had not broken loose from their tethers, for a food supply, and settled down to his one-dragon siege of the city.

X

Chee Lan had no trouble reaching the east wall unseen. The Katandarans hadn't been close enough to trample the shrubs, nor had the Rangakorans gone out to prune and weed. There was plenty of tall growth to hide her approach. Crouched at the foot, she looked up a sheer dark cliff; a cloud scudded through the purple sky above and made it seem toppling on her. Pungent tarry smells of vegetation filled her nose. The wind blew cold. From the opposite side she heard the cataract roar.

Here in the shadow it was hard to make out details. But slowly she picked a route. As usual, the stones were not dressed except where they fitted together, and the rains and frosts of several thousand years had pitted them. She could climb.

Her sinews tautened. She sprang, grabbed finger- and toeholds, reached for the next and the next. Chill and rough, the surface scratched her belly. She was handicapped by her loot from the empty camp, two daggers at her waist and a rope coiled around her. Nonetheless, unemotionally, she climbed.

When her fingers grasped the edge of a crenel, she did hesitate a moment. Guards were posted at intervals here. But—she pulled herself over, hunched down between the merlons, and peeped out. Some meters to left and right she saw the nearest watchers. One was human, one Ikranankan. Their cloaks fluttered as wildly as the banners atop the more distant towers. But they were looking straight outward.

Quick, now! Chee darted across the parapet. As expected—any competent military engineer would have designed things thus—several meters of empty paving stretched between the inside foot of the wall and the nearest houses. With commerce to the outer world suspended, no traffic moved on it. She didn't stop to worry about chance passersby, but spidered herself down with reckless speed. The last few meters she dropped. Low gravity was helpful.

Once she had streaked into the nearest alley, she took a while to pant. No longer than she must, though. She could hear footfalls and croaking voices. Via a window frame, she got onto the roof of one house.

There she had a wide view. The bloated red sun slanted long rays over streets where gratifyingly few natives were abroad. Hours after Adzel's coming, they must still be too shaken to work. *Let's see . . . David's sure to be kept in the palace, which must be that pretentious object in the middle of town.* She plotted a path, roof to roof as much as possible, crossing the narrowest lanes when they were deserted, and started off.

Wariness cost time; but cheap at the price. The worst obstacle lay at the end. Four spacious avenues bordered the royal grounds, and they were far from deserted. Besides a trickle of workaday errands, they milled with anxious clusters of Ikranankans, very humanlike in seeking what comfort they could get from the near presence of their rulers. Chee spent a couple of hours behind a chimney, studying the scene, before a chance came by.

A heavy wagon was trundling down the street in front of her at the same time as an aged native in sweeping official robes was headed for the palace. Chee leaped down into the gut between this house and the next. She had counted on buildings being crowded. The karikuts clopped past, the wagon creaked and rumbled behind, its bulk screened her. She zipped underneath it and trotted along on all fours. At closest approach, she had about three meters to go to the Ikranankan gaffer. If she was noticed, the gardens were immediately beyond, with lots of hedges and bowers to skulk in. But she hoped that wouldn't be necessary.

It wasn't, since she crossed the open space in half a second flat. Twitching up the back of the old fellow's skirt, she dove beneath and let the cloth fall over her.

He stopped. "What? What?" she heard, and turned with him, careful not to brush against his shins. "Krrr-ek? What? Swear I felt . . . no, no . . . uk-k-k. . . ." He shambled on. When she judged they were well into the grounds, Chee abandoned him for the nearest bush. Through the leaves she saw him stop again, feel his garments, scratch his head, and depart mumbling.

So far, so good. The next stage could really get merry. Chee prowled the garden for some while, hiding as only a forester can hide when anyone passed near, until the permutations of perambulation again offered her an opportunity.

She had worked her way around to a side of the palace. A stand of pseudobamboo veiled her from it, with a hedge at right angles for extra cover, and nobody was in sight: except a native guard, scrunching down the gravel path in breastplate and greaves. He ought to know. Chee let him go by and pounced. A flying tackle brought him onto his stomach with a distressing clatter. At once she was on his shoulders, left arm choking off his breath and right hand drawing a knife.

She laid the point against his throat and whispered cheerfully: "One squeak out of you, my friend, and you're cold meat. I wouldn't like that either. You can't be very tasty."

Slacking the pressure, she let him turn his head till he glimpsed her, and decided to pardon the gargle he emitted. It must be disturbing to be set on by a gray-masked demon, even a small one. "Quick, now, if you want to live," she ordered. "Where is the prisoner Ershokh?"

"Ak-k-k—uk-k-k—"

"No stalling." Chee pinked him. "You know who I mean. The tall yellow-haired beardless person. Tell me or die!"

"He—he is in—" Words failed. The soldier made a gallant attempt to rise. Chee throttled him momentarily insensible. She had taken care, while at Haijakata, to get as good a knowledge of Ikranankan anatomy as was possible without dissection. And this was a comparatively feeble species.

When the soldier recovered, he was quite prepared to cooperate. Or anyhow, he was too terrified to invent a lie; Chee had done enough interrogation in her time to be certain of that. She got exact directions for finding the suite. Two Ershoka watched it, but outside a solid bronze door.

"Thank you," she said, and applied pressure again. Cutting some lengths of rope and a strip of his cloak for a gag, she immobilized her informant and rolled him in among the plumed stalks. He was regaining consciousness as she left. "You'll be found before too long, I'm sure," she said. "Probably before they water the garden."

She slipped off. Now there was indeed need to hurry. And she couldn't. Entering the capitol of this damned nightless city unnoticed made everything that had gone before look like tiddlywinks. An open window gave access to a room she had seen was empty. But then it was to get from tapestry to settee to ornamental urn to statue, while aleph-null servants and guards and bureaucrats and tradespeople and petitioners and sisters and cousins and aunts went back and forth through the long corridors; and take a ramp at the moment it was deserted, on the hope that no one would appear before she found her next hiding place; and on and on—By the time she reached the balcony she wanted, whose slender columns touched the eaves, even her nerves were drawn close to breaking.

She shinnied up, swung herself over the roof edge, and crawled to a point directly above a window that must belong to Falkayn's apartment. Her prisoner had told her it was between the second and third north-side balconies. And two stories down, with a wall too smooth for climbing. But she had plenty of rope left, and plenty of chimneys poked from the tiles. She made a loop around the nearest. After a glance to be sure no one was gauping from the ground, she slid.

Checked, she peered in the window. An arabesque grille of age-greened bronze would let her pass, but not a man. Why hadn't she thought to search the Katandaran litter for a hacksaw? She reached through and rapped on the glass behind. There was no response. With a remark that really shouldn't have come out of such fluffy white fur, she broke the pane with a dagger butt and crept inside. While she looked around, she pulled in the rope.

The rooms were well furnished, if you were an Ikranankan. For a man they were dark and cold, and Falkayn lay asleep curled up like a hawser. Chee padded to the bed, covered his mouth—humans were so ridiculously emotional—and shook him.

He started awake. "Huh? Whuff, whoo, ugh!" Chee laid a finger on her muzzle. His eyes cleared, he nodded and she let him go.

"Chee!" he breathed shakenly. His hands closed around hers. "How the devil?"

"I sneaked in, you idiot. Did you expect me to hire a band? Now let's figure some way to get you out."

Falkayn gasped. "You mean you don't know?"

"How should I?"

He rose to his feet, but without vigor. "Me too," he said.

Chee's courage sank. She slumped down on the floor.

With a rush of love, Falkayn stooped, lifted her, and cradled her in his arms. "Just knowing you tried is enough," he murmured.

Her tail switched. The vinegar returned to her voice. "Not for me it isn't." After a moment: "All we need is an escape from here. Then we can wait in the outback for the relief expedition."

Falkayn shook his head. "Sorry, no. How'd we get in touch? They'd spot *Muddlin' Through,* sure, but as soon as we reached that area, we'd be filled with ironmongery, so Jadhadi could throw the blame for our disappearance on Thorn. He'd probably get away with it, too. Think how these natives would stick together in the face of an alien."

Chee reflected awhile. "I could try to slip within voice range of our ship's detectors."

"M-m-m." Falkayn ran a hand through his hair. "You know you'd never manage that, as witness the fact you didn't try in the first place. No cover worth itemizing." Rage welled in him. "Damn that chance that Adzel's transceiver got smashed! If we could have called the ship—"

And then his mind rocked. He stumbled back and sat down on the bed. Chee jumped clear and watched with round yellow eyes. The silence grew huge.

Until Falkayn smashed fist into palm and said, "Judas on Mercury! Yes!"

The discipline of his boyhood came back. He'd been drugged and kidnapped and given one figurative belly kick after another, and been unable to do a thing about it, and that had shattered him. Now, as the idea took shape, he knew he was a man yet. The possibility that he would get killed mattered not a hoot in a vacuum. Under the thrumming consciousness, his soul laughed for joy.

"Listen," he said. "You could get out of town again, even if I can't. But your chance of surviving very long, and Adzel's, wouldn't be worth much. Your chance of being rescued would be still smaller. If you're willing to throw the dice right now—go for broke—then—"

Chee did not argue with his plan. She pondered, made a few calculations in her head, and nodded. "Let us."

Falkayn started to put on his clothes but paused. "Wouldn't you like a nap first?"

"No, I feel quite ready. Yourself?"

Falkayn grinned. His latest sleep had restored him. The blood tingled in his flesh. "Ready to fight elephants, my friend."

Dressed, he went to the door and pounded on it. "Hey!" he shouted. "Help! Emergency! Urgency! Top secret! Priority One! Handle with care! Open this door, you scratchbrains!"

A key clicked in the lock. The door swung wide. A large Ershokh stood in the entrance with drawn sword. His companion waited a discreet distance behind. "Well?"

"I've got to see your boss," Falkayn babbled. Anything to get within arm's length. He stepped closer, waving his hands. "I've thought of something terrible."

"What?" growled from the beard.

"This." Falkayn snatched at the man's cloak, on either side of the brooch, with wrists crossed. He pulled his hands together. The backs of them closed on his victim's larynx. Simultaneously, Chee hurtled into the hall and over the clothes of the other guard.

Falkayn's man slashed downward with his saber, but Falkayn's leg wasn't there any more. That knee had gone straight up. The soldier doubled in anguish. Then strangulation took him. Falkayn let him fall and bounded to the next Ershokh. Chee swarmed on that one, and had so far kept him from uttering more than a few snorts and grunts, but she couldn't overpower him. Falkayn chopped with the blade of a hand. The guard collapsed.

He wasn't badly injured either, Falkayn saw with some relief. He stooped, to drag them both inside and don a uniform. But there had been too much ruckus. A female Ikranankan stuck her head out of an entrance further down the hall and began to scream. Well, you couldn't have everything. Falkayn grabbed a saber and sped off. Chee loped beside him. The screams hit high C and piled on the decibels.

Down yonder ramp! A courtier was headed up. Falkayn stiff-armed him and continued. Several more were in the corridor below. He waved his sword. "Blood and bones!" he yelled. "Boo!" They cleared a path, falling over each other and clamoring.

And here was the electrical shop. Falkayn stormed in. Across workbenches crammed with quaintly designed apparatus, two scientists and several assistants gaped at him. "Everybody out," Falkayn said. When they didn't move fast enough, he paddled the Grand Chief Philosopher of Royal Rangakora with the flat of his blade. They got the message. He slammed the door and shot the bolt.

The uproar came through that heavy metal, louder by the minutes, voices, feet, weapon clatter, and alarm drums. He glanced around. The windows gave no access, but another door opened at the far end of the long room. He bolted that, too, and busied himself shoving furniture against it. If he piled everything there that wasn't nailed down and used Chee's rope to secure the mass further, he could probably make it impasssable to anyone short of the army engineers. And they wouldn't likely be called, when the other approach looked easier.

He ended his task and returned, breathing hard. Chee had also been busy. She squatted on the floor amid an incredible clutter of batteries and assorted junk, coiling a wire into a helix while she frowned at a condenser jar. She could do no more than guess at capacitances, resistances, inductances, voltages, and amperages. However, the guess would be highly educated.

Both doors trembled under fists and boots. Falkayn watched the one he had not reinforced. He stretched, rocked a little on his feet, willed the tension out of his muscles. Behind him, Chee fiddled with a spark gap; he heard the slight frying noise.

A human voice bawled muffled: "Clear the way! Clear the way! We'll break the obscenity thing down, if you'll get out of our obscenity way!" Chee didn't bother to look from her work.

The racket outside died. After a breathless moment, feet pounded and a weight smashed at the bronze. It rang and buckled. Again the ram struck. This time a sound of splintering was followed by hearty curses. Falkayn grinned. They must have used a balk of glued-together timber, which had proved less than satisfactory. He went to a gap where the door had been bent a little clear of the jamb and had a look. Several Ershoka could be seen, in full canonicals, fury alive on their faces. "Peekaboo," Falkayn said.

"Get a smith!" He thought he recognized Hugh Padrick's cry. "You, there, get an obscenity smith. And hammers and cold chisels."

That would do the job, but time would be needed. Falkayn returned to help Chee. "Think we've got ample juice in those batteries?" he asked.

"Oh yes." She kept eyes at the single workbench not manning the barricade, where she improvised a telegraph key out of scrap metal. "Only four hundred kilometers or so, right? Even that slue-footed Adzel made it in a few standard days. What worries me is getting the right frequency."

"Well, estimate as close as you can, and then use different values. You know, make a variable contact along a wire."

"Of course I know! Didn't we plan this in your rooms? Stop yattering and get useful."

"I'm more the handsome type," said Falkayn. He wielded a pair of pliers awkwardly—they weren't meant for a human grasp—to hook the batteries in series. And a Leyden jar, though you really should call it a Rangakora jar. . . .

The door belled and shuddered. Falkayn kept half his mind in that direction. Probably somewhat less than an hour had passed since he crashed out. Not a hell of a lot of time to play Heinrich Hertz. But Chee had put on the last touches. She squatted before the ungainly sprawl of apparatus, tapped her key, and nodded. A spark sizzled across a gap. She went into a rattle of League code. Invisible, impalpable, the radio waves surged forth.

Now everything depended on her finding the waveband of the late lamented transceivers, somewhere among those she could blindly try. She hadn't long, either. The door would give way in another minute or two. Falkayn left her for his post.

The bolt sprang loose. The door sagged open. An Ershokh pushed in, sword a-shimmer.

Falkayn crossed blades. Steel chimed. As expected, the man was a sucker for scientific fencing. Falkayn could have killed him in thirty seconds. But he didn't want to. Besides, while he held this chap in the doorway, no others could get past. "Having fun?" he called across the whirring edges. Rage snarled back at him.

Dit-dit-dah-dit. . . . Come to Rangakora. Land fifty meters outside the south gate. Dit-dah-dah. Clash, rattle, clang!

The Ershokh got his back to the jamb. Abruptly he sidled past the entrance, and another man was there. Falkayn held the first one by sheer energy while his foot lashed out in an epical savate kick. The second man yelped agony and lurched back into the arms of his fellows. Whirling, Falkayn deflected the blade of the first one with a quick beat and followed with a glide. His point sank into the forearm. He twisted deftly, ripping through tissue, and heard the enemy saber clank on the floor.

Not stopping to pull his own weapon free, he turned and barely avoided the slash of a third warrior. He took one step forward and grabbed, karate-style. A tug—a rather dreadful snapping noise—the Ershokh went to his knees, gray-faced and broken-armed, and Falkayn had his blade. It rang on the next.

The Hermetian's eyes flicked from side to side. The man he had cut was hunched over. Blood spurted from his wound, an impossibly brilliant red. The other casualty sat slumped against the wall. Falkayn looked into the visage that confronted him (a downy-cheeked kid, as he'd been himself not so long ago) and said, "If you'll hold off a bit, these busters can crawl out and get help."

The boy cursed and hacked at him. He caught the sword with his own in a bind and held fast. "Do you want your chum to bleed to death?" he asked. "Relax. I won't bite you. I'm really quite peaceful as long as you feed me."

He disengaged and poised on guard. The boy stared at him an instant, then backed off, into the crowd of humans and Ikranankans that eddied in the corridor behind him. Falkayn nudged the hurt men with a foot. "Go on," he said gently. They crept past him, into a descending hush.

Hugh Padrick trod to the forefront. His blade was out, but held low. His features worked. "What're you about?" he rasped.

"Very terrible magic," Falkayn told him. "We'll save trouble all around if you surrender right now."

Dit-dah-dah-dah!

"What do you want of us?" Padrick asked.

"Well, to start with, a long drink. After that we can talk." Falkayn tried to moisten his lips, without great success. Damn this air! No wonder the natives didn't go in for rugs. Life would become one long series of static shocks. Maybe that was what had first gotten the Rangakorans interested in electricity.

"We might talk, yes." Padrick's saber drooped further. Then in a blinding split second it hewed at Falkayn's calf.

The Hermetian's trained body reacted before his mind had quite engaged gears. He leaped straight up, under two-thirds of a Terrestrial gee. The whetted metal hissed beneath his boot soles. He came down before it could withdraw. His weight tore the weapon from Padrick's grasp. "Naughty!" he cried. His left fist rocketed forward. Padrick went on his bottom, nose a red ruin. Falkayn made a mental note that he be charged through that same nose for plastic surgery, if and when van Rijn's factors got around to offering such services.

An Ikranankan poked a spear at him. He batted it aside and took it away. That gained him a minute.

He got another while Padrick reeled erect and vanished in the mob. And still another passed while they stared and shuffled their feet. Then he heard Bobert Thorn trumpet, "Clear the way! Crossbows!"—and knew that the end was on hand.

The crowd parted, right and left, out of his view. Half a dozen Ikranankan archers tramped into sight and took their stance before him, across the hall. But he put on the most daredevil grin in his repertory when Stepha ran ahead of them.

She stopped and regarded him with wonder. "David," she breathed. "No other man in the world could've—and I never knew."

"You do now." Since her dagger was sheathed, he risked chucking her under the chin. "They teach us more where I've been than how to handle machines. Not that I'd mind a nice safe armored vehicle."

Tears blurred the gray eyes. "You've got to give up, though," she begged. "What more can anyone do?"

"This," he said, dropped his saber and grabbed her. She yelled and fought back with considerable strength, but his was greater. He pinioned her in front of him and said to the archers, "Go away, you ugly people." The scent of her hair was warm in his nostrils.

Imperturbably, Chee continued to signal.

Stepha stopped squirming. He felt her stiffen in his grip. She said with an iron pride, "No, go 'head and shoot."

"You don't mean that!" he stammered.

"Sure do." She gave him a forlorn smile. "Think an Ershokh's less ready to die than you are?"

The archers took aim.

Falkayn shook his head. "Well," he said, and even achieved a laugh, "when the stakes are high, people bluff." A howl, a babble, distant but rising and nearing, didn't seem very important. "Of course I wouldn't've used you for a shield. I'm an awful liar, and you have better uses." He kissed her. She responded. Her hands moved over his back and around his neck.

Which was fun, and moreover gained a few extra seconds. . . .

"*The demon, the demon!*" Men and Ikranankans pelted by. A thunderclap was followed by the sound of falling masonry.

Stepha didn't join the stampede. But she pulled free, and the dagger flashed into her hand. "What's that?" she cried.

Falkayn gusted the air from his lungs. His head swam. Somehow he kept his tone level. "That," he said, "was our ship. She landed and took Adzel on for a pilot, and now he's aloft, losing merit but having a ball with a mild demonstration of strength." He took her hand. "Come on, let's go out where he can see us and get taken aboard. I'm overdue for a dry martini."

XI

The conference was held on neutral ground, an autonomous Chakoran village between the regions claimed of old by Katandara and Rangakora. (Autonomy meant that it paid tribute to both of them.) Being careful to observe every possible formality and not hurt one party's feelings more than another's, Falkayn let its head preside at the opening ceremonies. They were interminable. His eyes must needs wander, around the reddish gloom of the council hut, over the patterns of the woven walls, across the local males who squatted with their spears as a sort of honor guard, and back to the large stone table at which the conference was benched. He wished he could be outside. A cheerful bustle and chatter drifted to him through the open door, where Adzel lay so patiently; the soldiers who had escorted their various chiefs here were fraternizing.

You couldn't say that for the chiefs themselves. King Ursala had finished droning through a long list of his grievances and desires, and now fidgeted while Emperor Jadhadi embarked on his own. Harry Smit glared at Bobert Thorn, who glared back. The Ershoka senior still blamed his phratry's troubles on the rebellion. His honor the mayor of this town rustled papers, doubtless preparing an introduction to the next harangue.

Well, Falkayn thought, *this was your idea, lad. And your turn has got to come sometime.*

When the spaceship hovered low above them and a giant's voice boomed forth, suggesting a general armistice and treaty-making, the factions had agreed. They didn't know they had a choice. Falkayn would never have fired on them, but he saw no reason to tell them that. No doubt Chee Lan, seated before the pilot board in the sky overhead, had more to do now with keeping matters orderly than Adzel's overwhelming presence. But why did they have to make these speeches? The issues were simple. Jadhadi wanted Rangakora and felt he could no longer trust the Ershoka. A large number of the Ershoka wanted Rangakora, too; the rest wished for the *status quo ante*, or a reasonable substitute, but didn't see how to get it; each group felt betrayed by the other. Ursala wanted all foreign devils out of his town, plus a whopping indemnity for damages suffered. And Falkayn wanted—well, he'd tell them. He lit his pipe and consoled himself with thoughts of Stepha, who awaited him in the village. Quite a girl, that, for recreation if not for a lifetime partner.

An hour passed.

"—the distinguished representative of the merchant adventurers from Beyond-the-World, Da'id 'Alkayn."

His boredom evaporated. He rose to his feet in a tide of eagerness that he could barely mask with a smile and a casual drawl.

"Thank you, most noble," he said. "After listening to these magnificent orations, I won't even try to match them. I'll state my position in a few simple words." That should win him universal gratitude!

"We came here in good faith," he said, "offering to sell you goods such as I have demonstrated at unbelievably reasonable prices. What happened? We were assaulted with murderous intent. I myself was imprisoned and humiliated. Our property was illegally sequestered. And frankly, most nobles, you can be plaguey thankful none of us was killed." He touched his blaster. "Remember, we do represent a great power, which has a fixed policy of avenging harm done to its people." *When expedient,* he added, and saw how Jadhadi's ruff rose with terror and Smit's knuckles stood white on his fist.

"Relax, relax," he urged. "We're in no unfriendly mood. Besides, we want to trade, and you can't trade during a war. That's one reason I asked for this get-together. If the differences between us can be settled, why, that's to the League's advantage. And to yours, too. You do want what we have to sell, don't you?

"So." He leaned forward, resting his fingertips on the table. "I think a compromise is possible. Everybody will give up something, and get something, and as soon as trade starts you'll be so wealthy that what you lost today will make you laugh. Here's a rough outline of the general agreement I shall propose.

"First, Rangakora will be guaranteed complete independence, but drop claims to indemnification—"

"Most noble!" Jadhadi and Ursala sprang up and yelled into each other's beaks.

Falkayn waved them to silence. "I yield for a question to King Ursala," he said, or the equivalent thereof.

"Our casualties . . . crops ruined . . . dependent villages looted . . . buildings destroyed—" Ursala stopped, collected himself, and said with more dignity: "We were not the aggressors."

"I know," Falkayn said, "and I sympathize. However, weren't you prepared to fight for your freedom? Which you now have. That should be worth something. Don't forget, the League will be a party to any treaty we arrive at here. If that treaty guarantees your independence, the League will back the guarantee." *Not strictly true. Only Solar Spice & Liquors is to be involved. Oh, well, makes no practical difference.* He nodded at Jadhadi. "By my standards, most noble, you should pay for the harm you did. I'm passing that in the interests of reconciliation."

"But my borders," the Emperor protested. "I must have strong borders. Besides, I have a rightful claim to Rangakora. My great ancestor, the first Jadhadi—"

Falkayn heroically refrained from telling him what to do to his great ancestor and merely answered in his stiffest voice: "Most noble, please consider yourself let off very lightly. You did endanger the lives of League agents. You cannot expect the League not to exact some penalty. Yielding Rangakora is mild indeed." He glanced at his blaster, and Jadhadi shivered. "As for your border defenses," Falkayn said, "the League can help you there. Not to mention the fact that we will sell you firearms. You won't need your Ershoka any more."

Jadhadi sat down. One could almost see the wheels turning in his head.

Falkayn looked at Thorn, who was sputtering. "The loss of Rangakora is your penalty, too," he said. "Your followers did seize me, you know."

"But what shall we do?" cried old Harry Smit. "Where shall we go?"

"Earth?" Thorn growled. Falkayn had been laying it on thick of late, how alien Earth was to these castaways. They weren't interested in repatriation any more. He didn't feel guilty about that. They would in fact be happier here, where they had been born. And if they were staying of their own free choice, van Rijn's traders could be trusted to keep silence. In the course of the next generation or two—the secret wouldn't last longer in any event—their children and grandchildren could gradually be integrated into galactic civilization, much as Adzel had been.

"No, if you don't want to," Falkayn said. "But what has your occupation been? Soldiering. Some of you keep farms, ranches, or town houses. No reason why you can't continue to do so; foreigners have often owned property in another country. Because what you should do is establish a nation in your own right. Not in any particular territory. Everything hereabouts is already claimed. But you can be an itinerant people. There are precedents, like nomads and Gypsies on ancient Earth. Or, more to the point, there are those nations on Cynthia which are trade routes rather than areas. My friend Chee Lan can explain the details of organization to you. As for work—well, you are warriors, and the planet is full of barbarians, and once the League gets started here there are going to be more caravans to protect than fighters to protect them. You can command high prices for your service. You'll get rich."

He beamed at the assembly. "In fact, we'll all get rich."

"Missionaries," said Adzel into the pensive silence.

"Uh, yes, I'd forgotten," Falkayn said. "I don't imagine anyone will object if the ships bring an occasional teacher? We would like to explain our beliefs to you."

The point looked so minor that no one argued. Yet it would bring more changes in the long run than machinery or medicine. The Katandarans would surely leap at Buddhism, which was infinitely more comfortable than their own demonology. Together with what scientific knowledge trickled down to them, the religion would wean them from their hostility complex. Result: a stable culture with which Nicholas van Rijn could do business.

Falkayn spread his hands. "That's the gist of my suggestions," he finished. "What I propose is what an Earthman once called an equality of dissatisfaction. After which the League traders will bring more satisfactions to you than you can now imagine."

Thorn bit his lip. He wouldn't easily abandon his dream of kingship. "Suppose we refuse?" he said.

"Well," Falkayn reminded him, "the League has been offended. We must insist on some retribution. My demands are nominal. Aren't they?"

He had them, he knew. The carrot of trade and the stick of war; they didn't know the war threat was pure bluff. They'd make the settlement he wanted.

But of course they'd do so with endless bargaining, recrimination, quibbles over details, speeches—oh, God, the speeches! Falkayn stepped back. "I realize this is a lot to swallow at once," he said. "Why don't we recess? After everyone's had time to think, and had a good sleep, we can talk to more purpose."

Mainly, he wanted to get back to Stepha. He'd promised her a jaunt in the spaceship; and Adzel and Chee could jolly well wait right here. When the assembly agreed to break, Falkayn was the first one out the door.

Metal hummed. The viewport blazed with stars in an infinite night. That red spark which was Ikrananka's sun dwindled swiftly toward invisibility.

Staring yonder, Falkayn sighed. "A whole world," he mused. "So many lives and hopes. Seems wrong for us to turn them over to somebody else."

"I know why you would go back," Chee Lan clipped. "But Adzel and I have no such reason. We've a long way to Earth—"

Falkayn brightened. He had analogous motives for looking forward to journey's end.

"—so move your lazy legs," Chee said.

Falkayn accompanied her to the saloon. Adzel was already there, arranging chips in neat stacks. "You know," Falkayn remarked as he sat down, "we're a new breed. Not troubleshooters. Trouble twisters. I suspect our whole career is going to be a sequence of ghastly situations that somehow we twist around to our advantage."

"Shut up and shuffle," Chee said. "First jack deals."

A pair of uninteresting hands went by, and then Falkayn got a flush. He bet. Adzel folded. Chee saw him. The computer raised. Falkayn raised back. Chee quit and the computer raised again. This went on for some time before the draw. Muddlehead must have a good hand, Falkayn knew, but considering its style of play, a flush was worth staying on. He stood pat. The computer asked for one card.

Judas in a nova burst! The damned machine must have gotten four of a kind! Falkayn tossed down his own. "Never mind," he said. "Take it."

Somewhat later, Chee had a similar experience, still more expensive. She made remarks that ionized the air.

Adzel's turn came when the other two beings dropped out. Back and forth the raises went, between dragon and computer, until he finally got nervous and called.

"You win," said the mechanical voice. Adzel dropped his full house, along with his jaw.

"*What?*" Chee screamed. Her tail stood vertical and bottled. "You were bluffing?"

"Yes," said Muddlehead.

"But, no, wait, you play on IOUs and we limit you," Falkayn rattled. "You can't bluff!"

"If you will inspect the No. 4 hold," said Muddlehead, "you will find a considerable amount of furs, jewels, and spices. While the value cannot be set exactly until the market involved has stabilized, it is obviously large. I got them in exchange for calculating probability tables for the native Gujgengi, and am now prepared to purchase chips in the normal manner."

"But, but, but you're a machine!"

"I am not programmed to predict how a court would adjudicate title to those articles," said Muddlehead. "However, my understanding is that in a commercially and individualistically oriented civilization, any legitimate earnings belong to the earner."

"Good Lord," said Falkayn weakly, "I think you're right."

"You're not a person!" Chee shouted. "Not even in fact, let alone the law!"

"I acquired those goods in pursuit of the objective you have programmed into me," Muddlehead replied, "namely, to play poker. Logic indicates that I can play better poker when properly staked."

Adzel sighed. "That's right, too," he conceded. "If we want the ship to give us an honest game, we have to take the syllogistic consequences. Otherwise the programming would become impossibly complicated. Besides . . . sportsmanship, you know."

Chee riffled the deck. "All right," she said grimly. "I'll win your stake the hard way."

Of course she didn't. Nobody did. With that much wealth at its disposal, Muddlehead could afford to play big. It didn't rake in their entire commissions for Operation Ikrananka in the course of the Earthward voyage, but it made a substantial dent in them.

INTRODUCTION

A book such as this would be rattlewing indeed did it not tell anything about Falkayn himself. Yet there seems no lift in repeating common knowledge or reprinting tales which, in their different versions, are as popular and available as ever aforetime.

Therefore Hloch reckons himself fortunate in having two stories whereof the fullness is well-nigh unknown, and which furthermore deal with events whose consequences are still breeding winds.

The first concerns Merseia. Although most folk, even here on far Avalon, have caught some awareness of yonder world and the strange fate that stooped upon it, the part that the Founder-to-be took has long been shadowed, as has been the very fact that he was there at all. For reasons of discretion, he never spoke publicly of the matter, and his report was well buried in League archives. Among his descendants, only a vague tradition remained that he had passed through such air.

Hearing this, Rennhi set herself to hunt down the truth. On Falkayn's natal planet Hermes she learned that, several years after the Babur War, he and van Rijn had quietly transferred many data units thither, putting them in care of the Grand Ducal house and his own immediate kin. The feeling was that they would be more secure than in the Solar System, now when a time of storms was so clearly brewing. After the League broke up, there was no decipherment program anymore, and the units lay virtually forgotten in storage. Rennhi won permission to transfer the molecular patterns. Once home again, she instigated a code-breaking effort. It was supported by the armed forces in hopes of snatching useful information, for by that time war with the Empire had become a thunderhead threat.

This hope was indirectly fulfilled. Nothing in the records had military value, but the cracking of a fiendishly clever cipher developed cryptographic capabilities. Nor does much in them have any particular bearing on Avalon. Nearly everything deals with details of matters whose bones grew white centuries ago. Interrupted by hostilities, the study has only been completed lately.

A few treasures did come forth, bright among them a full account of what happened on Merseia. Hloch and Arinnian together have worked it into narrative form.

—Hloch of the Stormgate Choth
The Earth Book of Stormgate

DAY OF BURNING

For who knows how long, the star had orbited quietly in the wilderness between Betelgeuse and Rigel. It was rather more massive than average—about half again as much as Sol—and shone with corresponding intensity, white-hot, corona and prominences a terrible glory. But there are no few like it. A ship of the first Grand Survey noted its existence. However, the crew were more interested in a neighbor sun which had planets, and could not linger long in that system either. The galaxy is too big; their purpose was to get some hint about this spiral arm which we inhabit. Thus certain spectroscopic omens escaped their notice.

No one returned thither for a pair of centuries. Technic civilization had more than it could handle, let alone comprehend, in the millions of stars closer to home. So the fact remained unsuspected that this one was older than normal for its type in its region, must indeed have wandered in from other parts. Not that it was very ancient, astronomically speaking. But the great childless suns evolve fast and strangely.

By chance, though, a scout from the Polesotechnic League, exploring far in search of new markets, was passing within a light-year when the star exploded.

Say instead (insofar as simultaneity has any meaning across interstellar distances) that the death agony had occurred some months before. Ever more fierce, thermonuclear reaction had burned up the last hydrogen at the center. Unbalanced by radiation pressure, the outer layers collapsed beneath their own weight. Forces were released which triggered a wholly different order of atomic fusions. New elements came into being, not only those which may be found in the planets but also the short-lived transuranics; for a while, technetium itself dominated that anarchy. Neutrons and neutrinos flooded forth, carrying with them the last balancing energy. Compression turned into catastrophe. At the brief peak, the supernova was as radiant as its entire galaxy.

So close, the ship's personnel would have died had she not been in hyperdrive. They did not remain there. A dangerous amount of radiation was still touching them between quantum microjumps. And they were not equipped to study the phenomenon. This was the first chance in our history to observe a new supernova. Earth was too remote to help. But the scientific colony on Catawrayannis could be reached fairly soon. It could dispatch laboratory craft.

Now to track in detail what was going to happen, considerable resources were demanded. Among these were a place where men could live and instruments be made to order as the need for them arose. Such things could not well be sent from the usual factories. By the time they arrived, the wave front carrying information about rapidly progressing events would have traveled so far that inverse-square enfeeblement would create maddening inaccuracies.

But a little beyond one parsec from the star—an excellent distance for observation over a period of years—was a G-type sun. One of its planets was terrestroid to numerous points of classification, both physically and biochemically. Survey records showed that the most advanced culture on it was at the verge of an industrial-scientific revolution. Ideal!

Except, to be sure, that Survey's information was less than sketchy, and two centuries out of date.

"No."

Master Merchant David Falkayn stepped backward in startlement. The four nearest guards clutched at their pistols. Peripherally and profanely, Falkayn wondered what canon he had violated now.

"Beg, uh, beg pardon?" he fumbled.

Morruchan Long-Ax, the Hand of the Vach Dathyr, leaned forward on his dais. He was big even for a Merseian, which meant that he overtopped Falkayn's rangy height by a good fifteen centimeters.

Long, shoulder-flared orange robes and horned miter made his bulk almost overwhelming. Beneath them, he was approximately anthropoid, save for a slanting posture counterbalanced by the tail which, with his booted feet, made a tripod for him to sit on. The skin was green, faintly scaled, totally hairless. A spiky ridge ran from the top of his skull to the end of that tail. Instead of earflaps, he had deep convolutions in his head. But the face was manlike, in a heavy-boned fashion, and the physiology was essentially mammalian.

How familiar the mind was, behind those jet eyes, Falkayn did not know.

The harsh basso said: "You shall not take the rule of this world. If we surrendered the right and freehold they won, the God would cast back the souls of our ancestors to shriek at us."

Falkayn's glance flickered around. He had seldom felt so alone. The audience chamber of Castle Afon stretched high and gaunt, proportioned like nothing men had ever built. Curiously woven tapestries on the stone walls, between windows arched at both top and bottom, and battle banners hung from the rafters, did little to stop echoes. The troopers lining the hall, down to a hearth whose fire could have roasted an elephant, wore armor and helmets with demon masks. The guns which they added to curved swords and barbed pikes did not seem out of place. Rather, what appeared unattainably far was a glimpse of ice-blue sky outside.

The air was chill with winter. Gravity was little higher than Terrestrial, but Falkayn felt it dragging at him.

He straightened. He had his own sidearm, no chemical slugthrower but an energy weapon. Adzel, abroad in the city, and Chee Lan aboard the ship, were listening in via the transceiver on his wrist. And the ship had power to level all Ardaig. Morruchan must realize as much.

But he had to be made to cooperate.

Falkayn picked his words with care: "I pray forgiveness, Hand, if perchance in mine ignorance I misuse thy . . . uh . . . your tongue. Naught was intended save friendliness. Hither bring I news of peril impending, for the which ye must busk yourselves betimes lest ye lose everything ye possess. My folk would fain show your folk what to do. So vast is the striving needed, and so scant the time, that perforce ye must take our counsel. Else can we be of no avail. But never will we act as conquerors. 'Twere not simply an evil deed, but 'twould boot us naught, whose trafficking is with many worlds. Nay, we would be brothers, come to help in a day of sore need."

Morruchan scowled and rubbed his chin. "Say on, then," he replied. "Frankly, I am dubious. You claim Valenderay is about to become a supernova—"

"Nay, Hand, I declare it hath already done so. The light therefrom will smite this planet in less than three years."

The time unit Falkayn actually used was Merseian, a trifle greater than Earth's. He sweated and swore to himself at the language problem. The Survey xenologists had gotten a fair grasp of Eriau in the several months they spent here, and Falkayn and his shipmates had acquired it by synapse transform while en route. But now it turned out that, two hundred years back, Eriau had been in a state of linguistic overturn. He wasn't even pronouncing the vowels right.

He tried to update his grammar. "Would ye, uh, I mean if your desire is . . . if you want confirmation, we can take you or a trusty member of your household so near in our vessel that the starburst is beheld with living eyes."

"No doubt the scientists and poets will duel for a berth on that trip," Morruchan said in a dry voice. "But I believe you already. You yourself, your ship and companions, are proof." His tone sharpened. "At the same time, I am no Believer, imagining you half-divine because you come from outside. Your civilization has a technological head start on mine, nothing else. A careful reading of the records from that other brief period when aliens dwelt among us shows they had no reason more noble than professional curiosity. And that was fitful; they left, and none ever returned. Until now.

"So: what do you want from us?"

Falkayn relaxed a bit. Morruchan seemed to be his own kind despite everything, not awestruck, not idealistic, not driven by some incomprehensible nonhuman motivation, but a shrewd and skeptical politician of a pragmatically oriented culture.

Seems to be, the man cautioned himself. *What do I really know about Merseia?*

Judging by observation made in orbit, radio monitoring, initial radio contact, and the ride here in an electric groundcar, this planet still held a jumble of societies, dominated by the one which surrounded the Wilwidh Ocean. Two centuries ago, local rule had been divided among aristocratic clans. He supposed that a degree of continental unification had since been achieved, for his request for an interview with the highest authority had gotten him to Ardaig and a confrontation with this individual. But could Morruchan speak for his entire species? Falkayn doubted it.

Nevertheless, you had to start somewhere.

"I shall be honest, Hand," he said. "My crew and I are come as naught but preparers of the way. Can we succeed, we will be rewarded with a share in whatever gain ensueth. For our scientists wish to use Merseia and its moons as bases wherefrom to observe the supernova through the next dozen years. Best for them would be if your folk could provide them with most of their needs, not alone food but such instruments as they tell you how to fashion. For this they will pay fairly; and in addition, ye will acquire knowledge.

"Yet first must we assure that there remaineth a Merseian civilization. To do that, we must wreak huge works. And ye will pay us for our toil and goods supplied to that end. The price will not be usurious, but it will allow us a profit. Out of it, we will buy whatever Merseian wares can be sold at home for further profit." He smiled. "Thus all may win and none need fear. The Polesotechnic League compriseth nor conquerors nor bandits, naught save merchant adventurers who seek to make their"—more or less—"honest living."

"*Hunh!*" Morruchan growled. "Now we bite down to the bone. When you first communicated and spoke about a supernova, my colleagues and I consulted the astronomers. We are not altogether savages here; we have at least gone as far as atomic power and interplanetary travel. Well, our astronomers said that such a star reaches a peak output about fifteen billion times as great as Korych. Is this right?"

"Close enough, Hand, if Korych be your own sun."

"The only nearby one which might burst in this manner is Valenderay. From your description, the brightest in the southern sky, you must be thinking of it too."

Falkayn nodded, realized he wasn't sure if this gesture meant the same thing on Merseia, remembered it did, and said: "Aye, Hand."

"It sounded terrifying," Morruchan said, "until they pointed out that Valenderay is three and a half light-years distant. And this is a reach so enormous that no mind can swallow it. The radiation, when it gets to us, will equal a mere one-third of what comes daily from Korych. And in some fifty-five days" (Terrestrial) "it will have dwindled to half . . . and so on, until before long we see little except a bright nebula at night.

"True, we can expect troublesome weather, storms, torrential rains, perhaps some flooding if sufficient of the south polar ice cap melts. But that will pass. In any case, the center of civilization is here, in the northern hemisphere. It is also true that, at peak, there will be a dangerous amount of ultraviolet and X radiation. But Merseia's atmosphere will block it.

"Thus." Morruchan leaned back on his tail and bridged the fingers of his oddly humanlike hands. "The peril you speak of scarcely exists. What do you really want?"

Falkayn's boyhood training, as a nobleman's son on Hermes, rallied within him. He squared his shoulders. He was not unimpressive, a tall, fair-haired young man with blue eyes bright in a lean, high-cheekboned face. "Hand," he said gravely, "I perceive you have not yet had time to consult your folk who are wise in matters—"

And then he broke down. He didn't know the word for "electronic."

Morruchan refrained from taking advantage. Instead, the Merseian became quite helpful. Falkayn's rejoinder was halting, often interrupted while he and the other worked out what a phrase must be. But, in essence and in current language, what he said was:

"The Hand is correct as far as he goes. But consider what will follow. The eruption of a supernova is violent beyond imagining. Nuclear processes are involved, so complex that we ourselves don't yet understand them in detail. That's why we want to study them. But this much we do know, and your physicists will confirm it.

"As nuclei and electrons recombine in that supernal fireball, they generate asymmetrical magnetic pulses. Surely you know what this does when it happens in the detonation of an atomic weapon. Now think of it on a stellar scale. When those forces hit, they will blast straight through Merseia's own magnetic field, down to the very surface. Unshielded electric motors, generators, transmission lines . . . oh, yes, no doubt you have surge arresters, but your circuit breakers will be tripped, intolerable voltages will be induced, the entire system will be wrecked. Likewise telecommunications lines. And computers.

If you use transistors—ah, you do—the flipflop between *p* and *n* type conduction will wipe every memory bank, stop every operation in its tracks.

"Electrons, riding that magnetic pulse, will not be long in arriving. As they spiral in the planet's field, their synchrotron radiation will completely blanket whatever electronic apparatus you may have salvaged. Protons should be slower, pushed to about half the speed of light. Then come the alpha particles, then the heavier matter: year after year after year of cosmic fallout, most of it radioactive, to a total greater by orders of magnitude than any war could create before civilization was destroyed. Your planetary magnetism is no real shield. The majority of ions are energetic enough to get through. Nor is your atmosphere any good defense. Heavy nuclei, sleeting through it, will produce secondary radiation that does reach the ground.

"I do not say this planet will be wiped clean of life. But I do say that, without ample advance preparation, it will suffer ecological disaster. Your species might or might not survive; but if you do, it will be as a few starveling primitives. The early breakdown of the electric systems on which your civilization is now dependent will have seen to that. Just imagine. Suddenly no more food moves into the cities. The dwellers go forth as a ravening horde. But if most of your farmers are as specialized as I suppose, they won't even be able to support themselves. Once fighting and famine have become general, no more medical service will be possible, and the pestilences will start. It will be like the aftermath of an all-out nuclear strike against a country with no civil defense. I gather you've avoided that on Merseia. But you certainly have theoretical studies of the subject, and—I have seen planets where it did happen.

"Long before the end, your colonies throughout this system will have been destroyed by the destruction of the apparatus that keeps the colonists alive. And for many years, no spaceship will be able to move.

"Unless you accept our help. We know how to generate force screens, small ones for machines, gigantic ones which can give an entire planet some protection. Not enough—but we also know how to insulate against the energies that get through. We know how to build engines and communications lines which are not affected. We know how to sow substances which protect life against hard radiation. We know how to restore mutated genes. In short, we have the knowledge you need for survival.

"The effort will be enormous. Most of it you must carry out yourselves. Our available personnel are too few, our lines of interstellar transportation too long. But we can supply engineers and organizers.

"To be blunt, Hand, you are very lucky that we learned of this in time, barely in time. Don't fear us. We have no ambitions toward Merseia. If nothing else, it lies far beyond our normal sphere of operation, and we have millions of more profitable planets much closer to home. We want to save you, because you are sentient beings. But it'll be expensive, and a lot of the work will have to be done by outfits like mine, which exist to make a profit. So, besides a scientific base, we want a reasonable economic return.

"Eventually, though, we'll depart. What you do then is your own affair. But you'll still have your civilization. You'll also have a great deal of new equipment and new knowledge. I think you're getting a bargain."

Falkayn stopped. For a while, silence dwelt in that long dim hall. He grew aware of odors which had never been on Earth or Hermes.

Morruchan said at last, slowly: "This must be thought on. I shall have to confer with my colleagues, and others. There are so many complications. For example, I see no good reason to do anything for the colony on Ronruad, and many excellent reasons for letting it die."

"What?" Falkayn's teeth clicked together. "Meaneth the Hand the next outward planet? But meseems faring goeth on apace throughout this system."

"Indeed, indeed," Morruchan said impatiently. "We depend on the other planets for a number of raw materials, like fissionables, or complex gases from the outer worlds. Ronruad, though, is of use only to the Gethfennu."

He spoke that word with such distaste that Falkayn postponed asking for a definition. "What recommendations I make in my report will draw heavily upon the Hand's wisdom," the human said.

"Your courtesy is appreciated," Morruchan replied: with how much irony, Falkayn wasn't sure. He was taking the news more coolly than expected. But then, he was of a different race from men, and a soldierly tradition as well. "I hope that, for now, you will honor the Vach Dathyr by guesting us."

"Well—" Falkayn hesitated. He had planned on returning to his ship. But he might do better on the spot. The Survey crew had found Merseian food nourishing to men, in fact tasty. One report had waxed ecstatic about the ale.

"I thank the Hand."

"Good. I suggest you go to the chambers already prepared, to rest and refresh yourself. With your leave, a messenger will come presently to ask what he should bring you from your vessel. Unless you wish to move it here?"

"Uh, best not . . . policy—" Falkayn didn't care to take chances. The Merseians were not so far behind the League that they couldn't spring a nasty surprise if they wanted to.

Morruchan raised the skin above his brow ridges but made no comment. "You will dine with me and my councillors at sunset," he said. They parted ceremoniously.

A pair of guards conducted Falkayn out, through a series of corridors and up a sweeping staircase whose bannister was carved into the form of a snake. At the end, he was ushered into a suite. The rooms were spacious, their comfort-making gadgetry not greatly below Technic standards. Reptile-skin carpets and animal skulls mounted on the crimson-draped walls were a little disquieting, but what the hell. A balcony gave on a view of the palace gardens, whose austere good taste was reminiscent of Original Japanese, and on the city.

Ardaig was sizeable, must hold two or three million souls. This quarter was ancient, with buildings of gray stone fantastically turreted and battlemented. The hills which ringed it were checkered by the estates of the wealthy. Snow lay white and blue-shadowed between. Ramparted with tall modern structures, the bay shone like gunmetal. Cargo ships moved in and out, a delta-wing jet whistled overhead. But he heard little traffic noise; nonessential vehicles were banned in the sacred Old Quarter.

"Wedhi is my name, Protector," said the short Merseian in the black tunic who had been awaiting him. "May he consider me his liegeman, to do as he commands." Tail slapped ankles in salute.

"My thanks," Falkayn said. "Thou mayest show me how one maketh use of facilities." He couldn't wait to see a bathroom designed for these people. "And then, mayhap, a tankard of beer, a textbook on political geography, and privacy for some hours."

"The Protector has spoken. If he will follow me?"

The two of them entered the adjoining chamber, which was furnished for sleeping. As if by accident, Wedhi's tail brushed the door. It wasn't automatic, merely hinged, and closed under the impact. Wedhi seized Falkayn's hand and pressed something into the palm. Simultaneously, he caught his lips between his teeth. A signal for silence?

With a tingle along his spine, Falkayn nodded and stuffed the bit of paper into a pocket.

When he was alone, he opened the note, hunched over in case of spy eyes. The alphabet hadn't changed.

Be wary, star dweller. Morruchan Long-Ax is no friend. If you can arrange for one of your company to come tonight in secret to the house at the corner of Triau's Street and Victory Way which is marked by twined fylfots over the door, the truth shall be explained.

As darkness fell, the moon Neihevin rose full, Luna size and copper color, above eastward hills whose forests glistened with frost. Lythyr was already up, a small pale crescent. Rigel blazed in the heart of that constellation named the Spear Bearer.

Chee Lan turned from the viewscreen with a shiver and an unladylike phrase. "But I am not equipped to do that," said the ship's computer.

"The suggestion was addressed to my gods," Chee answered.

She sat for a while, brooding on her wrongs. Ta-chih-chien-pih—O_2 Eridani A II or Cynthia to humans—felt even more distant than it was, warm ruddy sunlight and rustling leaves around treetop homes lost in time as well as space. Not only the cold outside daunted her. Those Merseians were so bloody *big!*

She herself was no larger than a medium-sized dog, though the bush of her tail added a good deal. Her arms, almost as long as her legs, ended in delicate six-fingered hands. White fur fluffed about her, save where it made a bluish mask across the green eyes and round, blunt-muzzled face. Seeing her for the first time, human females were apt to call her darling.

She bristled. Ears, whiskers, and hair stood erect. What was she—descendant of carnivores who chased their prey in five-meter leaps from branch to branch, xenobiologist by training, trade pioneer by choice, and pistol champion because she liked to shoot guns—what was she doing, feeling so much as respect for a gaggle of slewfooted bald barbarians? Mainly she was irritated. While standing by aboard the ship, she'd hoped to complete her latest piece of sculpture. Instead, she must hustle into that pustulent excuse for weather, and skulk through a stone garbage dump that its perpetrators called a city, and hear some yokel drone on for hours about some squabble between drunken cockroaches which he thought was politics . . . and pretend to take the whole farce seriously!

A narcotic cigarette soothed her, however ferocious the puffs in which she consumed it. "I guess the matter is important, at that," she murmured. "Fat commissions for me if the project succeeds."

"My programming is to the effect that our primary objective is humanitarian," said the computer. "Though I cannot find that concept in my data storage."

"Never mind, Muddlehead," Chee replied. Her mood had turned benign. "If you want to know, it relates to those constraints you have filed under Law and Ethics. But no concern of ours, this trip. Oh, the bleeding hearts do quack about Rescuing a Promising Civilization, as if the galaxy didn't have too chaos many civilizations already. Well, if they want to foot the bill, it's their taxes. They'll have to work with the League, because the League has most of the ships, which it won't hire out for nothing. And the League has to start with us, because trade pioneers are supposed to be experts in making first contacts and we happened to be the sole such crew in reach. Which is our good luck, I suppose."

She stubbed out her cigarette and busied herself with preparations. There was, for a fact, no alternative. She'd had to admit that, after a three-way radio conversation with her partners. (They didn't worry about eavesdroppers, when not a Merseian knew a word of Anglic.) Falkayn was stuck in what's-his-name's palace. Adzel was loose in the city, but he'd be the last one you'd pick for an undercover mission. Which left Chee Lan.

"Maintain contact with all three of us," she ordered the ship. "Record everything coming in tonight over my two-way. Don't stir without orders—in a galactic language—and don't respond to any native attempts at communication. Tell us at once whatever unusual you observe. If you haven't heard from any of us for twenty-four hours at a stretch, return to Catawrayannis and report."

No answer being indicated, the computer made none.

Chee buckled on a gravity harness, a tool kit, and two guns, a stunner and a blaster. Over them she threw a black mantle, less for warmth than concealment. Dousing the lights, she had the personnel lock open just long enough to let her through, jumped, and took to the air.

It bit her with chill. Flowing past, it felt liquid. An enormous silence dwelt beneath heaven; the hum of her grav was lost. Passing above the troopers who surrounded *Muddlin' Through* with armor and artillery—a sensible precaution from the native standpoint, she had to agree, sensibly labelled an honor guard—she saw the forlorn twinkle of campfires and heard a snatch of hoarse song. Then a hovercraft whirred near, big and black athwart the Milky Way, and she must change course to avoid being seen.

For a while she flew above snow-clad wilderness. On an unknown planet, you didn't land downtown if you could help it. Hills and woods gave way at length to a cultivated plain where the lights of villages huddled around tower-jagged castles. Merseia—this continent, at least—appeared to have retained feudalism even as it swung into an industrial age. Or had it?

Perhaps tonight she would find out

The seacoast hove in view, and Ardaig. That city did not gleam with illumination and brawl with traffic as most Technic communities did. Yellow windows strewed its night, like fireflies trapped in a web of phosphorescent paving. The River Oiss gleamed dull where it poured through town and into the bay, on which there shone a double moonglade. No, triple; Wythna was rising now. A murmur of machines lifted skyward.

Chee dodged another aircraft and streaked down for the darkling Old Quarter. She landed behind a shuttered bazaar and sought the nearest alley. Crouched there, she peered forth. In this section, the streets were decked with a hardy turf which ice had blanketed, and lit by widely spaced lamps. A Merseian went past, riding a horned gwydh. His tail was draped back across the animal's rump; his cloak fluttered behind him to reveal a quilted jacket reinforced with glittering metal discs, and a rifle slanted over his shoulder.

No guardsman, surely; Chee had seen what the military wore, and Falkayn had transmitted pictures of Morruchan's household troops to her via a hand scanner. He had also passed on the information that those latter doubled as police. So why was a civilian going armed? It bespoke a degree of lawlessness that fitted ill with a technological society . . . unless that society was in more trouble than Morruchan had admitted. Chee made certain her own guns were loose in the holsters.

The clop-clop of hooves faded away. Chee stuck her head out of the alley and took bearings from street signs. Instead of words, they used colorful heraldic emblems. But the Survey people had compiled a good map of Ardaig, which Falkayn's gang had memorized. The Old Quarter ought not to have changed much. She loped off, seeking cover whenever she heard a rider or pedestrian approach. There weren't many.

This corner! Squinting through murk, she identified the symbol carved in the lintel of a lean gray house. Quickly, she ran up the stairs and rapped on the door. Her free hand rested on the stunner.

The door creaked open. Light streamed through. A Merseian stood silhouetted against it. He carried a pistol himself. His head moved back and forth, peering into the night. "Here I am, thou idiot," Chee muttered.

He looked down. A jerk went through his body. "*Hu-ya!* You are from the star ship?"

"Nay," Chee sneered, "I am come to inspect the plumbing." She darted past him, into a wainscoted corridor. "If thou wouldst preserve this chickling secrecy of thine, might one suggest that thou close yon portal?"

The Merseian did. He stood a moment, regarding her in the glow of an incandescent bulb overhead. "I thought you would be . . . different."

"They were Terrans who first visited this world, but surely thou didst not think every race in the cosmos is formed to those ridiculous specifications. Now I've scant time to spare for whatever griping ye have here to do, so lead me to thine acher."

The Merseian obeyed. His garments were about like ordinary street clothes, belted tunic and baggy trousers, but a certain precision in their cut—as well as blue-and-gold stripes and the double fylfot embroidered on the sleeves—indicated they were a livery. Or a uniform? Chee felt the second guess confirmed when she noted two others, similarly attired, standing armed in front of a door. They saluted her and let her through.

The room beyond was baronial. Radiant heating had been installed, but a fire also roared on the hearth. Chee paid scant attention to rich draperies and carven pillars. Her gaze went to the two who sat awaiting her.

One was scarfaced, athletic, his tailtip restlessly aflicker. His robe was blue and gold, and he carried a short ceremonial spear. At sight of her, he drew a quick breath. The Cynthian decided she'd better be polite. "I hight Chee Lan, worthies, come from the interstellar expedition in response to your kind invitation."

"*Khraich.*" The aristocrat recovered his poise and touched finger to brow. "Be welcome. I am Dagla, called Quick-to-Anger, the Hand of the Vach Hallen. And my comrade: Olgor hu Freylin, his rank Warmaster in the Republic of Lafdigu, here in Ardaig as agent for his country."

That being was middle-aged, plump, with skin more dark and features more flat than was common around the Wilwidh Ocean. His garb was foreign too, a sort of toga with metal threads woven into the purple cloth. And he was soft-spoken, imperturbable, quite without the harshness of these lands. He crossed his arms—gesture of greeting?—and said in accented Eriau:

"Great is the honor. Since the last visitors from your high civilization were confined largely to this region, perhaps you have no knowledge of mine. May I therefore say that Lafdigu lies in the southern hemisphere, occupying a goodly part of its continent. In those days we were unindustrialized, but now, one hopes, the situation has altered."

"Nay, Warmaster, be sure our folk heard much about Lafdigu's venerable culture and regretted they had no time to learn therefrom." Chee got more tactful the bigger the lies she told. Inwardly, she groaned: *Oh, no! We haven't troubles enough, there has to be international politicking too!*

A servant appeared with a cut-crystal decanter and goblets. "I trust that your race, like the Terran, can partake of Merseian refreshment?" Dagla said.

"Indeed," Chee replied. "'Tis necessary that they who voyage together use the same stuffs. I thank the Hand."

"But we had not looked for, *hurgh,* a guest your size," Olgor said. "Perhaps a smaller glass? The wine is potent."

"This is excellent." Chee hopped onto a low table, squatted, and raised her goblet two-handed. "Galactic custom is that we drink to the health of friends. To yours, then, worthies." She took a long draught. The fact that alcohol does not affect the Cynthian brain was one she had often found it advantageous to keep silent about.

Dagla tossed off a yet larger amount, took a turn around the room, and growled: "Enough formalities, by your leave, Shipmaster." She discarded her cloak. "Shipmistress?" He gulped. His society had a kitchen-church-and-kids attitude toward females. "We—*kh-h-h*—we've grave matters to discuss."

"The Hand is too abrupt with our noble guest," Olgor chided.

"Nay, time is short," Chee said. "And clearly the business hath great weight, sith ye went to the length of suborning a servant in Morruchan's very stronghold."

Dagla grinned. "I planted Wedhi there eight years ago. He's a good voice-tube."

"No doubt the Hand of the Vach Hallen hath surety of all his own servitors?" Chee purred.

Dagla frowned. Olgor's lips twitched upward.

"Chances must be taken." Dagla made a chopping gesture. "All we know is what was learned from your first radio communications, which said little. Morruchan was quick to isolate you. His hope is plainly to let you hear no more of the truth than he wants. To use you! Here, in this house, we may speak frankly with each other."

As frankly as you two klongs choose, Chee thought. "I listen with care," she said.

Piece by piece, between Dagla and Olgor, the story emerged. It sounded reasonable, as far as it went.

When the Survey team arrived, the Wilwidh culture stood on the brink of a machine age. The scientific method had been invented. There was a heliocentric astronomy, a post-Newtonian, pre-Maxwellian physics, a dawning chemistry, a well-developed taxonomy, some speculations about evolution. Steam engines were at work on the first railroads. But political power was fragmented among the Vachs. The scientists, the engineers, the teachers were each under the patronage of one or another Hand.

The visitors from space had too much sense of responsibility to pass on significant practical information. It wouldn't have done a great deal of good anyway. How do you make transistors, for instance, before you can refine ultrapure semimetals? And why should you want to, when you don't yet have electronics? But the humans had given theoretical and experimental science a boost by what they related—above all, by the simple and tremendous fact of their presence.

And then they left.

A fierce, proud people had their noses rubbed in their own insignificance. Chee guessed that here lay the root of most of the social upheaval which followed. And belike a more urgent motive than curiosity or profit began to drive the scientists: the desire, the need to catch up, to bring Merseia in one leap onto the galactic scene.

The Vachs had shrewdly ridden the wave. Piecemeal they shelved their quarrels, formed a loose confederation, met the new problems well enough that no movement arose to strip them of their privileges. But rivalry persisted, and cross purposes, and often a reactionary spirit, a harking back to olden days when the young were properly respectful of the God and their elders.

And meanwhile modernization spread across the planet. A country which did not keep pace soon found itself under foreign domination. Lafdigu had succeeded best. Chee got a distinct impression that the Republic was actually a hobnail-booted dictatorship. Its own imperial ambitions clashed with those of the Hands. Nuclear war was averted on the ground, but space battles had erupted from time to time, horribly and inconclusively.

"So here we are," Dagla said. "Largest, most powerful, the Vach Dathyr speak loudest in this realm. But others press upon them, Hallen, Ynvory, Rueth, yes, even landless Urdiolch. You can see what it would mean if any one of them obtained your exclusive services."

Olgor nodded. "Among other things," he said, "Morruchan Long-Ax would like to contrive that my country is ignored. We are in the southern hemisphere. We will get the worst of the supernova blast. If unprotected, we will be removed from his equations."

"In whole truth, Shipmistress," Dagla added, "I don't believe

Morruchan wants your help. *Khraich,* yes, a minimum, to forestall utter collapse. But he has long ranted against the modern world and its ways. He'd not be sorry to see industrial civilization reduced so small that full-plumed feudalism returns."

"How shall he prevent us from doing our work?" Chee asked. "Surely he is not fool enough to kill us. Others will follow."

"He'll bet the knucklebones as they fall," Dagla said. "At the very least, he'll try to keep his position—that you work through him and get most of your information from his sources—and use it to increase his power. At the expense of every other party!"

"We could predict it even in Lafdigu, when first we heard of your coming," Olgor said. "The Strategic College dispatched me here to make what alliances I can. Several Hands are not unwilling to see my country continue as a force in the world, as the price for our help in diminishing their closer neighbors."

Chee said slowly: "Meseems ye make no few assumptions about us, on scant knowledge."

"Shipmistress," said Olgor, "civilized Merseia has had two centuries to study each word, each picture, each legend about your people. Some believe you akin to gods—or demons—yes, whole cults have flowered from the expectation of your return, and I do not venture to guess what they will do now that you are come. But there have also been cooler minds; and that first expedition was honest in what it told, was it not?

"Hence: the most reasonable postulate is that none of the starfaring races have mental powers we do not. They simply have longer histories. And as we came to know how many the stars are, we saw how thinly your civilization must be spread among them. You will not expend any enormous effort on us, in terms of your own economy. You cannot. You have too much else to do. Nor have you time to learn everything about Merseia and decide every detail of what you will effect. The supernova will flame in our skies in less than three years. You must cooperate with whatever authorities you find, and take their words for what the crucial things are to save and what others must be abandoned. Is this not truth?"

Chee weighed her answer. "To a certain degree," she said carefully, "ye have right."

"Morruchan knows this," Dagla said. "He'll use the knowledge as best he can." He leaned forward, towering above her. "For our part, we will not tolerate it. Better the world go down in ruin, to be rebuilt by us, than that the Vach Dathyr engulf what our ancestors wrought. No planetwide effort can succeed without the help of a majority. Unless we get a full voice in what decisions are made, we'll fight."

"Hand, Hand," reproved Olgor.

"Nay, I take no offense," Chee said. "Rather, I give thanks for so plain a warning. Ye will understand, we bear ill will toward none on Merseia, and have no partisanship—" *in your wretched little jockeyings.* "If ye have prepared a document stating your position, gladly will we ponder on the same."

Olgor opened a casket and took out a sheaf of papers bound in something like snakeskin. "This was hastily written," he apologized. "At another date we would like to give you a fuller account."

"'Twill serve for the nonce." Chee wondered if she should stay a while. No doubt she could learn something further. But chaos, how much propaganda she'd have to strain out of what she heard! Also, she'd now been diplomatic as long as anyone could expect. Hadn't she?

They could call the ship directly, she told them. If Morruchan tried to jam the airwaves, she'd jam him, into an unlikely posture. Olgor looked shocked. Dagla objected to communication which could be monitored. Chee sighed. "Well, then, invite us hither for a private talk," she said. "Will Morruchan attack you for that?"

"No . . . I suppose not . . . but he'll get some idea of what we know and what we're doing."

"My belief was," said Chee in her smoothest voice, "that the Hand of the Vach Hallen wished naught save an end to these intrigues and selfishnesses, an openness in which Merseians might strive together for the common welfare."

She had never cherished any such silly notion, but Dagla couldn't very well admit that his chief concern was to get his own relatives on top of everybody else. He made wistful noises about a transmitter which could not be detected by Merseian equipment. Surely the galactics had one? They did, but Chee wasn't about to pass on stuff with that kind of potentialities. She expressed regrets—nothing had been brought along—so sorry—goodnight, Hand, goodnight, Warmaster.

The guard who had let her in escorted her to the front door. She wondered why her hosts didn't. Caution, or just a different set of mores? Well, no matter. Back to the ship. She ran down the frosty street, looking for an alley from which her takeoff wouldn't be noticed. Someone might get trigger happy.

An entrance gaped between two houses. She darted into darkness. A body fell upon her. Other arms clasped tight, pinioning. She yelled. A light gleamed briefly, a sack was thrust over her head, she inhaled a sweet-sick odor and whirled from her senses.

Adzel still wasn't sure what was happening to him, or how it had begun. There he'd been, minding his own business, and suddenly he was the featured speaker at a prayer meeting. If that was what it was.

He cleared his throat. "My friends," he said.

A roar went through the hall. Faces and faces and faces stared at the rostrum which he filled with his four and a half meters of length. A thousand Merseians must be present: clients, commoners, city proletariat, drably clad for the most part. Many were female; the lower classes didn't segregate sexes as rigidly as the upper. Their odors made the air thick and musky. Being in a new part of Ardaig, the hall was built plain. But its proportions, the contrasting hues of paneling, the symbols painted in scarlet across the walls, reminded Adzel he was on a foreign planet.

He took advantage of the interruption to lift the transceiver hung around his neck up to his snout and mutter plaintively, "David, what *shall* I tell them?"

"Be benevolent and noncommittal," Falkayn's voice advised. "I don't think mine host likes this one bit."

The Wodenite glanced over the seething crowd, to the entrance. Three of Morruchan's household guards stood by the door and glowered.

He didn't worry about physical attack. Quite apart from having the ship for a backup, he was too formidable himself: a thousand-kilo centauroid, his natural armorplate shining green above and gold below, his spine more impressively ridged than any Merseian's. His ears were not soft cartilage but bony, a similar shelf protected his eyes, his rather crocodilian face opened on an alarming array of fangs. Thus he had been the logical member of the team to wander around the city today, gathering impressions. Morruchan's arguments against this had been politely overruled. "Fear no trouble, Hand," Falkayn said truthfully. "Adzel never seeketh any out. He is a Buddhist, a lover of peace who can well afford tolerance anent the behavior of others."

By the same token, though, he had not been able to refuse the importunities of the crowd which finally cornered him.

"Have you got word from Chee?" he asked.

"Nothing yet," Falkayn said. "Muddlehead's monitoring, of course. I imagine she'll contact us tomorrow. Now don't you interrupt me either, I'm in the middle of an interminable official banquet."

Adzel raised his arms for silence, but here that gesture was an encouragement for more shouts. He changed position, his hooves clattering on the platform, and his tail knocked over a floor candelabrum. "Oh, I'm sorry," he exclaimed. A red-robed Merseian named Gryf, the chief nut of this organization—Star Believers, was that what they called themselves?—picked the thing up and managed to silence the house.

"My friends," Adzel tried again. "Er . . . my friends. I am, er, deeply appreciative of the honor ye do me in asking for some few words." He tried to remember the political speeches he had heard while a student on Earth. "In the great fraternity of intelligent races throughout the universe, surely Merseia hath a majestic part to fulfill."

"Show us—show us the way!" howled from the floor. "The way, the truth, the long road futureward!"

"Ah . . . yes. With pleasure." Adzel turned to Gryf. "But perchance first your, er, glorious leader should explain to me the purposes of this—this—" What was the word for "club?" Or did he want "church"?

Mainly he wanted information.

"Why, the noble galactic jests," Gryf said in ecstasy. "You know we are those who have waited, living by the precepts the galactics taught, in loyal expectation of their return which they promised us. We are your chosen instrument for the deliverance of Merseia from its ills. Use us!"

Adzel was a planetologist by profession, but his large bump of curiosity had led him to study in other fields. His mind shuffled through books he had read, societies he had visited . . . yes, he identified the pattern. These were cultists, who'd attached a quasi-religious significance to what had actually been quite a casual stopover. Oh, the jewel in the lotus! What kind of mess had ensued?

He had to find out.

"That's, ah, very fine," he said. "Very fine indeed. Ah . . . how many do ye number?"

"More than two million, Protector, in twenty different nations. Some high ones are among us, yes, the Heir of the Vach Isthyr. But most belong to the virtuous poor. Had they all known the Protector was to walk forth this day—well, they'll come as fast as may be, to hear your bidding."

An influx like that could make the pot boil over, Adzel foresaw. Ardaig had been restless enough as he quested through its streets. And what little had been learned about basic Merseian instincts, by the Survey psychologists, suggested they were a combative species. Mass hysteria could take ugly forms.

"No!" the Wodenite cried. The volume nearly blew Gryf off the podium. Adzel moderated his tone. "Let them stay home. Calm, patience, carrying out one's daily round of duties, those are the galactic virtues."

Try telling that to a merchant adventurer. Adzel checked himself. "I fear we have no miracles to offer."

He was about to say that the word he carried was of blood, sweat, and tears. But no. When you dealt with a people whose reactions you couldn't predict, such news must be released with care. Falkayn's first radio communications had been guarded, on precisely that account.

"This is clear," Gryf said. He was not stupid, or even crazy, except in his beliefs. "We must ourselves release ourselves from our oppressors. Tell us how to begin."

Adzel saw Morruchan's troopers grip their rifles tight. *We're expected to start some kind of social revolution?* he thought wildly. *But we can't! It's not our business. Our business is to save your lives, and for that we must not weaken but strengthen whatever authority can work with us, and any revolution will be slow to mature, a consequence of technology—dare I tell them this tonight?*

Pedantry might soothe them, if only by boring them to sleep. "Among those sophonts who need a government," Adzel said, "the basic requirement for a government which is to function well is that it be legitimate, and the basic problem of any political innovator is how to continue, or else establish anew, a sound basis for that legitimacy. Thus newcomers like mineself cannot—"

He was interrupted (later he was tempted to say "rescued") by a noise outside. It grew louder, a harsh chant, the clatter of feet on pavement. Females in the audience wailed. Males snarled and moved toward the door. Gryf sprang from the platform, down to what Adzel identified as a telecom, and activated the scanner. It showed the street, and an armed mob. High over them, against snow-laden roofs and night sky, flapped a yellow banner.

"Demonists!" Gryf groaned. "I was afraid of this."

Adzel joined him. "Who be they?"

"A lunatic sect. They imagine you galactics mean, have meant from the first, to corrupt us to our destruction. . . . I was prepared, though. See." From alleys and doorways moved close-ranked knots of husky males. They carried weapons.

A trooper snapped words into the microphone of a walkie-talkie. Sending for help, no doubt, to quell the oncoming riot. Adzel returned to the rostrum and filled the hall with his pleas that everyone remain inside.

He might have succeeded, by reverberation if not reason. But his own transceiver awoke with Falkayn's voice: "Get here at once! Chee's been nabbed!"

"What? Who did it? Why?" The racket around became of scant importance.

"I don't know. Muddlehead just alerted me. She'd left this place she was at. Muddlehead received a yell, sounds of scuffling, then no more from her. I'm sending him aloft, to try and track her by the carrier wave. He says the source is moving. You move too, back to Afon."

Adzel did. He took part of the wall with him.

Korych rose through winter mists that turned gold as they smoked past city towers and above the river. Kettledrums rolled their ritual from Eidh Hill. Shutters came down off windows and doors, market circles began to fill, noise lifted out of a hundred small workshops. Distantly, but deeper and more portentous, sounded the buzz of traffic and power from the new quarters, hoot of ships on the bay, whine of jets overhead, thunder of rockets as a craft left the spaceport for the moon Seith.

Morruchan Long-Ax switched off the lights in his confidence chamber. Dawnglow streamed pale through glass, picking out the haggardness of faces. "I am weary," he said, "and we are on a barren trail."

"Hand," said Falkayn, "it had better not be. Here we stay until we have reached some decision."

Morruchan and Dagla glared. Olgor grew expressionless. They were none of them accustomed to being addressed thus. Falkayn gave them stare for stare, and Adzel lifted his head from where he lay coiled on the floor. The Merseians slumped back onto their tails.

"Your whole world may be at stake, worthies," Falkayn said. "My people will not wish to spend time and treasure, aye, some lives, if they look for such ungrateful treatment."

He picked up the harness and kit which lay on Morruchan's desk and hefted them. Guided by Muddlehead, searchers from this household had found the apparatus in a ditch outside town and brought it here several hours ago. Clearly Chee's kidnappers had suspected a signal was being emitted. The things felt pitifully light in his hand.

"What more can be said?" Olgor argued. "We have each voiced a suspicion that one of the others engineered the deed to gain a lever for himself. Or yet a different Vach, or another nation, may have done it; or the Demonists; or even the Star Believers, for some twisted reason." He turned to Dagla. "Are you certain you have no inkling who that servant of yours may have been working for?"

"I told you before, no," said the Hallen chief. "It's not our way in this country to pry into lives. I know only that Dwyr entered my service a few years ago, and gave satisfaction, and now has also vanished. So I presume he was a spy for someone else, and told his masters of a chance to seize a galactic. A telecom call would be easy to make, and they needed only to cover the few possible routes she could take on leaving me."

"In sum," Morruchan declared, "he acted just like your spy who betrayed my doings to you."

"Enough, worthies," Falkayn sighed. "Too stinking often this night have we tracked the same ground. Perchance investigation will give some clues to this Dwyr, whence he came and so forth. But such taketh time. We must needs look into every possibility at once. Including your very selves. Best ye perform a mutual checking."

"And who shall do the like for you?" Morruchan asked.

"What meaneth the Hand?"

"This might be a trick of your own."

Falkayn clutched his hair. "For what conceivable reason?" He wanted to say more, but relations were strained already.

"How should I know?" Morruchan retorted. "You are unknowns. You *say* you have no imperial designs here, but your agents have met with rivals of mine, with a cult whose main hope is to upset the order of things—and with how many else? The Gethfennu?"

"Would the Hand be so gracious as to explain to me who those are?" said Adzel in an oil-on-the-waves voice.

"We described them already," Dagla answered.

"Then 'twas whilst I was out, Hand, directing our ship in its search and subsequent return to base. Indulge a humble fool's request, I beg you."

The idea of someone equipped like Adzel calling himself a humble fool took the Merseians so much aback that they forgot to stay angry. Falkayn added: "I'd not mind hearing about them again. Never suspected I their existence erenow."

"They are the criminal syndicate, spread across the world and on into space," Morruchan said. "Thieves, assassins, harlots, tricksters, corrupters of all good."

He went on, while Falkayn analyzed his words. No doubt the Gethfennu were a bad influence. But Morruchan was too prejudiced, and had too little historical sense, to see why they flourished. The industrial revolution had shaken foundation stones loose from society. Workers flocking to the cities found themselves cut off from the old feudal restrictions . . . and securities. Cultural and material impoverishment bred lawlessness. Yet the baronial tradition survived, in a distorted form; gangs were soon gathered into a network which offered members protection and purpose as well as loot.

The underground kingdom of the Gethfennu could not be

destroyed by Vachs and nations divided against each other. It fought back too effectively, with money and influence more often than with violence. And, to be sure, it provided some safety valve. A commoner who went to one of its gambling dens or joyhouses might get fleeced, but he would not plot insurrection.

So a tacit compromise was reached, the kind that many planets have known, Earth not least among them. Racketeering and vice were held to a tolerable level, confined to certain areas and certain classes, by the gang lords. Murder, robbery, and shakedown did not touch the aristocratic palace or the high financial office. Bribery did, in some countries, and thereby the Gethfennu was strengthened.

Of late, its tentacles had stretched beyond these skies. It bought into established interplanetary enterprises. And then there was Ronruad, the next planet out. Except for scientific research, it had scant intrinsic value, but bases upon it were of so great strategic importance that they had occasioned wars. Hence the last general peace treaty had neutralized it, placed it outside any jurisdiction. Soon afterward, the Gethfennu took advantage of this by building a colony there, where anything went. A spaceship line, under the syndicate's open-secret control, offered passenger service. Luridor became the foremost town for respectable Merseians to go in search of unrestrained, if expensive fun. It also became a hatchery of trouble, and Falkayn could understand why Morruchan didn't want it protected against the supernova.

Neither, he found, did Dagla. Probably few if any Hands did. Olgor was less emphatic, but agreed that, at best, Ronruad should get a very low priority.

"The Gethfennu may, then, have seized Chee Lan for ransom?" Adzel said.

"Perhaps," Dagla said. "Though the ransom may be that you galactics help them. If they've infiltrated Hand Morruchan's service too, they could know what the situation is."

"In that case," Falkayn objected, "they are scarcely so naive as to think—"

"I will investigate," Morruchan promised. "I may make direct inquiry. But channels of communication with the Gethfennu masters are devious, therefore slow."

"In any event," Falkayn said bleakly, "Adzel and I do not propose to leave our partner in the grip of criminals—for years, after which, they may cut her throat."

"You do not know they have her," Olgor reminded him.

"True. Yet may we prowl somewhat through space, out toward their colony. For little can we do on Merseia, where our knowledge is scant. Here must ye search, worthies, and contrive that all others search with you."

The command seemed to break Morruchan's thin-stretched patience. "Do you imagine we've nothing better to do than hunt for one creature? We, who steer millions?"

Falkayn lost his temper likewise. "If ye wish to keep on doing thus, best ye make the finding of Chee Lan your foremost concern!"

"Gently, gently," Olgor said. "We are so tired that we are turning on allies. And that is not well." He laid a hand on Falkayn's shoulder. "Galactic," he said, "surely you can understand that organizing a systemwide hunt, in a world as diverse as ours, is a greater task than the hunt itself. Why, no few leaders of nations, tribes, clans, factions will not believe the truth if they are told. Proving it to them will require diplomatic skill. Then there are others whose main interest will be to see if they cannot somehow maneuver this affair to give them an advantage over us. And yet others hope you do go away and never return; I do not speak merely of the Demonists."

"If Chee be not returned safely," Falkayn said, "those last may well get their wish."

Olgor smiled. The expression went no deeper than his lips. "Galactic," he murmured, "let us not play word games. Your scientists stand to win knowledge and prestige here, your merchants a profit. They will not allow an unfortunate incident, caused by a few Merseians and affecting only one of their fold . . . they will not let that come between them and their objectives. Will they?"

Falkayn looked into the ebony eyes. His own were the first to drop. Nausea caught at his gullet. The Warmaster of Lafdigu had identified his bluff and called it.

Oh, no doubt these who confronted him would mount some kind of search. If nothing else, they'd be anxious to learn what outfit had infiltrated agents onto their staffs, and to what extent. No doubt, also, various other Merseians would cooperate. But the investigation would be ill-coordinated and lackadaisical. It would hardly succeed against beings as wily as those who captured Chee Lan.

These three here—nigh the whole of Merseia—just didn't give a damn about her.

She awoke in a cell.

It was less than three meters long, half that in width and height: windowless, doorless, comfortless. A coat of paint did not hide the basic construction, which was of large blocks. Their unresponsiveness to her fist-pounding suggested a high density. Brackets were bolted into the walls, to hold equipment of different sorts in place. Despite non-Technic design, Chee recognized a glowlamp, a thermostated air renewer, a waste unit, an acceleration couch . . . space gear, by Cosmos!

No sound, no vibration other than the faint whirr of the air unit's fan, reached her. The walls were altogether blank. After a while, they seemed to move closer. She chattered obscenities at them.

But she came near weeping with relief when one block slid aside. A Merseian face looked in. Behind was polished metal. Rumble, clangor, shouted commands resounded through what must be a spaceship's hull, from what must be a spaceport outside.

"Are you well?" asked the Merseian. He looked still tougher than average, but he was trying for courtesy, and he wore a neat tunic with insignia of rank.

Chee debated whether to make a jump, claw his eyes out, and bolt for freedom. No, not a chance. But neither was she going to embrace him. "Quite well, I thank thee," she snarled, "if thou'lt set aside trifles such as that thy heart-rotten varlets have beaten and gassed me, and I am athirst and anhungered. For this outrage, methinks I'll summon my mates to blow thy pesthole of a planet from the universe it defileth."

The Merseian laughed. "You can't be too sick, with that kind of spirit. Here are food and water." He passed her some containers. "We blast off soon for a voyage of a few days. If I can supply you with anything safe, I will."

"Where are we bound? Who art thou? What meaneth—"

"*Hurh,* little one, I'm not going to leave this smugglehole open very long, for any spillmouth to notice. Tell me this instant what you want, so I can try to have it sent from the city."

Later Chee swore at herself, more picturesquely than she had ever cursed even Adzel. Had she specified the right things, they might have been a clue for her partners. But she was too foggy in the head, too dazed by events. Automatically, she asked for books and films which might help her understand the Merseian situation better. And a grammar text, she added in haste. She was tired of sounding like a local Shakespeare. The Merseian nodded and pushed the block back in place. She heard a faint click. Doubtless a tongue-and-groove lock, operated by a magnetic key.

The rations were revivifying. Before long, Chee felt in shape to make deductions. She was evidently in a secret compartment, built into the wall of a radiation shelter.

Merseian interplanetary vessels ran on a thermonuclear-powered ion drive. Those which made landings—ferries tending the big ships, or special jobs such as this presumably was—set down in deep silos and departed from them, so that electromagnetic fields could contain the blast and neutralize it before it poisoned the neighborhood. And each craft carried a blockhouse for crew and passengers to huddle in, should they get caught by a solar storm. Altogether, the engineering was superb. Too bad it would go by the board as soon as gravity drive and force screens became available.

A few days, at one Merseian gee: hm, that meant an adjacent planet. Not recalling the present positions, Chee wasn't sure which. A lot of space traffic moved in the Korychan System, as instruments had shown while *Muddlin' Through* approached. From a distance, in magniscreens, she had observed some of the fleet, capacious cargo vessels and sleek naval units.

Her captor returned with the materials she had requested and a warning to strap in for blastoff. He introduced himself genially as Iriad the Wayfarer, in charge of this dispatch boat.

"Who are thou working for?" Chee demanded.

He hesitated, then shrugged. "The Gethfennu." The block glided back to imprison her.

Lift was nothing like the easy upward floating of a galactic ship. Acceleration rammed Chee down into her couch and sat on her chest. Thunder shuddered through the very blockhouse. Eternal minutes passed before the pressure slacked off and the boat fell into steady running.

After that, for a timeless time, Chee had nothing to do but study. The officers brought her rations. They were a mixed lot, from every part of Merseia; some did not speak Eriau, and none had much to say to her. She considered tinkering her life support apparatus into a weapon, but without tools the prospect was hopeless. So for amusement she elaborated the things she would like to do to Iriad, come the day. Her partners would have flinched.

Once her stomach, the only clock she had, told her she was far overdue for a meal. When finally her cell was opened, she leaped forward in a whirlwind of abuse. Iriad stepped back and raised a pistol. Chee stopped and said: "Well, what happened? Hadn't my swill gotten moldy enough?"

Iriad looked shaken. "We were boarded," he said low.

"How's that?" Acceleration had never varied.

"By . . . your people. They laid alongside, matching our vector as easily as one runner might pace another. I did not know what armament they had, so—he who came aboard was a dragon."

Chee beat her fists on the shelter deck. Oh, no, no, no! Adzel had passed within meters of her, and never suspected . . . the big, ugly, vacuum-skulled bumblemaker!

Iriad straightened. "But Haguan warned me it might happen," he said with a return of self-confidence. "We know somewhat about smuggling. And you are not gods, you galactics."

"Where did they go?"

"Away. To inspect other vessels. Let them."

"Do you seriously hope to keep me hidden for long?"

"Ronruad is full of Haguan's boltholes." Iriad gave her her lunch, collected the empty containers, and departed.

He came back several meals later, to supervise her transferral from the cell to a packing crate. Under guns, Chee obeyed his instructions. She was strapped into padding, alongside an air unit, and left in darkness. There followed hours of maneuver, landing, waiting, being unloaded and trucked to some destination.

Finally the box was opened. Chee emerged slowly. Weight was less than half a standard gee, but her muscles were cramped. A pair of workers bore the crate away. Guards stayed behind, with a

Merseian who claimed to be a medic. The checkup he gave her was expert and sophisticated enough to bear him out. He said she should rest a while, and they left her alone.

Her suite was interior but luxurious. The food brought her was excellent. She curled in bed and told herself to sleep.

Eventually she was taken down a long, panelled corridor and up a spiral ramp to meet him who had ordered her caught.

He squatted behind a desk of dark, polished wood that looked a hectare in area. Thick white fur carpeted the room and muffled footsteps. Pictures glowed, music sighed, incense sweetened the air. Windows gave a view outside; this part of the warren projected above-ground. Chee saw ruddy sand, strange wild shrubbery, a dust storm walking across a gaunt range of hills and crowned with ice crystals. Korych stood near the horizon, shrunken, but fierce through the tenuous atmosphere. A few stars also shone in that purple sky. Chee recognized Valenderay, and shivered a little. So bright and steady it looked; and yet, at this moment, death was riding from it on the wings of light.

"Greeting, galactic." The Eriau was accented differently from Olgor's. "I am Haguan Eluatz. Your name, I gather, is Chee Lan."

She arched her back, bottled her tail, and spat. But she felt very helpless. The Merseian was huge, with a belly that bulged forward his embroidered robe. He was not of the Wilwidh stock, his skin was shiny black and heavily scaled, his eyes almond-shaped, his nose a scimitar.

One ring-glittering hand made a gesture. Chee's guards slapped tails to ankles and left. The door closed behind them. But a pistol lay on Haguan's desk, next to an intercom.

He smiled. "Be not afraid. No harm is intended you. We regret the indignities you have suffered and will try to make amends. Sheer necessity forced us to act."

"The necessity for suicide?" Chee snorted.

"For survival. Now why don't you make yourself comfortable on yonder couch? We have talk to forge, we two. I can send for whatever refreshment you desire. Some arthberry wine, perhaps?"

Chee shook her head, but did jump onto the seat. "Suppose you explain your abominable behavior," she said.

"Gladly." Haguan shifted the weight on his tail. "You may not know what the Gethfennu is. It came into being after the first galactics had departed. But by now—" He continued for a while. When he spoke of a systemwide syndicate, controlling millions of lives and uncounted wealth, strong enough to build its own city on this planet and clever enough to play its enemies off against each other so that none dared attack that colony: he was scarcely lying. Everything that Chee had seen confirmed it.

"Are we in this town of yours now?" she asked.

"No. Elsewhere on Ronruad. Best I not be specific. I have too much respect for your cleverness."

"And I have none for yours."

"*Khraich?* You must. I think we operated quite smoothly, and on such short notice. Of course, an organization like ours must always be prepared for anything. And we have been on special alert ever since your arrival. What little we have learned—" Haguan's gaze went to the white point of Valenderay and lingered. "That star, it is going to explode. True?"

"Yes. Your civilization will be scrubbed out unless—"

"I know, I know. We have scientists in our pay." Haguan leaned forward. "The assorted governments on Merseia see this as a millennial chance to rid themselves of the troublesome Gethfennu. We need only be denied help in saving our colony, our shipping, our properties on the home planet and elsewhere. Then we are finished. I expect you galactics would agree to this. Since not everything can be shielded in time, why not include us in that which is to be abandoned? You stand for some kind of law and order too, I suppose."

Chee nodded. In their mask of dark fur, her eyes smoldered emerald. Haguan had guessed shrewdly. The League didn't much care who it dealt with, but the solid citizens whose taxes were to finance the majority of the rescue operations did.

"So to win our friendship, you take me by force," she sneered half-heartedly.

"What had we to lose? We might have conferred with you, pleaded our cause, but would that have wrought good for us?"

"Suppose my partners recommend that no help be given your whole coprophagous Merseian race."

"Why, then the collapse comes," Haguan said with chilling calm, "and the Gethfennu has a better chance than most organizations of improving its relative position. But I doubt that any such recommendation will be made, or that your overlords would heed it if it were.

"So we need a coin to buy technical assistance. You."

Chee's whiskers twitched in a smile of sorts. "I'm scarcely that big a hostage."

"Probably not," Haguan agreed. "But you are a source of information."

The Cynthian's fur stood on end with alarm. "Do you have some skewbrained notion that I can tell you how to do everything for yourself? I'm not even an engineer!"

"Understood. But surely you know your way about in your own civilization. You know what the engineers can and cannot do. More important, you know the planets, the different races and cultures upon them, the mores, the laws, the needs. You can tell us what to expect. You can help us get interstellar ships—hijacking under your advice should succeed, being unlooked for—and show us how to pilot them, and put us in touch with someone who, for pay, will come to our aid."

"If you suppose for a moment that the Polesotechnic League would tolerate—"

Teeth flashed white in Haguan's face. "Perhaps it won't, perhaps it will. With so many stars, the diversity of peoples and interests is surely inconceivable. The Gethfennu is skilled in stirring up competition among others. What information you supply will tell us how, in this particular case. I don't really visualize your League, whatever it is, fighting a war—at a time when every resource must be devoted to saving Merseia—to prevent someone else rescuing us."

He spread his hands. "Or possibly we'll find a different approach," he finished. "It depends on what you tell and suggest."

"How do you know you can trust me?"

Haguan said like iron: "We judge the soil by what crops it bears. If we fail, if we see the Gethfennu doomed, we can still enforce our policy regarding traitors. Would you care to visit my punishment facilities? They are quite extensive. Even though you are of a new species, I think we could keep you alive and aware for many days."

Silence dwelt a while in that room. Korych slipped under the horizon. Instantly the sky was black, strewn with the legions of the stars, beautiful and uncaring.

Haguan switched on a light, to drive away that too enormous vision. "If you save us, however," he said, "you will go free with a very good reward."

"But—" Chee looked sickly into sterile years ahead of her. And the betrayal of friends, and scorn if ever she returned, a lifetime's exile. "You'll keep me till then?"

"Of course."

No success. No ghost of a clue. She was gone into an emptiness less fathomable than the spaces which gaped around their ship.

They had striven, Falkayn and Adzel. They had walked into Luridor itself, the sin-bright city on Ronruad, while the ship hovered overhead and showed with a single, rock-fusing flash of energy guns what power menaced the world. They had ransacked, threatened, bribed, beseeched. Sometimes terror met them, sometimes the inborn arrogance of Merseia's lords. But nowhere and never had anyone so much as hinted he knew who held Chee Lan or where.

Falkayn ran a hand through uncombed yellow locks. His eyes stood bloodshot in a sunken countenance. "I still think we should've taken that casino boss aboard and worked him over."

"No," said Adzel. "Apart from the morality of the matter, I feel sure that everyone who has any information is hidden away. That precaution is elementary. We're not even certain the outlaw regime is responsible."

"Yeh. Could be Morruchan, Dagla, Olgor, or colleagues of theirs acting unbeknownst to them, or any of a hundred other governments, or some gang of fanatics, or—Oh, *Judas!*"

Falkayn looked at the after viewscreen. Ronruad's tawny-red crescent was dwindling swiftly among the constellations, as the ship drove at full acceleration back toward Merseia. It was a dwarf planet, an ocherous pebble that would not make a decent splash if it fell into one of the gas giants. But the least of planets is still a world: mountains, plains, valleys, arroyos, caves, waters, square kilometers by the millions, too vast and varied for any mind to grasp. And Merseia was bigger yet; and there were others, and moons, asteroids, space itself.

Chee's captors need but move her around occasionally, and the odds against a fleetful of League detectives finding her would climb for infinity.

"The Merseians themselves are bound to have some notion where to look, what to do, who to put pressure on," he mumbled for the hundredth time. "We don't know the ins and outs. Nobody from our cultures ever will—five billion years of planetary existence to catch up with! We've got to get the Merseians busy. I mean really busy."

"They have their own work to do," Adzel said.

Falkayn expressed himself at pungent length on the value of their work. "How about those enthusiasts?" he wondered when he had calmed down a trifle. "The outfit you were talking to."

"Yes, the Star Believers should be loyal allies," Adzel said. "But most of them are poor and, ah, unrealistic. I hardly expect them to be of help. Indeed, I fear they will complicate our problem by starting pitched battles with the Demonists."

"You mean the antigalactics?" Falkayn rubbed his chin. The bristles made a scratchy noise, in the ceaseless gentle thrum that filled the cabin. He inhaled the sour smell of his own weariness. "Maybe they did this."

"I doubt that. They must be investigated, naturally—a major undertaking in itself—but they do not appear sufficiently well organized."

"Damnation, if we don't get her back I'm going to push for letting this whole race stew!"

"You will not succeed. And in any event, it would be unjust to let millions die for the crime of a few."

"The millions jolly well ought to be tracking down the few. It's possible. There have to be some leads somewhere. If every single one is followed—"

The detector panel flickered. Muddlehead announced: "Ship observed. A chemical carrier, I believe, from the outer system. Range—"

"Oh, dry up," Falkayn said, "and blow away."

"I am not equipped to—"

Falkayn stabbed the voice cutoff button.

He sat for a while, then, staring into the stars. His pipe went out unnoticed between his fingers. Adzel sighed and laid his head down on the deck.

"Poor little Chee," Falkayn whispered at last. "She came a long way to die."

"Most likely she lives," Adzel said.

"I hope so. But she used to go flying through trees, in an endless forest. Being caged will kill her."

"Or unbalance her mind. She is so easily infuriated. If anger can find no object, it turns to feed on itself."

"Well . . . you were always squabbling with her."

"It meant nothing. Afterward she would cook me a special dinner. Once I admired a painting of hers, and she thrust it into my hands and said, 'Take the silly thing, then,' like a cub that is too shy to say it loves you."

"Uh-huh."

The cutoff button popped up. "Course adjustment required," Muddlehead stated, "in order to avoid dangerously close passage by ore carrier."

"Well, do it," Falkayn rasped, "and I wish those bastards joy of their ores. Destruction, but they've got a lot of space traffic!"

"Well, we are in the ecliptic plane, and as yet near Ronruad," Adzel said. "The coincidence is not great."

Falkayn clenched his hands. The pipestem snapped. "Suppose we strafe the ground," he said in a cold strange voice. "Not kill anyone. Burn up a few expensive installations, though, and promise more of the same if they don't get off their duffs and start a real search for her."

"No. We have considerable discretion, but not that much."

"We could argue with the board of inquiry later."

"Such a deed would produce confusion and antagonism, and weaken the basis of the rescue effort. It might actually make rescue impossible. You have observed how basic pride is to the dominant Merseian cultures. An attempt to browbeat them, with no face-saving formula possible, might compel them to refuse galactic assistance. We would be personally, criminally responsible. I cannot permit it, David."

"So we can't do anything, not anything, to—"

Falkayn's words chopped off. He smashed a fist down on the arm of his pilot chair and surged to his feet. Adzel rose also, sinews drawn taut. He knew his partner.

Merseia hung immense, shining with oceans, blazoned with

clouds and continents, rimmed with dawn and sunset and the deep sapphire of her sky. Her four small moons made a diadem. Korych flamed in plumage of zodiacal light.

Space cruiser *Yonuar,* United Fleet of the Great Vachs, swung close in polar orbit. Officially she was on patrol to stand by for possible aid to distressed civilian vessels. In fact she was there to keep an eye on the warcraft of Lafdigu, Wolder, the Nersan Alliance, any whom her masters mistrusted. And, yes, on the new-come galactics, if they returned hither. The God alone knew what they intended. One must tread warily and keep weapons close to hand.

On his command bridge, Captain Tryntaf Fangryf-Tamer gazed into the simulacrum tank and tried to imagine what laired among those myriad suns. He had grown up knowing that others flitted freely between them while his people were bound to this one system, and hating that knowledge. Now they were here once again . . . why? Too many rumors flew about. But most of them centered on the ominous spark called Valenderay.

Help; collaboration; were the Vach Isthyr to become mere clients of some outworld grotesque?

A signal fluted. The intercom said: "Radar Central to captain. Object detected on an intercept path." The figures which followed were unbelievable. No meteoroid, surely, despite an absence of jet radiation. Therefore, the galactics! His black uniform tunic grew taut around Tryntaf's shoulders as he hunched forward and issued orders. Battle stations: not that he was looking for trouble, but he was prudent. And if trouble came, he'd much like to see how well the alien could withstand laser blasts and nuclear rockets.

She grew in his screens, a stubby truncated raindrop, ridiculously tiny against the sea-beast hulk of *Yonuar.* She matched orbit so fast that Tryntaf heard the air suck in through his lips. Doom and death, why wasn't that hull broken apart and the crew smeared into a red layer? Some kind of counterfield. . . . The vessel hung a few kilometers off and Tryntaf sought to calm himself. They would no doubt call him, and he must remain steady of nerve, cold of brain.

For his sealed orders mentioned that the galactics had left Merseia in anger, because the whole planet would not devote itself to a certain task. The Hands had striven for moderation; of course they would do what they reasonably could to oblige their guests from the stars, but they had other concerns too. The galactics seemed unable to agree that the business of entire worlds was more important than their private wishes. Of necessity, such an attitude was met with haughtiness, lest the name of the bachs, of all the nations, be lowered.

Thus, when his outercom screen gave him an image, Tryntaf kept one finger on the combat button. He had some difficulty hiding his revulsion. Those thin features, shock of hair, tailless body, fuzzed brown skin, were like a dirty caricature of Merseiankind. He would rather have spoken to the companion, whom he could see in the background. That creature was honestly weird.

Nonetheless, Tryntaf got through the usual courtesies and asked the galactic's business in a level tone.

Falkayn had pretty well mastered modern language by now. "Captain," he said, "I regret this and apologize, but you'll have to return to base."

Tryntaf's heart slammed. Only his harness prevented him from jerking backward, to drift across the bridge in the dreamlike flight of zero gravity. He swallowed and managed to keep his speech calm. "What is the reason?"

"We have communicated it to different leaders," said Falkayn, "but since they don't accept the idea, I'll also explain to you personally.

"Someone, we don't know who, has kidnapped a crew member of ours. I'm sure that you, Captain, will understand that honor requires we get her back."

"I do," Tryntaf said, "and honor demands that we assist you. But what has this to do with my ship?"

"Let me go on, please. I want to prove that no offense is intended. We have little time to make ready for the coming disaster, and few personnel to employ. The contribution of each is vital. In particular, the specialized knowledge of our vanished teammate cannot be dispensed with. So her return is of the utmost importance to all Merseians."

Tryntaf grunted. He knew the argument was specious, meant to provide nothing but an acceptable way for his people to capitulate to the strangers' will.

"The search for her looks hopeless when she can be moved about in space," Falkayn said. "Accordingly, while she is missing, interplanetary traffic must be halted."

Tryntaf rapped an oath. "Impossible."

"Contrariwise," Falkayn said. "We hope for your cooperation, but if your duty forbids this, we too can enforce the decree."

Tryntaf was astonished to hear himself, through a tide of fury, say just: "I have no such orders."

"That is regrettable," Falkayn said. "I know your superiors will issue them, but that takes time and the emergency will not wait. Be so good as to return to base."

Tryntaf's finger poised over the button. "And if I don't?"

"Captain, we shouldn't risk damage to your fine ship—"

Tryntaf gave the signal.

His gunners had the range. Beams and rockets vomited forth.

Not one missile hit. The enemy flitted aside, letting them pass, as if they were thrown pebbles. A full-power ray struck: but not her hull. Energy sparked and showered blindingly off some invisible barrier.

The little vessel curved about like an aircraft. One beam licked briefly from her snout. Alarms resounded. Damage Control cried, near hysteria, that armorplate had been sliced off as a knife might cut soft wood. No great harm done; but if the shot had been directed at the reaction-mass tanks—

"How very distressing, Captain," Falkayn said. "But accidents will happen when weapons systems are overly automated, don't you agree? For the sake of your crew, for the sake of your country whose ship is your responsibility, I do urge you to reconsider."

"Hold fire," Tryntaf gasped.

"You will return planetside, then?" Falkayn asked.

"I curse you, yes," Tryntaf said with a parched mouth.

"Good. You are a wise male, Captain. I salute you. Ah . . . you may wish to notify your fellow commanders elsewhere, so they can take steps to assure there will be no further accidents. Meanwhile, though, please commence re-entry."

Jets stabbed into space. *Yonuar,* pride of the bachs, began her inward spiral.

And aboard *Muddlin' Through,* Falkayn wiped his brow and grinned shakily at Adzel. "For a minute," he said, "I was afraid that moron was going to slug it out."

"We could have disabled his command with no casualties," Adzel said, "and I believe they have lifecraft."

"Yes, but think of the waste; and the grudge." Falkayn shook himself. "Come on, let's get started. We've a lot of others to round up."

"Can we—a lone civilian craft—blockade an entire globe?" Adzel wondered. "I do not recall that it has ever been done."

"No, I don't imagine it has. But that's because the opposition has also had things like grav drive. These Merseian rowboats are something else again. And we need only watch this one planet. Everything funnels through it." Falkayn stuffed tobacco into a pipe. "Uh, Adzel, suppose you compose our broadcast to the public. You're more tactful than I am."

"What shall I say?" the Wodenite asked.

"Oh, the same guff as I just forked out, but dressed up and tied with a pink ribbon."

"Do you really expect this to work, David?"

"I've pretty high hopes. Look, all we'll call for is that Chee be left some safe place and we be notified where. We'll disavow every intention of punishing anybody, and we can make that plausible by pointing out that the galactics have to prove they're as good as their word if their mission is to have any chance of succeeding. If the kidnappers don't oblige—well, first, they'll have the entire population out on a full-time hunt after them. And second, they themselves will be suffering badly from the blockade meanwhile. Whoever they are. Because you wouldn't have as much interplanetary shipping as you do, if it weren't basic to the economy."

Adzel shifted in unease. "We must not cause anyone to starve."

"We won't. Food isn't sent across space, except gourmet items; too costly. How often do I have to explain to you, old thickhead? What we will cause is that everybody loses money. Megacredits per diem. And Very Important Merseians will be stranded in places like Luridor, and they'll burn up the maser beams ordering their subordinates to remedy that state of affairs. And factories will shut down, spaceports lie idle, investments crumble, political and military balances get upset. . . . You can fill in the details."

Falkayn lit his pipe and puffed a blue cloud. "I don't expect matters will go that far, actually," he went on. "The Merseians are as able as us to foresee the consequences. Not a hypothetical disaster three years hence, but money and power eroding away right now. So they'll put it first on their agenda to find those kidnappers and take out resentment on them. The kidnappers will know this and will also, I trust, be hit in their personal breadbasket. I bet in a few days they'll offer to swap Chee for an amnesty."

"Which I trust we will honor," Adzel said.

"I told you we'll have to. Wish we didn't."

"Please don't be so cynical, David. I hate to see you lose merit."

Falkayn chuckled. "But I make profits. Come on, Muddlehead, get busy and find us another ship."

The teleconference room in Castle Afon could handle a sealed circuit that embraced the world. On this day it did.

Falkayn sat in a chair he had brought, looking across a table scarred by the daggers of ancestral warriors, to the mosaic of screens which filled the opposite wall. A hundred or more Merseian visages lowered back at him. On that scale, they had no individuality. Save one: a black countenance ringed by empty frames. No lord would let his image stand next to that of Haguan Eluatz.

Beside the human, Morruchan, Hand of the Vach Dathyr, rose and said with frigid ceremoniousness: "In the name of the God and the blood, we are met. May we be well met. May wisdom and honor stand shield to shield—" Falkayn listened with half an ear. He was busy rehearsing his speech. At best, he was in for a cobalt bomb's worth of trouble.

No danger, of course. *Muddlin' Through* hung plain in sight above Ardaig. Television carried that picture around Merseia. And it linked him to Adzel and Chee, who waited at the guns. He was protected.

But what he had to say could provoke a wrath so great that his mission was wrecked. He must say it with infinite care, and then he must hope.

"—obligation to a guest demands we hear him out," Morruchan finished brusquely.

Falkayn stood up. He knew that in those eyes he was a monster, whose motivations were not understandable and who had proven himself dangerous. So he had dressed in his plainest gray zipsuit, and was unarmed, and spoke in soft words.

"Worthies," he said, "forgive me that I do not use your titles, for you are of many ranks and nations. But you are those who decide for your whole race. I hope you will feel free to talk as frankly as I shall. This is a secret and informal conference, intended to explore what is best for Merseia.

"Let me first express my heartfelt gratitude for your selfless and successful labors to get my teammate returned unharmed. And let me also thank you for indulging my wish that the, uh, chieftain Haguan Eluatz participate in this honorable assembly, albeit he has no right under law to do so. The reason shall soon be explained. Let me, finally, once again express my regret at the necessity of stopping your space commerce, for however brief a period, and my thanks for your cooperation in this emergency measure. I hope that you will consider any losses made good, when my people arrive to help you rescue your civilization.

"Now, then, it is time we put away whatever is past and look to the future. Our duty is to organize that great task. And the problem is, how shall it be organized? The galactic technologists do not wish to usurp any Merseian authority. In fact, they could not. They will be too few, too foreign, and too busy. If they are to do their work in the short time available, they must accept the guidance of the powers that be. They must make heavy use of existing facilities. That, of course, must be authorized by those who control the facilities. I need not elaborate. Experienced leaders like yourselves, worthies, can easily grasp what is entailed."

He cleared his throat. "A major question, obviously, is: with whom shall our people work most closely? They have no desire to discriminate. Everyone will be consulted, within the sphere of his time-honored prerogatives. Everyone will be aided, as far as possible. Yet, plain to see, a committee of the whole would be impossibly large and diverse. For setting overall policy, our people require a small, unified Merseian council, whom they can get to know really well and with whom they can develop effective decision-making procedures.

"Furthermore, the resources of this entire system must be used in a coordinated way. For example, Country One cannot be allowed to hoard minerals which Country Two needs. Shipping must be free to go from any point to any other. And all available shipping must be pressed into service. We can furnish radiation screens for your vessels, but we cannot furnish the vessels themselves in the numbers that are needed. Yet at the same time, a certain amount of ordinary activity must continue. People will still have to eat, for instance. So—how do we make a fair allocation of resources and establish a fair system of priorities?

"I think these considerations make it obvious to you, worthies, that an international organization is absolutely essential, one which can *impartially* supply information, advice, and coordination. If it has facilities and workers of its own, so much the better.

"Would that such an organization had legal existence! But it does not, and I doubt there is time to form one. If you will pardon me for saying so, worthies, Merseia is burdened with too many old hatreds and jealousies to join overnight in brotherhood. In fact, the international group must be watched carefully, lest it try to aggrandize itself or diminish others. We galactics can do this with one organization. We cannot with a hundred.

"So." Falkayn longed for his pipe. Sweat prickled his skin. "I have no plenipotentiary writ. My team is merely supposed to make recommendations. But the matter is so urgent that whatever scheme we propose will likely be adopted, for the sake of getting on with the job. And we have found one group which transcends the rest. It pays no attention to barriers between people and people. It is large, powerful, rich, disciplined, efficient. It is not exactly what my civilization would prefer as its chief instrument for the deliverance of Merseia. We would honestly rather it went down the drain, instead of becoming yet more firmly entrenched. But we have a saying that necessity knows no law."

He could feel the tension gather, like a thunderstorm boiling up; he heard the first rageful retorts; he said fast, before the explosion came: "I refer to the Gethfennu."

What followed was indescribable.

But he was, after all, only warning of what his report would be. He could point out that he bore a grudge of his own, and was setting it aside for the common good. He could even, with considerable enjoyment, throw some imaginative remarks about ancestry and habits in the direction of Haguan—who grinned and looked smug. In the end, hours later, the assembly agreed to take the proposal under advisement. Falkayn knew what the upshot would be. Merseia had no choice.

The screens blanked.

Wet, shaking, exhausted, he looked across a stillness into the face of Morruchan Long-Ax. The Hand loomed over him. Fingers twitched longingly near a pistol butt. Morruchan said, biting off each word: "I trust you realize what you are doing. You're not just perpetuating that gang. You're conferring legitimacy on them. They will be able to claim they are now a part of recognized society."

"Won't they, then, have to conform to its laws?" Falkayn's larynx hurt, his voice was husky.

"Not them!" Morruchan stood brooding a moment. "But a reckoning will come. The Vachs will prepare one, if nobody else does. And afterward—are you going to teach us how to build stargoing ships?"

"Not if I have any say in the matter," Falkayn replied.

"Another score. Not important in the long run. We're bound to learn a great deal else, and on that basis . . . well, galactic, our grandchildren will see."

"Is ordinary gratitude beneath your dignity?"

"No. There'll be enough soft-souled dreambuilders, also among my race, for an orgy of sentimentalism. But then you'll go home again. I will abide."

Falkayn was too tired to argue. He made his formal farewells and called the ship to come get him.

Later, hurtling through the interstellar night, he listened to Chee's tirade: "—I still have to get back at those greasepaws. They'll be sorry they ever touched me."

"You don't aim to return, do you?" Falkayn asked.

"Pox, no!" she said. "But the engineers on Merseia will need recreation. The Gethfennu will supply some of it, gambling especially, I imagine. Now if I suggest our lads carry certain miniaturized gadgets which can, for instance, control a wheel—"

Adzel sighed. "In this splendid and terrible cosmos," he said, "why must we living creatures be forever perverse?"

A smile tugged at Falkayn's mouth. "We wouldn't have so much fun otherwise," he said.

Men and not-men were still at work when the supernova wavefront reached Merseia.

Suddenly the star filled the southern night, a third as brilliant as

Korych, too savage for the naked eye to look at. Blue-white radiance flooded the land, shadows were etched sharp, trees and hills stood as if illuminated by lightning. Wings beat upward from forests, animals cried through the troubled air, drums pulsed and prayers lifted in villages which once had feared the dark for which they now longed. The day that followed was lurid and furious.

Over the months, the star faded, until it became a knife-keen point and scarcely visible when the sun was aloft. But it waxed in beauty, for its radiance excited the gas around it, so that it gleamed amidst a whiteness which deepened at the edge to blue-violet and a nebular lacework which shone with a hundred faerie hues. Thence also, in Merseia's heaven, streamed huge shuddering banners of aurora, whose whisper was heard even on the ground. An odor of storm was blown on every wind.

Then the nuclear rain began. And nothing was funny any longer.

A loftier Argo cleaves the main,
Fraught with a later prize;
Another Orpheus sings again,
And loves, and weeps, and dies.
A new Ulysses leaves once more
Calypso for his native shore.

—Shelley

THE MASTER KEY

Once upon a time there was a king who set himself above the foreign merchants. What he did is of no account now; it was long ago and on another planet, and besides, the wench is dead. Harry Stenvik and I hung him by the seat of his trousers from his tallest minaret, in sight of all the people, and the name of the Polesotechnic League was great in the land. Then we made inroads on the stock-in-trade of the Solar Spice & Liquors Company factor and swore undying brotherhood.

Now there are those who maintain that Nicholas van Rijn has a cryogenic computer in that space used by the ordinary Terran for storing his heart. This may be so. But he does not forget a good workman. And I know no reason why he should have invited me to dinner except that Harry would be there, and—this being the briefest of business trips to Earth for me—we would probably have no other chance of meeting.

The flitter set me off atop the Winged Cross, where Van Rijn keeps what he honestly believes is a modest little penthouse apartment. A summer's dusk softened the mass of lesser buildings that stretched to the horizon and beyond; Venus had wakened in the west and Chicago Integrate was opening multitudinous lights. This high up, only a low machine throb reached my ears. I walked among roses and jasmine to the door. When it scanned me and dilated, Harry was waiting. We fell into each other's arms and praised God with many loud violations of His third commandment.

Afterward we stood apart and looked. "You haven't changed

much," he lied. "Mean and ugly as ever. Methane in the air must agree with you."

"Ammonia, where I've been of late," I corrected him. "S.O.P.: occasional bullets and endless dickering. *You're* disgustingly sleek and contented. How's Sigrid?" As it must to all men, domesticity had come to him. In his case it lasted, and he had built a house on the cliffs above Hardanger Fjord and raised mastiffs and sons. Myself—but that also is irrelevant.

"Fine. She sends her love and a box of her own cookies. Next time you must wangle a longer stay and come see us."

"The boys?"

"Same." The soft Norse accent roughened the least bit. "Per's had his troubles, but they are mending. He's here tonight."

"Well, great." The last I'd heard of Harry's oldest son, he was an apprentice aboard one of Van Rijn's ships, somewhere in the Hercules region. But that was several years ago, and you can rise fast in the League if you survive. "I imagine he has master's rank by now."

"Yes, quite newly. Plus an artificial femur and a story to tell. Come, let's join them."

Hm, I thought, so Old Nick was economizing on his bird-killing stones again. He had enough anecdotes of his own that he didn't need to collect them, unless they had some special use to him. A gesture of kindness might as well be thrown into the interview.

We passed through the foyer and crossed a few light-years of trollcat rug to the far end of the living room. Three men sat by the viewer wall, at the moment transparent to sky and city. Only one of them rose. He had been seated a little to one side, in a tigery kind of relaxed alertness—a stranger to me, dark and lean, with a blaster that had seen considerable service at his hip.

Nicholas van Rijn wallowed his bulk deeper into his lounger, hoisted a beer stein and roared, "Ha! Welcome to you, Captain, and you will maybe have a small drink like me before dinner?" After which he tugged his goatee and muttered, "Gabriel will tootle before I get your bepestered Anglic through this poor old noggin. I think I have just called myself a small drink."

I bowed to him as is fitting to a merchant prince, turned, and gave Per Stenvik my hand. "Excuse my staying put," he said. His face was still pale and gaunt; health was coming back, but youth never would. "I got a trifle clobbered."

"So I heard," I answered. "Don't worry, it'll heal up. I hate to think how much of me is replacement by now, but as long as the important parts are left . . ."

"Oh, yes, I'll be okay. Thanks to Manuel. Uh, Manuel Felipe Gómez y Palomares of Nuevo México. My ensign."

I introduced myself with great formality, according to what I knew of the customs of those poor and haughty colonists from the far side of Arcturus. His courtesy was equal, before he turned to make sure the blanket was secure around Per's legs. Nor did he go back to his seat and his glass of claret before Harry and I lowered ourselves. A human servant—male, in this one van Rijn establishment—brought us our orders, *akvavit* for Harry and a martini for me. Per fiddled with a glass of Ansan vermouth.

"How long will you be home?" I asked him after the small talk had gone by.

"As long as needful," Harry said quickly.

"No more, though," van Rijn said with equal speed. "Not one millimoment more can he loaf than nature must have; and he is young and strong."

"Pardon, *señor,*" Manuel said—how softly and deferentially, and with what a clang of colliding stares. "I would not gainsay my superiors. But my duty is to know how it is with my captain, and the doctors are fools. He shall rest not less than till the Day of the Dead; and then surely, with the Nativity so near, the *señor* will not deny him the holidays at home?"

Van Rijn threw up his hands. "Everyone, they call me apocalyptic beast," he wailed, "and I am only a poor lonely old man in a sea of grievances, trying so hard to keep awash. One good boy with promises I find, I watch him from before his pants dry out for I know his breed. I give him costly schooling in hopes he does not turn out another curdlebrain, and no sooner does he not but he is in the locker and my fine new planet gets thrown to the wolves!"

"Lord help the wolves," Per grinned. "Don't worry, sir, I'm as anxious to get back as you are."

"Hoy, hoy, I am not going. I am too old and fat. Ah, you think you have troubles now, but wait till time has gnawed you down to a poor old wheezer like me who has not even any pleasures left. Abdul! Abdul, you jellylegs, bring drink, you want we should dry up and puff away? . . . What, only me ready for a refill?"

"Do you really want to see that Helheim again?" Harry asked, with a stiff glance at van Rijn.

"Judas, yes," Per said. "It's just waiting for the right man. A whole *world*, Dad! Don't you remember?"

Harry looked through the wall and nodded. I made haste to intrude on his silence. "What were you there after, Per?"

"Everything," the young man said. "I told you it's an entire planet. Not one percent of the land surface has been mapped."

"Huh? Not even from orbit?"

Manuel's expression showed me what they thought of orbital maps.

"But for a starter, what attracted us in the first place, furs and herbs," Per said. Wordlessly, Manuel took a little box from his pocket, opened it, and handed it to me. A bluish-green powder of leaves lay within. I tasted. There was a sweet-sour flavor with wild overtones, and the odor went to the oldest, deepest part of my brain and roused memories I had not known were lost.

"The chemicals we have not yet understood and synthesized," van Rijn rumbled around the cigar he was lighting. "Bah! What do my chemists do all day but play happy fun games in the lab alcohol? And the furs, *ja,* I have Lupescu of the Peltery volcanomaking that he must buy them from me. He is even stooping to spies, him, he has the ethics of a paranoid weasel. Fifteen thousand he spent last month alone, trying to find where that planet is."

"How do you know how much he spent?" Harry asked blandly.

Van Rijn managed to look smug and hurt at the same time.

Per said with care, "I'd better not mention the coordinates myself. It's out Pegasus way. A G-nine dwarf star, about half as luminous as Sol. Eight planets, one of them terrestroid. Brander came upon it in the course of a survey, thought it looked interesting, and settled down to learn more. He'd really only time to tape the language of the locality where he was camped, and do the basic-basic planetography and bionics. But he did find out about the furs and herbs. So I was sent to establish a trading post."

"His first command," Harry said, unnecessarily on anyone's account but his own.

"Trouble with the natives, eh?" I asked.

"Trouble is not the word," van Rijn said. "The word is not for polite ears." He dove into his beer stein and came up snorting. "After all I have done for them, the saints keep on booting me in the soul like this."

"But we seem to have it licked," Per said.

"Ah. You think so?" Van Rijn waggled a hairy forefinger at him. "That is what we should like to be more sure of, boy, before we send out and maybe lose some expensive ships."

"*Y algunos hombres buenos,*" Manuel muttered, so low he could scarcely be heard. One hand dropped to the butt of his gun.

"I have been reading the reports from Brander's people," van Rijn said. "Also your own. I think maybe I see a pattern. When you have been swindling on so many planets like me, new captain, you will have analogues at your digits for much that is new. . . . Ah, pox and pity it is to get jaded!" He puffed a smoke ring that settled around Per's bright locks. "Still, you are never sure. I think sometimes God likes a little practical joke on us poor mortals, when we get too cockish. So I jump on no conclusions before I have heard from your own teeth how it was. Reports, even on visitape, they have no more flavor than what my competition sells. In you I live again the fighting and merrylarks, everything that is now so far behind me in my doting."

This from the single-handed conqueror of Borthu, Diomedes, and t'Kela!

"Well—" Per blushed and fumbled with his glass. "There really isn't a lot to tell, you know. I mean, each of you freemen has been through so much more than—uh—one silly episode. . . ."

Harry gestured at the blanketed legs. "Nothing silly there," he said.

Per's lips tightened. "I'm sorry. You're right. Men died."

Chiefly because it is not good to dwell overly long on those lost from a command of one's own, I said, "What's the planet like? 'Terrestroid' is a joke. They sit in an Earthside office and call it that if you can breathe the air."

"And not fall flat in an oof from the gravity for at least half an hour, and not hope the whole year round you have no brass-monkey ancestors." Van Rijn's nod sent the black ringlets swirling around his shoulders.

"I generally got assigned to places where the brass monkeys melted," Harry complained.

"Well, Cain isn't too bad in the low latitudes," Per said. His face relaxed, and his hands came alive in quick gestures that reminded me of his mother. "It's about Earth-size, average orbital radius a little over one A.U. Denser atmosphere, though, by around fifteen percent, which makes for more greenhouse effect. Twenty-hour rotation period; no moons. Thirty-two degrees of axial tilt, which does rather complicate the seasons. But we were at fifteen-forty north, in fairly low hills, and it was summer. A nearby pool was frozen every morning, and snowbanks remained on the slopes—but really, not bad for the planet of a G-nine star."

"Did Brander name it Cain?" I asked.

"Yes. I don't know why. But it turned out appropriate. Too damned appropriate." Again the bleakness. Manuel took his captain's empty glass and glided off, to return in a moment with it filled. Per drank hurriedly.

"Always there is trouble," van Rijn said. "You will learn."

"But the mission was going so well!" Per protested. "Even the language and the data seemed to . . . to flow into my head on the voyage out. In fact, the whole crew learned easily." He turned to me. "There were twenty of us, on the *Miriam Knight.* She's a real beauty, Cheland-class transport, built for speed rather than capacity, you know. More wasn't needed, when we were only supposed to erect the first post and get the idea of regular trade across to the autochthones. We had the usual line of goods, fabrics, tools, weapons, household stuff like scissors and meat grinders. Not much ornament, because Brander's xenologists hadn't been able to work out any consistent pattern for it. Individual Cainites seemed to dress and decorate themselves any way they pleased. In the Ulash area, at least, which of course was the only one we had any details on."

"And damn few there," Harry murmured. "Also as usual."

"Agriculture?" I inquired.

"Some primitive cultivation," Per said. "Small plots scratched out of the forest, tended by the Lugals. In Ulash a little metallurgy has begun, copper, gold, silver, but even they are essentially neolithic. And essentially hunters—the Yildivans, that is—along with such

Lugals as they employ to help. The food supply is mainly game. In fact, the better part of what farming is done is to supply fabric."

"What do they look like, these people?"

"I've a picture here." Per reached in his tunic and handed me a photograph. "That's old Shivaru. Early in our acquaintance. He was probably scared of the camera but damned if he'd admit it. You'll notice the Lugal he has with him is frankly in a blue funk."

I studied the image with an interest that grew. The background was harsh plutonic hillside, where grass of a pale yellowish turquoise grew between dark boulders. But on the right I glimpsed a densely wooded valley. The sky overhead was wan, and the orange sunlight distorted colors.

Shivaru stood very straight and stiff, glaring into the lens. He was about two meters tall, Per said, his body build much like that of a long-legged, deep-chested man. Tawny, spotted fur covered him to the end of an elegant tail. The head was less anthropoid: a black ruff on top, slit-pupiled green eyes, round mobile ears, flat nose that looked feline even to the cilia around it, full-lipped mouth with protruding tushes at the corners, and jaw that tapered down to a V. He wore a sort of loincloth, gaudily dyed, and a necklace of raw semiprecious stones. His left hand clutched an obsidian-bladed battle-ax and there was a steel trade-knife in his belt.

"They're mammals, more or less," Per said, "though with any number of differences in anatomy and chemistry, as you'd expect. They don't sweat, however. There's a complicated system of exo- and endothermic reactions in the blood to regulate temperature."

"Sweating is not so common on cold terrestroids," Van Rijn remarked. "Always you find analogs to something you met before, if you look long enough. Evolution makes parallels."

"And skew lines," I added. "Uh—Brander got some corpses to dissect, then?"

"Well, not any Yildivans," Per said. "But they sold him as many dead Lugals as he asked for, who're obviously of the same genus." He winced. "I hope to hell they didn't kill the Lugals especially for that purpose."

My attention had gone to the creature that cowered behind Shivaru. It was a squat, short-shanked, brown-furred version of the other Cainite. Forehead and chin were poorly developed and the muzzle had not yet become a nose. The being was nude except for a heavy pack, a quiver of arrows, a bow, and two spears piled on its muscular back. I could see that the skin there was rubbed naked and calloused by such burdens. "This is a Lugal?" I pointed.

"Yes. You see, there are two related species on the planet, one farther along in evolution than the other. As if Australopithecus had survived till today on Earth. The Yildivans have made slaves of the Lugals—certainly in Ulash, and as far as we could find out by spot checks, everywhere on Cain."

"Pretty roughly treated, aren't they, the poor devils?" Harry said. "I wouldn't trust a slave with weapons."

"But Lugals are completely trustworthy," Per said. "Like dogs. They do the hard, monotonous work. The Yildivans—male and female—are the hunters, artists, magicians, everything that matters. That is, what culture exists is Yildivan." He scowled into his drink. "Though I'm not sure how meaningful 'culture' is in this connection."

"How so?" Van Rijn lifted brows far above his small black eyes.

"Well . . . they, the Yildivans, haven't anything like a nation, a tribe, any sort of community. Family groups split up when the cubs are old enough to fend for themselves. A young male establishes himself somewhere, chases off all comers, and eventually one or more young females come join him. Their Lugals tag along, naturally—like dogs again. As near as I could learn, such families have only the most casual contact. Occasional barter, occasional temporary gangs formed to hunt extra-large animals, occasional clashes between individuals, and that's about it."

"But hold on," I objected. "Intelligent races need more. Something to be the carrier of tradition, something to stimulate the evolution of brain, a way for individuals to communicate ideas to each other. Else intelligence hasn't got any biological function."

"I fretted over that too," Per said. "Had long talks with Shivaru, Fereghir, and others who drifted into camp whenever they felt like it. We really tried hard to understand each other. They were as curious about us as we about them, and as quick to see the mutual advantage in trade relations. But what a job! A whole different planet—two or three billion years of separate evolution—and we had only pidgin Ulash to start with, the limited vocabulary Brander's people had gotten. We couldn't go far into the subtleties. Especially when they, of course, took everything about their own way of life for granted.

"Toward the end, though, I began to get a glimmering. It turns out that in spite of their oafish appearance, the Lugals are not stupid. Maybe even as bright as their masters, in a different fashion; at any rate, not too far behind them. And—in each of these family groups, these patriarchal settlements in a cave or hut, way off in the forest, there are several times as many Lugals as Yildivans. Every member of the family, even the kids, has a number of slaves. Thus you may not get Yildivan clans or tribes, but you do get the numerical equivalent among the Lugals.

"Then the Lugals are sent on errands to other Yildivan preserves, with messages or barter goods or whatever, and bring back news. And they get traded around; the Yildivans breed them deliberately, with a shrewd practical grasp of genetics. Apparently, too, the Lugals are often allowed to wander off by themselves when there's no work for them to do—much as we let our dogs run loose—and hold powwows of their own.

"You mustn't think of them as being mistreated. They are, by our standards, but Cain is a brutal place and Yildivans don't exactly have an easy life either. An intelligent Lugal is valued. He's made straw boss over the others, teaches the Yildivan young special skills and songs and such, is sometimes even asked by his owner what he thinks ought to be done in a given situation. Some families let him eat and sleep in their own dwelling, I'm told. And remember, his loyalty is strictly to the masters. What they may do to other Lugals is nothing to him. He'll gladly help cull the weaklings, punish the lazy, anything.

"So, to get to the point, I think that's your answer. The Yildivans do have a community life, a larger society—but indirectly, through their Lugals. The Yildivans are the creators and innovators, the Lugals the communicators and preservers. I daresay the relationship has existed for so long a time that the biological evolution of both species has been conditioned by it."

"You speak rather well of them," said Harry grimly, "considering what they did to you."

"But they were very decent people at first." I could hear in Per's voice how hurt he was by that which had happened. "Proud as Satan, callous, but not cruel. Honest and generous. They brought gifts whenever they arrived, with no thought of payment. Two or three offered to assign us Lugal laborers. That wasn't necessary or feasible when we had machinery along, but they didn't realize it then. When they did, they were quick to grasp the idea, and mightily impressed. I think. Hard to tell, because they couldn't or wouldn't admit anyone else might be superior to them. That is, each individual thought of himself as being as good as anyone else anywhere in the world. But they seemed to regard us as their equals. I didn't try to explain where we were really from. 'Another country' looked sufficient for practical purposes.

"Shivaru was especially interested in us. He was middle-aged, most of his children grown and moved away. Wealthy in local terms, progressive—he was experimenting with ranching as a supplement to hunting—and his advice was much sought after by the others. I took him for a ride in a flitter and he was happy and excited as any child; brought his three mates along next time so they could enjoy it too. We went hunting together occasionally. Lord, you should have seen him run down those great horned beasts, leap on their backs, and brain them with one blow of that tremendous ax! Then his Lugals would butcher the game and carry it home to camp. The meat tasted damn good, believe me. Cainite biochemistry lacks some of our vitamins, but otherwise a human can get along all right there.

"Mainly, though, I remember how we'd talk. I suppose it's old hat to you freemen, but I had never before spent hour after hour with another being, both of us at work trying to build up a vocabulary and an understanding, both getting such a charge out of it that we'd forget even to eat until Manuel or Cherkez—that was his chief Lugal, a gnarly, droll old fellow, made me think of the friendly gnomes in my fairy tale books when I was a youngster—until one of them would tell us. Sometimes my mind wandered off and I'd come back to earth realizing that I'd just sat there admiring his beauty. Yildivans are as graceful as cats, as pleasing in shape as a good gun. And as deadly, when they want to be. I found that out!

"We had a favorite spot, in the lee of a cottage-sized boulder on the hillside above camp. The rock was warm against our backs; seemed even more so when I looked at that pale shrunken sun and my breath smoking out white across the purplish sky. Far, far overhead a bird of prey would wheel, then suddenly stoop—in the thick air I could hear the whistle through its wing feathers—and vanish into the treetops down in the valley. Those leaves had a million different shades of color, like an endless autumn.

"Shivaru squatted with his tail curled around his knees, ax on the ground beside him. Cherkez and one or two other Lugals hunkered at a respectful distance. Their eyes never left their Yildivan. Sometimes Manuel joined us, when he wasn't busy bossing some phase of construction. Remember, Manuel? You really shouldn't have kept so quiet."

"Silence was fitting, Captain," said the Nuevo Méxican.

"Well," Per said, "Shivaru's deep voice would go on and on. He was full of plans for the future. No question of a trade treaty—no organization for us to make a treaty with—but he foresaw his people bringing us what we wanted in exchange for what we offered. And he was bright enough to see how the existence of a central mart like this, a common meeting ground, would affect them. More joint undertakings would be started. The idea of close cooperation would take root. He looked forward to that, within the rather narrow limits he could conceive. For instance, many Yildivans working together could take real advantage of the annual spawning run up the Mukushyat River. Big canoes could venture across a strait he knew of, to open fresh hunting grounds. That sort of thing.

"But then in a watchtick his ears would perk, his whiskers vibrate, he'd lean forward and start to ask about my own people. What sort of country did we come from? How was the game there? What were our mating and child-rearing practices? How did we ever produce such beautiful things? Oh, he had the whole cosmos to explore! Bit by bit, as my vocabulary grew, his questions got less practical and more abstract. So did mine, naturally. We were getting at each other's psychological foundations now, and were equally fascinated.

"I was not too surprised to learn that his culture had no religion. In fact, he was hard put to understand my questions about it. They practiced magic, but looked on it simply as a kind of technology. There was no animism, no equivalent of anthropomorphism. A Yildivan knew too damn well he was superior to any plant or animal. I think, but I'm not sure, that they had some vague concept of reincarnation. But it didn't interest them much, apparently, and the problem of origins hadn't occurred. Life was what you had, here and now. The world was a set of phenomena, to live with or master or be defeated by as the case might be.

"Shivaru asked me why I'd asked him about such a self-evident thing."

Per shook his head. His glance went down to the blanket around his lap and quickly back again. "That may have been my first mistake."

"No, Captain," said Manuel most gently. "How could you know they lacked souls?"

"Do they?" Per mumbled.

"We leave that to the theologians," van Rijn said. "They get paid to decide. Go on, boy."

I could see Per brace himself. "I tried to explain the idea of God," he said tonelessly. "I'm pretty sure I failed. Shivaru acted puzzled and . . . troubled. He left soon after. The Yildivans of Ulash use drums for long-range communication, have I mentioned? All that night I heard the drums mutter in the valley and echo from the cliffs. We had no visitors for a week. But Manuel, scouting around in the area, said he'd found tracks and traces. We were being watched.

"I was relieved, at first, when Shivaru returned. He had a couple of others with him, Fereghir and Tulitur, important males like himself. They came straight across the hill toward me. I was supervising the final touches on our timber-cutting system. We were to use local lumber for most of our construction, you see. Cut and trim in the woods with power beams, load the logs on a gravsled for the sawmill, then snake them directly through the induration vats to the site, where the foundations had now been laid. The air was full of whine and crash, boom and chug, in a wind that cut like a laser. I could hardly see our ship or our sealtents through dust, tinged bloody in the sun.

"They came to me, those three tall hunters, with a dozen armed Lugals hovering behind. Shivaru beckoned. 'Come,' he said. 'This is no place for a Yildivan.' I looked him in the eyes and they were filmed over, as if he'd put a glass mask between me and himself. Frankly, my skin prickled. I was unarmed—everybody was except Manuel, you know what Nuevo Méxicans are—and I was afraid I'd precipitate something by going for a weapon. In fact, I even made a point of speaking Ulash as I ordered Tom Bullis to take over for me and told Manuel to come along uphill. If the autochthones had taken some notion into their heads that we were planning harm, it wouldn't do for them to hear us use a language they didn't know.

"Not another word was spoken till we were out of the dust and racket, at the old place by the boulder. It didn't feel warm today. Nothing did. 'I welcome you,' I said to the Yildivans, 'and bid you dine and sleep with us.' That's the polite formula when a visitor arrives. I didn't get the regular answer.

"Tulitur hefted the spear he carried and asked—not rudely, understand, but with a kind of shiver in the tone—'Why have you come to Ulash?'

"'Why?' I stuttered. 'You know. To trade.'

"'No, wait, Tulitur,' Shivaru interrupted. 'Your question is blind.' He turned to me. 'Were you sent?' he asked. And what I would like to ask you sometime, freemen, is whether it makes sense to call a voice black.

"I couldn't think of any way to hedge. Something had gone awry, but I'd no feeblest notion what. A lie or a stall was as likely, *a priori,* to make matters worse as the truth. I saw the sunlight glisten along that dark ax head and felt most infernally glad to have Manuel beside me. Even so, the noise from the camp sounded faint and distant. Or was it only that the wind was whittering louder?

"I made myself stare back at him. 'You know we are here on behalf of others like us at home,' I said. The muscles tightened still more under his fur. Also . . . I can't read nonhuman expressions especially well. But Fereghir's lips were drawn off his teeth as if he confronted an enemy. Tulitur had grounded his spear, point down. Brander's reports observed that a Yildivan never did that in the presence of a friend. Shivaru, though, was hardest to understand. I could have sworn he was grieved.

"'Did God send you?' he asked.

"That put the dunce's cap on the whole lunatic business. I actually laughed, though I didn't feel at all funny. Inside my head it went click-click-click. I recognized a semantic point. Ulash draws some fine distinctions between various kinds of imperative. A father's command to his small child is entirely different—in word and concept both—from a command to another Yildivan beaten in a fight, which is different in turn from a command to a

Lugal, and so on through a wider range than our psycholinguists have yet measured.

"Shivaru wanted to know if I was God's slave.

"Well, this was no time to explain the history of religion, which I'm none too clear about anyway. I just said no, I wasn't; God was a being in Whose existence some of us believed, but not everyone, and He had certainly not issued me any direct orders.

"That rocked them back! The breath hissed between Shivaru's fangs, his ruff bristled aloft and his tail whipped his legs. 'Then who did send you?' he nearly screamed. I could translate as well by: 'So who is your owner?'

"I heard a slither alongside me as Manuel loosened his gun in the holster. Behind the three Yildivans, the Lugals gripped their own axes and spears at the ready. You can imagine how carefully I picked my words. 'We are here freely,' I said, 'as part of an association.' Or maybe the word I had to use means 'fellowship'—I wasn't about to explain economics either. 'In our home country,' I said, 'none of us is a Lugal. You have seen our devices that work for us. We have no need of Lugalhood.'

"'Ah-h-h,' Fereghir sighed, and poised his spear. Manuel's gun clanked free. 'I think best you go,' he said to them, 'before there is a fight. We do not wish to kill.'

"Brander had made a point of demonstrating guns, and so had we. No one stirred for a time that went on eternally, in that Fimbul wind. The hair stood straight on the Lugals. They were ready to rush us and die at a word. But it wasn't forthcoming. Finally the three Yildivans exchanged glances. Shivaru said in a dead voice, 'Let us consider this thing,' They turned on their heels and walked off through the long, whispering grass, their pack close around them.

"The drums beat for days and nights.

"We considered the thing ourselves at great length. What was the matter, anyhow? The Yildivans were primitive and unsophisticated by Commonwealth standards, but not stupid. Shivaru had not been surprised at the ways we differed from his people. For instance, the fact that we lived in communities instead of isolated families had only been one more oddity about us, intriguing rather than shocking. And, as I've told you, while large-scale cooperation among Yildivans wasn't common, it did happen once in a while; so what was wrong with our doing likewise?

"Igor Yuschenkoff, the captain of the *Miriam,* had a reasonable suggestion. 'If they have gotten the idea that we are slaves,' he said, 'then our masters must be still more powerful. Can they think we are preparing a base for invasion?'

"'But I told them plainly we are not slaves,' I said.

"'No doubt,' He laid a finger alongside his nose. 'Do they believe you?'

"You can imagine how I tossed awake in my sealtent. Should we haul gravs altogether, find a different area and start afresh? That would mean scrapping nearly everything we'd done. A whole new language to learn was the least of the problems. Nor would a move necessarily help. Scouting trips by flitter had indicated pretty strongly that the same basic pattern of life prevailed everywhere on Cain, as it did on Earth in the paleolithic era. If we'd run afoul, not of some local taboo, but of some fundamental . . . I just didn't know. I doubt if Manuel spent more than two hours a night in bed. He was too busy tightening our system of guards, drilling the men, prowling around to inspect and keep them alert.

"But our next contact was peaceful enough on the surface. One dawn a sentry roused me to say that a bunch of natives were here. Fog had arisen overnight, turned the world into wet gray smoke where you couldn't see three meters. As I came outside I heard the drip off a trac parked close by, the only clear sound in the muffledness. Tulitur and another Yildivan stood at the edge of camp, with about fifty male Lugals behind. Their fur sheened with water, and their weapons were rime-coated. 'They must have traveled by night, Captain,' Manuel said, 'for the sake of cover. Surely others wait beyond view.' He led a squad with me.

"I made the Yildivans welcome, ritually, as if nothing had happened. I didn't get any ritual back. Tulitur said only, 'We are here to trade. For your goods we will return those furs and plants you desire.'

"That was rather jumping the gun, with our post still less than half built. But I couldn't refuse what might be an olive branch. 'That is well,' I said. 'Come, let us eat while we talk about it.' Clever move, I thought. Accepting someone's food puts you under the same sort of obligation in Ulash that it used to on Earth.

"Tulitur and his companion—Bokzahan, I remember the name now—didn't offer thanks, but they did come into the ship and sit at the mess table. I figured this would be more ceremonious and impressive than a tent; also, it was out of that damned raw cold. I ordered stuff like bacon and eggs that the Cainites were known to like. They got right to business. 'How much will you trade to us?'

"'That depends on what you want, and on what you have to give in exchange,' I said, to match their curtness.

"'We have brought nothing with us,' Bokzahan said, 'for we knew not if you would be willing to bargain.'

"'Why should I not be?' I answered. 'That is what I came for. There is no strife between us.' And I shot at him: 'Is there?'

"None of those ice-green eyes wavered. 'No,' Tulitur said, 'there is not. Accordingly, we wish to buy guns.'

"'Such things we may not sell,' I answered. Best not to add that policy allowed us to as soon as we felt reasonably sure no harm would result. 'However, we have knives to exchange, as well as many useful tools.'

"They sulked a bit, but didn't argue. Instead, they went right to work, haggling over terms. They wanted as much of everything as we'd part with, and really didn't try to bargain the price down far. Only they wanted the stuff on credit. They needed it now, they said, and it'd take time to gather the goods for payment.

"That put me in an obvious pickle. On the one hand, the Yildivans had always acted honorably and, as far as I could check, always spoken truth. Nor did I want to antagonize them. On the other hand—but you can fill that in for yourself. I flatter myself I gave them a diplomatic answer. We did not for an instant doubt their good intentions, I said. We knew the Yildivans were fine chaps. But accidents could happen, and if so, we'd be out of pocket by a galactic sum.

"Tulitur slapped the table and snorted, 'Such fears might have been expected. Very well, we shall leave our Lugals here until payment is complete. Their value is great. But then you must carry the goods where we want them.'

"I decided that on those terms they could have half the agreed amount right away."

Per fell silent and gnawed his lip. Harry leaned over to pat his hand. Van Rijn growled, "*Ja,* by damn, no one can foretell everything that goes wrong, only be sure that some bloody-be-plastered thing will. You did hokay, boy. . . . Abdul, more drink, you suppose maybe this is Mars?"

Per sighed. "We loaded the stuff on a gravsled," he went on. "Manuel accompanied in an armed flitter, as a precaution. But nothing happened. Fifty kilometers or so from camp, the Yildivans told our men to land near a river. They had canoes drawn onto the bank there, with a few other Yildivans standing by. Clearly they intended to float the goods further by themselves, and Manuel called me to see if I had any objections. 'No,' I said. 'What difference does it make? They must want to keep the destination secret. They don't trust us any longer.' Behind him, in the screen, I saw Bokzahan watching. Our communicators had fascinated visitors before now. But this time, was there some equivalent of a sneer on his face?

"I was busy arranging quarters and rations for the Lugals, though. And a guard or two, nothing obtrusive. Not that I really expected trouble. I'd heard their masters say, 'Remain here and do as the *Erziran* direct until we come for you.' But nevertheless it felt queasy, having that pack of dog-beings in camp.

"They settled down in their animal fashion. When the drums began again that night they got restless, shifted around in the pavilion we'd turned over to them and mewled in a language Brander hadn't recorded. But they were quite meek next morning. One of them even asked if they couldn't help in our work. I had to laugh at the thought of a Lugal behind the controls of a five hundred kilowatt trac, and told him no, thanks, they need only loaf and watch us. There were good at loafing.

"A few times, in the next three days, I tried to get them into conversation. But nothing came of that. They'd answer me, not in the deferential style they used to a Yildivan but not insolently either. However, the answers were meaningless. 'Where do you live?' I would say. 'In the forest yonder,' the slave replied, staring at his toes. 'What sort of tasks do you have to do at home?' 'That which my Yildivan sets for me.' I gave up.

"Yet they weren't stupid. They had some sort of game they played, involving figures drawn in the dirt, that I never did unravel. Each sundown they formed ranks and crooned, an eerie minor-key chant, with improvisations that sometimes sent a chill along my nerves.

Mostly they slept, or sat and stared at nothing, but once in a while several would squat in a circle, arms around their neighbors' shoulders, and whisper together.

"Well . . . I'm making the story too long. We were attacked shortly before dawn of the fourth day.

"Afterward I learned that something like a hundred male Yildivans were in that party, and heaven knows how many Lugals. They'd rendezvoused from everywhere in that tremendous territory called Ulash, called by the drums and, probably, by messengers who'd run day and night through the woods. Our pickets were known to their scouts, and they laid a hurricane of arrows over those spots, while the bulk of them rushed in between. Otherwise I can't tell you much. I was a casualty." Per grimaced. "What a damn fool thing to happen. On my first command!"

"Go on," Harry urged. "You haven't told me any details."

"There aren't many," Per shrugged. "The first screams and roars slammed me awake. I threw on a jacket and stuffed feet into boots while my free hand buckled on a gun belt. By then the sirens were in full cry. Even so, I heard a blaster beam sizzle past my tent.

"I stumbled out into the compound. Everything was one black, boiling hell-kettle. Blasters flashed and flashed, sirens howled and voices cried battle. The cold stabbed at me. Starlight sheened on snowbanks and hoarfrost over the hills. I had an instant to think how bright and many the stars were, out there and not giving a curse.

"Then Yuschenkoff switched on the floodlamps in the *Miriam's* turret. Suddenly an artificial sun stood overhead, too bright for us to look at. What must it have been to the Cainites? Blue-white incandescence, I suppose. They swarmed among our tents and machines, tall leopard-furred hunters, squat brown gnomes, axes, clubs, spears, bows, slings, our own daggers in their hands. I saw only one man—sprawled on the earth, gun still between his fingers, head a broken horror.

"I put the command mike to my mouth—always wore it on my wrist as per doctrine—and bawled out orders as I pelted toward the ship. We had the atom itself to fight for us, but we were twenty, no, nineteen or less, against Ulash.

"Now our dispositions were planned for defense. Two men slept in the ship, the others in sealtents ringed around her. The half dozen on guard duty had been cut off, but the rest had the ship for an impregnable retreat. What we must do, though, was rally to the rescue of those guards, and quick. If it wasn't too late.

"I saw the boys emerge from their strong point under the landing jacks. Even now I remember how Zerkowsky hadn't fastened his parka, and what a low-comedy way it flapped around his bottom. He didn't use pajamas. You notice the damnedest small things at such times, don't you? The Cainites had begun to mill about, dazzled by the light. They hadn't expected that, nor the siren, which is a terrifying thing to hear at close range. Quite a few of them were already strewn dead or dying.

"Then—but all I knew personally was a tide that bellowed and yelped and clawed. It rolled over me from behind. I went down under their legs. They pounded across me and left me in the grip of a Lugal. He lay on my chest and went for my throat with teeth and hands. Judas, but that creature was strong! Centimeter by centimeter he closed in against my pushing and gouging. Suddenly another one got into the act. Must have snatched a club from some fallen Cainite and attacked whatever part of me was handiest, which happened to be my left shin. It's nothing but pain and rage after that, till the blessed darkness came.

"The fact was, of course, that our Lugal hostages had overrun their guards and broken free. I might have expected as much. Even without specific orders, they wouldn't have stood idle while their masters fought. But doubtless they'd been given advance commands. Tulitur and Bokzahan diddled us very nicely. First they got a big consignment of our trade goods, free, and then they planted reinforcements for themselves right in our compound.

"Even so, the scheme didn't work. The Yildivans hadn't really comprehended our power. How could they have? Manuel himself dropped the two Lugals who were killing me. He needed exactly two shots for that. Our boys swept a ring of fire, and the enemy melted away.

"But they'd hurt us badly. When I came to, I was in the *Miriam's* sick bay. Manuel hovered over me like an anxious raven. 'How'd we do?' I think I said.

"'You should rest, *señor,*' he said, 'and God forgive me that I made the doctor rouse you with drugs. But we must have your decision quickly. Several men are wounded. Two are dead. Three are missing. The enemy is back in the wilderness, I believe with prisoners.'

"He lifted me into a carrier and took me outside. I felt no physical pain, but was lightheaded and half crazy. You know how it is when you're filled to the cap with stimulol. Manuel told me straight out that my legbone was pretty well pulverized, but that didn't seem to matter at the time. . . . What do I mean, 'seem'? Of course it didn't! Gower and Muramoto were dead. Bullis, Cheng, and Zerkowsky were gone.

"The camp was unnaturally quiet under the orange sun. My men had policed the grounds while I was unconscious. Enemy corpses were laid out in a row. Twenty-three Yildivans—that number's going to haunt me for the rest of my life—and I'm not sure how many Lugals, a hundred perhaps. I had Manuel push me along while I peered into face after still, bloody face. But I didn't recognize any.

"Our own prisoners were packed together in our main basement excavation. A couple of hundred Lugals, but only two wounded Yildivans. The rest who were hurt had been carried off by their friends. With so much construction and big machines standing around for cover, that hadn't been too hard to do. Manuel explained that he'd stopped the attack of the hostages with stunbeams. Much the best weapon. You can't prevent a Lugal fighting for his master with a mere threat to kill him.

"In a corner of the pit, glaring up at the armed men above, were the Yildivans. One I didn't know. He had a nasty blaster burn, and our medics had given him sedation after patching it, so he was pretty much out of the picture anyway. But I recognized the other, who was intact. A stunbeam had taken him. It was Kochihir, an adult son of Shivaru, who'd visited us like his father a time or two.

"We stared at each other for a space, he and I. Finally, 'Why?' I asked him. 'Why have you done this?' Each word puffed white out of my mouth and the wind shredded it.

"'Because they are traitors, murderers, and thieves by nature, that's why,' Yuschenkoff said, also in Ulash. Brander's team had naturally been careful to find out whether there were words corresponding to concepts of honor and the reverse. I don't imagine the League will ever forget the Darborian Semantics!

"Yuschenkoff spat at Kochihir. 'Now we shall hunt down your breed like the animals they are,' he said. Gower had been his brother-in-law.

"'No,' I said at once, in Ulash, because such a growl had risen from the Lugals that any insane thing might have happened next. 'Speak thus no more.' Yuschenkoff shut his mouth, and a kind of ripple went among those packed, hairy bodies, like wind dying out on an ocean. 'But Kochihir,' I said, 'your father was my good friend. Or so I believed. In what wise have we offended him and his people?'

"He raised his ruff, the tail lashed his ankles, and he snarled, 'You must go and never come back. Else we shall harry you in the forests, roll the hillsides down on you, stampede horned beasts through your camps, poison the wells, and burn the grass about your feet. Go, and do not dare return!'

"My own temper flared—which made my head spin and throb, as if with fever—and I said, 'We shall certainly not go unless our captive friends are returned to us. There are drums in camp that your father gave me before he betrayed us. Call your folk on those, Kochihir, and tell them to bring back our folk. After that, perhaps we can talk. Never before.'

"He fleered at me without replying.

"I beckoned to Manuel. 'No sense in stalling unnecessarily,' I said. 'We'll organize a tight defense here. Won't get taken by surprise twice. But we've got to rescue those men. Send flitters aloft to search for them. The war party can't have gone far.'

"You can best tell how you argued with me, Manuel. You said an airflit was an utter waste of energy which was badly needed elsewhere. Didn't you?"

The Nuevo Méxican looked embarrassed. "I did not wish to contradict my captain," he said. His oddly delicate fingers twisted together in his lap as he stared out into the night that had fallen. "But, indeed, I thought that aerial scouts would never find anyone in so many, many hectares of hill and ravine, water and woods. They could have dispersed, those devils. Surely, even if they traveled away in company, they would not be in such a clump that infrared detectors could see them through the forest roof. Yet I did not like to contradict my captain."

"Oh, you did, you," Per said. A corner of his mouth bent upward.

"I was quite daft by then. Shouted and stormed at you, eh? Told you to jolly well obey orders and get those flitters in motion. You saluted and started off, and I called you back. You mustn't go in person. Too damned valuable here. Yes, that meant I was keeping back the one man with enough wilderness experience that he might have stood a chance of identifying spoor, even from above. But my brain was spinning down and down the sides of a maelstrom. 'See what you can do to make this furry bastard cooperate,' I said."

"It pained me a little that my captain should appoint me his torturer," Manuel confessed mildly. "Although from time to time, on various planets, when there was great need—No matter."

"I'd some notion of breaking down morale among our prisoners," Per said. "In retrospect, I see that it wouldn't have made any difference if they had cooperated, at least to the extent of drumming for us. The Cainites don't have our kind of group solidarity. If Kochihir and his buddy came to grief at our hands, that was their hard luck. But Shivaru and some of the others had read our psychology shrewdly enough to know what a hold on us their three prisoners gave.

"I looked down at Kochihir. His teeth gleamed back. He hadn't missed a syllable or a gesture, and even if he didn't know any Anglic, he must have understood almost exactly what was going on. By now I was slurring my words as if drunk. So, also like a drunk, I picked them with uncommon care. 'Kochihir,' I said, 'I have commanded our fliers out to hunt down your people and fetch our own whom they have captured. Can a Yildivan outrun a flying machine? Can he fight when its guns flame at him from above? Can he hide from its eyes that see from end to end of the horizon? Your kinfolk will dearly pay if they do not return our men of their own accord. Take the drums, Kochihir, and tell them so. If you do not, it will cost *you* dearly. I have commanded my man here to do whatever may be needful to break your will.'

"Oh, that was a vicious speech. But Cower and Muramoto had been my friends. Bullis, Cheng, and Zerkowsky still were, if they lived. And I was on the point of passing out. I did, actually, on the way back to the ship. I heard Doc Leblanc mutter something about how could he be expected to treat a patient whose system was abused with enough drugs to bloat a camel, and then the words kind of trailed off in a long gibber that went on and on, rising and falling until I thought I'd been turned into an electron and was trapped in an oscilloscope . . . and the darkness turned green and . . . and they tell me I was unconscious for fifty hours.

"From there on it's Manuel's story."

At this stage, Per was croaking. As he sank back in his lounger, I saw how white he had become. One hand picked at his blanket, and the vermouth slopped when he raised his glass. Harry watched him, with a helpless anger that smoldered at van Rijn. The merchant said, "There, there, so soon after his operation and I make him lecture us, ha? But shortly comes dinner, no better medicine than a real *rijstaffel,* and so soon after that he can walk about, he comes to my place in Djakarta for a nice old-fashioned orgy."

"Oh, hellfire!" Per exploded in a whisper. "Why're you trying to make me feel good? I ruined the whole show!"

"Whoa, son," I ventured to suggest. "You were in good spirits half an hour ago, and half an hour from now you'll be the same. It's only that reliving the bad moments is more punishment than Jehovah would inflict. I've been there too." Blindly, the blue gaze sought mine. "Look, Per," I said, "if Freeman van Rijn thought you'd botched a mission through your own fault, you wouldn't be lapping his booze tonight. You'd be selling meat to the cannibals."

A ghost of a grin rewarded me.

"Well, Don Manuel," van Rijn said, "now we hear from you, *nie?*"

"By your favor, *señor,* I am no Don," the Nuevo Méxican said, courteously, academically, and not the least humbly. "My father was a huntsman in the Sierra de los Bosques Secos, and I traveled in space as a mercenary with Rogers' Rovers, becoming sergeant before I left them for your service. No more." He hesitated. "Nor is there much I can relate of the happenings on Cain."

"Don't make foolishness," van Rijn said, finished his third or fourth liter of beer since I arrived, and signaled for more. My own glass had been kept filled too, so much so that the stars and the city lights had begun to dance in the dark outside. I stuffed my pipe to help me ease off. "I have read the official reports from your expeditioning," van Rijn continued. "They are scum-dreary. I need details—the little things nobody thinks to record, like Per has used up his lawrence in telling—I need to make a planet real for me before this cracked old pot of mine can maybe find a pattern. For it is my experience of many other planets, where I, even I, Nicholas van Rijn, got my nose rubbed in the dirt—which, ho, ho! takes a lot of dirt—it is on that I draw. Evolutions have parallels, but also skews, like somebody said tonight. Which lines is Cain's evolution parallel to? Talk, Ensign Gómez y Palomares. Brag. Pop jokes, sing songs, balance a chair on your head if you want but talk!"

The brown man sat still a minute. His eyes were steady on us, save when they moved to Per and back.

"As the *señor* wishes," he began. Throughout, his tone was level, but the accent could not help singing.

"When they bore my captain away I stood in thought, until Igor Yuschenkoff said, 'Well, who is to take the flitters?'

"'None,' I said.

"'But we have orders,' he said.

"'The captain was hurt and shaken. We should not have roused him,' I answered, and asked of the men who stood near, 'Is this not so?'

"They agreed, after small argument. I leaned over the edge of the pit and asked Kochihir if he would beat the drums for us. 'No,' he said, 'whatever you do.'

"'I shall do nothing, yet,' I said. 'We will bring you food presently.' And that was done. For the rest of the short day I wandered about among the snows that lay in patches on the grass. Ay, this was a stark land, where it swooped down into the valley and then rose again at the end of sight in saw-toothed purple ranges. I thought of home and of one Dolores whom I had known, a long time ago. The men did no work; they huddled over their weapons, saying little, and toward evening the breath began to freeze on their parka hoods.

"One by one I spoke to them and chose them for those tasks I had in mind. They were all good men of their hands, but few had been hunters save in sport. I myself could not trail the Cainites far, because they had crossed a broad reach of naked rock on their way downward and once in the forest had covered their tracks. But Hamud ibn Rashid and Jacques Ngolo had been woodsmen in their day. We prepared what we needed. Then I entered the ship and looked on my captain—how still he lay!

"I ate lightly and slept briefly. Darkness had fallen when I returned to the pit. The four men we had on guard stood like deeper shadows against the stars which crowd that sky. 'Go now,' I said, and took out my own blaster. Their footfalls crunched away.

"The shapes that clotted the blackness of the pit stirred and mumbled. A voice hissed upward, 'Ohé, you are back. To torment me?' Those Cainites have eyes that see in the night like owls. I had thought, before, that they snickered within themselves when they watched us blunder about after sunset.

"'No,' I said, 'I am only taking my turn to guard you.'

"'You alone?' he scoffed.

"'And this.' I slapped the blaster against my thigh.

"He fell silent. The cold gnawed deeper into me. I do not think the Cainites felt it much. As the stars wheeled slowly overhead, I began to despair of my plan. Whispers went among the captives, but otherwise I stood in a world where sound was frozen dead.

"When the thing happened, it went with devil's haste. The Lugals had been shifting about a while, as if restless. Suddenly they were upon me. One had stood on another's shoulders and leaped. To death, as they thought—but my shot missed, a quick flare and an amazed gasp from him that he was still alive. Had I not missed, several would have died to bring me down.

"As it was, two fell upon me. I went under, breaking hands loose from my throat with a judo release but held writhing by their mass. Hard fists beat me on head and belly. A palm over my mouth muffled my yells. Meanwhile the prisoners helped themselves out and fled.

"Finally I worked a leg free and gave one of them my knee. He rolled off with pain rattling in his throat. I twisted about on top of the other and struck him below the skull with the blade of my hand. When he went limp, I sprang up and shouted.

"Siren and floodlights came to life. The men swarmed from ship and tents. 'Back!' I cried. 'Not into the dark!' Many Lugals had not yet escaped, and those retreated snarling to the far side of the pit as our troop arrived. With their bodies they covered the wounded Yildivan from the guns. But we only fired, futilely, after those who were gone from sight.

"Guards posted themselves around the cellar. I scrabbled over the earth, seeking my blaster. It was gone. Someone had snatched it up: if not Kochihir, then a Lugal who would soon give it to him. Jacques Ngolo came to me and saw. 'This is bad,' he said.

"'An evil turn of luck,' I admitted, 'but we must proceed anyhow.' I rose and stripped off my parka. Below were the helmet and space-suit torso which had protected me in the fight. I threw them down, for they would only hinder me now, and put the parka back on. Hamud ibn Rashid joined us. He had my pack and gear and another blaster for me. I took them, and we three started our pursuit.

"By the mercy of God, we had never found occasion to demonstrate night-seeing goggles here. They made the world clear, though with a sheen over it like dreams. Ngolo's infrared tracker was our compass, the needle trembling toward the mass of Cainites that loped ahead of us. We saw them for a while, too, as they crossed the bare hillside, in and out among tumbled boulders; but we kept ourselves low lest they see us against the sky. The grass was rough in my face when I went all-fours, and the earth sucked heat out through boots and gloves. Somewhere a hunter beast screamed.

"We were panting by the time we reached the edge of trees. Yet in under their shadows we must go, before the Cainites fled farther than the compass would reach. Already it flickered, with so many dark trunks and so much brake to screen off radiation. But thus far the enemy had not stopped to hide his trail. I moved through the underbrush more carefully than him—legs brought forward to part the stems that my hands then guided to either side of my body—reading the book of trampled bush and snapped branch.

"After an hour we were well down in the valley. Tall trees gloomed everywhere about; the sky was hidden, and I must tune up the photomultiplier unit in my goggles. Now the book began to close. The Cainites were moving at a natural pace, confident of their escape, and even without special effort they left little spoor. And since they were now less frantic and more alert, we must follow so far behind that infrared detection was of no further use.

"At last we came to a meadow, whose beaten grass showed that they had paused here a while. And that was seen which I feared. The party had broken into three or four, each bound a different way. 'Which do we choose?' Ngolo asked.

"'Three of us can follow three of them,' I said.

"'*Bismillah!*' Hamud grunted. 'Blaster or no, I would not care to face such a band alone. But what must be, must be.'

"We took so much time to ponder what clues the forest gave that the east was gray before we parted. Plainly, the Lugals had gone toward their masters' homes, while Kochihir's own slaves had accompanied him. And Kochihir was the one we desired. I could only guess that the largest party was his, because most likely the first break had been made under his orders by his own Lugals, whose capabilities he knew. That path I chose for myself. Hamud and Ngolo wanted it too, but I used my rank to seize the honor, that folk on Nuevo México might never say a Gómez lacked courage.

"So great a distance was now between that there was no reason not to use our radios to talk with each other and with the men in camp. That was often consoling, in the long time which was upon me. For it was slow, slow, tracing those woods-wily hunters through their own land. I do not believe I could have done it, had they been only Yildivans and such Lugals as are regularly used in the chase. But plain to see, the attack had been strengthened by calling other Lugals from fields and mines and household tasks, and those were less adept.

"Late in the morning, Ngolo called. 'My gang just reached a cave and a set of lean-tos,' he said. 'I sit in a tree and watch them met by some female and half-grown Yildivans. They shuffle off to their own shed. This is where they belong, I suppose, and they are not going farther. Shall I return to the meadow and pick up another trail?'

"'No,' I said, 'it would be too cold by now. Backtrack to a spot out of view and have a flitter fetch you.'

"Some hours later, the heart leaped in my breast. For I came upon a tree charred by unmistakable blaster shots. Kochihir had been practicing.

"I called Hamud and asked where he was. 'On the bank of a river,' he said, 'casting about for the place where they crossed. That was a bitter stream to wade!'

"'Go no farther,' I said. 'My path is the right one. Have yourself taken back to camp.'

"'What?' he asked. 'Shall we not join you now?'

"'No,' I said. 'It is uncertain how near I am to the end. Perhaps so near that a flitter would be seen by them as it came down and alarm them. Stand by.' I confess it was a lonely order to give.

"A few times I stopped to eat and rest. But stimulants kept me going in a way that would have surprised my quarry who despised me. By evening his trail was again so fresh that I slacked my pace and went on with a snake's caution. Down here, after sunset, the air was not so cold as on the heights; yet every leaf glistened hoar in what starlight pierced through.

"Not much into the night, my own infrared detector began to register a source, stronger than living bodies could account for. I whispered the news into my radio and then ordered no more communication until further notice, lest we be overheard. Onward I slipped. The forest rustled and creaked about me, somewhere far off a heavy animal broke brush in panic flight, wings whirred overhead, yet *Santa María,* how silent and alone it was!

"Until I came to the edge of a small clearing.

"A fire burned there, throwing unrestful shadows on the wall of a big, windowless log cabin which nestled under the trees beyond. Two Yildivans leaned on their spears. And light glimmered from the smoke hole in the roof.

"Most softly, I drew my stun gun. The bolt snicked twice, and they fell in heaps. At once I sped across the open ground, crouched in the shadow under that rough wall, and waited.

"But no one had heard. I glided to the doorway. Only a leather curtain blocked my view. I twitched it aside barely enough that I might peer within.

"The view was dimmed by smoke, but I could see that there was just one long room. It did not seem plain, so beautiful were the furs hung and draped everywhere about. A score or so of Yildivans, mostly grown males, squatted in a circle around the fire, which burned in a pit and picked their fierce flat countenances out of the dark. Also there were several Lugals hunched in a corner. I recognized old Cherkez among them, and was glad he had outlived the battle. The Lugals in Kochihir's party must have been sent to barracks. He himself was telling his father Shivaru of his escape.

"As yet the time was unripe for happiness, but I vowed to light many candles for the saints. Because this was as I had hoped: Kochihir had not gone to his own home, but sought an agreed rendezvous. Zerkowsky, Cheng, and Bullis were here. They sat in another corner at the far end of the room, coughing from the smoke, skins drawn around them to ward off the cold.

"Kochihir finished his account and looked at his father for

approval. Shivaru's tail switched back and forth. 'Strange that they were so careless about you,' he said.

"'They are like blind cubs,' Kochihir scoffed.

"'I am not so sure,' the old Yildivan murmured. 'Great are their powers. And . . . we know what they did in the past.' Then suddenly he grew stiff, and his whisper struck out like a knife. 'Or did they do it? Tell me again, Kochihir, how the master ordered one thing and the rest did another.'

"'No, now, that means nothing,' said a different Yildivan, scarred and grizzled. 'What we must devise is a use for these captives. You have thought they might trade our Lugals and Gumush, whom Kochihir says they still hold, for three of their own. But I say, Why should they? Let us instead place the bodies where the *Erziran* can find them, in such condition that they will be warned away.'

"'Just so,' said Bokzahan, whom I now spied in the gloom. 'Tulitur and I proved they are weak and foolish.'

"'First we should try to bargain,' said Shivaru. 'If that fails. . . . 'His fangs gleamed in the firelight.

"'Make an example of one, then, before we talk,' Kochihir said angrily. 'They threatened the same for me.'

"A rumble went among them, as from a beast's cage in the zoo. I thought with terror of what might be done. For my captain has told you how no Yildivan is in authority over any other. Whatever his wishes, Shivaru could not stop them from doing what they would.

"I must decide my own course immediately. Blaster bolts could not destroy them all fast enough to keep them from hurling the weapons that lay to hand upon me—not unless I set the beam so wide that our men must also be killed. The stun gun was better, yet it would not overpower them either before I went down under axes and clubs. By standing to one side I could pen them within, for they had only the single door. But Bullis, Cheng, and Zerkowsky would remain hostages.

"What I did was doubtless stupid, for I am not my captain. I sneaked back to the edge of the woods and called the men in camp. 'Come as fast as may be,' I said, and left the radio going for them to home on. Then I circled about and found a tree overhanging the cabin. Up I went, and down again from a branch to the sod roof, and so to the smoke hole. Goggles protected my eyes, but nostrils withered in the fumes that poured forth. I filled my lungs with clean air and leaned forward to see.

"Best would have been if they had gone to bed. Then I could have stunned them one by one as they slept, without risk. But they continued to sit about and quarrel over what to do with their captives. How hard those poor men tried to be brave, as that dreadful snarling broke around them, as slit eyes turned their way and hands went stroking across knives!

"The time felt long, but I had not completed the Rosary in my mind when thunder awoke. Our flitters came down the sky like hawks. The Yildivans roared. Two or three of them dashed out the door to see what was afoot. I dropped them with my stunner, but not before one had screamed, 'The *Erziran* are here!'

"My face went back to the smoke hole. It was turmoil below. Kochihir screeched and pulled out his blaster. I fired but missed. Too many bodies in between, *señores.* There is no other excuse for me.

"I took the gun in my teeth, seized the edge of the smoke hole, and swung myself as best I could before letting go. Thus I struck the dirt floor barely outside the firepit, rolled over and bounced erect. Cherkez leaped for my throat. I sent him reeling with a kick to the belly, took my gun, and fired around me.

"Kochihir could not be seen in the mob which struggled from wall to wall. I fought my way toward the prisoners. Shivaru's ax whistled down. By the grace of God, I dodged it, twisted about and stunned him point-blank. I squirmed between two others. A third got on my back. I snapped my head against his mouth and felt flesh give way. He let go. With my gun arm and my free hand I tossed a Lugal aside and saw Kochihir. He had reached the men. They shrank from him, too stupefied to fight. Hate was on his face, in his whole body, as he took unpracticed aim.

"He saw me at his sight's edge and spun. The blaster crashed, blinding in that murk. But I had dropped to one knee as I pulled trigger. The beam scorched my parka hood. He toppled. I pounced, got the blaster, and whirled to stand before our people.

"Bokzahan raised his ax and threw it. I blasted it in mid-air and then killed him. Otherwise I used the stunner. And in a minute or two more, the matter was finished. A grenade brought down the front wall of the cabin. The Cainites fell before a barrage of knockout beams. We left them to awaken and returned to camp."

Again silence grew upon us. Manuel asked if he might smoke, politely declined van Rijn's cigars, and took a vicious-looking brown cigarette from his own case. That was a lovely, grotesque thing, wrought in silver on some planet I could not identify.

"Whoof!" van Rijn gusted. "But this is not the whole story, from what you have written. They came to see you before you left."

Per nodded. "Yes, sir," he said. A measure of strength had rearisen in him. "We'd about finished our preparations when Shivaru himself arrived, with ten other Yildivans and their Lugals. They walked slowly into the compound, ruffs erect and tails held stiff, looking neither to right nor left. I guess they wouldn't have been surprised to be shot down. I ordered such of the boys as were covering them to holster guns and went out on my carrier to say hello with due formality.

"Shivaru responded just as gravely. Then he got almost tongue-tied. He couldn't really apologize. Ulash doesn't have the phrases for it. He beckoned to Cherkez. 'You were good to release our people whom you held,' he said."

Per chuckled. "Huh! What else were we supposed to do, keep feeding them? Cherkez gave him a leather bag. 'I bring a gift,' he told me, and pulled out Tulitur's head. 'We shall return as much of the goods he got from you as we can find,' he promised, 'and if you will give us time, we shall bring double payment for everything else.'

"I'm afraid that after so much blood had gone over the dam, I didn't find the present as gruesome as I ought. I only sputtered that we didn't require such tokens.

"'But we do,' he said, 'to cleanse our honor.'

"I invited them to eat, but they declined. Shivaru made haste to explain that they didn't feel right about accepting our hospitality until their debt was paid off. I told them we were pulling out. Though that was obvious from the state of the camp, they still looked rather dismayed. So I told them we, or others like us, would be back, but first it was necessary to get our injured people home.

"Another mistake of mine. Because being reminded of what they'd done to us upset them so badly that they only mumbled when

I tried to find out why they'd done it. I decided best not press that issue—the situation being delicate yet—and they left with relief branded on them.

"We should have stuck around a while, maybe, because we've got to know what the trouble was before committing more men and equipment to Cain. Else it's all too likely to flare up afresh. But between our being shorthanded, and having a couple of chaps who needed first-class medical treatment, I didn't think we could linger. All the way home we wondered and argued. What had gone wrong? And what, later, had gone right? We still don't know."

Van Rijn's eyes glittered at him. "What is your theory?" he demanded.

"Oh—" Per spread his hands. "Yuschenkoff's, more or less. They were afraid we were the spearhead of an invasion. When we acted reasonably decently—refraining from mistreatment of prisoners, thanks to Manuel, and using stunners rather than blasters in the rescue operation—they decided they were mistaken."

Manuel had not shifted a muscle in face or body, as far as I could see. But van Rijn's battleship prow of a nose swung toward him and the merchant laughed, "You have maybe a little different notion, ha? Come, spew it out."

"My place is not to contradict my captain," said the Nuevo Méxican.

"So why you make fumblydiddles against orders, that day on Cain? When you know better, then you got a duty, by damn, to tell us where to stuff our heads."

"If the *señor* commands. But I am no learned man. I have no book knowledge of studies made on the psychonomy. It is only that . . . that I think I know those Yildivans. They seem not so unlike men of the barranca country on my home world, and again among the Rovers."

"How so?"

"They live very near death, their whole lives. Courage and skill in fighting, those are what they most need to survive, and so are what they most treasure. They thought, seeing us use machines and weapons that kill from afar, seeing us blinded by night and most of us clumsy in the woods, hearing us talk about what our life is like at home—they thought we lacked *cojones.* So they scorned us. They owed us nothing, since we were spiritless and could never understand their own spirit. We were only fit to be the prey, first of their wits and then of their weapons." Manuel's shoulders drew straight. His voice belled out so that I jumped in my seat. "When they found how terrible men are, that they themselves are the weak ones, we changed in their eyes from peasants to kings!"

Van Rijn sucked noisily on his cigar. "Any other shipboard notions?" he asked.

"No, sir, those were our two schools of thought," Per said.

Van Rijn guffawed. "So! Take comfort, freemen. No need for angelometrics on pinheads. Relax and drink. You are both wrong."

"I *beg* your pardon," Harry rapped. "You were not there, may I say."

"No, not in the flesh." Van Rijn slapped his paunch. "Too much flesh for that. But tonight I have been on Cain up here, in this old brain, and it is rusty and afloat in alcohol but it has stored away more information about the universe than maybe the universe gets credit for holding. I see now what the parallels are. Xanadu, Dunbar, Tametha, Disaster Landing . . . oh, the analogue is never exact and on Cain the thing I am thinking of has gone far and far . . . but still I see the pattern, and what happened makes sense.

"Not that we have got to have an analogue. You gave us so many clues here that I could solve the puzzle by logic alone. But analogues help, and also they show my conclusion is not only correct but possible."

Van Rijn paused. He was so blatantly waiting to be coaxed that Harry and I made a long performance out of refreshing our drinks. Van Rijn turned purple, wheezed a while, decided to keep his temper for a better occasion, and chortled.

"Hokay, you win," he said. "I tell you short and fast, because very soon we eat if the cook has not fallen in the curry. Later you can study the formal psychologies.

"The key to this problem is the Lugals. You have been calling them slaves, and there is your mistake. They are not. They are domestic animals."

Per sat bolt upright. "Can't be!" he exclaimed. "Sir. I mean, they have language and—"

"*Ja, ja, ja,* for all I care they do mattress algebra in their heads.

They are still tame animals. What is a slave, anyhows? A man who has got to do what another man says, willy-billy. Right? Harry said he would not trust a slave with weapons, and I would not either, because history is too pocked up with slave revolts and slaves running away and slaves dragging their feet and every such foolishness. But your big fierce expensive dogs, Harry, you trust them with their teeth, *nie?* When your kids was little and wet, you left them alone in rooms with a dog to keep watches. There is the difference. A slave may or may not obey. But a domestic animal has got to obey. His genes won't let him do anything different.

"Well, you yourselves figured the Yildivans had kept Lugals so long, breeding them for what traits they wanted, that this had changed the Lugal nature. Must be so. Otherwise the Lugals would be slaves, not animals, and could not always be trusted the way you saw they were. You also guessed the Yildivans themselves must have been affected, and this is very sleek thinking only you did not carry it so far you ought. Because everything you tell about the Yildivans goes to prove by nature they are wild animals.

"I mean wild, like tigers and buffalos. They have no genes for obediences, except to their parents when they are little. So long have they kept Lugals to do the dirty work—before they really became intelligent, I bet, like ants keeping aphids; for remember, you found no Lugals that was not kept—any gregarious-making genes in the Yildivans, any inborn will to be led, has gone foof. This must be so. Otherwise, from normal variation in ability, some form of Yildivan ranks would come to exist, *nie?*

"This pops your fear-of-invasion theory, Per Stenvik. With no concept of a tribe or army, they can't have any notions about conquest. And wild animals don't turn humble when they are beat, Manuel Gómez y Palomares, the way you imagine. A man with a superiority complexion may lick your boots when you prove you are his better; but an untamed carnivore hasn't got any such pride in the first place. He is plain and simple independent of you.

"Well, then, what did actual go on in their heads?

"Recapitalize. Humans land and settle down to deal. Yildivans have no experience of races outside their own planet. They natural assume you think like them. In puncture of fact, I believe they could not possible imagine anything else, even if they was told.

Your findings about their culture structure shows their half-symbiosis with the Lugals is psychological too; they are specialized in the brains, not near so complicated as man.

"But as they get better acquaintanced, what do they see? People taking orders. How can this be? No Yildivan ever took orders, unless to save his life when an enemy stood over him with a sharp thing. Ah, ha! So some of the strangers is Lugal type. Pretty soon, I bet, old Shivaru decides all of you is Lugal except young Stenvik, because in the end all orders come from him. Some others, like Manuel, is straw bosses maybe, but no more. Tame animals.

"And then Per mentions the idea of God."

Van Rijn crossed himself with a somewhat irritating piety. "I make no blasfuming," he said. "But everybody knows our picture of God comes in part from our kings. If you want to know how Oriental kings in ancient days was spoken to, look in your prayer book. Even now, we admit He is the Lord, and we is supposed to do His will, hoping He will not take too serious a few things that happen to anybody like anger, pride, envy, gluttony, lust, sloth, greed, and the rest what makes life fun.

"Per said this. So Per admitted he had a master. But then he must also be a Lugal—an animal. No Yildivan could possible confess to having even a mythical master, as shown by the fact they have no religion themselves though their Lugals seem to.

"Give old boy Shivaru his credits, he came again with some friends to ask further. What did he learn? He already knew everybody else was a Lugal, because of obeying. Now Per said he was no better than the rest. This confirmed Per was also a Lugal. And what blew the cork out of the bottle was when Per said he nor none of them had any owners at home!

"Whup, whup, slow down, youngster. You could not have known. Always we make discoveries the hard way. Like those poor Yildivans.

"They was real worried, you can imagine. Even dogs turn on people now and then, and surely some Lugals go bad once in a while on Cain and make big trouble before they can get killed. The Yildivans had seen some of your powers, knew you was dangerous . . . and your breed of Lugal must have gone mad and killed off its own Yildivans. How else could you be Lugals and yet have no masters?

"So. What would you and I do, friends, if we lived in lonely country houses and a pack of wild dogs what had killed people set up shop in our neighborhood?"

Van Rijn gurgled beer down his throat. We pondered for a while. "Seems pretty farfetched," Harry said.

"No." Per's cheeks burned with excitement. "It fits. Freeman Van Rijn put into words what I always felt as I got to know Shivaru. A—a single-mindedness about him. As if he was incapable of seeing certain things, grasping certain ideas, though his reasoning faculties were intrinsically as good as mine. Yes . . ."

I nodded at my pipe, which had been with me when I clashed against stranger beings than that.

"So two of them first took advantage of you," van Rijn said, "to swindle away what they could before the attack because they wasn't sure the attack would work. No shame there. You was outside the honor concept, being animals. Animals whose ancestors must have murdered a whole race of true humans, in their views. Then the alarmed males tried to scrub you out. They failed, but hoped maybe to use their prisoners for a lever to pry you off their country. Only Manuel fooled them."

"But why'd they change their minds about us?" Per asked.

Van Rijn wagged his finger. "Ha, there you was lucky. You gave a very clear and important order. Your men disobeyed every bit of it. Now Lugals might go crazy and kill off Yildivans, but they are so bred to being bossed that they can't stand long against a leader. Or if they do, it's because they is too crazy to think straight. Manuel, though, was thinking straight like a plumber line. His strategy worked five-four-three-two-one-zero. Also, your people did not kill more Yildivans than was needful, which crazy Lugals would do.

"So you could not be domestic animals after all, gone bad or not. Therefore you had to be wild animals. The Cainite mind—a narrow mind like you said—can't imagine any third horn on that special bull. If you had proved you was not Lugal type, you must be Yildivan type. Indications to the contrariwise, the way you seemed to take orders or acknowledge a Lord, those must have been misunderstandings on the Cainites' part.

"Once he had time to reason this out, Shivaru saw his people had done yours dirty. Partway he felt bad about it in his soul, if he has one stowed somewhere; Yildivans do have some notion about upright behavior to other Yildivans. And besides, he did not want to lose a chance at your fine trade goods. He convinced his friends. They did what best they could think about to make amendments."

Van Rijn rubbed his palms together in glee. "Oh, ho, ho, what customers they will be for us!" he roared.

We sat still for another time, digesting the idea, until the butler announced dinner. Manuel helped Per rise. "We'll have to instruct everybody who goes to Cain," the young man said. "I mean, not to let on that we aren't wild animals, we humans."

"But, Captain," Manuel said, and his head lifted high, "we are."

Van Rijn stopped and looked at us a while. Then he shook his own head violently and shambled bearlike to the viewer wall. "No," he growled. "Some of us are."

"How's that?" Harry wondered.

"We here in this room are wild," van Rijn said. "We do what we do because we want to or because it is right. No other motivations, *nie?* If you made slaves of us, you would for sure not be wise to let us near a weapon.

"But how many slaves has there been, in Earth's long history, that their masters could trust? Quite some! There was even armies of slaves, like the Janissaries. And how many people today is domestic animals at heart? Wanting somebody else should tell them what to do, and take care of their needfuls, and protect them not just against their fellow men but against themselves? Why has every free human society been so shortlived? Is this not because the wild-animal men are born so heartbreaking seldom?"

He glared out across the city, where it winked and glittered beneath the stars, around the curve of the planet. "Do you think they yonder is free?" he shouted. His hand chopped downward in scorn.

SATAN'S WORLD

✲I✲

Elfland is the new section of Lunograd. So it is written, and therefore believed by the computers of administrative authority. Living beings know better. They see marvels, beauties, gaieties, a place for pleasure and heartbreak. They experience a magic that is unique.

But in the old town underground, the machines are always working.

Near a post on the frontier between these two universes, David Falkayn halted. "Well, my love," he said, "here's a pleasant spot for an adios."

The girl who called herself Veronica lifted one hand to her lips. "Do you mean that?" she asked in a stricken voice.

A little taken aback, Falkayn regarded her closely. She made enjoyable looking anyhow: piquant features, flowing dark hair in which synthetic diamonds twinkled like stars, spectacular figure in a few wisps of iridescent cloth. "Oh, not permanently, I hope." He smiled. "I simply had better get to work. Shall I see you again this evenwatch?"

Her mouth quivered upward. "That's a relief. You startled me. I thought we were strolling, and then with no warning you—I didn't know what to imagine. Were you getting rid of me or what?"

"Why in the galaxy should I do any such ridiculous thing? I've known you, let's see, just three standard days, isn't it, since Theriault's party?"

She flushed and did not meet his gaze. "But you might want a lot of variety in women, as well as everything else you've missed in space," she said low. "You must realize you can take your pick. You're the glamour man, the cosmopolitan in the real sense of the word. We may follow the latest gossip and the newest fashion here, but none of us girls has traveled past Jupiter. Hardly any of the men we know have, either. Not a one of them compares to you. I've been so happy, so envied, and so afraid it will come to a sudden end."

Falkayn's own blood beat momentarily high. Smugness tempted him. Few indeed had won their Master Merchant's certificates as young as he, let alone become confidential associates of an uncrowned prince like Nicholas van Rijn, or served as fate's instrument for entire planets. He reckoned himself fairly good-looking, too: face rather snub-nosed, but high in the cheekbones and hard in the jaw, eyes a startling blue against tanned skin, curly yellow hair bleached by foreign suns. He stood an athletic 190 centimeters tall; and he might be newly arrived from the outermost bourn of known space, but Luna's best clothier had designed his pearl-gray tunic and gold culottes.

Whoa, there, son. An animal alertness, developed in countries for which man was never meant, stirred to life within him. *She isn't performing for free, remember. The reason I didn't tell her in advance that today I return to the job still holds good: I'd prefer not to have to worry about prearranged shadowings.*

"You flatter me outrageously," he said, "especially by giving me your company." His grin turned impudent. "In exchange, I'd love to continue outraging you. Dinner first, though. Maybe we'll have time for the ballet too. But dinner for certain. After my long while outside the Solar System, exploring wild new planets, I'm most anxious to continue exploring wild new restaurants"—he bowed—"with such a delightful guide."

Veronica fluttered her lashes. "Native scout glad-glad servem big captain from Polesotechnic League."

"I'll join you soon's I can manage after 1800 hours."

"Please do." She tucked an arm beneath his. "But why part at once? If I've declared myself on holiday—for you—I can keep on with you to wherever you're bound."

His animal showed teeth. He must remind himself to stay relaxed. "Sorry, not possible. Secrecy."

"Why?" She arched her brows. "Do you actually need theatricals?" Her tone half bantered, half challenged his manhood. "I'm told you stand high in the Solar Spice & Liquors Company, which stands high in the Polesotechnic League, which stands above planetary law—even the Commonwealth's. What are you afraid of?"

If she's trying to provoke me, flashed through Falkayn's mind, *might be worth provoking right back at her.* "The League isn't a unity," he said as if to a child. "It's an association of interstellar merchants. If it's more powerful than any single government, that's simply because of the scale on which star traders necessarily operate. Doesn't mean the League is a government too. It organizes cooperative, mutual-benefit activities, and it mediates competition that might otherwise become literally cutthroat. Believe me, however, rival members don't use outright violence on each other's agents, but chicanery is taken for granted."

"So?" Though a lecture on the obvious was perhaps insulting, he thought the resentment that nickered in her expression came too fast to be uncalculated.

He shrugged. "So, with all proper immodesty, I'm a target figure. Right-hand man and roving troubletwister for Old Nick. Any hint as to what I'll be doing next could be worth mega-credits to somebody. I have to watch out for, shall we say, commercial intelligence collectors."

Veronica released him and stepped back. Her fists clenched. "Are you implying I'm a spy?" she exclaimed.

As a matter of fact, Falkayn thought, *yes.*

He wasn't enjoying this. In search of inner peace, he let his gaze travel past her for a second. The setting was as lovely and not altogether real as she was.

Elfland was not the first unwalled community built on the Lunar surface. But on that account, its designers could take advantage of previous engineering experience. The basic idea was simple. Spaceships employ electromagnetic screens to ward off particle radiation. They employ artificially generated positive and negative gravity fields not only for propulsion, not only for constant weight inside the hull at every acceleration, but also for tractor and pressor beams. Let us scale up these systems until they maintain a giant bubble of air on an otherwise empty surface.

In practice, the task was monumental. Consider problems like leakage, temperature regulation, and ozone layer control. But they were solved; and their solution gave to the Solar System one of its most beloved resorts.

Falkayn saw a park around the girl and himself, greensward, arbors, flowerbeds that were a riot of rainbows. In Lunar gravity, trees soared through heights and arcs no less fantastic than the splashing fountains; and people walked with that same marvelous bounding lightness. Behind the crowds, towers and colonnades lifted in fanciful filigree multitudinously hued. Birds and elevated streets flew between them. Perfumes, laughter, a drift of music, a pervasive murmur of engines wove through the warm air.

But beyond and above stood Luna. Clocks ran on GMT; a thousand small suns hanging from bronze vines created morning. Yet the true hour neared midnight. Splendid and terrible, darkness struck through. At zenith, the sky was black, stars icily visible. South swelled the cloudy-bright-blue shield of Earth. A close observer could see twinkles on its unlit quarter, the megalopolises, dwarfed to sparks by that least astronomical distance. The Avenue of Sphinxes gave a clear westward view to the edge of air, an ashen crater floor, Plato's ringwall bulking brutally over the near horizon.

Falkayn's attention went back to Veronica. "I'm sorry," he said. "Of course I don't intend anything personal."

Of course I do. I may range in the galactic outback, but that doesn't mean I'm an especially simple or trusting soul. Contrariwise. When a lady this desirable and sophisticated locks onto me, within hours of my making planetfall . . . and obliges me in every possible way except telling me about herself—a little quiet checking up by Chee Lan proves that what vague things she does say are not in precise one-one correspondence with truth—what am I supposed to think?

"I should hope not!" Veronica snapped.

"I've sworn fealty to Freeman van Rijn," Falkayn said, "and his orders are to keep everything belowdecks. He doesn't want the competition to get in phase with him." He took both her hands. "It's for your own sake too, heartlet," he added gently.

She let her wrath fade. Tears came forth and trembled on her lids with what he considered admirable precision. "I did want to . . . to share with you . . . more than a few days' casual pleasure, David," she whispered. "And now you call me a spy at worst, a blabbermouth at"—she gulped—"at best. It hurts."

"I did nothing of the sort. But what you don't know can't get you in trouble. Which is the last place I'd want you to be in."

"But you said th-there wasn't any—violence—"

"No, no, absolutely not. Murder, kidnapping, brainscrub . . . Polesotechnic League members don't indulge in such antics. They know better. But that doesn't mean they're tin saints. They, or certain of their hirelings, have been known to use fairly nasty ways of getting what's wanted. Bribery you could laugh at, Veronica." *Ha!* Falkayn thought. "*Jump at" is the correct phrase, I suspect. What retainer were you paid, and what're you offered for solid information about me?* "But worse approaches are possible. They're frowned on, but sometimes used. Every kind of snooping, for instance; don't you value your privacy? A hundred ways of pressure, direct and indirect, subtle and unsubtle. Blackmail—which often catches the innocent. You do a favor for somebody, and one thing leads to another, and suddenly the somebody has fastened the screws on you and begun tightening them."

As you probably figure to do with me, his mind added. Wryly: *Why shouldn't I let you try? You're the devil I know. You'll keep off the devils I don't know, and meanwhile provide me some gorgeous fun. A dirty trick, perhaps, for a cunning unscrupulous yokel like me to play on a naive city operator like you. But I believe you get honest enjoyment out of my company. And when I leave, I'll give you an inscribed fire stone bracelet or something.*

She pulled loose from his grasp. Her tone stiffened again. "I never asked you to violate your oath," she said. "I do ask not to be treated like a spineless, brainless toy."

Ah, so. We put frost back in the voice, eh? Hoarfrost, to be exact. Well, I can't argue for the rest of this week. If she won't reverse vectors, forget her, son.

Falkayn snapped to virtual attention. His heels clicked. A machine might have used his throat. "Freelady, my apologies for inflicting my society upon you under conditions you appear to find intolerable. I shall not trouble you further. Good day." He bowed, wheeled, and strode off.

For a minute he thought it hadn't worked. Then she uttered

almost a wail, and ran after him, and spent a tearful time explaining how she had misunderstood, and was sorry, and would never, never get off orbit again, if only he—

She might even be partly sincere. Twenty-five percent, maybe?

It helped, being a scion of a baronial house in the Grand Duchy of Hermes, Falkayn reflected. To be sure, he was a younger son; and he'd left at an early age, after kicking too hard against the traces that aristocrats were supposed to carry; and he hadn't visited his home planet since. But some of that harsh training had alloyed with the metal of him. He knew how to deal with insolence.

Or how to stick with a job when he'd really rather prolong his vacation. He got rid of Veronica as fast as was consistent with a reconciliation scene, and proceeded on his way.

II

First he passed through a large sporting goods store on the other side of the park. He should be able to shake off any followers among the wares on exhibition. The vac suits and vehicles were less bulky than he had counted on. But then, a jaunt into the Lunar mountains, rescue flitters available within minutes of a radio call, was not like hiking off on an unmapped world where you were the sole human being for several light-years. The collapsible boats with their gaudy sails were more helpful. He wondered how popular they were. Lake Leshy was small, and low-weight sailing tricky until you got the hang of it—as he had learned beyond the Solar System.

Emerging from a rear door, he found a kiosk and entered the dropshaft. The few people floating down the gee-beam with him seemed like ordinary citizens.

Maybe I'm being overcautious, he thought. *Does it matter if our competitors know I've paid a visit to Serendipity, Incorporated? Shouldn't I try to remember this isn't some nest of nonhuman barbarians? This is Terra's own moon, at the heart of the Commonwealth! The agents of the companies don't fight for naked survival, no holds barred; essentially, they play a game for money, and the losers don't lose anything vital. Relax and enjoy it.* But habit was too strong, reminding him of the context in which that last bit of advice had originally been given.

He got off at the eighth sublevel and made his way along the corridors. Wide and high, they were nonetheless crowded with traffic: freightways, robotic machines, pedestrians in workaday coveralls. Their facings were in plain pastel tones, overlaid by an inevitable thin film of grime and oil. The doors opened on factories, warehouses, shipping depots, offices. Rumble and rattle filled the air, odors of crowded humanity, chemicals, electrical discharges. Hot gusts struck out of fenced-off grilles. A deep, nearly subliminal vibration quivered through rock and floor and shinbones, the toil of the great engines. Elfland was a pretty mask; here, in the industrial part of old Lunograd, were the guts.

Gagarin Corridor ended, like many others, at Titov Circus. The hollow cylinder of space, reaching from a skylighting dome where Earth and stars gleamed, down to the depths of excavation, was not as big as Falkayn's impression had been from its fame. But it was built in early days, he reflected. And certainly the balconies which encircled it on every level were thronged enough. He must weave his way through the crowds. They were local people mostly, workers, businessmen, officials, monitors, technicians, housewives, showing more in their gait and mannerisms than in their bodies the effects of generations on Luna. But there were plenty of outsiders, merchants, spacemen, students, tourists, including a wild variety of nonhumans.

He noted that the prestigious stores, like Ivarsen Gems, occupied cubbyholes compared to newer establishments. Really big money has no need to advertise itself. Boisterous noises from the Martian Chop House tempted him to stop in for a mug of its ale, which he'd heard about as far away as Betelgeuse. But no . . . maybe later . . . duty was calling, "in a shrill unpleasant voice," as van Rijn often said. Falkayn proceeded around the balcony.

The door he reached at length was broad, of massive bronze, decorated with an intricate bas-relief circuit diagram. Stereoprojection spelled SERENDIPITY, INC. a few centimeters in front. But the effect remained discreet. You might have supposed this outfit to have been in operation these past two centuries. And instead, in—fifteen years, was that the figure?—it had rocketed from nowhere to the very firmament of the Polesotechnic League.

Well, Falkayn thought, *in a free-market economy, if you see a widespread need and can fill it, you get rich fast. Actually, when Old Nick organized his trade pioneer teams, like mine, he set them to doing in a physical way what Serendipity was already doing in its computers.*

A certain irony here. Adzel, Chee Lan, and I are supposed to follow up whatever interesting reports our robot probes bring back from hitherto unvisited planets. If we see potentially valuable resources or markets, we report back to van Rijn, very much on the q.t., so he can exploit them before the rest of the League learns they exist. And yet I, the professional serendipitist, have come to Serendipity, Inc., like any hopeful Earth-lubber businessman.

He shrugged. His team had been overdue for a visit to the Solar System. Having arrived, they might as well see if the data-processing machines could free-associate them with an item that pointed in some profitable direction. Van Rijn had agreed to pay the fees, without bellowing very much.

The door opened. Instead of a lobby, Falkayn entered a room, luxuriously draped but miniature, from which several other doors led. A vocolyre sang, "Good day, sir. Please take Number Four." That led down a short, narrow passage to still another door, and thus finally to an office. Unlike most chambers in Lunograd, this one did not compensate for lack of windows with some landscape film played on a wall screen. In fact, though the carpeting was deep and rich blue, walls azure, ceiling mother-of-pearl, air flower-scented, furniture comfortable, the total effect was somehow stark. At one end, a woman sat behind a large desk. The battery of secretarial gadgets around her suggested a barricade.

"Welcome," she said.

"Thanks," he replied with an attempted grin. "I felt as if I were invading a fortress."

"In a way, sir, that was correct." Her voice could have been pleasantly husky, the more so when she spoke Anglic with a guttural accent that not even his widely traveled ear could identify. But it was too crisp, too sexless; and her smile gave the same impression of having been learned. "Protection of privacy is a major element of our service. Many do not wish it known they have consulted us on a specific occasion. We partners receive each client in person, and usually need not call on our staff to help."

That better be the case, Falkayn thought, *seeing what a whopping sum you charge just for an appointment.*

She offered her hand without rising. "I am Thea Beldaniel." The clasp was perfunctory on both sides. "Please be seated, Freeman Kubichek."

He lowered his frame into a lounger. It extended an arm, offering excellent cigars. He took one. "Thanks," he repeated. "Uh, now that I'm here, I can drop the *nom du phone.* Most visitors do, I'm sure."

"Actually, no. There is seldom any reason, until they are alone with the machines. Of course, we are bound to recognize many because they are prominent." Thea Beldaniel paused before adding, with a tactfulness that appeared equally studied, "Prominent in this galactic neighborhood, that is. No matter how important some beings may be, no living brain can recognize them all, when civilization extends across scores of light-years. You, sir, for example, are obviously from a colonized planet. Your bearing suggests that its social structure is aristocratic, yourself born into the nobility. The Commonwealth does not have hereditary distinctions. Therefore your home world must be autonomous. But that leaves quite a few possibilities."

Since he had long been curious about this organization, he tried to strike up a genuine conversation. "Right, Freelady. I'm not on political business, though. I work for an Earth-based company, Solar Spice & Liquors. My real name's David Falkayn. From Hermes, to be exact."

"Everyone knows of Nicholas van Rijn." She nodded. "I have met him personally a few times."

I must confess to myself he's the main reason I've been lionized, Falkayn thought. *Reflected glory. By now, high society is abuzz about me. Invitations are pouring in, from the emperors of industry, their wives, daughters, hangers-on, to the bold space ranger and his partners, in honor of our (largely unspecified) exploits among the far stars. But that's because we aren't just any bold space rangers, we're Old Nick's bold space rangers.*

A paradox remains. The Beldaniel sisters, Kim Yoon-Kun, Anastasia, Herrera, Freeman and Freelady Latimer—the founders and owners of Serendipity, Inc., which aims to correlate all the information in known space—they haven't heard about us. They don't go out in society. They keep to themselves, in these offices and in that castle where outsiders never visit. . . . I truly would like to get a rise out of this woman.

She wasn't bad-looking, he realized piecemeal. Indeed, she could be called handsome: tall, lithe, well formed, no matter how much the severe white slacksuit tried to conceal that fact. Her hair was cut short, but this only emphasized a good shape of head; her face was practically classic, except that you thought of Athena as showing a bit more warmth. Her age was hard to guess. She must be at least in her forties. But having taken care of her body and, doubtless, advantage of the best anti-senescence treatments, she might be older by a decade, and yet show merely the same gray streak in brown tresses, slight dryness in the clear pale skin, crow's-feet about the eyes. Those eyes were her best feature, Falkayn decided, wide-spaced, large, luminous green.

He started his cigar and rolled the smoke about his tongue. "We may find ourselves bargaining," he said. "Don't you buy information, either for cash or for remittance of fees?"

"Certainly. The more the better. I must warn you that we set our own prices, and sometimes refuse to pay anything, even after the item has been given us. You see, its value depends on what is already stored in the memory banks. And we can't let others see this. That would risk betrayal of secrets entrusted to us. If you wish to sell, Freeman Falkayn, you must rely on our reputation for fair dealing."

"Well, I've visited a lot of planets, species, cultures—"

"Anecdotal material is acceptable, but not highly paid for. What we most desire is thorough, accurate, documented, quantitative facts. Not necessarily about new discoveries in space. What is going on on the major civilized worlds is often of greater interest."

"Look," he said bluntly, "no offense meant, but I've been wondering. I work for Freeman van Rijn, and in an important capacity. Suppose I offered you details about his operations that he didn't want released. Would you buy them?"

"Probably. But we would not then release them to others. Our whole position in the Polesotechnic League depends on our trustworthiness. This is one reason why we have so few employees: a minimal staff of experts and technicians—all nonhuman—and otherwise our machines. In part, it is a good reason for us to be notoriously asocial. If Freeman van Rijn knows we have not been partying with Freeman Harleman of Venusian Tea & Coffee, he has the fewer grounds for suspecting us of collusion with the latter."

"Coffee grounds?" Falkayn murmured.

Thea Beldaniel folded her hands in her lap, sat back, and said, "Perhaps, coming from the frontier as you do, Freeman, you don't quite understand the principle on which Serendipity, Inc., works. Let me put it in oversimplified language.

"The problem of information retrieval was solved long ago, through electronic data storage, scanning, coding, and replication. But the problem of information usage continues acute. The perceptual universe of man and other space-traveling species is expanding still more rapidly than the universe of their exploration. Suppose you were a scientist or an artist, with what you believed was a new idea. To what extent has the thought of countless billions of other sophonts, on thousands of known worlds, duplicated your own? What might you learn from them? What might you contribute that is genuinely new? Well, you could ransack libraries and data centers, and get more information on any subject than is generally realized. Too much more! Not only could you not read it all in your lifetime, you could not pick out what was relevant. Still worse is the dilemma of a company planning a mercantile venture. What developments elsewhere in space will collide, compete, conceivably nullify their efforts? Or what positive opportunities are being overlooked, simply because no one can comprehend the total picture?"

"I've heard those questions asked," Falkayn said. He spoke dryly, with puzzlement rather than resentment at being patronized. Was this woman so insensitive to human feelings—hell, to ordinary human common sense—that she must lecture a client as if he were some six-legged innocent newly hauled out of his planet's Stone Age?

"Obvious, of course," she said imperturbably. "And in principle, the answer is likewise obvious. Computers should not merely scan, but sift data. They should identify possible correlations, and test them, with electronic speed and parallel-channel capacity. You might say they should make suggestions. In practice, this was difficult. Technologically, it required a major advance in cybernetics. Besides . . . the members of the League guarded their hard-won knowledge jealously. Why tell anything you knew to your rival? Or to public data centers, and thus indirectly to your rival? Or to a third party who was not your competitor but might well make a deal with your rival—or might decide to diversify his interests and himself become your rival?

"Whether or not you could use a datum, it had cost you something to acquire. You would soon go bankrupt if you made a free gift of every item. And while secrets were traded, negotiations about this were slow and awkward.

"Serendipity, Inc., solved the problem with improved systems—not only better robotics, but a better idea for exchanging knowledge."

Falkayn sat back with his cigar. He felt baffled, fascinated, the least bit frightened. This female was even weirder than he had been told the partners were. Giving a basic sales pitch to a man who'd already bought an appointment . . . in God's name, *why?* Stories were rife about the origin of these people. But what story might account for the behavior he was observing?

Beneath her quick, level words, intensity gathered: "The larger the information pool, the greater the probability of making a correlation that is useful to a given individual. Thus the creation of such a pool was to the general benefit, provided that no one gained a special advantage. This is the service that we have offered. We draw on ordinary sources, of course. And that in itself is valuable, there being so many libraries and memory banks scattered on so many planets. But in addition, we buy whatever anyone cares to tell, if it is worthwhile. And we sell back whatever other data may be of interest to him. The important point is, this is done anonymously. We founders of the business do not know or wish to know what questions you ask, what answers you get, what you relate, how the computers appraise it, what additional conclusions their logic circuits draw. Such things stay in the machines. We only concern ourselves or our staff with a specific problem if we are requested to. Otherwise our sole attention is on the statistics, the input-output average. Our firm has grown as trust in us has grown. Innumerable private investigations have shown that we favor no one, do not blurt anything out, and cannot be corrupted. So has the accumulated experience of doing business with us."

She leaned forward. Her gaze was unblinking on him. "For example," she said, "imagine that you did wish to sell us confidential information about your company. Mere word-of-mouth assertions would be filed, since a rumor or a falsehood is also a datum, but would probably not be believed. The usual precautions against commercial espionage should safeguard documentary evidences. But if this fails—yes, we will buy it. Crosschecks will quickly show that we have bought thief's goods, which fact is noted. If your employer was the only one who possessed the information, it will not be given out until somebody else has registered the same thing with us. But it will be taken into account by the logic circuits in preparing their recommendations—which they do impersonally for any client. That is to say, they might advise your employer's rival against a certain course of action, because they know from the stolen information that this will be futile. But they will not tell him why they offer such counsel."

Falkayn got a word in fast while she caught up on her breathing. "That makes it to everybody's advantage to consult you on a regular basis. And the more your machines are told during consultations, the better the advice they can give. Uh-huh. That's how you grow."

"It is one mechanism of growth for us," Thea Beldaniel said. "Actually, however, information theft is very minor. Why should Freeman van Rijn not sell us the fact that, say, one of his trading ships happened upon a planet where there is a civilization that creates marvelous sculptures? He is not in the art business to any significant extent. In exchange, he pays a much reduced fee to learn that a crew of hydrogen-breathing explorers have come upon an oxygen-atmosphere planet that produces a new type of wine."

"I'm not clear about one thing," Falkayn said. "My impression is he'd have to come in person to be told any important fact. Is this true?"

"Not in that particular case," she answered. "His needs would be obvious. But we must safeguard privacy. You, for example—" She paused. The strangeness left her eyes; she said shrewdly, "I would guess that you plan to sit down before the machine and say, 'My name is David Falkayn. Tell me whatever might be of special interest to me.' No doubt you have good reason to expect that the memory banks include something about you. Now don't you realize, sir, for your own protection, we can't let anyone do this? We must ask for positive identification."

Falkayn reached into his pocket. She raised a palm. "No, no," she said, "not to me. I don't have to know whether you really are who you claim to be. But to the machine—retinal scan, fingerprints, the usual procedures if you are registered in the Commonwealth. If not, it will suggest other ways to establish yourself to its satisfaction." She rose. "Come, I'll take you there and demonstrate its operation."

Following her and watching, Falkayn could not decide whether she walked like a frigid woman.

No matter. A more interesting thought had struck him. He believed he could tell why she behaved the way she did, dwelt on elementary details though she must realize he knew most of them already. He'd encountered that pattern elsewhere. It was usually called fanaticism.

III

Seated alone—and yet not alone, for the great quasi-brain was there and had already spoken to him—Falkayn took a moment to consider his surroundings. Though he had spent his life with robots, including his beloved Muddlehead, this one felt eerie. He tried to understand why.

He sat in an ordinary self-adjusting chair before an ordinary desk with the standard secretarial apparatus. Around him were bare gray walls, white fluorolight, odorless recycled air, a faint humming through stillness. Confronting him was a basic control panel and a large 3D screen, blank at the moment. What was strange?

It must be subjective, he decided, his own reaction to the mystery about this organization. The detectives of a wary League had verified that the founder-owners of Serendipity, Inc., had no special ties to any other group—or, for that matter, to anyone or anything, human or nonhuman, throughout known space. But their origin remained obscure. Their chilly, graceless personalities (Thea Beldaniel was evidently typical of the whole half-dozen) and aloofness from society only emphasized that basic isolation.

Their secret could not be ferreted out. Quite apart from the regard for privacy inherent in today's individualism, it wasn't feasible. The universe is too big. This tiny segment of the fringe of one spiral arm of a single galaxy which we have somewhat explored and exploited . . . is too big. In going to thousands of suns that intrigue us, we have passed by literally millions of others. It will take centuries even to visit them, let alone begin to understand them a little. And meanwhile, and forever, beyond the outermost radius of our faring will lie nearly all the suns that exist.

The partners had entered the Solar System in a cargo vessel loaded with heavy metals. Selling that for a good price, they established their information enterprise. Though they ordered many parts on Earth, the basic logic and memory units were brought from elsewhere. Once, out of curiosity, Nicholas van Rijn had bribed a Commonwealth customs inspector; but that man merely said, "Look, sir, I verify that imports aren't dangerous. I make sure they don't carry disease, and aren't going to blow up, that sort of thing. What else can we stop, under a free trade law? What Serendipity got was just a shipment of computer-type stuff. Not human-made, I'm sure. You get an eye for, uh, style, after a few years in my job. And if, like you tell me, nobody can quite duplicate the kind of work it's been doing since it was installed . . . well, jingles, sir, isn't the answer plain to see? These people found a planet that can do tricks we aren't up to yet, nobody we know about. They made a deal. They kept quiet. Wouldn't you? *Don't* you, sir?"

Falkayn started from his reverie. The machine had spoken again. "Pardon?" he said. Instantly: *What the devil am I doing, apologizing to a gadget?* He picked his cigar from the rack above the disposer and took a nervous puff.

"David Falkayn of Hermes and the Solar Spice & Liquors Company, your identity has been verified." The voice was not the flat baritone of most human-built robots; it was high, with a curious whistling quality, and varied both pitch and speed in a way hard to describe. "Your name is associated with a number of accounts in these data banks, most notably the episodes involving Beta Centauri, Ikrananka, and Merseia." *Judas priest!* Falkayn thought. *How did it learn about Ikrananka?* "Many items are logically connected with each of these, and in turn connected with other facts. You will understand that the total ramifications are virtually infinite. Thus it is necessary to select a point and search the association chains radiating from it in a limited number of directions. If none of them are productive, other lines are tried, and eventually other starting points, until a satisfactory result is obtained." *Or until I run out of money.* "What type of search do you wish conducted?"

"Well—I—" Falkayn rallied his shaken wits. "How about new markets on extrasolar planets?"

"Since confidential information is not released here, you are asking no service which ordinary data centers cannot provide."

"Now, wait. I want you to do what you're uniquely built to do. Take the points Me and Cash, and see what association chains exist between 'em."

"Commenced."

Did the humming louden, or did the silence deepen? Falkayn leaned back and struggled to relax. Behind that panel, these walls, electrons and quanta hurtled through vacuum; charges and the absence of charges moved through crystal lattices; distorted molecules interacted with magnetic, electric, gravitational, nuclear fields; the machine thought.

The machine dreamed.

He wondered if its functioning was continuous, building immense webs of correlation and inference whether or not a client sat here. Quite probably; and in this manner, it came closer than any other entity to comprehending our corner of the universe. And yet the facts must be too many, the possible interconnections between them uncountable. The fruitful few were buried in that sheer mass. Every major discovery has involved a recognition of such rare meaningful associations. (Between the water level in a bath and the weight of gold; between the pessimism of a small-town parson and the mechanism of organic evolution; between the Worm Ouroboros, that biteth its own tail, and the benzene molecule—) Living creatures like Falkayn, coming from the living cosmos to the cave where this engine dwelt, must be what triggered its real action, made it perceive the significance of what had hitherto looked like another isolated fact.

"David Falkayn of Hermes!"

"Yes?" He sat bolt upright and tensed.

"A possibility. You will recall that, a number of years ago, you showed that the star Beta Centauri has planets in attendance."

Falkayn couldn't help crowing, uselessly save that it asserted his importance in contrast to the huge blind brain. "I should forget? That was what really attracted the notice of the higher-ups and started me to where I am. Blue giant suns aren't supposed to have planets. But this one does."

"That is recorded, like most news," said the machine, unimpressed. "Your tentative explanation of the phenomenon was later verified. While the star was condensing, a nucleus still surrounded by an extensive nebular envelope, a swarm of rogue planets chanced by. Losing energy to friction with the nebula, they were captured.

"Sunless planets are common. They are estimated to number a thousand or more times the stars. That is, nonluminous bodies, ranging in size from superjovian to asteroidal, are believed to occupy interstellar space in an amount greater by three orders of magnitude than the nuclear-reacting self-luminous bodies called stars. Nevertheless, astronomical distances are such that the probability of an object like this passing near a star is vanishingly small. Indeed, explorers have not come upon many rogues even in mid-space. An actual capture must be so rare that the case you found may well be unique in the galaxy.

"However, your discovery excited sufficient interest that an expedition set forth not long afterward, from the Collectivity of Wisdom in the country of Kothgar upon the planet Lemminkainen. Those are the Anglic names, of course. Herewith a transcript of the full report." A slot extruded a spooled micro-reel which Falkayn automatically pocketed.

"I know of them," he said. "Nonhuman civilization, but they do have occasional relations with us. And I followed the story. I had somewhat of a personal interest, remember. They checked out every giant within several hundred light-years that hadn't been visited before. Results negative, as expected—which is why no one else bothered to try."

"At that time, you were on Earth to get your Master's certificate," the machine said. "Otherwise you might never have heard. And, while Earth's data-processing and news facilities are unsurpassed in known space, they are nonetheless so overloaded that details which seem of scant importance are not sent in. Among those filtered-out items was the one presently under consideration.

"It was by chance that Serendipity, Inc., obtained a full account several years later. A Lemminkainenite captain who had been on that voyage tendered the data in exchange for a reduction of fee for his own inquiries. Actually, he brought information and records pertaining to numerous explorations he had made. This one happened to be among them. No significance was noticed until the present moment, when your appearance stimulated a detailed study of the fact in question."

The man's pulse quickened. His hands clenched on the chair arms.

"Preliminary to your perusal of the transcript, a verbal summary is herewith offered," whistled the oracle. "A rogue planet was found to be approaching Beta Crucis. It will not be captured, but the hyperbola of its orbit is narrow and it will come within an astronomical unit."

The screen darkened. Space and the stars leaped forth. One among them burned a steady steel blue. It waxed as the ship that had taken the pictures ran closer.

"Beta Crucis lies approximately south of Sol at an approximate distance of two hundred and four light-years." The dry recital, in that windful tone, seemed to make cold strike out of the moving view. "It is of type B_1, with a mass of approximately six, radius four, luminosity eight hundred and fifty times Sol's. It is quite young, and its total residence time on the main sequence will be on the order of a hundred million standard years."

The scene shifted. A streak of light crossed the wintry stellar background. Falkayn recognized the technique. If you cruise rapidly along two or three orthogonal axes, recording photo-multipliers will pick up comparatively nearby objects like planets, by their apparent motion, and their location can be triangulated.

"In this instance, only a single object was detected, and that at a considerable distance out," said the machine. "Since it represented the lone case of passage that the expedition found, closer observation was made."

The picture jumped to a strip taken from orbit. Against the stars hung a globe. On one side it was dark, constellations lifting over its airless horizon as the ship moved. On the other side it shimmered wan bluish white. Irregular markings were visible, where the steeper uplands reared naked. But most of the surface was altogether featureless.

Falkayn shivered. *Cryosphere,* he thought.

This world had condensed, sunless, from a minor knot in some primordial nebula. Dust, gravel, stones, meteoroids rained together during multiple megayears; and in the end, a solitary planet moved off between the stars. Infall had released energy; now radioactivity did, and the gravitational compression of matter into denser allotropes. Earthquakes shook the newborn sphere; volcanoes spouted forth gas, water vapor, carbon dioxide, methane, ammonia, cyanide, hydrogen sulfide . . . the same which had finally evolved into Earth's air and oceans.

But here was no sun to warm, irradiate, start the chemical cookery that might at last yield life. Here were darkness and the deep, and a cold near absolute zero.

As the planet lost heat, its oceans froze. Later, one by one, the gases of the air fell out solid upon those immense glaciers, a Fimbul blizzard that may have gone for centuries. In a sheath of ice—ice perhaps older than Earth herself—the planet drifted barren, empty, nameless, meaningless, through time to no harbor except time's end.

Until—

"The mass and diameter are slightly greater than terrestrial, the gross density somewhat less," said the brain that thought without being aware. "Details may be found in the transcript, to the extent that they were ascertained. They indicate that the body is quite ancient. No unstable atoms remain in appreciable quantity, apart from a few of the longest half-life.

"A landing party made a brief visit."

The view jumped again. Through the camera port of a gig, Falkayn saw bleakness rush toward him. Beta Crucis rose. Even in the picture, it was too savagely brilliant to look near. But it was nonetheless a mere point—distant, distant; for all its unholy radiance, it threw less light than Sol does on Earth.

That was ample, however, reflected off stiffened air and rigid seas. Falkayn must squint against dazzle to study a ground-level scene.

That ground was a plain, flat to the horizon save where the spaceboat and crew had troubled it. A mountain range thrust above the world's rim, dark raw stone streaked with white. The gig cast a blue shadow across diamond snow-glitter, under the star-crowded black sky. Some Lemminkainenites moved about, testing and taking samples. Their otter shapes were less graceful than ordinarily, hampered by the thick insulating soles that protected them and the materials of their spacesuits from the heat sink that such an environment is. Falkayn could imagine what hush enclosed them, scarcely touched by radio voices or the seething of cosmic interference.

"They discovered nothing they considered to be of value," said the computer. "While the planet undoubtedly has mineral wealth, this lay too far under the cryosphere to be worth extracting. Approaching Beta Crucis, solidified material would begin to sublime, melt, or vaporize. But years must pass until the planet came sufficiently near for this effect to be noticeable."

Unconsciously, Falkayn nodded. Consider the air and oceans of an entire world, chilled to equilibrium with interstellar space. What a Dante's hell of energy you'd need to pour in before you observed so much as a little steam off the crust!

The machine continued. "While periastron passage would be accompanied by major geological transformations, there was no reason to suppose that any new order of natural phenomena would be disclosed. The course of events was predictable on the basis of the known properties of matter. The cryosphere would become atmosphere and hydrosphere. Though this must cause violent readjustments, the process would be spectacular rather than fundamentally enlightening—or profitable; and members of the dominant culture on Lemminkainen do not enjoy watching catastrophes. Afterward the planet would recede. In time, the cryosphere would re-form. Nothing basic would have happened.

"Accordingly, the expedition reported what it had found, as a mildly interesting discovery on an otherwise disappointing cruise. Given little emphasis, the data were filed and forgotten. The negative report that reached Earth did not include what appeared to be an incidental."

Falkayn smote the desk. It thrummed within him. *By God,* he thought, *the Lemminkainenites for sure don't understand us humans. We won't let the thawing of an ice world go unwatched!*

Briefly, fantasies danced in his mind. Suppose you had a globe like that, suddenly brought to a livable temperature. The air would be poisonous, the land raw rock . . . but that could be changed. You could make your own kingdom—

No. Quite aside from economics (a lot cheaper to find uninhabited planets with life already on them), there were the dull truths of physical reality. Men can alter a world, or ruin one; but they cannot move it one centimeter off its ordained course. That requires energies of literally cosmic magnitude.

So you couldn't ease this planet into a suitable orbit around Beta Crucis. It must continue its endless wanderings. It would not freeze again at once. Passage close to a blue giant would pour in unbelievable quantities of heat, which radiation alone is slow to shed. But the twilight would fall within years; the dark within decades; the Cold and the Doom within centuries.

The screen showed a last glimpse of the unnamed sphere, dwindling as the spaceship departed. It blanked. Falkayn sat shaken by awe.

He heard himself say, like a stranger, with a flippancy that was self-defensive, "Are you proposing I organize excursions to watch this object swing by the star? A pyrotechnic sight, I'm sure. But how do I get an exclusive franchise?"

The machine said, "Further study will be required. For example, it will be needful to know whether the entire cryosphere is going to become fluid. Indeed, the very orbit must be ascertained with more precision than now exists. Nevertheless, it does appear that this planet may afford a site of unprecedented value to industry. That did not occur to the Lemminkainenites, whose culture lacks a dynamic expansionism. But a correlation has just been made here with the fact that, while heavy isotopes are much in demand, their production has been severely limited because of the heat energy and lethal waste entailed. Presumably this is a good place on which to build such facilities."

The idea hit Falkayn in the belly, then soared to his head like champagne bubbles. The money involved wasn't what brought him to his feet shouting. Money was always pleasant to have; but he could get enough for his needs and greeds with less effort. Sheer instinct roused him. He was abruptly a Pleistocene hunter again, on the track of a mammoth.

"Judas!" he yelled. "*Yes!*"

"Because of the commercial potentialities, discretion would be advantageous at the present stage," said the voice which knew no glories. "It is suggested that your employer pay the fee required to place this matter under temporary seal of secrecy. You may discuss that with Freelady Beldaniel upon leaving today, after which you are urged to contact Freeman van Rijn." It paused, for a billion nanoseconds; what new datum, suddenly noticed, was it weaving in? "For reasons that may not be given, you are most strongly advised to refrain from letting out the truth to anyone whatsoever before you have left Luna. At present, since you are here, it is suggested that the matter be explored further, verbally, in the hope that lines of association will open to more data that are relevant."

—Emerging, two hours later, in the office, Falkayn stopped before the woman's desk. "Whew!" he said, triumphant and weary.

She smiled back, with something akin to pleasure. "I trust you had a successful time?"

"And then some. Uh, I've got a thing or two to take up with you."

"Please sit down." Thea Beldaniel leaned forward. Her gaze grew very bright and level. "While you were in there, Captain Falkayn, I used another outlet to get from the bank what data it has about you. Only what is on public record, of course, and only in the hope of serving you better. It is quite astonishing what you have accomplished."

So it is, Falkayn agreed. "Thank you," he said.

"The computers do not do all the computing in this place." By heaven, she did have a little humor! "The idea occurred to me that you and we might cooperate in certain ways, to great mutual advantage. I wonder if we could talk about that too?"

IV

From Lunograd, the Hotel Universe challenges a galaxy: "No oxygen-breathing sophont exists for whom we cannot provide suitable accommodation. Unless every room is already occupied, we will furnish any such visitor with what is necessary for health, safety, and satisfaction. If equipment and supplies on hand are insufficient, we will obtain them upon reasonable advance notice and payment of a reasonable extra charge. If we fail to meet the terms of this guarantee, we will present the disappointed guest with the sum of one million credits of the Solar Commonwealth."

Many attempts are made to collect, by spacemen in collusion with the most outlandish beings they can find. Twice the cost of fulfilling the promise has exceeded the megacredit. (In one case, research and development were needed for the molecular synthesis of certain dietary materials; in the other case, the management had to fetch a symbiotic organism from the visitor's home planet.) But the publicity is well worth it. Human tourists especially will pay ten prices in order to stay here and feel cosmopolitan.

Chee Lan afforded no problems. The most advanced trade routes on her world—"trade route" comes nearer to translating the concept than does "nation"—have been in close contact with man since the first expedition to O_2 Eridani A II discovered them. Increasing numbers of Cynthians arrive at the Solar System as travelers, merchants, delegates, specialists, students. Some go on to roam space professionally. Chee was given a standardized suite.

"No, I am not comfortable," she had snapped when Falkayn called to ask if she was. "But I shouldn't have expected them to produce a decent environment for me, when they can't even get the name of my planet right."

"Well, true, you call it Lifehome-under-Sky," Falkayn answered blandly; "but over on the next continent they—"

"I know, I know! That's exactly the trouble. Those klongs forget Tah-chih-chien-pi is a complete world, with geography and seasons. They've booked me into the next continent, and it's bloody cold!"

"So ring up and bitch," Falkayn said. "You're good at that."

Chee sputtered but later followed his advice.

An Earthling would probably not have noticed the adjustments that were made. He would have continued to be aware simply of a gravity 0.8 standard; a reddish-orange illumination that varied through a fifty-five-hour diurnal-nocturnal period; hot wet air, full of musky odors; pots of giant flowers scattered about the floor, a vine-draped tree, a crisscrossing set of bars used not merely for exercise but for getting from place to place within the rooms. (The popular impression is wrong, that Cynthians are arboreal in the sense that monkeys are. But they have adapted and adjusted to the interwoven branches of their endless forests, and often prefer these to the ground.) The Earthling would have observed that the animated picture which gave the illusion of a window showed jungle, opening on a savanna where stood the delicate buildings of a caravanserai. He would have paid attention to the scattered books and the half-finished clay sculpture with which Chee had been amusing herself while she waited for Falkayn to carry out the business that brought the team here.

At this moment, he would have seen her turn from the phone, where the man's image had just faded, and squat in arch-backed tension.

Tai Tu, with whom she had also been amusing herself, tried to break the thickening silence. "I take it that was one of your partners?" He knew Espanish, not Anglic.

"Yes, do take it," Chee clipped. "Take it far away."

"I beg your gracious elucidation?"

"Get out," Chee said. "I've got thinking to do."

Tai Tu gasped and goggled at her.

The hypothetical observer from Earth would probably have called her cute, or actually beautiful; many of his species did. To Tai Tu, she was desirable, fascinating, and more than a little terrifying.

When erect, she stood some ninety centimeters tall, and her bushy tail curled upward a full half that length. Lustrous white angora fur covered her otherwise naked form. A long-legged biped, she nonetheless had five prehensile toes on either foot, and walked digitigrade. The arms, scarcely less long and muscular, ended in hands that each possessed five four-jointed, rosy-nailed fingers and a thumb. The round, pointed-eared head carried a short-muzzled face whose flat nose and dainty mouth were fringed with whiskers like a cat's. Above, the enormous emerald eyes were emphasized by a mask of the same blue-gray hue as feet, hands, and ears. Though hirsute, viviparous, and homeothermic, she was not a mammal. The young of her race eat flesh from birth, using their lips to suck out the blood.

Tai Tu was smaller and a less aggressive carnivore. During their evolution, male Cynthians were never required to carry the cubs through the trees and fight for them. He had been flattered when Chee Lan told him—a humble visiting professor at Lomonosov University, whereas she was a xenologist in the service of Nicholas van Rijn—to move in with her.

Still, he had his pride. "I cannot accept this treatment," he said.

Chee bared her fangs. They were white and very sharp. She jerked her tail at the door. "Out," she said. "And stay."

Tai Tu sighed, packed his belongings, and returned to his former quarters.

Chee sat for a while alone, scowling ever more blackly. At last she punched a number on the phone. There was no response. "Damnation, I know you're in!" she yelled. The screen remained blank. Presently she was hopping up and down with rage. "You and your stupid Buddhist meditations!" After a hundred or so rings, she snapped the switch and went out the airlock.

The corridors beyond were Earth-conditioned. She adjusted to the change without effort. Of necessity, members of the same space team have much the same biological requirements. The slideways were too slow for her. She bounded along them. En route, she bowled over His Excellency, the Ambassador of the Epopoian Empire. He cawed his indignation. She flung such a word back over her shoulder that His Excellency's beak hung open and he lay voiceless where he had fallen for three minutes by the clock.

Meanwhile Chee reached the entrance to Adzel's single room. She leaned on the doorchime button. It produced no results. He must really be out of this continuum. She punched dots and dashes, emergency code signals. SOS. *Help. Engine failure. Collision. Shipwreck. Mutiny. Radiation. Famine. Plague. War. Supernova.* That untranced him. He activated the valves and she cycled through the lock. The quick change of pressure made her eardrums hurt.

"Dear me," rumbled his mild basso profundo. "What language. I am afraid that you are further from attaining enlightenment than I had estimated."

Chee looked up toward Adzel's countenance, and up, and up. A weight of two and a half Terran gees, the hellish white blaze of a simulated F-type sun, the loudness of every sound in this dense, parched, thunder-smelling atmosphere, struck her and quelled her. She crawled under a table for shelter. The chamber's austerity was unrelieved by a film view of illimitable windy plains on that planet which men call Woden, or by the mandala that Adzel had hung from the ceiling or the scroll of Mahayana text he had posted on a wall.

"I trust your news is of sufficient importance to justify interrupting me at my exercises," he went on, as severely as possible for him.

Chee paused, subdued. "I don't know," she confessed. "But it concerns us."

Adzel composed himself to listen.

She studied him for a moment, trying to anticipate his response to what she had to say. No doubt he would feel she was overreacting. And maybe that was right. But she'd be flensed and gutted if she'd admit it to him!

He bulked above her. With the powerful tail, his centauroid body had a length of four and a half meters and mass exceeding a ton. A barndoor-broad torso, carrying a pair of arms and quadridigital hands in proportion, lifted the head more than two meters above the four cloven hoofs, at the end of a longish neck. That head was almost crocodilian, the snout bearing flared nostrils and an alarming array of teeth. The external ears were solid bony material, like the row of triangular dorsal plates which made a serration from the top of his pate to the end of his tail. Yet the skull bulged far backward to hold a considerable brain, and beneath overhanging brow ridges, his eyes were large and brown and rather wistful. Scutes armored his throat and belly, scales the rest of him. Yet they were a lovely, shimmering dark-green on top, shading to gold underneath. He was respected in his field of planetology, or had been before he quit academe to take sordid commercial employment. And in some ways, he was biologically closer to human than Chee. Besides being warm-blooded and omnivorous, he came of a species whose females give live birth and suckle their infants.

"Dave phoned me," Chee said. Feeling a bit more her usual self, she added with a snort, "He finally dragged himself away for a few hours from that hussy he's been wasting our time on."

"And went to Serendipity, Inc., as per plan? Excellent, excellent. I hope material of interest was revealed to him." Adzel's rubbery lips formed League Latin rather than the Anglic Chee was using, in order to stay in practice.

"He was certainly skyhooting excited about it," the Cynthian replied. "But he wouldn't mention details."

"I should think not, over an unsealed circuit." Adzel's tone grew disapproving. "In this town, I understand, every tenth being is somebody's spy."

"I mean he wouldn't come here either, or have us come to his hotel, and talk," Chee said. "The computer warned him against it, without giving a reason."

The Wodenite rubbed his jaw. "Now that is curious. Are not these quarters proof against snooping devices?"

"They ought to be, at the rates we pay. But maybe a new kind of bug has come along, and the machine's learned about it confidentially. You know SI's policy on that, don't you? Dave wants us to radio the home office for more money and buy a 'restricted' tag for whatever he was told today. He says once we're back on Earth, he can safely chatter."

"Why not beforehand? If he cannot leave Luna immediately, at least we could take a jaunt in our ship with him. That won't be gimmicked, not while Muddlehead is active."

"Listen, you glorified bulligator, I can see the obvious quicker than you, including the obvious fact that of course I'd suggest the ship. But he said no, not right away, at least. You see, one of the partners in SI invited him to spend a while at that castle of theirs."

"Strange. I had heard they never entertain guests."

"For once you heard right. But he said this anthro wants to discuss business with him, wouldn't tell him what but hinted at large profits. The chance looked too good to miss. Only, the invitation was for immediately. He'd just time to duck back to his place for a clean shirt and a toothbrush."

"Will Freeman van Rijn's affair wait?" Adzel asked.

"Presumably," Chee said. "At any rate, Dave wasn't sure the socializing mood of the partners would last if he stalled them. By every account, their souls consist of printed circuits. If nothing else comes of visiting them at home, he felt this was a unique chance for an inside view of their outfit."

"Indeed." Adzel nodded. "Indeed. David acted quite correctly, when the opportunity concerns an organization so powerful and enigmatic. I do not see what makes you feel any urgency. We two shall simply have to spend a few more days here."

Chee bristled. "I don't have your stone-brained calm. The computer put Dave onto something big. I mean astronomical—money by the planetful. I could tell that by his manner. Suppose his hosts aim to do him in, for the sake of getting at that thing themselves?"

"Now, now, my little friend," Adzel chided. "Serendipity, Inc., does not meddle in the business of its clients. It does not reveal their secrets. As a rule, the partners do not even know what those secrets are. They have no ties to other organizations. Not only repeated private investigations, but the experience of years has confirmed this. If ever they had violated their own announced ethic, ever shown special favor or prejudice, the repercussions would soon have laid the deed bare. No other member of the Polesotechnic League—no group throughout the whole of known space—has proven itself more trustworthy."

"Always a first time, sonny."

"Well, but think. If the strain is not excessive," Adzel said with rare tartness. "For the sake of argument, let us make the ridiculous assumption that Serendipity did in fact eavesdrop on David's conference with the computer, and has in fact decided to break its word never to seize private advantage.

"It remains bound by the covenant of the League, a covenant which was established and is enforced for good pragmatic reasons. Imprisonment, murder, torture, drugs, brainscrub, every kind of direct attack upon the psychobiological integrity of the individual, is banned. The consequences of transgression are atavistically severe. As the saying goes on Earth, the game is not worth the lantern. Hence the resources of espionage, temptation, and coercion are limited. David is immune to bribery and blackmail. He will reveal nothing to hypothetical surveillance, nor will he fall into conversational traps. If female bait is dangled before him, he will delightedly accept it without touching the fishhook. Has he not already—"

At that point, in a coincidence too outrageous for anything other than real life, the phone buzzed. Adzel pressed the Accept button. The image of Falkayn's latest girlfriend appeared. His partners recognized her; they had both met her, briefly, and were too experienced to believe the old cliche that all humans look alike.

"Good evenwatch, Freelady," Adzel said. "May I be of assistance?"

Her expression was unhappy, her tone unsteady. "I apologize for disturbing you," she said. "But I'm trying to get hold of Da—Captain Falkayn. He's not come back. Do you know—?"

"He isn't here either, I am sorry to say."

"He promised he'd meet me . . . before now . . . and he hasn't, and—" Veronica swallowed. "I'm worried."

"A rather urgent matter arose. He lacked time in which to contact you," Adzel lied gallantly. "I was asked to convey his sincere regrets."

Her smile was forlorn. "Was the urgent matter blond or brunette?"

"Neither, Freelady. I assure you it involves *his* profession. He may be gone for a few standard days. Shall I remind him to phone you upon his return?"

"I'd be so grateful if you would, sir." She twisted her fingers together. "Th-thank you."

Adzel blanked the screen. "I am reluctant to state this of a friend," he murmured, "but occasionally David impresses me as being rather heartless in certain respects."

"Huh!" Chee said. "That creature's only afraid he'll get away without spilling information to her."

"I doubt it. Oh, I grant you such a motive has been present, and probably continues in some degree. But her distress looks genuine, insofar as I can read human behavior. She appears to have conceived a personal affection for him." Adzel made a commiserating noise. "How much more conducive to serenity is a fixed rutting season like mine."

Chee had been calmed by the interruption. Also, her wish to get out of this lead-weighting bake oven that Adzel called home grew stronger each minute. "That is a good-looking specimen, by Dave's standards," she said. "No wonder he delayed getting down to work. And I don't suppose he'll be overly slow about returning to her, until he's ready to haul gravs off Luna altogether. Maybe we needn't really fret on his account."

"I trust not," Adzel said.

V

By flitter, the castle in the Alps was not many minutes from Lunograd. But those were terrible kilometers that lay between; mountaineering parties never ventured so far. And a wide reach of land and sky around the site was forbidden—patrolled by armed men, guarded by robot gun emplacements—with that baronial absoluteness the great may claim in a civilization which exalts the rights of privacy and property.

A nonhuman labor force had built it, imported for the purpose from a dozen remote planets and afterward returned, totally dispersed. For a while, local resentment combined with curiosity to yield fantastic rumors. Telescopic pictures were taken from orbit, and published, until half the Commonwealth knew about gaunt black towers, sheer walls, comings and goings of ships at a special spaceport, in the Lunar mountains.

But gossip faded with interest. Large estates were common enough among the lords of the Polesotechnic League—most of whom carried on in a far more colorful fashion than these recluses. Furtiveness and concealment were a frequent part of normal business practice. For years, now, Serendipity, Inc., had been taken for granted.

To be sure, Falkayn thought, *if the society news learns I've been chauffeured out here, actually gotten inside*—A sour grin tugged at his mouth. *Wouldn't it be cruel to tell the poor dears the truth?*

The scenery was spectacular, from this upper-level room where he stood. A wide viewport showed the downward sweep of rock, crags, cliffs, talus slopes, to a gash of blackness. Opposite that valley, and on either side of the castle plateau, peaks lifted raw into the constellations. Earth hung low in the south, nearly full, nearly blinding in its brilliance; interminable shadows surrounded the bluish spotlight that it cast.

But you could watch the same, or better, from a number of lodges: where there would be merriment, music, decoration, decent food and decent talk. The meal he had just finished, shortly after his arrival, had been as grimly functional as what he saw of the many big chambers. Conversation, with the four partners who were present, had consisted of banalities punctuated by silences. He excused himself as soon as he could. That was obviously sooner than they wished, but he knew the glib phrases and they didn't.

Only in the office had he been offered a cigar. He decided that was because the gesture was programmed into the kind of lounger they had bought. He reached inside his tunic for pipe and tobacco. Kim Yoon-Kun, a small neat expressionless man in a pajama suit that managed to resemble a uniform, had followed him. "We don't mind if you smoke at the table, Captain Falkayn," he said, "though none of us practice the . . . amusement."

"Ah, but I mind," Falkayn answered. "I was strictly raised to believe that pipes are not allowed in dining areas. At the same time, I crave a puff. Please bear with me."

"Of course," said the accented voice. "You are our guest. Our sole regret is that Freeman Latimer and Freelady Beldaniel cannot be present."

Odd, Falkayn thought, not for the first time. *Hugh Latimer leaves his wife here, and goes off with Thea's sister.* Mentally, he shrugged. Their pairing arrangements were their own affair. If they had any. By every account, Latimer was as dry a stick as Kim, despite being an accomplished space pilot. The wife, like Anastasia Herrera and no doubt the sister of Thea, succeeded in being more old-maidish than the latter. Their attempt to make small talk with the visitor would have been pathetic had it been less dogged.

What matters, Falkayn thought, *is getting out of here, back to town and some honest fun. E.g., with Veronica.*

"This is not an ideal room for you, though," Kim said with a starched smile. "You observe how sparsely furnished it is. We are six people and a few nonhuman servants. We built this place large with a view to eventual expansion, bringing in more associates, perhaps spouses and children in time, if that proves feasible. But as yet we, ah, rattle around. I believe you and we should converse in a more amenable place. The others are already going there. We can serve coffee and brandy if you wish. May I conduct you?"

"Thanks," Falkayn said. The doubtless rehearsed speech did not quench his hope of soon being able to leave what had proven to be a citadel of boredom. "We can start talking business?"

"Why—" Startled, Kim searched for words. "It was not planned for this evenwatch. Is not the custom that social activity precede . . . that one get acquainted? We assume you will stay with us for several days, at least. Some interesting local excursions are possible from here, for example. And we will enjoy hearing you relate your adventures in distant parts of space."

"You're very kind," Falkayn said, "but I'm afraid I haven't time."

"Did you not tell the younger Freelady Beldaniel—"

"I was mistaken. I checked with my partners, and they told me my boss has started to sweat rivets. Why don't you sketch out your proposition right away, to help me decide how long he might let me stay in connection with it?"

"Proper discussion requires material we do not keep in our dwelling." Impatience, a touch of outright nervousness, cracked slightly the mask that was Kim Yoon-Kun. "But come, we can lay your suggestion before the others."

The knowledge hit Falkayn: *He's almighty anxious to get me out of this particular room, isn't he?* "Do you mean we'll discuss the commencement of discussions?" he hedged. "That's a funny one. I didn't ask for documentation. Can't you simply explain in a general way what you're after?"

"Follow me." Kim's tone jittered. "We have problems of security, the preservation of confidences, that must be dealt with in advance."

Falkayn began enjoying himself. He was ordinarily a genial, obliging young man; but those who push a merchant adventurer, son of a military aristocrat, must expect to be pushed back, hard. He donned hauteur. "If you do not trust me, sir, your invitation was a mistake," he said. "I don't wish to squander your valuable time with negotiations foredoomed to fruitlessness."

"Nothing of the sort." Kim took Falkayn's arm. "Come along, if you please, and all shall be made clear."

Falkayn stayed put. He was stronger and heavier; and the gravity field was set at about Earth standard, the usual practice in residences on dwarf worlds where muscles would otherwise atrophy. His resistance to the tug did not show through his tunic. "In a while, Freeman," he said. "Not at once, I beg of your indulgence. I came here to meditate."

Kim let go and stepped back. The black eyes grew still narrower. "Your dossier does not indicate any religious affiliation," he said slowly.

"Dossier?" Falkayn raised his brows with ostentation.

"The integrated file of material our computer has about you—nothing except what is on public record," Kim said in haste. "Only in order that our company may serve you better."

"I see. Well, you're right, except that one of my shipmates is a Buddhist—converted years ago, while studying on Earth—and he's gotten me interested. Besides," Falkayn said, warming up, "it's quite a semantic quibble whether the purer sects of Buddhism are religions, in the ordinary sense. Certainly they are agnostic with respect to gods or other hypothetical animistic elements in the reality-complex; their doctrine of karma does not require reincarnation as that term is generally used; and in fact, nirvana is not annihilation, but rather is a state that may be achieved in this life and consists of—"

And then it was too late for Kim.

The spaceship slanted across the view, a lean cylinder that glowed under Earthlight and shimmered within the driving grav-fields. She swung into vertical ascent and dwindled from sight until lost in the cold of the Milky Way.

"Well," Falkayn murmured. "Well, well."

He glanced at Kim. "I suppose Latimer and Beldaniel are crewing her?" he said.

"A routine trip," Kim answered, fists knotted at sides.

"Frankly, sir, I doubt that." Falkayn remembered the pipe he held and began to stuff it. "I know hyperdrive craft when I see them. They are not used for interplanetary shuttling; why tie up that much capital when a cheaper vessel will do? For the same reason, common carriers are employed interstellar wherever practical. And full partners in a big company don't make long voyages as a matter of routine. Clear to see, this job is on the urgent side."

And you didn't want me to know, he added unspoken. His muscles grew taut. *Why not?*

Wrath glittered at him. He measured out a chuckle. "You needn't have worried about me, if you did," he said. "I wouldn't pry into your secrets."

Kim eased a trifle. "Their mission is important, but irrelevant to our business with you," he said.

Is it? Falkayn thought. *Why didn't you tell me at the beginning, then, instead of letting me grow suspicious?—I believe I know why. You're so isolated from the human mainstream, so untrained in the nuances of how people think and act, that you doubted your own ability to convince me this takeoff is harmless as far as I'm concerned . . . when it probably isn't!*

Again Kim attempted a smile. "But pardon me, Captain Falkayn. We have no desire to intrude upon your religious practices. Please remain, undisturbed, as long as you wish. When you desire company, you may employ the intercom yonder, and one of us will come to guide you to the other room." He bowed. "May you have a pleasant spiritual experience."

Touché! Falkayn thought, staring after the man's back. *Since the damage has been done, he turns my yarn right around on me—his aim being to keep me here for some time, and my navel-watching act presenting him with an extra hour—but what's the purpose of it all?*

He lit his pipe and made volcano clouds, strode to and fro, looked blindly out the viewport, flung himself into chairs and bounced up again. Was he nursing an empty, automatic distrust of the merely alien, or did he feel a real wrongness in his bones?

The idea was not new with him, that information given the computers at Serendipity did not remain there. The partners had never let those circuits be traced by an independent investigator. They could easily have installed means for playing back an item or listening in on a conversation. They could instruct a machine to slant its advice as they desired. And—cosmos—once faith in them had developed, once the masters of the League started making full use of their service, what a spy they had! What a saboteur!

Nevertheless the fact stood: not one of those wary, wily enterprisers had ever found the least grounds for believing that Serendipity was in unfair collaboration with any of his rivals, or attempting to sneak in on anyone's operations, not even to the extent of basing investments on advance knowledge.

Could be they've decided to change their policy. That planet of mine could tempt the most virtuous into claim-jumping. . . . But sunder it, that doesn't feel right either. Six personalities as rigid as these don't switch from information broker to pirate on an hour's notice. They don't.

Falkayn checked his watch. Thirty minutes had passed, sufficient time for his pretense. (Which probably wasn't believed anyway.) He strode to the intercom, found it set for its station number 14, flipped the switch and said, "I'm done now."

Scarcely had he turned when Thea Beldaniel was in the doorway. "That was quick!" he exclaimed.

"I happened to be near. The message was relayed to me."

Or were you waiting this whole while?

She approached, halting when they both reached the viewport. Her walk was more graceful, in a high-necked long-sleeved gown, and her smile more convincingly warm than before. A gawkiness remained, and she poised stiffly after she had entered his arm's length. But he felt himself attracted for some odd reason. Maybe she was a challenge, or maybe she was just a well-formed animal.

He knocked out his pipe. "I hope I didn't give offense," he said.

"Not in the least. I quite sympathize. The outlook inspires you, does it not?" She gestured at a control panel. Lights dimmed; the eldritch moonscape stood forth before their vision.

No pressure on me now, Falkayn thought cynically. *Contrariwise. The longer I dawdle before reporting to Old Nick, the happier they'll be. Well, no objections from my side for the nonce. This has suddenly gotten interesting. I have a lot of discreet curiosity to satisfy.*

"Glory out there," she whispered.

He regarded her. Earthlight lifted her profile from shadow and poured softly downward. Stars glimmered in her eyes. She looked into their wintry myriads with a kind of hunger.

He blurted, caught by an abrupt compassion that surprised him, "You feel at home in space, don't you?"

"I can't be sure." Still she gazed skyward. "Not here, I confess. Never here. You must forgive us if we are poor company. It comes from shyness, ignorance . . . fear, I suppose. We live alone and work with data—abstract symbols—because we are fit to do nothing else."

Falkayn didn't know why she should reveal herself to him. But wine had been served at dinner. The etiquette book could have told them this was expected, and the drink could have gone to her inexperienced head.

"I'd say you've done fine, beginning as complete strangers," he told her. "You did, am I right? Strangers to your whole species?"

"Yes." She sighed. "You may as well know. We declined to state our background originally because, oh, we couldn't foresee what the reaction might be. Later, when we were more familiar with this culture, we had no reason to tell; people had stopped asking, and we were set in our asocial ways. Besides, we didn't want personal publicity. Nor do we now." She glanced at him. In this blue elflight, the crisp middle-aged businesswoman had become a young girl again, who asked for his mercy. "You won't speak . . . to the news . . . will you?"

"On my honor," he said, and meant it.

"The story is simple, really," said her muted voice. "A ship, bound from one of the colonized planets in search of her own world. I understand those aboard left because of a political dispute; and yet I don't understand. The whole thing seems utterly meaningless. Why should rational beings quarrel about—no matter. Families sold everything they had, pooled the money, bought and outfitted a large ship with the most complete and modern robotic gear available. And they departed."

"Into the complete unknown?" Falkayn asked, incredulous. "Not one preliminary scouting expedition?"

"The planets are many where men can live. They were sure they would find one. They wanted to leave no hint to their enemies where it was."

"But—I mean, they must have known how tricky a new world can be—tricks of biochemistry, disease, weather, a million unpredictable tricks and half of them lethal if you aren't on your guard—"

"I said this was a large, fully stocked, fully equipped vessel," she retorted. The sharpness left her as she went on. "They were prepared to wait in orbit while tests proceeded. That was well for us. You see, en route the radiation screens broke down in a bad sector. Apart from the nursery, where we infants were, which had an auxiliary generator, every part of the ship got a fatal dose. The people might have been saved in a hospital, but they could never reach one in time, especially since the autopilot systems were damaged too. Supportive treatment kept them functional barely long enough to fix the screens and program some robots. Then they died. The machines cared for us children; raised us, in a loveless mechanical fashion. They educated those who survived—willy-nilly, a hodgepodge of mainly technical information crammed into our brains. We didn't mind that too much, however. The ship was such a barren environment that any distractions were welcome. We had nothing else except each other.

"Our ages ranged from twelve to seventeen when we were found. The vessel had kept going under low hyperdrive, in the hope she would finally pass within detection range of somebody. The somebodies proved to be nonhuman. But they were kindly, did what they were able for us. They were too late, of course, for the shaping of normal personalities. We stayed with our rescuers, on their planet, for several years.

"Never mind where," she added quickly. "They know about the League—there have been occasional brief encounters—but their leaders don't want an ancient civilization corrupted by exposure to your cannibal capitalism. They mind their own lives and avoid drawing attention to themselves.

"But the physical environment was not good for us. Besides, the feeling grew that we should attempt to rejoin our race. What they learned from our ship had advanced our hosts technologically in several fields. As a fair exchange—they have an unbendable moral code—they helped us get a start, first with a valuable cargo of metal and later with the computer units we decided we could use. Also, they are glad to have friends who are influential in the League; sooner or later, increased contact is unavoidable. And that," Thea Beldaniel finished, "is the story behind Serendipity, Inc."

Her smile went no deeper than her teeth. Her voice held a tinge of the fanaticism he had met in her office.

Only a tinge? But what she'd been relating here was not operational procedure; it was her life!

Or was it? Parts of the account rang false to him. At a minimum, he'd want more details before he agreed it could be the absolute truth. No doubt some fact was interwoven. But how much, and how significant to his purposes?

"Unique," was all he could think to say.

"I don't ask for pity," she said with a firmness he admired. "Obviously, our existence could have been far worse. I wondered, though, if—perhaps"—voice and eyes dropped, fluttered in confusion—"you, who've seen so much, done so much beyond these bounds—if you might understand."

"I'd like to try," Falkayn said gently.

"Would you? Can you? I mean . . . suppose you stayed a while . . . and we could talk like this, and do, oh, the little things—the big things—whatever is human—you might be able to teach me how to be human. . . ."

"Is that what you wanted me for? I'm afraid I—"

"No. No. I realize you . . . you must put your work first. I think—

taking what we know, we partners—exchange ideas with you—we might develop something really attractive. No harm in exploring each other's notions for a while, is there? What can you lose? And at the same time—you and I—" She half turned. One hand brushed against his.

For an instant, Falkayn almost said yes. Among the greatest temptations that beset mankind is Pygmalion's. Potentially, she was quite a woman. The rogue could wait.

The rogue! Awareness crashed into him. *They do want to keep me here. It's their whole purpose. They have no definite proposals to make, only vague things they hope will delay me. I must not let them.*

Thea Beldaniel flinched back. "What's wrong?" she cried low. "Are you angry?"

"Eh?" Falkayn gathered his will, laughed and relaxed, picked his pipe off the viewport embrasure and took forth his tobacco pouch. The briar hadn't cooled, but he needed something to do. "No. Certainly not, Freelady. Unless I'm angry at circumstance. You see, I'd like to stay, but I have no choice. I have got to go back tomorrow mornwatch, kicking and screaming maybe, but back."

"You said you could spend several days."

"As I told Freeman Kim, that was before I learned old van Rijn's gnawing his whiskers."

"Have you considered taking a position elsewhere? Serendipity can make you a good offer."

"He has my contract and my fealty," Falkayn rapped. "I'm sorry. I'll be glad to confer with you people this whole night-watch, if you desire. But then I'm off." He shrugged, though his skin prickled. "And what's your rush? I can return at another date, when I do have leisure."

Her look was desolate. "You cannot be persuaded?"

"I'm afraid not."

"Well . . . follow me to the meeting room, please." She thumbed the intercom and spoke a few words he did not recognize. They went down a high, stone-flagged corridor. Her feet dragged, her head drooped.

Kim met them halfway. He stepped from an intersecting hall with a stun pistol in his grip. "Raise your hands, Captain," he said unemotionally. "You are not leaving soon."

VI

After touching at Djakarta, Delfinburg proceeded by way of Makassar Strait and the Celebes into Pacific waters. At that point, an aircar deposited Nicholas van Rijn. He did not own the town; to be precise, his rights in it consisted of one house, one dock for a largish ketch, and seventy-three percent of the industry. But mayor and skipper agreed with his suggestion that they change course and pass nearer the Marianas than was usual on their circuit.

"Be good for the poor toilers, visiting those nice islands, *nie?*" he beamed, rubbing hairy hands together. "Could be they might also like a little holiday and come cheer their old honorific uncle when he enters the Micronesia Cup regatta on twenty-fourth of this month. That is, I will if we chance to be by the right place no later than twenty-second noon, and need to lay over a few days. I don't want to be you any bother."

The skipper made a quick calculation. "Yes, sir," he reported, "it so happens we'll arrive on the twenty-first." He signaled for an additional three knots. "And you know, you're right, it would be a good idea to stop a while and clean out the catalyst tanks or something."

"Good, good! You make a poor old lonely man very happy, how much he is in need of rest and recreation and maybe right now a gin and tonic to settle his stomach. A lot of settlement to make, hey?" Van Rijn slapped his paunch.

He spent the next week drilling his crew to a degree that would have appalled Captain Bligh. The men didn't really mind—sails dazzling against living, limitless, foam-laced blue across which the sun flung diamond dust; surge, pitch, thrum, hiss at the bows and salt on the lips, while the wind filled lungs with purity—except that he acted hurt when they declined to carouse with him every night. At length he gave them a rest. He wanted them tuned to an exact pitch for the race, not overstrained. Besides, a business operating across two hundred light-years had inevitably accumulated problems requiring his personal attention. He groaned, cursed, and belched most piteously, but the work did not go away.

"Bah! Pox and pestilence! Work! Four-letter Angular-Saxon

word! Why must I, who should be having my otium, should at my age be serene and spewing wisdom on younger generations, why must I use up grindstones against my nose? Have I not got a single deputy whose brain is not all thumbs?"

"You could sell out, for more money than you can spend in ten lifetimes," answered his chief secretary, who was of a warrior caste in a tigerish species and thus required to be without fear. "Or you would finish your tasks in half the time if you stopped whining."

"I let my company, that I built from scratches and got maybe millions of what claim to be thinking beings hanging off it, I let that go crunch? Or I sit meek like my mouth won't smelt butter, and not say pip about vacuum-conscience competitors, subordinates with reverse peristalsis, guilds, brotherhoods, unions, leeches, and"—van Rijn gathered his breath before shouting the ultimate obscenity—"*bureaucrats*? No, no, old and tired and feeble and lonesome I am, but I wield my sword to the last bullet. We get busy, ha?"

An office had been established for him in an upper-level solarium of his mansion. Beyond the ranked phones, computers, recorders, data retrievers, and other portable business equipment, the view was broad, from one many-tiered unit to the next, of that flotilla which comprised Delfinburg. There was not much overt sign of production. You might notice turbulence around the valves of a minerals-extraction plant, or the shadow traces of submarines herding fish, or the appetizing scents from a factory that turned seaweeds into condiments. But most of the work was interior, camouflaged by hanging gardens, shops, parks, schools, recreation centers. Few sportboats were out; the ocean was choppy today, although you could not have told that blindfolded on these stabilized superbarges.

Van Rijn settled his huge body into a lounger. He was clad only in a sarong and a lei; why not be comfortable while he suffered? "Commence!" he bawled. The machines chattered, regurgitating facts, calculations, assessments, summaries, and proposals. The principal phone screen flickered with the first call, from a haggard man who had newly escaped a war ten parsecs distant. Meanwhile a set of loudspeakers emitted Mozart's Eighth Symphony; a scarcely clothed young woman fetched beer; another lit the master's Trichinopoly cigar; a third set forth a trayful of fresh Danish sandwiches in case he got hungry. She came incautiously near, and he swept her to him with one gorilla arm. She giggled and ran her fingers through the greasy black ringlets that fell to his shoulders.

"What you making fumblydiddles about?" van Rijn barked at the image. "Some piglet of a king burns our plantations, we give troops to his enemies what beat him and make terms allowing us poor sat-upon exploited meeters of inflated payrolls enough tiny profit we can live. *Nie?*" The man objected. Van Rijn's beady eyes popped. He tugged his goatee. His waxed mustaches quivered like horns. "What you mean, no local troops can face his? What you been doing these years, selling them maybe jackstraws for deadly weapons?—Hokay, hokay, I authorize you should bring in a division outplanet mercenaries. Try Diomedes. Grand Admiral Delp hyr Orikan, in Drak'ho Fleet, will remember me and maybe spare a few restless young chaps what like adventure and booties. In six months, I hear everything is loverly-doverly, or you go find yourself a job scrubbing somebody else's latrines. *Tot weerziens!*" He waved his hand, and an assistant secretary switched to the next caller. Meanwhile he buried his great hook nose in his tankard, came up snorting and blowing foam, and held out the vessel for another liter.

A nonhuman head appeared in the screen. Van Rijn replied by the same eerie set of whistles and quavers. Afterward, his sloping forehead corrugated with thought, he rumbled, "I hate like taxes admitting it, but that factor is almost competent, him. He settles his present trouble, I think we can knock him up to sector chief, ha?"

"I couldn't follow the discussion," said his chief secretary. "How many languages do you speak, sir?"

"Twenty-thirty bad. Ten-fifteen good. Anglic best of all." Van Rijn dismissed the girl who had been playing with his hair; though friendly meant, his slap to the obvious target as she started off produced a bombshell crack and a wail. "Hu, hu, little chickpea, I am sorry. You go buy that shimmerlyn gown you been wheedling at me about, and maybe tonight we trot out and show you off—you show plenty, shameless way such things is cut, oh, what those bandits charge for a few square centimeters cloth!" She squealed and scampered away before he changed his mind. He glowered at the other members of his current harem. "Don't you waggle at me too. You wait your turns to bleed a poor foolish old man out of what he's got left between him and beggary. . . . Well, who's next?"

The secretary had crossed the deck to study the phone in person. He turned about. "The agenda's been modified, sir. Direct call, Priority Two."

"Hum. Hum-hum." Van Rijn scratched the pelt that carpeted his chest, set down his beer, reached for a sandwich and engulfed it. "Who we got in these parts now, authoritied for using Priority Two?" He swallowed, choked, and cleared his throat with another half-liter draught. But thereafter he sat quite still, cigar to lips, squinting through the smoke, and said with no fuss whatsoever, "Put them on."

The screen flickered. Transmission was less than perfect, when a scrambled beam must leave a moving spaceship, punch through the atmosphere, and stay locked on the solitary station that could unscramble and relay. Van Rijn identified the control cabin of his pioneer vessel *Muddlin' Through,* Chee Lan in the foreground and Adzel behind her. "You got problems?" he greeted mildly.

The pause was slight but noticeable, while electromagnetic radiation traversed the distance between. "I believe we do," Adzel said. Interference hissed around his words. "And we cannot initiate corrective measures. I would give much for those machines and flunkies that surround you to have allowed us a direct contact before today."

"I'll talk," Chee said. "You'd blither for an hour." To van Rijn: "Sir, you'll remember we told you, when reporting on Earth, that we'd proceed to Lunograd and look in on Serendipity, Inc." She described Falkayn's visit there and subsequently to the castle. "That was two weeks ago. He hasn't come back yet. One call arrived after three standard days. Not a real talk—a message sent while he knew we'd be asleep. We kept the record, of course. He said not to worry; he was on to what might be the most promising lead of his career, and he might be quite some time following it up. We needn't stay on Luna, he could take a shuttle-boat to Earth." Her fur stood out, a wild aureole around her countenance. "It wasn't his style. We had voice and somatic analysis done at a detective agency, using several animations of him from different sources. It's him, beyond reasonable doubt. But it's *not* his style."

"Playback," van Rijn ordered. "Now. Before you go on." He watched unblinkingly, as the blond young man spoke his piece and signed off. "By damn, you have right, Chee Lan. He should at least grin and ask you give his love to three or four girls."

"We've been pestered by one, for certain," the Cynthian declared. "A spy set on him, who found she couldn't cope with his technique or whatever the deuce he's got. Last call, she actually admitted she'd been on a job, and blubbered she was sorry and she'd never, never, never—you can reconstruct the sequence."

"Play her anyhow." Veronica wept. "*Ja,* a bouncy wench there. Maybe I interview her personal, ho-ho! Somebody got to. Such a chance to get a look inside whoever hired her!" Van Rijn sobered. "What happened next?"

"We fretted," Chee said. "At last even this big lard statue of a saint here decided that enough was too furious much. We marched into the SI office itself and said if we didn't get a more satisfactory explanation, from Dave himself, we'd start disassembling their computers. With a pipe wrench. They quacked about the covenant, not to mention the civil police, but in the end they promised he'd phone us." Grimly: "He did. Here's the record."

The conversation was long. Chee yelled, Adzel expostulated, Falkayn stayed deadpan and unshakable. "—I am sorry. You may never guess how sorry I am, old friends. But nobody gets a choice about how the lightning's going to strike him. Thea's my woman, and there's an end on the matter.

"We'll probably go aroving after we get married. I'll be working for SI. But only in a technical sense. Because what we're really after, what's keeping me here, is something bigger, more fundamental to the whole future, than—no. I can't say more. Not yet. But think about making liaison with a genuinely superior race. The race that's been dreamed about for centuries, and never found—the Elders, the Wise Ones, the evolutionary step beyond us—

"—Yes!" A flicker of irritation. "Naturally SI will refund Solar S & L's wretched payments. Maybe SI should double the sum. Because a fact that I supplied was what started our whole chain of discovery. Though what possible reward could match the service?

"—Good-bye. Good faring."

Silence dwelt, under the wash of sea waves and whisper of stars. Until van Rijn shook himself, animal fashion, and said, "You took into space and called me today when I got available."

"What else could we do?" Adzel groaned. "David may be under psychocontrol. We suspect it, Chee and I. But we have no proof. For anyone who does not know him personally, the weight of credibility is overwhelming on the opposite side, so great that I myself can reach no firm conclusion about what has really happened. More is involved than Serendipity's established reputation. There is the entire covenant. Members of the League do not kidnap and drug each other's agents. Not ever!"

"We did ask the Lunar police about a warrant," Chee said. She jerked her tail at the Wodenite. "Tin Pan Buddha insisted. We were laughed at. Literally. We can't propose a League action—strike first, argue with the law afterward—not us. We aren't on the Council. You are."

"I can propose it," van Rijn said carefully. "After a month's wringle-wrangle, I get voted no. They won't believe either, SI would do something so bad like that, for some sternly commercial reason."

"I doubt if we have a month, regardless," Chee said. "Think. Suppose Dave has been brainscrubbed. They'll've done it to keep him from reporting to you what he learned from their damned machine. They'll pump him for information and advice too. Might as well. But he is evidence against them. Any medic can identify his condition and cure it. So as soon as possible—or as soon as necessary—they'll get rid of the evidence. Maybe send him off in a spaceship, with his new fiançée to control him. Maybe kill him and disintegrate the body. I don't see where Adzel and I had any alternative except to investigate as we did. Nevertheless, our investigations will probably cause SI to speed up whatever timetable it's laid out for Captain Falkayn."

Van Rijn smoked through an entire minute. Then: "Your ship is loaded for bear, also elephant and walrus. You could maybe blast in, you two, and snatch him?"

"Maybe," Adzel said. "The defenses are unknown. It would be an act of piracy."

"Unless he was a prisoner. In what case, we can curry ruffled fur afterward. I bet curried fur tastes terrible. But you turn into heroes."

"What if he is there voluntarily?"

"You turn into pumpkins."

"If we strike, we risk his life," said Adzel. "Quite possibly, if he is not a prisoner, we take several innocent lives. We are less concerned with our legal status than with our shipmate. But however deep our affection for him, he is of another civilization, another species, yes, a wholly different evolution. We cannot tell whether he was in a normal state when he called us. He acted peculiarly, true. But might that have been due to the emotion known as love? Coupled, perhaps, with a sense of guilt at breaking his contract? You are human, we are not. We appeal to your judgment."

"And mix me—old, tired, bothered, sorrowful me, that wants nothing except peace and a little, little profit—you mix me right in with the glue," van Rijn protested.

Adzel regarded him steadily. "Yes, sir. If you authorize us to attack, you commit yourself and everything you own, for the sake of one man who may not even need help. We realize that."

Van Rijn drew on his cigar till the end glowed volcanic. He pitched it aside. "Hokay," he growled. "Is a flousy boss does not stand by his people. We plan a raid, us, ha?" He tossed off his remaining beer and threw the tankard to the deck. "God damn," he bellowed, "I wish I was going along!"

VII

Adzel paused at the airlock. "You will be careful, won't you?" he asked.

Chee bristled. "You're the one to worry about, running around without a keeper. Watch yourself, you oversized clatterbrain." She blinked. "Rats and roaches! Something in my eyes. Get started—out of my way."

Adzel closed his faceplate. Encased in space armor, he could just fit inside the lock. He must wait until he had cycled through before securing his equipment on his back. It included a small, swivel-mounted automatic cannon.

Muddlin' Through glided from him, low above soaring, jagged desolation. Mottled paint made her hard to see against that patchwork of blinding noon and ink-black shadow. When past the horizon, she climbed.

Adzel stayed patiently put until the seething in his radio earplugs was broken by the Cynthian's voice: "Hello, do you read me?"

"Like a primer," he said. Echoes filled his helmet. He was aware of the mass he carried, protective but heavy; of the smells, machine and organic, already accumulating; of temperature that began to mount and prickle him under the scales.

"Good. This beam's locked onto you, then. I'm stabilized in position, about a hundred and fifty kilometers up. No radar has fingered me yet. Maybe none will. All check, sir?"

"*Ja.*" Van Rijn's words, relayed from a hired maser in Lunograd, sounded less distinct. "I have talked with the police chief here and he is not suspecting. I got my boys set to start a fracas that will make distractions. I got a judge ready to hand out injunctions if I tell him. But he is not a very high judge, even if he is expensive like Beluga caviar, so he can't make long stalls either. Let the Lunar federal police mix in this affair and we got troubles. Ed Garver would sell the soul he hasn't got to jail us. You better be quick like kissing a viper. Now I go aboard my own boat, my friends, and light candles for you in the shrine there, to St. Dismas, and St. Nicholas, and especial to St. George, by damn."

Adzel couldn't help remarking, "In my studies of Terrestrial culture, I have encountered mention of that latter personage. But did not the Church itself, as far back as the twentieth century, decide he was mythical?"

"Bah," said van Rijn loftily. "They got no faith. I need a good fighting saint, who says God can't improve the past and make me one?"

Then there was no time, or breath, or thought for anything except speed.

Adzel could have gone quicker and easier on a gravsled or some such vehicle. But the radiations would have given him away. Afoot, he could come much nearer before detection was certain. He bounded up the Alpine slopes, over razorback ridges, down into ravines and out their other sides, around crater walls and crags. His heart slugged, his lungs strained, in deep steady rhythm. He used the forward tendency of his mass—great inertia at low weight—and the natural pendulum-periods of his legs, to drive himself. Sometimes he overleaped obstacles, soaring in an arc and landing with an impact that beat through his bones. He kept to the shade wherever possible. But pitilessly, at each exposure to sunlight, heat mounted within his camouflaged armor faster than his minimal cooling system could shed it. Glare filters did not entirely protect his eyes from the raw sun-dazzle. No human could have done what he did—hardly anyone, indeed, of any race, except the children of a fiercer star than Sol and a vaster planet than Earth.

Twice he crouched where he could and let a patrol boat slip overhead. After an hour, he wormed his way from shadow to shadow, evading a watchpost whose radar and guns stood skeletal against the sky. And he won to the final peak unheralded.

The castle loomed at the end of an upward road, black witch-hatted towers above battlemented walls. With no further chance of concealment, Adzel started openly along the path. For a moment, the spatial silence pressed in so huge that it well-nigh smothered pulse, breath, airpump, foot-thuds. Then: "Who goes there? Halt!" on the standard band.

"A visitor," Adzel replied without slacking his even trot. "I have an urgent matter to discuss and earnestly request admittance."

"Who are you? How did you get here?" The voice was female human, accented, and shrill with agitation. "Stop, I tell you! This is private property. No trespassing."

"I humbly beg pardon, but I really must insist on being received."

"Go back. You will find a gatehouse at the foot of the road. You may shelter there and tell me what you have to say."

"Thank you for your kind offer." Adzel kept advancing. "Freelady . . . ah . . . Beldaniel, I believe? It is my understanding that your partners are presently at their office. Please correct me if I am wrong."

"I said go back!" she screamed. "Or I open fire! I have the right. You have been warned."

"Actually, my business is with Captain Falkayn." Adzel proceeded. He was quite near the main portal. Its outer valve bulked broad in the fused-stone wall. "If you will be good enough to inform him that I wish to talk to him, viva voce, we can certainly hold our discussion outdoors. Permit me to introduce myself. I am one of his teammates. My claim upon his attention therefore takes precedence over the seclusion of your home. But I have no real wish to intrude, Freelady."

"You're not his companion. Not any more. He resigned. He spoke to you himself. He does not want to see you."

"With profoundest regret and sincerest apologies for any

inconvenience caused, I am compelled to require a direct confrontation."

"He . . . he isn't here. I will have him call you later."

"Since you may conceivably be in error as to his whereabouts, Freelady, perhaps you will graciously allow me to search your premises?"

"No! This is your last warning! Stop this instant or you'll be killed!"

Adzel obeyed; but within the armor, his muscles bunched. His left hand worked the cannon control. In his palm lay a tiny telescreen whose cross hairs centered on the same view as the muzzle. His right hand loosened his blast pistol in its holster.

"Freelady," he said, "violence and coercion are deplorable. Do you realize how much merit you have lost? I beg of you—"

"Go back!" Half hysterical, the voice broke across. "I'll give you ten seconds to turn around and start downhill. One. Two."

"I was afraid of this." Adzel sighed. And he sprang—but forward. His cannon flung three shaped charges at the main gate. Fire spurted, smoke puffed, shrapnel flew, eerily soundless except for a quiver through the ground.

Two energy beams flashed at him, out of the turrets that flanked the entry port. He had already bounded aside. His cannon hammered. One emplacement went down in a landslide of rubble. Smoke and dust whirled, veiling him from the other. By the time it had settled, he was up to the wall, beneath the gun's reach.

The outer valve sagged, twisted metal. "I'm headed in," he said to Chee Lan, and fired through the chamber. A single shell tore loose the second, less massive barrier. Air gushed forth, momentarily white as moisture froze, vanishing as fog dissipated under the cruel sun.

Inside, an illumination now undiffused fell in puddles on a disarrayed antechamber. Through its shadows, he noticed a few pictures and a brutally massive statue. The artistic conventions were foreign to anything he had encountered in all his wanderings. He paid scant attention. Which way to David, in this damned warren? Like a great steel hound, he cast about for clues. Two hallways led off in opposite directions. But one held empty rooms; the chambers fronting on the other were furnished, albeit sparsely. *Hm, the builders plan on enlarging the castle's population sometime. But with whom, or what?* He galloped down the inhabited corridor. Before long he encountered a bulkhead that had automatically closed when pressure dropped.

Beldaniel's retainers were probably on the other side of it, spacesuited, expecting to give him a full barrage when he cracked through. She herself was no doubt on the phone, informing her partners in Lunograd of the invasion. With luck and management, van Rijn could tie up the police for a while. They must be kept off, because they were bound to act against the aggressor, Adzel. No matter what allegations he made, they would not ransack the castle until warrants had been issued. By that time, if it ever came, the Serendipity gang could have covered their tracks as regarded Falkayn in any of numerous ways.

But Beldaniel herself might attempt that, if Adzel didn't get busy. The Wodenite retreated to the foreroom and unlimbered his working gear. No doubt another chamber, belonging to the adjacent airseal section, lay behind this one. Though gas-tight, the interior construction was nowhere near as ponderous as the outworks. What he must do was enter unnoticed. He spread out a plastic bubblecloth, stood on it, and stuck its edges to the wall. His cutting torch flared. He soon made a hole, and waited until air had leaked through and inflated to full pressure the tent that now enclosed him. Finishing the incision, he removed the panel he had burned out and stepped into an apartment.

It was furnished with depressing austerity. He took a moment to pull the door off a closet—yes, female garb—and inspect a bookshelf. Many volumes were in a format and symbology he did not recognize; others, in Anglic, were texts describing human institutions for the benefit of visiting extraterrestrials. Boddhisattva! What sort of background did this outfit have, anyway?

He opened his faceplate, removed an earplug, and cautiously stuck his muzzle out into the hall. Clanks and rattles came to him from around a corner where the bulkhead must be. Hoarse words followed. The servants hadn't closed their helmets yet. . . . They were from several scarcely civilized planets, and no doubt even those who were not professional guards were trained in the use of modern weapons as well as household machinery. Cat-silent in his own armor, Adzel went the opposite way.

This room, that room, nothing. *Confound it—yes, I might go so far as to say curse it—David must be somewhere near. . . . Hold!* His wilderness-trained hearing had picked up the least of sounds. He entered a boudoir and activated its exterior scanner.

A woman went by, tall, slacksuited, vigorous-looking in a lean fashion. Her face was white and tense, her breath rapid. From van Rijn's briefing, Adzel recognized Thea Beldaniel. She passed. Had she looked behind her, she would have seen four and a half meters of dragon following on tiptoe.

She came to a door and flung it wide. Adzel peeked around the jamb. Falkayn sat in the chamber beyond, slumped into a lounger. The woman hurried to him and shook him. "Wake up!" she cried. "Oh, hurry!"

"Huh? Uh. Whuzza?" Falkayn stirred. His voice was dull, his expression dead.

"Come along, darling. We must get out of here."

"Uhhh. . . ." Falkayn shambled to his feet.

"Come, I say!" She tugged at his arm. He obeyed like a sleepwalker. "The tunnel to the spaceport. We're off for a, a little trip, my dear. But run!"

Adzel identified the symptoms. Brainscrub drugs, yes, in their entire ghastliness. You submerged the victim into a gray dream where he was nothing but what you told him to be. You could focus an encephaloductor beam on his head and a subsonic carrier wave on his middle ear. His drowned self could not resist the pulses thus generated; he would carry out whatever he was told, looking and sounding almost normal if you operated him skillfully but in truth a marionette. Otherwise he would simply remain where you stowed him.

In time, you could remodel his personality.

Adzel trod full into the entrance. "Now that is too bloody much!" he roared.

Thea Beldaniel sprang back. Her scream rose, went on and on. Falkayn stood hunched.

A yell answered, through the hallways. *My mistake,* Adzel realized. *Perhaps not avoidable. But the guards have been summoned, and they have more armament than I do. Best we escape while we may.*

Nonetheless, van Rijn's orders had been flat and loud. "You get films of our young man, right away, and you take blood and spit samples, before anything else. Or I take them off you, hear me, and not in so polite a place neither!" It seemed foolish to the Wodenite, when death must arrive in a minute or two. But so rarely did the old man issue so inflexible a directive that Adzel decided he'd better obey.

"Excuse me, please." His tail brushed the shrieking woman aside and pinned her gently but irresistibly to the wall. He tabled his camera, aimed it at Falkayn, set it on Track, and left it to work while he used needle and pipette on the flesh that had been his comrade. (And would be again, by everything sacred, or else be honorably dead!) Because he was calm about it, the process took just a few seconds. He stowed the sample tubes in a pouch, retrieved the camera, and gathered Falkayn in his arms.

As he came out the door, half a dozen retainers arrived. He couldn't shoot back, when he must shield the human with his own body. He plowed through, scattering a metallic bow wave. His tail sent two of the opposition off on an aerial somersault. Bolts and bullets smote. Chaos blazed around him. Some shots were deflected, some pierced the armor—but not too deeply, and it was self-sealing and he was tough.

None could match his speed down the hall and up the nearest rampway. But they'd follow. He couldn't stand long against grenades or portable artillery. Falkayn, unprotected, would be torn to pieces sooner than that. It was necessary to get the devil out of this hellhole.

Up, up, up! He ended in a tower room, bare and echoing, its viewports scanning the whole savage moonscape. Beldaniel, or someone, must have recovered wits and called in the patrols, because several boats approached swift above the stonelands. At a distance, their guns looked pencil thin, but those were nasty things to face. Adzel set Falkayn down in a corner. Carefully, he drilled a small hole in a viewport through which he could poke the transmitter antenna on his helmet.

Since Chee Lan's unit was no longer locked on his, he broadened the beam and increased the power. "Hello, hello. Adzel to ship. Are you there?"

"No." Her reply was half-sneer, half-sob. "I'm on Mars staging a benefit for the Sweet Little Old Ladies' Knitting and Guillotine Watching Society. What have you bungled now?"

Adzel had already established his location with reference to published photographs of the castle's exterior and van Rijn's arbitrary nomenclature. "David and I are in the top of Snoring Beauty's Tower. He is indeed under brainscrub. I estimate we will be attacked from the ramp within five minutes. Or, if they decide to sacrifice this part of the structure, their flitters can demolish it in about three minutes. Can you remove us beforehand?"

"I'm halfway there already, idiot. Hang on!"

"You do not go aboard, Adzel," van Rijn cut in. "You stay outside and get set down where we agreed, hokay?"

"If possible," Chee clipped. "Shut up."

"I shut up to you," van Rijn said quietly. "Not right away to God."

Adzel pulled back his antenna and slapped a sealing patch on the hole. Little air had bled out. He looked over Falkayn. "I have a spacesuit here for you," he said. "Can you scramble into it?"

The clouded eyes met his without recognition. He sighed. No time to dress a passive body. From the spiraling rampwell, barbaric yells reached his ears. He couldn't use his cannon; in this narrow space, concussion would be dangerous to an unarmored Falkayn. The enemy was not thus restricted. And the patrols were converging like hornets.

And *Muddlin' Through* burst out of the sky.

The spaceship was designed for trouble—if need be, for war. Chee Lan was not burdened by any tenderness. Lightnings flashed, briefly hiding the sun. The boats rained molten down the mountain. The spaceship came to a halt on gravfields alongside the turret. She could have sliced through, but that would have exposed those within to hard radiation. Instead, with tractor and pressor beams, she took the walls apart.

Air exploded outward. Adzel had clashed shut his own faceplate. He fired his blaster down the ramp, to discourage the servants, and collected Falkayn. The human was still unprotected, and had lost consciousness. Blood trickled from his nostrils. But momentary exposure to vacuum is not too harmful; deep-sea divers used to survive greater decompressions, and fluids do not begin to boil instantaneously. Adzel pitched Falkayn toward an open airlock. A beam seized him and reeled him in. The valve snapped shut behind him. Adzel sprang. He was caught likewise and clutched to the hull.

Muddlin' Through stood on her tail and grabbed herself some altitude.

Shaken, buffeted, the castle and the mountains spinning beneath him, Adzel still received van Rijn's orders to Chee Lan:

"—You let him down by where I told you. My yacht fetches him inside five minutes and takes us to Lunograd. But you, you go straight on with Falkayn. Maybe he is thick in the noodle, but he can tell you what direction to head in."

"Hoy, wait!" the Cynthian protested. "You never warned me about this."

"Was no time to make fancy plans, critchety-crotchety, for every possible outgo of happenings. How could I tell for sure what would be the circlestances? I thought probable it would be what it is, but maybe could have been better, maybe worse. Hokay. You start off."

"Look here, you fat pirate, my shipmate's drugged, hurt, sick! If you think for one picosecond he's going anywhere except to a hospital, I suggest you pull your head—the pointed one, that is—out of a position I would hitherto have sworn was anatomically impossible, and—"

"Whoa down, my furry friendling, easy makes it. From what you describe, his condition is nothing you can't cure en route. We fixed you with a complete kit and manual for unscrubbing minds and making them dirty again, not so? And what it cost, yow, would stand your hair on end so it flew out of the follicles! Do listen. This is big. Serendipity puts its whole existing on stake for whatever this is. We got to do the same."

"I like money as well as you do," Chee said with unwonted slowness. "But there are other values in life."

"*Ja, ja.*" Adzel grew dizzy from the whirling away of the land beneath. He closed his eyes and visualized van Rijn in the transmitter room, churchwarden in one fist, chins wobbling as he ripped off words, but somehow acrackle. "Like what Serendipity is after. Got to be more than money.

"Think hard, Chee Lan. You know what I deducted from the facts? Davy Falkayn *had* to be under drugs, a prisoner chained worse than with irons. Why? Because a lot of things, like he wouldn't quit on me sudden . . . but mainly, he is human and I is human, and I say a healthy lecherous young man that would throw over

Veronica—even if he didn't think Veronica is for anything except fun—what would throw over a bouncer-bouncer like that for a North Pole like Thea Beldaniel, by damn, he got something wrong in his upper story and maybe in his lower story too. So it looked probabilistic he was being mopped in the head.

"But what follows from this? Why, Serendipity was breaking the covenant of the Polesotechnic League. And that meant something big was on foot, worth the possible consequentials. Maybe worth the end of Serendipity itself—which is for sure now guaranteed!

"And what follows from that, little nuffymuff? What else, except the purpose was not commercial? For money, you play under rules, because the prize is not worth breaking them if you got the sense you need to be a strong player. But you could play for different things—like war, conquest, power—and those games is not nice, ha? The League made certain Serendipity was not doing industrial espionaging. But there is other kinds. Like to some outsider—somebody outside the whole of civilizations we know about—somebody hidden and ergo very, very likely our self-appointed enemy. *Nie?*"

Adzel's breath sucked in between his teeth.

"We got no time for fumblydiddles," van Rijn went on. "They sent off a messenger ship two weeks ago. Leastwise, Traffic Control records clearing it from the castle with two of the partners aboard personal. Maybe you can still beat their masters to wherever the goal is. In every case, you and Falkayn makes the best we got, right now in the Solar System, to go look. But you wait one termite-bitten hour, the police is in action and you is detained for material witnesses.

"No, get out while you can. Fix our man while you travel. Learn what gives, yonderwards, and report back to me, yourselfs or by robocourier. Or mail or passenger pigeon or whatever is your suits. The risk is big but maybe the profit is in scale. Or maybe the profit is keeping our lives or our freedom. Right?"

"Yes," said Chee faintly, after a long pause. The ship had crossed the mountains and was descending on the rendezvous. Mare Frigoris lay darkling under a sun that stood low in the south. "But we're a team. I mean, Adzel—"

"Can't go, him," van Rijn said. "Right now, we are also ourselfs making crunch of the covenant and the civil law. Bad enough you and Falkayn leave. Must be him, not Adzel, because he's the one of the team is trained special for working with aliens, new cultures, diddle and counterdiddle. Serendipity is clever and will fight desperate here on Luna. I got to have evidences of what they done, proofs, eye-witnessing. Adzel was there. He can show big, impressive testimonials."

"Well—" The Wodenite had never heard Chee Lan speak more bleakly. "I suppose. I didn't expect this."

"To be alive," said van Rijn, "is that not to be again and again surprised?"

The ship set down. The tractor beam released Adzel. He stumbled off over the lava. "Fare you well," said Chee. He was too shaken for any articulate answer. The ship rose anew. He stared after her until she had vanished among the stars.

Not much time passed before the merchant's vessel arrived; but by then, reaction was going at full tide through Adzel. As if in a dream, he boarded, let the crew divest him of his gear and van Rijn take over his material from the castle. He was only half conscious when they made Lunograd port, and scarcely heard the outraged bellows of his employer—was scarcely aware of anything except the infinite need for sleep and sleep and sleep—when he was arrested and led off to jail.

VIII

The phone announced, "Sir, the principal subject of investigation has called the office of Méndez and is demanding immediate conference with him."

"Exactly as I expected," Edward Garver said with satisfaction, "and right about at the moment I expected, too." He thrust out his jaw. "Go ahead, then, switch him to me."

He was a short man with thinning hair above a pugdog face; but within a severe gray tunic, his shoulders were uncommonly wide. The secretarial machines did not merely surround him as they would an ordinary executive or bureaucrat; somehow they gave the impression of standing guard. His desk bore no personal items—he had never married—but the walls held numerous pictures, which he often animated, of himself shaking hands with successive

Premiers of the Solar Commonwealth, Presidents of the Lunar Federation, and other dignitaries.

His words went via wire to a computer, which heard and obeyed. A signal flashed through electronic stages, became a maser beam, and leaped from a transmitter perched above Selenopolis on the ringwall of Copernicus. It struck a satellite of Earth's natural satellite and was relayed north, above barren sun-beaten ruggedness, until it entered a receiver at Plato. Coded for destination, it was shunted to another computer, which closed the appropriate connections. Because this moon is a busy place with heavy demands on its communication lines, the entire process took several milliseconds.

A broad countenance, mustached and goateed, framed in the ringleted mane that had been fashionable a generation ago, popped into Carver's phone screen. Little jet eyes, close set to an enormous crag of a nose, widened. "Pox and pestilence!" exclaimed Nicholas van Rijn. "I want Hernando Méndez, police chief for Lunograd. What you doing here, you? Not enough busybodying in the capital for keeping you happy?"

"I am in the capital . . . still," Garver said. "I ordered any call from you to him passed directly to me."

Van Rijn turned puce. "You the gobblehead told them my Adzel should be arrested?"

"No *honest* police official would let a dangerous criminal like that go loose."

"Who you for calling him criminals?" van Rijn sputtered. "Adzel got more milk of human kindness, *ja,* with plenty butterfat too, than what thin, blue, sour yechwater ever oozes from you, by damn!"

The director of the Federal Centrum of Security and Law Enforcement checked his temper. "Watch your language," he said. "You're in bad trouble yourself."

"We was getting out of trouble, us. Self-defense. And besides, was a local donnerblitz, no business of yours." Van Rijn tried to look pious. "We come back, landed in my yacht, Adzel and me, after he finished. We was going straight like arrows with crow feathers to Chief Méndez and file complaints. But what happened? He was busted! Marched off the spacefield below guard! By whose commandments?"

"Mine," Garver said. "And frankly, I'd have given a lot to include you, Freeman."

He paused before adding as quietly as possible, "I may get what I need for that very shortly, too. I'm coming to Lunograd and take personal charge of investigating this affair. Consider yourself warned. Do not leave Federation territory. If you do, my office will take it as *prima facie* evidence sufficient for arrest. Maybe we won't be able to extradite you from Earth, or wherever you go, on a Commonwealth warrant—though we'll try. But we'll slap a hold on everything your Solar Spice & Liquors Company owns here, down to the last liter of vodka. And your Adzel will serve a mighty long term of correction whatever you do, Freeman. Likewise his accomplices, if they dare come back in reach."

His voice had gathered momentum as he spoke. So had his feelings. He knew he was being indiscreet, even foolish, but the anger of too many years was upon him, now when at least a small victory was in sight. Almost helpless to do otherwise, he leaned forward and spoke staccato:

"I've been waiting for this chance. For years I've waited. I've watched you and your fellow plutocrats in your Polesotechnic League make a mockery of government—intrigue, bribe, compel, corrupt, ignore every inconvenient law, make your private deals, set up your private economic systems, fight your private battles, act like barons of an empire that has no legal existence but that presumes to treat with whole civilizations, make vassals of whole worlds—bring back the rawest kind of feudalism and capitalism! This 'freedom' you boast about, that your influence has gotten written into our very Constitution, it's nothing but license. License to sin, gamble, indulge in vice . . . and the League supplies the means, at a whopping profit!

"I can't do much about your antics outside the Commonwealth. Nor much about them anyplace, I admit, except on Luna. But that's a beginning. If I can curb the League here in the Federation, I'll die glad. I'll have laid the cornerstone of a decent society everywhere. And you, van Rijn, are the beginning of the beginning. You have finally gone too far. I believe I've got you!"

He sat back, breathing hard.

The merchant had turned impassive. He took his time about

opening a snuffbox, inhaling, sneezing, and dribbling a bit on the lace of his shirtfront. Finally, mild as the mid-oceanic swell of a tsunami, he rumbled, "Hokay. You tell me what you think I done wrong. Scripture says sinful man is prone to error. Maybe we can find out whose error."

Garver had gathered calm. "All right," he said. "No reason why I should not have the pleasure of telling you personally what you could find out for yourself.

"I've always had League activities watched, of course, with standing orders that I'm to be told about anything unusual. Slightly less than a week ago, Adzel and the other xeno teamed with him—yes, Chee Lan of Cynthia—applied for a warrant against the information brokers, Serendipity, Inc. They said their captain, David Falkayn, was being held prisoner under brainscrub drugs in that Alpine castle the SI partners keep for a residence. Naturally, the warrant was refused. It's true the SI people are rather mysterious. But what the flame, you capitalists are the very ones who make a fetish of privacy and the right to keep business details confidential. And SI is the only member of the League that nothing can be said against. All it does, peacefully and lawfully, is act as a clearinghouse for data and a source of advice.

"But the attempt did alert me. Knowing what you freebooters are like, I thought violence might very well follow. I warned the partners and suggested they call me directly at the first sign of trouble. I offered them guards, but they said they had ample defenses." Carver's mouth tightened. "That's another evil thing you Leaguers have brought. Self-defense, you call it! But since the law does say a man may keep and use arms on his own property—" He sighed. "I must admit SI has never abused the privilege."

"Did they tell you their story about Falkayn?" van Rijn asked.

"Yes. In fact, I talked to him myself on the phone. He explained he wanted to marry Freelady Beldaniel and join her outfit. Oh, sure, he *could* have been drugged. I don't know his normal behavior pattern. Nor do I care to. Because it was infinitely more plausible that you simply wanted him snatched away before he let his new friends in on your dirtier secrets.

"So." Garver bridged his fingers and grinned. "Today, about three hours ago, I got a call from Freeman Kim at the SI offices. Freelady Beldaniel had just called him. A space-armored Wodenite, obviously

Adzel, had appeared at the castle and demanded to see Falkayn. When this was denied him, he blasted his way in, and was rampaging loose at that moment.

"I instructed Chief Méndez to send out a riot detachment. He said he was already preoccupied with a riot—a brawl, at least—among men of yours, van Rijn, at a warehouse of yours. Don't tell me that was coincidence!"

"But it was," van Rijn said. "Ask them. They was bad boys. I will scold them."

"And slip them a fat bonus after they get out of jail."

"Well, maybe for consoling them. Thirty days on britches of the peace charges makes them so sad my old gray heart is touched. . . . But go on, Director. What did you do?"

Garver turned livid. "The next thing I had to do was get an utterly baseless injunction quashed. One of your kept judges? Never mind now; another thing to look into. The proceedings cost me a whole hour. After that, I could dispatch some men from my Lunograd division. They arrived too late. Adzel had already gotten Falkayn. The damage was done."

Again he curbed his wrath and said with bitter control, "Shall I list the different kinds of damage? SI's private, but legitimate, patrollers had been approaching the tower where Adzel was, in their gravboats. Then a spaceship came down. Must have been a spaceship, fully armed, acting in closely planned coordination with him. It wiped out the boats, broke apart the tower, and fled. Falkayn is missing. So is his one-time partner Chee Lan. So is the vessel they habitually used—cleared from Lunograd spaceport several standard days ago. The inference is obvious, don't you agree? But somehow, Adzel didn't escape. He must have radioed you to pick him up, because you did, and brought him back. This indicates that you have also been in direct collusion, van Rijn. I know what a swarm of lawyers you keep, so I want a little more evidence before arresting you yourself. But I'll get it. I'll do it."

"On what charges?" the other man asked tonelessly.

"For openers, those brought by the Serendipity partners, with eyewitness corroboration from Freelady Beldaniel and the castle staff. Threat. Mayhem. Invasion of privacy. Malicious mischief. Extensive destruction of property. Kidnapping. Murder."

"Whoa, horsey! Adzel told me, maybe he banged up those servants and guards a little, but he's a Buddhist and was careful not to kill anybody. That gun tower he shot out, getting in, was a standard remote-control type."

"Those patrol boats were not. Half a dozen one-seaters, smashed by energy beams. Okay, the pilots, like the rest of the castle staff, were nonhuman, noncitizen hirelings. But they were sophonts. Killing them in the course of an illegal invasion was murder. Accessories are equally guilty. This brings up the charge of conspiracy and—"

"Never mind," van Rijn said. "I get a notion somehow you don't like us much. When you coming?"

"I leave as soon as I can set matters in order here. A few hours." Garver peeled lips up from his teeth again. "Unless you care to record a confession at once. You'd save us trouble and might receive a lighter sentence."

"No, no. I got nothings to confess. This is such a terrible mistake. You got the situation all arsey-free versey. Adzel is gentle like a baby, except for some babies I know what are frightening ferocious. And me, I am a poor lonely old fat man only wanting a tiny bit profit so he does not end up like a burden on the welfare."

"Stow it," Garver said, and moved to break the connection.

"Wait!" van Rijn cried. "I tell you, everything is upwhirled. I got to unkink things, I see, because I try hard for being a good Christian that loves his fellow man and not let you fall on your ugly flat face and get laughed at like you deserve. I go talk with Adzel, and with Serendipity, too, before you come, and maybe we straighten out this soup you have so stupid-like brewed."

A muscle jumped at the corner of Garver's mouth. "I warn you," he said, "if you attempt any threat, bribery, blackmail—"

"You call me names," van Rijn huffed. "You implicate my morals. I don't got to listen at your ungentlemanly language. Good day for you, Gorgonzola brain." The screen blanked.

Luna being a focal point for outsystem traffic, the jails of the Federation's member cities are adjustable to the needs of a wide variety of species. Adzel's meticulous fairness compelled him to admit that with respect to illumination, temperature, humidity, pressure, and weight, he was more at home in his cell than under

Earth conditions. But he didn't mind the latter. And he did mind the food here, a glutinous swill put together according to what some fink of a handbook said was biologically correct for Wodenites. Still more did he suffer from being too cramped to stretch his tail, let alone exercise.

The trouble was, individuals of his race were seldom met off their planet. Most were primitive hunters. When he was brought in, by an understandably nervous squad of policemen, the warden had choked. "*Allahu akbar!* We must house this cross between a centaur and a crocodile? And every elephant-size unit already filled because of that cursed science fiction convention—"

Thus it was with relief, hours later, that Adzel greeted the sergeant in the phonescreen who said, "Your, uh, legal representative is here. Wants a conference. Are you willing?"

"Certainly. High time! No reflection on you, officer," the prisoner hastened to add. "Your organization has treated me with correctness, and I realize you are bound to your duty as to the Wheel of Karma." The sergeant in his turn made haste to switch over.

Van Rijn's image squinted against a glare too faithfully reproduced. Adzel was surprised. "But . . . but I expected a lawyer," he said.

"Got no time for logic choppers," his boss replied. "We chop our own logics, *ja,* and split and stack them. I mainly should tell you, keep your turnip hatch dogged tight. Don't say one pip. Don't even claim you is innocent. You are not legally requisitioned to tell anybody anything. They want the time of day, let them send out their flatfeetsers and investigate."

"But what am I doing in this kennel?" Adzel protested.

"Sitting. Loafing. Drawing fat pay off me. Meanwhiles I run around sweating my tired old legs down to the knees. Do you know," van Rijn said pathetically, "for more than an hour I have had absolute no drink? And it looks like I might miss lunch, that today was going to be Limfjord oysters and stuffed Pacific crab a la—"

Adzel started. His scales crashed against unyielding walls. "But I don't belong here!" he cried. "My evidence—"

Van Rijn achieved the amazing feat for a human of out-shouting him. "*Quiet!* I said upshut you! Silence!" He dropped his tone. "I know this is supposed to be a sealed circuit, but I do not put past that Garver he plugs one of his trained seals in the circuit. We keep what trumps we hold a while yet, play them last like Gabriel. Last trump—Gabriel—you understood me? Ha, ha!"

"Ha," said Adzel hollowly, "ha."

"You got privacy for meditating, plenty chances to practice asceticisms. I envy you. I wish I could find a chance for sainthood like you got there. You sit patient. I go talk with the people at Serendipity. Toodle oodle." Van Rijn's features vanished.

Adzel crouched motionless for a long while.

But I had the proof! he thought, stunned. *I took those photographs, those body-fluid samples, from David in the castle . . . exactly as I'd been told to . . . proof that he was, indeed, under brainscrub. I handed the material over to Old Nick when he asked for it, before we landed. I assumed he'd know best how to use it. For certainly that would justify my breaking in. This civilization has a horror of personality violations. But he—the leader I trusted—he hasn't mentioned it!*

When Chee Lan and a cured Falkayn returned they could testify, of course. Without the physical evidence Adzel had obtained, their testimony might be discounted, even if given torporifically. There were too many ways of lying under those drugs and electropulses that interrogators were permitted to use on volunteers: immunization or verbal conditioning, for instance.

At best, the situation would remain difficult. How could you blink the fact that intelligent beings had been killed by unauthorized raiders? (Though Adzel had more compunctions about fighting than the average roamer of today's turbulent frontiers, he regretted this particular incident only mildly in principle. A private war remained a war, a type of conflict that was occasionally justifiable. The rescue of a shipmate from an especially vile fate took priority over hard-boiled professional weapon-wielders who defended the captors of that shipmate. The trouble was, however, Commonwealth law did not recognize private wars.) But there was a fair chance the authorities would be sufficiently convinced that they would release, or convict and then pardon, the raiders.

If the proof of brainscrubbing was laid before them. And if Chee and Falkayn came back to tell their story. They might not. The unknowns for whom Serendipity had been an espionage front might find them and slay them before they could learn the truth. *Why did van Rijn not let me go too?* Adzel chafed. *Why, why, why?*

Alone, the exhibits would at least get him out on bail. For they would show that his attack, however illegal, was no wanton banditry. It would also destroy Serendipity by destroying the trust on which that organization depended—overnight.

Instead, van Rijn was withholding the proof. He was actually off to dicker with Falkayn's kidnappers.

The walls seemed to close in. Adzel was born to a race of rangers. A spaceship might be cramped, but outside burned the stars. Here was nothing other than walls.

Oh, the wide prairies of Zatlakh, earthquake hoof beats, wind whooping off mountains ghost-blue above the great horizon! After dark, fires beneath a shaken aurora; the old songs, the old dances, the old kinship that runs deeper than blood itself. Home is freedom. Ships, outfarings, planets, and laughter. Freedom is home. Am I to be sold for a slave in his bargain?

Shall I let him sell me?

IX

Puffing like an ancient steam locomotive, Nicholas van Rijn entered the central office. He had had previous dealings with Serendipity, in person as well as through subordinates. But he had never been in this particular room before, nor did he know anyone besides the owners who had.

Not that it differed much from the consultation cubicles, except for being larger. It was furnished with the same expensive materials in the same cheerlessly functional style, and the same strong white light spilled from its fluoropanels. Instead of a desk there was a large table around which several beings could sit; but this was equipped with a full battery of secretarial machines. Weight was set at Earth standard, atmosphere a little warmer.

Those partners who remained on Luna awaited him in a row behind the table. Kim Yoon-Kun was at the middle, slight, stiff, and impassive. The same wary expressionlessness marked Anastasia Herrera and Eve Latimer, who flanked him. Thea Beldaniel showed a human touch of weariness and shakenness—eyes dark-shadowed, the fine lines deepened in her face, hands not quite steady—but less than was normal for a woman who, a few hours ago, had seen her castle stormed by a dragon.

Van Rijn halted. His glance flickered to the pair of great gray-furred four-armed tailed bipeds, clad alike in traditional mail and armed alike with modern blasters, who stood against the rear wall. Their yellow eyes, set beneath bony prominences that looked like horns, glowered back out of the coarse faces. "You did not need to bring your Gorzuni goons," he said. His cloak swirled as he spread his hands wide, then slapped them along his tight plum-colored culottes. "I got no arsenal, me, and I come alone, sweet and innocent like a pigeon of peace. You know how pigeons behave."

"Colonel Melkarsh heads the patrol and outpost crews on our grounds," Kim stated. "Captain Urugu commands the interior guards and therefore the entire household servant corps. They have the right to represent their people, on whom your agents have worked grievous harm."

Van Rijn nodded. You can preserve secrets by hiring none except nonhumans from barbarian cultures. They can be trained in their jobs and in no other aspects of Technic civilization. Hence they will keep to themselves, not mix socially with outsiders, blab nothing, and at the end of their contracts go home and vanish into the anonymity of their seldom-visited planets. But if you do this, you must also accept their codes. The Siturushi of Gorzun make fine mercenaries—perhaps a little too fierce—and one reason is the bond of mutual loyalty between commanders and troops.

"Hokay," the merchant said. "Maybe best. Now we make sure everybody gets included in the settlement we reach." He sat down, extracted a cigar, and bit off the end.

"We did not invite you to smoke," Anastasia Herrera said frigidly.

"Oh, that's all right, don't apologize, I know you got a lot on your minds." Van Rijn lit the cigar, leaned back, crossed his legs, and exhaled a blue cloud. "I am glad you agreed to meet private with me. I would have come out to your home if you wanted. But better here, *nie?* What with police swarming around grounds and trying to look efficient. Here is maybe the one place in Lunograd we can be sure nobody is dropping eaves."

Melkarsh growled, deep in his throat. He probably knew some

Anglic. Kim said, "We are leaning backward to be accommodating, Freeman van Rijn, but do not overstrain our patience. Whatever settlement is reached must be on our terms and must have your full cooperation. And we cannot guarantee that your agents will go unpunished by the law."

The visitor's brows climbed, like black caterpillars, halfway up his slanted forehead. "Did I hear you right?" He cupped one ear. "Maybe, in spite of what extrarageous fees I pay for antisenescence treating, maybe at last in my old age I grow deaf? I hope you are not crazy. I hope you know this wowpow is for your sakes, not mine, because I don't want to squash you flat. Let us not beat around the barn." He pulled a stuffed envelope from his waistcoat pocket and threw it on the table. "Look at the pretty pictures. They are duplicates, natural. Originals I got someplace else, addressed to police and will be mailed if I don't come back in a couple hours. Also biological specimens—what can positive be identified for Falkayn's, because on Earth is medical records of him what include his chromosome patterns. Radioisotope tests will prove samples was taken not many hours ago."

The partners handed the photographs around in a silence that grew deeper and colder. Once Melkarsh snarled and took a step forward, but Urugu restrained him and both stood glaring.

"You had Falkayn under brainscrub," van Rijn said. He wagged a finger. "That was very naughty. No matter what we Solar Spicers may be guilty of, police going to investigate you from guzzle to zorch. And no matter what is then done with you, Serendipity is finished. Just the suspicion that you acted not so nice will take away your customers and their money."

They looked back at him. Their faces were metal-blank, aside from Thea Beldaniel's, on which there flickered something akin to anguish. "We *didn't*—" she half sobbed; and then, slumping back: "Yes. But I . . . we . . . meant him no real harm. We had no choice."

Kim waved her to silence. "You must have had some reason for not introducing this material officially at the outset," he said, syllable by syllable.

"*Ja, ja,*" van Rijn answered. "Don't seem my boy was permanent hurt. And Serendipity does do a real service for the whole Polesotechnic League. I carry no big grudge. I try my best to spare you the worst. Of course, I can't let you go without some loss. Is not possible. But you was the ones brought in the policemen, not me."

"I admit no guilt," Kim said. His eyes kindled. "We serve another cause than your ignoble money-grubbing."

"I know. You got bosses somewhere out in space don't like us. So we can't so well let your outfit continue for a spy and maybe someday a saboteur. But in spirit of charity, I do want to help you escape terrible results from your own foolishness. We start by calling off the law dogs. Once they got their big sticky teeth out of our business—"

"Can they be called off . . . now?" Thea Beldaniel whispered.

"I think maybe so, if you cooperate good with me. After all, your servants inside the castle did not suffer more from Adzel than some bruises, maybe a bone or two broken, right? We settle damage claims out of court with them, a civil and not a criminal matter." Van Rijn blew a thoughtful smoke ring. "You do the paying. Now about those patrol boats got clobbered, who is left that saw any spaceship hit them? If we—"

Melkarsh shook off his companion's grasp, jumped forward, raised all four fists and shouted in the dog Latin that has developed from the League's common tongue, "By the most foul demon! Shall my folks' heads lie unavenged?"

"Oh, you get weregild you can take to their relatives," van Rijn said. "Maybe we add a nice sum for you personal, ha?"

"You believe everything is for sale," Melkarsh rasped. "But honor is not. Know that I myself saw the spaceship from afar. It struck and was gone before I could arrive. But I know the type for one that you companies use, and I will so declare to the Federation's lawmen."

"Now, now," van Rijn smiled. "Nobody is asking you should perjure. You keep your mouth shut, don't volunteer information you saw anything, and nobody will ask you. Especial since your employers is going to send you home soon—next available ship, or maybe I myself supply one—with pay for your entire contract and a fat bonus." He nodded graciously at Urugu. "Sure, my friend, you too. Don't you got generous employers?"

"If you expect I will take your filthy bribe," Melkarsh said, "when I could avenge my folk by speaking—"

"Could you?" van Rijn answered. "Are you sure you pull me

down? I don't pull down easy, with my big and heavy foundation. You will for certain destroy your employers here, what you gave your word to serve faithful. Also, you and yours will be held for accessories to kidnap and other bad behavings. How you help your folk, or your own honor, in a Lunar jail? Ha? Far better you bring back weregild to their families and story of how they fell nobly in battle like warriors should."

Melkarsh snatched for air but could speak no further. Thea Beldaniel rose, went to him, stroked his mane, and murmured, "He's right, you know, my dear old friend. He's a devil, but he's right."

The Gorzuni gave a jerky nod and stepped backward.

"Good, good!" van Rijn beamed. He rubbed his hands. "How glad I am for common sense and friendliness. I tell you what plans we make together." He looked around. "Only I'm terrible thirsty. How about you send out for a few bottles beer?"

X

Reaching Lunograd, Edward Garver went directly to the police complex. "Bring that Wodenite prisoner to an interrogation room," he ordered. With a nod at the three hard-countenanced men who accompanied him: "My assistants and I want to grill him ourselves. Make his environment as uncomfortable as the law allows—and if the law should happen to get stretched a trifle, this case is too big for recording petty details."

He did not look forward to the prospect. He was not a cruel man. And intellectually he despised his planned approach. Guilt should be determined by logical reasoning from scientifically gathered evidence. What could you do, though, when the League paid higher salaries than you were able to offer, thus getting technicians more skilled and reasoners more glib? He had spent a career building the Centrum into an efficient, high-morale organization. His pride was how well it now functioned against the ordinary criminal. But each time he saw his agents retreat, baffled and disheartened, from a trail that led to the League, that pride became ashen within him.

He had studied the apologetics of the modern philosophers. "Government is that organization which claims the right to command all individuals to do whatever it desires and to punish disobedience with loss of property, liberty, and ultimately life. It is nothing more. The fact is not changed by its occasional beneficence. Possessing equal or greater power, but claiming no such right of compulsion, the Polesotechnic League functions as the most effective check upon government which has yet appeared in known history." He did not believe a word of it.

Thus Adzel found himself in air stranglingly thin and wet, cold enough for his scales to frost over, and in twice the gravity of his home planet. He was almost blind beneath the simulated light of a distant red dwarf sun, and could surely not look through the vitryl panel behind which Garver's team sat under Earth conditions. As time passed, no one offered food or drink. The incessant questions were projected shrill, on a frequency band painful to eardrums adapted for low notes.

He ignored them.

After half an hour, Garver realized this could go on indefinitely. He braced his mind for the next stage. It wouldn't be pleasant for anyone, but the fault was that monster's own.

Inflating his lungs, he roared, "Answer us, damn you! Or do you want to be charged with obstructing justice, on top of everything else?"

For the first time, Adzel replied. "In point of fact," he said, "yes. As I am merely standing upon my right to keep silent, such an accusation would cap the ridiculousness of these proceedings."

Garver jabbed a button. Adzel must needs wince. "Is something wrong?" asked the team member who had been assigned the kindliness role.

"I suffered quite a severe electric shock through the floor."

"Dear me. Perhaps a wiring defect. Unless it was your imagination. I realize you're tired. Why don't we finish this interview and all go get some rest?"

"You are making a dreadful mistake, you know," Adzel said mildly. "I admit I was somewhat irritated with my employer. Now I am far more irritated with you. Under no circumstances shall I cooperate. Fortunately, my spacefaring has accustomed me to exotic surroundings. And I regard this as an opportunity to gain merit by transcending physical discomfort." He assumed the quadrupedal equivalent of the lotus position, which is quite a sight. "Excuse me while I say my prayers."

"Where were you on the evenwatch of—"

"*Om mani padme hum.*"

An interrogator switched off the speaker system. "I don't know if this is worth our trouble, Chief," he said.

"He's a live organism," Garver growled. "Tough, yeh, but he's got his limits. We'll keep on, by God, in relays, till we grind him down."

Not long afterward, the phone buzzed in the chamber and Mendez's image said deferentially, "Sir, I regret the interruption, but we've received a call. From the Serendipity people." He gulped. "They . . . they're dropping their complaint."

"*What?*" Garver leaped from his chair. "No! They can't! I'll file the charges myself!" He stopped. The redness ebbed from his cheeks. "Put them on," he said coldly.

Kim Yoon-Kun looked out of the screen. Was he a shade less collected than before? At his back loomed van Rijn. Garver suppressed most of his automatic rage at glimpsing that man. "Well?" he said. "What is this nonsense?"

"My partners and I have conferred with the gentleman here," Kim said. Each word seemed to taste individually bad; he spat them out fast. "We find there has been a deplorable misunderstanding. It must be corrected at once."

"Including bringing the dead back to life?" Garver snorted. "Never mind what bribes you've been tempted by. I have proof that a federal crime was committed. And I warn you, sir, trying to conceal anything about it will make you an accessory after the fact."

"But it was no crime," Kim said. "It was an accident."

Garver stared past him, at van Rijn. If the old bastard tried to gloat—! But van Rijn only smiled and puffed on a large cigar.

"Let me begin from the beginning," Kim said, "My partners and I would like to retire. Because Serendipity, Inc., does satisfy a genuine need, its sale will involve considerable sums and many different interests. Negotiations are accordingly delicate. This is especially true when you consider that the entire value of our company lies in the fact that its services are rendered without fear or favor. Let its name be tainted with the least suspicion of undue influence from outside, and it will be shunned. Now everyone knows that we are strangers here, aloof from society. Thus we are unfamiliar with the emotional intricacies that may be involved. Freeman van Rijn generously"—Kim had a fight to get the adverb out—"offered us advice. But his counseling must be done with extreme discretion, lest his rivals assume that he will turn Serendipity into a creature of his own."

"You—you—" Garver heard himself squeak, as if still trying to grill Adzel, "you're selling out? To who?"

"That is the problem, Director," Kim said. "It must be someone who is not merely able to pay, but is capable of handling the business and above suspicion. Perhaps a consortium of non-humans? At any rate, Freeman van Rijn will, *sub rosa,* be our broker."

"At a fat commission," Garver groaned.

Kim could not refrain from groaning back, "Very fat." He gathered himself and plowed on:

"Captain Falkayn went as his representative to discuss matters with us. To preserve the essential secrecy, perforce he misled everyone, even his long-time shipmates. Hence that story about his betrothal to Freelady Beldaniel. I see now that this was a poor stratagem. It excited their suspicions to the point where they resorted to desperate measures. Adzel entered violently, as you know. But he did no real harm, and once Captain Falkayn had explained the situation to him, we were glad to accept his apologies. Damage claims will be settled privately. Since Captain Falkayn had completed his work at our home anyhow, he embarked with Chee Lan on a mission related to finding a buyer for us. There was nothing illegal about his departure, seeing that no laws had been broken. Meanwhile Freeman van Rijn was kind enough to fetch Adzel in his personal craft."

"No laws broken? What about the laws against murder?" Garver yelled. His fingers worked, as if closing on a throat. "I've got them—you—for that!"

"But no, Director," Kim said. "I agree the circumstances looked bad, for which reason we were much too prompt to prefer charges. By 'we' I mean those of us who were not present at the time. But now a discussion with Freelady Beldaniel, and a check of the original plans of the castle, have shown what actually happened.

"You know the place has automatic as well as manned defenses.

Adzel's disruptive entry alerted the robots in one tower, which then overreacted by firing on our own patrol boats as these came back to help. Chee Lan, in her spaceship, demolished the tower in a valiant effort to save our people, but she was too late.

"A tragic accident. If anyone is to blame, it is the contractor who installed those machines with inadequate discriminator circuits. Unfortunately, the contractor is nonhuman, living far beyond the jurisdiction of the Commonwealth. . . ."

Garver sat.

"You had better release Adzel immediately," Kim said. "Freeman van Rijn says he may perhaps be induced not to generate a great scandal about false arrest, provided that you apologize to him in person before a public newscaster."

"You have made your own settlement—with van Rijn?" Garver whispered.

"Yes," said Kim, like one up whom a bayonet has been rammed.

Garver rallied the fragments of his manhood. "All right," he got out. "So be it."

Van Rijn looked over Kim's shoulder. "Gloat," he said and switched off.

The space yacht lifted and swung toward Earth. Stars glittered in every viewport. Van Rijn leaned back in his lounger, hoisted a foamful mug, and said, "By damn, we better celebrate fast. No sooner we make planetfall but we will be tongue-dragging busy, you and me."

Adzel drank from a similar mug which, however, was filled with prime whisky. Being large has some advantages. His happiness was limited. "Will you let the Serendipity people go scot-free?" he asked. "They are evil."

"Maybe not evil. Maybe plain enemies, which is not necessarily same thing," van Rijn said. "We find out. For sure not scot-free, though, any more than what you glug down at my expense like it was beer is free Scotch. No, you see, they has lost their company, their spy center, which was their whole *raison d'être.* Off that loss, I make a profit, since I handle the selling."

"But you must have some goal besides money!" Adzel exclaimed.

"Oh, *ja, ja,* sure. Look, I did not know what would happen after you rescued Davy boy. I had to play on my ear. What happened was, Serendipity tried striking back at us through the law. This made special dangers, also special opportunities. I found four things in my mind."

Van Rijn ticked the points off on his fingers. "One," he said, "I had to get you and my other loyal friends off the hook. That was more important by itself than revenge. But so was some other considerates.

"Like two, I had to get the government out of this business. For a while at least. Maybe later we must call it back. But for now, these reasons to keep it out. Alpha, governments is too big and cumbersome for handling a problem with so many unknowns as we got. Beta, if the public in the Commonwealth learned they have a powerful enemy some place we don't know, they could get hysterical and this could be bad for developing a reasonable type policy, besides bad for business. Gamma, the longer we can work private, the better chance for cutting ourselves a share of whatever pies may be floating around in space, in exchange for our trouble."

He paused to breathe and gulp. Adzel looked from this comfortable saloon, out the viewport to the stars that were splendid but gave no more comfort than life could seize for itself; and no life was long, compared to the smallest time that any of those suns endured. "What other purposes have you?" he asked mutedly.

"Number three," van Rijn said, "did I not make clear Serendipity is in and for itself a good idea, useful to everybody? It should not be destroyed, only passed on into honest hands. Or tentacles or paws or flippers or whatever. Ergo, we do not want any big hurray about it. For that reason too, I must bargain with the partners. I did not want them to feel like Samson, no motive not to pull down the whole barbershop.

"And four." His tone turned unwontedly grave. "Who are these X beings? What do they want? Why are they secret? Can we maybe fix a deal with them? No sane man is after a war. We got to learn more so we can know what is best to do. And Serendipity is our one lonesome lead to its masters."

Adzel nodded. "I see. Did you get any information?"

"No. Not really. That I could not push them off of. They would die first. I said to them, they must go home and report to their bosses. If nothings else, they got to make sure their partners who has already left is not seized on returning to Luna and maybe put in the question. So hokay, they start, I have a ship that trails theirs, staying in detection range the whole way. Maybe they can lure her into a trap, maybe not. Don't seem worth the trouble, I said, when neither side is sure it can outfox the other. The most thickly sworn enemies always got *some* mutual interests. And supposing you intend to kill somebody, why not talk at him first? For worst, you have wasted a little time; for best, you learn you got no cause to kill him."

Van Rijn drained his mug. "Ahhhh! Well," he said, "we made a compromise. They go away, except one of them, in a ship that is not followed. Their own detectors can tell them this is so. The one stays behind and settles legal details of transferring ownership. That is Thea Beldaniel. She was not too unwilling, and I figure she is maybe more halfway human than her friends. Later on, she guides one ship of ours to a rendezvous agreed on, some neutral spot, I suppose, where maybe we can meet her bosses. They should be worth meeting, what made so brilliant a scheme like Serendipity for learning all about us. *Nie?*"

Adzel lifted his head with a jerk. "I beg your pardon?" he exclaimed. "Do you mean that you personally and—and I—"

"Who else?" van Rijn said. "One reason I kept you back. I need to be sure some fellow besides me will be around I can trust. It is going to be a cold journey, that one. Like they used to say in Old Norse and such places, 'Bare is brotherless back.'" He pounded the table. "Cabin boy!" he thundered. "Where in hell's name is more beer?"

XI

In the decade or so that had passed since the Lemminkainenites found it, the rogue had fallen a long way. Watching Beta Crucis in the bow viewscreen, Falkayn whistled, low and awed. "Can we even get near?" he asked. Seated amidst the control boards, flickering and blinking and clicking instruments, soft power-throb and quiver, of *Muddlin' Through*'s bridge, he did not look directly at the star, nor at a true simulacrum. Many astronomical units removed, it would still have burned out his eyes. The screen reduced brightness and magnified size for him. He saw an azure circle, spotted like a leopard, wreathed in an exquisite filigree of ruby, gold, and opal, a lacework that stretched outward for several times its diameter. And space behind was not dark, but shimmered with pearliness through a quarter of the sky before fading into night.

Falkayn's grip tautened on the arms of his chair. The heart thuttered in him. Seeking comfort for a rising, primitive dread, he pulled his gaze from the screen, from all screens, to the homely traces of themselves that his team had put on used patches of bulkhead. Here Chee Lan had hung one of those intricate reticulations that her folk prized as art; there he himself had pasted up a girlie picture; yonder Adzel kept a bonsai tree on a shelf—*Adzel, friend, now when we need your strength, the strength in your very voice, you are two light-centuries behind us.*

Stop that, you nit! Falkayn told himself. *You're getting spooked. Understandable, when Chee had to spend most of our voyage time nursing me out of half-life—*

His mind halted. He gasped for air. The horror of what had been done to him came back in its full strength. All stars receded to an infinite radius. He crouched alone in blackness and ice.

And yet he could not remember clearly what the enslavement of his mind had been like. It was as if he tried to reconstruct a fever dream. Everything was vague and grotesque; time twisted smokily about, dissolved and took new evanescent shapes; he had been trapped in another universe and another self, and they were not his own, and he could not bring himself to confront them again in memory, even were he able. He had desired Thea Beldaniel as he had desired no other woman since his first youth; he had adored the undefined Elder Race as he had adored no gods in his life; he had donned a cool surface and a clear logical mind at need, and afterward returned to his dim warm abyss. Yet somehow it was not he who did these things, but others. They used him, entered and wore him. . . . How could he find revenge for so inward a rape?

That last thought was born as a solitary spark in his night. He seized it, held it close, blew his spirit upon it and nursed it to flame. Fury followed, blinding as yonder great sun, burning him clean again. He might have been reliving ancient incarnations as he swung a Viking ax, galloped torch in hand on a Tartar pony, unleashed the guns that smash cities to rubble. It gave strength, which in turn gave sanity.

Minutes after the seizure began, he was calm once more. His muscles slackened their hurtful knots, pulse and breath slowed, the sweat dried on him though he was aware of its lingering sourness.

He thought harshly: *Let's get on with the work we've got here. And to begin with, let's not be so bloody reverential about it. I've seen bigger, brighter stars than this one.*

Only a few, of course. The blue giants are also monsters in their rarity. And the least of them is terrifying to contemplate. Those flecks on the photosphere were vortices that could each have swallowed a planet like Jupiter. That arabesque of filaments comprised the prominences—the mass equivalents of whole Earths, vaporized, ionized, turned to incandescent plasma, spewed millions of kilometers into space, some forever lost and some raining back—yet given its faerie patterns by magnetic fields great enough to wrestle with it. The corona fluoresced across orbital distances because its gas was sleeted through and through by the particles, stripped atoms, hard and soft quanta of a star whose radiance was an ongoing storm, eight hundred and fifty times the measure of Sol's, a storm so vast that it could endure no longer than a hundred megayears before ending in the thunderclap of a supernova. Falkayn looked upon its violence and shivered.

He grew aware that the ship's computer had spoken. "I beg your pardon?" he said automatically.

"I am not programmed to take offense; therefore apologies to me are superfluous," said the flat artificial voice. "However, I have been instructed to deal as circumspectly with you as my data banks and ideational circuits allow, until you have fully recovered your nervous equilibrium. Accordingly, it is suggested that you consider indulgence as having been granted you as requested."

Falkayn relaxed. His chuckle grew into a guffaw. "Thanks, Muddlehead," he said. "I needed that." Hastily: "Don't spoil it by telling me you deduced the need and calculated your response. Just start over."

"In reply to your question as to whether we can come near, the answer depends upon what is meant by 'near.' Context makes it obvious that you wish to know whether we can reach the planet of destination with an acceptable probability of safety. Affirmative."

Falkayn turned to Chee Lan, who hunkered in her own chair—it looked more like a spiderweb—on his right. She must have sensed it when the horror came upon him but, characteristically, decided not to intervene. Because he still needed distraction, he said:

"I distinctly remember telling Muddlehead to lay off that stupid 'affirmative, negative' business, when a plain 'yes' or 'no' was good enough for Churchill. Why did you countermand?"

"I didn't," the Cynthian answered. "I don't care either way. What are the nuances of the Anglic language to me? If it has any," she sneered. "No, blame Adzel."

"Why him?"

"The ship came new to us from the yard, you recall, so the computer's vocabulary was engineerese. It's gotten modified in the course of work with us. But you may recall too that while we were on Luna, we ordered a complete inspection. You were hot on the tail of your Veronica creature, which left Adzel and me to make arrangements. Old butterheart was afraid the feelings of the engineers would be hurt, if they noticed how little use we have for their dialect. He instructed Muddlehead—"

"Never mind," Falkayn said. He felt he had now gotten enough distraction to last him for quite a while. To the ship: "Revert to prior linguistic pattern and give us some details about our next move."

"Instrumental observation appears to confirm what you were told of the planet itself," said the machine. Falkayn nodded. Though he had only recovered the full use of his free will in the past several days, Chee had been able to get total-recollection answers from him very early in the trip. "However, the noise level is too high for exactitude at our present distance. On the other hand, I have determined the orbit with sufficient precision. It is, indeed, a hyperbola of small eccentricity. At present, the rogue is near periastron, the radius vector having a length of approximately one-point-seven-five astronomical units. It will make the closest approach, approximately zero-point-nine-three astronomical units, in approximately twenty-seven-point-three-seven days, after which it will naturally return to outer space along the other arm of the hyperbola. There is no evidence of any companion body of comparable size. Thus the dynamics of the situation are simple and the orbit almost perfectly symmetrical."

Chee put a cigarette in an interminable ivory holder and puffed it alight. Her ears twitched, her whiskers bristled. "What a time to arrive!" she snarled. "It couldn't be when the planet's decently far off from that bloated fire balloon. Oh, no! That'd be too easy. It'd put the gods to the trouble of finding somebody else to dump their garbage on. We get to go in while the radiation peaks."

"Well," Falkayn said, "I don't see how the object could've been found at all, if it hadn't happened to be coming in, close enough to reflect a detectable amount of light off its cryosphere. And then there was the galactic communications lag. Sheer luck that I ever heard about the discovery."

"You could have heard a few years earlier, couldn't you?"

"In that event," Muddlehead said, "the necessity would have remained of making later, short-range observations, in order to ascertain whether surface conditions are indeed going to become suitable for an industrial base. The amount and the composition of frozen material could not have been measured accurately. Nor could its behavior have been computed beforehand in sufficient detail. The problem is too complex, with too many unknowns. For example, once a gaseous atmosphere has begun to form, other volatile substances will tend to recondense at high altitudes, forming clouds which will in time disappear but which, during their existence, may reflect so much input radiation that most of the surface remains comparatively cold."

"Oh, dry up," Chee said.

"I am not programmed or equipped to—"

"And blow away." Chee faced the human. "I see your point, Dave, as well as Muddlehead's. And of course the planet's accelerating as it moves inward. I got a preliminary orbital estimate a few watches back, while you were asleep, that says the radius vector changes from three to one a.u. in about ten standard weeks. So little time, for the irradiation to grow ninefold!—But I do wish we could've arrived later, anyhow, when the thing's outward bound and cooling off."

"Although not prepared for detailed meteorological calculations," Muddlehead said, "I can predict that the maximum atmospheric instability will occur after periastron passage. At present, most of the incident stellar energy is being absorbed by heats of fusion, vaporization, et cetera. Once this process has been completed, energy input will continue large. For example, at thirty astronomical units the planet will still be receiving approximately as much irradiation as Earth; and it will not get that far out for a number of years. Thus temperatures can be expected to soar, and storms of such magnitude will be generated that no vessel dares land. Ground observation may as yet be feasible for us, given due precautions."

Falkayn grinned. He felt better by the minute: if not able to whip the cosmos, at least to let it know it had been in a fight. "Maybe our luck is the best possible," he said.

"I wouldn't be the least bit surprised," Chee replied sourly. "Well, Muddlehead, how do we make rendezvous?"

"The force-screens can of course ward off more particle radiation than we will receive, even if a stellar storm occurs," said the computer. "Electromagnetic input is the real problem. Our material shielding is insufficient to prevent an undesirable cumulative X-ray dosage in the period required for adequate study. The longer wavelengths could similarly overload our thermostatting capabilities. Accordingly, I propose to continue under hyperdrive."

Falkayn drew his pipe from a pocket of his gray coveralls. "That's a pretty close shave, so few a.u. at faster-than-light," he warned. He left unspoken the possibilities: imperfect inter-mesh with the star's gravitational field tearing the ship asunder; a brush with a solid body, or a moderately dense gas, producing a nuclear explosion as atoms tried to occupy the same volume.

"It is within the one percent safety margin of this vessel and myself," Muddlehead declared. "Besides spending less time in transit, during that transit we will not interact significantly with ambient photons or material particles."

"Good enough," Chee said. "I don't fancy the nasty little things buzzing through my personal cells. But what about when we reach the planet? We can take station in its shadow cone and let its bulk protect us—obviously—but what can we then observe of the surface?"

"Adequate instruments are available. As a trained planetologist, Adzel could make the most effective use of them. But no doubt you two with my assistance can manage. Furthermore, it should be possible to pay brief visits to the daylight side."

"Bully-o," Falkayn said. "We'll grab some lunch and a nap and be on our way."

"You can stuff your gut and wiggle your epiglottis later," Chee said. "We proceed *now.*"

"Huh? Why?"

"Have you forgotten that we have rivals? That messengers departed weeks ago to inform them? I don't know how long the word took to get back there, or how fast they can send an expedition here, but I don't expect them to dawdle very much or be overly polite if they find us." Chee jerked her tailtip and spread her hands, a shrugging gesture. "We might or might not be able to take them in a fight, but I'd really rather delegate the job to a League battle fleet. Let's get our data and out."

"M-m-m . . . yes. I read. Carry on, Muddlehead. Keep every sensor alert for local dangers, though. There're bound to be some unpredictable ones." Falkayn loaded his pipe. "I'm not sure van Rijn would call for a fleet action at that," he murmured to the Cynthian. "It might impair his claim to the planet. He might have to share some of the profit."

"He'll squeeze every millo he can out of this," she said. "Of course. But for once, he's seen something bigger than money. And it scares him. He thinks the Commonwealth—maybe the whole of Technic civilization—is at war and doesn't realize the fact. And if this rogue is important enough to the enemy that they risked, and lost, a spy organization they'd spent fifteen years developing, it's equally important to us. He'll call in the League; even the different governments and their navies, if he must. I talked to him, after we'd hooked you from the castle."

The humor dropped out of Falkayn. His mouth drew taut. *I know what kind of conflict this is!*

Barely in time, he choked the mood. *No more blue funks. I* did *get free. I* will *get revenge. Let's think about what's to be done now.*

He forced lightness back into voice and brain. "If Old Nick really does end up having to settle for a fraction of the wealth, hoo-hah! They'll hear his screams in the Magellanic Clouds. But maybe we can save his bacon—and French toast and scrambled eggs and coffee royal and, uh, yes, it was coconut cake, last time I had breakfast with him. Ready, Muddlehead?"

"Stand by for hyperdrive," said the computer.

The power-hum deepened. Briefly, the screened sky became a blur. Then the system adjusted, to compensate for billions of quantum micro jumps per second. Stars aft assumed their proper colors and configurations. Forward, where Beta Crucis drowned them out, its disc swelled, until it seemed to leap with its flames into the ship. Falkayn crouched back in his seat and Chee Lan bared her fangs.

The moment passed. The vessel resumed normal state. She must swiftly attain the proper position and kinetic velocity, before the heightened power of the sun blasted through her defenses. But her internal gee-fields were manipulated with such suppleness by the computer that the two beings aboard felt no change of weight. In minutes, a stable condition was established. The ship lay two radii from the rogue's ground level, balancing gravitational and centrifugal forces with her own thrust. Her riders peered forth.

The wide-angle screen showed an immense black circle, rimmed with lurid white where the star's rays were refracted through the atmosphere. Behind this, in turn, glowed corona, and wings of zodiacal light. The planetary midnight was not totally unrelieved. Auroras flung multicolored banners from the poles; a wan bluishness flickered elsewhere, as the atoms and ions of sun-split molecules recombined in strange ways; lightning, reflected by immense cloud banks farther down, created the appearance of running will-o'-the-wisps; here and there glowered a red spark, the throat of a spouting volcano.

In the near-view screens, mere fractions of the globe appeared, shouldering into heaven. But there you saw, close and clear, the pattern of weather, the rage of rising mountains and newborn oceans. Almost, Falkayn imagined he could hear the wind-shriek, rain-roar, thunder-cannonade, that he could feel the land shake and split beneath him, the gales whirl boulders through a blazing sky. It was long before he could draw his gaze free of that scene.

But work was on hand, and in the watches that followed, he inevitably lost some of his awe amidst the instruments. With it vanished the weakness that his imprisonment had left in him. The basic anger, the drive to scrub out his humiliation in blood, did not go; but he buried it deep while he studied and calculated. What he was witnessing must be unique in the galaxy—perhaps in the cosmos—and fascinated him utterly.

As the Lemminkainenites had concluded, this was an ancient world. Most of its natural radioactivity was long spent, and the chill had crept near its heart. But part of the core must remain molten, to judge from the magnetism. So stupendous an amount of heat, insulated by mantle and crust and frozen oceans and a blanket of frozen atmosphere averaging ten or twenty meters thick, was slow to dissipate. Nevertheless, for ages the surface had lain at a temperature not far above absolute zero.

Now the cryosphere was dissolving. Glaciers became torrents, which presently boiled away and became stormwinds. Lakes and seas, melting, redistributed incredible masses. Pressures within the globe were shifted; isostatic balance was upset; the readjustments of strata, the changes of allotropic structure, released catastrophic, rock-melting energy. Quakes rent the land and shocked the waters. Volcanoes awoke by the thousands. Geysers spouted above the ice sheath that remained. Blizzard, hail, and rain scourged the world, driven by tempests whose fury mounted daily until words like "hurricane" could no more name them. Hanging in space, Falkayn and Chee Lan took measurements of Ragnarok.

And yet—and yet—what a prize this was! What an incredible all-time treasure house!

XII

"Frankly," Chee Lan said, "speaking between friends and meaning no offense, you're full of fewmets. How can one uninhabitable piece of thawed hell matter that much to anybody?"

"Surely I explained, even in my wooze," Falkayn replied. "An industrial base, for the transmutation of elements."

"But they do that at home."

"On a frustratingly small scale, compared to the potential market." Falkayn poured himself a stiff whisky and leaned back to enjoy digesting his dinner. He felt he had earned a few hours' ease in the saloon. "Tomorrow" they were to land, having completed their investigations from orbit, and things could get shaggy. "How about a poker game?"

The Cynthian, perched on the table, shook her head. "No, thanks! I've barely regained my feeling for four-handed play, after Muddlehead got rich enough in its own right to bluff big. Without Adzel, the development's apt to be too unfamiliar. The damned machine'll have our hides." She began grooming her silken fur. "Stick to business, you. I'm a xenologist. I never paid more attention than I could help to your ugly factories. I'd like a proper explanation of why I'm supposed to risk my tailbone down there."

Falkayn sighed and sipped. He would have taken for granted that she could see the obvious as readily as he. But to her, with her biological heritage, cultural background, and special interests, it was not obvious. *I wonder what she sees that I miss? How could I even find out?* "I don't have the statistics in my head," he admitted. "But you don't need anything except a general knowledge of the situation. Look, there isn't an element in the periodic table, nor hardly a single isotope, that doesn't have some use in modern technology. And when that technology operates on hundreds of planets, well, I don't care how minor a percentage of the consumption is Material Q. The total amount of Q needed annually is going to run into tons at a minimum—likelier into megatons.

"Now nature doesn't produce much of some elements. Even in the peculiar stars, transmutation processes have a low yield of nuclei like rhenium and scandium—two metals I happen to know are in heavy demand for certain alloys and semiconductors. Didn't you hear about the rhenium strike on Maui, about twenty years ago? Most fabulous find in history, tremendous boom; and in three years the lodes were exhausted, the towns deserted, the price headed back toward intergalactic space. Then there are the unstable heavy elements, or the shorter-lived isotopes of the lighter ones. Again, they're rare, no matter how you scour the galaxy. When you do find some, you have to mine the stuff under difficult conditions, haul it a long way home . . . and that also drives up the cost."

Falkayn took another swallow. He had been very sober of late, so this whisky, on top of cocktails before dinner and wine with, turned him loquacious. "It isn't simply a question of scarcity making certain things expensive," he added. "Various projects are *impossible* for us, because we're bottlenecked on materials. We could progress a lot faster in interstellar exploration, for instance—with everything that that implies—if we had sufficient hafnium to make sufficient polyergic units to make sufficient computers to pilot a great many more spaceships than we can build at present. Care for some other examples?"

"N-no. I can think of several for myself," Chee said. "But any kind of nucleus can be made to order these days. And is. I've seen the bloody transmutation plants with my own bloody eyes."

"What had you been doing the night before to make your eyes bloody?" Falkayn retorted. "Sure, you're right as far as you go. But those were pygmy outfits you saw. They can't ever keep up with the demand. Build them big enough, and their radioactive waste alone would sterilize whatever planets they're on. Not to mention the waste heat. An exothermic reaction gives it off directly. But so does an endothermic one . . . indirectly, via the power-source that furnishes the energy to make the reaction go. These are nuclear processes, remember. E equals mc squared. One gram of difference, between raw material and final product, means nine times ten to the thirteenth joules. A plant turning out a few tons of element per day would probably take the Amazon River in at one end of its cooling system and blow out a steam jet at the other end. How long before Earth became too hot for life? Ten years, maybe? Or any life-bearing world? Therefore we can't use one, whether or not it's got sophont natives. It's too valuable in other ways—quite apart from interplanetary law, public opinion, and common decency."

"I realize that much," Chee said. "This is why most existing transmuters are on minor, essentially airless bodies. Of course."

"Which means they have to install heat exchangers, feeding into the cold mass of the planetoid." Falkayn nodded. "Which is expensive. Worse, it puts engineering limitations on the size of a plant, and prohibits some operations that the managers would dearly love to carry out."

"I hadn't thought about the subject before," Chee said. "But why not use sterile worlds—new ones, for instance, where life has not begun to evolve—that have reasonable atmospheres and hydrospheres to carry off the heat for you?"

"Because planets like that belong to suns, and circle 'em fairly close," Falkayn answered. "Otherwise their air would be frozen, wouldn't it? If they have big orbits, they might retain hydrogen and helium in a gaseous state. But hydrogen's nasty. It leaks right in between the molecules of any material shielding you set up, and bollixes your nuclear reactions good. Therefore you need a world about like Earth or Cynthia, with reasonably dense air that does not include free hydrogen, and with plenty of liquid water. Well, as I said, when you have a nearby sun pouring its own energy into the atmosphere, a transmutation industry of any size will cook the planet. How can you use a river if the river's turned to vapor? Oh, there have been proposals to orbit a dust cloud around such a world, raising the albedo to near 100. But that'd tend to trap home-grown heat. Cost-effectiveness studies showed it would never pay. And furthermore, new-formed systems have a lot of junk floating around. One large asteroid, plowing into your planet, stands a good chance of wrecking every operation on it."

Falkayn refreshed his throat. "Naturally," he continued, "once a few rogues had been discovered, people thought about using them. But they were *too* cold! Temperatures near absolute zero do odd things to the properties of matter. It'd be necessary to develop an entire new technology before a factory could be erected on the typical rogue. And then it wouldn't accomplish anything. Remember, you need liquid water and gaseous atmosphere—a planet's worth of both—for your coolants. And you can't fluidify an entire cryosphere. Not within historical time. No matter how huge an operation you mount. The energy required is just plain too great. Figure it out for yourself sometime. It turns out to be as much as all Earth gets from Sol in quite a few centuries."

Falkayn cocked his feet on the table and elevated his glass. "Which happens to be approximately what our planet here will have received, in going from deep space to Beta C. and back again," he finished. He tossed off his drink and poured another.

"Don't sound that smug," Chee grumbled. "You didn't cause the event. You are not the Omnipotent: a fact which often reconciles me to the universe."

Falkayn smiled. "You'd prefer Adzel, maybe? Or Muddlehead? Or Old Nick? Hey, what a thought, creation operated for profit!—But at any rate, you can see the opportunity we've got now, if the different factors do turn out the way we hope; and it looks more and more like they will. In another ten years or so, this planet ought to have calmed down. It won't be getting more illumination than your home world or mine; the cold, exposed rocks will have blotted up what excess heat didn't get reradiated; temperature will be reasonable, dropping steadily but not too fast. The transmutation industry can begin building, according to surveys and plans already made. Heat output can be kept in balance with heat loss: the deeper into space the planet moves, the more facilities go to work on it. Since the air will be poisonous anyway, and nearly every job will be automated, radioactive trash won't pose difficulties either.

"Eventually, some kind of equilibrium will be reached. You'll have a warm surface, lit by stars, lamps here and there, radio beacons guiding down the cargo shuttles; nuclear conversion units on every suitable spot; tons of formerly rare materials moving out each day, to put some real muscle in our industry—" The excitement caught him. He was still a young man. His fist smacked into his other palm. "And *we* brought it about!"

"For a goodly reward," Chee said. "It had better be goodly."

"Oh, it will be, it will be," Falkayn burbled. "Money in great, dripping, beautiful gobs. Only think what a franchise to build here will be worth. Especially if Solar S & L can maintain rights of first reconnaissance and effective occupation."

"As against commercial competitors?" Chee asked. "Or against the unknown rivals of our whole civilization? I think they'll make rather more trouble. The kind of industry you speak of has war potentials, you know."

The planet rotated in a little over thirteen hours. Its axis was tilted about eleven degrees from the normal to the plane of its hyperbolic orbit. *Muddlin' Through* aimed for the general area of the arctic circle, where the deadly day would be short, though furnishing periodic illumination, and conditions were apparently less extreme than elsewhere.

When the ship spiraled the globe at satellite altitude and slanted downward, Falkayn drew a sharp breath. He had glimpsed the sun side before, but in brief forays when he was preoccupied with taking accurate measurements. And Beta Crucis had not been this near. At wild and ever mounting velocity, the rogue would soon round the blue giant. They were not much farther apart now than are Earth and Sol.

With four times the angular diameter, this sun raged on the horizon, in a sky turned incandescent. Clouds roiled beneath, now steaming white, now gray and lightning-riven, now black with the smoke of volcanoes seen through rents in their reaches. Elsewhere could be glimpsed stony plains, lashed by terrible winds, rain, earthquake, flood, under mountain ranges off whose flanks cascaded the glacial melt. Vapors decked half a continent, formed into mist by the chill air, until a tornado cut them in half and a pack of gales harried the fragments away. On a gunmetal ocean, icebergs the size of islands crashed into each other; but spume and spindrift off monstrous waves hid most of their destruction. As the spaceship pierced the upper atmosphere, thin though it was, she rocked with its turbulence, and the first clamor keened through her hull plates. Ahead were stacked thunderstorms.

Falkayn said between his teeth, "I've been wondering what we should name this place. Now I know." But then they were in blindness and racket. He lacked any chance to speak further.

The internal fields held weight steady, but did not keep out repeated shocks nor the rising, raving noise. Muddlehead did the essential piloting—the integration of the whole intricate system which was the ship—while the team waited to make any crucial decisions. Straining into screens and meters, striving to make sense of the chaos that ramped across them, Falkayn heard the computer speak through yells, roars, whistles, and bangs:

"The condition of clear skies over the substellar point and in early tropical afternoons prevails as usual. But this continues to be followed by violent weather, with wind velocities in excess of 500 kilometers per hour and rising daily. I note in parentheses that it would already be dangerous to enter such a meteorological territory, and that at any moment it could become impossible even for the most well-equipped vessel. Conditions in the polar regions are much as previously observed. The antarctic is undergoing heavy rainfall with frequent supersqualls. The north polar country remains comparatively cold; thus a strong front, moving southward, preserves a degree of atmospheric tranquillity at its back. I suggest that planetfall be made slightly below the arctic circle, a few minutes in advance of the dawn line, on a section of the larger northern continent which appears to be free of inundation and, judging from tectonic data, is likely to remain stable."

"All right," Chee Lan said. "You pick it. Only don't let the instruments overload your logic circuits. I guess they're feeding you information at a fantastic rate. Well, don't bother processing and evaluating it for now. Just stash it in your memory and concentrate on getting us down safe!"

"Continuous interpretation is necessary, if I am to understand an unprecedented environment like this and conduct us through it," Muddlehead answered. "However, I am already deferring consideration of facts that do not seem to have immediate significance, such as the precise reflection spectra off various types of ice fields. It is noteworthy that—" Falkayn didn't hear the rest. A bombardment of thunder half deafened him for minutes.

And they passed through a wild whiteness, snow of some kind driven by a wind that made the ship reel. And they were in what felt, by contrast, like utter peace. It was night, very dark. Scanner beams built up the picture of a jagged highland, while the ship flew on her own inorganic senses.

And landed.

Falkayn sagged a moment in his chair, simply breathing. "Cut fields," he said, and unharnessed himself. The change to planetary weight wasn't abrupt; it came within five percent of Earth pull, and he was used to bigger differences. But the silence rang in his ears. He stood, working the tension out of his muscles, before he considered the viewscreens again.

Around the ship lay a rough, cratered floor of dark rock. Mountains rose sheer in the north and east. The former began no more than four kilometers away, as an escarpment roofed with crags and streaked with the white of glaciers. Stars lit the scene, for the travelers had passed beneath the clouds, which bulked swart in the south. Alien constellations shone clear, unwavering, through wintry air. Often across them streaked meteors; like other big, childless suns, Beta Crucis was surrounded by cosmic debris. Aurora danced glorious over the cliffs, and southeastward the first luster of morning climbed into heaven.

Falkayn examined the outside meters. The atmosphere was not

breathable—CO, CO_2, CH_4, NH_4, H_2S, and such. There was some oxygen, broken loose from water molecules by solar irradiation, retained when the lighter hydrogen escaped into space, not yet recombined with other elements. But it was too little for him, and vilely cold to boot, not quite at minus 75 degrees Celsius. The ground was worse than that, below minus 200. The tropics had warmed somewhat more. But an entire world could not be brought from death temperature to room temperature in less than years—not even by a blue giant—and conditions upon it would always vary from place to place. No wonder its weather ran amok.

"I'd better go out," he said. His voice dropped near a whisper in the frozen quietness.

"Or I." Chee Lan seemed equally subdued.

Falkayn shook his head. "I thought we'd settled that. I can carry more gear, accomplish more in the available time. And somebody's got to stand by in case of trouble. You take the next outing, when we use a gravsled for a wider look around."

"I merely wanted to establish my claim to an exterior mission before I go cage-crazy," she snapped.

That's more like the way we ought to be talking. Heartened, Falkayn proceeded to the airlock. His suit and his equipment were ready for him. Chee helped him into the armor. He cycled through and stood upon a new world.

An old one, rather: but one that was undergoing a rebirth such as yonder stars had never seen before.

He breathed deeply of chemical-tainted recycled air and strode off. His movements were a trifle clumsy, he stumbled now and then, on the thick soles attached to his boots. But without them, he would probably have been helpless. *Muddlin' Through* could pump heat from her nuclear powerplant into her landing jacks, to keep them at a temperature their metal could stand. But the chill in these rocks would suck warmth straight through any ordinary space brogan. His feet could freeze before he knew it. Even with extra insulation, his stay outdoors was sharply limited.

The sun bounded him more narrowly, though. Day was strengthening visibly, fire and long shadows across desolation. The shielding in his armor allowed him about half an hour in the full radiance of Beta Crucis.

"How are things?" Chee's voice sounded faint in his earplugs, through a rising buzz of static.

"Thing-like." Falkayn unlimbered a counter from his backpack and passed it above the ground. The readoff showed scant radioactivity. Much of what there was, was probably induced by solar wind in the past decade, before the atmosphere thickened. (Not that its insignificant ozone layer was a lot of protection at present.) No matter, men and the friends of men would make their own atoms here. Falkayn hammered in a neutron-analysis spike and continued on his way.

That looked like an interesting outcrop. He struck loose a sample.

The sun lifted into view. His self-darkening faceplate went almost black. Gusts moaned down off the mountains, and vapors began to swirl above the glacial masses.

Falkayn chose a place for a sonic probe and began to assemble the needful tripod. "Better not dawdle," said Chee's distorted tone. "The radiation background's getting foul."

"I know, I know," the Hermetian said. "But we want some idea about the underlying strata, don't we?" The combination of glare and protection against it handicapped his eyes, making delicate adjustments difficult. He swore picturesquely, laid tongue on lip, and slogged ahead with the job. When at last he had the probe in action, transmitting data back to the ship, his safety margin was ragged.

He started his return. The vessel looked unexpectedly small, standing beneath those peaks that also enclosed him on the right. Beta Crucis hurled wave upon wave of heat at his back, to batter past reflecting paint and refrigerating unit. Sweat made his undergarments soggy and stank in his nostrils. Simultaneously, cold stole up into his boots, until toenails hurt. He braced himself, beneath the weight of armor and gear, and jog-trotted.

A yell snatched his gaze around. He saw the explosion on the clifftop, like a white fountain. A moment later, the bawl of it echoed in his helmet and the earth shock threw him to his knees. He staggered erect and tried to run. The torrent—part liquid flood, part solid avalanche—roared and leaped in pursuit. It caught him halfway to the ship.

✲XIII✲

Reflex cast him down and rolled him into a ball an instant before the slide arrived. Then he was in darkness and bass noise, tumbled about, another object among the boulders and ice chunks that smashed against his armor.

Concussion struck through metal and padding. His head rocked in the helmet. Blow after blow kicked him loose from awareness.

The cataract ground to a halt. Falkayn realized dazedly that he was buried in it. His knees remained next his belly, his arms across the faceplate. He mumbled at the pain that throbbed through him, and tried to stir. It was impossible. Terror smote. He yelled and strained. No use. Sheer surrounding bulk locked him into his embryonic crouch.

The freezing began. Radiation is not an efficient process. Conduction is, especially when the stuff around drinks every calorie that a far higher temperature will supply. Falkayn's heating coils drained their powerpack before he had recovered consciousness. He could not thresh about to keep warm by effort. He tried to call on his radio, but it seemed to be knocked out; silence filled his skull, darkness his vision, cold his body.

The thought trickled: *I'm helpless. There is not one goddamned thing in the continuum I can do to save myself. It's an awful feeling.*

Defiance: *At least my mind is my own. I can go out thinking, reliving memories, like a free man.* But nothing came to mind save blackness, stillness, and cold.

He clamped his jaws together against the clatter of teeth and hung bulldog-wise onto the resolution that he would not panic again.

He was lying thus, no more than a spark left in his brain, when the glacial mass steamed away from him. He sprawled stupid in fog and evaporating liquid. Beta Crucis burned off the mists and beat on his armor. Elsewhere the avalanche was boiling more gradually off the valley floor. But *Muddlin' Through* cruised overhead, slowly, fanning a low-level energy beam across the snows. When her scanners detected Falkayn, a tractor beam extended. He was snatched up, hauled through a cargo port, and dumped on deck for Chee Lan's profane ministrations.

A couple of hours later he sat in his bunk, nursing a bowl of soup, and regarded her with clear eyes. "Sure, I'm fine now," he said. "Give me a nightwatch's sleep and I'll be my old self."

"Is that desirable?" the Cynthian snorted. "If I were so tube-headed as to go out on dangerous terrain without a gravbelt to flit me aloft, I'd trade myself in on a newer model."

Falkayn laughed. "You never suggested it either," he said. "It'd have meant I could carry less gear. What did happen?"

"*Ying-ng-ng* . . . the way Muddlehead and I reconstruct it, that glacier wasn't water. It was mostly dry ice—solid carbon dioxide—with some other gases mixed in. Local temperature has finally gotten to the sublimation point, or a touch higher. But the heat of vaporization must be fed in. And this area chills off fast after dark; and daylight lasts just a few hours; and, too, I suspect the more volatile components were stealing heat from the main frozen mass. The result was an unstable equilibrium. It happened to collapse precisely when you were outside. How very like the fates! A major part of the ice pack sublimed, explosively, and dislodged the rest from the escarpment. If only we'd thought to take reflection spectra and thermocouple readings—"

"But we didn't," Falkayn said, "and I for one don't feel too guilty. We can't think of everything. Nobody can. We're bound to do most of our learning by trial and error."

"Preferably with someone standing by to retrieve us when it really hits the fan."

"Uh-huh. We ought to be part of a regular exploratory fleet. But under present circumstances, we aren't, that's all." Falkayn chuckled. "At least I've had my opinion strengthened as to what this planet should be named. Satan."

"Which means?"

"The enemy of the divine, the source of evil, in one of our terrestrial religions."

"But any reasonable being can see that the divine itself is—Oh, well, never mind. I thought you humans had run out of mythological names for planets. Surely you've already christened one Satan."

"M-m, I don't remember. There's Lucifer, of course, and Ahriman, and Loki, and—Anyhow, the traditional Satan operates an underworld of fire, except where it's icy, and amuses himself thinking up woes for wicked souls. Appropriate, no?"

"If he's like some other antigods I've met," Chee said, "he can make you rich, but you always find in the end that it was not a good idea to bargain with him."

Falkayn shrugged. "We'll see. Where are we at the moment?"

"Cruising over the night side, taking readings and pictures. I don't see any point in lingering. Every indication we've gotten, every extrapolation we can make, indicates that the course of events will gladden van Rijn to the clinkered cockles of his greedy heart. That is, the whole cryosphere will fluidify, and in a decade or so conditions will be suitable for industry. Meanwhile, however, things are getting more dangerous by the hour."

As if to underline Chee's words, the ship lurched and her wind-smitten hull plates belled. She was through the storm in a minute or two. But Falkayn reflected what that storm must be like, thus to affect a thermonuclear-powered, gravity-controlling, force-screened, sensor-guided, and computer-piloted vessel capable of crossing interstellar space and fighting a naval engagement.

"I agree," he said. "Let's collect as much more data as we safely can in—oh, the next twenty-four hours—and then line out for home. Let somebody else make detailed studies later. We'll need a combat group here anyway, I suppose, to mount guard on this claim."

"The sooner Old Nick learns it's worth his while to send that group, the better." Chee switched her tail. "If enemy pickets are posted when it arrives, we've all got troubles."

"Don't worry," Falkayn said. "Our distinguished opponents must live quite a ways off, seeing they haven't even gotten a scout here yet."

"Are you certain their advance expedition did not come and go while we were en route?" Chee asked slowly.

"It'd still be around. We spent a couple of weeks in transit and a bit longer at work. We're quitting early because two beings in one ship can only do so much—not because we've learned everything we'd like to know—and because we've a sense of urgency. The others, having no reason to suspect we're on to their game, should logically have planned on a more leisurely and thorough survey." Falkayn scratched his chin. The stubble reminded him that he was overdue for a dose of antibeard enzyme. "Of course," he said, "their surveyors may have been around, detected us approaching, and run to fetch Daddy. Who might be on his way as of now, carrying a rather large stick." He raised his voice, jocularly. "You don't spot any starships, do you, Muddlehead?"

"No," said the computer.

"Good." Falkayn eased back on his pillows. This craft was equipped to register the quasi-instantaneous "wake" of troubled space that surrounded an operating hyperdrive, out almost to the theoretical limit of about one light-year. "I hardly expected—"

"My detectors are turned off," Muddlehead explained.

Falkayn jerked upright. The soup spilled from his bowl, across Chee Lan, who went into the air with a screech. "*What?*" the man cried.

"Immediately before our run to take orbit, you instructed me to keep every facility alert for local dangers," Muddlehead reminded him. "It followed that computer capability should not be tied up by monitoring instruments directed at interstellar space."

"Judas in a reactor," Falkayn groaned. "I thought you'd acquired more initiative than that. What'd those cookbook engineers on Luna do when they overhauled you?"

Chee shook herself, dog fashion, spraying soup across him. "*Ya-t'in-chai-ourh,*" she snarled, which will not bear translation. "Get cracking on those detectors!"

For a moment, silence hummed, under the shriek outside. The possessions that crowded Falkayn's cabin—pictures, books, taper and spools and viewer, a half-open closet jamful of elegant garments, a few souvenirs and favorite weapons, a desk piled with unanswered letters—became small and fragile and dear. Human and Cynthian huddled together, not noticing that they did so, her fangs shining within the crook of his right arm.

The machine words fell: "Twenty-three distinct sources of pulsation are observable in the direction of Circinus."

Falkayn sat rigid. It leaped through him: *Nobody we know lives out that way. They must be headed here. We won't be sure of their course or distance unless we run off a base line and triangulate, or wait and see how they behave. But who can doubt they are the enemy?*

As if across an abyss he heard Chee Lan whisper, "Twenty . . . mortal . . . three of them. That's a task force! Unless—Can you make any estimates?"

"Signal-to-noise ratio suggests they are within one-half light-year," the computer said, with no more tone in its voice than ever before. "Its time rate of change indicates a higher pseudo-speed than a Technic shipmaster would consider wise in approaching a star like Beta Crucis that is surrounded by an unusual density of gas and solid material. The ratio of the separate signal amplitudes would appear to fit the hypothesis of a fleet organized around one quite large vessel, approximately equivalent to a League battleship, three light cruisers or similar units, and nineteen smaller, faster craft. But of course these conclusions are tentative, predicated on assumptions such as that it is indeed an armed force and is actually bound our way. Even under that class of hypotheses, the probable error of the data is too large at present to allow reliable evaluations."

"If we wait for those," Chee growled, deep in her throat, "we'll be reliably dead. I'll believe it's *not* a war fleet sent by our self-appointed enemies, with orders to swat anybody it finds, when the commander invites us to tea." She moved away from Falkayn, crouched before him on the blanket, tail bottled and eyes like jade lamps. "Now what's our next move?"

The man drew a breath. He felt the damp cold leave his palms, the heartbeat within him drop back to a steady slugging, a military officer take command of his soul. "We can't stay on Satan, or nearby," he declared. "They'd pick up our engines on neutrino detectors, if nothing else, and blast us. We could run away on ordinary gravitics, take an orbit closer to the sun, hope its emission would screen us till they go away. But that doesn't look any good either. They'll hardly leave before we'd've taken a lethal cumulative radiation dose . . . if they intend to leave at all. We might, alternatively, assume a very large orbit around Beta. Our minimal emission would be detectable against the low background; but we could pray that no one happens to point an instrument in our direction. I don't like that notion either. We'd be stuck for some indefinite time, with no way to get a message home."

"We'd send a report in a capsule, wouldn't we? There's a full stock of four aboard." Chee pondered. "No, effectively two, because we'd have to rob the others of their capacitors if those two are going to have the energy to reach Sol—or anyplace from which the word could go on to Sol, I'm afraid. Still, we do have a pair."

Falkayn shook his head. "Too slow. They'd be observed—"

"They don't emit much. It's not as if they had nuclear generators."

"A naval-type detector can nevertheless spot a capsule under hyperdrive at farther range than we've got available, Chee. And the thing's nothing more than a tube, for Judas's sake, with an elementary sort of engine, a robopilot barely able to steer where it's programmed for and holler, 'Here I am, come get me,' on its radio at journey's end. No, any pursuer can zero in, match phase, and either blow the capsule up or take it aboard."

The Cynthian eased her thews somewhat. Having assimilated the fact of crisis, she was becoming as coldly rational as the Hermetian. "I gather you think we should run for home ourselves," she said. "Not a bad idea, if none of those units can outpace us."

"We're pretty fast," he said.

"Some kinds of combat ship are faster. They fill space with powerplants and oscillators that we reserve for cargo."

"I know. It's uncertain what the result of a race would be. Look, though." Falkayn leaned forward, fists clenched on knees. "Whether we have longer legs than they, or vice versa, a half light-year head start will scarcely make any difference across two hundred. We don't much increase the risk by going out to meet them. And we just might learn something, or be able to do something, or—I don't know. It's a hand we'll have to play as it is dealt. Mainly, however, think of this. If we go hyper with a powerful surge of 'wake,' we'll blanket the takeoff of a tiny message capsule. It'll be out of detection range before anybody can separate its emission from ours . . . especially if we're headed toward him. So whatever happens to us, we'll've got our information home. We'll've done the enemy that much damage, at least!"

Chee regarded him for a while that grew quite silent, until she murmured, "I suspect your emotions are speaking. But today they make sense."

"Start preparing for action," Falkayn rapped. He swung his feet to the deck and stood up. A wave of giddiness went through him. He rested against the bulkhead until it passed. Exhaustion was a luxury he couldn't afford. He'd take a stim pill and pay the metabolic price later, if he survived.

Chee's words lingered at the back of his mind. *No doubt she's right. I'm being fueled by anger at what they did to me. I want revenge on them.* A jag went along his nerves. He gasped. *Or is it fear . . . that they might do the thing to me again?*

I'll die before that happens. And I'll take some of them with me to—to Satan!

XIV

Stars glittered in their prismatic colors and multiple thousands, Beta Crucis little more than the brightest among them; the Milky Way spilled around crystal darkness; the far cold whirlpools of a few sister galaxies could be seen, when the League ship made contact with the strangers.

Falkayn sat in the bridge, surrounded by outside views and engine murmur. Chee Lan was aft, in the fire control center. Either one could have been anywhere aboard, to receive information from the computer and issue it orders. Their separation was no more than a precaution in case of attack, and no wider than a hull permeated by light-speed electronic webs. But loneliness pressed in on Falkayn. The uniform he wore beneath his space armor, in place of a long john, was less a diplomatic formality than a defiance.

He stared through his helmet, which was still open, first at the screens and then at the instruments. His merely flesh-and-blood organism could not apprehend and integrate the totality of data presented, as the computer could. But an experienced eye took in a general picture.

Muddlin' Through was plunging along a curve that would soon intercept one of the fleet's outriders. She must have been detected, from the moment she went on hyperdrive. But none of those vessels had altered course or reckless pseudospeed. Instead, they proceeded as before, in a tighter formation than any Technic admiral would have adopted.

It looked as if the alien commander wouldn't grant his subordinates the least freedom of action. His entire group moved in a unit, one hammer hurled at target.

Falkayn wet his lips. Sweat prickled along his ribs. "Damnation," he said, "don't they want to parley? To find out who we are, if nothing else?"

They didn't have to, of course. They could simply let *Muddlin' Through* pass between them. Or they might plan on a quick phase-match and assault, the moment she came in ready range—so quick that her chance of shifting the phase of her own quantum oscillations, thus becoming transparent to whatever they threw at her, would be slight.

"They may not recognize our signal for what it is," Chee Lan suggested. Her voice on the intercom made Falkayn visualize her, small, furry, and deadly . . . yes, she'd insist on operating one gun by hand, if battle broke—

"They know enough about us to establish spies in our home territory. So they know our standard codes," Falkayn snapped. "Give 'em another toot, Muddlehead."

Viewscreens flickered with the slight alterations in hyper-velocity imposed by the outercom as it modulated drive vibrations to carry dots and dashes. That system was still new and crude (Falkayn could remember when, early in his career, he had been forced to turn his engines themselves on and off to transmit a message) but the call was simple. *Urgent. Assume normal state and prepare for radionic communication on standard band.*

"No response," the computer said after a minute.

"Cease transmission," Falkayn ordered. "Chee, can you think of any motive for their behavior?"

"I can imagine quite a number of different explanations," the Cynthian said. "That's precisely the trouble."

"Uh, yeh. Especially when none of 'em are apt to be right. One culture's rationality isn't quite the same as another's. Though I did think any civilization capable of space flight must necessarily—No matter. They obviously aren't going to detach a ship for talkie-talkie. So I don't propose to steer into a possible trap. Change course, Muddlehead. Run parallel to them."

Engines growled. Stars swung around the screens. The situation stabilized. Falkayn gazed toward the unseen strangers. They were crossing the clouded glory of Sagittarius. . . . "We may learn a bit by analyzing their 'wake' patterns, now that we're close enough to get accurate readings," he said. "But we hardly dare follow them clear to Satan."

"I don't like accompanying them any distance," Chee said. "They travel too bloody-be-gibbeted fast for this kind of neighborhood."

Falkayn reached out an ungauntleted hand for the pipe he had laid on a table. It had gone cold. He made a production of rekindling it. The smoke gave tongue and nostrils a comforting love-bite. "We're safer than they are," he said. "We know more about the region, having been here a while. For instance, we've charted several asteroid orbits, remember?"

"You don't believe, then, they had a scout like ours, who paid a visit before we arrived?"

"No. That'd imply their home sun—or at least a large outpost of their domain—is nearby, as cosmic distances go. Now the Beta Crucis region isn't what you'd call thoroughly explored, but some expeditions have come through, like the one from Lemminkainen. And explorers always keep a weather eye out for signs of atomic-powered civilizations. I feel sure that somebody, sometime, would've identified the neutrino emission from any such planet within fifty light-years of here. True, conceivably those nuclear generators weren't yet built fifty years ago and the neutrinos haven't arrived yet. But on the other hand, voyages have been made beyond this star. Altogether, every probability says these characters have come a considerable ways. The messenger ship from Luna must barely have had time to notify them about the existence of the rogue."

"And they committed a whole fleet immediately—with no preliminary investigation—and it's roaring down on goal as if this were clear one-hydrogen-atom-per-c.c. space—and not even trying to discover who we are? *Ki-yao!*"

Falkayn's grin was taut and brief. "If a Cynthian says an action is too impulsive, then by my battered halidom, it is."

"But these same beings . . . presumably the same . . . they organized Serendipity . . . one of the longest-range, most patience-demanding operations I've ever heard of."

"There are parallels in human history, if not in yours. And, hm, humans—more or less humans—were involved in our case—"

The computer said, "Incoming hypercode." The display screen blinked with a series that Falkayn recognized: *Request for talk acknowledged. Will comply. Propose we rendezvous ten astronomical units hence, five hundred kilometers apart.*

He didn't stop to inform Chee—the ship would do that—nor shout his own astonishment, nor feel it except for an instant. Too much work was on hand. Orders rapped from him: Send agreement. Lay appropriate course. Keep alert for treachery, whether from the vessel that would stop and parley or from the rest of the fleet, which might double back under hyper-drive.

"The entire group remains together," Muddlehead interrupted. "Evidently they will meet us as one."

"What?" he choked. "But that's ridiculous."

"No." Chee's voice fell bleak. "If twenty-three of them fire on us simultaneously, we're dead."

"Perhaps not." Falkayn clamped the pipe more firmly between his jaws. "Or they may be honest. We'll know in another thirty seconds."

The ships cut off their quantum oscillators and flashed into the relativistic state of matter-energy. There followed the usual period of hastily calculated and applied thrust, until kinetic velocities were matched. Falkayn let Muddlehead take care of that and Chee stand by the defenses. He concentrated on observing what he might about the strangers.

It was little. A scanner could track a ship and magnify the image for him, but details got lost across those dimly lighted distances. And details were what mattered; the laws of nature do not allow fundamental differences between types of spacecraft.

He did find that the nineteen destroyers or escort pursuers, or whatever you wanted to call them, were streamlined for descent into atmosphere: but radically streamlined, thrice the length of his vessel without having appreciably more beam. They looked like stiffened conger eels. The cruisers bore more resemblance to sharks, with gaunt finlike structures that must be instrument or control turrets. The battleship was basically a huge spheroid, but this was obscured by the steel towers, pillboxes, derricks, and emplacements that covered her hull.

You might as well use naval words for yonder craft, even though none corresponded exactly to such classes in the League. They bristled with guns, missile launchers, energy projectors. Literally, they bristled. Falkayn had never before encountered vessels so heavily armed. With the machinery and magazines that that entailed . . . where the devil was room left for a crew?

Instruments said that they employed force screens, radars, fusion power—the works. It was hardly a surprise. The unorthodox, tight formation was. If they expected trouble, why not disperse? One fifty-megaton warhead exploding in their midst would take out two or three of them directly, and fill the rest with radiation. Maybe that wouldn't disable their computers and other electronic apparatus—depended on whether they used things like transistors—but it would give a lethal dose to a lot of crewfolk, and put the rest in hospital.

Unless the aliens didn't mind X-rays and neutrons. But then they couldn't be protoplasmic. With or without drugs, the organic molecule can only tolerate a certain bombardment before it shatters. Unless they'd developed some unheard-of screen to deflect uncharged particles. Unless, unless, unless!

"Are you in communication with any of their mechanisms?" Falkayn asked.

"No," Muddlehead answered. "They are simply decelerating as they would have had to sooner or later if they wish to take orbit around Satan. The task of matching velocities is left to us."

"Arrogant bastards, aren't they?" Chee said.

"With an arsenal like theirs, arrogance comes easy." Falkayn settled into his chair. "We can play their game. Hold off on the masers. Let them call us." He wondered if his pipe looked silly, sticking out of an open space helmet. To hell with it. He wanted a smoke. A beer would have been still more welcome. The strain of wondering if their weapons were about to cut loose on him was turning his mouth dry.

An energy blast would smite before it could be detected. It might not penetrate the armor too fast for *Muddlin' Through* to go hyper and escape. That would be determined by various unpredictables, like its power and the exact place it happened to strike. *But if the aliens want to kill us, why bother to revert? They can overhaul us, maybe not their capital ships, but those destroyers must be faster. And we can't stay out of phase with nineteen different enemies, each trying to match us, for very long.*

Yet if they want to talk, why didn't they answer our call earlier?

As if she had read her companion's mind, Chee Lan said, "I have an idea that may account for parts of their behavior, Dave. Suppose they are wildly impulsive. Learning about Satan, they dispatch a task force to grab it. The grabbing may be away from members of their own race. We don't know how unified they are. And they can't have learned that Serendipity's cover is blown. Nor can they be sure that it isn't.

"Under those circumstances, most sophonts would be cautious. They'd send an advance party to investigate and report back, before committing themselves substantially. Not these creatures, though. These charge right ahead, ready to blast their way through any opposition or die in the attempt.

"And they do find someone waiting for them: us, one small ship, cheekily running out to make rendezvous. You or I would wonder if more vessels, bigger ones, aren't lying doggo near Satan. Our first thought would be to talk with the other. But they don't emote that way. They keep on going. Either we are alone and can safely be clobbered, or we have friends and there will be a battle. The possibility of retreat or negotiation isn't considered. Nor do they alter any vectors on our account. After all, we're headed straight for them. We'll bring ourselves in killing range.

"Well, we fool them, changing over to a parallel course. They decide they'd better hear us out; or, at least, that they might as well do so. Maybe it occurs to them that we could perhaps get away, bring word back to Earth, in spite of everything. You see, they'd have to detach one or more destroyers to chase us down. And their formation suggests that, for some reason, they're reluctant to do this.

"In short, another lightning decision has been made, regardless of what may be at hazard."

"It sounds altogether crazy," Falkayn objected.

"To you, not me. Cynthians are less stodgy than humans. I grant you, my people—my own society—is forethoughtful. But I know other cultures on my planet where berserk action is normal."

"But those're technologically primitive, Chee. Aren't they? Hang it, you can't operate an atomic-powered civilization that way.

Things'd fall apart on you. Even Old Nick doesn't have absolute authority in his own outfit. He has to work with advisers, executives, people of every kind and rank. The normal distribution curve guarantees enough naturally cautious types to put the brakes on an occasional reckless—"

Falkayn broke off. The central receiver was flickering to life.

"They're calling us," he said. His belly muscles tightened. "Want an auxiliary screen to watch?"

"No," Chee Lan answered starkly. "I'll listen, but I want my main attention on our weapons and theirs."

The maser beams locked on. Falkayn heard the report, "Their transmission is from the battleship," with half an ear. The rest of him focused on the image that appeared before him.

A man! Falkayn almost lost his pipe. A man, lean, with gray-speckled hair, smoldering eyes, body clad in a drab coverall. . . . *I should've guessed. I should've been prepared.* Scant background was visible: an instrument console of obviously non-Technic manufacture, shining beneath a hard white light.

Falkayn swallowed. "Hello, Hugh Latimer," he said most softly.

"We have not met," the accented, unemotional Anglic replied.

"No. But who else might you be?"

"Who are you?"

Falkayn's mind scrambled. His name was a hole card in a wild game. He wasn't about to turn it up for the enemy to make deductions from. "Sebastian Tombs," he replied. The alias was unoriginal, but Latimer would scarcely have come upon the source. Mere chance had put those books in the library of Duke Robert for an inquisitive boy to find, and thus discover that ancient languages weren't all classics and compositions but were sometimes fun—"Master merchant and captain in the Polesotechnic League." Asserting his rank should do no harm, and possibly a little good. "Are you in command of your group?"

"No."

"Then I'd like to speak with whoever is in charge."

"You shall," Hugh Latimer told him. "He has ordered it."

Falkayn bridled. "Well, connect him."

"You do not understand," said the other. Still his voice had no inflection, and his eyes stared directly out of the hollow-cheeked, deeply tanned face. "Gahood wants you to come here."

The pipestem snapped between Falkayn's teeth. He cast it aside and exclaimed, "Are you living in the same universe as me? Do you expect I'd—" He curbed himself. "I have a few suggestions for your commander," he said, "but I'll reserve them, because his anatomy may not be adapted for such things. Just ask him if he considers it reasonable for me, for anyone in my crew, to put himself at your mercy that way."

Did the least hint of fear cross Latimer's rigid features? "My orders have been given me. What value for you if I went back, argued, and was punished?" He hesitated. "You have two choices, I think. You can refuse. In that case, I imagine Gahood will start firing. You may or may not escape; he does not seem to care greatly. On the other hand, you can come. He is intrigued at the thought of meeting a . . . wild human. You may accomplish something. I do not know. Perhaps you and I can work out conditions beforehand that will give you assurance of being able to return. But we mustn't take long, or he will grow impatient. Angry." His fear was now unmistakable. "And then anything might happen."

XV

The danger in coming near the enemy was obvious. Not only an energy beam, but a material missile could hit before effective reaction was possible. However, the danger was mutual. *Muddlin' Through* might be a gnat compared to the battlewagon, but she was every bit as mean. Falkayn didn't fancy leaving five hundred kilometers between him and her. He was dismayed when Latimer insisted.

"Do not forget, my life's work was learning everything I could about Technic civilization," the gaunt man said. "I know the capabilities of a vessel like yours. Besides an assortment of small arms, and several light guns for dogfights, she mounts four heavy blast cannon and carries four nuclear torpedoes. At close range, such armament makes us too nearly equal. Let a dispute arise, and we could doubtless kill you, but ships of ours might also perish."

"If my crew are too far off to strike effectively, what'll stop you from taking me prisoner?" Falkayn protested.

"Nothing," Latimer said, "except lack of motive. I think Gahood merely wants to interrogate you, and perhaps give you a message to take back to your masters. If you delay, though, he'll lose patience and order you destroyed."

"All right!" Falkayn said harshly. "I'll come as fast as I can. If I don't report back within an hour of entering, my crew will assume treachery on your part and act accordingly. In that case, you might get a rude surprise." He broke the connection and sat for a moment, clenching the arms of his chair, trying not to shudder.

Chee Lan padded in, squatted at his feet and looked upward. "You don't want to go," she said with uncommon gentleness. "You're afraid of being drugged again."

Falkayn nodded, a jerk of his head. "You can't imagine what it's like," he said through a tightened gullet.

"I can go."

"No. I am the skipper." Falkayn rose. "Let's get me ready."

"If nothing else," Chee said, "we can guarantee you won't be captured."

"What? How?"

"Of course, the price might be death. But that's one fear you've been trained to control."

"Oh-h-h," Falkayn breathed. "I see what you mean." He snapped his fingers. His eyes sparked. "Why didn't I think of it?"

And so presently he departed.

He wore an impeller on his space armor, but this was reserve. His actual transportation was a gravsled. He kept the canopy down, the cockpit filled with air, as another reserve; in case his helmet got cracked or something, he needn't spend time preparing this minimal, skeletal vehicle for departure. But atmosphere or no, he rode in ghostly silence, naught save a faint tug of acceleration making his broomstick flight feel real. The stars had dimmed and withdrawn in his vision. That was prosaically due to the panel lights, their greenish glow desensitizing his retinae. Nevertheless, he missed the stars. He grasped his controls more tightly than required and whistled up a tune for company.

Oh, a tinker came a-strollin',
A-strollin' down the Strand—

It didn't seem inappropriate for what might be the last melody ever to pass his lips. Solemnity had no appeal. His surroundings, that mountain of a ship bulking closer and closer before him, furnished as much seriousness as anybody could want.

Latimer's radio voice chopped off his bawdy little ballad. "You will be guided to an airlock by a beam at 158.6 megahertz. Park your sled in the chamber and wait for me."

"What?" Falkayn gibed. "You don't aim to pipe me aboard?"

"I do not understand."

"You wouldn't. Forget it. I'm not ambitious to become a haggis anyway." Falkayn tuned in the signal and set the sled to home on it. He got busy photographing the battleship as he neared, studying the fortress-like superstructures himself, stowing every possible datum in memory. But part of his mind freewheeled, wondering.

That Latimer is sure one overworked chap. He acts like a kind of executive officer for Gahood, whatever Gahood is. But he also acts like the communications officer, boatswain . . . everything!

Well, given sufficient automation, you don't need much crew. The all-around Renaissance man has come back these days, with a battery of computers to specialize for him. But some jobs remain that machines don't do well. They haven't the motivation, the initiative, the organismic character of true sophonts. We—each civilized species man's encountered—we've never succeeded in building a hundred percent robotic vessel for more than the elementary, cut-and-dried jobs. And when you're exploring, trading, conducting a war, anything that takes you into unpredictable situations, the size of crew you need goes up. Partly to meet psychological necessities, of course; but partly to fulfill the mission itself in all its changing complexity.

Look how handicapped Chee and I have been, in being just two. That was because of an emergency, which Gahood did not face. Why is Latimer the only creature I've spoken to in yonder armada?

His approach curve brought Falkayn near a cruiser. More than ever he was struck by the density of her armament. And those fin-shaped turrets were thinner than he had imagined. They were fine for instruments, with that much surface area, and indeed they appeared to be studded with apparatus. But it was hard to see how an animal of any plausible size and shape could move around inside them. Or, for that matter, inside the hull, considering how packed it must be.

The thought did not jolt Falkayn. It had grown in him for a while and was quietly born. He plugged the jack on his helmet into the maser unit locked on *Muddlin' Through.* "You read me, Chee Lan?" he asked.

"Aye. What report?"

Falkayn switched to the Eriau they had learned on Merseia. Latimer would scarcely know it, if he had ways to monitor. The Hermetian described what he had seen. "I'm damn near convinced that everything except the battleship is strictly robot," he finished. "That'd account for a lot of things. Like their formation. Gahood has to keep closer tabs on them than he would on live captains. And he cares less about losses in battle. They're merely machines. Probably radiation-proof anyhow. And if he's got a single crewed ship, it'd be easy—even natural—for him to charge off the way he did. Of course, no matter how his race has organized its economy, a fleet like this is expensive. But it's more replaceable than several hundred or thousand highly skilled crewpeople. For a prize like Satan, one might well take the gamble."

"*I-yirh,* your idea sounds plausible, David. Especially if Gahood is something like a war lord, with a personal following ready to go anywhere at any moment. Then he might not have needed to consult others. . . . I feel a touch more hope. The enemy isn't quite as formidable as he seemed."

"Formidable enough. If I don't report back to you in the hour, or if you have any other reason to suspect something's fused, don't you play Loyal Retainer. Get the devil out of here."

She started to object. He overrode her words with the reminder: "I'll be dead. Nothing you can do for me, except whatever revenge may come from getting our information home."

She paused. "Understood," she said finally.

"You have a fifty-fifty chance of eluding pursuit, I'd say, if there is any," he told her. "Nineteen destroyers can phase-match you by sheer random trying if nothing else. But if they're robots, you might outfox them first. Or at least send another message capsule off without their noticing. . . . Well, I'm closing in now. Will be out of touch. Good faring, Chee."

He could not follow her answer. It was in an archaic version of her native language. But he caught a few words, like "blessing," and her voice was not altogether steady.

The battleship loomed sheer before him. He cut off his autopilot and proceeded on manual. As he left the shadow of a turret, light spilled blindingly into his view. It came from a circle big as a cargo hatch, the airlock he must be supposed to use. He steered with care past the thick coaming and outer gate. The inner valve was shut. Ship's gravity caught at him, making it a little tricky to set down. Having done so, he cycled out through the cockpit minilock as fast as he was able.

Quickly, then, he unhooked the thing at his belt and made it ready. Held in his left hand, it gave him a frosty courage. Waiting for Latimer, he examined the sled's instrument panel through the canopy. Gravpull felt higher than Earth standard, and the scale confirmed this with a value of 1.07. Illumination was more than a third again what he was used to. Spectral distribution indicated an F-type home star, though you couldn't really tell from fluorescents. . . .

The inner valve opened. Little air whiffed through; the lock was compound, with another chamber behind the first. A space-suited human figure trod in. Behind the faceplate, Latimer's austere features showed in highlights and darknesses. He carried a blaster. It was an ordinary pistol type, doubtless acquired on Luna. But at his back moved a metal shape, tall, complex, a multitude of specialized limbs sprouting from the cylindrical body to end in sensors and effectors: a robot.

"What a rude way to receive an ambassador," Falkayn said. He did not raise his hands.

Latimer didn't ask him to. "Precaution," he explained matter-of-factly. "You are not to enter armed. And first we check for bombs or other surprises you may have brought."

"Go ahead," Falkayn answered. "My vehicle's clean and, as agreed, I left my guns behind. I do have this, however." He elevated his left fist, showing the object it grasped.

Latimer recoiled. "*Jagnath hamman!* What is that?"

"Grenade. Not nuclear, only an infantry make. But the stuffing is tordenite, with colloidal phosphorus for seasoning. It could mess things up rather well within a meter or two radius right here. Much nastier in an oxygenous atmosphere, of course. I've pulled the pin, and counted almost the whole five seconds before driving the plunger back in. Nothing except my thumb keeps it from going off. Oh, yes, it spits a lot of shrapnel too."

"But—you—no!"

"Don't fret yourself, comrade. The spring isn't too strong for me to hold down for an hour. I don't want to be blown up. It's just that I want even less to be taken prisoner, or shot, or something like that. You abide by the diplomatic courtesies and we won't have any problems."

"I must report," Latimer said thickly. He plugged into what was evidently an intercom. Emotionless, the robot checked out the sled as it had been ordered, and waited.

Latimer said, "He will see you. Come." He led the way, his movements still jerky with outrage. The robot brought up the rear.

Falkayn felt walled between them. His grenade was no defense against anything except capture. If the others wished, they could maneuver him into destruction without suffering undue damage. Or their ship wouldn't be harmed in the least if they potted him on his return, after he was well clear.

Forget it. You came here to learn what you might. You're no hero. You'd one hell of a lot rather be quite far away, a drink in your grip and a wench on your knee, prevaricating about your exploits. But this could be a war brewing. Whole planets could get attacked. A little girl, as it might be your own kid niece, could lie in an atom-blasted house, her face a cinder and her eyeballs melted, screaming for her daddy who's been killed in a spaceship and her mother who's been smashed against the pavement. Maybe matters aren't really that bad. But maybe they are. How can you pass up a chance to do something? You've got to inhabit the same skin as yourself.

It itches. And I can't scratch. A grin bent one corner of Falkayn's mouth. The second lock chamber had been closed, pressure had been restored, the inner valve was opening. He stepped through.

There was not much to see. A corridor led off, bare metal, blazingly lit. Footfalls rang on its deck. Otherwise a quiver of engines, hoarse murmur of forced-draft ventilation, were the sole relief in its blankness. No doors gave on it, merely grilles, outlets, occasional enigmatic banks of instruments or controls. Another robot passed through a transverse hall several meters ahead: a different model, like a scuttling disc with tentacles and feelers, doubtless intended for some particular kind of maintenance work. But the bulk of the ship's functioning must be integrated, even more than on a human-built vessel; she was herself one vast machine.

Despite the desertion, Falkayn got a sense of raw, overwhelming vitality. Perhaps it came from the sheer scale of everything, or the ceaseless throbbing, or a more subtle clue like the proportions of that which he saw, the sense of masses huge and heavy but crouched to pounce.

"The atmosphere is breathable," Latimer's radio voice said. "Its density is slightly above Earth sea level." Falkayn imitated him with his free hand, opening the bleeder valve to let pressures equalize gradually before he slid back his faceplate and filled his lungs.

Except for the added information, he wished he hadn't. The air was desert hot, desert dry, with enough thunder-smelling ozone to sting. Other odors blew on those booming currents, pungencies like spice and leather and blood, strengthening as the party approached what must be living quarters. Latimer didn't seem to mind the climate or the glare. But he was used to them. Wasn't he?

"How big a crew do you have?" Falkayn asked.

"Gahood will put the questions." Latimer looked straight before him, one muscle twitching in his cheek. "I advise you in the strongest terms, give him full and courteous answers. What you did with that grenade is bad already. You are fortunate that his wish to meet you is high and his irritation at your insolence slight. Be very careful, or his punishment may reach beyond your own death."

"What a jolly boss you've got." Falkayn edged closer, to watch his guide's expression. "If I were you, I'd've quit long ago. Spectacularly."

"Would you quit your world—your race and everything it means—because its service grew a little difficult?" Latimer retorted scornfully. His look changed, his voice dropped. "Hush! We are coming there."

The layout was not too strange for Falkayn to recognize a gravshaft rising vertically. Men and robot were conveyed up a good fifteen meters before they were deposited on the next deck.

Anteroom? Garden? Grotto? Falkayn looked around in bewilderment. An entire cabin, ballroom big, was filled with planters. The things grown in them ranged from tiny, sweet-scented quasi-flowers, through tall many-branched succulents, to whole trees with leaves that were spiky or fringed or intricately convoluted. The dominant hue was brownish gold, as green is dominant on Earth. Near the center splashed a fountain. Its stone basin must have stood outdoors for centuries, so weathered was it. Regardless of the wholly foreign artistic conventions, Falkayn could see that the shape and what remained of the carvings were exquisite. In startling contrast were the bulkheads. Enormous raw splashes of color decorated them, nerve-jarring, tasteless by almost any standards.

Latimer led the way to an arched door at the end. Beyond lay the first stateroom of a suite. It was furnished—overfurnished—with barbaric opulence. The deck was carpeted in pelt that might almost have belonged to angora tigers. One bulkhead was sheathed in roughly hammered gold plate, one was painted like the outer compartment, one was draped in scaly leather, and one was a screen whereon jagged abstract shapes flashed in a lightning dance to the crash of drums and bray of horns. The skull of a dinosaur-sized animal gaped above the entrance. From several four-legged stands wafted a bitter smoke. Two of the censers were old: time-worn, delicate, beautiful as the fountain. The rest were hardly more than iron lumps. Seating arrangements consisted of a pair of striped daises, each with space for three humans to lie on, and cushions scattered about the deck. A lot of other stuff lay carelessly heaped in odd places or on shelves. Falkayn didn't try to identify most of those objects. He thought some might be containers, musical instruments, and toys, but he'd need acquaintance with the owner before he could make anything except wild guesses.

And here we go!

A thick sheet of transparent material, possibly vitryl, had been leaned against the inner doorway. It would shield whoever stood behind, if the grenade went off. The someone would have been safer yet, talking to him via telecom. But no, Gahood didn't have that kind of mentality. He trod into view. Falkayn had seen more than his share of nonhumans, but he must suppress an oath. He confronted the Minotaur.

XVI

No . . . not that exactly . . . any more than Adzel was exactly a dragon.

The impression was archetypical rather than literal. Yet as such it was overwhelming.

The creature was a biped, not unlike a man. Of course, every proportion was divergent, whether slightly, as in the comparative shortness of legs, or grotesquely, as in the comparative length of arms. Few if any humans had so stocky a build, and the muscles made different ripples across the limbs and bands across the abdomen. The feet were three-toed and padded, the hands four-fingered; and these digits were stubby, with greenish nails. The same tint was in the skin, which sprouted bronze hairs as thickly as the shaggiest of men though not enough to be called furred. Since the mouth, filled with flat yellow teeth, was flexible, but vestigial nipples were lacking, one couldn't tell offhand if the basic type was mammalian in a strict sense or not. However, the being was grossly male and surely warm-blooded.

The head—comparisons between species from separate planets are nearly always poor. But that massive head, with its short broad snout, dewlapped throat, black-smoldering wide-set eyes under heavy brow ridges and almost no forehead, long mobile ears . . . was more tauroid than anthropoid, at least. Naturally, variances exceeded resemblances. There were no horns. A superb mane enclosed the face, swept backward, tumbled over the shoulders and halfway to the hips. Those hairs were white, but must have a microgroove structure, because rainbows of iridescence played across their waves.

Falkayn and Latimer were tall, but Gahood towered over them, an estimated 230 centimeters. Such height, together with the incongruous breadth and thickness and the hard muscularity, might well bring his mass to a couple of hundred kilos.

He wore nothing except a jeweled necklace, several rings and heavy gold bracelets, a belt supporting a pouch on one side and a knife, or small machete, on the other. His breathing was loud as the ventilators. A musky scent hung around him. When he spoke, it was like summer thunder.

Latimer brought his gun to his lips—a salute?—lowered it again and addressed Falkayn. "You meet Gahood of Neshketh." His vocal organs weren't quite right for pronouncing the names. "He will question you. I have already told him you are called Sebastian Tombs. Are you from Earth?"

Falkayn rallied his courage. The being behind the shield-screen was intimidating, yes: but hang it, mortal! "I'll be glad to swap information," he said, "on a two-way basis. Is Neshketh his planet, or what?"

Latimer looked agitated. "*Don't,*" he muttered. "For your own sake, answer as you are instructed."

Falkayn skinned his teeth at them. "You poor scared mamzer," he said. "It could go hard with you, couldn't it? I haven't such a terrible lot to lose. You're the one who'd better cooperate with me."

A bluff, he thought inwardly, tensely. *I don't want to provoke an attack that'd end with me getting blown up. How very, very, very much I don't want to. And Gahood obviously has a hair-trigger temper. But if I can walk the tightrope from here to there . . .* An imp in him commented: *What a majestic lot of metaphors. You are playing poker while doing a high-wire act above a loaded revolver.*

"After all," he went on, into the dismayed face and the blaster muzzle, "sooner or later you'll deal with the League, if only in war. Why not start with me? I come cheaper than a battle fleet."

Gahood grunted something. Latimer replied. Sweat glistened on his countenance. The master clapped hand to knife hilt, snorted, and spoke a few syllables.

Latimer said, "You don't understand, Tombs. As far as Gahood is concerned, you are trespassing on his territory. He is showing rare restraint in not destroying you and your ship on the spot. You must believe me. Not many of his kind would be this tolerant. He will not be for long."

"His" territory? Falkayn thought. *He acts insane, I admit; but he can't be so heisenberg that he believes one flotilla can keep the Polesotechnic League off Satan. Quite possibly, getting here first gives him a special claim under the law of his own people. But his group has got to be only the vanguard, the first hastily organized thing that could be sent. I imagine the woman—what's-her-name, Thea Beldaniel's sister—went on to notify others. Or maybe she's rejoined a different Minotaur. Latimer's attitude suggests Gahood is his personal* owner. . . . *I suspect I'm being counter bluffed. Gahood's natural impulse likely is to squash me: which makes Latimer nervous, considering he has no protection against what's in my fist. But Gahood's actually curbing his instinct, hoping to scare me too so I'll spill information.*

"Well," he said, "you being the interpreter, I don't see why you can't slip me a few answers. You aren't directly forbidden to, are you?"

"N-n-no. I—" Latimer drew a shaky breath. "I will tell you the, ah, place name mentioned refers to a . . . something like a domain." Gahood rumbled. "Now answer me! You came directly from Earth?"

"Yes. We were sent to investigate the rogue planet." A claim that *Muddlin' Through* had found it by accident was too implausible, and would not imply that the League stood ready to avenge her.

Gahood, through Latimer: "How did you learn of its existence?"

Falkayn, donning a leer: "Ah, that must have been a shock to you, finding us on tap when you arrived. You thought you'd have years to build impregnable defenses. Well, friends, I don't believe there is anything in the galaxy that we of the Polesotechnic League can't get pregnant. What's the name of your home planet?"

Gahood: "Your response is evasive. How did you learn? How many of you are here? What further plans have you?"

Falkayn: A bland stare.

Latimer, swallowing: "Uh . . . I can't see any harm in—The planet is called Dathyna, the race itself the Shenna. In General Phonetic, D-A-Thorn-Y-N-A and Sha-E-N-N-A. The singular is 'Shenn.' The words mean, roughly, 'world' and 'people.'"

Falkayn: "Names like that do, as a rule."

He noted that the Shenna seemed confined to their home globe, or to a few colonies at most. No surprise. Clearly, they didn't live at such a distance that they could operate on a large scale without Technic explorers soon chancing on spoor of them and tracking them down.

It did not follow from this that they were not, possibly, mortally dangerous. The information Serendipity must have fed them over the years—not to mention the capability demonstrated by their creating such an outfit in the first place—suggested they were. A single planet, heavily armed and cunningly led, might best the entire League through its ability to inflict unacceptable damage. Or, if finally defeated, it might first destroy whole worlds, their civilizations and sentient species.

And if Gahood is typical, the Shenna might seriously plan on just that, Falkayn thought. His scalp crawled.

Too damned many mysteries and contradictions yet, though.

Robotics won't explain every bit of the speed with which this group reacted to the news. And that, in turn, doesn't square with the far-reaching patience that built Serendipity—patience that suddenly vanished, that risked the whole operation (and, in the event, lost it) by kidnapping me.

"Speak!" Latimer cried. "Answer his questions."

"Eh? Oh. Those," Falkayn said slowly. "I'm afraid I can't. All I know is, our ships got orders to proceed here, check out the situation, and report back. We were warned someone else might show up with claim-jumping intentions. But no more was told us." He laid a finger alongside his nose and winked. "Why should the League's spies risk letting you find out how much they've found out about you . . . and where and how?"

Latimer gasped, whirled, and talked in fast, coughing gutturals. The suggestion that Dathynan society had itself been penetrated must be shocking even to Gahood. He wouldn't dare assume it was not true. Would he? But what he'd do was unpredictable. Falkayn balanced flex-kneed, every sense alert.

His training paid off. Gahood belched an order. The robot slipped unobtrusively to one side. Falkayn caught the movement in the corner of an eye. With his karate stance, he didn't need to jump. He relaxed the tension in one leg and was automatically elsewhere. Steel tendrils whipped where his left hand had been.

He bounded into the nearest corner. "Naughty!" he rapped. The machine whirred toward him. "Latimer, I can let go this switch before that thing can squeeze my fingers shut around it. Call off your iron dog or we're both dead."

The other man uttered something that halted the robot. Evidently Gahood endorsed the countermand, for at his word the machine withdrew until it no longer hemmed Falkayn in. Across the room he saw the Minotaur stamp, hungrily flex his hands, and blow through distended nostrils—furious behind his shield.

Latimer's blaster aimed at the Hermetian's midriff. It wavered, and the wielder looked ill. Though his life had been dedicated to the cause of Dathyna, or whatever the cause was, and though he was doubtless prepared to lay it down if need be, he must have felt a shock when his master so impulsively risked it. "Give up, Tombs," he well-nigh pleaded. "You cannot fight a ship."

"I'm not doing badly," Falkayn said. The effort was cruel to hold his own breathing steady, his voice level. "And I'm not alone, you know."

"One insignificant scoutcraft—No. You did mention others. How many? What kind? Where?"

"Do you seriously expect the details? Listen close, now, and translate with care. When we detected you, my ship went out to parley because the League doesn't like fights. They cut into profit. When fights become necessary, though, we make damn sure the opposition will never louse up our bookkeeping again. You spent enough time in the Commonwealth, Latimer, and maybe elsewhere in the territory covered by Technic civilization, to vouch for that. The message I have for you is this. Our higher-ups are willing to dicker with yours. Time and place can be arranged through any envoys you send to the League secretariat. But for the moment, I warn you away from Beta Crucis. We were here first, it's ours, and our fleet will destroy any intruders. I suggest you let me return to my ship, and go home yourselves and think it over."

Latimer looked yet more profoundly shaken. "I can't . . . address him . . . like that!"

"Then don't address him." Falkayn shrugged. Gahood lowered his ponderous head, stamped on the deck, and boomed. "But if you ask me, he's getting impatient."

Latimer began stumblingly to speak to the Dathynan.

I suspect he's shading his translation, Falkayn thought. *Poor devil. He acted boldly on Luna. But now he's back where he's property, physical, mental, spiritual property. Worse off than I was; he doesn't even need to be chained by drugs. I don't know when I've watched a ghastlier sight.* The thought was an overtone in a voiceless scream: *Will they play safe and release me? Or must I die?*

Gahood bellowed. It was no word, it was raw noise, hurting Falkayn's eardrums. Echoes flew. The creature hurled himself against the barricading slab. It weighed a ton or better in this gravity, but he tipped it forward. Leaning upon it, he boomed a command. Latimer sprang, clumsy in his spacesuit, toward him.

Falkayn understood: *He'll let his slave in, lean the shelter back, and when both of them are safe, he'll tell the robot to go after me. It's worth a robot and the treasures in this room, to kill me who insulted him—*

And Falkayn's body was already reacting. He was farther from the arch, and must sidestep the machine. But he was youthful, in hard condition, accustomed to wearing space armor . . . and driven by more love of life. He reached the slab simultaneously with Latimer, on the opposite side. It stood nearly vertical now, with a one-meter gap giving admittance to the room beyond. The ireful beast who upheld it did not at once notice what had happened. Falkayn got through along with the other man.

He skipped aside. Gahood let the slab crash into its tilted position again and whirled to grab him. "Oh, no!" he called. "Get him off me, Latimer, or he's the third chunk of hamburger here!"

Slave threw himself upon owner and tried to wrestle Gahood to a halt. The Dathynan tore him loose and pitched him to the deck. Space armor clanged where it struck. But then reason appeared to enter the maned head. Gahood stopped cold.

For a minute, tableau. Latimer sprawled, bloody-nosed and semiconscious, under the bent columns of Gahood's legs. The Minotaur stood with arms dangling, chest heaving, breath storming, and glared at Falkayn. The spaceman poised a few meters off, amidst another jumble of barbarous luxuries. Sweat plastered the yellow hair to his brow, but he grinned at his enemies and waved the grenade aloft.

"That's better," he said. "That's much better. Stand fast, you two. Latimer, I'll accept your gun."

In a dazed fashion, the slave reached for the blaster, which he had dropped nearby. Gahood put one broad foot on it and snorted a negative.

"Well . . . keep it, then," Falkayn conceded. The Dathynan was rash but no idiot. Had Falkayn gotten the weapon, he could have slain the others without dooming himself. As it was, there must be compromise. "I want your escort, both of you, back to my sled. If you summon your robots, or your merry men, or anything that makes my capture seem feasible, this pineapple goes straight up."

Latimer rose, painfully. "Merry men—?" he puzzled. His gaze cleared. "Oh. The rest of our officers and crew. No, we will not call them." He translated.

Falkayn kept impassive. But a new excitement boiled within him. Latimer's initial reaction confirmed what had already begun to seem probable, after no one heard the racket here and came to investigate, or even made an intercom call.

Gahood and Latimer were alone. Not just the other craft, the flagship too was automatic.

But that was impossible!

Maybe not. Suppose Dathyna—or Gahood's Neshketh barony, at least—suffered from an acute "manpower" shortage. Now the Shenna did not expect that anyone from the League would be at Beta Crucis. They had no reason to believe Serendipity had been exposed. Assuming a rival expedition did appear, it would be so small that robots could dispose of it. (Serendipity must have described this trait in Technic society, this unwillingness to make large commitments sight unseen. And, of course, it *was* the case. No League ship except *Muddlin' Through* was anywhere near the blue star.) Rather than go through the tedious business of recruiting a proper complement—only to tie it up needlessly, in all apparent likelihood—Gahood had taken what robots he commanded. He had gone off without other live companionship than the dog-man who brought him the word.

What kind of civilization was this, so poor in trained personnel, so careless about the requirements for scientific study of a new planet, and yet so rich and lavish in machines?

Gahood cast down the barrier. Probably robots had raised it for him; but none came in response to its earthquake fall, and the one in the cabin stood as if frozen. In the same eerie wordlessness, Falkayn trailed his prisoners: out the antechamber, down the gravshaft, through the corridor to the airlock.

There the others stopped and glowered defiance. The Hermetian had had time to make a plan. "Now," he said, "I'd like to take you both hostage, but my vehicle's too cramped and I won't risk the chances that Gahood's riding along might give him. You'll come, Latimer."

"No!" The man was appalled.

"Yes. I want some assurance of not being attacked en route to my fleet."

"Don't you understand? M-my information . . . what I know . . . you could learn. . . . He'll have to sacrifice me."

"I thought of that already. I don't reckon he's anxious to vaporize you. You're valuable to him, and not simply as an interpreter. Else you wouldn't be here." *You had the name in the Solar System of being an uncommonly good spaceman, Hugh Latimer. And at the moment, though I hope he doesn't know I know, you're half his party. Without you, never mind how good his robots are, he's got big problems. He could return home, all right; but would he dare do anything else, as long as the possibility exists I did not lie about having an armada at my back? Besides—who knows?—there may well be a kind of affection between you two.* "He won't attack a vessel with you aboard if he can avoid it. Correct? Well, you're already space-suited. Ride with me as far as my ship. I'll let you off there. His radar can confirm that I do, and he can pick you up in space. If he does not spot you separating from my sled, shortly before it joins my ship, then he can open fire."

Latimer hesitated. "Quick!" Falkayn barked. "Translate and give me his decision. My thumb's getting tired."

The truth was, he aimed to keep them both off balance, not give them a chance to think. The exchange was brief, under his profane urging. "Very well." Latimer yielded sullenly. "But I keep my blaster."

"And I our mutual suicide pact. Fair enough. Cycle us through."

Latimer instructed the airlock by voice. Falkayn's last glimpse of Gahood, as the inmost valve closed again, was of the huge form charging up and down the corridor, pounding the bulkheads with fists until they clamored, and bellowing.

The sled waited. Falkayn sent Latimer first through its mini-lock in order that he, entering afterward, would present the full menace of the grenade. It was awkward, squeezing one spacesuit past another in the tiny cockpit, and guiding the sled by one hand was worse. He made a disgraceful liftoff. Once in motion, he let the vehicle do as it would while he broadcast a call.

"Dave!" Chee Lan's voice shuddered in his earplugs. "You're free—*Yan-tai-i-lirh-ju.*"

"We may have to run hard, you and I," he said in Anglic, for Latimer's benefit. "Give my autopilot a beam. Stand by to reel me in and accelerate the moment I'm in tractor range. But, uh, don't pay attention when I first discharge a passenger."

"Hostage, eh? I understand. Muddlehead, get off your fat electronic duff and lock onto him!"

A minute later, Falkayn could let go the main stick. The sled flew steadily, the ominous shape of the battleship dwindled aft. He glanced at Latimer, crowded more or less beside him. In the dim glow of stars and instrument panel, he saw a shadow bulk and a gleam off the faceplate. The blaster muzzle was poked almost in his belly.

"I don't imagine Gahood will shoot at us," he said low.

"I think not, now." Latimer's reply sounded equally exhausted.

"Whoo-oo. How about relaxing? We've a tedious ride ahead of us."

"How can you relax, with that thing in your hand?"

"Sure, sure. We keep our personal deterrents. But can't we take it easy otherwise? Open our helmets, light each other's cigarettes."

"I do not smoke," Latimer said. "However—" He undogged and slid back his faceplate concurrently with Falkayn. A sigh gusted from him. "Yes. It is good to . . . to uncramp."

"I don't bear you any ill will, you know," Falkayn said, not quite truthfully. "I'd like to see this dispute settled without a fight."

"Me too. I must admire your courage. It's almost like a Shenn's."

"If you could give me some idea what the quarrel is about—"

"No." Latimer sighed, "I'd better not say anything. Except . . . how are they, back on Luna? My friends of Serendipity?"

"Well, now—"

Latimer shifted position and Falkayn saw his chance. He had been prepared to wait for it as long as need be, and do nothing if it didn't happen to materialize. But the sled had already gotten so far away from the battleship that no scanner could give a clue as to what went on in this cockpit. There was no contact in either direction, apart from Muddlehead's beam and Gahood's tracking radar. In the low weight of acceleration, Latimer's tired body had settled into his seat harness. The blaster rested laxly on one knee and the face lolled in its frame of helmet near Falkayn's right shoulder.

"—it's like this," the Hermetian continued. *Here goes—for broke!* His left fist, with the grenade to lend mass, swept about, battered the gun barrel aside and pinned it against the cockpit wall. His right hand darted through the faceplate opening and closed on Latimer's throat.

✡XVII✡

The blaster flared once, while the man tried to struggle. Then both were still.

Panting, Falkayn released the judo strangle. "Got to work fast," he muttered aloud, as if to offset the hiss of escaping air. But that hole was sealing itself while the reserve tanks brought pressure back up. He stuffed the blaster into his tool belt and strained his eyes aft. Nothing stirred in the Shenn fleet. Well, it had always been unlikely that one little flash and brief puff of water mist would be seen.

Getting rid of the grenade was more tricky. Falkayn cut the main drive and swiveled the sled transversely to its path, so that the minilock faced away from the battleship. On this model, the valves had been simplified to a series of sphinctered diaphragms on either side of a rigid cylinder. It meant some continuous gas leakage, and comparatively high loss whenever you went in or out. But it compensated with speed and flexibility of use; and the sled wasn't intended for long hops through space anyway. Helmet reclosed, Falkayn braced feet against the opposite side of the cockpit and pushed head and shoulders out into the void. He tossed the grenade, flat and hard. It exploded at a reasonably safe distance. A few shrapnel chunks ricocheted off the vehicle, but no serious damage was done.

"Wowsers!" His left hand ached. He flexed the fingers, trying to work some tension out, as he withdrew to the interior. Latimer was regaining consciousness. With a bit of reluctance—rough way to treat a man—Falkayn choked him again. Thus the Hermetian won the extra few seconds he needed, undisturbed, to put his sled back on acceleration before Gahood should notice anything and grow suspicious.

He placed himself with care vis-a-vis Latimer, leveled the blaster, opened his helmet, and waited. The captive stirred, looked around him, shuddered, and gathered himself for a leap. "Don't," Falkayn advised, "or you're dead. Unharness; back off to the rear; get out of your suit."

"What? *Logra doadam!* You swine—"

"Oink," Falkayn said. "Listen, I don't want to shoot you. Quite apart from morals and such, you've got a lot of hostage value. But you're most certainly not returning to help Gahood. I have my whole people to worry about. If you cause me any trouble, I'll kill you and sleep quite well, thank you. Get moving."

Still dazed, by his stunning reversal as well as physically, the other man obeyed. Falkayn made him close up the spacesuit. "We'll eject it at the right moment and your boss will think it's you," he explained. "His time loss collecting it is my gain."

A growl and glare through the shadows: "It is true what I was told about your sort, what I observed for myself. Evil, treacherous—"

"Desiccate it, Latimer. I signed no contract, swore no oath. Earlier, you types weren't exactly following the usual rules of parley. I didn't enjoy the hospitality I received in your Lunar castle, either."

Latimer jerked backward. "Falkayn?" he whispered.

"Right. Captain David Falkayn, M.M.P.L., with a hydrocyanic personal grudge and every reason to believe your gang is out for blood. Can you prove this is a pillow fight we're in? If it is, then you've put bricks in your pillow. Which led me to put nails in mine. Be quiet, now, before I get so mad I fry you!"

The last sentence was roared. Latimer crouched rather than cowered, but he was certainly daunted. Falkayn himself was astounded. *I really pushed that out, didn't I? The idea was to keep him stampeded, so he won't think past the moment, guess my real intentions, and become desperate. But Judas, the fury I feel!* He trembled with it.

Time passed. The enemy receded farther, *Muddlin' Through* came nearer. When they were quite close, Falkayn ordered Latimer to shove the empty spacesuit through the minilock: an awkward job, eardrum-popping if one had no armor, but performed in tight-lipped silence.

"Haul us in, Chee," Falkayn said.

A tractor beam clamped on. The drive was shut off. A cargo hatch stood open to one of the after holds. No sooner was the sled inboard, protected by the ship's gee-field from acceleration pressures, than Chee started off under full drive. The hum and bone-deep vibration could be felt.

She scurried below to meet the humans. They had just emerged, and stood glaring at each other in the coldly lit cavern. Chee hefted the stun pistol she carried. "Ah, s-s-so," she murmured. Her tail waved. "I rather expected you'd do that, Dave. Where shall we lock this klong up?"

"Sick bay," Falkayn told her. "The sooner we begin on him, the better. We may be hounded down, you see, but if we can launch our other capsule with something in it—"

He should not have spoken Anglic. Latimer divined his intention, screamed, and hurled himself straight at the blaster. Hampered by his spacesuit, Falkayn could not evade the charge; and he did not share the prisoner's desire that he shoot. They went to the deck, rolling over and over in their struggle. Chee Lan eeled between them and gave Latimer a judicious jolt.

He sprawled limp. Falkayn rose, breathing hard, shaking. "How long'll he be out?"

"Hour; maybe two," the Cynthian answered. "But I'll need a while to prepare anyway." She paused. "I'm not a psychotechnician, you realize, and we don't have a full battery of drugs, electroencephalic inducers, all that junk they use. I don't know how much I can wring out of him."

"You can get him to babble something, I'm sure," Falkayn said. "What with the stuff left over from curing me, and the experience you got then. Just the coordinates of Dathyna—of the enemy's home system—would be invaluable."

"Haul him topside and secure him for me. After which, if you aren't too shredded in the nerves, you'd better take the bridge."

Falkayn nodded. Weariness, reaction, had indeed begun to invade him. Latimer's body was a monstrous weight over his shoulders. The thin face looked tormented even in slumber. And what waited was a will-less half-consciousness. . . . *Tough,* Falkayn thought sarcastically.

Coffee, a sandwich, a quick shower, grabbed while he related via intercom what had happened, made him feel better. He entered the bridge with his pipe at a jaunty angle. "What's the situation, Muddlehead?" he asked.

"As respects ourselves, we are bound back toward the rogue planet at maximum thrust," said the computer. It was the only way to continue the bluff of armed support. "Our systems check satisfactory, although a fluctuation in line voltage on circuit 47 is symptomatic of malfunction in a regulator that should be replaced next we make port."

"Repaired," Falkayn corrected automatically.

"Replaced," Muddlehead maintained. "While data do indicate that Freeman van Rijn is describable, in terms of the vocabulary you instructed me to use, as a cheapskate bastard, it is illogical that my operations should be distracted, however slightly, by—"

"Great Willy! We may be radioactive gas inside an hour, and you indent for a new voltage regulator! Would you like it gold-plated?"

"I had not considered the possibility. Obviously, only the casing could be. It would lead to a pleasing appearance, provided of course that every similar unit is similarly finished."

"Up your rectifier," Falkayn said. His teeth clamped hard on the pipe bit. "What readings on the enemy?"

"A destroyer has put a tractor beam on the suit and is bringing it near the battleship."

"Which'll take it aboard," Falkayn predicted without difficulty. Things were going as he'd anticipated . . . thus far. The Dathynan ships were delayed in their recovery operation by the need to get detailed instructions from Gahood.

They had electronic speed and precision, yes, but not full decision-making capacity. No robot built in any known civilization does. This is not for lack of mystic vital forces. Rather, the biological creature has available to him so much more physical organization. Besides sensor-computer-effector systems comparable to those of the machine, he has feed-in from glands, fluids, chemistry reaching down to the molecular level—the integrated ultracomplexity, the entire battery of *instincts*—that a billion-odd years of ruthlessly selective evolution have brought forth. He perceives and thinks with a wholeness transcending any possible symbolism; his purposes arise from within, and therefore are infinitely flexible. The robot can only do what it was designed to do. Self-programming has extended these limits, to the point where actual consciousness may occur if desired. But they remain narrower than the limits of those who made the machines.

To be sure, given an unequivocal assignment of the type for which it is built, the robot is superior to the organism. Let Gahood order his fleet to annihilate *Muddlin' Through,* and the contest became strictly one between ships, weapons, and computers.

Didn't it?

Falkayn sat down, drummed fingers on his chair arm, blew acrid clouds at the star images that enclosed him.

Chee's voice pulled him from his brown study: "I've got your boy nicely laid out, intravenous insertions made, brain and vagus nerve monitored, life-support apparatus on standby, everything I can do with what's available. Should I jolt him awake with a stim shot?"

"M-m-m, no, wait a while. It'd be hard on his body. We don't want to damage him if we can possibly help it."

"Why not?"

Falkayn sighed. "I'll explain some other time. But practically speaking, we can pump him drier if we treat him carefully."

"They can do still better in a properly equipped lab."

"Yeh, but that's illegal. So illegal that it's a toss-up whether anyone would do the job for us on the q.t. Let's get what we can, ourselves. We're also violating law, but that can be winked at if we're well beyond civilization. . . . Of course, we can't predict whether Gahood will give us the days you need for a thorough and considerate job of quizzing."

"You met him. What do you think?"

"I didn't get exactly intimate with him. And even if I knew his inner psychology, which I don't except for his tendency to make all-out attacks at the first sign of opposition—even then, I wouldn't know what pragmatic considerations he might have to take into account. On the one hand, we have his trusty man for a hostage, and he has at least some reason to believe we may have husky friends waiting at Satan. He should cut his losses, return, and report. On the other hand, he may be so bold, or so angry, or so afraid Latimer will reveal something vital to us, that he'll strike."

"Supposing he does?"

"We run like hell, I guess. A stern chase is a long chase. We may throw him off the scent, like in Pryor's Nebula. Or we may outrun his heavy ships altogether, and he recall his destroyers rather than—Whoops! Hang on!"

Muddlehead spoke what flickered on the 'scope faces: "They are starting after us."

"Rendezvous point?" Chee demanded.

"Data cannot yet be evaluated with precision, considering especially the velocity we have already gained. But." For an instant, it hummed. "Yes, the destroyers are lining out on courses effectively parallel to ours, with somewhat greater acceleration. Under such conditions, they will overhaul us in slightly less than one astronomical unit."

"Their shooting can overhaul us sooner than that," Chee stated. "I'm going ahead on Latimer."

"I suppose you must," Falkayn said reluctantly, half wishing he had not captured the man.

"Commence hyperdrive," Chee ordered from sick bay.

"No," Falkayn said. "Not right now."

"*Chi'in-pao?*"

"We're safe for a little while. Keep driving toward Satan, Muddlehead. They might just be testing our bluff."

"Do you really believe that?" the Cynthian asked.

"No," Falkayn said. "But what can we lose?"

Not much, he answered himself. *I knew the chances of our coming out of this web alive aren't good. But as of this moment, I can't do anything but sit and feel the fact.*

Physical courage was schooled into him, but the sense of life's sweetness was born in. He spent a time cataloguing a few of the myriad awarenesses that made up his conscious being. The stars burned splendid across night. The ship enclosed him in a lesser world, one of power-thrum, ventilator breath, clean chemical odors, music if he wanted it, the battered treasures he had gathered in his wanderings. Smoke made a small autumn across his tongue. Air blew into his nostrils, down into the lungs, as his chest expanded. The chair pressed back against the weight of his body; and it had texture; and seated, he nevertheless operated an interplay of muscles, an unending dance with the universe for his lady. A sleeve of the clean coverall he had donned felt crisp, and tickled the hair on one arm. His heart beat faster than usual, but steadily, and that pleased him.

He summoned memories from the deeps: mother, father, sisters, brothers, retainers, old weather-beaten soldiers and landsmen, in the windy halls of the castle on Hermes. Hikes through the woods; swims in the surf; horses, boats, aircraft, spaceships. Gourmet dinners. A slab of black bread and cheese, a bottle of cheap wine, shared one night with the dearest little tart. . . . Had there actually been so many women? Yes. How delightful. Though of late he had begun to grow wistful about finding some one girl who—well, had the same quality of friendship that Chee or Adzel did—who would be more than a partner in a romp—but hadn't he and his comrades enjoyed their own romps, on world after wild world? Including this latest, perhaps last mission to Satan. If the rogue was to be taken away, he hoped the conquerors would at least get pleasure from it.

How can they tell if they will? None of them have been there yet. In a way, you can't blame Gahood for charging in. He must be eager too, I think, to see what the place is like. The fact that I know, that I've landed there already, must hone the edge of his impatience. . . .

Wait! Drag that thought by slowly. You'd started playing with it before, when Chee interrupted—

Falkayn sat rigid, oblivious, until the Cynthian grew nervous and shouted into the intercom, "What ails you?"

"Oh." The man shook himself. "Yes. That. How're we doing?"

"Latimer is responding to me, but deliriously. He's in worse shape than I realized."

"Psychic stress," Falkayn diagnosed without paying close attention. "He's being forced to betray his master—his owner, maybe his god—against a lifetime's conditioning."

"I think I can haul him back into orbit long enough at a time to put a question or two. What about the enemy, Muddlehead?"

"The destroyers are closing the gap," reported the ship. "How soon they will be prepared to fire on us depends on their armament, but I would expect it to be soon."

"Try to raise the battleship by radio," Falkayn ordered. "Maybe they—he—will talk. Meanwhile, prepare to go hyper at the first sign of hostile action. Toward Satan."

Chee had evidently not heard him, or was too intent to comment. The mutter of her voice, Latimer's incoherence, the medical machines, drifted unpleasantly over the intercom. "Shall I revert to normal when we reach the planet?" Muddlehead inquired.

"Yes. Starting at once, change our acceleration. I want nearly zero kinetic velocity with respect to goal," Falkayn said.

"That, in effect, involves deceleration," Muddlehead warned. "The enemy will come in effective firing range correspondingly faster."

"Never mind. Do you think you can find a landing spot, once we're there?"

"It is uncertain. Meteorological violence, and diastrophism, appeared to be increasing almost exponentially when we left."

"Still, you've got a whole world to pick and choose from. And you know something about it. I can't guess how many billion bits of information regarding Satan you've got stashed away. Prepare to devote most of your computer capacity to them, as well to observation on the spot. I'll give you generalized instructions—make the basic decisions for you—as we proceed. Clear?"

"I presume you wish to know whether your program has been unambiguously comprehended. Yes."

"Good." Falkayn patted the nearest console and smiled through his gathering, half-gleeful tension. "We come through this, and you can have your gold-plated regulators. If need be, I'll pay for them out of my own account."

There was no perceptible change of forces within the ship, nor in the configuration of light-years-remote stars or the luridness of Beta Crucis. But meters said the ship was slowing down. Magnifying viewscreens showed the glints that were Gahood's vessels growing into slivers, into toys, into warcraft.

"I've got it!" ripped from Chee.

"Huh?" Falkayn said.

"The coordinates. In standard values. But he's spinning off into shock. I'd better concentrate on keeping him alive."

"Do. And, uh, don safety harness. We may dive right into Satan's atmosphere. The compensators may get overloaded."

Chee was quiet a moment before she said, "I see your plan. It is not a bad one."

Falkayn gnawed on his pipe. This was the worst part, now, this waiting. Gahood must have detected the change of vector, must see what was like an attempt to rendezvous, must know about at least one of the communication beams on different bands that probed toward his flagship. But his fleet plunged on, and nothing spoke to Falkayn save a dry cosmic hiss.

If he'll try to talk . . . if he'll show any sign of goodwill . . . Judas, we don't want *a battle—*

Whiteness flared in the screens, momentarily drowning the constellations. Alarm bells rang. "We were struck by an energy bolt," Muddlehead announced. "Dispersion was sufficient at this range that damage was minimal. I am taking evasive action. A number of missiles are being released from the fleet. They behave like target-seekers."

Doubts, terrors, angers departed from Falkayn. He became entirely a war animal. "Go hyper to Satan as instructed," he said without tone. "One-tenth drive."

The wavering sky, the keening noises, the shifting forces: then steadiness again, a low throb, Beta Crucis swelling perceptibly as the ship ran toward it faster than light.

"So slow?" Chee Lan's voice asked.

"For the nonce," Falkayn said. "I want to keep a close watch on what they do."

Only instruments could tell, the fleet being already lost in millions of kilometers. "They aren't going hyper immediately," Falkayn said. "I expect they're matching our kinetic velocity first, more or less. Which suggests they intend to start shooting again at their earliest opportunity."

"Whether or not we have reinforcements at Satan?"

"Whether or not. I imagine the battleship will bring up the rear, though, at a goodly distance, and wait to see how things develop before making any commitment." Falkayn laid his pipe aside. "No matter how hot-tempered he is, I doubt if Gahood will rush into an unknown danger right along with his robots. They're more expendable than him. Under present conditions, this fact works in our favor."

"Hyperdrive pulses detected," the computer said a few minutes later.

Falkayn whistled. "Can they normal-decelerate that fast? Very well, open up, flat out. We don't want them to overtake us and maybe phase-match before we reach Satan."

The engine pulse became a drumbeat, a current, a cataract. The flames of Beta Crucis seemed to stretch and seethe outward. The computer said, "All but one unit, presumably the largest, are in pursuit. The cruisers are lagging behind us but the destroyers are gaining. However, we will reach goal several minutes in advance of them."

"How much time do you want for scanning the planet and picking us a course down?"

Click. Click-click. "A hundred seconds should suffice."

"Reduce speed so we'll arrive, let's see, three minutes before the leading destroyer. Commence descent one hundred seconds after we're back to normal state. Make it as quick as possible."

The power-song dropped a touch lower. "Are you in your own harness, Dave?" Chee asked.

"Uh . . . why, no," Falkayn suddenly realized.

"Well, get into it! Do you think I want to scrub the deck clean of that clabbered oatmeal you call brains? Take care of yourself!"

Falkayn smiled for half a second. "Same to you, fluffykins."

"*Fluffykins—*" Oaths and obscenities spattered the air. Falkayn sat down and webbed in. Chee needed something to take her mind off the fact that in this hour she could do nothing about her own fate. It was a condition harder for a Cynthian to endure than a human.

Then they were upon the rogue. Then they flashed into relativistic state. Then engines roared, hull structure groaned and shuddered, while the last adjustments in velocity were made, within seconds.

They were not far out, just enough so that most of the daylit hemisphere could be observed. Satan loomed frightful, filling the screens, stormclouds, lightnings, winds gone crazy, volcanoes, avalanches, floods, mountainous waves raised on the oceans and torn into shreds of spume, air nearly solid with rain and hail and flung stones, one immense convulsion beneath the demon disc of the star. Momentarily Falkayn did not believe there was any spot anywhere on the globe where a ship might descend, and he readied himself for death.

But the League vessel sprang ahead. On a comet-like trajectory, she arced toward the north pole. Before reaching it, she was in the upper atmosphere. Thin it might be, but it smote her so the hull rang.

Darkness, lit with explosions of lightning, rolled beneath. Falkayn glanced aft. Did the screens truly reveal to him the shark-shape destroyers of Gahood? Or was that an illusion? Torn clouds whipped across sun and stars. Thunder and shrieking and the cry of metal filled his ship, his skull, his being. The interior field regulators could not handle every shock, as *Muddlin' Through* staggered downward. The deck pitched, yawed, swayed, fell away, rose savagely again. Something crashed off something else and broke. Lights flickered.

He tried to understand the instruments. Nuclear sources, behind, coming nearer . . . yes, the whole nineteen, stooping on their quarry!

They were meant for aerodynamic work. They had orders to catch and kill a certain vessel. They were robots.

They did not have sophontic judgment, nor any data to let them estimate how appalling these totally unprecedented conditions were, nor any mandate to wait for further instructions if matters looked doubtful. Besides, they observed a smaller and less powerful craft maneuvering in the air.

They entered at their top atmospheric speed.

Muddlehead had identified a hurricane and plotted its extent and course. It was merely a hurricane—winds of two or three hundred kilometers per hour—a kind of back eddy or dead spot in the storm that drove across this continent with such might that half an ocean was carried before it. No matter how thoroughly self-programmed, on the basis of how much patiently collected data, no vessel could hope to stay in the comparatively safe region long.

The destroyers blundered into the main blast. It caught them as a November gale catches dead leaves in the northlands of Earth. Some it bounced playfully between cloud-floor and wind-roof, for whole minutes, before it cast them aside. Some it peeled open, or broke apart with the meteoroidal chunks of solid matter it bore along, or drowned in the spume-filled air farther down. Most it tossed at once against mountainsides. The pieces were strewn, blown away, buried, reduced in a few weeks to dust, mud, atoms locked into newly forming rock strata. No trace of the nineteen warships would ever be found.

"Back aloft!" Falkayn had already cried. "Locate those cruisers. Use cloud cover. With this kind of electric noise background, they aren't likely to detect us fast."

A roll and lurch rattled his teeth together. Slowly, fighting for every centimeter, *Muddlin' Through* rose. She found a stratospheric current she could ride for a while, above the worst weather though beneath a layer where boiled-off vapors were recondensing in vast turbulent masses that, from below, turned heaven Stygian. Her radars could penetrate this, her detectors pick up indications that came to her. The three cruisers were not supposed to make planetfall. Obviously, they were to provide cover against possible space attack. Their attention must be almost wholly directed outward. They orbited incautiously close, in inadvisably tight formation. But they were also robots, whose builders had more faith in strength than in strategy.

Falkayn sent off three of his nuclear torpedoes. Two connected. The third was intercepted in time by a countermissile. Reluctantly, he ordered the fourth and last shot. It seemed to achieve a near miss and must have inflicted heavy damage, judging by what the meters recorded.

And . . . the cruiser was limping off. The battleship, whose mass made ominous blips on half a dozen different kinds of screen, was joining her. They were both on hyperdrive—retreating—dwindling toward the Circinus region whence they came.

Falkayn whooped.

After a while, he recovered his wits sufficiently to order, "Get us into clear space again, Muddlehead. Barely outside the atmosphere. Take orbit, with systems throttled down to minimum. We don't want to remind Gahood of us. He could change his mind and return before he's too far off ever to catch us."

"What does he believe happened?" Chee asked, so weakly she could barely be heard.

"I don't know. How does his psyche work? Maybe he thinks we have a secret weapon. Or maybe he thinks we lured his destroyers down by a suicide dive, and we've got friends who fired those torps. Or maybe he's guessed the truth, but figures that with his fleet essentially gone, and the possibility that a League force might soon arrive, he'd better go home and report."

"Lest we outfox him again, eh?" Exhausted and battered though she was, Chee began to have a note of exultation in her voice.

Likewise Falkayn. "What do you mean, 'we,' white puss?" he teased.

"I obtained those coordinates for you, didn't I? Bloodiest important thing we've accomplished this whole trip."

"You're right," Falkayn said, "and I apologize. How's Latimer?"

"Dead."

Falkayn sat straight. "What? How?"

"The life-support apparatus got knocked out of kilter, that battering we took. And in his weakened condition, with his whole organism fighting itself—too long a time has passed now for resuscitation to mean anything." Falkayn could imagine Chee Lan's indifferent gesture, her probable thoughts. *Pity for us. Oh, well, we got something out of him; and we're alive.*

His went, surprisingly to himself: *Poor, damned devil. I have my revenge, I've been purged of my shame; and I find it didn't really matter that much.*

Quietness grew around the ship, the stars trod forth, and she reentered open space. Falkayn could not stay sorry. He felt he ought to, but the knowledge of deliverance was too strong. They'd give their foeman an honorable burial, an orbit straight into yonder terrible, glorious sun. And they'd steer for Earth.

No. The realization struck like a fist. *Not that. We can't go home yet.*

The work of survival had barely been started.

XVIII

Well-established laws of nature are seldom overthrown by new scientific discovery. Instead, they turn out to be approximations, or special cases, or in need of rephrasing. Thus—while a broader knowledge of physics permits us to do things he would have considered impossible, like traversing a light-year in less than two hours—Einstein's restrictions on the concept of simultaneity remain essentially valid. For no matter how high a pseudo-velocity we reach, it is still finite.

So did Adzel argue. "You may not correctly ask what our friends are doing 'now,' when interstellar distances separate us from them. True, after they have rejoined us, we can compare their clocks with ours, and find the same time lapse recorded. But to identify any moment of our measured interval with any moment of theirs is to go beyond the evidence, and indeed to perpetrate a meaningless statement."

"Hokay!" Nicholas van Rijn bawled. He windmilled his arms in the air. "Hokay! Then give me a meaningless answer! Four weeks, close as damn, since they left. Couldn't need much more than two for getting at Beta Crosseyes, ha? They maybe finding thawed-out glaciers of beer and akvavit, we haven't heard diddly-dong from them yet?"

"I understand your concern," Adzel said quietly. "Perhaps I feel a little more of it than you do. But the fact is that a message capsule is slower than a ship like *Muddlin' Through*. Had they dispatched one immediately upon arrival, it would barely have gotten to the Solar System by today. And they would not logically do so. For surely David, after he recovered, credited you with the ability to pry as much out of the SI computer as it gave him. Why, then, should he waste a capsule to confirm the mere fact of the rogue's existence? No, he and Chee Lan will first have gathered ample data. With luck, they need not have taken the trouble and risk of interception involved in sending any written report. They ought to be returning home . . . quite soon . . . if at all."

His huge scaly form got off the deck where he rested. His neck must bend under the overhead, his tail curl past a corner. Hoofs rattled on steel. He took several turns around the command bridge before he stopped and gazed into the simulacrum of the sky that made a black, bejeweled belt for this compartment.

The ship was on gravdrive, accelerating outward. Earth and Luna had shrunk to a double star, blue and gold, and Sol had visibly dwindled. Ahead glistened the southern stars. An X etched into the bow section of the continuous screen centered on a region near the constellation Circinus. But Adzel's gaze kept straying to another point of brilliance, second brightest in the Cross.

"We could return and wait," he suggested. "Maybe Freelady Beldaniel can nonetheless be induced to withdraw her threat to cancel the meeting. Or maybe the threat was always an empty one."

"No," said van Rijn from the chair he overflowed, "I think not. She is tough, I found out while we haggled. *Ja*, I bet she puts spaghetti sauce on barbed wire. And best we believe her when she says her bosses is not terrible anxious to talk with us anyways, and she can't guarantee they will come to the rendezvous, and if we do anything they don't like—or she don't like so she is not enthusiastic about telling them they should negotiate—why, then they go home in a huff-puff."

He drew on his churchwarden, adding more blue reek to that which already filled the air. "We know practicalistically nothings about them, they know lots about us," he went on. "Ergo, where it comes to meetings and idea exchanges, we is buyers in a seller's market and can't do a lot else than ask very polite if they mind using not quite so big a reamer on us. Q.," he finished gloomily, "E. D."

"If you worry about David and Chee," Adzel said, "you might get on the radio before we go hyper, and dispatch another ship or two for reinforcement to them."

"No pointing in that unless we get a holler for help from them, or a long time has gone by with no word. They are good experienced pioneers what should could handle any planet by their own selfs. Or if they got hurt, too late now, I am afraid."

"I was thinking of assistance against hostile action. They may encounter armed forces, alerted by the first two Serendipity partners who left several weeks ago."

"To fight, how much power we need send? No telling, except got to be plenty." Van Rijn shook his head. "They don't give out second prizes for combat, dragon boy. We send less fighting power than the enemy, we don't likely get none back. And we can't spare enough warcraft for making sure of victories over these unknown villains trying to horn us out of our hard-begotten profit."

"Profit!" Adzel's tailtip struck the deck with a thud and a dry rattle. Unwonted indignation roughened his basso. "We'd have plenty of available power if you'd notify the Commonwealth, so regular naval forces could be mobilized. The more I think about your silence, the more I realize with horror that you are deliberately letting whole planets, a whole civilization, billions upon billions of sentient beings, lie unsuspecting and unprepared . . . lest you miss your chance at a monopoly!"

"Whoa, whoa, horsey." Van Rijn lifted one palm. "Is not that bad. Look here, I don't make no money if my whole society goes down guggle-guggle to the bottom. Do I? And besides, I got a conscience. Bent and tobacco-stained, maybe, but a conscience. I got to answer to God my own poor self, someday." He pointed to the little Martian sandroot statuette of St. Dismas that usually traveled with him. It stood on a shelf; candles had been overlooked in the haste of departure, but numerous IOUs for them were tucked under its base. He crossed himself.

"No," he said, "I got to decide what gives everybody his best chance. Not his certainty—is no such thing—but his best chance. With this tired old brain, all soggy and hard to light, I got to decide our action. Even if I decide to let you do the deciding, that is a deciding of mine and I got to answer for it. Also, I don't think you would want that responsibility."

"Well, no," Adzel admitted. "It is frightful. But you show dangerous pride in assuming it unilaterally."

"Who else is better? You is too naive, too trusting, for one exemplar. Most others is stupids, or hysterics, or toot some political theory they chop up the universe to fit, or is greedy or cruel or— Well, me, I can ask my friend yonder to make interceding in Heaven for me. And I make connections in this life too, you understand. I am not playing every card alone; no, no, I got plenty good people up my sleeve, who is being told as much as they need to know."

Van Rijn leaned back. "Adzel," he said, "down the corridor you find a cooler with beer. You bring me one like a good fellow and I review this whole affair with you what has mostly waited patient and not sat in on the talks I had. You will see what a bucket of worms I must balance on each other—"

Those who are not afraid of death, even at their own hands, may get power beyond their real strength. For then their cooperation has to be bargained for.

The partners in Serendipity had not suffered total defeat. They held several counters. For one, there was the apparatus they had built up, the organization, the computers and memory banks. It would be difficult, perhaps impossible, to keep them from destroying this before its sale went through, if they chose. And more was involved here than someone's money. Too many key enterprises were already too dependent on the service; many others were potentially so; though the loss would be primarily economic, it would give a severe shock to the League, the Commonwealth, and allied peoples. In effect, while untold man-years would not be lost as lives, their productivity would be.

Of course, the system contained no information about its ultimate masters. A few deductions might perhaps be made, e.g., by studying the circuits, but these would be tentative and, if correct, not very important. However, perusal of the accumulated data would have some value as an indicator of the minimum amount of knowledge that those masters had about Technic civilization.

Hence the partners could exact a price for sparing their machines. The price included their own free departure, with no one trailing them: a fact they could verify for themselves.

Van Rijn, in his turn, could demand some compensation for helping to arrange this departure. He was naturally anxious to learn something, anything concerning the Shenna (as he soon did worm out that they were called in at least one of their languages). He wanted a meeting between their people and his. Before Kim Yoon-Kun, Anastasia Herrera, and Eve Latimer left the Solar System, he got their promise to urge their lords to send a delegation. Where it would be sent they did not specify. Thea Beldaniel, who stayed behind, was to reveal this at the appropriate time if she saw fit.

Another mutual interest lay in preserving discretion. Neither Serendipity nor van Rijn wanted Technic governments directly involved . . . as yet, anyhow. But if either got disgusted with these private chafferings, that party could stop them by making a public statement of the facts. Since van Rijn probably had less to lose from any such outcome, this was a more powerful chess piece in his hand than in Thea's. Or so he apparently convinced her. She bought his silence initially by helping him get the information from the computers, about Beta Crucis and the rogue, that Falkayn had gotten earlier.

Nevertheless, negotiations between him and her dragged on. This was partly because of the legal formalities involved in the sale of the company, and tussles with news agencies that wanted to know more. Partly, too, it was due to his own stalling. He needed time. Time for *Muddlin' Through* to report back. Time to decide what word should be quietly passed to whom, and what should then be done in preparation against an ill-defined danger. Time to begin those preparations, but keep them undercover, yet not too well hidden. . . .

In contrast, Thea's advantage—or that of her masters—lay in making an early start for the rendezvous. This should not be too soon for the Shenna to have received ample warning from Kim's party. But neither should it give van Rijn more time to organize his forces than was unavoidable.

She told him that the Shenna had no overwhelming reason to dicker with anybody. Their spy system being wrecked, they might wish to meet with someone well informed like van Rijn, feel out the changed situation, conceivably work toward an agreement about spheres of influence. But then again, they might not. Powerful as they were, why should they make concessions to inferior races like man? She proposed that the merchant go unaccompanied to the rendezvous, in a spaceship chosen by her, viewports blanked. He refused.

Abruptly she broke off the talks and insisted on leaving in less than a week. Van Rijn howled to no avail. This was the deadline she and her partners had agreed on, when they also set the meeting place they would suggest to their lords. If he did not accept it, he would simply not be guided.

He threatened not to accept. He had other ways to trace down the Shenna, he said. The haggling went back and forth. Thea did have some reason for wanting the expedition to go. She believed it would serve the ends of her masters; at a minimum, it ought to give them an extra option. And, a minor but real enough consideration, it would carry her home, when otherwise she was doomed to suicide or lifelong exile. She gave in on some points.

The agreement reached at last was for her to travel alone, van Rijn with none but Adzel. (He got a partner in exchange for the fact that his absence would, he claimed, badly handicap the League.) They were to leave at the time she wanted. However, they would not travel blind. Once they went hyper, she would instruct the robopilot, and he might as well listen to her as she specified the coordinates. The goal wasn't a Shenn planet anyway.

But she would not risk some booby trap, tracing device, clandestine message ejector, or whatever else he might put into a ship he had readied beforehand. Nor did he care to take corresponding chances. They settled on jointly ordering a new-built vessel from a nonhuman yard—there happened to be one that had just completed her shakedown cruise and was advertising for buyers—with an entire supply stock. They boarded immediately upon Solar System delivery, each having inspected the other's hand baggage, and started the moment that clearance was granted.

This much Adzel knew. He had not been party to van Rijn's other activities. It came as no surprise to him that confidential couriers had been dispatched from end to end of the Solar Spice & Liquors trading territory, carrying orders for its most reliable factors, district chiefs, "police" captains, and more obscure employees. But he had not realized the degree to which other merchant princes of the League were alerted. True, they were not told everything. But the reason for that was less to keep secret the existence of the rogue than it was to head off shortsighted avarice and officiousness that must surely hamper a defense effort. The magnates were warned of a powerful, probably hostile civilization beyond the rim of the known. Some of them were told in more detail about the role Serendipity had played. They must gather what forces they had.

And this was sufficient to bring in governments! A movement of Polesotechnic fighting units could not escape notice. Inquiries would be rebuffed, more or less politely. But with something clearly in the wind, official military-naval services would be put on the qui vive. The fact that League ships were concentrating near the important planets would cause those charged with defense to apportion their own strength accordingly.

Given out-and-out war, this would not serve. The merchant lords must work as closely as might be with the lords spiritual and temporal that legal theory (the different, often wildly different legal theories of the various races and cultures) said were set over them in any of the innumerable separate jurisdictions. But in the immediate situation, where virtually everything was unknown—where the very existence of a dangerous enemy remained unproven—such an alliance was impossible. The rivalries involved were too strong. Van Rijn could get more action faster by complicated flimflammery than by any appeal to idealism or common sense.

At that, the action was far too slow. Under perfect conditions, with everyone concerned a militant angel, it would still be too slow. The distances involved were so immense, lines of communication so thin, planets so scattered and diverse. No one had ever tried to rally all of those worlds at once. Not only had it never been necessary, it did not look feasible.

"I done what I could," van Rijn said, "not even knowing what I should. Maybe in three-four months—or three-four years, I don't know—the snowball I started rolling will bear fruit. Maybe then everybody is ready to ride out whatever blow will go bang on them. Or maybe not.

"I left what information I didn't give out in a safe place. It will be publicated after a while if I don't come back. After that, hoo-hoo, me I can't forespeak what happens! Many players then come in the game, you see, where now is only a few. It got demonstrated centuries back, in early days of theory, the more players, the less of a stable is the game.

"We go off right now, you and me, and try what we can do. If we don't do nothing except crash, well, we begun about as much battering down of hatches as I think could have been. Maybe enough. Maybe not. *Vervloekt,* how hard I wish that Beldaniel witch did not make us go away so soon like this!"

XIX

The ship went under hyperdrive and raced through night. She would take about three weeks to reach her destination.

In the beginning Thea held aloof, stayed mainly in her cabin, said little beyond the formulas of courtesy at mealtimes and chance encounters. Van Rijn did not press her. But he talked at the table, first over the food and afterward over large bottles of wine and brandy. It sounded like idle talk, reminiscence, free association, genial for the most part though occasionally serious. Remarks of Adzel's often prompted these monologues; nonetheless, van Rijn seemed to take for granted that he was addressing the thin, jittery, never-smiling woman as well as the mild-mannered dracocentauroid.

She excused herself immediately after the first few meals. But soon she stayed, listening till all hours. There was really nothing else to do; and a multiple billion light-years of loneliness enclosed this thrumming metal shell; and van Rijn's tongue rambled through much that had never been public knowledge, the stuff of both science and saga.

"—we could not come near that white dwarf star, so bad did it radiate . . . *ja,* hard X-ray quanta jumping off it like fleas abandoning a sinking dog . . . only somehow we had got to recover the derelict or our poor little new company would be bankruptured. Well, I thought, fate had harpooned me in the end. But by damn, the notion about a harpoon made me think maybe we could—"

What she did not know was that Adzel received his instructions prior to each such occasion. What he was to say, ask, object to, and confirm was listed for him. Thus van Rijn had a series of precisely planned conversations to try on Thea Beldaniel.

He soon developed a pretty good general idea of what subjects interested and pleased her, what bored or repelled. No doubt she was storing away in memory everything that might possibly be useful to the Shenna. But she must recognize that usefulness was marginal, especially when she had no way of telling how much truth lay in any given anecdote. It followed that her reaction to whatever he told her came chiefly from her own personality, her own emotions. Even more self-revealing were her reactions to the various styles he used. A story might be related in a cold, impersonal, calculating manner; or with barbaric glee; or humorously; or philosophically; or tenderly; or poetically, when he put words in the mouth of someone else; or in any number of other ways. Of course, he did not spring from one method straight to another. He tried different proportions.

The voyage was not half over when he had learned what face to adopt for her. Thereafter he concentrated on it. Adzel was no longer needed. She responded directly, eagerly to the man.

They were enemies yet. But he had become a respected opponent—or more than respected—and the hope was pathetic to see growing in her, that peace might be made between him and her lords.

"Natural, I want peace myself," he boomed benevolently. "What we got to fight for? Two or three hundred billion stars in our galaxy. Plenty room, *nie?*" He gestured at Adzel, who, well rehearsed, trotted off to fetch more cognac. When it arrived, he made a fuss—"Wa-a-agh! Not fit for pouring in burned-out chemosensors, this, let alone our lady friend what don't drink a lot and keeps a fine palate. Take it back and bring me another what better be decent! No, don't toss it out neither! You got scales on your brain like on your carcass? We take this home and show it to the dealer and make him consume it in a most unlikely way!"—although it was a perfectly good bottle which he and the Wodenite would later share in private. The act was part of the effect he was creating. Jove must loose occasional thunders and lightnings.

"Why is your Shenna scared of us?" he asked another time.

Thea bristled. "They are not! Nothing frightens them!" (Yes, they must be Jove and she their worshiper. At least to a first approximation. There were hints that the relationship was actually more subtle, and involved a master-figure which was actually more primitive.) "They were being careful . . . discreet . . . wise . . . to study you b-b-beforehand."

"So, so, so. Don't get angry, please. How can I say right things about them when you won't tell me none?"

"I can't." She gulped. Her hands twisted together. "I mustn't." She fled to her cabin.

Presently van Rijn followed. He could drift along like smoke when he chose. Her door was shut and massive; but he had worn a button in his ear, hidden by the ringlets, when he embarked. It was a transistorized sound amplifier, patterned after hearing aids from the period before regenerative techniques were developed. He listened to her sobs for a while, neither bashfully nor gloatingly. They confirmed that he had her in psychological retreat. She would not surrender, not in the mere days of travel which remained. But she would give ground, if he advanced with care.

He jollied her, the next watch they met. And at the following supper, he proceeded to get her a little drunk over dessert. Adzel left quietly and spent half an hour at the main control board, adjusting the color and intensity of the saloon lights. They became a romantic glow too gradually for Thea to notice. Van Rijn had openly brought a player and installed it that they might enjoy dinner music. "Tonight's" program ran through a calculated gamut of pieces like *The Last Spring, Là Ci Darem La Mano, Isoldes Liebestod, Londonderry Air, Evenstar Blues.* He did not identify them for her. Poor creature, she was too alienated from her own people for the names to mean anything. But they should have their influence.

He had no physical designs on her. (Not that he would have minded. She was, if not beautiful, if far less well filled out than he liked, rather attractive—despite her severe white suit—now that she had relaxed. Interest turned her finely boned features vivid and kindled those really beautiful green eyes. When she spoke with a smile, and with no purpose except the pleasure of speaking to a fellow human, her voice grew husky.) Any such attempt would have triggered her defenses. He was trying for a more rarefied, and vital, kind of seduction.

"—they raised us," she said dreamily. "Oh, I know the Earthside jargon. I know it gave us deviant personalities. But what is the norm, honestly, Nicholas? We're different from other humans, true. But human nature is plastic. I don't believe you can call us warped, any more than you yourself are because you were brought up in a particular tradition. We are healthy and happy."

Van Rijn raised one eyebrow.

"We are!" she said louder, sitting erect again. "We're glad and proud to serve our . . . our saviors."

"'The lady doth protest too much, methinks,'" he murmured.

"What?"

"A line in Old Anglic. You would not recognize. Pronunciation has changed. It means I am very interested. You never told nobody about your background before, the shipwreck and all."

"Well, I did tell Davy Falkayn . . . when he was with us—" Tears gleamed suddenly on her lashes. She squeezed the lids together, shook her head, and drained her glass. Van Rijn refilled it.

"He's a sweet young man," she said fast. "I never wanted to harm him. None of us did. Not our fault he was, was, was sent off to danger. By you! I do hope he'll be lucky."

Van Rijn did not pursue the point she had inadvertently verified: that Latimer and her sister had carried word to the Shenna, who would promptly have organized a Beta Crucis expedition of their own. It was a rather obvious point. Instead, the merchant drawled:

"If he was a friend like you say, you must have hurt when you lied to him."

"I don't know what you mean." She looked shocked.

"You spun him one synthetic yarn, you." Van Rijn's mild tone took the edge off his words. "That radiation accident, and you getting found later, is too big, spiky a coincidence for me to swallow. Also, if the Shenna only wanted to return you home, with a stake, they would not set you up for spies. Also, you is too well trained, too loyal, for being raised by utter aliens from adolescence. You might have been grateful to them for their help, but you would not be their agents against your own race what never harmed you—not unless you was raised from pups. No, they got you sooner in life than you tell. *Nie?*"

"Well—"

"Don't get mad." Van Rijn raised his own glass and contemplated the colors within. "I am simple-minded, good-hearted trying to come at some understandings, so I can figure how we settle this trouble and not have any fights. I don't ask you should pass out no real secrets from the Shenna. But things like, oh, what they call their home planet—"

"Dathyna," she whispered.

"Ah. See? That did not hurt you nor them for saying, did it? And makes our talking a lot handier, we don't need circumlocomotions. Hokay, you was raised from babies, for a purpose, as might be because the Shenna wanted special ambassadors. Why not admit it? How you was raised, what the environment was like, every little friendly datum helps me understand you and your people, Thea."

"I can't tell you anything important."

"I know. Like the kind of sun Dathyna got is maybe too good a clue. But how about the kind of living? Was your childhood happy?"

"Yes. Yes. My earliest memory is . . . Isthayan, one of my master's sons, took me exploring . . . he wanted someone to carry his weapons, even their toddlers have weapons. . . . We went out of the household, into the ruined part of the huge old, old building . . . we found some machinery in a high tower room, it hadn't rusted much, the sunlight struck through a hole in the roof like white fire, off metal, and I laughed to see it shine. . . . We could look out, across the desert, like forever—" Her eyes widened. She laid a hand across her lips. "No. I'm talking far too freely. I'd better say goodnight."

"*Verweile doch, du bist so schön,*" van Rijn said, "what is another old Earth quotation and means stay a while and have some Madeira, my dear. We discuss safe things. For instance, if you babies didn't come off no colonizer ship, then where?"

The color left her cheeks. "Goodnight!" she gasped, and once again she ran. By now he could have shouted an order to stay and she would have heeded; for the reflex of obedience to that kind of stimulus had become plain to see in her. He refrained, though. Interrogation would only produce hysteria.

Instead, when he and Adzel were alone in the Wodenite's stateroom—which had been prepared by ripping out the bulkhead between two adjoining ones—he rumbled around a nightcap:

"I got a few information bits from her. Clues to what kind of world and culture we is colliding with. More about the psychologies than the outside facts. But that could be helpful too." His mustaches rose with the violence of his grimace. "Because what we face is not just troublesome, it is nasty. Horrible."

"What have you learned, then?" the other asked calmly.

"Obvious, the Shenna made slaves—no, dogs—out of humans on purpose that they got from babies. Maybe other sophonts too, but anyways humans."

"Where did they obtain the infants?"

"I got no proof, but here is a better guess than Beldaniel and her partners maybe thought I could make. Look, we can assume pretty safe the rendezvous planet we is bound for is fairly near Dathyna so they got the advantage of short communications while we is far from home and our nice friends with guns. Right?"

Adzel rubbed his head, a bony sound. "'Near' is a relative term. Within a sphere of fifty or a hundred light-years' radius there are so many stars that we have no reasonable chance of locating the centrum of our opponents before they have mounted whatever operation they intend."

"*Ja, ja, ja.* What I mean is, though, somewhere around where we aim at is territory where Shenna been active for a longish while. Hokay? Well, happens I remember, about fifty years back was an attempt for planting a human colony out this way. A little Utopian group like was common in those days. Late type G star, but had one not bad planet what they called, uh, *ja,* Leandra. They wanted to get away from anybody interrupting their paradise. And they was successful. No profit for traveling that far to trade. They had one ship for their own what would visit Ifri or Llynathawr maybe once a year and buy things they found they needed, for money they had along.

Finally was a long time with no ship. Somebody got worried and went to see. Leandra stood abandoned. The single village was pretty burned—had been a forest fire over everywhere for kilometers around—but the ship was gone. Made a big mystery for a while. I heard about it because happened I was traveling by Ifri some years afterward. Of course, it made no splash on Earth or any other important planet."

"Did no one think of piracy?" Adzel asked.

"Oh, probable. But why should pirates sack a tiny place like that? Besides, had been no later attacks. Whoever heard of one-shot pirates? Logical theory was, fire wiped out croplands, warehouses, everything the Leandrans needed to live. They went after help, all in their ship, had troubles in space and never made port. The matter is pretty well forgot now. I don't believe nobody has bothered with Leandra since. Too many better places closer to home." Van Rijn scowled at his glass as if it were another enemy. "Tonight I guess different. Could be Shenna work. They could of first landed, like friendly explorers from a world what lately begun space travel. They could learn details and figure what to do. Then they could kidnap everybody and set a fire for covering the evidence."

"I believe I see the further implications," Adzel said softly. "Some attempt, perhaps, to domesticate the older captive humans. Presumably a failure, terminated by their murder, because the youngest ones don't remember natural parents. No doubt many infants died too, or were killed as being unpromising material. Quite possibly the half-dozen of Serendipity are the sole survivors. It makes me doubt that any nonhumans were similarly victimized. Leandra must have represented a unique opportunity."

"What it proves is bad enough," van Rijn said. "I can't push Beldaniel about her parents. She must feel suspicions, at least, but not dare let herself think about them. Because her whole soul is founded on being a creature of the Shenna. In fact, I got the impression of she being the special property of one among them—like a dog."

His hand closed around the tumbler with force that would have broken anything less strong than vitryl. "They want to make us the same, maybe?" he snarled. "No, by eternal damn! *Liever dood dan slaaf!*" He drained the last whisky. "What means, I'll see them in Hell first . . . if I got to drag them down behind me!" The tumbler crashed warheadlike on the deck.

✡XX✡

The rendezvous site was listed in Technic catalogues. Scanning its standard memory units, the ship's computer informed van Rijn that this system had been visited once, about a century ago. A perfunctory survey revealed nothing of interest, and no one was recorded as having gone back. (Nothing except seven planets, seven worlds, with their moons and mysteries, life upon three of them, and one species that had begun to chip a few stones into handier shapes, look up at the night sky and gropingly wonder.) There were so uncountably many systems.

"I could have told you that," Thea said.

"Ha?" Van Rijn turned, planet-ponderous himself, as she entered the command bridge.

Her smile was shy, her attempt at friendliness awkward from lack of practice. "Obviously we couldn't give you a hint at anything you didn't already know. We picked a sun arbitrarily, out of deserted ones within what we guessed is a convenient volume of space for the Shenna."

"Hm-hm." Van Rijn tugged his goatee. "I wouldn't be an ungentleman, but wasn't you never scared I might grab you and pump you, I mean for where Dathyna sits?"

"No. The information has been withheld from me. Only the men, Latimer and Kim, were ever told, and they received deep conditioning against revealing it." Her gaze traveled around the stars which, in this craft built by nonhumans, showed as a strip engirdling the compartment. "I can tell you what you must have guessed, that some of the constellations are starting to look familiar to me." Her voice dropped. She reached her arms forth, an unconscious gesture of yearning. "They, the Shenna, will take me home. Moath himself may be waiting. *Eyar wathiya grazzan tolya. . . .*"

Van Rijn said quietly, into her growing rapture, "Suppose they do not come? You said they might not. What do you do?"

She drew a quick breath, clenched her fists, stood for a moment as the loneliest figure he remembered seeing, before she turned to him. Her hands closed around his, cold and quick. "Then will you help me?" she begged. Fire mounted in her countenance. She withdrew. "But Moath will not abandon me!" She turned on her heel and walked out fast.

Van Rijn glowered at the star that waxed dead ahead, and took out his snuffbox for what consolation was in it.

But his hunch was right, that Thea had no real reason for worry. Sweeping inward, the ship detected emanations from a sizable flotilla, at an initial distance indicating those vessels had arrived two or three days ago. (Which meant they had departed from a point not much over a hundred light-years hence—unless Shenna craft could travel a great deal faster than Technic ones—and this was unlikely, because if the Shenna were not relative newcomers to space, they would surely have been encountered already by explorers—not to mention the fact that today's hyperdrive oscillator frequencies were crowding the maximum which quantum theory allowed—) They accelerated almost at the instant van Rijn came within detection range. Some fanned out, doubtless to make sure he didn't have followers. The rest converged on him. A code signal, which the Shenna must have learned from human slaves, flashed. Van Rijn obeyed, dropped into normal state, assumed orbit around the sun, and let the aliens position themselves however they chose.

Gathered again in the bridge before the main outercom, all three waited. Thea shivered, her face now red and now white, staring and staring at the ships which drew closer. Van Rijn turned his back on her. "I don't know why," he muttered to Adzel in one of the languages they were sure she did not have in common with them, "but I get some feeling I can't name from the sight of her like that."

"Embarrassment, probably," the Wodenite suggested.

"Oh, is that how it feels?"

"She is unlike me, of course, in her deepest instincts as well as her upbringing," Adzel said. "Regardless, I do not find it decent either to observe a being stripped so naked."

He concentrated his attention on the nearest Shenn craft. Its gaunt high-finned shape was partly silhouetted black upon the Milky Way, partly asheen by the distant orange sun. "A curious design," he said. "It does not look very functional."

Van Rijn switched to Anglic. "Could be hokay for machines, that layout," he remarked. "And why this many of them—fifteen, right?—big and hedgehoggy with weapons and would need hundreds in the crews—to meet one little unarmed speedster like us, unless they is mostly robots? I think they is real whizzards at robotics, those Shenna. Way beyond us. The SI computer system points likelywise."

Thea reacted in her joy as he had hoped. She could not keep from boasting, rhapsodizing, about the powerful and complex automatons whose multitudes were skeleton and muscle of the whole Dathynan civilization. Probably no more than three or four living Masters were in this group, she said. No more were needed.

"Not even for making dicker with us?" van Rijn asked.

"They speak for themselves alone," Thea said. "You don't have plenipotentiary powers either, you know. But they will confer with their colleagues after you have been interviewed." Her tone grew more and more absent-minded while she spoke, until it faded into a kind of crooning in the guttural Shenn tongue. She had never ceased staring outward.

"'They will confer with their colleagues,'" Adzel quoted slowly, in the private language. "Her phrase suggests that decision-making authority rests with an exceedingly small group. Yet it does not follow that the culture is an extreme oligarchy. Oligarchs would prefer live crews for most tasks, like us, and for the same reasons. No matter how effective a robot one builds, it remains a machine—essentially, an auxiliary to a live brain—because if it were developed so highly as to be equivalent to a biological organism, there would be no point in building it."

"*Ja,* I know that line of argument," van Rijn said. "Nature has already provided us means for making new biological organisms, a lot cheaper and more fun than producing robots. Still, how about the computer that has been speculated about, fully motivated but superior in every way to any being born from flesh?"

"A purely theoretical possibility in any civilization we have come upon thus far; and frankly, I am skeptical of the theory. But supposing it did exist, such a robot would rule, not serve. And the Shenna are obviously not subordinates. Therefore they have—well, on the whole, perhaps somewhat better robots than we do, perhaps not; certainly more per capita; nevertheless, only robots, with the usual inherent limitations. They employ them lavishly in order to compensate as best they can for those limitations. But why?"

"Little population? That would explain why they do not have many decision makers, if they do not."

"*Zanh-h-h* . . . maybe. Although I cannot offhand see how a society few in numbers could build—could even design—the vast, sophisticated production plant that Dathyna evidently possesses."

They had been talking largely to relieve their tension, quite well aware of how uncertain their logic was. When the ship said, "Incoming signal received," they both started. Thea choked a shriek. "Put them on, whoever they is," van Rijn ordered. He wiped sweat off his jowls with the soiled lace of one cuff.

The visiscreen flickered. An image sprang forth. It was half manlike; but swelling muscles, great bull head, iridescent mane, thunder that spoke from the open mouth were such embodied volcano power that Adzel stepped backward hissing.

"Moath!" Thea cried. She fell to her knees, hands outstretched toward the Shenn. Tears whipped down her face.

Life is an ill-arranged affair, where troubles and triumphs both come in lots too big to cope with, and in between lie arid stretches of routine and marking time. Van Rijn often spoke sharply to St. Dismas about this. He never got a satisfactory reply.

His present mission followed the pattern. After Thea said Moath her lord commanded her presence aboard the vessel where he was—largest of the flotilla, a dreadnaught in size, fantastically beweaponed—and entered a flitter dispatched for her, nothing happened for forty-seven hours and twenty-nine minutes by the clock. The Shenna sent no further word nor heeded any calls addressed to them. Van Rijn groaned, cursed, whined, stamped up and down the passages, ate six full meals a day, cheated at solitaire, overloaded the air purifiers with smoke and the trash disposal with empty bottles, and would not even be soothed by his Mozart symphonies. At last he exhausted Adzel's tolerance. The Wodenite locked himself in his own room with food and good books, and did not emerge until his companion yelled at the door that the damned female icicle with the melted brain was ready to interpret and maybe now something could be done to reward him, Nicholas van Rijn, for his Griselda-like patience.

Nonetheless, the merchant was showing her image a certain avuncular courtliness when Adzel galloped in. "—wondered why you left us be when everybody traveled this far for meeting."

Seated before a transmitter pickup on the battleship, she was changed. Her garb was a loose white robe and burnoose and her eyes bore dark contact lenses, protection from the harsh light in that cabin. She was altogether self-possessed again, her emotional needs fulfilled. Her answer came crisp: "My lords the Shenna questioned me in detail, in preparation for our discussions. No one else from Serendipity was brought along, you see."

Below the viewfield of his own sender, van Rijn kept a scrib on his lap. Like fast hairy sausages, his fingers moved across the noiseless console. Adzel read an unrolling tape: *That was foolish. How could they be sure nothing would have happened to her, their link with us? More proof they rush into things, not stopping for thought.*

Thea was continuing. "Furthermore, before I could talk rationally, I must get the *haaderu.* I had been so long away from my lord Moath. You would not understand *haaderu.*" She blushed the faintest bit, but her voice might have described some adjustment to a machine. "Consider it a ceremony in which he acknowledges my loyalty to him. It requires time. Meanwhile, the scoutships verified no one else had treacherously accompanied us at a distance."

Van Rijn wrote: *Not Jove. The Minotaur. Raw power and maleness.*

"I do not identify the reference," Adzel breathed in his ear.

What that Shenn beast really is to her. She is only somewhat a slave. I have known many women like her in offices, spinsters fanatically devoted to a male boss. No wonder the SI gang were four women, two men. Men seldom think quite that way. Unless first they are conditioned, broken. I doubt if those people have had any sex relationship. The Latimer marriage was to prevent gossip. Their sexuality has been directed into the channel of serving the Shenna. Of course, they don't realize that.

"My lords will now hear you," Thea Beldaniel said. For an instant, humanness broke through. She leaned forward and said, low and urgent, "Nicholas, be careful. I know your ways, and I'll translate what you mean, not what you say. But be careful what you mean, too. I won't lie to them. And they are more easily angered than you might think. I—" She paused a second. "I want you to go home unhurt. You are the, the only man who was ever kind to me."

Bah, he wrote, *I played Minotaur myself, once I saw she wished for something like that, though I supposed at the time that it was Jove. She responded, not conscious of what moved her. Not but what she doesn't deserve to be led back into her own species. That is a filthy thing they have done to her.*

Thea gestured. A robot responded. The view panned back, revealing a great conference chamber where four Shenna sat on cushions. Van Rijn winced and mumbled an oath when he saw the decor. "No taste, not by no standards nowhere in the universe or Hell! They skipped right past civilization, them, gone straight from barbarism to decadence." It was Adzel who, as the conference progressed and the focus of view shifted about, remarked on a few ancient-looking objects in that overcrowded room which were lovely.

A voice rolled from one shaggy deep chest. Dwarfed and lost-looking, but her glance forever straying back to adore the Shenn called Moath, Thea interpreted: "You have come to speak of terms between your people and mine. What is the dispute?"

"Why, nothings, really," van Rijn said, "except could be a few pieces of dirt we divvy up like friends instead of blowing our profit on squabbles. And maybe we got things we could trade, or teach each other, like how about one of us has a fine new vice?"

Thea's translation was interrupted halfway through. A Shenn asked something at some length which she rendered as: "What is your alleged complaint against us?"

She must have shaded her interpretation from that side also, but van Rijn and Adzel were both too taken aback to care. "Complaint?" the Wodenite nearly bleated. "Why, one scarcely knows where to begin."

"I do, by damn," van Rijn said, and commenced.

The argument erupted. Thea was soon white and shaking with nerves. Sweat plastered her hair to her brow. It would be useless to detail the wranglings. They were as confused and pointless as the worst in human history. But piece by piece, through sheer stubbornness and refusal to be outshouted, van Rijn assembled a pattern.

Item: Serendipity had been organized to spy upon the Polesotechnic League and the whole Technic civilization.

Answer: The Shenna had provided the League with a service it was too stupid to invent for itself. The forced sale of Serendipity was a bandit act for which the Shenna demanded compensation.

Item: David Falkayn had been kidnapped and drugged by Shenn agents.

Answer: One inferior organism was not worth discussing.

Item: Humans had been enslaved, and probably other humans had been massacred, by Shenna.

Answer: The humans were given a nobler life in service to a higher cause than could ever have been theirs otherwise. Ask them if this was not true.

Item: The Shenna had tried to keep knowledge of a new planet from those who were entitled to it.

Answer: The ones entitled were the Shenna. Let trespassers beware.

Item: Despite their espionage, the Shenna did not seem to appreciate the strength of the Technic worlds and especially the League, which was not in the habit of tolerating menaces.

Answer: Neither were the Shenna.

—About that time, Thea collapsed. The being called Moath left his place and went to stoop over her. He looked, briefly, into the screen. His nostrils were dilated and his mane stood erect. He snorted a command. Transmission ended.

It was probably just as well.

Van Rijn woke so fast that he heard his own final snore. He sat up in bed. His stateroom was dark, murmurous with ventilation, a slight sugary odor in the air because no one had adjusted the chemosystem. The mechanical voice repeated, "Incoming signal received."

"Pestilence and pustules! I heard you, I heard you, let me haul my poor tired old body aloft, by damn." The uncarpeted deck was cold under his feet. From a glowing clock face he saw he had been asleep for not quite six hours. Which made over twenty hours since the conference broke off. If you could dignify that slanging match by that name. What ailed those shooterbulls, anyhow? A high technological culture such as was needed to build robots and spaceships ought to imply certain qualities—a minimum level of diplomacy and caution and enlightened self-interest—because otherwise you would have wrecked yourself before you progressed that far. . . . Well, maybe communications had stayed off until now because the Shenna were collecting their tempers. . . . Van Rijn hurried down the corridor. His nightgown flapped around his ankles.

The bridge was another humming emptiness. Taking its orders literally, the computer had stopped annunciating when it got a response. Adzel, his ears accustomed to denser air, was not roused in that short time. The machine continued as programmed by reporting, "Two hours ago, another spacecraft was detected in approach from the Circinus region. It is still assuming orbit but is evidently in contact with those already present—"

"Shut up and put me on," van Rijn said. His gaze probed the stars. An eel-like destroyer, a more distant cruiser, a point of light that that could be the Shenn flagship, drifted across his view. No visible sign of the newcomer. But he did not doubt that was what had caused this summons.

The viewscreen came on. Thea Beldaniel stood alone in the harsh-lit, machine-murmurous cavern of the conference chamber. He had never seen her so frantic. Her eyes were white-rimmed, her mouth was stretched out of shape.

"Go!" Nor was her voice recognizable. "Escape! They're talking with Gahood. They haven't thought of ordering the robots to watch you. You can leave quietly—maybe—get a head start, or lose them in space—but they'll kill you if you stay!"

He stood altogether unmoving. His deepened tone rolled around her. "Please to explain me more."

"Gahood. He came . . . alone . . . Hugh Latimer's dead or—I sleep in my lord Moath's cabin by the door. An intercom call. Thellam asked him to come to the bridge, him and everyone. He said Gahood was back from Dathyna, Gahood who went to the giant star where the rogue is, and something happened so Gahood lost Latimer. They should meet, hear his full story, decide—" Her fingers made claws in the air. "I don't know any more, Nicholas. Moath gave me no command. I w-w-would not betray him . . . them . . . never . . . but what harm if you stay alive? I could hear the fury gather, *feel* it; I know them; whatever this is, they'll be enraged. They'll have the guns fire on you. Get away!"

Still van Rijn had not stirred. He was quiet until some measure of control returned to her. She shuddered, her breath was uneven, but she regarded him half sanely. Then he asked, "Would they for sure kill Adzel and me? Hokay, they are mad and don't feel like more jaw-jaw right now. But would not sense be for them, they take us home? We got information. We got hostage value."

"You don't understand. You'd never be freed. You might be tortured for your knowledge, you'd surely be drugged. And I would have to help them. And in the end, when you're no further use—"

"They knock me on the head. *Ja, ja,* is clear. But I got a hard old noggle." Van Rijn leaned forward, resting his fingertips lightly on a chairback and his weight on them, catching her look and not letting go. "Thea, if we run, maybe we get away, maybe we don't. I think chances is not awesome good. Those destroyers, at least, I bet can outrun me, what is fat in the shanks. But if we go to Dathyna, well, maybe we can talk after your bosses cool down again. Maybe we strike a bargain yet. What they got to lose, anyhows, taking us along? Can you get them not to kill us, only capture us?"

"I . . . well, I—"

"Was good of you to warn me, Thea. I know what it cost you, I think. But you shouldn't get in trouble, neither, like you might if they find we skedoodled and guessed it was your fault. Why don't you go argue at your Moath? You remind him here we is and he better train guns on us and you better tell us we is prisoners and got to come to Dathyna. Think he does?"

She could not speak further. She managed a spastic nod.

"Hokay, run along." He blew her a kiss. The effect would have been more graceful if less noisy. The screen blanked. He stumped off to find a bottle and Adzel, in that order. But first he spent a few minutes with St. Dismas. If rage overrode prudence among the Shenna, despite the woman's pleas and arguments, he would not be long alive.

XXI

At full pseudospeed, from the nameless star to the sun of Dathyna took a bit under a week. The prisoner ship must strain to keep pace with the warcraft that surrounded her. But she succeeded, which told Earthman and Wodenite something about Shenn space capabilities.

They gathered quite a few other facts en route. This did not include the contents of Gahood's message, nor the reason why it sent the team plunging immediately homeward. But their captors questioned them at irregular intervals, by hypercom. The interrogation was unsystematic and repetitive, seemingly carried out whenever some individual Shenn got the impulse, soon degenerating into boasts and threats. Van Rijn gave many truthful answers, because the aliens could generally have obtained them directly from Thea—population, productivity, etc., of the major Technic worlds; nature and activities of the Polesotechnic League; picturesque details about this or that life form, this or that culture—she was plainly distressed at the behavior of her lords, and tried to recast their words into something better organized. By playing along with her, van Rijn was able to draw her out. For example:

"Lord Nimran wants to hear more about the early history of Earth," she told the merchant. Computers on either vessel converted between dot-dash transmission and voice. "He is especially interested in cases where one civilization inherited from another."

"Like Greeks taking over from Minoans, or Western Christendom from Roman Empire, or Turks from Byzantines?" van Rijn asked. "Cases are not comparable. And was long ago. Why should he care?"

He could imagine how she flushed. "It suffices that he does care."

"Oh, I don't mind making lectures at him. Got nothings else to do except pour me another beer. Speaking about which—" Van Rijn leaned over and fumbled in the cooler that Adzel had carried to the bridge for him. "Ah, there you are, fishie."

The computer turned this into hyperimpulses. The receiving computer was not equipped to translate, but its memory bank now included an Anglic vocabulary. Thea must have told Nimran that he had not properly replied. Did the Minotaur growl and drop hand to gun? Her plea was strained through the toneless artificial voice: "Do not provoke him. They are terrible when they grow angry."

Van Rijn opened the bottle and poured into a tankard. "*Ja*, sure, sure. I only try for being helpful. But tell him I got to know where he wants his knowledge deepened before I can drill in the shaft. And why. I feel the impression that Shenn culture does not produce scientists what wants to know things from pure curiosity."

"Humans overrate curiosity. A monkey trait."

"Uh-huh, uh-huh. Every species got its own instincts, sometimes similar at some other race's but not necessary so. I try now to get the basic instinct pattern for your . . . owners . . . because elsewise what I tell them might not be what they want, might not make any sense to them whatsomever. Hokay, you tell me there is no real science on Dathyna. No interest in what isn't practical or edible or drinkable *(Aaahhh!)* or salable or useful in other ways I should not mention to a lady."

"You oversimplify."

"I know. Can't describe one single individual being in a few words, let alone a whole intelligent race. Sure. But speaking rough, have I right? Would you say this society is not one for abstracted science and odd little facts what aren't relevancy right away?"

"Very well, agreed." There came a pause, during which Thea was probably calming Nimran down again.

Von Rijn wiped foam off his nose and said, "I collect from this, is only one Shenn civilization?"

"Yes, yes. I must finish talking to him." After a couple of minutes: "If you do not start answering, the consequences may be grave."

"But I told you, sweetling, I'm not clear what is his question. He has not got a scientific curiosity, so he asks about successions of culture on Earth because might be is something useful to his own recent case on Dathyna. True?"

After hesitation: "Yes."

"All right, let us find out what kind of succession he is interested in. Does he mean how does a supplanter like Hindu appear, or a hybrid like Technic or Arabic, or a segue of one culture into another like Classical into Byzantine, or what?"

No doubt forlornness crossed her eyes. "I don't know anything myself about Earth's history."

"Ask him. Or better I should ask him through you."

In this manner, von Rijn got confirmation of what he suspected. The Shenna had not created the magnificent cybernetic structure they used. They took it over from an earlier race, along with much else. Still more appeared to have been lost, for the Shenna were conquerors, exterminators, savages squatting in a house erected by civilized beings whom they had murdered. (How was this possible?)

They were not less dangerous on that account, or because they were herbivorous. (What kind of evolution could produce warlike herbivores?)

They had the wit to heed the recommendation of the Serendipity computer as regards the planet at Beta Crucis. They could see its industrial potential. But they were more concerned with denying this to others than with making intensive use of it themselves. For they were not traders or manufacturers on any significant scale. Their robots produced for them the basic goods and services they required, including construction and maintenance of the machinery itself. They had no desire for commercial or intellectual relations with Technic societies. Rather, they believed that coexistence was impossible. (Why?)

The Serendipity operation typified them. When they first happened upon other races that traveled and colonized through space, out on the fringe of the existing Technic sphere, they proceeded to study these. Their methods were unspecified, and doubtless varied from place to place and time to time, but need not always have been violent. A Shenn could be cunning. Since no one can remember all the planets whose natives may go aroving, he need not admit he came from Outside, and he could ask many natural-sounding questions.

Nevertheless, they could not secretly get the detailed information they wanted by such hit-and-run means. One brilliant male among them conceived the idea of establishing spies in the heart of the other territory: spies who could expect the eager cooperation of their victims. His fellows agreed to help start the enterprise. No Shenn had the patience to run that shop in Lunograd. But computers and dog-humans did.

Even so, the basic program for the machines and doctrine for the people were drawn up by Shenna. And here the nature of the beast again revealed itself. *When something important and urgent comes up, react aggressively—fast!* Most species would have given an agency more caution, more flexibility. The Shenna could not endure to. Their instinct was such that to them, in any crisis, action was always preferable to wait-and-see. The pieces could be picked up later.

The Shenna did have a rationale for their distrust of other spacegoing races. (Which distrust automatically produced murderous hatred in them.) They themselves were not many. Their outplanet colonies were few, small, and none too successful. Four-fifths of their adults must be counted out as significant help—because the females outnumbered the polygynous males by that fraction, and were dull-brained subservient creatures. Their political structure was so crude as to be ridiculous. Baronial patriarchs, operating huge estates like independent kingdoms, might confer or cooperate at need, on a strictly voluntary basis; and this constituted the state. Their economics was equally primitive. (How had a race like this gone beyond the Paleolithic, let alone destroyed another people who had covered the planet with machines and were reaching for the stars?)

The companies of the League could buy and sell them for peanuts. The outward wave of Technic settlement would not necessarily sweep over them when it got that far—why bother?—but would certainly engulf every other desirable world around Dathyna. At best, with enormous effort, the Shenna might convert themselves into one more breed of spacefarers among hundreds. To natures like theirs, that prospect was intolerable.

However their society was describable, they were not ridiculous themselves. On the contrary, they were as ominous as the plague bacillus when first it struck Europe. Or perhaps more so; Europe did survive.

XXII

The sun of Dathyna looked familiar to Adzel—middle F-type, 5.4 times as luminous as Sol, white more than gold—until he studied it with what instruments he had available. Astonished, he repeated his work, and got the same results. "That is not a normal star," he said.

"About to go nova?" van Rijn asked hopefully.

"No, not that deviant." Adzel magnified the view, stepping down the brilliance, until the screen showed a disc. The corona gleamed immense, a beautiful serene nacre; but it was background for the seething of flares and prominences, the dense mottling of spots. "Observe the level of output. Observe likewise the intricate patterns. They show a powerful but inconstant magnetic field. . . . Ah." A pinpoint of eye-hurting light flashed and died on the surface.

"A nuclear explosion, taking place within the photosphere. Imagine what convection currents and plasma effects were required. Spectroscopy is consistent with visual data, as is radiation metering. Even at our present distance, the solar wind is powerful; and its pattern as we move inward is highly changeable." He regarded the scene with his rubbery lips pulled into a disconcerting smile. "I had heard of cases like this, but they are rare and I never thought I would have the good fortune to see one."

"I'm glad you get fun out of now," van Rijn grumbled. "Next funeral I attend, I want you along for doing a buck and wing while you sing hey nonny nonny. So what we got here?"

"A sun not only massive, but of unusual composition, extremely rich in metals. Probably it condensed in the neighborhood of a recent supernova. Besides the normal main-sequence evolution, a number of other fusion chains, some of which terminate in fission, go on during its life. This naturally influences interior phenomena, which in turn determine the output. Consider it an irregularly variable star. It isn't really, but the pattern is so complex that it does not repeat within epochs. If I interpret my findings correctly, it is at present receding from a high peak which occurred—*zanh-h-h,* several thousand years ago, I would guess."

"But did not wipe out life on Dathyna?"

"Obviously not. The luminosity will never become that great, until the sun leaves the main sequence altogether. Nevertheless, there must have been considerable biological effect, especially since the charged-particle emission did reach an extreme."

Van Rijn grunted, settled deeper in his chair, and reached for his churchwarden. He usually smoked it when he wanted to think hard.

The flotilla approached Dathyna. The computer of the captive ship kept all sensors open as instructed, and reported much activity in surrounding space—ships in orbit, ships coming and going, ships under construction. Adzel took readings on the globe itself.

It was the fourth one out from its sun, completing a period of 2.14 standard years at a mean distance of two a.u. In mass it likewise resembled Mars: 0.433 Terrestrial, the diameter only 7950 kilometers at the equator. Despite this, and a third again the heat and light which Earth receives, Dathyna had an extensive oxynitrogen atmosphere. Pressure dropped off rapidly with altitude, but at sea level was slightly greater than Terrestrial. Such an amount of gas was surely due to the planetary composition, an abundance of heavy elements conferring an overall specific gravity of 9.4 and thus a surface acceleration of 1057 cm/sec^2. The metal-rich core must have produced enormous outgassing through vulcanism in the world's youth. Today, in combination with the fairly rapid spin—once around in seventeen and a quarter hours—it generated a strong magnetic field which screened off most of the solar particles that might otherwise have kicked air molecules free. The fact was also helpful that Dathyna had no moons.

Visually, swelling upon blackness and stars, the planet was equally strange. It had far less hydrosphere than Earth; quanta from the ultraviolet-spendthrift sun had split many a water molecule. But because mountains and continental masses were less well defined, the surface flatter on the average, water covered about half. Shallow, virtually tideless, those seas were blanketed with algae-like organisms, a red-brown-yellow mat that was sometimes ripped apart to show waves, sometimes clotted into floating islands.

With slight axial tilt and comparatively small edge effect, the polar regions did not differ spectacularly from the equatorial. But with a steep air pressure gradient, the uplands were altogether unlike the valleys beneath—were glacier and naked rock. Some lowlands, especially along the oceans, appeared to be fertile. The brownish-gold native vegetation colored them; forests, meadows, croplands showed in the magniscreen. But enormous regions lay desert, where dust storms scoured red rock. And their barrenness was geologically new—probably not historically too old—because one could identify the towers and half-buried walls of many great dead cities, the grid of highways and power pylons that a large population once required.

"Did the sun burn the lands up when it peaked?" For once, van Rijn almost whispered a question.

"No," Adzel said. "Nothing that simple, I think."

"Why not?"

"Well, increased temperature would cause more evaporation, more clouds, higher albedo, and thus tend to control itself. Furthermore, while it might damage some zones, it would benefit others. Life should migrate poleward and upward. But you can see that the high latitudes and high altitudes have suffered as badly as anyplace. . . . Then too, a prosperous, energetic machine culture ought to have found ways of dealing with a mere change in climate—a change which did not come about overnight, remember."

"Maybe they held a war what got rough?"

"I see no signs of large-scale misuse of nuclear energies. And would any plausible biological or chemical agents wreck the entire ecology of an entire planet, right down to the humble equivalents of grass? I think," said Adzel grimly, "that the catastrophe had a much larger cause and much deeper effects."

He got no chance to elaborate then, for the ship was ordered into atmosphere. A pair of destroyers accompanied. Moath and Thea directed the robots from a tender. The group landed near the Shenn's ancestral castle. An armed swarm ran forth to meet them.

In the next three days, van Rijn and Adzel were given a look around. Thea guided them. "My lord permits this on my recommendation, while he is away at the Grand Council that's been called," she said. "By giving you a better comprehension of our society, we make you better able to help us with information." Pleadingly, not meeting their eyes: "You will help, won't you? You can't do anything else, except die. My lord will treat you well if you serve him well."

"So let's see what it's like where we got to pass our lives," van Rijn said.

The party was heavily guarded, by young males—the sons, nephews, and retainers who comprised Moath's fighting cadre—and robot blastguns that floated along on gravity platforms. Adzel's size inspired caution, though he acted meek enough. Youngsters and idle servants trailed after. Females and workers goggled as the outworlders passed by. The Shenn race was not absolutely devoid of curiosity; no vertebrate is, on any known planet. They simply lacked the intensity of it that characterizes species like Homo or Dracocentaurus sapiens. They were quite analogous in their love of novelty.

"Castle" was a misleading word for the establishment. Once there had been an interlinked set of buildings, an enormous block, five or six kilometers on a side, a full tenth as high—yet for all that mass, graceful, many-colored, with columns of crystal that were nonfunctional but a joy to the eye, with towers that soared so far above the walls that their petal-shaped spires nearly vanished in heaven. It had been a place where millions lived and worked, a community which was an engineered unit, automated, nuclear-powered, integrated through traffic and communication with the whole planet.

Now half of it was a ruin. Pillars were fallen, roofs gaped to the sky, machines had corroded away, creatures like birds nested in the turrets and creatures like rats scuttered through the apartments. Though destruction had passed the rest by, and the patient self-maintaining robots kept it in repair, the echoing hollowness of too many corridors, the plundered bareness of too many rooms and plazas and terraces, were more oppressive than the broken sections.

Thea refused to say what had happened, centuries past. "Are you forbidden to tell us?" Adzel asked.

She bit her lip. "No," she said in a sad little voice, "not exactly. But I don't want to." After a moment: "You wouldn't understand. You'd get the wrong idea. Later, when you know our lords the Shenna better—"

About half of the functional half of the complex was occupied today. The dwellers were not haunted by the past. They seemed to regard its overwhelming shell as part of their landscape. The ruins were quarried—that was one reason they were in poor condition—and the remainder would be taken over as population grew. A busy, lusty, brawling life surged between the walls and across the country-side. While robots did most of the essential work, Moath's folk had plenty of tasks left to do, from technical supervision to their crude arts and crafts, from agriculture and forestry to prospecting and hunting, from education for one's state in a hierarchical society to training for war. Aircraft bore passengers and cargo from other domains. Gravships shuttled between the planets of this system; hyperships trafficked with colonies newly planted among the nearer stars, or prowled farther in exploration and imperialism. Even the peaceful routines of Dathyna had that thunderous vigor which is the Minotaur's.

Nonetheless, here was a life-impoverished world—metal-rich but life-impoverished. The crops grew thin in dusty fields. A perpetual faint stench hung in the air, blown from the nearby ocean, where the vast sea-plant blanket was dying and rotting faster than it replenished itself. The eastern hills were wooded, but with scrubby trees growing among the traces of fallen giants. At night, a hunter's trumpet sounded from them lonelier than would have been the howl of the last wolf alive.

Adzel was astounded to learn that the Shenna hunted and, in fact, kept meat animals. "But you said they are herbivorous," he protested.

"Yes, they are," Thea replied. "This sunlight causes plants to form high-energy compounds which will support a more active, hence intelligent, animal than on the world of a Sol-type star."

"I know," Adzel said. "I am native to an F_5 system myself—though on Zatlakh, Woden, animals generally spend the extra energy on growing large, and we sophonts are omnivorous. I suppose the Shenna must process meat before they can digest it?"

"Correct. Of course, I am sure you know better than I how vague the line is between 'carnivore' and 'herbivore.' I have read, for instance, that on Earth, ungulates habitually eat their own placentas after bringing forth young, whereas cats and dogs often eat grass. Here on Dathyna, a further possibility exists. Certain fruit juices make meat nourishing for any normally vegetarian creature, through enzyme action. The treatment process is simple. It was discovered in—in early times, by the primitive ancestors of today's Shenna. Or perhaps even earlier."

"And on a planet which has suffered ecological disaster like this one, every food source must be utilized. I see." Adzel was satisfied.

Until van Rijn said, "But the Shenna goes hunting, tally-hoo, for fun. I'm sure they does. I watched that young buck ride home yesterday wearing the horns off his kill. He'd used a bow, too, when he got a perfect good gun. That was sport."

Thea arched her brow. "And why not?" she challenged. "I'm told most intelligent species enjoy hunting. And combat. Including your own."

"*Ja, ja.* I don't say is bad, unless they start chasing me. But where do we get the instinct that makes us feel good when we catch and kill? Maybe just catch a photograph . . . though very few people what would never kill a deer do not get happy to swat a fly. How come?" Van Rijn wagged a finger. "I tell you. You and me is descended from hunters. Preman in Africa was a killer ape. Those what was not natural-born killers, they did not live to pass on their squeamery. But ancestors of Shenna was browsers and grazers! Maybe they had fights at mating season, but they did not hunt down other animals. Yet Shenna now, they do. How come *that?*"

Thea changed the subject. It was easy to do, with so much to talk about, the infinite facets of a planet and a civilization. One must admit the Shenna were civilized in the technical sense of the word. They had machines, literacy, a worldwide culture which was becoming more than worldwide. To be sure, they were inheritors of what the earlier society had created. But they had made a comeback from its destruction, restored part of what it had been, added a few innovations.

And their patriarchs aimed to go farther. Elsewhere on Dathyna, they met in stormy debate to decide—what? Van Rijn shivered in a gathering dusk. The nights of this semi-desert were cold. It would be good to enter the warmth and soft light of his ship.

He had won that concession after the first night, which he and Adzel spent locked in a room of the castle. The next morning he had been at the top of his form, cursing, coughing, wheezing, weeping, swearing by every human and nonhuman saint in or out of the catalogue that one more bedtime without respite from the temperatures, the radiation, the dust, the pollen, the heavy metals whose omnipresence not only forced outworlders to take chelating pills lest they be poisoned but made the very air taste bad, the noises, the stinks, the everything of this planet whose existence was a potent argument for the Manichaean heresy because he could not imagine why a benevolent God would wish it on the universe: another night must surely stretch his poor old corpse out stiff and pitiful—Finally Thea grew alarmed and took it upon herself to change their quarters. A couple of engineer officers with robot assistance disconnected the drive units of the League vessel. It was a thorough job. Without parts and tools, the captives had no possibility of lifting that hull again. They might as well sleep aboard. A guard or two with a blastcannon could watch outside.

Late on the third day, Moath returned.

Van Rijn and Adzel observed the uproar from a distance, as his folk boiled around the overlord. He addressed them from an upper airlock chamber in his personal spaceflitter. His voice rolled like surf and earthquake. Hurricane answered from the ground. The young Shenna roared, capered, danced in rings, hammered on the boat's side till it rang, lifted archaic swords and fired today's energy weapons into the air. From the highest remaining tower, a banner was raised, the color of new blood.

"What's he say?" van Rijn asked. Thea stood moveless, eyes unfocused, stunned as if by a blow to the head. He seized her arm and shook her. "Tell me what he said!" A guard tried to intervene. Adzel put his bulk between long enough for van Rijn to trumpet loud as Moath himself, "Tell me what is happening! I order you!"

Automatically in her shock, she obeyed the Minotaur.

Soon afterward, the prisoners were herded into their ship. The lock valves hissed shut behind them. Viewscreens showed frosty stars above a land turned gray and shadowful, the castle ablaze with light and immense bonfires leaping outside. Sound pickups brought the distant wail of wind, the nearby bawling, bugling, clangor, and drum-thud of the Shenna.

Van Rijn said to Adzel, "You do what you like for an hour. I will be with St. Dismas. Got to confess to somebody." He could not refrain from adding, "Ho, ho, I bet he never heard a hotter confession than he's going to!"

"I shall relive certain memories and meditate upon certain principles," Adzel said, "and in one hour I will join you in the command bridge."

That was where van Rijn had explained why he surrendered to the enemy, back in the system of the nameless sun.

"But we could perhaps give them the slip," Adzel had protested. "Granted, the chance of our success is not good. At worst, though, they will overtake and destroy us. A quick, clean death, in freedom, almost an enviable death. Do you really prefer to become a slave on Dathyna?"

"Look," van Rijn answered with rare seriousness, "is necessary, absolute necessary our people learn what these characters is up to, and as much as possible about what they is like. I got a hunch what smells like condemned Limburger, they may decide on war. Maybe they win, maybe they lose. But even one surprise attack on a heavy-populated planet, with nuclear weapons—millions dead? Billions? And burned, blind, crippled, mutated. . . . I am a sinful man, but not that sinful I wouldn't do what I could for trying to stop the thing."

"Of course, of course," Adzel said; and he was unwontedly impatient. "But if we escape, we can convey an added warning, to emphasize what will be read when your papers are released on Earth. If we go to Dathyna, though—oh, granted, we probably will gather extremely valuable information. But what good will it do our people? We will surely not have access to spacecraft. The great problem of military intelligence has always been less its collection than its transmission home. This is a classic example."

"Ah," said van Rijn. "You would ordinary be right. But you see, we will probable not be alone there."

"*Yarru!*" Adzel said. That relieved him sufficiently that he sat down, curled his tail around his haunches, and waited for an explanation.

"See you," van Rijn said around a glass of gin and a cigar, "this Gahood fellow was Hugh Latimer's owner. We know that from Thea. We know too Latimer's lost to him. And we know he brought news what has got eggbeaters going in everybody's guts here. That is all we know for sure. But we can deduce a snorky lot from it, I tell you.

"Like from the timing. Dathyna got to be about one week from this star. We can assume a straight line Sol-here-there, and not be too far off. Beta Crucis is like two weeks from Sol. Do a little trigonometrizing, angle between Southern Cross and Compass—is very rough approximations, natural, but timing works out so close it makes sense, like follows.

"Latimer would report straight to his boss, Gahood, on Dathyna. Gahood would go straight to Beta Crucis for a look—we seen how these Shenna is bulls in a china shop, and life is the china shop—and Latimer would go along. Takes them maybe two and a half weeks. So they arrive when Davy Falkayn and Chee Lan is still there. Our friends could not get decent data on the rogue in less time, two of them in one ship. Right away, though, Gahood returns to Dathyna. When he comes there, he learns about this meeting with you and me. He runs here and tells his chumsers about something. The timing is right for that land of Gahood-trek, and it fits the pattern for everything else."

"Yes-s-s," Adzel breathed. His tailtip stirred. "Gahood arrives in great agitation, and without Latimer, who is gone."

"Gone—where else but at Beta Crucis?" van Rijn said. "If he was lost anyplace else, nobody would care except maybe Gahood. Looks like Gahood tangled with our friends yonder. And he was the one got knotted. Because if he had won over them, he would hardly come out here to brag about it . . . and for sure the other Shenna would not react with anger and preturbation.

"Also: it would not matter if Latimer got killed in a fight. Only another slave, *nie?* But if he got captured, now—ho-ho! That changes a whole picture. From him can be squeezed many kinds fine information, starting with where is Dathyna. No wondering that Gahood galloped straight out here! These Shenna got to be warned about a changed situation before they maybe make a deal with us. Not so?" Van Rijn swigged deep.

"It appears plausible, then, that *Muddlin' Through* is bound home with her gains." Adzel nodded. "Do you think, therefore, we may be liberated by friendly forces?"

"I would not count on it," van Rijn said, "especial not when we is held by people like these, what would likely take out their irritations at being defeated on us. Besides, we don't know for sure a war is fermenting. And we want to prevent one if we can. I don't think, though, neither, that *Muddlin' Through* is homeheaded. I just hope the Shenna assume so, like you."

"What else?" Adzel asked, puzzled again.

"You is not human, and you don't always follow human mental processing. Likewise Shenna. Has you forgot, Falkayn can send a message capsule back with his data? Meanwhile, he sees Gahood going off. He knows Gahood will alert Dathyna. Will soon be very hard to scout that planet. But if he goes there direct, fast, to a world what has relied on its whereabouts not being known to us and therefore probably has not got a lot in the way of pickets—he should could sneak in."

"And be there yet?"

"I am guessing it. Takes time to study a world. He'll have a way planned for outsneaking too, of course." Van Rijn lifted his head, straightened his back, squared his shoulders, and protruded his belly. "Maybe he can get us away. Maybe he can't. But *Deo volente,* he might be able to carry home extra information, or urgent information, we slip to him. There is lots of ugly little ifs in my logic, I know. The odds is not good. But I don't think we got any choice except taking the bet."

"No," said Adzel slowly, "we do not."

The celebration was fading at the castle when Wodenite met human in the bridge. As the fires burned low, the stars shone forth more coldly bright.

"We are fortunate that they did not dismantle our communicators," Adzel said. There was no reason to speak otherwise than impersonally. What they were about to do might bring immediate death upon them. But they considered themselves doomed already, they had made their separate peaces, and neither was given to sentimentalism. When van Rijn sat down, though, the dragon laid one great scaly hand on his shoulder; and the man patted it briefly.

"No reason they should," van Rijn said. "They don't think Davy and Chee might be doing a skulkabout somewhere near. Besides, I told Beldaniel it would help me understand the Shenna if I could tune in their programs." He spat. "Their programs is terrible."

"What waveband will you use?"

"Technic Standard Number Three, I guess. I been monitoring, and don't seem like the Shenna use it often. *Muddlin' Through* will have one receiver tuned in on it automatic."

"If *Muddlin' Through* is, indeed, free, functional, and in range. And if our transmission does not happen to be intercepted."

"Got to assume somethings, boy. Anyhow, a Shenn radio operator what chances to hear us making our code might well assume it is ordinary QRN. It was made up with that in mind. Open me a beer, will you, and fill my pipe yonder? I should start sending."

His hand moved deftly across the keyboard.

Nicholas van Rijn, Master Merchant of the Polesotechnic League, calling. . . .

The following has been learned about Dathyna and its inhabitants. . . .

Now stand by for my primary message.

Realizing that the location of their planet is, with fair probability, no longer a secret, the Shenna have not reacted as most sophonts would, by strengthening defenses while searching for ways and means of accommodation with us. Instead, their Grand Council has decided to hazard all on an offensive launched before the sprawling, ill-organized Technic sphere can gather itself.

From what little we have learned of it, the idea is militarily not unsound. Though inefficient, Shenn warships are numerous, and each has more firepower than any of ours in the corresponding class. From the Serendipity operation, their naval intelligence has an enormous amount of precise information about those races and societies we lump together as "Technic." Among other things, the Shenna know the Commonwealth is the heart of that complex, and that the Commonwealth has long been at peace and does not dream any outsiders would dare attack. Hostile fleets could pass through its territory unbeknownst; when they did come in detection range, it would be too late for a world that was not heavily defended.

The Shenn scheme is for a series of massive raids upon the key planets of the Commonwealth, and certain others. This will create general chaos, out of which Dathyna may hope to emerge dominant if not absolutely supreme. Whether the Shenna succeed or not, obviously whole civilizations will be wiped out, perhaps whole intelligent species, surely untold billions of sophonts.

It will doubtless take the enemy some time to marshal his full strength, plan the operation, and organize its logistics. The time will be increased above a minimum by the arrogance of the Shenn lords and the half-anarchic character of their society. On the other hand, their built-in aggressiveness will make them cut corners and accept deficiencies for the sake of getting on with the assault.

The League should be able to take appropriate countermeasures, without calling upon governmental assistance, if it is warned soon enough. That warning must be delivered at once. To David Falkayn, Chee Lan, and/or any other entities who may be present: Do not spend a minute on anything else. Go home immediately and inform the leadership of the League.

✡XXIII✡

Night was younger where the Cynthian lurked. But the desert was fast radiating the day's heat outward to the stars. Their swarms, and the shimmer of a great aurora, were sufficiently bright for crags and dunes to stand ghost-gray, for the walls she gazed upon to cast shadows. She fluffed her fur in the chill. For minutes after landing she waited behind the thorny bush she had chosen from aloft. No scent came to her but its own acridity, no sound but a wind-whimper, no sight but a veil of blowing dust.

Her caution was only partly because animals laired in abandoned places. The guns she wore—blaster, slugthrower, needler, and stunner—could handle any beast of prey; against the possibility of venomous creatures she put her senses and reflexes. But most of the ruins she had seen thus far were inhabited by Dathynans, and correspondingly dangerous. While those little groups appeared to be semibarbaric hunters and herders—she and Falkayn were still too ignorant about conditions to try spying on the larger and more advanced communities—they owned firearms. Worse, Muddlehead reported detecting electronic transceivers in their huddling places, doubtless supplied by traders from the "baronies."

It had not been difficult for the ship to descend secretly, or to flit around after dark and hole up in the wastelands by day. The lords of this world had not expected its location to become known and had thus not done much about posting sentinels in orbit. Nor had they installed anything like an atmospheric traffic monitor. Let some sheik relate an encounter with an alien, though, and matters would change in a hurry.

Falkayn dared not visit any settlement. He was too big and awkward. Chee Lan could fly close with a gravity impeller, then work her little self into a position from which she observed what went on.

The present location, however, was empty. She had rather expected that. The interwoven buildings stood in the middle of a region which erosion had scoured until it could probably support none except a few nomads. She saw signs of them, cairns, charcoal, scattered trash. But nothing was recent. The tribe—no, patriarchal clan was probably more accurate—must be elsewhere on its annual round. Good; Falkayn could bring the ship here and work. This site looked richer than the one he was currently studying. More and more, it seemed that the key to Dathyna's present and future lay in its near past, in the downfall of a mighty civilization.

Of an entire species. Chee was becoming convinced of that.

She left her concealment and approached the ruins. Shards of masonry, broken columns, rust-eaten machines thrust from the sand like tombstones. Walls loomed high above her; but they were worn, battered, smashed open in places, their windows blind and their doors agape. Few if any Dathynan communities had simply been left when their hinterlands failed them. No, they were burst into, plundered and vandalized. Their people were massacred.

Something stirred in the shadows. Chee arched her back, bottled her tail, dropped hand to gun belt. But it was only a beast with several pairs of legs, which ran from her.

The entry, lobby, whatever you wanted to call the section behind the main gate, had been superb, a vista of pillars and fountains and sculpture, exquisitely veined marble and malachite that soared a hundred meters aloft. Now it was an echoing black cave. Sand and nomad rubbish covered the floor; the stonework was chipped, the grand mosaics hidden under soot from centuries of campfires. But when Chee sent a beam upward from her lamp, color glowed back. She activated her impeller and rose for a closer look. Winged things fled, thinly chittering.

The walls were inlaid to the very ceiling. No matter how strange the artistic conventions, Chee could not but respond to an intrinsic nobility. The hues were at once rich and restrained, the images at once heroic and gentle. She did not know what facts or myths or allegories were portrayed; she knew she never would, and that knowledge was an odd small pain. Partly for anodyne, she bent her whole attention to the factual content.

Excitement sprang to life in her. This was the clearest portrayal she had ever found of the Old Dathynans. Falkayn was digging up their bones where the ship rested, noting crushed skulls and arrowheads lodged in rib cages. But here, by the lamp's single shaft of light, surrounded by limitless night and cold and wind and beating wings and death, here they themselves looked forth. And a tingle went along Chee Lan's nerves.

The builders were not unlike Shenna. Falkayn could not prove from his relics that they were not as close as Mongoloid is to Negroid on Earth. In their wordless language, these pictures said otherwise.

It was not mere typological difference. You could get a scale from objects that were shown, like still-extant plants and animals. They indicated the ancients were smaller than today's race, none over 180 centimeters tall, more slender, more hairy, though lacking the male mane. Within those limits, however, many variants appeared. In fact, the section that Chee was looking at seemed to make a point of depicting every kind of autochthon, each wearing native costume and holding something that was most likely emblematic of his or her land. Here came a burly golden-furred long-headed male with a sickle in one hand and an uprooted sapling in the other; there stood a tiny dark female in an embroidered robe, a distinct epicanthic fold in her eyelids, playing a harp; yonder a kilted baldpate with a large and curved muzzle raised his staff, as if in protection, over a bearer of ripe fruits whose face was almost solar in its roundness. The loving spirit and the expert hand which put together this scene had been guided by a scientifically trained eye.

Today one solitary race existed. That was so unusual—so disturbing—that Chee and Falkayn had made it their special business to verify the fact as they slunk about the planet.

And yet the Shenna, altogether distinct in appearance and culture, were shown nowhere on a mosaic which had tried to represent everybody. Nowhere!

A taboo, a dislike, a persecution? Chee spat in contempt of the thought. Every sign pointed to the lost civilization as having been unified and rationalistic. A particular series of pictures on this wall doubtless symbolized progress up from savagery. A nude male was vividly shown defending his female against a large predatory beast—with a broken branch. Later on, edged metal implements appeared: but always tools, never weapons. Masses of Dathynans were seen working together: never fighting. But this could not be because the topic excluded strife. Two scenes of individual combat did appear; they must be key incidents in a history or legendry forever vanished. The earliest had one male wielding a kind of brush knife, the other an unmistakable wood ax. The second armed the enemies with primitive matchlock guns which were surely intended for help against dangerous animals . . . seeing that the background depicted steam vehicles and electric power lines.

Occupations through the ages were likewise re-created here. Some were recognizable, like agriculture and carpentry. Others could only be guessed at. (Ceremonial? Scientific? The dead cannot tell us.) But hunting was not among them, nor herding except for a species that obviously provided wool, nor trapping, nor fishing, nor butchering.

Everything fitted together with the most basic clue of all: diet. Intelligence on Dathyna had evolved among herbivores. Though not common, this occurs often enough for certain general principles to be known. The vegetarian sophonts do not have purer souls than omnivores and carnivores. But their sins are different. Among other things, while they may sometimes institutionalize the duello or accept a high rate of crimes of passion, they do not independently invent war, and they find the whole concept of the chase repugnant. As a rule they are gregarious and their social units—families, clans, tribes, nations, or less nameable groups—merge easily into larger ones as communication and transportation improve.

The Shenna violated every such rule. They killed for sport, they divided their planet into patriarchies, they built weapons and warships, they menaced a neighbor civilization which had never given them offense. . . . *In short,* thought Chee Lan, *they act like humans. If we can understand what brought them forth, out of this once promising world, maybe we'll understand what to do about them.*

Or, at least, what they want to do about us.

Her communicator interrupted. It was a bone-conduction device, so as not to be overheard; the code clicks felt unnaturally loud in her skull. "Return without delay." Neither she nor Falkayn would have transmitted except in emergency. Chee switched her impeller to lift-and-thrust, and streaked out the doorway.

The stars glittered frigid, the aurora danced in strange figures, the desert rolled stark beneath her. With no hostiles around, and no warning about them near the ship, she lowered her facemask and flew at top speed. Wind hooted and cut at her. That was a long hundred kilometers.

Muddlin' Through lay in the bottom of a dry, brush-grown canyon, hidden from above. Chee slanted past the snags of that minor community on its edge which Falkayn was excavating. Descending into shadow, she switched both her lamp and her goggles to infrared use. There was still no observable reason for caution, but to a carnivore like her it was instinctive. Twigs clawed at her, leaves rustled, she parted the branches and hovered before an airlock. Muddlehead's sensors identified her and the valves opened. She darted inside.

"Dave!" she yelled. "What in Tsucha's flaming name's the matter?"

"Plenty." His intercom voice had never been bleaker. "I'm in the bridge."

She could have flitted along the hall and companionway, but it was almost as quick and more satisfying to use her muscles. Quadrupedal again, tail erect, fangs agleam, eyes a green blaze, she sped through the ship and soared into her chair. "*Niaor!*" she cried.

Falkayn regarded her. Since he didn't sleep while she was out, he wore the dusty coveralls of his day's work, which had begrimed his nails and leathered his skin. A sun-bleached lock of hair hung past one temple. "Word received," he told her.

"What?" She tensed till she quivered. "From who?"

"Old Nick in person. He's on this planet . . . with Adzel." Falkayn turned his face to the main control board, as if the ship herself lived there. "Read back the message in clear," he ordered.

The phrases fell curt and flat.

They were followed by a silence which went on and on.

At last Chee stirred. "What do you propose to do?" she asked quietly.

"Obey, of course," Falkayn said. His tone was as bare as the computer's. "We can't get the message home too soon. But we'd better discuss first how to leave. Muddlehead keeps getting indications of more and more ships on picket. I suppose the Shenna are finally worried about spies like us. Question is, should we creep out, everything throttled down to minimum, and hope we won't be noticed? Or should we go at full power and rely on surprise and a head start and possible evasive action in deep space?"

"The latter," Chee said. "Our rescue operation will already have alerted the enemy. If we time it right, we can jump between their patrollers and—"

"Huh?" Falkayn sat straight. "What rescue operation?"

"Adzel," Chee said. Her manner was forbearing but her whiskers vibrated. "And van Rijn, no doubt. We have to pick up Adzel, you know."

"No, I do not know! Listen, you spinheaded catamonkey—"

"We have squabbled, he and I," Chee said, "but he remains my shipmate and yours." She cocked her head and considered the man. "I always took you for a moral person, Dave."

"Well, but—but I am, God damn it!" Falkayn yelled. "Didn't you listen? Our orders are to start directly for home!"

"What has that got to do with the price of eggs? Don't you want to rescue Adzel?"

"Certainly I do! If it cost me my own life, I'd want to. But—"

"Will you let a few words from that potgutted van Rijn stop you?"

Falkayn drew a shaken breath. "Listen, Chee," he said. "I'll explain slowly. Van Rijn wants us to abandon him too. He hasn't even told us where he's at. Since he necessarily used a waveband that would bounce around the planet, he could be anywhere on it."

"Muddlehead," asked Chee, "can you work out the source of his transmission?"

"By the pattern of reflections off the ionosphere, yes, to a fair approximation," answered the computer. "It corresponds to one of the larger communities, not extremely far from here, which we identified as such during our atmospheric entry."

Chee turned back to Falkayn. "You see?" she said.

"You're the one that doesn't see!" he protested. "Adzel and van Rijn aren't important compared to what's at stake. Neither are you and me. It merely happens they can't warn the League but we can."

"As we shall, after we fetch Adzel."

"And risk getting shot down, or caught ourselves, or—" Falkayn paused. "I know you, Chee. You're descended from beasts of prey that operated alone, or in minimum-size groups. You get your instincts from that. Your world never knew any such thing as a nation. The idea of universal altruism is unreal to you. Your sense of duty is as strong as mine, maybe stronger, but it stops with your kinfolk and friends. All right. I realize that. Now suppose you exercise your imagination and realize what I'm getting at. Hell's balls, just use arithmetic! One life is not equal to a billion lives!"

"Certainly not," Chee said. "However, that doesn't excuse us from our obligation."

"I tell you—"

Falkayn got no farther. She had drawn her stun pistol and aimed it between his eyes. He might have attempted to swat it from her, had she been human, but he knew she was too fast for him. He sat frozenly and heard her say:

"I'd rather not knock you out and tie you up. Lacking your help, I may well fail to get our people out. I'll try anyhow, though. And really, Dave, be honest. Admit we have a reasonable chance of pulling the job off. If we didn't, against these Shenn yokels, we ought to turn ourselves in at the nearest home for the feeble-minded."

"What do you want of me?" he whispered.

"Your promise that we'll try our best to take Adzel with us."

"Can you trust me?"

"If not, one of us shall have to kill the other." Her gun remained steady, but her head drooped. "I would hate that, Dave."

He sat a whole minute, unmoving. Then his fist smote the chair arm and his laughter stormed forth. "All right, you little devil! You win. It's pure blackmail . . . but Judas, I'm glad of it!"

Her pistol snicked back into its holster. She sprang to his lap. He rubbed her back and tickled her beneath the jaws. Her tail caressed his cheek. Meanwhile she said, "We need their help too, starting with a full description of the layout where they are. I expect they'll refuse at first. Point out to them in your message that they have no choice but to cooperate with us. If we don't go home together, none of us will."

XXIV

Again Chee Lan worked alone. *Muddlin' Through* had come down below the horizon. Other spacecraft stood ahead, a pair of destroyers, a flitter, the disabled vessel where the prisoners were kept. Hulls glimmered hoarfrosted in the dying night. Behind them, Moath's stronghold lifted like a mountain. It was very quiet now.

Ghosting from rock to bush to hillock, Chee neared. The guards were said to be a pair. She could make out one, a shaggy-maned shadow, restlessly apace near the barrel of a mobile cannon. His breath smoked, his metal jingled. She strained her eyes, tasted the predawn wind, listened, felt with every hair and whisker. Nothing came to her. Either van Rijn and Adzel had been mistaken in what they related, or the guard's mate had gone off duty without a replacement—or, in an environment for which she was not evolved, she missed the crucial sensory cues.

No more time! They'll be astir in that castle before long. Ay-ah, let's go.

She launched herself across the final sandy stretch. It would have been better to strike from above. But her impeller, like close-range radio conversation with those in the ship, might trip some damned detector. No matter. The sentry was not aware of the white shape that flowed toward him. The instant she came in range, she flattened to earth, drew her stunner and fired. She would rather have killed, but that might be noisy. The supersonic bolt spun the Shenn around on his heel. He toppled with a doomsday racket. Or did he? Sounded like that, anyhow. Chee flashed her light at the ship, blink-blink-blink. They'd better be watching their screens, those two!

They were. An airlock slid open, a gangway protruded. Adzel came out, himself huge and steel-gray by starlight. On his back, where a dorsal plate had been removed for riders, sat Nicholas van Rijn. Chee bounded to meet them. Hope fluttered in her. If they could really make this break unnoticed—

A roar blasted from the darkness near the warships. A moment later, there sizzled an energy beam. "Get going . . . yonder way!" Chee yelled. Her flashbeam pointed toward unseen Falkayn. Whizzing upward on antigrav, she activated her communicator. "We've been seen, Dave. Muck-begotten guard must've strolled off to take a leak." She curved down again, to meet the shooter.

"Shall I come get you?" Falkayn's voice sounded.

"Hold back for a minute. Maybe—" A firebeam stabbed at her. She had been noticed too. She dodged, feeling its heat, smelling its ozone and ions, half dazzled by its brightness. The Shenn could have taken cover and tried to pick her off, but that was not his nature. He dashed forth. Chee dove at full power, pulled out of her screaming arc a few centimeters above his head, gave him a jolt as she did. He collapsed. She barely avoided smashing into the ship before her.

Alarms gonged through the castle. Its black mass woke with a hundred lights. Shenna streamed from the gate. Most were armed; they must sleep with their cursed weapons. Four of them were donning flit-harness. Chee headed after Adzel's galloping form. He couldn't outrun such pursuers. She'd provide air cover. . . . "What's wrong?" Falkayn barked. "Shouldn't I come?"

"No, not yet. We'll keep you for a surprise." Chee unholstered her own blaster. Enough of these la-de-da stun pistols. The enemy were aloft, lining out after Wodenite and human. They hadn't noticed her. She got altitude on them, aimed, and fired twice. One crashed, in a cloud of dust. The other flew on, but did not stir any longer save as the wind flapped his limbs.

The third angled after her. He was good. They started a dogfight. She could do nothing about the fourth, who stooped upon the escapers.

Adzel slammed to a halt, so fast that van Rijn fell off and rolled yammering through the thornbushes. The Wodenite picked up a rock and threw. It struck with a clang. Impeller disabled, the Shenn fluttered to the ground.

His mates, incredibly swift on their feet, were not far behind. They opened fire. Adzel charged them, bounding from side to side, taking an occasional bolt or bullet in his scales but suffering no serious wound. He was mortal, of course. A shot sufficiently powerful or sufficiently well placed would kill him. But he got in among the Shenna first. Hoofs, hands, tail, fangs ripped into action.

The downed flier was not badly hurt either. He saw his gun lying where he had dropped it and ran to retrieve the weapon. Van Rijn intercepted him. "Oh, no, you don't, buddy-chum," the merchant panted. "I take that thing home and see if you got new ideas in it I can patent." Taller, broader, muscles like cables, the Minotaur sprang at the fat old man. Van Rijn wasn't there any more. Somehow he had flicked aside. He delivered a karate kick. The Shenn yelled. "Ha, is a tender spot for you too?" van Rijn said.

The Dathynan circled away from him. They eyed each other, and the blaster that sheened on the sand between them. The Shenn lowered his head and charged. Knowing he faced an opponent with some skill, he kept his hands in a guarding position. But no Earthling would survive on whom they closed. Van Rijn sped to meet him. At the last breath before collision, he sidestepped again, twirled, and was at the back of the onrushing giant warrior. "God send the right!" bawled van Rijn, reached into his tunic, drew forth St. Dismas, and sapped his foe. The Shenn went down.

"Whoo-hoo," van Rijn said, blowing out his cheeks above the

dazed colossus. "I'm not so young like I used to be." He returned the statuette to its nesting place, collected the gun, studied it until he had figured out its operation, and looked around for targets.

There were none immediately on hand. Chee Lan had overcome her adversary. Adzel trotted back. The Shenn mob was scattered, fleeing toward the castle. "I hoped for that result," the Wodenite remarked. "It accords with their psychology. The instinct to assail rashly should, by and large, be coupled with an equal tendency to stampede. Otherwise the ancestral species could not long have survived."

Chee descended. "Let's travel before they gather their wits," she said.

"*Ja,* they isn't really stupids, them, I am afraid," van Rijn said. "When they tell their robots to stop loafing—"

A deep hum cut through the night. One of the destroyers trembled on her landing jacks. "They just did," Chee said. Into her communicator: "Come and eat them, friends."

Muddlin' Through soared above the horizon. "Down!" Adzel called. He sheltered the other two with his body, which could better stand heat and radiation.

Beams flashed. Had either warcraft gotten off the ground, Falkayn and Muddlehead would have been in trouble. Their magazines were depleted after the battle of Satan. But they were forewarned, warmed up, ready and ruthless to exploit the advantage of surprise. The first destroyer loosed no more than a single ill-aimed shot before she was undercut. She fell, struck her neighbor, both toppled with an earth-shaking metal roar. The League vessel disabled Moath's flitter—three bolts were needed, and the sand ran molten beneath—and landed.

"*Donder op!*" van Rijn cried. Adzel tucked him under one arm. "*Wat drommel?*" he protested. The Wodenite grabbed Chee by the tail and pounded toward the airlock.

He must squint into lightning dazzle, stagger from thunders, gasp in smoke and vapor, as the ship bombarded the castle. In the bridge, Falkayn protested, "We don't want to hurt noncombatants."

Muddlehead replied, "In conformity with your general directive, I am taking the precaution of demolishing installations whose radio resonances suggest that they are heavy guns and missile racks."

"Can you get me through to somebody inside?" Falkayn asked.

"I shall tune in what we have noted as the usual Dathynan communication bands. . . . Yes. An attempt is being made to call us."

The screen flickered. Streaked, distorted, static-crazed, the image of Thea Beldaniel appeared. Her face was a mask of horror. Behind her, the room where she sat trembled and cracked under the ship's blows. By now, Falkayn could no longer see the castle facade. Nothing showed but dust, pierced through and through by the nuclear flames and the bursting shells. His skull shivered; he was himself half deafened by the violence he unleashed. Faintly he heard her: "Davy, Davy, are you doing this to us?"

He gripped the arms of his chair and said through clenched jaws, "I didn't want to. You force me. Listen, though. This is a taste of war for you and yours. The tiniest, gentlest, most carefully administered dose of the poison we can give. We're bound away soon. I'd hoped to be far off before you realized what'd happened. But maybe this is best. Because I don't think you can summon help from elsewhere in time to catch us. And you know what to expect."

"Davy . . . my lord Moath . . . is dead . . . I saw a bolt hit him, he went up in a spurt of fire—" She could not go on.

"You're better off without a lord," Falkayn said. "Every human being is. But tell the others. Tell them the Polesotechnic League bears no grudge and wants no fight. However, if we must, we will do the job once for all. Your Shenna won't be exterminated; we have more mercy than they showed the Old Dathynans. But let them try resisting us, and we'll strip the machinery from them and turn them into desert herders. I suggest you urge them to consider what terms they might make instead. Show them what happened here and tell them they were fools to get in the way of freemen!"

She gave him a shattered look. Pity tugged at him, and he might have said more. But Adzel, Chee Lan, Nicholas van Rijn were aboard. The stronghold was reduced: with few casualties, he hoped, nevertheless a terrible object lesson. He cut his transmission. "Cease barrage," he ordered. "Lift and make for Earth."

XXV

"There has been no trace of any hyperdrive except our own for a continuous twenty-four hours," Muddlehead reported.

Falkayn gusted a sigh. His long body eased into a more comfortable position, seated half on the spine, feet on the saloon table. "I reckon that settles it." He smiled. "We're home safe."

For in the illimitable loneliness that reaches between the stars, how shall a single mote be found, once it has lost itself and the lives it carries? Dathyna's sun was no more than the brightest glitter in those hordes that filled the cabin viewscreens. The engines murmured, the ventilators blew odors suggesting flowery meadows, tobacco was fragrant, one could look for peace throughout the month of flight that lay ahead.

And Judas, but they needed a rest!

A point of anxiety must first be blunted. "You're sure you didn't take undue radiation exposure while you were outside?" Falkayn asked.

"I tell you, I have checked each of us down to the chromosomes," Chee snapped. "I *am* a xenobiologist, you know—you do know, don't you?—and this vessel is well equipped for that kind of studies. Adzel got the largest dose, because he shielded us, but even in his case, no damage was done that available pharmaceuticals will not repair." She turned from her curled-up placement on a bench, jerked her cigarette holder at the Wodenite where he sprawled on the deck, and added, "Of course, I shall have to give you your treatments en route, when I might be painting or sculpting or—you big slobbersoul, why didn't you bring a chunk of lead to lie under?"

Adzel leered. "You had all the lead in your own possession," he said. "Guess where."

Chee sputtered. Van Rijn slapped the table—his beer glass leaped—and guffawed: "*Touché!* I did not think you was a wit."

"That's wit?" the Cynthian grumbled. "Well, I suppose for him it is."

"Oh, he needs to learn," van Rijn conceded, "but what makes matter is, he has begun. We will have him play at drawing room comedies yet. How about in *The Importance of Being Earnest?* Haw!"

The merchant's classical reference went by the others. "I'd suggest a party to celebrate," Falkayn said. "Unfortunately—"

"Right," van Rijn said. "Business before pleasure, if not too bloomering long before. We should assemble our various informations while they is fresh in our minds, because if we let them begin to rot and stink in our minds, we could lose parts of what they imply."

"Huh?" Falkayn blinked. "What do you mean, sir?"

Van Rijn leaned forward, cradling his chins in one great paw. "We need keys to the Shenn character so we know how to handle them."

"But isn't that a job for professionals?" inquired Adzel. "After the League has been alerted to the existence of a real threat, it will find ways to carry out a detailed scientific study of Dathyna and draw conclusions much more certain and complete than we possibly could on the basis of our inadequate data."

"*Ja, ja, ja,*" van Rijn said, irritated, "but our time is shortening. We don't know for sure what the Shenna do next. Could be they decide they will attack fast as they possible can, try and beat us to the rum punch, in spite of what you taught them, Muddlehead."

"I was not programmed to deliver formal instruction," the computer admitted.

Van Rijn ignored it. "Maybe they don't be that suicidal," he went on. "Anyhowever, we got to have some theory about them to start on. Maybe it is wrong, but even then it is better than nothing, because it will set xenological teams looking for something definite. When we know what the Shenna want in their bottom, then we can talk meaningful to them and maybe make peace."

"It is not for me to correct a Terrestrial's use of Terrestrial idiom," Adzel said, "but don't you wish to discuss what they *basically* want?"

Van Rijn turned red. "Hokay, hokay, you damn pedagoggle! What is the base desires of the Shenna? What drives them, really? We get insight—oh, not scientific, Chee Lan, not in formulas—but we get a feel for them, a poet's empathizing, and they is no longer senseless monsters to us but beings we can reason with. The specialists from the League can make their specials later. Time is so precious, though. We can save a lot of it, and so maybe save a lot of lives, if we bring back with us at Earth a tantivvy . . . a tentacle . . . *dood ook ondergang,* this Anglic! . . . a tentative program for research and even for action."

He drained his beer. Soothed thereby, he lit his pipe, settled back, and rumbled, "We got our experience and information. Also we got analogues for help. I don't think any sophonts could be total unique, in this big a universe. So we can draw on our understanding about other races.

"Like you, Chee Lan, for instance: we know you is a carnivore—but a small one—and this means you got instincts for being tough and aggressive within reason. You, Adzel, is a big omnivore, so big your ancestors didn't never need to carry chips on their shoulders, nor fish either; your breed tends more to be peaceful, but hellish independent too, in a quiet way; somebody tries for dictating your life, you don't kill him like Chee would, no, you plain don't listen at him. And we humans, we is omnivores too, but our primate ancestors went hunting in packs, and they got built in a year-around sex drive; from these two roots springs everything what makes a man a human being. Hokay? I admit this is too generalistic, but still, if we could fit what we know about the Shenna in one broad pattern—"

Actually, the same idea had been germinating in each of them. Talking, they developed several facets of it. These being mutually consistent, they came to believe their end result, however sketchy, was in essence true. Later xenological studies confirmed it.

Even a world like Earth, blessed with a constant sun, has known periods of massive extinction. Conditions changed in a geological overnight, and organisms that had flourished for megayears vanished. Thus, at the end of the Cretaceous, ammonites and dinosaurs alike closed their long careers. At the end of the Pliocene, most of the large mammals—those whose names, as bestowed afterward, usually terminate in *-therium*—stopped bumbling across the landscape. The reasons are obscure to this day. The raw fact remains: existence is precarious.

On Dathyna, the predicament was worse. The solar bombardment was always greater than Earth receives. At the irregular peaks of activity, it was very much greater. Magnetic field and atmosphere could not ward off everything. Belike, mutations which occurred during an earlier maximum led to the improbable result of talking, dreaming, tool-making herbivores. If so, a cruel natural selection was likewise involved: for the history of such a planet must needs be one of ecological catastrophes.

The next radiation blizzard held off long enough for the race to attain full intelligence; to develop its technology; to discover the scientific method; to create a worldwide society which was about to embark for the stars, had perhaps already done it a time or two. Then the sun burned high again.

Snows melted, oceans rose, coasts and low valleys were inundated. The tropics were scorched to savanna or desert. All that could be survived. Indeed, quite probably its harsh stimulus was what produced the last technological creativity, the planetary union, the reaching into space.

But again the assault intensified. This second phase was less an increase of electromagnetic energy, heat and light, than it was a whole new set of processes, triggered when a certain threshold was passed within the waxing star. Protons were hurled forth; electrons; mesons; X-ray quanta. The magnetosphere glowed with synchrotron radiation, the upper atmosphere with secondaries. Many life forms must have died within a year or two. Others, interdependent, followed them. The ecological pyramid crumbled. Mutation went over the world like a scythe, and everything collapsed.

No matter how far it had progressed, civilization was not autonomous. It could not synthesize all its necessities. Croplands became dustbowls, orchards stood leafless, sea plants decayed into scum, forests parched and burned, new diseases arose. Step by step, population shrank, enterprises were abandoned for lack of personnel and resources, knowledge was forgotten, the area of the possible shrank. A species more fierce by nature might have made a stronger effort to surmount its troubles—or might not—but in any event, the Dathynans were not equal to the task. More and more of those who remained sank gradually into barbarism.

And then, among the barbarians, appeared a new mutation.

A favorable mutation.

Herbivores cannot soon become carnivores, not even when they can process meat to make it edible. But they can shed the instincts which make them herd together in groups too large for a devastated country to support. They can acquire an instinct to hunt the animals that supplement their diet—to defend, with absolute fanaticism, a territory that will keep them and theirs alive—to move if that region is no longer habitable, and seize the next piece of land—to perfect the weapons, organization, institutions, myths, religions, and symbols necessary—

—to become killer herbivores.

And they will go farther along that line than the carnivora, whose fang-and-claw ancestors evolved limits on aggressiveness lest the species dangerously deplete itself. They might even go farther than the omnivora, who, while not so formidable in body and hence with less original reason to restrain their pugnacity, have borne arms of some kind since the first proto-intelligence developed in them, and may thus have weeded the worst berserker tendencies out of their own stock.

Granted, this is a very rough rule-of-thumb statement with many an exception. But the idea will perhaps be clarified if we compare the peaceful lion with the wild boar who may or may not go looking for a battle and him in turn with the rhinoceros or Cape buffalo.

The parent stock on Dathyna had no chance. It could fight bravely, but not collectively to much effect. If victorious in a given clash, it rarely thought about pursuing; if defeated, it scattered. Its civilization was tottering already, its people demoralized, its politico-economic structure reduced to a kind of feudalism. If any groups escaped to space, they never came back looking for revenge.

A gang of Shenna would invade an area, seize the buildings, kill and eat those Old Dathynans whom they did not castrate and enslave. No doubt the conquerors afterward made treaties with surrounding domains, who were pathetically eager to believe the aliens were now satisfied. Not many years passed, however, before a new land-hungry generation of Shenna quarreled with their fathers and left to seek their fortunes.

The conquest was no result of an overall plan. Rather, the Shenna took Dathyna in the course of several centuries because they were better fitted. In an economy of scarcity, where an individual needed hectares to support himself, aggressiveness paid off; it was how you acquired those hectares in the first place and retained them later. No doubt the sexual difference, unusual among sophonts, was another mutation which, being useful too, became linked. Given a high casualty rate among the Shenn males, the warriors, reproduction was maximized by providing each with several females. Hunting and fighting were the principal jobs; females, who must conserve the young, could not take part in this; accordingly, they lost a certain amount of intelligence and initiative. (Remember that the original Shenn population was very small, and did not increase fast for quite a while. Thus genetic drift operated powerfully. Some fairly irrelevant characteristics like the male mane became established in that way—plus some other traits that might actually be disadvantageous, though not crippling.)

At length the parricidal race had overrun the planet. Conditions began to improve as radiation slacked off, new life forms developed, old ones returned from enclaves of survival. It would be long before Dathyna had her original fertility back. But she could again bear a machine culture. From relics, from books, from traditions, conceivably from a few last slaves of the first species, the Shenna began rebuilding what they had helped destroy.

But here the peculiar set of drives which had served them well during the evil millennia played them false. How shall there be community, as is required for a high technology, if each male is to live alone with his harem, challenging any other who dares enter his realm?

The answer is that the facts were never that simple. There was as much variation from Shenn to Shenn as there is from man to man. The less successful had always tended to attach themselves to the great, rather than go into exile. From this developed the extended household—a number of polygynous families in strict hierarchy under a patriarch with absolute authority—that was the "fundamental" unit of Shenn society, as the tribe is of human, the matrilineal clan of Cynthian, or the migratory band of Wodenite society.

The creation of larger groups out of the basic one is difficult on any planet. The results are all too likely to be pathological organizations, preserved more and more as time goes on by nothing except naked force, until finally they disintegrate. Consider, for example, nations, empires, and world associations on Earth. But it need not always be thus.

The Shenna were reasoning creatures. They could grasp the necessity for cooperation intellectually, as most species can. If they were not emotionally capable of a planet-wide government, they were of an interbaronial confederacy.

Especially when they saw their way clear to an attack—the Minotaur's charge—upon the stars!

✲ ✲ ✲

"*Ja,*" nodded van Rijn, "if they are like that, we can handle them hokay."

"By kicking them back into the Stone Age and sitting on them," Chee Lan growled.

Adzel raised his head. "What obscenity did you speak? I won't have it!"

"You'd rather let them run loose, with nuclear weapons?" she retorted.

"Now, now," said van Rijn. "Now, now, now. Don't let's say bad things about a whole race. I am sure they can do much good if they is approached right." He beamed and rubbed his hands together. "Sure, much fine money to make off them Shenna." His grin grew broader and smugger. "Well, friends, I think we finished our duty for today. We has clubbed our brains and come up with understandings and we deserve a little celebration. Davy, lad, suppose you start by bringing in a bottle Genever and a few cases beer—"

Falkayn braced himself. "I tried to tell you earlier, sir," he said. "That brew you drank was the end of our supply."

Van Rijn's prawnlike eyes threatened to leap from their sockets.

"This ship left Luna without taking on extra provisions," Falkayn said. "Nothing aboard except the standard rations. Including some beverages, of course . . . but, well, how was I to know you'd join us and—" His voice trailed off. The hurricane was rising.

"Wha-a-a-at?" Echoes flew around van Rijn's scream. "You mean . . . you mean . . . a month in space . . . and nothings for drinking except—*Not even any beer?*"

The next half-hour was indescribable.

✡XXVI✡

But half an Earth year after that—

Chandra Mahasvany, Assistant Minister of Foreign Relations of the Terrestrial Commonwealth, looked out at the ocher-and-gold globe which the battleship was orbiting, and back again, and said indignantly, "You cannot do it! You, a mere mutual-benefit alliance of . . . of capitalists . . . enslaving a species, a world!"

Fleet Admiral Wiaho of the Polesotechnic League gave him a chill stare. "What do you think the Shenna were planning to do to us?" He was born on Ferra; saber tusks handicapped him in speaking human languages. But his scorn was plain to hear.

"You hadn't even the decency to notify us. If Freeman Garver's investigations had not uncovered evidence strong enough to bring me here in person—"

"Why should the League consult the Commonwealth, or any government?" Wiaho jerked a claw at Dathyna, where it spun in the viewscreen. "We are quite beyond their jurisdictions. Let them be glad that we are dealing with a menace and not charging them for the service."

"Dealing?" Mahasvany protested. "Bringing an overwhelming armada here . . . with no overt provocation . . . forcing those poor, ah, Shenna to surrender everything they worked so hard to build, their space fleet, their key factories . . . tampering with their sovereignty . . . reducing them to economic servitude—do you call that dealing with the situation? Oh, no, sir. I assure you otherwise. It is nothing but the creation of a hatred which will soon explode in greater conflict. The Commonwealth government must insist on a policy of conciliation. Do not forget, any future war will involve us too."

"Won't be any," Wiaho said. "We're seeing to that. Not by 'enslavement,' either. I give you, *zuga-ya,* we have taken the war-making capability out of their hands, we supervise their industry, we weave their economy together with ours till it cannot function independently. But the precise reason for this is to keep revanchism from having any chance of success. Not that we expect it to arise. The Shenna don't deeply resent being ordered about—by someone who's proven to them he's stronger."

A human female passed by the open door, memotape in one hand. Wiaho hailed her. "Would you come in for a minute, pray? . . . Freelady Beldaniel, Freeman Mahasvany from Earth. . . . Freelady Beldaniel is our most valuable liaison with the Shenna. She was raised by them, have you heard? Don't you agree, what the League is doing is best for their entire race?"

The thin, middle-aged woman frowned, not in anger but in concentration. "I don't know about that, sir," she answered frankly. "But I don't know what better can be done, either, than turn them into another member of Technic civilization. The alternative would be to destroy them." She chuckled. On the whole, she must enjoy her job. "Seeing that the rest of you insist on surviving too."

"But what about the economics?" Mahasvany protested.

"Well, naturally we cannot operate for nothing," Wiaho said. "But we are not pirates. We make investments, we expect a return on them. Remember, though, business is not a zero-sum game. By improving this world, we benefit its dwellers."

Mahasvany flushed. "Do you mean . . . your damned League, sir, has the eternal gall to arrogate to itself the functions of a government?"

"Not exactly," Wiaho purred. "Government couldn't accomplish this much." He uncoiled his length from the settee he occupied. "Now, if you will excuse Freelady Beldaniel and myself, we have work to do."

On Earth, in a garden, palm trees overhead, blue water and white surf below, girls fetching him drink and tobacco, Nicholas van Rijn turned from the screen on which was projected a view brought home by the latest expedition to Satan. The great star had dwindled; highlands were beginning to stand calm above the storms that yet harried oceans and plains. He smiled unctuously at a boardful of lesser screens, wherein showed human and nonhuman faces, the mightiest industrialists in the known galaxy.

"Hokay, friends," he said, "you seen what I got a full clear claim on, namely you by the short hairs. However, I is a tired old man what mainly wants only sitting in the sun scratching his memories and having maybe just one more Singapore sling before evening—hurry it up, will you, my dear?—and anyhows is a dealer in sugar and spice and everything nice, not in dark Satanic mills. I don't want no managing for myself, on this fine planet where is money to make by the shipload every second. No, I will be happy with selling franchises . . . naturally, we make a little profit-sharing arrangement too, nothing fancy, a token like maybe thirty or forty percent of net . . . I is very reasonable. You want to start bidding?"

Beyond the Moon, *Muddlin' Through* accelerated outward. Falkayn looked long in the after screen. "What a girl she was," he murmured.

"Who, Veronica?" Chee asked.

"Well, yes. Among others." Falkayn lit his pipe. "I don't know why we're starting out again, when we're rich for life. I honestly don't."

"I know why you are," Chee said. "Any more of the kind of existence you've been leading, and you'd implode." Her tail switched. "And me, I grew bored. It'll be good to get out under fresh skies again."

"And find new enlightenments," Adzel said.

"Yes, of course," Falkayn said. "I was joking. It sounded too pretentious, though, to declaim that the frontier is where we belong."

Muddlehead slapped down a pack of cards and a rack of poker chips onto the table, with the mechanical arms which had been installed for such purposes. "In that event, Captain," it said, "and pursuant to the program you outlined for us to follow during the next several hours, it is suggested that you shut up and deal."

INTRODUCTION

As a dewdrop may reflect the glade wherein it lies, even so does the story which follows give a glimpse into some of the troubles which Technic civilization was bringing upon itself, among many others. Ythrians, be not overly proud; only look back, from the heights of time, across Ythrian history, and then forward to the shadow of God across the future.

This tale appears at first glance to have no bearing on the fate-to-be of Avalon. Yet consider: It shows a kindred spirit. Ythri was not the sole world that responded to the challenge which, wittingly or no, humans and starflight had cried. Like the countless tiny influences which, together, draw a hurricane now this way, now that, the actions of more individuals than we can ever know did their work upon history. Also, Paradox and Trillia are not galactically distant from us; they may yet come to be of direct import.

The tale was brought back to Ythri lifetimes ago by the xenologist Fluoch of Mistwood. Arinnian of Stormgate, whose human name is Christopher Holm and who has rendered several Ythrian works into Anglic, prepared this version for the book you behold.

—Hloch of the Stormgate Choth
The Earth Book of Stormgate

A LITTLE KNOWLEDGE

They found the planet during the first Grand Survey. An expedition to it was organized very soon after the report appeared; for this looked like an impossibility.

It orbited its G9 sun at an average distance of some three astronomical units, thus receiving about one-eighteenth the radiation Earth gets. Under such a condition (and others, e.g., the magnetic field strength which was present) a subjovian ought to have formed; and indeed it had fifteen times the terrestrial mass. But—that mass was concentrated in a solid globe. The atmosphere was only half again as dense as on man's home, and breathable by him.

"Where 'ave h'all the H'atoms gone?" became the standing joke of the research team. Big worlds are supposed to keep enough of their primordial hydrogen and helium to completely dominate the chemistry. Paradox, as it was unofficially christened, did retain some of the latter gas, to a total of eight percent of its air. This posed certain technical problems which had to be solved before anyone dared land. However, land the men must; the puzzle they confronted was so delightfully baffling.

A nearly circular ocean basin suggested an answer which studies of its bottom seemed to confirm. Paradox had begun existence as a fairly standard specimen, complete with four moons. But the largest of these, probably a captured asteroid, had had an eccentric orbit. At last perturbation brought it into the upper atmosphere, which at that time extended beyond Roche's limit. Shock waves, repeated each time one of these ever-deeper grazings was made, blew vast quantities of gas off into space: especially the lighter molecules. Breakup of the moon hastened this process and made it more violent, by presenting more solid surface. Thus at the final crash, most of those meteoroids fell as one body, to form that gigantic astrobleme. Perhaps metallic atoms, thermally ripped free of their ores and splashed as an incandescent fog across half the planet, locked onto the bulk of what hydrogen was left, if any was.

Be that as it may, Paradox now had only a mixture of what had hitherto been comparatively insignificant impurities, carbon dioxide, water vapor, methane, ammonia, and other materials. In short, except for a small amount of helium, it had become rather like the young Earth. It got less heat and light, but greenhouse effect kept most of its water liquid. Life evolved, went into the photosynthesis business, and turned the air into the oxynitrogen common on terrestrials.

The helium had certain interesting biological effects. These were not studied in detail. After all, with the hyperdrive opening endless wonders to them, spacefarers tended to choose the most obviously glamorous. Paradox lay a hundred parsecs from Sol. Thousands upon thousands of worlds were more easily reached; many were more pleasant and less dangerous to walk on. The expedition departed and had no successors.

First it called briefly at a neighboring star, on one of whose planets were intelligent beings that had developed a promising set of civilizations. But, again, quite a few such lay closer to home.

The era of scientific expansion was followed by the era of commercial aggrandizement. Merchant adventurers began to appear in the sector. They ignored Paradox, which had nothing to make a profit on, but investigated the inhabited globe in the nearby system. In the language dominant there at the time, it was called something like Trillia, which thus became its name in League Latin. The speakers of that language were undergoing their equivalent of the First Industrial Revolution, and eager to leap into the modern age.

Unfortunately, they had little to offer that was in demand elsewhere. And even in the spacious terms of the Polesotechnic League, they lived at the far end of a long haul. Their charming arts and crafts made Trillia marginally worth a visit, on those rare occasions when a trader was on such a route that the detour wasn't great. Besides, it was as well to keep an eye on the natives. Lacking the means to buy the important gadgets of Technic society, they had set about developing these for themselves.

Bryce Harker pushed through flowering vines which covered an otherwise doorless entrance. They rustled back into place behind him, smelling like allspice, trapping gold-yellow sunlight in their leaves. That light also slanted through ogive windows in a curving wall, to glow off the grain of the wooden floor. Furniture was sparse: a few stools, a low table bearing an intricately faceted piece of rock crystal. By Trillian standards the ceiling was high; but Harker, who was of average human size, must stoop.

Witweet bounced from an inner room, laid down the book of poems he had been reading, and piped, "Why, be welcome, dear boy—Oo-oo-ooh!"

He looked down the muzzle of a blaster.

The man showed teeth. "Stay right where you are," he commanded. The vocalizer on his breast rendered the sounds he made into soprano cadenzas and arpeggios, the speech of Lenidel. It could do nothing about his vocabulary and grammar. His knowledge did include the fact that, by omitting all honorifics and circumlocutions without apology, he was uttering a deadly insult.

That was the effect he wanted—deadliness.

"My, my, my dear good friend from the revered Solar Commonwealth," Witweet stammered, "is this a, a jest too subtle for a mere pilot like myself to comprehend? I will gladly laugh if you wish, and then we, we shall enjoy tea and cakes. I have genuine Lapsang Souchong tea from Earth, and have just found the most darling recipe for sweet cakes—"

"Quiet!" Harker rapped. His glance flickered to the windows. Outside, flower colors exploded beneath reddish tree trunks; small bright wings went fluttering past; The Waterfall That Rings Like Glass Bells could be heard in the distance. Annanna was akin to most cities of Lenidel, the principal nation on Trillia, in being spread through an immensity of forest and parkscape. Nevertheless, Annanna had a couple of million population, who kept busy. Three aircraft were crossing heaven. At any moment, a pedestrian or cyclist might come along The Pathway Of The Beautiful Blossoms And The Bridge That Arches Like A Note Of Music, and wonder why two humans stood tense outside number 1337.

Witweet regarded the man's skinsuit and boots, the pack on his shoulders, the tightly drawn sharp features behind the weapon. Tears blurred the blue of Witweet's great eyes. "I fear you are engaged in some desperate undertaking which distorts the natural goodness that, I feel certain, still inheres," he quavered. "May I beg the honor of being graciously let help you relieve whatever your distress may be?"

Harker squinted back at the Trillian. *How much do we really know about his breed, anyway? Damned nonhuman thing—though I never resented his existence till now*—His pulse knocked; his skin was wet and stank, his mouth was dry and cottony-tasting.

Yet his prisoner looked altogether helpless. Witweet was an erect biped; but his tubby frame reached to barely a meter, from the padded feet to the big, scalloped ears. The two arms were broomstick thin, the four fingers on either hand suggested straws. The head was practically spherical, bearing a pug muzzle, moist black nose, tiny mouth, quivering whiskers, upward-slanting tufty brows. That, the tail, and the fluffy silver-gray fur which covered the whole skin, had made Olafsson remark that the only danger to be expected from this race was that eventually their cuteness would become unendurable.

Witweet had nothing upon him except an ornately embroidered kimono and a sash tied in a pink bow. He surely owned no weapons, and probably wouldn't know what to do with any. The Trillians were omnivores, but did not seem to have gone through a hunting stage in their evolution. They had never fought wars, and personal violence was limited to an infrequent scuffle.

Still, Harker thought, *they've shown the guts to push into deep space. I daresay even an unarmed policeman—Courtesy Monitor—could use his vehicle against us, like by ramming.*

Hurry!

"Listen," he said. "Listen carefully. You've heard that most intelligent species have members who don't mind using brute force, outright killing, for other ends than self-defense. Haven't you?"

Witweet waved his tail in assent. "Truly I am baffled by that statement, concerning as it does races whose achievements are of incomparable magnificence. However, not only my poor mind, but those of our most eminent thinkers have been engaged in fruitless endeavors to—"

"Dog your hatch!" The vocalizer made meaningless noises and Harker realized he had shouted in Anglic. He went back to Lenidellian-equivalent. "I don't propose to waste time. My partners and I did not come here to trade as we announced. We came to get a Trillian spaceship. The project is important enough that we'll kill if we must. Make trouble, and I'll blast you to greasy ash. It won't bother me. And you aren't the only possible pilot we can work through, so don't imagine you can block us by sacrificing yourself. I admit you are our best prospect. Obey, cooperate fully, and you'll live. We'll have no reason to destroy you." He paused. "We may even send you home with a good piece of money. We'll be able to afford that."

The bottling of his fur might have made Witweet impressive to another Trillian. To Harker, he became a ball of fuzz in a kimono, an agitated tail and a sound of coloratura anguish. "But this is insanity . . . if I may say that to a respected guest. . . . One of *our* awkward, lumbering, fragile, unreliable prototype ships—when you came in a vessel representing centuries of advancement—? Why, why, why, in the name of multiple sacredness, why?"

"I'll tell you later," the man said. "You're due for a routine supply trip to, uh, Gwinsai Base, starting tomorrow, right? You'll board this afternoon, to make final inspection and settle in. We're coming along. You'd be leaving in about an hour's time. Your things must already be packed. I didn't cultivate your friendship for nothing, you see! Now, walk slowly ahead of me, bring your luggage back here and open it so I can make sure what you've got. Then we're on our way."

Witweet stared into the blaster. A shudder went through him. His fur collapsed. Tail dragging, he turned toward the inner rooms.

Stocky Leo Dolgorov and ash-blond Einar Olafsson gusted simultaneous oaths of relief when their leader and his prisoner came out onto the path. "What took you that time?" the first demanded. "Were you having a nap?"

"Nah, he entered one of their bowing, scraping, and unction-smearing contests." Olafsson's grin held scant mirth.

"Trouble?" Harker asked.

"N-no . . . three, four passersby stopped to talk—we told them the story and they went on," Dolgorov said. Harker nodded. He'd put a good deal of thought into that excuse for his guards' standing around—that they were about to pay a social call on Witweet but were waiting until the pilot's special friend Harker had made him a gift. A lie must be plausible, and the Trillian mind was not human.

"We sure hung on the hook, though." Olafsson started as a bicyclist came around a bend in the path and fluted a string of complimentary greetings.

Dwarfed beneath the men, Witweet made reply. No gun was pointed at him now, but one rested in each of the holsters near his brain. (Harker and companions had striven to convince everybody that the bearing of arms was a peaceful but highly symbolic custom in *their* part of Technic society, that without their weapons they would feel more indecent than a shaven Trillian.) As far as Marker's wire-taut attention registered, Witweet's answer was routine. But probably some forlornness crept into the overtones, for the neighbor stopped.

"Do you feel quite radiantly well, dear boy?" he asked.

"Indeed I do, honored Pwiddy, and thank you in my prettiest thoughts for your ever-sweet consideration," the pilot replied. "I . . . well, these good visitors from the starfaring culture of splendor have been describing some of their experiences—oh, I simply must relate them to you later, dear boy!—and naturally, since I am about to embark on another trip, I have been made pensive by this." Hands, tail, whiskers gesticulated. *Meaning what?* wondered Harker in a chill; and clamping jaws together: *Well, you knew you'd have to take risks to win a kingdom.* "Forgive me, I pray you of your overflowing generosity, that I rush off after such curt words. But I have promises to keep, and considerable distances to go before I sleep."

"Understood." Pwiddy spent a mere five minutes bidding farewell all around before he pedaled off. Meanwhile several others passed by. However, since no well-mannered person would interrupt a conversation even to make salute, they created no problem.

"Let's go." It grated in Dolgorov's throat.

Behind the little witch-hatted house was a pergola wherein rested Witweet's personal flitter. It was large and flashy—large enough for three humans to squeeze into the back—which fact had become an element in Harker's plan. The car that the men had used during their stay on Trillia, they abandoned. It was unmistakably an off-planet vehicle.

"Get started!" Dolgorov cuffed at Witweet.

Olafsson caught his arm and snapped: "Control your emotions! Want to tear his head off?"

Hunched over the dashboard, Witweet squeezed his eyes shut and shivered till Harker prodded him. "Pull out of that funk," the man said.

"I . . . I beg your pardon. The brutality so appalled me—" Witweet flinched from their laughter. His fingers gripped levers and twisted knobs. Here was no steering by gestures in a light-field, let alone simply speaking an order to an autopilot. The overloaded flitter crawled skyward. Harker detected a flutter in its grav unit, but decided nothing was likely to fail before they reached the spaceport. And after that, nothing would matter except getting off this planet.

Not that it was a bad place, he reflected. Almost Earthlike in size, gravity, air, deliciously edible life forms—an Earth that no longer was and perhaps never had been, wide horizons and big skies, caressed by light and rain. Looking out, he saw woodlands in a thousand hues of green, meadows, river-gleam, an occasional dollhouse dwelling, grainfields ripening tawny and the soft gaudiness of a flower ranch. Ahead lifted The Mountain Which Presides Over Moonrise In Lenidel, a snowpeak pure as Fuji's. The sun, yellower than Sol, turned it and a few clouds into gold.

A gentle world for a gentle people. Too gentle.

Too bad. For them.

Besides, after six months of it, three city-bred men were about ready to climb screaming out of their skulls. Harker drew forth a cigarette, inhaled it into lighting and filled his lungs with harshness. *I'd almost welcome a fight,* he thought savagely.

But none happened. Half a year of hard, patient study paid richly off. It helped that the Trillians were—well, you couldn't say lax about security, because the need for it had never occurred to them. Witweet radioed to the portmaster as he approached, was informed that everything looked okay, and took his flitter straight through an open cargo lock into a hold of the ship he was to pilot.

The port was like nothing in Technic civilization, unless on the remotest, least visited of outposts. After all, the Trillians had gone in a bare fifty years from propeller-driven aircraft to interstellar spaceships. Such concentration on research and development had necessarily been at the expense of production and exploitation. What few vessels they had were still mostly experimental. The scientific bases they had established on planets of next-door stars needed no more than three or four freighters for their maintenance.

Thus a couple of buildings and a ground-control tower bounded a stretch of ferrocrete on a high, chilly plateau; and that was Trillia's spaceport. Two ships were in. One was being serviced, half its hull plates removed and furry shapes swarming over the emptiness within. The other, assigned to Witweet, stood on landing jacks at the far end of the field. Shaped like a fat torpedo, decorated in floral designs of pink and baby blue, it was as big as a Dromond-class hauler. Yet its payload was under a thousand tons. The primitive systems for drive, control, and life support took up that much room.

"I wish you a just too, too delightful voyage," said the portmaster's voice from the radio. "Would you honor me by accepting an invitation to dinner? My wife has, if I may boast, discovered remarkable culinary attributes of certain sea weeds brought back from Gwinsai; and for my part, dear boy, I would be so interested to hear your opinion of a new verse form with which I am currently experimenting."

"No . . . I thank you, no, impossible, I beg indulgence—" It was hard to tell whether the unevenness of Witweet's response came from terror or from the tobacco smoke that had kept him coughing. He almost flung his vehicle into the spaceship.

Clearance granted, *The Serenity of the Estimable Philosopher Ittypu* lifted into a dawn sky. When Trillia was a dwindling cloud-marbled sapphire among the stars, Harker let out a breath. "We can relax now."

"Where?" Olafsson grumbled. The single cabin barely allowed three humans to crowd together. They'd have to take turns sleeping in the hall that ran aft to the engine room. And their voyage was going to be long. Top pseudovelocity under the snail-powered hyper-drive of this craft would be less than one light-year per day.

"Oh, we can admire the darling murals," Dolgorov fleered. He kicked an intricately painted bulkhead.

Witweet, crouched miserable at the control board, flinched. "I beg you, dear, kind sir, do not scuff the artwork," he said.

"Why should you care?" Dolgorov asked. "You won't be keeping this junkheap."

Witweet wrung his hands. "Defacement is still very wicked. Perhaps the consignee will appreciate my patterns? I spent *such* a time on them, trying to get every teensiest detail correct."

"Is that why your freighters have a single person aboard?" Olafsson laughed. "Always seemed reckless to me, not taking a backup pilot at least. But I suppose two Trillians would get into so fierce an argument about the interior décor that they'd each stalk off in an absolute snit."

"Why, no," said Witweet, a trifle calmer. "We keep personnel down to one because more are not really needed. Piloting between stars is automatic, and the crewbeing is trained in servicing functions. Should he suffer harm en route, the ship will put itself into orbit around the destination planet and can be boarded by others. An extra would thus uselessly occupy space which is often needed for passengers. I am surprised that you, sir, who have set a powerful intellect to prolonged consideration of our astronautical practices, should not have been aware—"

"I was, I was!" Olafsson threw up his hands as far as the overhead permitted. "Ask a rhetorical question and get an oratorical answer."

"May I, in turn, humbly request enlightenment as to your reason for . . . sequestering . . . a spacecraft ludicrously inadequate by every standards of your oh, so sophisticated society?"

"You may." Harker's spirits bubbled from relief of tension. They'd pulled it off. They really had. He sat down—the deck was padded and perfumed—and started a cigarette. Through his bones beat the throb of the gravity drive: energy wasted by a clumsy system. The weight it made underfoot fluctuated slightly in a rhythm that felt wavelike.

"I suppose we may as well call ourselves criminals," he said; the Lenidellian word he must use had milder connotations. "There are people back home who wouldn't leave us alive if they knew who'd done certain things. But we never got rich off them. Now we will."

He had no need for recapitulating except the need to gloat: "You know we came to Trillia half a standard year ago, on a League ship that was paying a short visit to buy art. We had goods of our own to barter with, and announced we were going to settle down for a while and look into the possibility of establishing a permanent trading post with a regular shuttle service to some of the Technic planets. That's what the captain of the ship thought too. He advised us against it, said it couldn't pay and we'd simply be stuck on Trillia till the next League vessel chanced by, which wouldn't likely be for more than a year. But when we insisted, and gave him passage money, he shrugged," as did Harker.

"You have told me this," Witweet said. "I thrilled to the ecstasy of what I believed was your friendship."

"Well, I did enjoy your company," Harker smiled. "You're not a bad little osco. Mainly, though, we concentrated on you because we'd learned you qualified for our uses—a regular freighter pilot, a bachelor so we needn't fuss with a family, a chatterer who could be pumped for any information we wanted. Seems we gauged well."

"We better have," Dolgorov said gloomily. "Those trade goods cost us everything we could scratch together. I took a steady job for two years, and lived like a lama, to get my share."

"And now we'll be living like fakirs," said Olafsson. "But afterward—afterward!"

"Evidently your whole aim was to acquire a Trillian ship," Witweet said. "My bemusement at this endures."

"We don't actually want the ship as such, except for demonstration purposes," Harker said. "What we want is the plans, the design. Between the vessel itself, and the service manuals aboard, we have that in effect."

Witweet's ears quivered. "Do you mean to publish the data for scientific interest? Surely, to beings whose ancestors went on to better models centuries ago—if, indeed, they ever burdened themselves with something this crude—surely the interest is nil. Unless . . . you think many will pay to see, in order to enjoy mirth at the spectacle of our fumbling efforts?" He spread his arms. "Why, you could have bought complete specifications most cheaply; or, indeed, had you requested of me, I would have been bubbly-happy to obtain a set and make you a gift." On a note of timid hope: "Thus you see, dear boy, drastic action is quite unnecessary. Let us return. I will state you remained aboard by mistake—"

Olafsson guffawed. Dolgorov said, "Not even your authorities can be that sloppy-thinking." Harker ground out his cigarette on the deck, which made the pilot wince, and explained at leisured length:

"We want this ship precisely because it's primitive. Your people weren't in the electronic era when the first human explorers contacted you. They, or some later visitors, brought you texts on physics. Then your bright lads had the theory of such things as gravity control and hyperdrive. But the engineering practice was something else again.

"You didn't have plans for a starship. When you finally got an opportunity to inquire, you found that the idealistic period of Technic civilization was over and you must deal with hardheaded entrepreneurs. And the price was set 'way beyond what your whole planet could hope to save in League currency. That was just the price for diagrams, not to speak of an actual vessel. I don't know if you are personally aware of the fact—it's no secret—but this is League policy. The member companies are bound by an agreement.

"They won't prevent anyone from entering space on his own. But take your case on Trillia. You had learned in a general way about, oh, transistors, for instance. But that did not set you up to manufacture them. An entire industrial complex is needed for that and for the million other necessary items. To design and build one, with the inevitable mistakes en route, would take decades at a minimum, and would involve regimenting your entire species and living in poverty because every bit of capital has to be reinvested. Well, you Trillians were too sensible to pay that price. You'd proceed more gradually. Yet at the same time, your scientists, all your more adventurous types were burning to get out into space.

"I agree your decision about that was intelligent too. You saw you couldn't go directly from your earliest hydrocarbon-fueled engines to a modern starship—to a completely integrated system of thermonuclear powerplant, initiative-grade navigation and engineering computers, full-cycle life support, the whole works, using solid-state circuits, molecular-level and nuclear-level transitions, force-fields instead of moving parts—an *organism,* more energy than matter. No, you wouldn't be able to build that for generations, probably.

"But you could go ahead and develop huge, clumsy, but workable fission-power units. You could use vacuum tubes, glass rectifiers, kilometers of wire, to generate and regulate the necessary forces. You could store data on tape if not in single molecules, retrieve with a cathode-ray scanner if not with a quantum-field pulse, compute with miniaturized gas-filled units that react in microseconds if not with photon interplays that take a nanosecond.

"You're like islanders who had nothing better than canoes till someone happened by in a nuclear-powered submarine. They couldn't copy that, but they might invent a reciprocating steam engine turning a screw—they might attach an airpipe so it could submerge—and it wouldn't impress the outsiders, but it would cross the ocean too, at its own pace; and it would overawe any neighboring tribes."

He stopped for breath.

"I see," Witweet murmured slowly. His tail switched back and forth. "You can sell our designs to sophonts in a proto-industrial stage of technological development. The idea comes from an excellent brain. But why could you not simply buy the plans for resale elsewhere?"

"The damned busybody League." Dolgorov spat.

"The fact is," Olafsson said, "spacecraft—of advanced type—have been sold to, ah, less advanced peoples in the past. Some of those weren't near industrialization, they were Iron Age barbarians, whose only thought was plundering and conquering. They could do that, given ships which are practically self-piloting, self-maintaining, self-everything. It's cost a good many lives and heavy material losses on border planets. But at least none of the barbarians have been able to duplicate the craft thus far. Hunt every pirate and warlord down, and that ends the problem. Or so the League hopes. It's banned any more such trades."

He cleared his throat. "I don't refer to races like the Trillians, who're obviously capable of reaching the stars by themselves and unlikely to be a menace when they do," he said. "You're free to buy anything you can pay for. The price of certain things is set astronomical mainly to keep you from beginning overnight to compete with the old-established outfits. They prefer a gradual phasing-in of newcomers, so they can adjust.

"But aggressive, warlike cultures, that'd not be interested in reaching a peaceful accommodation—they're something else again. There's a total prohibition on supplying their sort with anything that might lead to them getting off their planets in less than centuries. If League agents catch you at it, they don't fool around with rehabilitation like a regular government. They shoot you."

Harker grimaced. "I saw once on a telescreen interview," he remarked, "Old Nick van Rijn said he wouldn't shoot that kind of offenders. He'd hang them. A rope is reusable."

"And this ship *can* be copied," Witweet breathed. "A low industrial technology, lower than ours, could tool up to produce a modified design, in a comparatively short time, if guided by a few engineers from the core civilization."

"I trained as an engineer," Harker said. "Likewise Leo; and Einar spent several years on a planet where one royal family has grandiose ambitions."

"But the horror you would unleash!" wailed the Trillian. He stared into their stoniness. "You would never dare go home," he said.

"Don't want to anyway," Harker answered. "Power, wealth, yes, and everything those will buy—we'll have more than we can use up in our lifetimes, at the court of the Militants. Fun, too." He smiled. "A challenge, you know, to build a space navy from zero. I expect to enjoy my work."

"Will not the, the, the Polesotechnic League . . . take measures?"

"That's why we must operate as we have done. They'd learn about a sale of plans, and then they wouldn't stop till they'd found and suppressed our project. But a non-Technic ship that never reported in won't interest them. Our destination is well outside their sphere of normal operations. They needn't discover any hint of what's going on—till an interstellar empire too big for them to break is there. Meanwhile, as we gain resources, we'll have been modernizing our industry and fleet."

"It's all arranged," Olafsson said. "The day we show up in the land of the Militants, bringing the ship we described to them, we'll become princes."

"Kings, later," Dolgorov added. "Behave accordingly, you xeno. We don't need you much. I'd soon as not boot you through an airlock."

Witweet spent minutes just shuddering.

The Serenity, etc. moved on away from Trillia's golden sun. It had to reach a weaker gravitational field than a human craft would have needed, before its hyperdrive would function.

Harker spent part of that period being shown around, top to

bottom and end to end. He'd toured a sister ship before, but hadn't dared ask for demonstrations as thorough as he now demanded. "I want to know this monstrosity we've got, inside out," he said while personally tearing down and rebuilding a cumbersome oxygen renewer. He could do this because most equipment was paired, against the expectation of eventual in-flight down time.

In a hold, among cases of supplies for the research team on Gwinsai, he was surprised to recognize a lean cylindroid, one hundred twenty centimeters long. "But here's a Solar-built courier!" he exclaimed.

Witweet made eager gestures of agreement. He'd been falling over himself to oblige his captors. "For messages in case of emergency, magnificent sir," he babbled. "A hyperdrive unit, an autopilot, a radio to call at journey's end till someone comes and retrieves the enclosed letter—"

"I know, I know. But why not build your own?"

"Well, if you will deign to reflect upon the matter, you will realize that anything we could build would be too slow and unreliable to afford very probable help. Especially since it is most unlikely that, at any given time, another spaceship would be ready to depart Trillia on the instant. Therefore this courier is set, as you can see if you wish to examine the program, to go a considerably greater distance—though nevertheless not taking long, your human constructions being superlatively fast—to the planet called, ah, Oasis . . . an Anglic word meaning a lovely, cool, refreshing haven, am I correct?"

Harker nodded impatiently. "Yes, one of the League companies does keep a small base there."

"We have arranged that they will send aid if requested. At a price, to be sure. However, for our poor economy, as ridiculous a hulk as this is still a heavy investment, worth insuring."

"I see. I didn't know you bought such gadgets—not that there'd be a pegged price on them; they don't matter any more than spices or medical equipment. Of course, I couldn't find out every detail in advance, especially not things you people take so for granted that you didn't think to mention them." On impulse, Harker patted the round head. "You know, Witweet, I guess I do like you. I will see you're rewarded for your help."

"Passage home will suffice," the Trillian said quietly, "though I do not know how I can face my kinfolk after having been the instrument of death and ruin for millions of innocents."

"Then don't go home," Harker suggested. "We can't release you for years in any case, to blab our scheme and our coordinates. But we could smuggle in whatever and whoever you wanted, same as for ourselves."

The head rose beneath his palm as the slight form straightened. "Very well," Witweet declared.

That fast? jarred through Harker. *He is nonhuman, yes, but*—The wondering was dissipated by the continuing voice:

"Actually, dear boy, I must disabuse you. We did not buy our couriers, we salvaged them."

"What? Where?"

"Have you heard of a planet named, by its human discoverers, Paradox?"

Harker searched his memory. Before leaving Earth he had consulted every record he could find about this entire stellar neighborhood. Poorly known though it was to men, there had been a huge mass of data—suns, worlds. . . . "I think so," he said. "Big, isn't it? With, uh, a freaky atmosphere."

"Yes." Witweet spoke rapidly. "It gave the original impetus to Technic exploration of our vicinity. But later the men departed. In recent years, when we ourselves became able to pay visits, we found their abandoned camp. A great deal of gear had been left behind, presumably because it was designed for Paradox only and would be of no use elsewhere, hence not worth hauling back. Among these machines we came upon a few couriers. I suppose they had been overlooked. Your civilization can afford profligacy, if I may use that term in due respectfulness."

He crouched, as if expecting a blow. His eyes glittered in the gloom of the hold.

"Hm." Harker frowned. "I suppose by now you've stripped the place."

"Well, no." Witweet brushed nervously at his rising fur. "Like the men, we saw no use in, for example, tractors designed for a gravity of two-point-eight terrestrial. They can operate well and cheaply on Paradox, since their fuel is crude oil, of which an abundant supply exists near the campsite. But we already had electric-celled grav motors, however archaic they are by your standards. And we do not need weapons like those we found, presumably for protection against animals. We certainly have no intention of colonizing Paradox!"

"Hm." The human waved, as if to brush off the chattering voice. "Hm." He slouched off, hands in pockets, pondering.

In the time that followed, he consulted the navigator's bible. His reading knowledge of Lenidellian was fair. The entry for Paradox was as laconic as it would have been in a Technic reference; despite the limited range of their operations, the Trillians had already encountered too many worlds to allow flowery descriptions. Star type and coordinates, orbital elements, mass density, atmospheric composition, temperature ranges, and the usual rest were listed. There was no notation about habitability, but none was needed. The original explorers hadn't been poisoned or come down with disease; Trillian metabolism was similar to theirs.

The gravity field was not too strong for this ship to make landing and, later, ascent. Weather shouldn't pose any hazards, given reasonable care in choosing one's path; that was a weakly energized environment. Besides, the vessel was meant for planetfalls, and Witweet was a skilled pilot in his fashion. . . .

Harker discussed the idea with Olafsson and Dolgorov. "It won't take but a few days," he said, "and we might pick up something really good. You know I've not been too happy about the Militants' prospects of building an ample industrial base fast enough to suit us. Well, a few machines like this, simple things they can easily copy but designed by good engineers . . . could make a big difference."

"They're probably rustheaps," Dolgorov snorted. "That was long ago."

"No, durable alloys were available then," Olafsson said. "I like the notion intrinsically, Bryce. I don't like the thought of our tame xeno taking us down. He might crash us on purpose."

"That sniveling faggot?" Dolgorov gibed. He jerked his head backward at Witweet, who sat enormous-eyed in the pilot chair listening to a language he did not understand. "By accident, maybe, seeing how scared he is!"

"It's a risk we take at journey's end," Harker reminded them. "Not a real risk. The ship has some ingenious failsafes built in. Anyhow, I intend to stand over him the whole way down. If he does a single thing wrong, I'll kill him. The controls aren't made for me, but I can get us aloft again, and afterward we can re-rig."

Olafsson nodded. "Seems worth a try," he said. "What can we lose except a little time and sweat?"

Paradox rolled enormous in the viewscreen, a darkling world, the sky-band along its sunrise horizon redder than Earth's, polar caps and winter snowfields gashed by the teeth of mountains, tropical forest and pampas a yellow-brown fading into raw deserts on one side and chopped off on another side by the furious surf of an ocean where three moons fought their tidal wars. The sun was distance-dwarfed, more dull in hue than Sol, nevertheless too bright to look near. Elsewhere, stars filled illimitable blackness.

It was very quiet aboard, save for the mutter of powerplant and ventilators, the breathing of men, their restless shuffling about in the cramped cabin. The air was blued and fouled by cigarette smoke; Witweet would have fled into the corridor, but they made him stay, clutching a perfume-dripping kerchief to his nose.

Harker straightened from the observation screen. Even at full magnification, the rudimentary electro-optical system gave little except blurriness. But he'd practiced on it, while orbiting a satellite, till he felt he could read those wavering traces.

"Campsite and machinery, all right," he said. "No details. Brush has covered everything. When were your people here last, Witweet?"

"Several years back," the Trillian wheezed. "Evidently vegetation grows apace. Do you agree on the safety of a landing?"

"Yes. We may snap a few branches, as well as flatten a lot of shrubs, but we'll back down slowly, the last hundred meters, and we'll keep the radar, sonar, and gravar sweeps going." Harker glanced at his men. "Next thing is to compute our descent pattern," he said. "But first I want to spell out again, point by point, exactly what each of us is to do under exactly what circumstances. I don't aim to take chances."

"Oh, no," Witweet squeaked. "I beg you, dear boy, I beg you the prettiest I can, please don't."

After the tension of transit, landing was an anticlimax. All at once the engine fell silent. A wind whistled around the hull. Viewscreens showed low, thick-boled trees; fronded brownish leaves; tawny undergrowth; shadowy glimpses of metal objects beneath vines and amidst tall, whipping stalks. The sun stood at late afternoon in a sky almost purple.

Witweet checked the indicators while Harker studied them over his head. "Air breathable, of course," the pilot said, "which frees us of the handicap of having to wear smelly old spacesuits. We should bleed it in gradually, since the pressure is greater than ours at present and we don't want earaches, do we? Temperature—" He shivered delicately. "Be certain you are wrapped up snug before you venture outside."

"You're venturing first," Harker informed him.

"What? Oo-ooh, my good, sweet, darling friend, no, please, no! It is *cold* out there, scarcely above freezing. And once on the ground, no gravity generator to help, why, weight will be tripled. What could I possibly, possibly do? No, let me stay inside, keep the home fires burning—I mean keep the thermostat at a cozy temperature—and, yes, I will make you the nicest pot of tea—"

"If you don't stop fluttering and do what you're told, I'll tear your head off," Dolgorov said. "Guess what I'll use your skin for."

"Let's get cracking," Olafsson said. "I don't want to stay in this Helheim any longer than you."

They opened a hatch the least bit. While Paradoxian air seeped in, they dressed as warmly as might be, except for Harker. He intended to stand by the controls for the first investigatory period. The entering gases added a whine to the wind-noise. Their helium content made speech and other sounds higher pitched, not quite natural; and this would have to be endured for the rest of the journey, since the ship had insufficient reserve tanks to flush out the new atmosphere. A breath of cold got by the heaters, and a rank smell of alien growth.

But you could get used to hearing funny, Harker thought. And the native life might stink, but it was harmless. You couldn't eat it and be nourished, but neither could its germs live off your body. If heavy weapons had been needed here, they were far more likely against large, blundering herbivores than against local tigers.

That didn't mean they couldn't be used in war.

Trembling, eyes squinched half-shut, tail wrapped around his muzzle, the rest of him bundled in four layers of kimono, Witweet crept to the personnel lock. Its outer valve swung wide. The gangway went down. Harker grinned to see the dwarfish shape descend, step by step under the sudden harsh hauling of the planet.

"Sure you can move around in that pull?" he asked his companions.

"Sure," Dolgorov grunted. "An extra hundred-fifty kilos? I can backpack more than that, and then it's less well distributed."

"Stay cautious, though. Too damned easy to fall and break bones."

"I'd worry more about the cardiovascular system," Olafsson said. "One can stand three gees a while, but not for a very long while. Fluid begins seeping out of the cell walls, the heart feels the strain too much—and we've no gravanol along as the first expedition must have had."

"We'll only be here a few days at most," Harker said, "with plenty of chances to rest inboard."

"Right," Olafsson agreed. "Forward!"

Gripping his blaster, he shuffled onto the gangway. Dolgorov followed. Below, Witweet huddled. Harker looked out at bleakness, felt the wind slap his face with chill, and was glad he could stay behind. Later he must take his turn outdoors, but for now he could enjoy warmth, decent weight—

The world reached up and grabbed him. Off balance, he fell to the deck. His left hand struck first, pain gushed, he saw the wrist and arm splinter. He screamed. The sound came weak as well as shrill, out of a breast laboring against thrice the heaviness it should have had. At the same time, the lights in the ship went out.

Witweet perched on a boulder. His back was straight in spite of the drag on him, which made his robes hang stiff as if carved on an idol of some minor god of justice. His tail, erect, blew jauntily in the bitter sunset wind; the colors of his garments were bold against murk that rose in the forest around the dead spacecraft.

He looked into the guns of three men, and into the terror that had taken them behind the eyes; and Witweet laughed.

"Put those toys away before you hurt yourselves," he said, using no circumlocutions or honorifics.

"You bastard, you swine, you filthy treacherous xeno, I'll kill you," Dolgorov groaned. "Slowly."

"First you must catch me," Witweet answered. "By virtue of being small, I have a larger surface-to-volume ratio than you. My bones, my muscles, my veins and capillaries and cell membranes suffer less force per square centimeter than do yours. I can move faster than you, here. I can survive longer."

"You can't outrun a blaster bolt," Olafsson said.

"No. You can kill me with that—a quick, clean death which does not frighten me. Really, because we of Lenidel observe certain customs of courtesy, use certain turns of speech—because our males in particular are encouraged to develop esthetic interests and compassion—does that mean we are cowardly or effeminate?" The Trillian clicked his tongue. "If you supposed so, you committed an elementary logical fallacy which our philosophers name the does-not-follow."

"Why shouldn't we kill you?"

"That is inadvisable. You see, your only hope is quick rescue by a League ship. The courier can operate here, being a solid-state device. It can reach Oasis and summon a vessel which, itself of similar construction, can also land on Paradox and take off again . . . in time. This would be impossible for a Trillian craft. Even if one were ready to leave, I doubt the Astronautical Senate would permit the pilot to risk descent.

"Well, rescuers will naturally ask questions. I cannot imagine any story which you three men, alone, might concoct that would stand up under the subsequent, inevitable investigation. On the other hand, I can explain to the League's agents that you were only coming along to look into trade possibilities and that we were trapped on Paradox by a faulty autopilot which threw us into a descent curve. I can do this *in detail,* which you could not if you killed me. They will return us all to Trillia, where there is no death penalty."

Witweet smoothed his wind-ruffled whiskers. "The alternative," he finished, "is to die where you are, in a most unpleasant fashion."

Harker's splinted arm gestured back the incoherent Dolgorov. He set an example by holstering his own gun. "I . . . guess we're outsmarted," he said, word by foul-tasting word. "But what happened? Why's the ship inoperable?"

"Helium in the atmosphere," Witweet explained calmly. "The monatomic helium molecule is ooh-how-small. It diffuses through almost every material. Vacuum tubes, glass rectifiers, electronic switches dependent on pure gases, any such device soon becomes poisoned. You, who were used to a technology that had long left this kind of thing behind, did not know the fact, and it did not occur to you as a possibility. We Trillians are, of course, rather acutely aware of the problem. I am the first who ever set foot on Paradox. You should have noted that my courier is a present-day model."

"I see," Olafsson mumbled.

"The sooner we get our message off, the better," Witweet said. "By the way, I assume you are not so foolish as to contemplate the piratical takeover of a vessel of the Polesotechnic League."

"Oh, no!" said they, including Dolgorov, and the other two blasters were sheathed.

"One thing, though," Harker said. A part of him wondered if the pain in him was responsible for his own abnormal self-possession. Counterirritant against dismay? Would he weep after it wore off? "You bargain for your life by promising to have ours spared. How do we know we want your terms? What'll they do to us on Trillia?"

"Entertain no fears," Witweet assured him. "We are not vindictive, as I have heard some species are; nor have we any officious concept of 'rehabilitation.' Wrongdoers are required to make amends to the fullest extent possible. You three have cost my people a valuable ship and whatever cargo cannot be salvaged. You must have technological knowledge to convey, of equal worth. The working conditions will not be intolerable. Probably you can make restitution and win release before you reach old age.

"Now, come, get busy. First we dispatch that courier, then we prepare what is necessary for our survival until rescue."

He hopped down from the rock, which none of them would have been able to do unscathed, and approached them through gathering cold twilight with the stride of a conqueror.

INTRODUCTION

Also in the records left on Hermes was information about an episode which had long been concealed: how Nicholas van Rijn came to the world which today we know as Mirkheim. The reasons for secrecy at the time are self-evident. Later they did not obtain. However, it is well known that Falkayn was always reluctant to mention his part in the origins of the Supermetals enterprise, and curt-spoken whenever the subject was forced upon him. Given all else there was to strive with in the beginning upon Avalon, it is no flaw of wind that folk did not press their leaders about this, and that the matter dropped from general awareness. Even before then, he had done what he could to suppress details.

Of course, the alatan facts are in every biography of the Founder. Yet this one affair is new to us. It helps explain much which followed, especially his reserve, rare in an otherwise cheerful and outgoing person. In truth, it gives us a firmer grip than we had before upon the reality of him.

The records contain only the ship's log for that voyage, plus some taped conversations, data lists, and the like. However, these make meaningful certain hitherto cryptic references in surviving letters written by Coya to her husband. Furthermore, with the identity of vessel and captain known, it became possible to enlist the aid of the Wryfields Choth on Ythri. Stirrok, its Wyvan, was most helpful in finding Hirharouk's private journal, while his descendants kindly agreed to waive strict rightness and allow it to be read.

From these sources, Hloch and Arinnian have composed the narrative which follows.

—Hloch of the Stormgate Choth
The Earth Book of Stormgate

LODESTAR

Lightning reached. David Falkayn heard the crack of torn air and gulped a rainy reek of ozone. His cheek stung from the near miss. In his eyes, spots of blue-white dazzle danced across night.

"Get aboard, you two," Adzel said. "I'll hold them."

Crouched, Falkayn peered after a target for his own blaster. He saw shadows move beneath strange constellations—that, and flames which tinged upward-roiling smoke on the far side of the spacefield, where the League outpost was burning. Shrieks resounded. "No, you start," he rasped. "I'm armed, you're not."

The Wodenite's bass remained steady, but an earthquake rumble entered it. "No more deaths. A single death would have been too much, of folk outraged in their own homes. David, Chee: *go*."

Half-dragon, half-centaur, four and a half meters from snout to tailtip, he moved toward the unseen natives. Firelight framed the hedge of bony plates along his back, glimmered off scales and belly-scutes.

Chee Lan tugged at Falkayn's trousers. "Come on," she spat. "No stopping that hairy-brain when he wambles off on an idealism binge. He won't board before us, and they'll kill him if we don't move fast." A sneer: "I'll lead the way, if that'll make you feel more heroic."

Her small, white-furred form shot from the hauler behind which they had taken refuge. (No use trying to get that machine aloft. The primitives had planned their attack shrewdly, must have hoarded stolen explosives as well as guns for years, till they could demolish everything around the base at the same moment as they fell upon the headquarters complex.) Its mask-markings obscured her blunt-muzzled face in the shuddering red light; but her bottled-up tail stood all too clear.

A Tamethan saw. On long thin legs, beak agape in a war-yell, he sped to catch her. His weapon was merely a spear. Sick-hearted, Falkayn took aim. Then Chee darted between those legs, tumbled the autochthon on his tocus and bounded onward.

Hurry! Falkayn told himself. Battle ramped around Adzel. The Wodenite could take a certain number of slugs and blaster bolts without permanent damage, he knew, but not many . . . and those mighty arms were pulling their punches. Keeping to shadow as well as might be, the human followed Chee Lan.

Their ship loomed ahead, invulnerable to the attackers. Her gangway was descending. So the Cynthian had entered audio range, had called an order to the main computer. . . . *Why didn't we tell Muddlehead to use initiative in case of trouble?* groaned Falkayn's mind. *Why didn't we at least carry radios to call for its help? Are we due for retirement? A sloppy trade pioneer is a dead trade pioneer.*

A turret gun flashed and boomed. Chee must have ordered that. It was a warning shot, sent skyward, but terrifying. The man gusted relief. His rangy body sped upramp, stopped at the open airlock, and turned to peer back. Combat seemed to have frozen. And, yes, here Adzel came, limping, trailing blood, but alive. Falkayn wanted to hug his old friend and weep.

No. First we haul mass out of here. He entered the ship. Adzel's hoofs boomed on the gangway. It retracted, the airlock closed, gravity drive purred, and *Muddlin' Through* ascended to heaven.

—Gathered on the bridge, her crew stared at a downward-viewing screen. The fires had become sparks, the spacefield a scar, in an illimitable night. Far off, a river cut through jungle, shining by starlight like a drawn sword.

Falkayn ran fingers through his sandy hair. "We, uh, well, do you think we can rescue any survivors?" he asked.

"I doubt there are any by now," Adzel said. "We barely escaped: because we have learned, over years, to meet emergencies as a team."

"And if there are," Chee added, "who cares?" Adzel looked

reproof at her. She bristled her whiskers. "We saw how those slime-souls were treating the aborigines."

"I feel sure much of the offense was caused simply by ignorance of basic psychology and mores."

"That's no excuse, as you flapping well know. They should've taken the trouble to learn such things. But no, the companies couldn't wait for that. They sent their bespattered factors and field agents right in, who promptly set up a little dunghill of an empire—*Ya-pu-yeh!*" In Chee's home language that was a shocking obscenity, even for her.

Falkayn's shoulders slumped. "I'm inclined to agree," he said. "Besides, we mustn't take risks. We've got to make a report."

"Why?" Adzel asked. "Our own employer was not involved."

"No, thanks be. I'd hate to feel I must quit. . . . This is League business, however. The mutual-assistance rule—"

"And so League warcraft come and bomb some poor little villages?" Adzel's tail drummed on the deck.

"With our testimony, we can hope not. The Council verdict ought to be, those klongs fell flat on their own deeds." Falkayn sighed. "I wish we'd been around here longer, making a regular investigation, instead of just chancing by and deciding to take a few days off on a pleasant planet." He straightened. "Well. To space, Muddlehead, and to—m-m-m, nearest major League base—Irumclaw."

"And you come along to sickbay and let me dress those wounds, you overgrown bulligator," Chee snapped at the Wodenite, "before you've utterly ruined this carpet, drooling blood on it."

Falkayn himself sought a washroom, a change of clothes, his pipe and tobacco, a stiff drink. Continuing to the saloon, he settled down and tried to ease away his trouble. In a viewscreen, the world dwindled which men had named Tametha—arbitrarily, from a native word in a single locality, which they'd doubtless gotten wrong anyway. Already it had shrunk in his vision to a ball, swirled blue and white: a body as big and fair as ever Earth was, four or five billion years in the making, uncounted swarms of unknown life forms, sentiences and civilizations, histories and mysteries, become a marble in a game . . . or a set of entries in a set of data banks, for profit or loss, in a few cities a hundred or more light-years remote.

He thought: *This isn't the first time I've seen undying wrong done.*

Is it really happening oftener and oftener, or am I just getting more aware of it as I age? At thirty-three, I begin to feel old.

Chee entered, jumped onto the seat beside him, and reported Adzel was resting. "You do need that drink, don't you?" she observed. Falkayn made no reply. She inserted a mildly narcotic cigarette in an interminable ivory holder and puffed it to ignition.

"Yes," she said, "I get irritated likewise, no end, whenever something like this befouls creation."

"I'm coming to think the matter is worse, more fundamental, than a collection of episodes." Falkayn spoke wearily. "The Polesotechnic League began as a mutual-benefit association of companies, true; but the idea was also to keep competition within decent bounds. That's breaking down, that second aspect. How long till the first does too?"

"What would you prefer to free enterprise? The Terran Empire, maybe?"

"Well, you being a pure carnivore, and coming besides from a trading culture that was quick to modernize—exploitation doesn't touch you straight on the nerves, Chee. But Adzel—he doesn't say much, you know him, but I've become certain it's a bitterness to him, more and more as time slides by, that nobody will help his people advance . . . because they haven't anything that anybody wants enough to pay the price of advancement. And—well, I hardly dare guess how many others. Entire worldsful of beings who look at yonder stars till it aches in them, and know that except for a few lucky individuals, none of them will ever get out there, nor will their descendants have any real say about the future, no, will instead remain nothing but potential victims—"

Seeking distraction, Falkayn raised screen magnification and swept the scanner around jewel-blazing blackness. When he stopped for another pull at his glass, the view happened to include the enigmatic glow of the Crab Nebula.

"Take that sentimentalism and stuff it back where it came from," Chee suggested. "The new-discovered species will simply have to accumulate capital. Yours did. Mine did soon after. We can't give a free ride to the whole universe."

"N-no. Yet you know yourself—be honest—how quick somebody already established would be to take away that bit of capital, whether by market manipulations or by thinly disguised piracy. Tametha's a minor example. All that those tribesbeings wanted was to trade directly with Over-the-Mountains." Falkayn's fist clamped hard around his pipe. "I tell you, lass, the heart is going out of the League, in the sense of ordinary compassion and helpfulness. How long till the heart goes out in the sense of its own survivability? Civilization *needs* more than the few monopolists we've got."

The Cynthian twitched her ears, quite slowly, and exhaled smoke whose sweetness blent with the acridity of the man's tobacco. Her eyes glowed through it, emerald-hard. "I sort of agree. At least, I'd enjoy listening to the hot air hiss out of certain bellies. How, though, Davy? How?"

"Old Nick—he's a single member of the Council, I realize—"

"Our dear employer keeps his hirelings fairly moral, but strictly on the principle of running a taut ship. He told me that himself once, and added, 'Never mind what the ship is taught, ho, ho, ho!' No, you won't make an idealist of Nicholas van Rijn. Not without transmuting every atom in his fat body."

Falkayn let out a tired chuckle. "A new isotope. Van Rijn-235, no, likelier Vr-235,000—"

And then his glance passed over the Nebula, and as if it had spoken to him across more than a thousand parsecs, he fell silent and grew tense where he sat.

This happened shortly after the Satan episode, when the owner of Solar Spice & Liquors had found it needful once more to leave the comforts of the Commonwealth, risk his thick neck on a cheerless world, and finally make a month-long voyage in a ship which had run out of beer. Returned home, he swore by all that was holy and much that was not: Never again!

Nor, for most of the following decade, had he any reason to break his vow. His business was burgeoning, thanks to excellently chosen personnel in established trade sites and to pioneers like the *Muddlin' Through* team who kept finding him profitable new lands. Besides, he had maneuvered himself into the overlordship of Satan. A sunless wandering planet, newly thawed out by a brush with a giant star, made a near-ideal site for the manufacture of odd isotopes on a scale commensurate with present-day demand. Such industry wasn't his cup of tea "or," he declared, "my glass Genever that molasses-on-Pluto-footed butler is supposed to bring me before I crumble away from thirst." Therefore van Rijn granted franchises, on terms calculated to be an ångström short of impossibly extortionate.

Many persons wondered, often in colorful language, why he didn't retire and drink himself into a grave they would be glad to provide, outsize though it must be. When van Rijn heard about these remarks, he would grin and look still harder for a price he could jack up or a competitor he could undercut. Nevertheless, compared to earlier years, this was for him a leisured period. When at last word got around that he meant to take Coya Conyon, his favorite granddaughter, on an extended cruise aboard his yacht—and not a single mistress along for him—hope grew that he was slowing down to a halt.

I can't say I like most of those money-machine merchant princes, Coya reflected, several weeks after leaving Earth; *but I really wouldn't want to give them heart attacks by telling them we're now on a nonhuman vessel, equipped in curious ways but unmistakably battle-ready, bound into a region that nobody is known to have explored.*

She stood before a viewport set in a corridor. A ship built by men would not have carried that extravagance; but to Ythrians, sky dwellers, ample outlook is a necessity of sanity. The air she breathed was a little thinner than at Terrestrial sea level; odors included the slight smokiness of their bodies. A ventilator murmured not only with draft but with a barely heard rustle, the distance-muffled sound of wingbeats from crewfolk off duty cavorting in an enormous hold intended for it. At 0.75 standard weight she still—after this long a trip—felt exhilaratingly light.

She was not presently conscious of that. At first she had reveled in adventure. Everything was an excitement; every day offered a million discoveries to be made. She didn't mind being the sole human aboard besides her grandfather. He was fun in his bearish fashion: had been as far back as she could remember, when he would roll roaring into her parents' home, toss her to the ceiling, half-bury her under presents from a score of planets, tell her extravagant stories and take her out on a sailboat or to a live performance or, later on, around most of the Solar System. . . . Anyhow, to make Ythrian friends, to discover a little of how their psyches worked and how one differed from another, to trade music, memories, and myths, watch their aerial dances and show them some ballet, that was an exploration in itself.

Today, however—they were apparently nearing the goal for which they had been running in a search helix, whatever it was. Van Rijn remained boisterous; but he would tell her nothing. Nor did the Ythrians know what was sought, except for Hirharouk, and he had passed on no other information than that all were to hold themselves prepared for emergencies cosmic or warlike. A species whose ancestors had lived like eagles could take this more easily than men. Even so, tension had mounted till she could smell it.

Her gaze sought outward. As an astrophysicist and a fairly frequent tourist, she had spent a total of years in space during the twenty-five she had been in the universe. She could identify the brightest individual stars amidst that radiant swarm, lacy and lethal loveliness of shining nebulae, argent torrent of Milky Way, remote glimmer of sister galaxies. And still size and silence, unknownness and unknowability, struck against her as much as when she first fared forth.

Secrets eternal . . . why, of course. They had run at a good pseudovelocity for close to a month, starting at Ythri's sun (which lies 278 light-years from Sol in the direction of Lupus) and aiming at the Deneb sector. That put them, oh, say a hundred parsecs from Earth. Glib calculation. Yet they had reached parts which no record said anyone had ever done more than pass through, in all the centuries since men got a hyperdrive. The planetary systems here had not been catalogued, let alone visited, let alone understood. Space is that big, that full of worlds.

Coya shivered, though the air was warm enough. *You're yonder somewhere, David,* she thought, *if you haven't met the inevitable final surprise. Have you gotten my message? Did it have any meaning to you?*

She could do nothing except give her letter to another trade pioneer whom she trusted. He was bound for the same general region as Falkayn had said *Muddlin' Through* would next go questing in. The crews maintained rendezvous stations. In one such turbulent place he might get news of Falkayn's team. Or he could deposit the letter there to be called for.

Guilt nagged her, as it had throughout this journey. A betrayal of her grandfather—No! Fresh anger flared. *If he's not brewing something bad, what possible harm can it do him that David knows what little I knew before we left—which is scarcely more than the old devil has let me know to this hour?*

And he did speak of hazards. I did have to force him into taking me along (because the matter seemed to concern you, David, oh, David). If we meet trouble, and suddenly you arrive—

Stop romancing, Coya told herself. *You're a grown girl now.* She found she could control her thoughts, somewhat, but not the tingle through her blood.

She stood tall, slender almost to boyishness, clad in plain black tunic, slacks, and sandals. Straight dark hair, shoulder-length, framed an oval face with a snub nose, mouth a trifle too wide but eyes remarkably big and gold-flecked green. Her skin was very white. It was rather freakish how genes had recombined to forget nearly every trace of her ancestry—van Rijn's Dutch and Malay; the Mexican and Chinese of a woman who bore him a girl-child and with whom he had remained on the same amicable terms afterward as, somehow, he did with most former loves; the Scots (from Hermes, David's home planet) plus a dash of African (via a planet called Nyanza) in that Malcolm Conyon who settled down on Earth and married Beatrix Yeo.

Restless, Coya's mind skimmed over the fact. Her lips could not help quirking. *In short, I'm a typical modern human.* The amusement died. *Yes, also in my life. My grandfather's generation seldom bothered to get married. My father's did. And mine, why, we're reviving patrilineal surnames.*

A whistle snapped off her thinking. Her heart lurched until she identified the signal. "All hands alert."

That meant something had been detected. Maybe not the goal; maybe just a potential hazard, like a meteoroid swarm. In uncharted space, you traveled warily, and van Rijn kept a candle lit before his little Martian sandroot statuette of St. Dismas.

A moment longer, Coya confronted the death and glory beyond the ship. Then, fists knotted, she strode aft. She was her grandfather's granddaughter.

✲ ✲ ✲

"Lucifer and leprosy!" bellowed Nicholas van Rijn. "You have maybe spotted what we maybe are after, at extreme range of your instruments tuned sensitive like an artist what specializes in painting pansies, a thing we cannot reach in enough hours to eat three good rijstaffels, and you have the bladder to tell me I got to armor me and stand around crisp saying, 'Aye-yi-yi, sir'?" Sprawled in a lounger, he waved a two-liter tankard of beer he clutched in his hairy left paw. The right held a churchwarden pipe, which had filled his stateroom with blue reek.

Hirharouk of the Wryfields Choth, captain of the chartered ranger *Gaiian (=Dewfall),* gave him look for look. The Ythrian's eyes were large and golden, the man's small and black and crowding his great hook nose; neither pair gave way, and Hirharouk's answer held an iron quietness: "No. I propose that you stop guzzling alcohol. You do have drugs to induce sobriety, but they may show side effects when quick decision is needed."

While his Anglic was fluent, he used a vocalizer to convert the sounds he could make into clearly human tones. The Ythrian voice is beautifully ringing but less flexible than man's. Was it to gibe or be friendly that van Rijn responded in pretty fair Planha? "Be not perturbed. I am hardened, which is why my vices cost me a fortune. Moreover, a body my size has corresponding capacity." He slapped the paunch beneath his snuff-stained blouse and gaudy sarong. The rest of him was huge in proportion. "This is my way of resting in advance of trouble, even as you would soar aloft and contemplate."

Hirharouk eased and fluted his equivalent of a laugh. "As you wish. I daresay you would not have survived to this date, all the sworn foes you must have, did you not know what you do."

Van Rijn tossed back his sloping brow. Long swarthy ringlets in the style of his youth, except for their greasiness, swirled around the jewels in his earlobes; his chins quivered beneath waxed mustaches and goatee; a bare splay foot smote the densely carpeted deck. "You mistake me," he boomed, reverting to his private version of Anglic. "You cut me to the quiche. Do you suppose I, poor old lonely sinner, *ja,* but still a Christian man with a soul full of hope, do you suppose *I* ever went after anything but peace—as many peaces as I could get? No, no, what I did, I was pushed into, self-defense against sons of mothers, greedy rascals who I may forgive though God cannot, who begrudge me what tiny profit I need so I not become a charge on a state that is only good for grinding up taxpayers anyway. Me, I am like gentle St. Francis, I go around ripping off olive branches and covering stormy seas with oil slicks and watering troubled fish."

He stuck his tankard under a spout at his elbow for a refill. Hirharouk observed him. And Coya, entering the disordered luxury of the stateroom, paused to regard them both.

She was fond of van Rijn. Her doubts about this expedition, the message she had felt she must try to send to David Falkayn, had been a sharp blade in her. Nonetheless she admitted the Ythrian was infinitely more sightly. Handsomer than her too, she felt, or David himself. That was especially true in flight; yet, slow and awkward though they were aground, the Ythrians remained magnificent to see, and not only because of the born hunter's inborn pride.

Hirharouk stood some 150 centimeters tall. What he stood on was his wings, which spanned five and a half meters when unfolded. Turned downward, they spread claws at the angle which made a kind of foot; the backward-sweeping alatan surface could be used for extra support. What had been legs and talons, geological epochs ago, were arms and three-fingered two-thumbed hands. The skin on those was amber-colored. The rest of him wore shimmering bronze feathers, save where these became black-edged white on crest and on fan-shaped tail. His body looked avian, stiff behind its jutting keel-bone. But he was no bird. He had not been hatched. His head, raised on a powerful neck, had no beak: rather, a streamlined muzzle, nostrils at the tip, below them a mouth whose lips seemed oddly delicate against the keen fangs.

And the splendor of these people goes beyond the sunlight on them when they ride the wind, Coya thought. *David frets about the races that aren't getting a chance. Well, Ythri was primitive when the Grand Survey found it. The Ythrians studied Technic civilization, and neither licked its boots nor let it overwhelm them, but took what they wanted from it and made themselves a power in our corner of the galaxy. True, this was before that civilization was itself overwhelmed by* laissez-faire *capitalism—*

She blinked. Unlike her, the merchant kept his quarters at Earth-standard illumination; and Quetlan is yellower than Sol. He was used to abrupt transitions. She coughed in the tobacco haze. The two males grew aware of her.

"Ah, my sweet bellybird," van Rijn greeted, a habit he had not shaken from the days of her babyhood. "Come in. Flop yourself." A gesture of his pipe gave a choice of an extra lounger, a desk chair, an emperor-size bed, a sofa between the liquor cabinet and the bookshelf, or the deck. "What you want? Beer, gin, whisky, cognac, vodka, arrack, akvavit, half-dozen kinds wine and liqueur, ansa, totipot, slumthunder, maryjane, ops, gait, Xanadu radium, or maybe—" he winced "—a soft drink? A soft, flabby drink?"

"Coffee will do, thanks." Coya drew breath and courage. "*Gunung Tuan,* I've got to talk with you."

"*Ja,* I outspected you would. Why I not told you more before is because—oh, I wanted you should enjoy your trip, not brood like a hummingbird on ostrich eggs."

Coya was unsure whether Hirharouk spoke in tact or truth: "Freeman van Rijn, I came to discuss our situation. Now I return to the bridge. For honor and life . . . *khr-r-r,* I mean please . . . hold ready for planlaying as information lengthens." He lifted an arm. "Freelady Conyon, hail and fare you well."

He walked from them. When he entered the bare corridor, his claws clicked. He stopped and did a handstand. His wings spread as wide as possible in that space, preventing the door from closing till he was gone, exposing and opening the gill-like slits below them. He worked the wings, forcing those antlibranchs to operate like bellows. They were part of the "supercharger" system which enabled a creature his size to fly under basically terrestroid conditions. Coya did not know whether he was oxygenating his bloodstream to energize himself for command, or was flushing out human stench. He departed. She stood alone before her grandfather.

"Do sit, sprawl, hunker, or how you can best relax," the man urged. "I would soon have asked you should come. Time is to make a clean breast, except mine is too shaggy and you do not take off your tunic." His sigh turned into a belch. "A shame. Customs has changed. Not that I would lech in your case, no, I got incest repellent. But the sight is nice."

She reddened and signalled the coffeemaker. Van Rijn clicked his tongue. "And you don't smoke neither," he said. "Ah, they don't put the kind of stuff in youngsters like when I was your age."

"A few of us try to exercise some forethought as well as our consciences," Coya snapped. After a pause: "I'm sorry. Didn't mean to sound self-righteous."

"But you did. I wonder, has David Falkayn influenced you that way, or you him?—Ho-ho, a spectroscope would think your face was receding at speed of light!" Van Rijn wagged his pipestem. "Be careful. He's a good boy, him, except he's not a boy no more. Could well be, without knowing it, he got somewhere a daughter old as you."

"We're friends," Coya said half-furiously. She sat down on the edge of the spare lounger, ignored its attempts to match her contours, twined fingers between knees, and glared into his twinkle. "What the chaos do you expect my state of mind to be, when you wouldn't tell me what we're heading for?"

"You did not have to come along. You shoved in on me, armored in black mail."

Coya did not deny the amiably made statement. She had threatened to reveal the knowledge she had gained at his request, and thereby give his rivals the same clues. He hadn't been too hard to persuade; after warning her of possible danger, he growled that he would be needing an astrophysicist and might as well keep things in the family.

I hope, God, how I hope he believes my motive was a hankering for adventure as I told him! He ought to believe it, and flatter himself I've inherited a lot of his instincts. . . . No, he can't have guessed my real reason was the fear that David is involved, in a wrong way. If he knew that, he need only have told me, "Blab and be damned," and I'd have had to stay home, silent. As is . . . David, in me you have here an advocate, whatever you may have done.

"I could understand your keeping me ignorant while we were on the yacht," she counterattacked. "No matter how carefully picked the crew, one of them might have been a commercial or government spy and might have managed to eavesdrop. But when, when in the Quetlan System we transferred to this vessel, and the yacht proceeded as if we were still aboard, and won't make any port for weeks—why didn't you speak?"

"Maybe I wanted you should for punishment be like a Yiddish brothel."

"What?"

"Jews in your own stew. Haw, haw, haw!" She didn't smile. Van Rijn continued: "Mainly, here again I could not be full-up sure of the crew. Ythrians is fearless and I suppose more honest by nature than men. But that is saying microbial little, *nie?* Here too we might have been overheard and—well, Hirharouk agreed, he could not either absolute predict how certain of them would react. He tried but was not able to recruit everybody from his own choth." The Planha word designated a basic social unit, more than a tribe, less than a nation, with cultural and religious dimensions corresponding to nothing human. "Some, even, is from different societies and belong to no choths at allses. Ythrians got as much variation as the Commonwealth—no, more, because they not had time yet for technology to make them into homogeneouses."

The coffeemaker chimed. Coya rose, tapped a cup, sat back down, and sipped. The warmth and fragrance were a point of comfort in an infinite space.

"We had a long trek ahead of us," the merchant proceeded, "and a lot of casting about, before we found what it *might* be we are looking for. Meanwhiles Hirharouk, and me as best I was able, sounded out those crewbeings not from Wryfields, got to understand them a weenie bit and—hokay, he thinks we can trust them, regardless how the truth shapes up or ships out. And now, like you know, we have detected an object which would well be the simple, easy, small dissolution to the riddle."

"What's small about a supernova?" Coya challenged. "Even an extinct one?"

"When people ask me how I like being old as I am," van Rijn said circuitously, "I tell them, 'Not bad when I consider the alternative.' Bellybird, the alternative here would make the Shenn affair look like a game of pegglety-mum."

Coya came near spilling her coffee. She had been adolescent when the sensation exploded: that the Polesotechnic League had been infiltrated by agents of a nonhuman species, dwelling beyond the regions which Technic civilization dominated and bitterly hostile to it; that war had barely been averted; that the principal rescuers were her grandfather and the crew of a ship named *Muddlin' Through.* On that day David Falkayn was unknowingly promoted to god (j.g.). She wondered if he knew it yet, or knew that their occasional outings together after she matured had added humanness without reducing that earlier rank.

Van Rijn squinted at her. "You guessed we was hunting for a supernova remnant?" he probed.

She achieved a dry tone: "Since you had me investigate the problem, and soon thereafter announced your plans for a 'vacation trip,' the inference was fairly obvious."

"Any notion why I should want a white dwarf or a black hole instead of a nice glass red wine?"

Her pulse knocked. "Yes, I think I've reasoned it out." *And I think David may have done so before either of us, almost ten years ago. When you, Grandfather, asked me to use in secret—*

—the data banks and computers at Luna Astrocenter, where she worked, he had given a typically cryptic reason. "Could be this leads to a nice gob of profit nobody else's nose should root around in because mine is plenty big enough." She didn't blame him for being close-mouthed, then. The League's self-regulation was breaking down, competition grew ever more literally cutthroat, and governments snarled not only at the capitalists but at each other. The Pax Mercatoria was drawing to an end and, while she had never wholly approved of it, she sometimes dreaded the future.

The task he set her was sufficiently interesting to blot out her fears. However unimaginably violent, the suicides of giant suns by supernova bursts, which may outshine a hundred billion living stars, are not rare cosmic events. The remains, in varying stages of decay—white dwarfs, neutron stars, in certain cases those eldritch not-quite-things known as black holes—are estimated to number fifty million in our galaxy alone. But its arms spiral across a hundred thousand light-years. In this raw immensity, the prospects of finding by chance a body the size of a smallish planet or less, radiating corpse-feebly if at all, are negligible.

(The analogy with biological death and decomposition is not morbid. Those lay the foundation for new life and further evolution. Supernovae, hurling atoms together in fusing fury, casting them forth into space as their own final gasps, have given us all the heavier elements, some of them vital, in our worlds and our bodies.)

No one hitherto had—openly—attempted a more subtle search.

The scientists had too much else to do, as discovery exploded outward. Persons who wished to study supernova processes saw a larger variety of known cases than could be dealt with in lifetimes. Epsilon Aurigae, Sirius B, and Valenderay were simply among the most famous examples.

Coya in Astrocenter had at her beck every fact which Technic civilization had ever gathered about the stellar part of the universe. From the known distribution of former supernovae, together with data on other star types, dust, gas, radiation, magnetism, present location and concentrations, the time derivatives of these quantities: using well-established theories of galactic development, it is possible to compute with reasonable probability the distribution of undiscovered dark giants within a radius of a few hundred parsecs.

The problem is far more complex than that, of course; and the best of self-programming computers still needs a highly skilled sophont riding close herd on it, if anything is to be accomplished. Nor will the answers be absolute, even within that comparatively tiny sphere to which their validity is limited. The most you can learn is the likelihood (not the certainty) of a given type of object existing within such-and-such a distance of yourself, and the likeliest (not the indubitable) direction. To phrase it more accurately, you get a hierarchy of decreasingly probable solutions.

This suffices. If you have the patience, and money, to search on a path defined by the equations, you *will* in time find the kind of body you are interested in.

Coya had taken for granted that no one before van Rijn had been that interested. But the completeness of Astrocenter's electronic records extended to noting who had run which program when. The purpose was to avoid duplication of effort, in an era when nobody could keep up with the literature in the smallest specialty. Out of habit rather than logic, Coya called for this information and—

—I found out that ten years earlier, David wanted to know precisely what you, Grandfather, now did. But he never told you, nor said where he and his partners went afterward, or anything. Pain: *Nor has he told me. And I have not told you. Instead, I made you take me along; and before leaving, I sent David a letter saying everything I knew and suspected.*

Resolution: *All right, Nick van Rijn! You keep complaining about how moralistic my generation is. Let's see how you like getting some cards off the bottom of the deck!*

Yet she could not hate an old man who loved her.

"What do you mean by your 'alternative'?" she whispered.

"Why, simple." He shrugged like a mountain sending off an avalanche. "If we do not find a retired supernova, being used in a way as original as spinning the peach basket, then we are up against a civilization outside ours, infiltrating ours, same as the Shenna did—except this one got technology would make ours let go in its diapers and scream, 'Papa, Papa, in the closet is a boogeyman!'" Unaccustomed grimness descended on him. "I think, in that case, really is a boogeyman, too."

Chill entered her guts. "Supermetals?"

"What else?" He took a gulp of beer. "Ha, you is guessed what got me started was Supermetals?"

She finished her coffee and set the cup on a table. It rattled loud through a stretching silence. "Yes," she said at length, flat-voiced. "You've given me a lot of hours to puzzle over what this expedition is for."

"A jigsaw puzzle it is indeed, girl, and us sitting with bottoms snuggled in front of the jigsaw."

"In view of the very, very special kind of supernova-and-companion you thought might be somewhere not too far from Sol, and wanted me to compute about—in view of that, and of what Supermetals is doing, sure, I've arrived at a guess."

"Has you likewise taken into account the fact Supermetals is not just secretive about everything like is its right, but refuses to join the League?"

"That's also its right."

"Truly true. Nonetheleast, the advantages of belonging is maybe not what they used to was; but they do outweigh what small surrender of anatomy is required."

"You mean autonomy, don't you?"

"I suppose. Must be I was thinking of women. A stern chaste is a long chaste. . . . But you never got impure thoughts." Van Rijn had the tact not to look at her while he rambled, and to become serious again immediately: "You better hope, you heathen, and I better pray, the supermetals what the agents of Supermetals is peddling do not come out of a furnace run by anybody except God Himself."

The primordial element, with which creation presumably began, is hydrogen-1, a single proton accompanied by a single electron. To this day, it comprises the overwhelming bulk of matter in the universe. Vast masses of it condensed into globes, which grew hot enough from that infall to light thermonuclear fires. Atoms melted together, forming higher elements. Novae, supernovae—and, less picturesquely but more importantly, smaller suns shedding gas in their red giant phase—spread these through space, to enter into later generations of stars. Thus came planets, life, and awareness.

Throughout the periodic table, many isotopes are radioactive. From polonium (number 84) on, none are stable. Protons packed together in that quantity generate forces of repulsion with which the forces of attraction cannot forever cope. Sooner or later, these atoms will break up. The probability of disintegration—in effect, the half-life—depends on the particular structure. In general, though, the higher the atomic number, the lower the stability.

Early researchers thought the natural series ended at uranium. If further elements had once existed, they had long since perished. Neptunium, plutonium, and the rest must be made artificially. Later, traces of them were found in nature: but merely traces, and only of nuclei whose atomic numbers were below 100. The creation of new substances grew progressively more difficult, because of proton repulsion, and less rewarding, because of vanishingly brief existence, as atomic number increased. Few people expected a figure as high as 120 would ever be reached.

Well, few people expected gravity control or faster-than-light travel, either. The universe is rather bigger and more complicated than any given set of brains. Already in those days, an astonishing truth was soon revealed. Beyond a certain point, nuclei become *more* stable. The periodic table contains an "island of stability," bounded on the near side by ghostly short-lived isotopes like those of 112 and 113, on the far side by the still more speedily fragmenting 123, 124 . . . etc. . . . on to the next "island" which theory says could exist but practice has not reached save on the most infinitesimal scale.

The first is amply hard to attain. There are no easy intermediate stages, like the neptunium which is a stage between uranium and plutonium. Beyond 100, a half-life of a few hours is Methuselan; most are measured in seconds or less. You build your nuclei by main force, slamming particles into atoms too hard for them to rebound—though not so hard that the targets shatter.

To make a few micrograms of, say, element 114, eka-platinum, was a laboratory triumph. Aside from knowledge gained, it had no industrial meaning.

Engineers grew wistful about that. The proper isotope of eka-platinum will not endure forever; yet its half-life is around a quarter million years, abundant for mortal purposes, a radioactivity too weak to demand special precautions. It is lustrous white, dense (31.7), of high melting point (ca. 4700°C.), nontoxic, hard and tough and resistant. You can only get it into solution by grinding it to dust, then treating it with H_2F_2 and fluorine gas, under pressure at 250°.

It can alloy to produce metals with a range of properties an engineer would scarcely dare daydream about. Or, pure, used as a catalyst, it can become a veritable Philosopher's Stone. Its neighbors on the island are still more fascinating.

When Satan was discovered, talk arose of large-scale manufacture. Calculations soon damped it. The mills which were being designed would use rivers and seas and an entire atmosphere for cooling, whole continents for dumping wastes, in producing special isotopes by the ton. But these isotopes would all belong to elements below 100. Not even on Satan could modern technology handle the energies involved in creating, within reasonable time, a ton of eka-platinum; and supposing this were somehow possible, the cost would remain out of anybody's reach.

The engineers sighed . . . until a new company appeared, offering supermetals by the ingot or the shipload, at prices high but economic. The source of supply was not revealed. Governments and the Council of the League remembered the Shenna.

To them, a Cynthian named Tso Yu explained blandly that the organization for which she spoke had developed a new process which it chose not to patent but to keep proprietary. Obviously, she said, new laws of nature had been discovered first; but Supermetals felt no obligation to publish for the benefit of science. Let science do its own sweating. Nor did her company wish to join the League, or put itself under any government. If some did not grant it license to operate in their territories, why, there was no lack of others who would.

In the three years since, engineers had begun doing things and building devices which were to bring about the same kind of revolution as did the transistor, the fusion converter, or the negagravity generator. Meanwhile a horde of investigators, public and private, went quietly frantic.

The crews who delivered the cargoes and the agents who sold them were a mixed lot, albeit of known species. A high proportion were from backward worlds like Diomedes, Woden, or Ikrananka; some originated in neglected colonies like Lochlann (human) or Catawrayannis (Cynthian). This was understandable. Beings to whom Supermetals had given an education and a chance to better themselves and help out their folk at home would be especially loyal to it. Enough employees hailed from sophisticated milieus to deal on equal terms with League executives.

This did not appear to be a Shenn situation. Whenever an individual's past life could be traced, it proved normal, up to the point when Supermetals engaged him (her, it, yx . . .)—and was not really abnormal now. Asked point blank, the being would say he didn't know himself where the factory was or how it functioned or who the ultimate owners were. He was merely doing a well-paid job for a good, *simpático* outfit. The evidence bore him out.

("I suspect, me, some detectiving was done by kidnaps, drugs, and afterward murder," van Rijn said bleakly. "I would never allow that, but fact is, a few Supermetals people have disappeared. And . . . as youngsters like you, Coya, get more prudish, the companies and governments get more brutish." She answered: "The second is part of the reason for the first.")

Scoutships trailed the carriers and learned that they always rendezvoused with smaller craft, built for speed and agility. Three or four of these would unload into a merchantman, then dash off in unpredictable directions, using every evasive maneuver in the book and a few that the League had thought were its own secrets. They did not stop dodging until their instruments confirmed that they had shaken their shadowers.

Politicians and capitalists alike organized expensive attempts to duplicate the discoveries of whoever was behind Supermetals. Thus far, progress was nil. A body of opinion grew, that that order of capabilities belonged to a society as far ahead of the Technic as the latter was ahead of the neolithic. Then why this quiet invasion?

"I'm surprised nobody but you has thought of the supernova alternative," Coya said.

"Well, it has barely been three years," van Rijn answered. "And the business began small. It is still not big. Nothing flashy-splashy: some kilotons arriving annually, of stuff what is useful and will get more useful after more is learned about the properties. Meanwhiles, everybody got lots else to think about, the usual skulduggeries and unknowns and whatnots. Finalwise, remember, I am pustulent—*dood en ondergang,* this Anglic!—I am postulating something which astronomically is hyperimprobable. If you asked a colleague offhand, his first response would be that it isn't possible. His second would be, if he is a sensible man, How would you like to come to his place for a drink?" He knocked the dottle from his pipe. "No doubt somebody more will eventual think of it too, and sic a computer onto the problem of: Is this sort of thing possible, and if so, where might we find one?"

He stroked his goatee. "Howsomever," he continued musingly, "I think a good whiles must pass before the idea does occur. You see, the ordinary being does not care. He buys from what is on the market without wondering where it come from or what it means. Besides, Supermetals has not gone after publicity, it uses direct contacts; and what officials are concerned about supermetals has been happy to avoid publicity themselves. A big harroo might too easy get out of control, lose them votes or profits or something."

"Nevertheless," Coya said, "a number of bright minds are worrying; and the number grows as the amount of supermetals brought in does."

"*Ja.* Except who wears those minds? Near-as-damn all is corporation executives, politicians, laboratory scientists, military officers, and—now I will have to wash my mouth out with Genever—bureaucrats. In shorts, they is planetlubbers. When they cross space, they go by cozy passenger ships, to cities where everything is known except where is a restaurant fit to eat in that don't charge as if the dessert was eka-platinum a la mode.

"Me, my first jobs was on prospecting voyages. And I traveled plenty after I founded Solar, troublepotshooting on the frontier and beyond in my own personals. I know—every genuine spaceman knows, down in his marrow like no deskman ever can—how God always makes surprises on us so we don't get too proud, or maybe just for fun. To me it came natural to ask myself: What joke might God have played on the theorists this time?"

"I hope it is only a joke," Coya said.

The star remained a titan in mass. In dimensions, it was hardly larger than Earth, and shrinking still, megayear by megayear, until at last light itself could no longer escape and there would be in the universe one more point of elemental blackness and strangeness. That process was scarcely started—Coya estimated the explosion had occurred some 500 millennia ago—and the giant-become-dwarf radiated dimly in the visible spectrum, luridly in the X-ray and gamma bands. That is, each square centimeter emitted a gale of hard quanta; but so small was the area in interstellar space that the total was a mere spark, undetectable unless you came within a few parsecs.

Standing in the observation turret, staring into a viewscreen set for maximum photoamplification, she discerned a wan-white speck amidst stars which thronged the sky and, themselves made to seem extra brilliant, hurt her eyes. She looked away, toward the instruments around her which were avidly gathering data. The ship whispered and pulsed, no longer under hyperdrive but accelerating on negagravity thrust.

Hirharouk's voice blew cool out of the intercom, from the navigation bridge where he was: "The existence of a companion is now confirmed. We will need a long baseline to establish its position, but preliminary indications are of a radius vector between forty and fifty a.u."

Coya marveled at a detection system which could identify the light-bending due to a substellar object at that distance. Any observatory would covet such equipment. Her thought went to van Rijn: *If you paid what it cost,* Gunung Tuan, *you were smelling big money.*

"So far?" came her grandfather's words. "By damn, a chilly ways out, enough to freeze your astronomy off."

"It had to be," she said. "This was an A-zero: radiation equal to a hundred Sols. Closer in, even a superjovian would have been cooked down to the bare metal—as happened when the sun detonated."

"*Ja,* I knows, I knows, my dear. I only did not foresee things here was on quite this big a scale. . . . Well, we can't spend weeks at sublight. Go hyper, Hirharouk, first to get your baseline sights, next to come near the planet."

"Hyperdrive, this deep in a gravitational well?" Coya exclaimed.

"Is hokay if you got good engines well tuned, and you bet ours is tuned like a late Beethoven quartet. Music, maestro!"

Coya shook her head before she prepared to continue gathering information under the new conditions of travel.

Again *Dewfall* ran on gravs. Van Rijn agreed that trying to pass within visual range of the ultimate goal, faster than light, when to them it was still little more than a mystery wrapped in conjectures, would be a needlessly expensive form of suicide.

Standing on the command bridge between him and Hirharouk, Coya stared at the meters and displays filling an entire bulkhead, as if they could tell more than the heavens in the screens. And they could, they could, but they were not the Earth-built devices she had been using; they were Ythrian and she did not know how to read them.

Poised on his perch, crested carnivore head lifted against the Milky Way, Hirharouk said: "Data are pouring in as we approach. We should make optical pickup in less than an hour."

"Hum-hum, better call battle stations," the man proposed.

"This crew needs scant notice. Let them slake any soul-thirst they feel. God may smite some of us this day." Through the intercom keened a melody, plangent strings and thuttering drums and shrilling pipes, like nothing Earth had brought forth but still speaking to Coya of hunters high among their winds.

Terror stabbed her. "You can't expect to fight!" she cried.

"Oh, an ordinary business precaution," van Rijn smiled.

"No! We mustn't!"

"Why not, if they are here and do rumblefumbles at us?"

She opened her lips, pulled them shut again, and stood in anguish. *I can't tell you why not. How can I tell you these may be David's people?*

"At least we are sure that Supermetals is not a *whinna* for an alien society," Hirharouk said. Coya remembered vaguely, through the racket in her temples, a demonstration of the *whinna* during her groundside visit to Ythri. It was a kind of veil, used by some to camouflage themselves, to resemble floating mists in the eyes of unflying prey; and this practical use had led to a form of dream-lovely airborne dance; and—*And here I was caught in the wonder of what we have found, a thing which must be almost unique even in this galaxy full of miracles . . . and everything's gotten tangled and ugly and, and, David, what can we do?*

She heard van Rijn: "Well, we are not total-sure. Could be our finding is accidental; or maybe the planet is not like we suppose. We got to check on that, and hope the check don't bounce back in our snoots."

"Nuclear engines are in operation around our quarry," Hirharouk said. "Neutrinos show it. What else would they belong to save a working base and spacecraft?"

Van Rijn clasped hands over rump and paced, slap-slap-slap over the bare deck. "What can we try and predict in advance? Forewarned is forearmed, they say, and the four arms I want right now is a knife, a blaster, a machine gun, and a rover missile, nothing fancy, maybe a megaton."

"The mass of the planet—" Hirharouk consulted a readout. The figure he gave corresponded approximately to Saturn.

"No bigger?" asked van Rijn, surprised.

"Originally, yes," Coya heard herself say. The scientist in her was what spoke, while her heart threshed about like any animal netted by a stooping Ythrian. "A gas giant, barely substellar. The supernova blew most of that away—you can hardly say it boiled the gases off; we have no words for what happened—and nothing was left except a core of nickel-iron and heavier elements."

She halted, noticed Hirharouk's yellow gaze intent on her, and realized the skipper must know rather little of the theory behind this venture. To him she had not been repeating banalities. And he was interested. If she could please him by explaining in simple terms, then maybe later—

She addressed him: "Of course, when the pressure of the outer layers was removed, that core must have exploded into new allotropes, a convulsion which flung away the last atmosphere and maybe a lot of solid matter. Better keep a sharp lookout for meteoroids."

"That is automatic," he assured her. "My wonder is why a planet should exist. I was taught that giant stars, able to become supernovae, do not have them."

"Well, they is still scratching their brains to account for Betelgeuse," van Rijn remarked.

"In this case," Coya told the Ythrian, "the explanation comes easier. True, the extremely massive suns do not in general allow planetary systems to condense around them. The parameters aren't right. However, you know giants can be partners in multiple star systems, and sometimes the difference between partners is quite large. So, after I was alerted to the idea that it might happen, and wrote a program which investigated the possibility in detail, I learned that, yes, under special conditions, a double can form in which one member is a large sun and one a superjovian planet. When I extrapolated backward things like the motion of dust and gas, changes in galactic magnetism, et cetera—it turned out that such a pair could exist in this neighborhood."

Her glance crossed the merchant's craggy features. *You found a clue in the appearance of the supermetals,* she thought. *David got the idea all by himself.* The lean snubnosed face, the Vega-blue eyes came between her and the old man.

Of course, David may not have been involved. This could be a coincidence. Please, God of my grandfather Whom I don't believe in, please make it a coincidence. Make those ships ahead of us belong not to harmless miners but to the great and terrible Elder Race.

She knew the prayer would not be granted. And neither van Rijn nor Hirharouk assumed that the miners were necessarily harmless.

She talked fast, to stave off silence: "I daresay you've heard this before, Captain, but you may like to have me recapitulate in a few words. When a supernova erupts, it floods out neutrons in quantities that I, I can put a number to, perhaps, but I cannot comprehend. In a full range of energies, too, and the same for other kinds of particles and quanta—do you see? Any possible reaction *must* happen.

"Of course, the starting materials available, the reaction rates, the yields, every quantity differs from case to case. The big nuclei which get formed, like the actinides, are a very small percentage of the total. The supermetals are far less. They scatter so thinly into space that they're effectively lost. No detectable amount enters into the formation of a star or planet afterward.

"Except—here—here was a companion, a planet-sized companion, turned into a bare metallic globe. I wouldn't try to guess how many quintillion tons of blasted-out incandescent gasses washed across it. Some of those alloyed with the molten surface, maybe some plated out—and the supermetals, with their high condensation temperatures, were favored.

"A minute fraction of the total was supermetals, yes, and a minute fraction of that was captured by the planet, also yes. But this amounted to—how much?—billions of tons? Not hard to extract from combination by modern methods; and a part may actually be lying around pure. It's radioactive; one must be careful, especially of the shorter-lived products, and a lot has decayed away by now. Still, what's left is more than our puny civilization can ever consume. It took a genius to think this might be!"

She grew aware of van Rijn's eyes upon her. He had stopped pacing and stood troll-burly, tugging his beard.

A whistle rescued her. Planha words struck from the intercom. Hirharouk's feathers rippled in a series of expressions she could not read; his tautness was unmistakable.

She drew near to the man's bulk. "What next?" she whispered. "Can you follow what they're saying?"

"*Ja,* pretty well; anyhow, better than I can follow words in an opera. Detectors show three ships leaving planetary orbit on an intercept course. The rest stay behind. No doubt those is the working vessels. What they send to us is their men-of-war."

Seen under full screen magnification, the supermetal world showed still less against the constellations than had the now invisible supernova corpse—a ball, dimly reflecting star-glow, its edge sharp athwart distant brightnesses. And yet, Coya thought: a world.

It could not be a smooth sphere. There must be uplands, lowlands, flatlands, depths, ranges and ravines, cliffs whose gloom was flecked with gold, plains where mercury glaciers glimmered; there must be internal heat, shudders in the steel soil, volcanoes spouting forth flame and radioactive ash; eternally barren, it must nonetheless mumble with a life of its own.

Had David Falkayn trod those lands? He would have, she knew, merrily swearing because beyond the ship's generated field he and his space gear weighed five or six times what they ought, and no matter the multitudinous death traps which a place so uncanny must hold in every shadow. Naturally, those shadows had to be searched out; whoever would mine the metals had first to spend years, and doubtless lives, in exploring, and studying, and the development and testing and redevelopment of machinery . . . but that wouldn't concern David. He was a charger, not a plowhorse. Having made his discovery, told chosen beings about it, perhaps helped them raise the initial funds and recruit members of races which could better stand high weight than men can—having done that, he'd depart on a new adventure, or stop off in the Solar Commonwealth and take Coya Conyon out dancing.

"*Iyan wherill-ll cha quellan.*"

The words, and Hirharouk's response, yanked her back to this instant. "What?"

"Shush." Van Rijn, head cocked, waved her to silence. "By damn, this sounds spiky. I should tell you, shush-kebab."

Hirharouk related: "Instruments show one of the three vessels is almost equal to ours. Its attendants are less, but in a formation to let them take full advantage of their firepower. If that is in proportion to size, which I see no reason to doubt, we are outgunned. Nor do they act as if they simply hope to frighten us off. That formation and its paths are well calculated to bar our escape spaceward."

"Can you give me details—? No, wait." Van Rijn swung on Coya. "Bellybird, you took a stonkerish lot of readings on the sun, and right here is an input-output panel you can switch to the computer system you was using. I also ordered, when I chartered the ship, should be a program for instant translation between Anglic language, Arabic numerals, metric units, whatever else kinds of ics is useful—translations back and forth between those and the Planha sort. Think you could quick-like do some figuring for us?" He clapped her shoulder, nearly felling her. "I know you can." His voice dropped. "I remember your grandmother."

Her mouth was dry, her palms were wet, it thudded in her ears. She thought of David Falkayn and said, "Yes. What do you want?"

"Mainly the pattern of the gravitational field, and what phenomena we can expect at the different levels of intensity. Plus radiation, electromagnetics, anything else you got time to program for. But we is fairly well protected against those, so don't worry if you don't get a chance to go into details there. Nor don't let outside talkings distract you—whoops!" Hirharouk was receiving a fresh report. "Speak of the devil and he gives you horns."

The other commander had obviously sent a call on a standard band, which had been accepted. As the image screen awoke, Coya felt hammerstruck. *Adzel!*

No . . . no . . . the head belonged to a Wodenite, but not the dear dragon who had given her rides on his back when she was little and had tried in his earnest, tolerant fashion to explain his Buddhism to her when she grew older. Behind the being she made out a raven-faced Ikranankan and a human in the garb of a colony she couldn't identify.

His rubbery lips shaped good Anglic, a basso which went through her bones: "Greeting. Commodore Nadi speaks."

Van Rijn thrust his nose toward the scanner. "Whose commodore?" he demanded like a gravel hauler dumping its load.

For a second, Nadi was shaken. He rallied and spoke firmly: "*Kho,* I know who you are, Freeman van Rijn. What an unexpected honor, that you should personally visit our enterprise."

"Which is Supermetals, *nie?*"

"It would be impolite to suggest you had failed to reach that conclusion."

Van Rijn signalled Coya behind his back. She flung herself at the chair before the computer terminal. Hirharouk perched imperturbable, slowly fanning his wings. The Ythrian music had ended. She heard a rustle and whisper through the intercom, along the hurtling hull.

Words continued. Her work was standardized enough that she could follow them.

"Well, you see, Commodore, there I sat, not got much to do no more, lonely old man like I am except when a girl goes wheedle-wheedle at me, plenty time for thinking, which is not fun like drinking but you can do it alone and it is easier on the kidneys and the hangovers next day are not too much worse. I thought, if the supermetals is not made by an industrial process we don't understand, must be they was made by a natural one, maybe one we do know a little about. That would have to be a supernova. Except a supernova blows everything out into space, and the supermetals is so small, proportional, that they get lost. Unless the supernova had a companion what could catch them?"

"Freeman, pray accept my admiration. Does your perspicacity extend to deducing who is behind our undertaking?"

"*Ja,* I can say, bold and bald, who you undertakers are. A consortium of itsy-bitsy operators, most from poor or primitive societies, pooling what capital they can scrape together. You got to keep the secret, because if they know about this hoard you found, the powerful outfits will horn themselves in and you out; and what chance you get afterward, in courts they can buy out of petty cash? No, you will keep this hidden long as you possible can. In the end, somebody is bound to repeat my sherlockery. But give you several more years, and you will have pumped gigacredits clear profit out of here. You may actual have got so rich you can defend your property."

Coya could all but see the toilers in their darkness—in orbital stations; aboard spacecraft; down on the graveyard surface, where robots dug ores and ran refineries, and sentient beings stood their watches under the murk and chill and weight and radiation and millionfold perils of Eka-World. . . .

Nadi, slow and soft: "That is why we have these fighting ships, Freeman and Captain."

"You do not suppose," van Rijn retorted cheerily, "I would come this far in my own precious blubber and forget to leave behind a message they will scan if I am not home in time to race for the Micronesia Cup?"

"As a matter of fact, Freeman, I suppose precisely that. The potential gains here are sufficient to justify virtually any risk, whether the game be played for money or . . . something else." Pause. "If you have indeed left a message, you will possess hostage value. Your rivals may be happy to see you a captive, but you have allies and employees who will exert influence. My sincere apologies, Freeman, Captain, everyone aboard your vessel. We will try to make your detention pleasant."

Van Rijn's bellow quivered in the framework. "*Wat drommel?* You sit smooth and calm like buttered granite and say you will make us prisoners?"

"You may not leave. If you try, we will regretfully open fire."

"You are getting on top of yourself. I warn you, always she finds nothing except an empty larder, Old Mother Hubris."

"Freeman, please consider. We noted your hyperdrive vibrations and made ready. You cannot get past us to spaceward. Positions and vectors guarantee that one of our vessels will be able to close in, engage, and keep you busy until the other two arrive." Reluctantly, van Rijn nodded. Nadi continued: "True, you can double back toward the sun. Evidently you can use hyperdrive closer to it than most. But you cannot go in that direction at anywhere near top pseudospeed without certain destruction. We, proceeding circuitously, but therefore able to go a great deal faster, will keep ahead of you. We will calculate the conoid in which your possible paths spaceward lie, and again take a formation you cannot evade."

"You is real anxious we should taste your homebrew, ha?"

"Freeman, I beg you, yield at once. I promise fair treatment—if feasible, compensation—and while you are among us, I will explain why we of Supermetals have no choice."

"Hirharouk," van Rijn said, "maybe you can talk at this slag-brain." He stamped out of scanner reach. The Ythrian threw him a dubious glance but entered into debate with the Wodenite. Van Rijn hulked over Coya where she sat. "How you coming?" he whispered, no louder than a Force Five wind.

She gestured at the summary projected on a screen. Her computations were of a kind she often handled. The results were shown in such terms as diagrams and equations of equipotential surfaces, familiar to a space captain. Van Rijn read them and nodded. "We got enough information to set out on," he decided. "The rest you can figure while we go."

Shocked, she gaped at him. "What? Go? But we're caught!"

"He thinks that. Me, I figured whoever squats on a treasure chest will keep guards, and the guards will not be glimmerwits but smart, trained oscos, in spite of what I called the Commodore. They might well cook for us a cake like what we is now baked in. Ergo, I made a surprise recipe for them." Van Rijn's regard turned grave. "It was for use only if we found we was sailing through dire straits. The surprise may turn around and bite us. Then we is dead. But better dead than losing years in the nicest jail, *nie?*" (And she could not speak to him of David.) "I said this trip might be dangerous." Enormous and feather-gentle, a hand stroked down her hair. "I is very sorry, Beatriz, Ramona." The names he murmured were of her mother and grandmother.

Whirling, he returned to Hirharouk, who matched pride against Nadi's patience, and uttered a few rapid-fire Planha words. The Ythrian gave instant assent. Suddenly Coya knew why the man had chosen a ship of that planet. Hirharouk continued his argument. Van Rijn went to the main command panel, snapped forth orders, and took charge of *Dewfall.*

At top acceleration, she sprang back toward the sun.

Of that passage, Coya afterward remembered little. First she glimpsed the flashes when nuclear warheads drove at her, and awaited death. But van Rijn and Hirharouk had adjusted well their vector relative to the enemy's. During an hour of negagrav flight, no missile could gather sufficient relative velocity to get past defensive fire; and that was what made those flames in heaven.

Then it became halfway safe to go hyper. That must be at a slower pace than in the emptiness between stars; but within an hour, the fleeing craft neared the dwarf. There, as gravitation intensified, she had to resume normal state.

Instead of swinging wide, she opened full thrust almost straight toward the disc.

Coya was too busy to notice much of what happened around her. She must calculate, counsel, hang into her seat harness as forces tore at her which were too huge for the compensator fields. She saw the undead supernova grow in the viewscreens till its baneful radiance filled them; she heard the ribs of the vessel groan and felt them shudder beneath stress; she watched the tale of the radiation meters mounting and knew how close she came to a dose whose ravages medicine could not heal; she heard orders bawled by van Rijn, fluted by Hirharouk, and whistling replies and storm of wingbeats, always triumphant though *Dewfall* flew between the teeth of destruction. But mainly she was part of the machinery.

And the hours passed and the hours passed.

They could not have done what they did without advance preparation. Van Rijn had foreseen the contingency and ordered computations made whose results were in the data banks. Her job was to insert numbers and functions corresponding to the reality on hand, and get answers by which he and Hirharouk might steer. The work filled her, crowded out terror and sometimes the memory of David.

Appalled, Nadi watched his quarry vanish off his telltales. He had followed on hyperdrive as close as he dared, and afterward at sublight closer than he ought to have dared. But for him was no possibility of plunging in a hairpin hyperbola around yonder incandescence. In all the years he had been stationed here, not he nor his fellows had imagined anyone would ever venture near the roiling remnant of a sun which had once burned brighter than its whole galaxy. Thus there were no precalculations in storage, nor days granted him to program them on a larger device than a ship might carry.

Radiation was not the barrier. It was easy to figure how narrow an approach a crew could endure behind a given amount of armor. But a mass of half a dozen Sols, pressed into the volume of an Earth, has stupendous gravitational power; the warped space around makes the laws of nature take on an eerie aspect. Moreover, a dwarf star spins at a fantastic rate: which generates relativistic forces, describable only if you have determined the precise quantities involved. And pulsations, normally found nowhere outside the atomic nucleus, reach across a million or more kilometers—

After the Ythrian craft whipped around the globe, into weirdness, Nadi had no way of knowing what she did, how she moved. He could not foretell where she would be when she again became detectable. And thus he could plan no interception pattern.

He could do nothing but hope she would never reappear. A ship flying so close, not simply orbiting but flying, would be seized, torn apart, and hauled into the star, unless the pilot and his computers knew exactly what they did.

Or almost exactly. That was a crazily chancy ride. When Coya could glance from her desk, she saw blaze in the screens, Hirharouk clutching his perch with both hands while his wings thundered and he yelled for joy, van Rijn on his knees in prayer. Then they ran into a meteoroid swarm (she supposed) which rebounded off their shield-fields and sent them careening off trajectory; and the man shook his fist, commenced on a mighty oath, glimpsed her and turned it into a Biblical "Damask rose and shittah tree!" Later, when something else went wrong—some interaction with a plasma cloud—he came to her, bent over and kissed her brow.

They won past reef and riptide, lined out for deep space, switched back into hyperdrive and ran on homeward.

Coincidences do happen. The life would be freakish which held none of them.

Muddlin' Through, bound for Eka-World in response to Coya's letter, passed within detection range of *Dewfall,* made contact, and laid alongside. The pioneers boarded.

This was less than a day after the brush with oblivion. And under no circumstances do Ythrians go in for tumultuous greetings. Apart from Hirharouk, who felt he must represent his choth, the crew stayed at rest. Coya, roused by van Rijn, swallowed a stimpill, dressed, and hastened to the flying hold—the sole chamber aboard which would comfortably accommodate Adzel. In its echoing dim space she threw her arms partway around him, took Chee Lan into her embrace, kissed David Falkayn and wept and kissed him and kissed him.

Van Rijn cleared his throat. "A-hem!" he grumbled. "Also bgr-rrm. I been sitting here hours on end, till my end is sore, wondering when everybody else's would come awake and make celebrations by me; and I get word about you three mosquito-ears is coming in, and by my own self I hustle stuff for a party." He waved at the table he had laid, bottles and glasses, platesful of breads, cheeses, sausage, lox, caviar, kanuba, from somewhere a vaseful of flowers. Mozart lilted in the background. "Well, ha, poets tell us love is enduring, but I tell us good food is not, so we take our funs in the right order, *nie?*"

Formerly Falkayn would have laughed and tossed off the first icy muglet of akvavit; he would have followed it with a beer chaser and an invitation to Coya that they see what they could dance to this music. Now she felt sinews tighten in the fingers that enclosed hers; across her shoulder he said carefully: "Sir, before we relax, could you let me know what's happened to you?"

Van Rijn got busy with a cigar. Coya looked a plea at Adzel, stroked Chee's fur where the Cynthian crouched on a chair, and found no voice. Hirharouk told the story in a few sharp words.

"A-a-ah," Falkayn breathed. "Judas priest. Coya, they ran you that close to that hellkettle—" His right hand let go of hers to clasp her waist. She felt the grip tremble and grew dizzy with joy.

"Well," van Rijn huffed, "I didn't want she should come, my dear tender little bellybird, *ja,* tender like tool steel—"

Coya had a sense of being put behind Falkayn, as a man puts a woman when menace draws near. "Sir," he said most levelly, "I know, or can guess, about that. We can discuss it later if you want. What I'd like to know immediately, please, is what you propose to do about the Supermetals consortium."

Van Rijn kindled his cigar and twirled a mustache. "You understand," he said, "I am not angry if they keep things under the posies. By damn, though, they tried to make me a prisoner or else shoot me to bits of lard what would go into the next generation of planets. And Coya, too, Davy boy, don't forget Coya, except she would make those planets prettier. For that, they going to pay."

"What have you in mind?"

"Oh . . . a cut. Not the most unkindest, neither. Maybe like ten percent of gross."

The creases deepened which a hundred suns had weathered into Falkayn's countenance. "Sir, you don't need the money. You stopped needing more money a long while back. To you it's nothing but a counter in a game. Maybe, for you, the only game in town. Those beings aft of us, however—they are not playing."

"What do they do, then?"

Surprisingly, Hirharouk spoke. "Freeman, you know the answer. They seek to win that which will let their peoples fly free." Standing on his wings, he could not spread gold-bronze plumes; but his head rose high. "In the end, God the Hunter strikes every being and everything which beings have made. Upon your way of life I see His shadow. Let the new come to birth in peace."

From Falkayn's hands, Coya begged: "*Gunung Tuan,* all you have to do is do nothing. Say nothing. You've won your victory. Tell them that's enough for you, that you too are their friend."

She had often watched van Rijn turn red—never before white. His shout came ragged: "*Ja! Ja!* Friend! So nice, so kind, maybe so far-sighted—Who, what I thought of like a son, broke his oath of fealty to me? Who broke kinship?"

He suspected, Coya realized sickly, *but he wouldn't admit it to himself till this minute, when I let out the truth.* She held Falkayn sufficiently hard for everyone to see.

Chee Lan arched her back. Adzel grew altogether still. Falkayn forgot Coya—she could feel how he did—and looked straight at his chief while he said, word by word like blows of a hammer: "Do you want a response? I deem best we let what is past stay dead."

Their gazes drew apart. Falkayn's dropped to Coya. The merchant watched them standing together for a soundless minute. And upon him were the eyes of Adzel, Chee, and Hirharouk the sky dweller.

He shook his head. "Hokay," said Nicholas van Rijn, well-nigh too low to hear. "I keep my mouth shut. Always. Now can we sit down and have our party for making you welcome?" He moved to pour from a bottle; and Coya saw that he was indeed old.

AFTERWORD

Nicholas van Rijn first appeared in 1956. He has come back on a number of occasions, among them two full-dress novels, but always in the same magazine, whether it was called *Astounding* or *Analog*. Likewise the exploratory team he organized—David Falkayn, Chee Lan, Adzel and Muddlehead, their ship's insufferable computer. They showed up because it wasn't logical that the old man should have all the adventures. But they too felt most at home with John Campbell.

While some readers cannot abide him, among a large majority Van Rijn seems to be the most popular character I've ever created. In fact, the series became study material for a graduate seminar in management! Campbell enjoyed him hugely. This alone was ample encouragement to write more—not the sales themselves, because after all it was just as easy to do something different, though less fun, but the approval of so genuinely great and greatly genuine a man.

The aim throughout was to tell colorful, fast-moving stories which would at the same time explore a few of the possible facets of this endlessly marvelous universe—and maybe a bit of philosophy. That last, by the way, was no mere dog-eat-dog anarchism. Campbell and I both knew better. Among the more moving experiences of my life was when an elderly lady, confined for years in a particularly grim hospital, wrote to say that something in one of the tales had given her the will to fight on.

What virtue they have is largely due to the Campbell influence, both as an electrifying atmosphere and, in a number of cases, as specific suggestions. Only those who wrote for him know what a fountainhead of ideas he was; he never claimed credit afterward. Mind you, though, he made suggestions, not commands. He delighted in seeing a thought of his carried further by someone else, or stood on its head and turned inside out.

The lodestar of the present yarn is due to him. He proposed it to me back in 1970. I put his letter aside to sparkle in a heap of similar communications from him, until an opportunity should come to use, not just the notion, but the considerable details of physics and chemistry which accompanied it.

Well, I waited too long. Now I can but hope that he would have liked what I've done, and wish he could know with what love I dedicate to him this ending of a saga on which so long we worked together.

Goodbye, John.

—Poul Anderson, 1973

CHRONOLOGY OF TECHIC CIVILIZATION

☼COMPILED BY SANDRA MIESEL☼

The Technic Civilization series sweeps across five millennia and hundreds of light-years of space to chronicle three cycles of history shaping both human and non-human life in our corner of the universe. It begins in the twenty-first century, with recovery from a violent period of global unrest known as the Chaos. New space technologies ease Earth's demand for resources and energy permitting exploration of the Solar system.

ca. 2055	"The Saturn Game" (*Analog Science Fiction*, hereafter *ASF*, February, 1981)
22nd C	The discovery of hyperdrive makes interstellar travel feasible early in the twenty-second century. The Breakup sends humans off to colonize the stars, often to preserve cultural identity or to try a social experiment. A loose government called the Solar Commonwealth is established. Hermes is colonized.
2150	"Wings of Victory" (*ASF*, April, 1972) The Grand Survey from Earth discovers alien races on Yithri, Merseia, and many other planets.
23rd C	The Polesetechnic League is founded as a mutual protection association of space-faring merchants.

Colonization of Aeneas and Altai.

24th C "The Problem of Pain" (*Fantasy and Science Fiction*, February, 1973)

2376 Nicholas van Rijn born poor on Earth.
Colonization of Vixen.

2400 Council of Hiawatha, a futile attempt to reform the League.
Colonization of Dennitza.

2406 David Falkayn born noble on Hermes, a breakaway human grand duchy.

2416 "Margin of Profit" (*ASF*, September, 1956) [van Rijn]
"How to Be Ethnic in One Easy Lesson" (in *Future Quest*, ed. Roger Elwood, Avon Books, 1974)

✲ ✲ ✲

2423 "The Three-Cornered Wheel" (*ASF*, April, 1966) [Falkayn]

✲ ✲ ✲

stories overlap
2420s "A Sun Invisible" (*ASF*, April, 1966) [Falkayn]
"The Season of Forgiveness" (*Boy's Life*, December, 1973) [set on same planet as "The Three-Cornered Wheel"]

The Man Who Counts (Ace Books, 1978 as *War of the Wing-Men,* Ace Books, 1958 from "The Man Who Counts," *ASF*, February-April,1958) [van Rijn]

"Esau" (as "Birthright," *ASF* February, 1970) [van Rijn]

"Hiding Place" (*ASF*, March, 1961) [van Rijn]

✲ ✲ ✲

stories overlap
2430s "Territory" (*ASF*, June, 1963) [van Rijn]
"The Trouble Twisters" (as "Trader Team," *ASF*, July-August, 1965) [Falkayn]

"Day of Burning" (as "Supernova," *ASF* January, 1967) [Falkayn]
Falkayn saves civilization on Merseia, mankind's

future foe.
"The Master Key" (*ASF* August, 1964) [van Rijn]

Satan's World (Doubleday, 1969 from *ASF*, May-August, 1968) [van Rijn and Falkayn]

"A Little Knowledge" *(ASF*, August, 1971)

The League has become a set of ruthless cartels.

✲ ✲ ✲

2446 "Lodestar" (in *Astounding: The John W. Campbell Memorial Anthology.* ed. Harry Harrison. Random House, 1973) [van Rijn and Falkayn]
Rivalries and greed are tearing the League apart. Falkayn marries van Rijn's favorite granddaughter.

2456 *Mirkheim* (Putnam Books, 1977) [van Rijn and Falkayn]
The Babur War involving Hermes gravely wounds the League. Dark days loom.

late 25th C Falkayn founds a joint human-Ythrian colony on Avalon ruled by the Domain of Ythri. [same planet—renamed—as "The Problem of Pain"]

26th C "Wingless" (as "Wingless on Avalon," *Boy's Life*, July, 1973) [Falkayn's grandson]
"Rescue on Avalon" (in *Children of Infinity*, ed. Roger Elwood. Franklin Watts, 1973)
Colonization of Nyanza.

2550 Dissolution of the Polesotechnic League.

27th C The Time of Troubles brings down the Commonwealth. Earth is sacked twice and left prey to barbarian slave raiders.

ca. 2700 "The Star Plunderer" (*Planet Stories*, hereafter *PS*, September, 1952)
Manuel Argos proclaims the Terran Empire with citizenship open to all intelligent species. The Principate phase of the Imperium ultimately brings peace to 100,000 inhabited worlds within a sphere of stars 400 light-years in diameter.

28th C Colonization of Unan Besar.

	"Sargasso of Lost Starships" (*PS*, January, 1952) The Empire annexes old colony on Ansa by force.
29th C	*The People of the Wind* (New American Library from *ASF*, February-April, 1973) The Empire's war on another civilized imperium starts its slide towards decadence. A descendant of Falkayn and an ancestor of Flandry cross paths.
30th C	The Covenant of Alfazar, an attempt at détente between Terra and Merseia, fails to achieve peace.
3000	Dominic Flandry born on Earth, illegitimate son of a an opera diva and an aristocratic space captain.
3019	*Ensign Flandry* (Chilton, 1966 from shorter version in *Amazing,* hereafter *AMZ*, October, 1966) Flandry's first collision with the Merseians.
3021	*A Circus of Hells* (New American Library, 1970, incorporates "The White King's War," *Galaxy*, hereafter *Gal*, October, 1969, Flandry is a Lieutenant (j.g.).
3022	Degenerate Emperor Josip succeeds weak old Emperor Georgios.
3025	*The Rebel Worlds* (New American Library, 1969) A military revolt on the frontier world of Aeneas almost starts an age of Barracks Emperors. Flandry is a Lt. Commander, then promoted to Commander.
3027	"Outpost of Empire" (*Gal*, December, 1967) [not Flandry] The misgoverned Empire continues fraying at its borders.
3028	*The Day of Their Return* (New American Library, 1973) [Aycharaych but not Flandry] Aftermath of the rebellion on Aeneas.
3032	"Tiger by the Tail" (*PS*, January, 1951) [Flandry] Flandry is a Captain and averts a barbarian invasion.
3033	"Honorable Enemies" (*Future Combined with Science Fiction Stories*, May, 1951) [Flandry] Captain Flandry's first brush with

enemy agent Aycharaych.

3035 "The Game of Glory" (*Venture*, March, 1958) [Flandry]
Set on Nyanza, Flandry has been knighted.

3037 "A Message in Secret" (as *Mayday Orbit*,
Ace Books, 1961 from shorter version,
"A Message in Secret," *Fantastic*, December, 1959)
[Flandry]
Set on Altai.

3038 "The Plague of Masters" (as *Earthman, Go Home!*,
Ace Books, 1961 from "A Plague of Masters,"
Fantastic, December, 1960- January, 1961.) [Flandry]
Set on Unan Besar.

3040 "Hunters of the Sky Cave" (as *We Claim These Stars!*,
Ace Books, 1959 from shorter version,
"A Handful of Stars, *Amz*, June, 1959)
[Flandry and Aycharaych]
Set on Vixen.

3041 Interregnum: Josip dies. After three years of civil war,
Hans Molitor will rule as sole emperor.

3042 "The Warriors from Nowhere"
(as "The Ambassadors of Flesh," *PS*, Summer, 1954.)
Snapshot of disorders in the war-torn Empire.

3047 *A Knight of Ghosts and Shadows* (New American
Library, 1975 from *If* September/October-
November/December, 1974) [Flandry]
Set on Dennitza, Flandry meets his illegitimate son
and has a final tragic confrontation with Aycharaych.

3054 Emperor Hans dies and is succeeded by his sons,
first Dietrich, then Gerhart.

3061 *A Stone in Heaven* (Ace Books, 1979) [Flandry]
Admiral Flandry pairs off with the daughter of his
first mentor from *Ensign Flandry*.

3064 *The Game of Empire* (Baen Books, 1985) [Flandry]
Flandry is a Fleet Admiral, meets his illegitimate
daughter Diana.

early 4th millennium The Terran Empire becomes more rigid and

	tyrannical in its Dominate phase. The Empire and Merseia wear each other out.
mid-4th millennium	The Long Night follows the Fall of the Terran Empire. War, piracy, economic collapse, and isolation devastate countless worlds.
3600	"A Tragedy of Errors" (*Gal*, February, 1968) Further fragmentation among surviving human worlds.
3900	"The Night Face" (Ace Books, 1978. as *Let the Spacemen Beware!*, Ace Books, 1963 from shorter version "A Twelvemonth and a Day," *Fantastic Universe*, January, 1960) Biological and psychological divergence among surviving humans.
4000	"The Sharing of Flesh" (*Gal*, December, 1968) Human explorers heal genetic defects and uplift savagery.
7100	"Starfog" (*ASF*, August. 1967) Revived civilization is expanding. A New Vixen man from the libertarian Commonalty meets descendants of the rebels from Aeneas.

Although Technic Civilization is extinct, another—and perhaps better—turn on the Wheel of Time has begun for our galaxy. The Commonalty must inevitably decline just as the League and Empire did before it. But the Wheel will go on turning as long as there are thinking minds to wonder at the stars.

✲ ✲ ✲

Poul Anderson was consulted about this chart
but any errors are my own.